WAC(

MW01285338

I Am Providence

One of the photos of H. P. Lovecraft
taken by Lucius Truesdell in De Land, Florida

I Am Providence
The Life and Times of H. P. Lovecraft: Volume 2

S. T. Joshi

Hippocampus Press

New York

Published by Hippocampus Press
P.O. Box 641, New York, NY 10156.
http://www.hippocampuspress.com

Hippocampus Press logo by Anastasia Damianakos.
Cover design by Barbara Briggs Silbert.

First Paperback Edition
1 3 5 7 9 8 6 4 2

ISBN 978-1-61498-052-0 (Volume 2)
ISBN 978-1-61498-053-7 (2 Volume Set)

The Library of Congress has cataloged the hardcover edition as follows:

Joshi, S. T., 1958-
  I am Providence : the life and times of H.P. Lovecraft / S. T. Joshi. -- 1st ed.
    p. cm.
  Complete in 2 volumes.
  In 1996, S. T. Joshi's H.P. Lovecraft: a life was published. The edition was abridged by more than 150,000 words. This new version I am Providence: the life and times of H.P. Lovecraft restores every word of Joshi's original manuscript. The text has been revised and updated in light of the new information on Lovecraft that has emerged since 1996--Provided by publisher.
  Includes bibliographical references and index.
  ISBN 978-0-9824296-7-9 (alk. paper)
  1. Lovecraft, H. P. (Howard Phillips), 1890-1937. 2. Authors, American--20th century--Biography. 3. Fantasy fiction--Authorship. 4. Horror tales--Authorship. I. Title.
  PS3523.O833Z72 2010
  813'.52--dc22
  [B]
                        2010028590

CONTENTS

ABBREVIATIONS

AD	August Derleth
AEPG	Annie E. P. Gamwell
CAS	Clark Ashton Smith
DW	Donald Wandrei
EHP	E. Hoffmann Price
FBL	Frank Belknap Long
JFM	James F. Morton
JVS	J. Vernon Shea
LDC	Lillian D. Clark
MWM	Maurice W. Moe
REH	Robert E. Howard
RHB	R. H. Barlow
RK	Rheinhart Kleiner
CoC	*Crypt of Cthulhu*
LS	*Lovecraft Studies*
AHT	Arkham House transcripts of Lovecraft's letters
JHL	John Hay Library of Brown University, Providence

I AM PROVIDENCE

16. THE ASSAULTS OF CHAOS
(1925–1926)

On December 31, 1924, I established myself in a large room of pleasing & tasteful proportions at 169 Clinton St., cor. of State, in the Heights or Borough Hall section of Brooklyn, in an house of early Victorian date with white classick woodwork & tall windows with panell'd seats. Two alcoves with portieres enable one to preserve the pure library effect, & the whole forms a pleasing hermitage for an old-fashion'd man, with its generous view of ancient brick houses in State & Clinton Sts.[1]

So begins one of the most unusual documents in Lovecraft's entire corpus: his "Diary" for 1925. If it is asked why this document, so seemingly vital for the understanding of his life in this critical year, has only recently been published (in the fifth volume [2006] of the *Collected Essays*), given that just about every other scrap of Lovecraft's work exclusive of his letters has seen print regardless of its merit or importance, the answer may lie in its somewhat mundane function. It does not have—and was not designed to have—the literary value of the diaries of Pepys or Evelyn, but was intended merely as a mnemonic aid. It is written in an appointment book for the year 1925, measuring about 2½" × 5¼", with only about four lines given for each date; Lovecraft, although not observing the ruled lines very well (he loathed ruled paper), has nevertheless written entries in such a cryptic and abbreviated fashion that some words or terms are still not clear to me. Here is a sample entry, for January 16:

Saw SH off—shopping for SL desk Fix SL room—trips to & fro—find SL & RK at 169—McN & GK arrive, converse cafeteria adjourn to SL's—surprise—break up 2 a m—GK McN & HPL subway—HP & GK to 106 St. Talk—sleep

Not exactly enthralling reading. But the fact is that this diary served a purely utilitarian purpose, namely as an aid to writing letters to Lillian. This practice may have developed years before: during his stay in New York in late summer 1922 Lovecraft, in the midst of a long letter to Lillian, writes: "This is a letter & a diary combined!"[2] In later years it appears that he kept a diary of this sort on all his trips, although none aside from this one have come to light. There may well have been a diary for 1924, and it would clarify much that remains cloudy and uncertain about his life in that year.

The diary for 1925 quite literally allows for a day-by-day chronicle of Lovecraft's activities for the year, but such a thing would serve little purpose. While it is true that some of his letters to both Annie and Lillian—where he elaborated, in great detail, the sketchy notes recorded in the diary—are missing, leaving us with only the skeletal diary entries as a guide to his daily life, it is less his activities on any single day than the general pattern of his existence that is of importance. For the first time in his life, Lovecraft was living alone without any relative—by blood or by marriage—with him. Of course, there were his friends, and 1925 was certainly the heyday of the Kalem Club, when the various members would flit in and out of each other's humble apartments as if they were a sort of literary commune; nevertheless, Lovecraft was on his own as he had never been before, having to prepare his own meals, take care of his laundry, purchase new items of clothing, and perform all the other tedious mundanities of life that most of us accept as a matter of course.

Lovecraft later admitted that 169 Clinton Street was selected "with the assistance of my aunt."[3] The search was clearly undertaken during Lillian's long stay in December, and Lovecraft's later mention of a trip he and Lillian took to Elizabeth in that month[4] suggests that that New Jersey haven was also considered as a residence; but perhaps a site more convenient to Manhattan was preferred. Lovecraft found the first-floor apartment itself pleasing, since the two alcoves—one for dressing and the other for washing—allowed him to preserve a study-like effect in the room proper. He supplies a plan of it in a letter to Maurice Moe:[5]

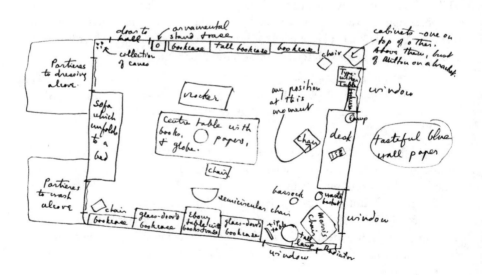

It is no surprise that bookshelves line the entirety of two walls of the room; and at that, a good number of his books were kept in storage. There were no cooking facilities in the apartment. He did his best, however, to keep the place neat, and in fact noted to Lillian that he was not spending any unwarranted amount of time in household chores: "I dust only once in three days, sweep only once a week, & eat so simply that I seldom have to do any dishwashing beyond a simple plate, or cup & saucer, plus one or two metallic utensils."[6] The only thing Lovecraft found disappointing, at least initially, was the seediness of the general area; but he knew that beggars could not be choosers. At $40 a month the place was a pretty good deal, especially as Sonia—during her infrequent visits there—could be accommodated well enough, as the sofa could be folded out into a double bed. When Sonia was not there, Lovecraft would frequently lie on the couch without opening it, or sometimes doze in the morris chair.

The peculiar thing about the locale is that the gentrification movement of the last three or four decades has markedly improved nearly the whole of Brooklyn Heights, so that it is now one of the more sought-after (and expensive) areas of the borough; conversely, the once-posh Flatbush area, where 259 Parkside Avenue lies, has suffered a deterioration as Flatbush Avenue has become the haven of a dismal array of tawdry discount stores. In other words, the socioeconomic status of the two areas of Brooklyn in which Lovecraft lived has been exactly reversed. Clinton Street, however, then as now provides easier access to Manhattan by subway, as it is far closer to Manhattan than Parkside Avenue, which is all the way on the other side of Prospect Park. Only a few blocks from 169 Clinton Street is Borough Hall, the governmental centre of Brooklyn and the hub for two of the three subway lines in the city, IRT (2, 3, 4, 5) and BMT (M, N, R); the F train (IND) stops at nearby Bergen Street. Most of these lines were already operating in Lovecraft's day, so that he could easily come home at any hour of day or night from almost any point in Manhattan—a fact worth noting in conjunction with his many late-night outings with the gang.

Let us first examine the precise degree to which, in the year 1925, Lovecraft was alone. Sonia's job at Mabley & Carew's, the Cincinnati department store, evidently allowed her to make monthly trips of a few days to New York. But as early as late February Sonia had either lost or had resigned from this position; Lovecraft wrote to Annie: ". . . despite a marked improvement in health since her last visit here, S H has at last found the hostile & exacting atmosphere of Mabley & Carew's intolerable; finally being virtually forced out of her position by quibbling executives & invidious inferiors."[7] Elsewhere Lovecraft noted that Sonia spent a short time on two separate occasions in a private hospital in Cincinnati.[8] Accordingly, Sonia returned to Brooklyn for an extended period in February and March, at that time deciding belatedly to take the six weeks' rest recommended to her by her doctors. She spent most of the period from late March to early June in the home of a woman physician in Saratoga Springs, in upstate New York; strangely enough, however, Lovecraft notes in April that there is a "child under her governance"[9] there, suggesting that her stay there involved some sort of work as a nanny. Perhaps this work was agreed upon in lieu of a fee or rent, since this was clearly a private household rather than a rest home or sanitarium. In May Lovecraft writes to Lillian: "She is holding out well at Saratoga; & though her last small hat venture did not succeed, is still looking about for better openings . . ."[10] I do not know what this hat venture was.

Sonia spent another extended period in June and July in Brooklyn. In mid-July she secured some sort of position with a hat shop or department store in Cleveland, leaving on the 24th and settling at a boarding house at 2030 East 81st Street for $45 a month.[11] In late August she moved to 1912 East 86th Street.[12] By mid-October, however, Sonia had again either lost or given up this position; Lovecraft reported: "The trouble with the new position is that it is only on a commission basis, so that during slack seasons the remuneration is next to nothing."[13] By mid-November at the latest, and probably somewhat earlier, Sonia had secured a new position, this time with Halle's, then (and, up to 1982, when it went out of business) the leading department store in Cleveland.[14] This position appears to have lasted well into 1926.

The upshot of all this is that Sonia was at 169 Clinton Street for a total of only 89 days of 1925, on nine different occasions as follows:

> January 11–16
> February 3–6
> February 23–March 19
> April 8–11
> May 2–5
> June 9–July 24
> August 15–20
> September 16–17
> October 16–18

She had wanted to come during the Christmas holidays, but evidently work at Halle's was too heavy to permit it. In the three and a half months that Lovecraft spent in Brooklyn in 1926, Sonia was there for a period of about three weeks, from roughly January 15 to February 5. In other words, for the fifteen and a half months of Lovecraft's stay at 169 Clinton Street in 1925–26, Sonia was present for a net total of just over three months at widely scattered intervals; the six weeks in June and July constituted the longest single visit.

If Sonia's record of employment during this period was chequered, Lovecraft's was completely hopeless. There is, in either the "Diary" of 1925 or the

160,000 words of correspondence to Lillian for 1925–26, only three references to looking through the Sunday *Times* want ads for work (in March, July, and September); none of these came to anything. It is evident that, with Sonia effectively out of the way, Lovecraft simply stopped looking very vigorously for work. I am not sure there is anything to criticise in this: many individuals who suffer prolonged unemployment become discouraged, and, in spite of the clumsiness and inexperience with which Lovecraft tried to find work in 1924, he did make the attempt with determination and zeal.

Lovecraft's job attempts in 1925 were largely a product of various tips he received from his friends. The one that seemed most promising was freelance work on a trade journal in which Arthur Leeds was involved with another man named Yesley. Lovecraft describes the nature of the project to Lillian in late May:

> The work in this Yesley establishment is simple, consisting wholly of writing up complimentary articles descriptive of striking business ventures or outstanding mercantile and professional personalities; each article to be about 1¼ to 1½ double-spaced typed pages in length. This writing is all from facts supplied— "leads", as they call them, culled from press notices or advertising matter.... [The] article, when done, is sent to the office; & unless too bad to be accepted is taken out by a trained salesman to the person or company whereof it treats. This salesman, after giving the interested party a chance to revise, urges the latter to order a quantity of the magazines mentioning him—for advertising purposes; & if he succeeds, (as he does in a surprising number of cases, since the sales force is a very expert one) the writer of the article receives 10% of the sum paid by the purchaser—amounts varying from $1.50 to over $30.00 according to the extent of the order.[15]

This does not exactly sound like work for which Lovecraft would be suited, but all it really takes is facility at writing, which he certainly had. Difficult as it may be to imagine Lovecraft writing advertising copy, we have the evidence in front of us in the form of five such pieces found among his effects (evidently unpublished). R. H. Barlow bestowed upon them the generic title of "Commercial Blurbs." The five items are titled as follows: "Beauty in Crystal" (about the "Steuben Glass" produced by the Corning Glass Works, Corning, New York); "The Charm of Fine Woodwork" (about the furniture made by the Curtis Companies, Clifton, Iowa); "Personality in Clocks" (about grandfather clocks from the Colonial Manufacturing Company, Zealand, Michigan); "A Real Colonial Heritage" (about the "Danersk" furniture made by the Erskine-Danforth Corporation in New York City); and "A True Home of Literature" (about the Alexander Hamilton Bookshop in Paterson, New Jersey). One extract will suffice:

> Curtis Woodwork embraces both the usual structural units and the cleverest contrivances of built-in or permanent furniture, such as bookcases, dressers, buf-

fets, and cupboards. Every model is conceived and created with the purest art, ripest scholarship, and mellowest craftsmanship which energetic enterprise can command; and made to conform rigidly to the architecture of each particular type of home. The cost, considering the quality, is amazingly low; and a trademark on the individual pieces prevents any substitution by careless contractors.

And so on. Those who have read these pieces have predictably subjected them to the same withering scorn that they have directed toward Lovecraft's application letter of 1924; but styles of advertising were very different seventy years ago, especially when dealing with the type of material Lovecraft was treating here. Many of these firms were clearly making an appeal to the pseudo-aristocratic tastes of the middle class, and Lovecraft's lofty tone would have been in keeping with this approach.

But, sadly, the venture did not pan out, and through no fault of Lovecraft's. By late July he was already reporting that the project is in difficulties, and it must have definitively collapsed shortly thereafter, for we hear nothing more of it. Lovecraft stated that both he and Long (who, along with Loveman, had attempted the work on a freelance or commission basis) would be paid for their articles, but it is doubtful whether they were.

In February Morton secured his position with the Paterson Museum; it would last the rest of his life. By mid-July Lovecraft was talking about the possibility that Morton might hire him as an assistant, and this rather dim prospect continued to be bruited about sporadically all the way up to Lovecraft's departure from New York in April 1926. The problem rested not with Lovecraft's lack of expert knowledge of natural history—Morton himself had had to do a considerable amount of last-minute boning up to pass an examination for the position—but rather with the fact that the trustees were not then in a position to expand the museum's functions or staff. The museum was at the time housed in a stable near the public library, and the trustees were impatiently waiting for the death of the aged occupant of a house adjoining the stable so that they could tear down both structures and erect an entirely new museum building on the spot; before all this could happen, no thought of increasing staff would be possible, and the matter failed to be resolved during Lovecraft's entire stay. After visiting Paterson in late August Lovecraft felt much less regret about the delay.

There was, of course, money trickling in from *Weird Tales*. Lovecraft had five stories published in the magazine in 1925 (as well as his revision of C. M. Eddy's "Deaf, Dumb, and Blind" [April 1925], for which he presumably received nothing). We know the amounts received for three of these: $35 for "The Festival" (January), $25 for "The Unnamable" (July), and $50 for "The Temple" (September); we do not know the amounts for the other two ("The Statement of Randolph Carter" [February] and "The Music of Erich Zann" [May]), but they each probably averaged in the $30 range. All these stories, of course, had been written years before and most had presumably been submitted in late 1924 or early 1925. In any case, these five sales make a rough total of $170 for the year—barely equivalent to four months' rent.

Where was the other money—for food, laundry, modest travel, clothing, household items, and of course the other eight months' rent—coming from? Clearly Sonia was largely supporting him, and his aunts were contributing as best they could. Sonia, however, spoke very bitterly on this subject in a letter to Samuel Loveman:

> When we lived at 259 Parkside, his aunts sent him five dollars ($5) a week. They expected me to support him. When he moved to Clinton St., they sent him $15 a week. His rent was $40 a month. Food, carfare, and laundry and writing materials cost more than $5 a week. It was this "more" that I supplied. And when I came into town to do the firm's buying, every two weeks, I paid all his expenses during those trips and for his entertainment also. And when I'd leave, I always left a generous sum with him . . .[16]

There is a similar passage in her memoir, written not only (as Sonia explicitly declares) to correct W. Paul Cook's account (he had written: "His income was almost nil, he was reduced to about twenty cents a day for food—and he usually spent that for stamps"[17]), but, implicitly, to rebuke his aunts posthumously for their lack of monetary support. And yet, Sonia has herself exaggerated a little. Lovecraft did ask for (and presumably received) $75 from Annie Gamwell for expenses during the month of December 1924, including moving;[18] and the phrasing of this letter suggests that this was by no means the first time such a request was made. A casual reference in a late February letter to Annie to "the ever-punctual cheques"[19] suggests that Annie, if not actually supplying the money, at least was the money manager for Lovecraft and perhaps for Lillian also. During Sonia's stay in Saratoga Springs in the spring, Lovecraft confessed to Lillian that "She cannot, of course, contribute her originally agreed quota to the rent," although he added that she was sending small amounts—varying from $2 to $5— whenever she could.[20] Lovecraft frequently acknowledged receipt of (mostly unspecified) sums from Lillian, and Annie was paying for his daily subscription to the *Providence Evening Bulletin*. In other words, there is every reason to believe that the aunts were contributing as best they could, although no doubt Sonia was still bearing the lion's share of Lovecraft's expenses.

How much could this amount have been? Rent was $40 per month; but in October Lovecraft's landlady, Mrs Burns, decided that tenants should now pay $10 per week, a net increase of about $3 per month. If we assume that this new rate went into effect by November 1, then Lovecraft's total rent for the year was $490. Around this time he stated that he was spending $5 per week for food (and perhaps other expenses),[21] making about $260 for the year. If we figure in at least $20 per month for additional expenses ($240 for the year), we find a total of $990 for the entire year, of which I cannot imagine that Lovecraft himself contributed much more than $250 ($170 from *Weird Tales* plus $74.16 from the mortgage payments of Mariano de Magistris), leaving about $750 to be supplied by Sonia and the aunts. I do not think the aunts could have contributed a full $15 a week, for Lovecraft would not have had to economise as he did; Sonia, not being around very much, could have had no first-hand knowledge of the matter. The aunts themselves, of course, were merely living off their own inheritance from Whipple Phillips, so I think Sonia is a little unfair in criticising them for their apparent lack of generosity.

The absence of remunerative work, of course, simply left Lovecraft that much more time to hang around with his friends. The year 1925 is the real pinnacle of the Kalem Club. Lovecraft and Kirk continued to be close; although Kirk was nominally employed as the owner of a bookstore, he could essentially set his own hours, and so made very congenial company for Lovecraft the night owl. An incident in January is typical. After putting Sonia on the train to Cincinnati on the afternoon of the 16th, Lovecraft went to Loveman's room (he had a key) and fixed it up with some presents Long had bought as a belated birthday gift; he returned home to receive the gang for their customary meeting, and then all hands went over to Loveman's to unveil the surprise. Later that night Lovecraft went to Kirk's apartment at 106th Street, where the two slept in their clothes before venturing out the next morning to fix up Kirk's room in a similar manner. Only a few days later, on the 20th, Kirk decided to move into Lovecraft's own boarding house at 169 Clinton Street, in the apartment directly above his. That evening Lovecraft and Kirk went back to Kirk's old room, dismantled it, and retired around 5 A.M. The next morning they finished packing, and the next day Kirk moved in. For a while Loveman considered moving into the building, but ultimately decided against it.

There is scarcely a day in the entire year when Lovecraft did not meet with one or the other of his friends—either as they came over to his place or as they met at various cafeterias in Manhattan or Brooklyn or at the formal Wednesday meetings, which still alternated between McNeil and Leeds gatherings because of the ongoing unresolved dispute between these two individuals. So much for Lovecraft the "eccentric recluse"! Indeed, so busy was he with these social obligations—as well as apparently voluminous correspondence relating to the UAPA—that he wrote almost nothing during the first seven months of the year save a handful of poems, and many of these were written to order for meetings of the Blue Pencil Club.

Kirk wrote to his fiancée on February 6 about the actual naming of the club: "Because all of the last names of the permanent members of our club begin with K, L or M, we plan to call it the KALEM KLYBB. Half a dozen friends are to be here tonight. Mostly they're bores. All but me and HPL . . ."[22] Kleiner, in an essay written a decade later, had a somewhat different account of the name: "'Kalem' was based upon the letters K, L, and M, which happened to be the initial letters in the names of the original group—McNeil, Long, and the writer—and of those who joined during the first six months of the club."[23] Whatever the case, I wonder whether the exact form of the name had anything to do with an old film company of 1905 called Kalem, formed on exactly the same principle by George Kleine, Samuel Long, and Frank Marion.[24] It is possible that one or more of the members subconsciously recollected this name in forming the name of their club. One wonders also when exactly this name was created. There was a large meeting on February 3 at the Milan restaurant (Eighth Avenue and 42nd Street), including Sonia, C. M. Eddy (who was in town for a few days), and Lillian (who, after leaving New York on January 10, had evidently spent some weeks with friends in Westchester County before returning to the city for a week beginning January 28), as well as Kirk, Kleiner, and Loveman; but this does not appear to have been a gang meeting, since Lovecraft much later announced that the gang had a "stag rule"[25] so that women were not allowed. The strange thing is that Lovecraft never refers to the group as the Kalems in the correspondence of this period, citing it merely as "the gang" or "The Boys."

Lovecraft at first did make the attempt to spend time with Sonia on her infrequent visits into town: he noted that he skipped a meeting of the Boys on February 4 because she was not feeling well.[26] But as time went on—and especially during Sonia's long stay in June and July—he became a little less conscientious. Even during her stay in February–March Lovecraft would stay out so late that he would come home well after Sonia was asleep and wake up late in the morning (or even early in the afternoon) to find that she had already gone out. Letters to the aunts for this period are scarce, so it is sometimes difficult to tell from the "Diary" what exactly is the state of affairs; but on March 1 there is the indication that after a gang meeting at Kirk's room some of the members went to the Scotch Bakery (only a block or two away), after which Kirk and Lovecraft came back to Kirk's room and talked till dawn. On the 10th Lovecraft and Kirk (without Sonia) visited Elizabeth, returning via Perth Amboy and Tottenville, Staten Island. The next day, after the regular Kalem meeting at Long's, Lovecraft and Kirk talked in the latter's room till 5.30 A.M.

The one thing Lovecraft could do during Sonia's absence is control his eating habits. He told Moe that after passing 193 pounds he refused to mount a pair of scales again; but in January his reducing plan began in earnest. The upshot is that in a few months Lovecraft went from close to 200 pounds to 146; from a 16 collar to 14½. All his suits had to be retailored, and each week he bought smaller and smaller collars. As Lovecraft put it:

> How the pounds flew! I helped the course along by exercise and outdoor walks, and everytime my friends saw me they were either pleased or frightened at the startling shrinkage. Fortunately I had not been fat for so many years that the skin must needs suffer radical distension. Instead, it shrunk neatly along with the tissue beneath, leaving a firm surface and simply restoring the lost outlines of 1915 and before. . . . It was dramatic—breathless—sensational—this reclamation of a decade-lost statue from the vile mud which had so long encrusted it.

What was the reaction by his friends, family, and wife?

> As you may imagine, my wife protested fearfully at what seemed an alarming decline. I received long scolding letters from my aunts, and was lectured severely by Mrs. Long every time I went up to see Little Belknap. But I knew what I was doing, and kept on like grim death. . . . I now publickly avow my personal mastery of my diet, and do not permit my wife to feed me in excess of it.[27]

Lovecraft's letters to his aunts elaborate considerably upon this account. It is, as I have stated before, very unfortunate that we do not possess a single scrap of correspondence from Lillian and only a few insignificant bits from Annie, even though it is abundantly evident from Lovecraft's responses that Lillian at least was writing fairly frequently. The topic of food does come up in late spring and early summer. Lovecraft writes:

> Diet & walking are the stuff—which reminds me that tonight I've begun my home dining programme, having spent *30¢* for a lot of food which ought to last about *3* meals:

$$\begin{array}{lr} \text{1 loaf bread} & 0.06 \\ \text{1 medium can beans} & 0.14 \\ \text{¼ lb cheese} & 0.10 \\ \hline \text{Total} & 0.30^{28} \end{array}$$

Lovecraft seems to have written the above in an effort to prove his skill at economising during lean times, and he no doubt expected to be praised for his frugality; but his next letter suggests that the response was very different:

> As to my dietary programme—bosh! I *am* eating enough! Just you take a medium-sized loaf of bread, cut it in four equal parts, & add to each of these ¼

can (medium) Heinz beans & a goodly chunk of cheese. If the result isn't a full-sized, healthy day's quota of fodder for an Old Gentleman, I'll resign from the League of Nations' dietary committee!! It only costs 8¢—but don't let that prejudice you! It's good sound food, & many vigorous Chinamen live on vastly less. Of course, from time to time I'll vary the "meat course" by getting something instead of beans—canned spaghetti, beef stew, corned beef, &c. &c. &c.—& once in a while I'll add a dessert of cookies or some such thing. Fruit, also, is conceivable.[29]

This is surely one of the most remarkable passages in all Lovecraft's correspondence. It suggests many things at once—the crippling poverty under which he was at this time living (and, although under somewhat less straitened circumstances, he would continue to live for the rest of his life, even back in Providence); the fact that he had largely abandoned restaurant meals, even at places like the automats, in the interest of economy; and the rather schoolboyish tone of the entire passage, as if he were a teenager attempting to justify his behaviour to his parents. The matter comes up for discussion again later on in the same letter, after Lovecraft had received another letter from Lillian:

> Great God! if you could see the engulfing plethora of needless nutriment which S H has been stuffing down me during her sojourn here!! Twice a day to—& beyond—my capacity; pressed beef, sliced ham, bread, American & swiss cheese, cake, lemonade, buns, cup puddings, (of her own manufacture . . .), &c. &c. &c.—indeed, I'll be shot if I don't wonder how in Pegāna's name I can get on my new 15 collars any more!

And so on.

And yet, in one sense Lovecraft's diet was being varied by experimentation with novel cuisines, either at restaurants with Sonia or on solitary excursions. Sonia took him to a Chinese restaurant in early July (probably not for the first time), although they had the disappointingly conventional chow mein.[30] In late August he sampled minestrone soup for the first time, liking it so much that on many subsequent occasions he would go to the Milan in Manhattan and make a meal of a huge tureen of minestrone for 15¢.[31] Around this time Lovecraft announced that his diet has become "prodigiously Italianised," but was quick to reassure Lillian that this is all to the good from the standpoint of health: ". . . I never order anything but spaghetti & minestrone except when those are not to be had—& they really contain an almost ideal balance of active nutritive elements, considering the wheaten base of spaghetti, the abundant vitamines in tomato sauce, the assorted vegetables in minestrone, & the profusion of powdered cheese common to both."[32]

There is, however, one depressing note in all this. In October Lovecraft was forced to buy an oil heater for the winter, since the heat provided by Mrs

Burns—especially in the wake of a nationwide coal strike organised by the United Mine Workers and lasting from September 1925 to February 1926—was quite insufficient. The heater came with a stove-top attachment, so that Lovecraft could now indulge in the high luxury of "the preparation of *hot dinners*. No more cold beans & spaghetti for me . . ."[33] Does this mean that, for the first nine and a half months of the year, Lovecraft was eating cold meals, mostly out of cans? In spite of an earlier remark about heating beans on a "sterno"[34] (a tin of a waxlike flammable substance), this seems to be a dismal probability—else why would he boast about the prospect of hot dinners?

The room at 169 Clinton Street really was rather dismal—in a run-down neighbourhood, with a dubious clientele, and infested with mice. For this last problem Lovecraft purchased 5¢ mousetraps, as recommended by Kirk, "since I can throw them away without removing the corpus delicti, a thing I should hate to do with a costlier bit of mechanism."[35] (Later he found even cheaper traps at two for 5¢.) Lovecraft has been ridiculed for this squeamishness, but I think unjustly. Not many of us are fond of handling the corpses of mice or any other pests. In his diary the mice are described as "invaders" or abbreviated as "inv." In September the light fixture in his washing alcove needed repairing, but Mrs Burns refused to fix it. Lovecraft expressed great irritation at this, noting that "I can't bathe myself, wash dishes, or black my boots in any comfort with only the feeble rays of outside illumination filtering in."[36] This situation dragged on into 1926, when—during Sonia's visit in mid-January—an electrician from a nearby appliance shop finally made the repairs. Perhaps this is another indication of Lovecraft's inability to deal with practical matters; but Mrs Burns had told him that a man from the Edison Co. would charge fabulous rates merely for inspecting the fixture, so perhaps this caused Lovecraft to delay until Sonia could deal definitively with the situation.

The final insult came on the morning of Sunday, May 24, when, while Lovecraft was sleeping on the couch after an all-night writing session, his dressing alcove was broken into from the connecting apartment and he was robbed of nearly all his suits, along with sundry other abstractions. The thieves had rented the adjoining apartment and, finding that the lock on the door leading into Lovecraft's alcove had no bolt, broke in and removed three of his suits (dating from 1914, 1921, and 1923), one overcoat (the fashionable 1924 coat that Sonia had purchased for him), a wicker suitcase of Sonia's (although the contents were later found in the thieves' apartment, which they had vacated without paying rent), and an expensive $100 radio set that Loveman had been storing in the alcove. All that Lovecraft was left with, in terms of suits, was a thin 1918 blue suit hanging on a chair in the main room, which the thieves did not enter. Lovecraft did not discover the robbery until 1.30 A.M. on Tuesday the 26th, since he had had no previous occasion to enter the alcove. His reaction was what one might have expected:

> I can't yet accustom myself to the shock—to the grim truth that I haven't a suit of clothes to my back save the thin, blue summer one. What I shall ever do if the property isn't recovered, Heaven alone knows!
> ... I could curse the atmosphere blue! Just as I had decided to try to look more respectable by keeping my clothes in good order, here comes this blasted, infernal thunderbolt to deprive me of the battery of four suits and one really decent overcoat needed as a minimum of neat appearance! To Hades with everything![37]

Of course, the property never was recovered, although a police detective came over and promised to do his best. And yet, Lovecraft managed to respond to the whole situation with surprising good humour, for only two days later he wrote a long letter to Lillian on the matter and in the process made light of the situation:

> Alas for the robes of my infancy, perennial in their bloom, & now cut off—or snatched off—in the finest flowering of their first few decades! They knew the slender youth of old, & expanded to accomodate [*sic*] the portly citizen of middle life—aye, & condensed again to shroud the wizened shanks of old age! And now they are gone—gone—& the grey, bent wearer still lives to bemoan his nudity; gathering around his lean sides as best he may the strands of his long white beard to serve him in the office of a garment![38]

Accompanying this mock-lament is a hilarious drawing of Lovecraft, wearing nothing but a belt around his own knee-length hair and beard, standing in front of a clothing store with suits priced at $35 and $45 and a placard in the window with the plea, "I want my clothes!" The mention of "the robes of my infancy" refers to Lovecraft's habit of keeping his suits and coats for years or even decades—he notes that among the pieces not taken was a 1909 light overcoat, a 1915 winter overcoat, and a 1917 light overcoat, along with sundry hats, gloves, shoes, etc. (not dated).

What now transpired was a five-month hunt for the cheapest but most tasteful suits Lovecraft could endure to wear, in the process of which he gained a considerable knowledge of discount clothing stores and even the rudiments of haggling. Lovecraft could not feel comfortable without four suits—two light and two dark, one each for summer and winter. He really did not think it possible—based on conversations with Long, Leeds, and others—to get a good suit for under $35, but he was going to make the effort. In early July, when Sonia was in town, he saw a sign in the shop of Monroe Clothes, a chain store, that intrigued him, and he managed to find a grey suit of sufficiently conservative cast for $25. "The suit in general," he remarked, "has a certain pleasing resemblance to my very first long-trouser outfit, purchased at Browning & King's in April 1904."[39]

This was a summer suit, and Lovecraft began wearing it immediately. In October he decided to buy a heavy suit for winter, since the weather was turning colder. This, he knew, would be a considerably more difficult proposition, for really good winter suits can rarely be secured at bargain prices. Moveover, Lovecraft had two absolute requirements for suits: they had to be entirely without pattern, and they had to have three buttons, in spite of the fact that the top button (usually under the lapel) is never used. To his dismay he found, on his weary peregrinations, that "In this age of well-heated houses men have stopped wearing the heavy clothing they used to wear . . . so that the unhappy victim of a menage in which the name *Burns* applies to the family instead of the fuel is very literally left out in the cold!"[40] The fabrics Lovecraft examined, both at Monroe's and at other stores, were scarcely heavier than those of his summer suit; and patternless three-button coats were simply not to be found. Lovecraft had learned to be scrupulous in his assessment of cloth and cut: "Anything under about $35.00 was either thin & slimpsy, [*sic*] or sportily cut, or of undesirable pattern, or of abominable texture & workmanship. . . . Fabricks seemed hewn with a blunt axe or hacked by a blind man with dull shears!"[41]

Finally he seemed to come across just what he wanted—except that the coat only had two buttons. This was at the Borough Clothiers in Fulton Street in Brooklyn. Lovecraft was shrewd in dealing with the salesman: he said that he really wanted only a provisional suit until he could get a better one, therefore implying that he might buy another suit from the place later (not mentioning that it might be more than a year before he did so); the salesman, accordingly, consulted with a superior and showed him a more expensive suit but priced it at only $25. Lovecraft, putting the thing on, found that it "vastly delighted me," but the absence of the third button gave him pause. He told the salesman to hold the suit while he checked more shops. The salesman told Lovecraft that it was unlikely he could get a better deal anywhere else, and after examinations of several more stores Lovecraft found that this was the case; he went back to Borough Clothiers and bought the suit for $25.

The long letter in which Lovecraft narrates this entire episode to Lillian certainly betrays more than a few indications of what would now be called obsessive-compulsive behaviour. The repeated emphasis on a three-button suit begins to sound almost manic; and when Lovecraft later found that the tailor who completed the alterations to the suit did not preserve the remnants (which Lovecraft wished to send to Lillian so that she could gauge the fineness of the material), he vowed to send the entire coat of the suit by express. Lillian clearly said no to this, eliciting the following complaint on Lovecraft's part:

> . . . hang it all, but *how* am I to let you know *just* what I've got? It is the precise *texture* I wish you to see—the smooth yet not hard surface, the well-bred dark-

ness of a patternless mixture wherein light & dark grey threads are made to fuse aristocratically to an homogeneous whole in which the diversity of 'pepper-&-saltness' is only faintly suggested as the eye strives to judge whether the fabrick is black, navy-blue, or very dark grey.[42]

Lovecraft took to calling this suit "the triumph." But he quickly came to the conclusion that he would need to buy a cheap winter suit in order not to wear out the good one, so in late October he undertook yet another long quest for a suit under $15 for everyday wear. The first place Lovecraft went was the row of stores on 14th Street between Sixth and Seventh Avenues in Manhattan, then (as now) the haven of discount clothing in the city. What he found, after trying "a dozen coats of varying degrees of impossibility," was a coat that was "a limp rag; crushed, dusty, twisted, & out-of-press, but I saw that cut, fabric, & fit were just right." It was part of a $9.95 sale; but the problem was that there was no exactly matching set of trousers. All that was left was one trouser that was too long and two that were too short. The salesman was trying to get Lovecraft to accept the short trousers, but Lovecraft wanted the long one; after considerable haggling he persuaded the salesman to sell him the coat, the long trousers, and one of the short trousers, all for $11.95. This was all pretty clever on Lovecraft's part, and a tailor repaired the coat and trousers the next day. This entire adventure, too, is narrated in a long and quite poignant letter to Lillian; in the course of which he indulges in a long tirade on the subject:

> . . . in general I think I have developed an eye for the difference between the clothing a gentleman wears & that which a gentleman doesn't. What has sharpened this sense is the constant sight of these accursed filthy rabbles that infest the N.Y. streets, & whose clothing presents such systematic differences from the normal clothing of real people along Angell St. & in Butler Ave. or Elmgrove Ave. cars that he comes to feel a tremendous homesickness & to pounce avidly on any gentleman whose clothes are proper & tasteful & suggestive of Blackstone Boulevard rather than Borough Hall or Hell's Kitchen. . . . Confound it, I'll be either in good Providence taste or in a bally bathrobe!! Certain lapel cuts, textures, & fits tell the story. It amuses me to see how some of these flashy young 'boobs' & foreigners spend fortunes on various kinds of expensive clothes which they regard as evidences of meritorious taste, but which in reality are their absolute social & aesthetic damnation—being little short of placards shrieking in bold letters: *"I am an ignorant peasant", "I am a mongrel gutter-rat",* or *"I am a tasteless & unsophisticated yokel."*

To which he added, with complete ingenuousness, "And yet perhaps these creatures are not, after all, seeking to conform to the absolute artistic standard of gentlefolk."[43] This remarkable passage—testifying to Lovecraft's inability to dissoci-

ate himself from the codes of attire and general social behaviour inculcated in him
in youth—goes on to say, rather touchingly:

> In my prime I could never have gotten so excited over clothes, but exile & old
> age make trifles dear to me. With my nervous hatred of slovenly & plebeian
> dressing, & after the maddening robbery which threatened to reduce *me* to ex-
> actly the thing I hate, you'll admit that apparel became very legitimately a
> "touchy" subject with me till such a time as I might again possess the four suits
> necessary for balanced dressing both in summer & in winter.

But now Lovecraft had his four suits, and he need think no more about the matter. All his letters are not quite as maniacal as this; he could still keep his good
humour even in the face of poverty and deprivation. He spoke in late August
about his shoes—"the good old Regals are about on the brink of spectacular disintegration"[44]—and then noted with satisfaction that the new Regal 2021 shoes
he secured in late October were a "veritable knockout"[45] at the next Kalem meeting.

Not having a job at least meant that Lovecraft could go out with the boys at almost any time and also indulge in modest travels. His diary and letters are full of
accounts of trips to Van Cortlandt Park, Fort Greene Park, Yonkers, and elsewhere; there were the usual walks through the colonial parts of Greenwich Village, and any number of walks across the Brooklyn Bridge. Here is how Lovecraft spent a few days in early April:

> I duly went [to Long's], had an excellent lunch, heard a fine new story & prose-
> poem of his, & later accompanied him & his mamma to the cinema at 95th St.,
> where we saw that much discussed German film, "The Last Laugh". . . . After
> the show I returned home, read, & retired; rising later the next day & cleaning
> my room in preparation for the Boys' meeting. Mortonius was the first to arrive,
> then Kleiner & Loveman together, & finally Leeds. Sonny couldn't come—but
> Kirk sent a telegram of regret from New Haven. The meeting was brisk, but
> Morton had to leave early for the last Paterson train—Loveman departing with
> him. Next Kleiner went—after which Leeds & I went upstairs to look over
> Kirk's books & pictures. Leeds left at 3 a.m., & I joined him in coffee & apricot
> pie at Johnson's. Then home—read—rest—& another day.[46]

Kirk described a session with Lovecraft later in April:

> HPL visited me and read while I toiled over cards. He is now sleeping on the
> lounge with *The Ghost Girl* open before him—no compliment to Saltus. . . .
> HPL awoke—uttered "Avernus!" and went back to Nirvana. . . . About mid-
> night we went to Tiffany's restaurant where I had a beautiful shrimp salad and
> coffee while H had a slice of cheesecake and two coffees. We sat around for 1½
> hours over meal and the morning papers. . . .[47]

Each Kalem member's home was, apparently, always open to the others. Indeed, there is a strange entry in Lovecraft's diary for March 15–16, unexplained by any existing letter, in which Lovecraft and Long walked along the Gowanus Expressway near the waterfront and then went over to Loveman's apartment, at which point Lovecraft writes: "carry FBL upstairs." I don't imagine Long was overcome by alcohol or anything of the sort; probably he had become tired after the long walk.

On the night of April 11 Lovecraft and Kirk, wishing to take advantage of a special $5 excursion fare to Washington, D.C., boarded the night train at Pennsylvania Station at midnight and arrived at dawn in the capital. They would have only a single morning and afternoon in the city, so they intended to make the most of it. There were two colleagues who could act as tour guides, Anne Tillery Renshaw and Edward L. Sechrist; and Renshaw had very obligingly offered to drive the visitors around in her car where possible. Lovecraft, Kirk, and Sechrist first made a walking tour of the important landmarks in the city centre, noting the Library of Congress (which failed to impress Lovecraft), the Capitol (which he thought inferior to Rhode Island's great marble-domed State Capitol), the White House, the Washington Monument, the Lincoln Memorial, and all the rest. Renshaw then drove them to Georgetown, the colonial town founded in 1751, years before Washington was ever planned or built. Lovecraft found it very rich in colonial houses of all sorts. They then crossed the Key Memorial Bridge into Virginia, going through Arlington to Alexandria, entering the Christ Church, an exquisite late Georgian (1772–73) structure where Washington worshipped, and other old buildings in the city. After this, they proceeded south to Washington's home, Mount Vernon, although they could not enter because it was Sunday. They drove back to Arlington, where, near the national cemetery, was the residence called Arlington, the manor of the Custis family. They also explored the cemetery, in particular the enormous Memorial Amphitheatre completed in 1920, which Lovecraft considered "one of the most prodigious and spectacular architectural triumphs of the Western World."[48] Naturally, Lovecraft was transported by this structure because it reminded him of classical antiquity—it was based upon the Dionysiac Theatre in Athens—and because of its enormous size (it covers 34,000 square feet). They then came back to Washington, seeing as much as possible before catching the 4.35 train back to New York, including the Brick Capitol (1815) and the Supreme Court Building. They caught the train just in time.

But by mid-May this endless round of socialising was becoming a little wearying to Lovecraft. He had, indeed, done singularly little creative work during the first four months of the year: his output consisted merely of five poems, two of which—"My Favourite Character" (January 31) and "Primavera" (March 27)—

were written for Blue Pencil Club meetings, for which members were to produce literary compositions on a given topic. "My Favourite Character" is a witty light poem that examines the gamut of fictional characters, from the classics ("Esmond, D. Copperfield, or Hiawatha, / Or anything from some nice high-school author") to the daring ("Jurgen, Clerk Nicholas, Boccaccio's misses, / And sundry things of Joyce's, from *Ulysses*") to childhood favourites ("Boyhood's own idols, whom the sages hear not— / Frank Merriwell, Nick Carter, and Fred Fearnot!"), and finally concludes:

> Now as for me, I am no man of learning
> To know just what I like and why I like it;
> Letters and hist'ry set my poor head turning
> Till not a choice can permanently strike it!
> My fav'rite? Fie on printed information—
> I'll frankly hand myself the nomination!

This is, to be sure, a weird anticipation of the future, for Lovecraft himself has indeed become a character in fiction. "Primavera," on the other hand, is a pensive nature poem that finds both wonder and horror in the non-human world:

> There are whispers from groves auroral
> To blood half-afraid to hear,
> While the evening star's faint choral
> Is an ecstasy touch'd with fear.
> And at night where the hill-wraiths rally
> Glows the far Walpurgis flame,
> Which the lonely swain in the valley
> Beholds, tho' he dare not name.

Of the other three poems, two are insignificant: there is the usual birthday poem to Jonathan E. Hoag, written this year only one day before Hoag's birthday on February 10, and an equally frivolous birthday poem to Sonia, "To Xanthippe" (March 16). This nickname is of some interest, and Sonia explains its origin: "The nomenclature of 'Socrates and Xantippe' [*sic*] was originated by me because as time marched on and our correspondence became more intimate, I either *saw* in Howard or endowed him with a Socratic wisdom and genius, so that in a jocular vein I subscribed myself as Xantippe."[49] Lovecraft may or may not have had Socratic wisdom; but Sonia evidently did not know that Xanthippe had a reputation in antiquity of being a shrew, hence is hardly a nickname someone ought to have chosen by design.

The final poem, "The Cats" (February 15), is an entirely different proposition. This daemoniac six-stanza poem in quatrains is one of his most effective weird verses—a wild, uncontrolled spasm bringing out all the shuddersome mystery of the feline species:

> Legions of cats from the alleys nocturnal,
>> Howling and lean in the glare of the moon,
> Screaming the future with mouthings infernal,
>> Yelling the burden of Pluto's red rune.

It is, incidentally, good to see Lovecraft avoiding the stereotyped heroic couplet in all these poems.

But that is the extent of Lovecraft's work as fiction writer, poet, and even essayist; and clearly he felt that the time had come to put a halt on what he called "the daily dropping-in and cafeteria loafing" to which he was so fatally tempted by the presence of so many of his friends in the city, but which he knew was "death to any personal intellectual life or creative accomplishment."[50] Accordingly, Lovecraft took to reading in the dressing alcove, leaving the light in the main room off so that he could pretend to be out if anyone came over. In many cases he knew that this skullduggery would not succeed: he and Kirk had set up a charming method of communication by banging on the radiator pipes, and there were times when Kirk knew Lovecraft was home, so that he would have to respond to the signal. But Lovecraft also adopted the stratagem of receiving visitors in his dressing-gown, with the bed unfolded, or with papers and manuscripts scattered all about, to discourage endless lounging around in his room. He would not cut out the weekly gang meetings yet, for this would seem too unusual, and in any case he really enjoyed them.

Lovecraft reported this resolve in a letter to Lillian of May 20. The robbery of May 25 augmented his efforts to some degree, if only because he now had only one decent suit to his name and had to be careful not to wear it out. But after a month or so his resolve appears—if the diary is any guide—to have weakened, and he is out gallivanting with the boys as much as before.

Amateur affairs were not quite over. The lack of a convention and election in 1924 meant that the existing editorial board continued in office by default, so that Lovecraft remained Official Editor. One thing he did during Sonia's long stay in June and July was to put together the July 1925 *United Amateur*—the only issue for the 1924–25 term. This, he knew, would be his farewell to the UAPA—and, indeed, his farewell to organised amateurdom in general until he was lured back into the affairs of the NAPA in the early 1930s—and he wished to go out in style. On June 4–6 he wrote an insubstantial and flattering essay, "The Poetry of John Ravenor Bullen," on the Anglo-Canadian poet and novelist who may or may not have introduced him to the Transatlantic Circulator in 1920, although this piece appeared only in the next issue of the *United Amateur* (September 1925). The July 1925 issue is full of contributions by the gang: Clark Ashton Smith's poem "Apologia"; a brief essay by Frank Long on Samuel Loveman's poetry, "Pirates and Hamadry-ades"; a review of two of Smith's books of poetry by Alfred Galpin (under the Consul Hasting pseudonym); two poems by Long, one of which, "A Man from Genoa," would be the title poem of his collection published early the next year; Samuel Loveman's delicate brief tale, "The One Who Found Pity"; and the usual "News Notes" (by Lovecraft), "Editorial" (by Lovecraft), and "President's Message" (by Sonia).

In some senses the "President's Message" is the most interesting of these, at least biographically. The piece is dated June 16, but as this is the very day on which (according to Lovecraft's diary) the issue was sent to the printer, it may have been written a day or two earlier. Sonia openly speaks of her difficulties during the official year:

> Outside responsibilities of unexpected magnitude, together with a failing health which culminated in my autumn sojourn at the Brooklyn Hospital, cut me off hopelessly from amateur work during the summer of 1924; a disastrous inter-regnum whose effects proved too profound to be shaken off during the balance of the year, especially since my energy and leisure have even since then been but fractional.

Both Sonia and Lovecraft in his "Editorial" spoke of the apathy overtaking all amateurdom and the frequent talk of consolidating the UAPA and NAPA for the sake of preserving the amateur movement; and both felt that this should be done only as a last resort, and that the UAPA ought to maintain a separate existence if at all possible. To that end, Sonia declared that a mail election would be held on July 15, with the ballots to be sent out shortly. Sure enough, Lovecraft wrote to Lillian that on July 3 he folded, addressed, and mailed the entire lot of 200 ballots.[51]

The results of the election were as follows: Edgar J. Davis, President; Paul Livingston Keil, First Vice-President; Grace M. Bromley, Second Vice-President. Davis appointed Victor E. Bacon Official Editor and (no doubt with additional cajoling from Lovecraft) Frank Long as chairman of the Department of Public Criticism. Lovecraft, hoping against hope, wrote to Moe that the Davis-Bacon tandem might somehow save the UAPA at the last moment:

> Don't you think there's a half-chance for the United to come back with two such cherubs as its leaders? With Davis's brains, & Bacon's restless egotism & energy to prod those brains into action, we certainly have a team whose possibilities are not to be sneez'd at. . . . [Bacon] stands a chance of rousing & getting together

enough surviving "live ones" to resist the decadent tendencies of the age . . .; so that we may be able to postpone hiring the mortician for a year or two more.[52]

Lovecraft accordingly spent the next several months attempting to get the board off the ground, but with indifferent success: a few slim issues of the *United Amateur* were indeed produced during 1925–26, but so far as I can tell no election was held in 1926, causing the association definitively to fold. I do not know how many other amateur journals were produced in this term; certainly Lovecraft had no intention of reviving his *Conservative,* even if he had had the finances to do so.

During Sonia's long stay Lovecraft did some travelling with her. The two of them went to Scott Park in Elizabeth on June 13. On the 28th they went to the Bryn Mawr Park section of Yonkers, where they had attempted to purchase the home lot the previous year; no account or explanation of this visit occurs in Lovecraft's letters to his aunts. His diary notes laconically: "charm still present." With Long, Lovecraft again visited the Cloisters in Fort Tryon Park, in the far northwest tip of Manhattan.

On July 2 Sonia and Lovecraft took a trip to Coney Island, where he had cotton candy for the first time. On this occasion Sonia had a silhouette of herself made by an African American named Perry; Lovecraft had had his own silhouette done on March 26. This silhouette has become very well known in recent years, and its very faithful (perhaps even a little flattering) rendition has caused Lovecraft's profile to become an icon; the silhouette of Sonia, on the other hand, is so little known that few have had any idea of its very existence.

On July 16 the couple took a hiking trip to the New Jersey Palisades—the wooded, hilly region directly facing northern Manhattan across the Hudson River. This proved a very pleasant outing:

> . . . we began the zigzag ascent of the majestic precipice by means of a winding route partly identical with the wagon road, partly a footpath through the verdant twilight of forest steeps, & partly a stone stairway which at one point tunnels under the road. The crest, which we attained in about a half-hour, commands the noblest possible view of the Hudson & its eastern shore; & along this we rambled—coming now on a patch of woods, now on a grassy pasture, & now on a chasm bordered by the jutting bed rock of the plateau itself.[53]

Lovecraft alternately read 5¢ Haldeman-Julius booklets and Stevenson's *Jekyll and Hyde.* They had lunch (tongue and cheese sandwiches and peaches, followed by ice cream and lemonade secured from a nearby pavilion), then returned home by ferry and subway.

Another thing Lovecraft and Sonia liked to do was to attend movies. Probably she was more interested in this form of entertainment than he was, but on occasion Lovecraft could become genuinely enthusiastic about a film that suited his tastes, either antiquarian or horrific. They were, of course, all silents at this time. In September he reports seeing *The Phantom of the Opera:*

> . . . what a spectacle it was!! It was about a *presence* haunting the great Paris opera house . . . but developed so slowly that I actually fell asleep several times during the first part. Then the second part began—horror lifted its grisly visage—& I could not have been made drowsy by all the opiates under heaven! Ugh!!! The *face* that was revealed when the mask was pulled off . . . & the nameless legion of *things* that cloudily appeared beside & behind the owner of that face when the mob chased him into the river at the last![54]

His diary records a viewing of *The Lost World* (an adaptation of the Conan Doyle novel) on October 6, but there is no corresponding letter testifying to his reaction to this remarkable film, a landmark in the use of special effects in its depiction of dinosaurs in South America. On a solitary outing Lovecraft saw a stirring documentary of whaling days in New Bedford, *Down to the Sea in Ships.* "The whole film is of inestimable historical value as a minute & authentic record of a dying yet gorgeously glamorous phase of American life & adventure."[55]

On July 24 Sonia returned to Cleveland, but she made Lovecraft promise to attend the Blue Pencil Club meeting in Brooklyn that evening. In the morning Lovecraft had written his literary contribution—the light verse "A Year Off," another fairly successful venture in *vers de société.* Lovecraft considers the possible choices for spending a year's vacation—"I'd look up ferries on the Nile, / And 'bus fares for the trip to Mecca"; "Arranging passage thro' Thibet / To dally with the Dalai Lama"—but concludes (somewhat predictably) that after this imaginative survey there is no need to go on the actual trip!

Now that Sonia was out of the way and his amateur work apparently finished, Lovecraft felt that the time had come to buckle down to some real creative work. On August 1 and 2 he wrote "The Horror at Red Hook," which he describes in a letter to Long (who was away on vacation) as follows: ". . . it deals with hideous cult-practices behind the gangs of noisy young loafers whose essential mystery has impressed me so much. The tale is rather long and rambling, and I don't think it is very good; but it represents at least an attempt to extract horror from an atmosphere to which you deny any qualities save vulgar commonplaceness."[56] Lovecraft is sadly correct in his analysis of the merits of the story, for it is one of the poorest of his longer efforts.

Red Hook is a small peninsula of Brooklyn facing Governor's Island, about two miles southwest of Borough Hall. Lovecraft could easily walk to the area from 169 Clinton Street, and indeed there is the laconic entry "Red Hook" in his diary for March 8, when he and Kleiner evidently strolled there. It was then and still remains one of the most dismal slums in the entire metropolitan area. In the story Lovecraft describes it not inaccurately, although with a certain jaundiced tartness:

> Red Hook is a maze of hybrid squalor near the ancient waterfront opposite Governor's Island, with dirty highways climbing the hill from the wharves to that higher ground where the decayed lengths of Clinton and Court Streets lead off toward the Borough Hall. Its houses are mostly of brick, dating from the first quarter of the middle of the nineteenth century, and some of the obscurer alleys and byways have that alluring antique flavour which conventional reading leads us to call "Dickensian".

Lovecraft is, indeed, being a little charitable (at least as far as present-day conditions are concerned), for I do not know of any quaint alleys there now. But of course it is not merely the physical decay that is of interest to him: "The population is a hopeless tangle and enigma; Syrian, Spanish, Italian, and negro elements impinging upon one another, and fragments of Scandinavian and American belts lying not far distant. It is a babel of sound and filth, and sends out strange cries to answer the lapping of oily waves at its grimy piers and the monstrous organ litanies of the harbour whistles." Here, in essence, is the heart of the story; for "The Horror at Red Hook" is nothing but a shriek of rage and loathing at the "foreigners" who have taken New York away from the white people to whom it presumably belongs. The mention of Syrians is interesting, and may perhaps relate to one of Lovecraft's neighbours at 169 Clinton, who played such strange music that it gave Lovecraft strange dreams; as he described it two years later, "once a *Syrian* had the room next to mine and played eldritch and whining monotones on a strange bagpipe which made me dream ghoulish and incredible things of crypts under Bagdad and limitless corridors of Eblis under the moon-cursed ruins of Istakhar."[57] One would think Lovecraft would be grateful for such imaginative stimulus, but he does not appear to have been.

Sonia in her memoir claims to supply the inspiration for the tale: "It was on an evening while he, and I think Morton, Sam Loveman and Rheinhart Kleiner were dining in a restaurant somewhere in Columbia Heights that a few rough, rowdyish men entered. He was so annoyed by their churlish behavior that out of this circumstance he wove 'The Horror at Red Hook.'"[58] Lovecraft may have mentioned this event in a letter to her; but I am not entirely convinced that it was any one incident that gave birth to the story, but rather the cumulative depression of New York after a year and a half of poverty and futility.

The plot of "The Horror at Red Hook" is simple, and is presented as an elementary good-vs.-evil conflict between Thomas Malone, an Irish police detective working out of the Borough Hall station, and Robert Suydam, a wealthy man of ancient Dutch ancestry who becomes the focus of horror in the tale. Suydam first attracts notice by "loitering on the benches around Borough Hall in conversation with groups of swarthy, evil-looking strangers." Later he realises that his clandestine activities must be masked by a façade of propriety; so he cleans up his act, foils the attempts of relatives to deem him legally incompetent by ceasing to be seen with those evil foreigners, and as a final coup marries Cornelia Gerritsen, "a young woman of excellent position" whose wedding attracts "a solid page from the Social Register." In all this there is a rather tart satire (entirely unintended by Lovecraft) on the meaninglessness of class distinctions. The wedding party following the ceremony, held aboard a steamer at the Cunard Pier, ends in horror as the couple are found horribly murdered and completely bloodless. Incredibly, officials follow the instructions written on a sheet of paper, signed by Suydam, and insouciantly hand his body over to a suspicious group of men headed by "an Arab with a hatefully negroid mouth."

From here the story takes a still more pulpish turn, and we are taken into the basement of a dilapidated church that has been turned into a dance-hall, where horrible rites to Lilith are being practised by loathsome monstrosities. The corpse of Suydam, miraculously revivified, resists being sacrificed to Lilith but instead somehow manages to overturn the pedestal on which she rests (with the result that the corpse sends "its noisome bulk floundering to the floor in a state of jellyish dissolution"), thereby somehow ending the horror. All this time detective Malone merely watches from a convenient vantage-point, although the sight so traumatises him that he is forced to spend many months recuperating in a small village in Rhode Island.

What strikes us about this tale, aside from the hackneyed supernatural manifestations, is the sheer poorness of its writing. The perfervid rhetoric that in other tales provides such harmless enjoyment here comes off sounding forced and bombastic: "Here cosmic sin had entered, and festered by unhallowed rites had commenced the grinning march of death that was to rot us all to fungous abnormalities too hideous for the grave's holding. Satan here held his Babylonish court, and in the blood of stainless childhood the leprous limbs of phosphorescent Lilith were laved." How the atheist Lovecraft could provide a satisfactory explanation for "cosmic sin" and the presence of Satan would be an interesting question; and the burden of this passage, as of the story as a whole, is the dread of being overwhelmed and "mongrelised" by those foreigners who by some miracle are increasingly ousting all the sturdy Anglo-Saxons who founded this great white nation of ours. Lovecraft cannot help ending the story on a note of dour ponderousness ("The soul of the beast is omnipresent and triumphant") and with a transparent indication that the horrors that were seemingly suppressed by the police raid will recur at some later date: the final scene shows Malone overhearing a "swarthy squinting hag" indoctrinating a small child in the same incantation he heard earlier in the tale. It is a fittingly stereotyped ending for a story that does nothing but deal in stereotypes—both of race and of weird fictional imagery.

The unoriginality and derivativeness of this story are encapsulated by the fact that much of the magical mumbo-jumbo was copied wholesale from the articles on "Magic" and "Demonology" (both by E. B. Tylor, celebrated author of the landmark anthropological work, *Primitive Culture* [1871]) from the 9th edition of the *Encyclopaedia Britannica,* which Lovecraft owned. He made no secret of this borrowing in a letter to Clark Ashton Smith, remarking: "I'd like to draw on less obvious sources if I knew of the right reservoirs to tap."[59] This comment is itself of interest, for it singlehandedly confounds the absurd claims of various occultists who have seen in Lovecraft a figure of great esoteric erudition. Many of his occultist allusions in later tales derive from Lewis Spence's handy *Encyclopaedia of Occultism* (1920), which he owned.

The borrowings from the *Encyclopaedia Britannica* in "The Horror at Red Hook" involve the Latin quotation from the mediaeval writer Antoine Delrio (or Del Rio), *An sint unquam daemones incubi et succubae, et an ex tali congressu proles nasci queat?* ("Have there ever been demons, incubi, and succubi, and from such a union can offspring be born?"), from the entry on "Demonology"; this citation evidently lent support to Lovecraft's otherwise peculiar usage of *succubus/i* as *succuba/ae* (even though, of course, a succubus is a female demon, parallel to an incubus). From the entry on "Magic" Lovecraft derived both the invocation uttered at the beginning and end of the story ("O friend and companion of night . . .") and the strange Graeco-Hebraic incantation which Malone finds on the wall of the dance-hall church. In a later letter he attempted to supply a translation of the formula, committing embarrassing errors in the process (the encyclopaedia entry provided no translation); for example, he rendered the celebrated Greek religious term *homousion* ("of the same substance"—referring usually to the belief that Christ is of the same substance as God) as "probably a decadent variant or compound involving the Greek *Homou—together.*"[60]

The figure of Malone is of some interest, at least autobiographically. This is not to say that Malone's character is based upon Lovecraft's; instead, it is possible that some (perhaps superficial) details of his character are drawn from Lovecraft's reigning literary mentors, Machen and Dunsany. The mere fact that Malone is Irish may link him to Dunsany; but it is also stated that he was "born in a Georgian villa near Phoenix Park," just as Dunsany was born, not in Ireland, but at 15 Park Square near Regent's Park in London. Malone's mysticism, conversely, seems a tip of the hat to Machen. Perhaps Lovecraft imagined that he was investing New York with the same sort of unholy witchery that Machen had done with London in *The Three Impostors* and other works.

Malone is interesting for another reason having to do with the possible genesis—or, at any rate, the particular form—of the story. Sometime before writing
"The Horror at Red Hook" Lovecraft had submitted "The Shunned House" to
Detective Tales, the magazine that had been founded together with *Weird Tales*
and of which Edwin Baird was the editor. Perhaps Lovecraft felt that Elihu
Whipple was enough of a detective figure that this tale might qualify for publication. And in spite of the fact that *Detective Tales* occasionally did print tales of
horror and the supernatural, Baird rejected the story.[61] By late July Lovecraft was
speaking of writing a "novel or novelette of Salem horrors which I may be able to
cast in a sufficiently 'detectivish' mould to sell to Edwin Baird for *Detective
Tales,*"[62] but he does not appear to have begun such a work. What this all suggests, however, is that Lovecraft was attempting to develop, however impracti-
cally, an alternative market to *Weird Tales*—and is calling upon the man who, as
editor of *Weird Tales,* accepted all his stories to aid him in the attempt. Sure
enough, in early August Lovecraft was speaking of sending "The Horror at Red
Hook" to *Detective Tales;*[63] whether he actually did so is unclear, but if he did,
the tale was obviously rejected. Lovecraft would later remark that the story was
consciously written with *Weird Tales* in mind,[64] and sure enough it appeared in
the January 1927 issue. But the figure of Malone—a much more orthodox detective than any character in previous tales of Lovecraft's, or for that matter in any
later ones—may perhaps have been fashioned at least in part with an eye toward
Detective Tales.

Otherwise "The Horror at Red Hook" is of interest only for some piquant
local colour derived from Lovecraft's growing familiarity with Brooklyn. The
dance-hall church is very likely modelled on an actual church (now destroyed)
near the waterfront in Red Hook. This church was, evidently, itself actually once
used as a dance hall.[65] Suydam's residence is said to be in Martense Street (very
close to 259 Parkside) and near the Dutch Reformed Church (on which "The
Hound" was based) with its "iron-railed yard of Netherlandish gravestones";
probably no specific house is intended, and I cannot find one on Martense Street
that might correspond to it. Another reference, not relating to topography, is to
the fact that some of the evil denizens of Red Hook are of a Mongoloid stock
originating in Kurdistan—"and Malone could not help recalling that Kurdistan
is the land of the Yezidis, last survivors of the Persian devil-worshippers." This, I
believe, is a borrowing from E. Hoffmann Price's fine tale "The Stranger from
Kurdistan," published in *Weird Tales* for July 1925, where mention is made of
the devil-worshipping Yezidis. Lovecraft would, however, not become personally
acquainted with Price for another seven years.

"The Horror at Red Hook" presents as good an opportunity as any for discussing the development (if it can be called that) of Lovecraft's racial attitudes

during this period. There is no question that his racism flared to greater heights at this time—at least on paper (as embodied in letters to his aunts)—than at any subsequent period in his life. I have already remarked that the seeming paradox of Lovecraft's marrying a Jewess when he exhibited marked anti-Semitic traits is no paradox at all, for Sonia in his mind fulfilled his requirement that aliens assimilate themselves into the American population, as did other Jews such as Samuel Loveman. Nevertheless, Sonia speaks at length about Lovecraft's attitudes on this subject. One of her most celebrated comments is as follows: "Although he once said he loved New York and that henceforth it would be his 'adopted state', I soon learned that he hated it and all its 'alien hordes'. When I protested that I too was one of them, he'd tell me I 'no longer belonged to these mongrels'. *'You are now Mrs. H. P. Lovecraft of 598 Angell St., Providence, Rhode Island!'*"[66] Let it pass that Lovecraft and Sonia never resided at 598 Angell Street. A later remark is still more telling: "Soon after we were married he told me that whenever we have company he would appreciate it if there were 'Aryans' in the majority."[67] This must refer to the year 1924, as they would not have done much entertaining in 1925. Sonia's final remark on the matter is more damning yet. Sonia claims that part of her desire to have Lovecraft and Loveman meet in 1922 was to "cure" Lovecraft of his bias against Jews by actually meeting one face to face. She continues:

> Unfortunately, one often judges a whole people by the character of the first ones he meets. But H. P. assured me that he was quite "cured"; that since I was so well assimilated into the American way of life and the American scene he felt sure our marriage would be a success. But unfortunately (and here I must speak of something I never intended to have publicly known), whenever he would meet crowds of people—in the subway, or, at the noon hour, on the sidewalks in Broadway, or crowds, wherever he happened to find them, and these were usually the workers of minority races—he would become livid with anger and rage.[68]

In a letter to Winfield Townley Scott, Sonia elaborates upon this comment:

> I reiterate once more, again on my solemn oath, that he became *livid with rage* at the foreign elements he would see in large number, especially at noontime, in the streets of New York City, and I would try to calm his outbursts by saying: "You don't have to love them; but hating them so outrageously can't do any good." It was then that he said: "It is more important to know what to hate than it is to know what to love."[69]

Again, there is nothing here that need surprise us; but Lovecraft's attitude is nonetheless dismaying to present-day sensibilities. And yet, in spite of what his previous biographer, L. Sprague de Camp, has suggested, comments on aliens are relatively rare in the correspondence to his aunts during this period. One notorious passage deals with a trip Sonia and Lovecraft took to Pelham Bay Park, an enormous park in the far northeast corner of the Bronx, on the fourth of July: ". . . we formed the highest expectations of the rural solitudes we were about to discover. Then came the end of the line—& disillusion. My Pete in Pegāna, but what crowds! And that is not the worst . . . for upon my most solemn oath, I'll be shot if three out of every four persons—nay, full nine out of every ten—weren't flabby, pungent, grinning, chattering **niggers!**"[70] It is interesting to note that both Sonia and Lovecraft decided to make a hasty retreat—perhaps Sonia herself was not, at this time at least, as free from all racial prejudice as she seems to suggest in her memoir. A long letter in early January goes on at length about the fundamental inassimilability of Jews in American life, maintaining that "vast harm is done by those idealists who encourage belief in a coalescence which never can be." When he went on to note that "On our side there is a shuddering physical repugnance to most Semitic types"[71] (the "our" is an interesting rhetorical ploy), he unwittingly reached the heart of the issue, at least as far as he himself was concerned: in spite of all Lovecraft's talk about cultural inassimilability, what he really found offensive about foreigners (or, more broadly, non-"Aryans," since many of the ethnics in New York were already first- or second-generation immigrants) is the fact that they looked funny to him.

But some words must be said in Lovecraft's defence at this juncture. Although I do not wish to treat his racism until a slightly later stage (for it is only in the early 1930s that he attempted a more broad-based philosophical and cultural justification of his brand of racism), it can be said here that this long letter about Jews is singular even in the correspondence to Lillian; nothing like it comes up again. In fact Lillian at some later date must have herself had some reservations on the subject, perhaps worrying that Lovecraft would take some sort of verbal or physical action against Jews or other non-Nordics; for in late March Lovecraft wrote: "Incidentally—don't fancy that my nervous reaction against alien N.Y. types takes the form of conversation likely to offend any individual. One knows when & where to discuss questions with a social or ethnic cast, & our group is not noted for *faux pas*'s or inconsiderate repetitions of opinion."[72]

It is on this latter point that Lovecraft's supporters base one of their own defences. Frank Long declares: "During all those talks on long walks through the streets of New York and Providence, I never once heard him utter a derogatory remark about any member of a minority group who passed him on the street or had occasion to engage him in conversation, whose cultural or racial antecedents differed from his own."[73] If this is a contradiction with what Sonia had said, it may simply be that Lovecraft did not feel it politic to say such things even in the presence of Long, in spite of the fact that Lovecraft in his early January letter to Lillian remarked:

The only company for a regular conservative American is that formed by regular conservative Americans—well-born, & comfortably nurtured in the old tradition. That's why Belknap is about the only one of the gang who doesn't irritate me at times. He is *regular*—he connects up with innate memories & Providence experiences to such an extent as to seem a real person instead of a two-dimensional shadow in a dream, as more Bohemian personalities do.[74]

I am not sure Long would have welcomed this presumed compliment. In any event, it seems clear to me that Lovecraft may have at least considered taking more forceful action against foreigners than merely fulminating against them in letters, as a startling remark made six years later attests: "The population [of New York City] is a mongrel herd with repulsive Mongoloid Jews in the visible majority, and the coarse faces and bad manners eventually come to wear on one so unbearably that one feels like punching every god damn bastard in sight."[75] Nevertheless, this supposed absence of demonstrative behaviour—verbal or physical—on Lovecraft's part in connexion with non-Aryans is at the heart of a defence that Dirk W. Mosig made in a letter to Long, quoted by Long in his memoir. Mosig adduces three mitigating circumstances: 1) ". . . the word 'racist' carries today connotations quite different from the meaning the term had in the first third of the century"; 2) "Lovecraft, like anyone else, deserves to be judged by his behavior, rather than by private statements made with no intention to injure another"; 3) "HPL presented different poses or 'personas' to his various correspondents . . . It is likely that he . . . appeared to his aunts as they wished him to be, that some of his 'racist' statements were made, not out of deep conviction, but out of a desire to be congenial with the views held by others."[76]

I fear that none of these defences amount to much. Of course racism took on different, and more sinister, connotations after World War II, but I shall argue later that Lovecraft was simply behind the times intellectually in adhering to such views as the biological inferiority of blacks, the radical cultural inassimilability of different ethnic groups, and the racial and cultural coherence of various races, nationalities, or cultural entities. The gauge for Lovecraft's beliefs is not the commonality of people of his time (who were, as are a good many today, frankly and openly racist) but the advanced intelligentsia, for most of whom the issue of race was simply of no consequence. And as for behaviour counting more than private statements, this is a truism; but Lovecraft cannot be acquitted of racism merely because he happened not to insult a Jew to his face or beat a black man with a baseball bat. The "private statements" conception carries over into Mosig's third point, which is that perhaps he was saying in his letters to his aunts only what they wished to hear; but this too can be seen to be quite false by anyone who reads the existing correspondence systematically. The long tirade about Jews in

January 1926 was clearly not a response to anything Lillian had said, but was triggered almost incidentally by some clipping she had sent regarding the racial origin of Jesus. It is quite likely that both Lillian and Annie, old-time Yankees that they were, were sympathetic to Lovecraft's remarks and generally in tune with his beliefs on the subject; but Lillian's own reservations, as reflected in Lovecraft's response of late March, suggests that she did not feel nearly as vehemently on the issue as he did.

And, of course, Lovecraft's hostility was exacerbated by his increasingly shaky psychological state as he found himself dragging out a life in an unfamiliar, unfriendly city where he did not seem to belong and where he had little prospects for work or permanent comfort. Foreigners made convenient scapegoats, and New York City, then and now the most cosmopolitan and culturally heterogeneous city in the country, stood in stark contrast to the homogeneity and conservatism he had known in the first thirty-four years of his life in New England. The city that had seemed such a fount of Dunsanian glamour and wonder had become a dirty, noisy, overcrowded place that dealt repeated blows to his self-esteem by denying him a job in spite of his abilities and by forcing him to hole up in a seedy, mice-infested, crime-ridden dump where all he could do was write racist stories like "The Horror at Red Hook" as a safety-valve for his anger and despair.

Lovecraft was, however, not finished with creative work. Eight days after writing the story, on August 10, he began a long, lone evening ramble that led through Greenwich Village to the Battery, then to the ferry to Elizabeth, which he reached at 7 A.M. He purchased a 10¢ composition book at a shop, went to Scott Park, and wrote a story:

> Ideas welled up unbidden, as never before for years, & the sunny actual scene soon blended into the purple & red of a hellish midnight tale—a tale of cryptical horrors among tangles of antediluvian alleys in Greenwich Village—wherein I wove not a little poetick description, & the abiding terror of him who comes to New-York as to a faery flower of stone & marble, yet finds only a verminous corpse—a dead city of squinting alienage with nothing in common either with its own past or with the background of America in general. I named it "He" . . .[77]

It is interesting that in this instance Lovecraft had to leave New York in order to write about it; he had, according to his diary, first gone to Scott Park on June 13, and it became a favourite haunt. And if the above description sounds autobiographical, it is by design; for "He," while much superior to "The Horror at Red Hook," is as heart-wrenching a cry of despair as its predecessor—quite avowedly so. Its opening is celebrated:

> I saw him on a sleepless night when I was walking desperately to save my soul and my vision. My coming to New York had been a mistake; for whereas I had looked for poignant wonder and inspiration in the teeming labyrinths of an-

cient streets that twist endlessly from forgotten courts and squares and waterfronts to courts and squares and waterfronts equally forgotten, and in the Cyclopean modern towers and pinnacles that rise blackly Babylonian under waning
moons, I had found instead only a sense of horror and oppression which threatened to master, paralyse, and annihilate me.

The power of this passage, of course, does not depend upon knowledge of Lovecraft's biography; but that knowledge will lend it an added poignancy in its transparent reflexion of Lovecraft's own mental state. The narrator goes on to say how
the gleaming towers of New York had first captivated him, but that

Garish daylight shewed only squalor and alienage and the noxious elephantiasis
of climbing, spreading stone where the moon had hinted of loveliness and elder
magic; and the throngs of people that seethed through the flume-like streets
were squat, swarthy strangers with hardened faces and narrow eyes, shrewd
strangers without dreams and without kinship to the scenes about them, who
could never mean aught to a blue-eyed man of the old folk, with the love of fair
green lanes and white New England village steeples in his heart.

Here is Lovecraft's sociology of New York: the immigrants who have clustered
there really have no "kinship" with it because the city was founded by the Dutch
and the English, and these immigrants are of a different cultural heritage altogether. This sophism allows Lovecraft to conclude that "this city of stone and stri-
dor is not a sentient perpetuation of Old New York as London is of Old London
and Paris of Old Paris, but that it is in fact quite dead, its sprawling body imper-
fectly embalmed and infested with queer animate things which have nothing to do
with it as it was in life." The immigrants are now considered to be on the level of
maggots.

Why, then, does not the narrator flee from the place? He gains some comfort
from wandering along the older portions of the town, but all he can say in accounting for his staying is that "I . . . refrained from going home to my people
lest I seem to crawl back ignobly in defeat." How faithful a reflection of Lovecraft's sentiments this is, it is difficult to say; but I shall have occasion to refer to
this passage at a later time, especially in connexion with Sonia's response to it.

The narrator, like Lovecraft, seeks out Greenwich Village in particular; and
it is here, at two in the morning one August night, that he meets "the man." This
person has an anomalously archaic manner of speaking and is wearing similarly
archaic attire, and the narrator takes him for a harmless eccentric; but the latter
immediately senses a fellow antiquarian. The man leads him on a circuitous tour
of old alleys and courtyards, finally coming to "the ivy-clad wall of a private estate," where the man lives. Can this place be specified? At the end of the story the
narrator finds himself "at the entrance of a little black court off Perry Street"; and
this is all the indication we need to realise that this segment of the tale was clearly

inspired by a very similar expedition Lovecraft took on August 29, 1924—a "lone tour of colonial exploration" that led to Perry Street, "in an effort to ferret out the nameless hidden court which the Evening Post had written up that day. . . . I found the place without difficulty, and enjoyed it all the more for having seen its picture. These lost lanes of an elder city have for me the utmost fascination . . ."[78] Lovecraft is referring to an article in the *New York Evening Post* for August 29, in a regular column entitled "Little Sketches About Town." This column contained both a line drawing of the "lost lane" in Perry Street and a brief writeup: "Everything about it is lost—name, country, identification of any sort. Its most prominent feature, an old oil lamp by a pair of crooked cellar steps, looks as if it came, after many years of shipwrecked isolation, from the Isle of Lost Ships, and feels more helplessly out of place than it can express."[79] A tantalising description indeed—no wonder Lovecraft promptly went out in search of it. He claimed to have found the lane or alley with ease; indeed, both the drawing and the mention in the article that the lane is on Perry Street past Bleecker make it quite clear that the reference is to what is now labelled 93 Perry Street, an archway that leads to a lane between three buildings still very much like that pictured in the article. What is more, according to an historical monograph on Perry Street, this general area was heavily settled by Indians (they had named it Sapohanican), and moreover, a sumptuous mansion was built in the block bounded by Perry, Charles, Bleecker, and West Fourth Streets sometime between 1726 and 1744, being the residence of a succession of wealthy citizens until it was razed in 1865.[80] Lovecraft almost certainly knew the history of the area, and he has deftly incorporated it into his tale.

And yet, it is critical to the logic of the tale that the man's residence itself cannot be found with ease. The man takes the narrator on a deliberately convoluted circuit that destroys the latter's sense of direction—at one point the two of them "crawled on hands and knees through a low, arched passage of stone whose immense length and tortuous twistings effaced at last every hint of geographical location I had managed to preserve." This action is vital to the incursion of fantasy, for in a story so otherwise realistic in its topography some zone of mystery is required for the unreal to be situated.

There is one further tantalising autobiographical connexion—the fact that Lovecraft and Sonia, on an earlier voyage of exploration of the colonial parts of Greenwich Village earlier in August 1924, actually met an elderly gentleman who led them to certain hidden sites they would otherwise not have seen. Here is Lovecraft's description:

> Falling into a conversation with the chrysostomic gentleman of leisure abovemention'd, we learned much of local history, including the fact that the houses in Milligan Court were originally put up in the late 1700's by the Methodist

Church, for the poorer but respectable families of the parish. Continuing his expositions, our amiable Mentor led us to a seemingly undistinguished door within the court, and through the dim hallway beyond to a back door. Whither he was taking us, we knew not; but upon emerging from the back door we paus'd in delighted amazement. There, excluded from the world on *every* side by sheer walls and house facades, was *a second hidden court or alley,* with vegetation growing here and there, and on the south side a row of simple Colonial doorways and small-pan'd windows!! . . . Beholding this ingulph'd and search-defying fragment of yesterday, the active imagination conjures up endless weird possibilities . . .[81]

The resemblance to the perambulation of the narrator of "He" into the hidden courtyard is uncanny—even if there was no crawling on hands and knees. And the "weird possibilities" of the site were certainly conveyed powerfully to Lovecraft, even if their expression was delayed a full year.

In the manor house the man begins to relate an account of his "ancestor," who practised some sort of sorcery, in part from knowledge gained from the Indians in the area; later he conveniently killed them with bad rum, so that he alone now had the secret information he had extracted from them. What is the nature of this knowledge? The man leads the narrator to a window and, parting the curtains, reveals an idyllic rural landscape—it can only be the Greenwich of the eighteenth century, magically brought in front of his eyes. The narrator, stunned, asks harriedly, "Can you—dare you—go *far?*" In scorn the man parts the curtains again and this time shows him a sight of the future:

> I saw the heavens verminous with strange flying things, and beneath them a hellish black city of giant stone terraces with impious pyramids flung savagely to the moon, and devil-lights burning from unnumbered windows. And swarming loathsomely on aërial galleries I saw the yellow, squint-eyed people of that city, robed horribly in orange and red, and dancing insanely to the pounding of fevered kettle-drums, the clatter of obscene crotala, and the maniacal moaning of muted horns whose ceaseless dirges rose and fell undulantly like the waves of an unhallowed ocean of bitumen.

It is not to be denied that there is a racialist element here also—the "yellow squint-eyed people" can be nothing more or less than Orientals, who have now apparently overrun the city either by conquest or (worse, in Lovecraft's view) interbreeding with whites—but the image is compelling for all that. My feeling is that this scenario was derived from Lord Dunsany's picaresque novel *The Chronicles of Rodriguez* (1922), in which Rodriguez and a companion make an arduous climb of a mountain to the house of a wizard, who in alternate windows unveils vistas of wars past and to come (the latter showing, of course, the titanic horrors of World War I, which lie far in the future from the mediaeval period in which the novel takes place).[82]

If Lovecraft had ended the tale here, it would have been a notable success; but he had the bad judgment to add a pulpish ending whereby the spirits of the murdered Indians, manifesting themselves in the form of a black slime, burst in on the pair and make off with the archaic man (who, of course, is himself the "ancestor"), while the narrator falls absurdly through successive floors of the building and then crawls out to Perry Street. It would still be a few years before Lovecraft would learn sufficient restraint to avoid bathos of this sort.

The final lines of the story are again poignant from an autobiographical perspective: "Whither *he* has gone, I do not know; but I have gone home to the pure New England lanes up which fragrant sea-winds sweep at evening." Thomas Malone of "The Horror at Red Hook" is sent to Chepachet, Rhode Island, on a vacation to recover from the shock of his ordeal; but here the narrator returns permanently to his home, and a more pitiable instance of wish-fulfilment would be hard to find. Nonetheless, "He" remains a quietly powerful tale for its brooding prose and its apocalyptic visions of a crazed future; and it is as tormented a cry from the heart as Lovecraft ever wrote.

Farnsworth Wright accepted "He," along with "The Cats of Ulthar," in early October, and it appeared in *Weird Tales* for September 1926. Strangely enough, Lovecraft had not yet submitted "The Shunned House" to Wright, but when he did so (probably in early September), Wright eventually turned it down on the grounds that it began too gradually.[83] Lovecraft did not make any notable comment on this rejection, even though it was the first rejection he had ever had from *Weird Tales* and the first (but by no means the last) that Farnsworth Wright had given. He spoke of retyping several earlier stories for Wright, and did send a batch of them in late September, and another batch in early October. Wright was also talking of compiling a volume of stories from *Weird Tales,* which would include "The Rats in the Walls";[84] but nothing came of this. The Popular Fiction Publishing Company did publish one book in 1927—*The Moon Terror,* with stories by A. G. Birch, Anthony M. Rud, Vincent Starrett, and Wright himself, all from early issues of *Weird Tales*—but it was such a commercial disaster that no more books of the sort were issued.

The writing of "He," however, did not put an entire end to Lovecraft's fictional efforts. The Kalem meeting on Wednesday, August 12, broke up at 4 A.M.; Lovecraft immediately went home and mapped out "a new story plot—perhaps a short novel" which he titled "The Call of Cthulhu."[85] Although he confidently reported that "the writing itself will now be a relatively simple matter," it would be more than a year before he would write this seminal story. It is a little sad to note how Lovecraft attempted to justify his state of chronic unemployment by suggesting to Lillian that a lengthy story of this sort "ought to bring in a very decent sized cheque"; he had earlier noted that the projected Salem novelette or novel, "if accepted, would bring in a goodly sum of cash."[86] It is as if he was desperately seeking to convince Lillian that he was not a drain on her (and Sonia's) finances in spite of his lack of a regular position and his continual cafeteria-lounging with the boys.

Sometime in August Lovecraft received a plot idea from C. W. Smith, editor of the *Tryout.* The idea is spelled out in a letter to Clark Ashton Smith: ". . . an undertaker imprisoned in a village vault where he was removing winter coffins for spring burial, & his escape by enlarging a transom reached by the piling-up of the coffins."[87] This does not sound very promising; and the mere fact that Lovecraft chose to write it up at this time, even with the addition of a supernatural element, may suggest the relative impoverishment of his creative imagination in the atmosphere of New York. The resulting tale, "In the Vault," written on September 18, is poorer than "He" but not quite as horrendously bad as "The Horror at Red Hook"; it is merely mediocre.

George Birch is the careless and thick-skinned undertaker of Peck Valley, an imaginary town somewhere in New England. On one occasion he finds himself trapped in the receiving-tomb—where coffins ready for burial are being stored for the winter, until the ground is soft enough to dig—by the slamming of the door in the wind and the breaking of the neglected latch. Birch realises that the only way to get out of the tomb is to pile the eight coffins up like a pyramid and get out through the transom. Although working in the dark, he is confident that he has piled up the coffins in the sturdiest possible manner; in particular, he is certain that he has placed the well-made coffin of the diminutive Matthew Fenner on the very top, rather than the flimsy coffin he had initially built for Fenner but which he later decided to use for the tall Asaph Sawyer, a vindictive man whom he had not liked in life. Ascending his "miniature Tower of Babel," Birch finds that he has to knock out some of the bricks around the transom in order for his large body to escape. As he is doing this, his feet fall through the top coffin and into the decaying contents within. He feels horrible pains in his ankles—they must be splinters or loose nails—but he manages to heave his body out the window and upon the ground. He cannot walk—his Achilles tendons have been cut—but he drags himself to the cemetery lodge, where he is rescued.

Later Dr Davis examines his wounds and finds them very unnerving. Going back to the receiving-tomb, he learns the truth: Asaph Sawyer was too big to fit into Matthew Fenner's coffin, so Birch had phlegmatically cut off Asaph's feet at the ankles to make the body fit; but he had not reckoned on Asaph's inhuman vengeance. The wounds in Birch's ankles are teeth marks.

This is nothing more than a commonplace tit-for-tat supernatural vengeance story. Clark Ashton Smith charitably wrote that "'In the Vault' . . . has the realistic grimness of Bierce";[88] there may well be a Bierce influence on this tale, but Bierce wrote nothing quite so simple-minded as this. Lovecraft attempts to write in a more homespun, colloquial vein—even going so far as to say, disingenuously, "Just where to begin Birch's story I can hardly decide, since I am no practiced teller of tales"—but the result is not successful. August Derleth developed an unfortunate fondness for this tale, so that it still stands embalmed among volumes of Lovecraft's "best" stories.

The tale's immediate fortunes were not very happy, either. Lovecraft dedicated the story to C. W. Smith, "from whose suggestion the central situation is taken," and it appeared in Smith's *Tryout* for November 1925. It was the last time that he would allow a new story (as opposed to an older, professionally rejected story) to appear first in an amateur journal. Of course Lovecraft also sought professional publication; and although it would seem that "In the Vault," in its limited scope and conventionally macabre orientation, would be ready-made for *Weird Tales,* Wright rejected it in November. The reason for the rejection, according to Lovecraft, is interesting: "its extreme gruesomeness would not pass the Indiana censorship."[89] The reference, of course, is to the banning of Eddy's "The Loved Dead," as Lovecraft makes clear in a later letter: "Wright's rejection of ["In the Vault"] was sheer nonsense—I don't believe any censor would have objected to it, but ever since the Indiana senate took action about poor Eddy's 'Loved Dead', he has been in a continual panic about censorship."[90] Here then is the first—but not the last—instance where the apparent uproar over "The Loved Dead," however much or little it may have helped "rescue" *Weird Tales* in 1924, had a negative impact upon Lovecraft.

There was, however, better news from Wright. Lovecraft had evidently sent him "The Outsider" merely for his examination, as it was already promised to W. Paul Cook—apparently for the *Recluse,* which Cook had conceived around September.[91] Wright liked the story so much that he pleaded with Lovecraft to let him print it. Lovecraft managed to persuade Cook to release the story, and Wright accepted it sometime around the end of the year; its appearance in *Weird Tales* for April 1926 would be a landmark.

The rest of the year was spent variously in activity with the Kalems, in receiving out-of-town guests, and in solitary travels of an increasingly wider scope in search of antiquarian oases. Some guests had come earlier in the year: John Russell, Lovecraft's erstwhile *Argosy* nemesis and now a cordial friend, came for several days in April; Albert A. Sandusky showed up for a few days in early June. Now, on August 18, Alfred Galpin's wife, a Frenchwoman whom Galpin had married the year before while studying music in Paris, arrived; she would stay until the 20th, when she would move on to Cleveland. Sonia was in town, so the two of them took her out to dinner and a play before returning to 169 Clinton, where Mrs Galpin had agreed to take a room during her stay. The next morning, however, she complained bitterly of bedbugs, and in the evening moved to the Hotel Brossert in Montague Street. But she took in the Kalem meeting that day, as did Sonia: evidently the presence of an overseas guest caused a suspension of the "stag rule."

Lovecraft continued to act conscientiously as host to the Kalems on occasion, and his letters display how much he enjoyed treating his friends to coffee, cake, and other humble delectables on his best blue china. Indeed, McNeil had complained that some of the other hosts did not serve refreshments even though he always did, and Lovecraft was determined not to be lax in this regard. On July 29 he bought an aluminum pail for 49¢ with which to fetch hot coffee from the deli at the corner of State and Court Streets. He was forced to do this because he could not make coffee at home—either because he did not know how or because he had no heating apparatus. He also invested in apple tarts, crumb cake (which Kleiner liked), and other comestibles. On one occasion Kleiner did not show up, and Lovecraft lugubriously noted: "The amount of crumb-cake remaining is prodigious, & there are four apple tarts—in fact, I can see my meals mapped out for me for two days!! Ironic circumstance—I got the crumb-cake especially for Kleiner, who adores it, & in the end he was absent; so that I, who don't particularly care for it at all, must swallow unending quantities of it in the interest of oeconomy!"[92] If any further indication of Lovecraft's poverty is needed, this must surely be it.

Some new colleagues emerged on Lovecraft's horizon about this time. One, Wilfred Blanch Talman (1904–1986), was an amateur who, while attending Brown University, had subsidised the publication of a slim volume of poetry entitled *Cloisonné and Other Verses* (1923)[93] and sent it to Lovecraft in July. (No copy of this book has, to my knowledge, surfaced.) The two met in late August, and Lovecraft took to him immediately: "He is a splendid young chap—tall, lean, light, & aristocratically clean-cut, with light brown hair & excellent taste in dress. . . . He is descended from the most ancient Dutch families of lower New York state, & has recently become a genealogical enthusiast."[94] Talman went on to become a reporter for the *New York Times* and later an editor of the *Texaco Star,* a paper issued by the oil company. He made random ventures into professional fiction, and would later have one of his stories subjected to (possibly unwanted) revision by Lovecraft. Talman was perhaps the first addition to the core membership of the Kalem Club, although he did not begin regular attendance until after Lovecraft had left New York.

A still more congenial colleague was Vrest Teachout Orton (1897–1986). Orton was a friend of W. Paul Cook and at this time worked in the advertising department of the *American Mercury*. Later he would achieve distinction as an editor at the *Saturday Review of Literature* and, still later, as the founder of the Vermont Country Store. For the time being he lived in Yonkers, but moved back to his native Vermont not long after Lovecraft's return to Providence. He visited Lovecraft at 169 Clinton on December 22, and they spent the rest of the afternoon and evening together—dining at Lovecraft's usual Brooklyn restaurant, John's, walking across the Brooklyn Bridge, and making their way to Grand Central Station, where Orton caught an 11.40 train back to Yonkers. Lovecraft was tremendously taken with him:

> No more likeable, breezy, & magnetic person ever existed than he. In person of smallish size; dark, slender, handsome, & dashing, he is clean-shaven of face & jauntily fastidious of dress . . . He confessed to 30 years, but does not look more than 22 or 23. His voice is mellow & pleasant . . . & his manner of delivery sprightly & masculine—the careless heartiness of a well-bred young man of the world. . . . A thorough Yankee to the bone, he hails from central Vermont, adores his native state and means to return thither in a year, & detests N.Y. as heartily as I do. His ancestry is uniformly aristocratic—old New England on his father's side, & on his mother's side New England, Knickerbocker Dutch, & French Huguenot.[95]

One almost gets the impression that Orton was the sort of person Lovecraft wished he were. Orton became perhaps the second honorary member of the Kalems, although his attendance at meetings was also irregular until after Lovecraft's departure from New York. Orton did a little literary work of his own—he compiled a bibliography of Theodore Dreiser, *Dreiserana* (1929), founded the *Colophon,* a bibliophiles' magazine, and later founded the Stephen Daye Press in Vermont, for which Lovecraft would do some freelance work—but he had little interest in the weird. Nevertheless, their mutual New England background and their loathing of New York gave the two men much to talk about.

Aside from activities with friends, Lovecraft engaged in much solitary travel in the latter half of 1925. Only three days after his all-night ramble that ended in Elizabeth on August 10–11, when he wrote "He," Lovecraft went there again on the night of August 14–15, this time proceeding on foot to the small towns of Union Center (now Union) and Springfield, several miles northwest of Elizabeth, and coming back through the communities of Galloping Hill Park, Roselle Park, and Rahway. (Lovecraft noted that, in returning to Scott Park in Elizabeth, he began another horror story;[96] but, if it was finished, as is unlikely, it does not survive.) This was an enormous distance to cover on foot, but Lovecraft was tireless in the hunt for antiquities.

On August 30 Lovecraft made his first visit to Paterson, to join Morton, Kleiner, and Ernest A. Dench in a nature hike with the Paterson Rambling Club. His response to the town itself was not favourable:

> Of the "beauty" of the town, nothing could be said without liberal draughts on the imagination—for it is certainly one of the dreariest, shabbiest, & most nondescript places it has ever been my misfortune to see. . . . Life seems mostly in the hands of Yankees & Germans, though a mongrel Italian & Slav element is indicated by the physiognomies of the repulsive rabble—the mill folk. . . . The town is said to have good parks, though I beheld none of them. Its hideous factory section is fortunately out of sight, across the river from the ordinary parts.[97]

I am not sure that things have gotten much better since. But the goal of the present journey was Buttermilk Falls, which proved to be no disappointment:

> There is a glorious picturesqueness & an ineffable majesty in such a spectacle— the precipitous cliff, the rifted rock, the limpid stream, & the titanic tiers of terraces flanked by massed slender columns of immemorial stone; all bathed in the abysmal hush & magical green twilight of the deep woods, where filtered sunlight dapples the leafy earth & transfigures the great wild boles into a thousand forms of subtle & evanescent wonder.

Once again Lovecraft demonstrates the keenest sensitivity to every sort of topographical stimulus—city or country, suburb or woodland, island or ocean. Only six days later, on September 5, Lovecraft, Loveman, and Kleiner undertook a late-night exploration into a region of Brooklyn not far from 169 Clinton— Union Place, a small cobblestoned street (now sadly demolished) that Lovecraft describes as follows:

> Litten only by the gibbous moon, & by a solitary lamp-post that flickered fantastically, there lay beyond that wooden tunnel a little realm apart—a brooding backwater of the 1850's, where in a quadrangle facing a central iron-railed bit of park stood side by side the high-stopped houses of elder days, each in its iron-fenced yard with garden or grass-plot, & totally innocent of the injudicious restorer's vandal touch. Silence rested soothingly on every hand, & the outer universe faded from consciousness as it retreated from sight. Here dreamed the past inviolate—leisurely, graceful & unperturbed; defying all that might occur in the seething hell of life beyond that protecting archway.[98]

Respites from New York could be found in the least expected places, and surprisingly close to home.

On September 9 Lovecraft and Loveman joined the Long family on a boat ride up the Hudson River to Newburgh, some twenty miles north of the city.

Along the way they sailed by such towns as Yonkers, Tarrytown, and Haver-straw—the area Washington Irving had vivified in "The Legend of Sleepy Hollow" and other works. They had only forty minutes to explore Newburgh ("where colonial gables & twisting byways supply an atmosphere hardly to be duplicated this side of Marblehead"[99]), but they made the most of it. The return trip, on a different boat, was uneventful. On the 20th Lovecraft took Loveman on a tour of Elizabeth.

One of his most extensive trips of the season was a three-day trip to Jamaica, Mineola, Hempstead, Garden City, and Freeport on Long Island. Jamaica was then a separate community but is now a part of Queens; the other towns are in Nassau County, east of Queens. On September 27 Lovecraft went to Jamaica, which "utterly astonisht" him: "There, all about me, lay a veritable New-England village; with wooden colonial houses, Georgian churches, & deliciously sleepy & shady streets where giant elms & maples stood in dense & luxurious rows."[100] Things are, I fear, very different now. Thereafter he went north to Flushing, also once separate and also now part of Queens. This was a Dutch settlement (the name is an Anglicisation of Vlissingen), and it too retained gratifying touches of colonialism. (Today, I fear, it is one unending succession of cheap brick apartment buildings.) One structure in particular—the Bowne house (1661) at Bowne Street and 37th Avenue—he was particularly anxious to find, and had to ask many policemen (who "were not very good antiquarians, for none of them had either seen or heard of the place") to locate it at last; it delighted him, but I cannot ascertain whether he actually entered the building. He may not have done so, for it may not have been open as a museum as it is now. He stayed in Flushing till twilight, then returned home.

The next day he returned to Flushing and Jamaica, examining both sites in greater detail. The 29th, however, was his great Long Island journey. He first came to Jamaica, whereupon he caught a trolley for Mineola; his ultimate goal was Huntington, but having no map and not knowing the trolley system, he was unsure how to get there. The route to Mineola he found quite dull (it was "lined almost continuously with modern real-estate developments testifying mournfully alike to the spread of the city & to the want of taste & ingenuity in the architects of small dwellings"[101]), and Mineola itself was scarcely less so. He proceeded to walk southward to Garden City, where he saw the extensive college-like brick buildings of Doubleday, Page & Co., now (after many years as Doubleday, Doran) simply Doubleday; the publisher has moved its editorial offices to Manhattan but still retains a considerable presence in its city of origin. Continuing southward on foot, he came to Hempstead, which captivated him utterly: "Enchantment reign'd supreme, for here dwelt the soul of antique New-England in all its fulness, unimpair'd by the tainting presence of a foreign Babylon some twenty or twenty-five miles to the east."[102] Once again it was the churches that delighted him—St George's Episcopal, Methodist, Christ's First Presbyterian, and others. He spent considerable time in Hempstead (which, alas, has changed quite considerably from the time Lovecraft saw it, and not for the better), then continued south on foot to Freeport, which he found pleasant but undistinguished from an antiquarian point of view. All this walking must have covered close to ten miles. Only at this point did he take a trolley for Jamaica and then an elevated back to Brooklyn. Five days later, on October 4, he took Loveman to Flushing and Hempstead (by trolley, this time).

With winter coming on, Lovecraft's trips perforce became fewer, although he visited Canarsie, Jamaica (where he saw the Rufus King Mansion, a magnificent 1750 gambrel-roofer with two ells that still stands), and Kew Gardens (a modern development in Queens with pleasing neo-Elizabethan architecture that still retains its charm today) on November 13, returning to Jamaica on the 14th and taking Loveman again to Flushing on the 15th.

The importance of these expeditions to Lovecraft's psyche can scarcely be overestimated. The shimmering skyscrapers of Manhattan had proven, upon closer examination, to be an oppressive horror; as he had noted when refusing the offer to edit *Weird Tales* in Chicago, "it is colonial atmosphere which supplies my very breath of life."[103] Lovecraft had, indeed, developed an uncanny nose for antiquity, whether it be in Manhattan, Brooklyn, or in the further reaches of the metropolitan area. The frequency with which he compares what he sees to New England may perhaps be understandable—New England always remained his frame of reference in these and most other matters—but can we detect an indirect plea to Lillian in them? Lovecraft had dutifully sent Lillian the three stories he had written in late summer, one of which ("In the Vault") is actually set in New England, and the other two—"The Horror at Red Hook" and "He"—feature characters who either temporarily or permanently end up there.

Sonia was not doing especially well herself. In October she had lost the position in Cleveland—whether she quit or was fired is unclear—but seems to have found another job fairly quickly. This too, however, was unsatisfactory, since like its predecessor it was on a commission basis and therefore engendered fierce rivalry among the various salespeople.[104] In November Lovecraft spent the better part of four days writing or revising an article on salesmanship for Sonia. He now reported that her new job was going better, Sonia having made "a decided 'hit' in the educational department of the store" with an earlier article.[105] What store is this? Lovecraft specified in a later letter that it was Halle's, the leading department store in Cleveland. Halle Brothers Company had been founded in 1891 by Salmon P. and Samuel H. Halle. It originally manufactured hats, caps, and furs, but later became a department store that merely sold these items. In 1910 a large building at the corner of Euclid and East 12th Street was built; Sonia presumably worked here. She was hoping to come home for Christmas, but the work was so heavy that she made no trip to New York between October 18 and the middle of January 1926.

Lovecraft accordingly spent a very pleasant Thanksgiving with the amateur Ernest A. Dench and his family in Sheepshead Bay, Brooklyn. In late August he had gone there for a Blue Pencil Club meeting; the purported literary topic was Dench's newborn son, and Lovecraft—by now becoming rather wearied of these artificial calls for literary production—wrote the unwontedly pensive, brooding poem "To an Infant," which in long Swinburnian Alexandrines tells of the grimness of waking life and the power of dreams to overcome it. At Thanksgiving there was no call for prose or poetic contributions, and Lovecraft had an entertaining time with McNeil, Kleiner, Morton, and Pearl K. Merritt, the amateur whom Morton would soon marry.

Christmas was spent with the Longs. He arrived at 1.30 in the afternoon, wearing his best grey suit (the "triumph"), finding McNeil and Loveman already there. The Long parents had purchased silk handkerchiefs for all, each in accordance with the guest's individual taste: Lovecraft's was a subdued grey, while Long's was a fiery purple. After a lavish turkey dinner, the party passed around a grab-bag consisting of useful items purchased from Woolworth's—things like shaving soap, a toothbrush (which Lovecraft later found too hard for his gums), talcum powder, and the like. After this there was a contest to see which guest could identify the greatest number of advertising illustrations taken from magazines. In spite of Lovecraft's avowed unfamiliarity with the popular magazines, he won the contest by identifying six out of twenty-five (Loveman and McNeil identified five, Long only three); as victor Lovecraft received a box of chocolate creams. All this sounds amusingly like a young boy's birthday party, but no doubt the guests took it in good spirit. A boring double-feature at the local cinema was followed by a light supper (with a lollypop on each plate!). Lovecraft came home at midnight.

After September Lovecraft lapsed again into literary quiescence. During the last three months of the year he wrote only an effective weird poem, "October" (October 18) and a pleasing birthday poem, "To George Willard Kirk" (November 24). Then, in mid-November, Lovecraft announced: "W. Paul Cook wants an article from me on the element of terror & weirdness in literature"[106] for his new magazine, the *Recluse*. He went on to say that "I shall take my time about preparing it," which was true enough: it would be close to a year and a half before he put the finishing touches on what would become "Supernatural Horror in Literature."

Lovecraft began the actual writing of the article in late December; by early January he had already written the first four chapters (on the Gothic school up to and including Maturin's *Melmoth and Wanderer*) and was reading Emily Brontë's *Wuthering Heights* preparatory to writing about it at the end of Chapter V;[107] by March he had written Chapter VII, on Poe;[108] and by the middle of April he had gotten "half through Arthur Machen" (Chapter X).[109] Lovecraft worked on the project in a somewhat peculiar way, alternately reading and writing on a given author or period. It is not entirely clear from his initial mention that Cook actually wished an historical monograph—an essay "on the element of terror & weirdness" could just as well have been theoretical or thematic—but Lovecraft clearly interpreted it this way. He justifies his compositional method—or, rather, declares it to be a matter of necessity—to Morton:

> With my rotten memory I lose the details of half the stuff I read in six months' or a year's time, so that in order to give any kind of intelligent comment on the high spots I selected, I had to give said spots a thorough re-reading. Thus I'd get as far as *Otranto* [Horace Walpole's *The Castle of Otranto*], and then have to rake the damn thing out and see what the plot really was. Ditto the *Old English Baron*. And when I came to *Melmoth* I carefully went over the two anthology fragments which constitute all I can get of it—it's a joke to consider the rhapsodies I've indulged in without having ever perused the opus as a whole! *Vathek* and the *Episodes of Vathek* came in for another once-over, and night before last I did *Wuthering Heights* again from kiver to kiver.[110]

Lovecraft was, indeed, at times scrupulous to a fault. He spent three days reading E. T. A. Hoffmann at the New York Public Library, even though he found him dull and, in his essay, dismissed him in half a paragraph as being more grotesque than genuinely weird. Of course, he took his short cuts, too: his remark above about the two "anthology excerpts" that were all he could get of Maturin's *Melmoth the Wanderer* refers to George Saintsbury's *Tales of Mystery* (1891), containing excerpts from Ann Radcliffe, M. G. Lewis, and Maturin, and Julian Hawthorne's magnificent ten-volume anthology, *The Lock and Key Library* (1909), which Lovecraft had obtained in one of his New York trips of 1922. He drew very heavily upon this latter compilation: the few scraps of Graeco-Roman weird literature he cites (insignificant things like the ghost story in Apuleius and Pliny's letter to Sura) come from this set, as do the four stories he cites by the French collaborators Erckmann-Chatrian.

Lovecraft had, of course, read much of the significant weird literature up to his time, but he was still making discoveries. Indeed, two of the writers whom he would rank very highly were encountered only at about this time. He first read

Algernon Blackwood (1869–1951) as early as 1920, at the recommendation of James F. Morton; curiously, however, he did not care for Blackwood at all at this time: "I can't say that I am very much enraptured, for somehow Blackwood lacks the power to create a really haunting atmosphere. He is too diffuse, for one thing; and for another thing, his horrors and weirdness are too obviously symbolical—symbolical rather than convincingly outré. And his symbolism is not of that luxuriant kind which makes Dunsany so phenomenal a fabulist."[111] Lovecraft next mentioned him in late September 1924, when he reported reading *The Listener and Other Stories* (1907), containing "The Willows," "perhaps the most devastating piece of supernaturally hideous suggestion which I have beheld in a decade."[112] In later years Lovecraft would unhesitatingly (and, I think, correctly) deem "The Willows" the single greatest weird story ever written, followed by Machen's "The White People." Blackwood does not come up for much mention again until early January 1926, but by then Lovecraft had read several of his other early collections—*The Lost Valley and Other Stories* (1910), *Incredible Adventures* (1914), and others. He had not yet read *John Silence—Physician Extraordinary* (1908), but would do so soon; finding some of the tales extremely powerful but in some cases marred by the stock use of the "psychic detective."

As with Machen and Dunsany, Blackwood is an author Lovecraft should have discovered earlier than he did. His first book, *The Empty House and Other Stories* (1906), is admittedly slight, although with a few notable items. *John Silence* became a bestseller, allowing Blackwood to spend the years 1908–14 in Switzerland, where he did most of his best work. *Incredible Adventures* (the very volume toward which Lovecraft was so lukewarm in 1920) is one of the great weird collections of all time; Lovecraft later said that it featured "a serious & sympathetic understanding of the human illusion-weaving process which makes Blackwood rate far higher as a creative artist than many another craftsman of mountainously superior word-mastery & general technical ability . . ."[113]

Blackwood was frankly a mystic. In his exquisite autobiography, *Episodes Before Thirty* (1923)—which completes that curious trilogy of great autobiographies by weird writers, with Machen's *Far Off Things* (1922) and Dunsany's *Patches of Sunlight* (1938)—he admitted to relieving the heavy and conventional religiosity of his household by an absorption of Buddhist philosophy, and he ultimately developed a remarkably vital and intensely felt pantheism that emerges most clearly in his novel *The Centaur* (1911), the central work in his corpus and the equivalent of a spiritual autobiography. In a sense Blackwood sought the same sort of return to the natural world as Dunsany. But because he was, unlike Dunsany, a mystic (and one who would, perhaps inevitably, later find himself attracted to occultism), he would see in the return to Nature a shedding of the moral and spiritual blinders which in his view modern urban civilisation places upon us; hence his ultimate goal was an expansion of consciousness that opened up to our perception the boundless universe with its throbbing presences. Several of his novels—notably *Julius LeVallon* (1916), *The Wave* (1916), and *The Bright Messenger* (1921)—deal explicitly with reincarnation, in such a way as to suggest that Blackwood himself clearly believed in it.

Philosophically, therefore, Blackwood and Lovecraft were poles apart; but the latter never let that bother him (he was just as hostile to Machen's general philosophy), and there is much in Blackwood to relish even if one does not subscribe to his world view. But this philosophical divergence may account for Lovecraft's lack of appreciation of some of Blackwood's less popular works. In particular, the emotion of love figures heavily in such works as *The Wave*, *The Garden of Survival* (1918), and others; and it is not surprising that Lovecraft remained cold to them. More seriously, Blackwood's interest in children—in spite, or perhaps because, of his lifelong bachelorhood—is exemplified in such delicate works of pure fantasy as *Jimbo* (1909), *The Education of Uncle Paul* (1909), and several others; Lovecraft, although appreciating *Jimbo* keenly, tended to dismiss the others as intolerably whimsical and namby-pamby. The accusation may stand when dealing with such weak novels as *A Prisoner in Fairyland* (1913) or *The Extra Day* (1915), but it is unjust to Blackwood's finest works in this vein. Horror, in fact, is frequently not an explicit goal in Blackwood, who much more often sought to evoke the sensation of awe; this is what makes *Incredible Adventures* the masterwork that it is. Lovecraft would, in the end, attempt—and perhaps succeed—in doing the same thing in his later work. It was not long before Lovecraft was ranking Blackwood—correctly—as the leading weird writer of his time, superior even to Machen.

Montague Rhodes James (1862–1936) is a much different proposition. Weird writing represents a quite small proportion of his writing, and was indeed merely a diversion from his work as educator, authority on mediaeval manuscripts, and biblical scholar. His edition of the *Apocryphal New Testament* (1924) long remained standard. James took to telling ghost stories while at Cambridge, and his first tales were recited at a meeting of the Chitchat Society in 1893. He later became Provost of Eton and began telling his tales to his young charges at Christmas. They were eventually collected in four volumes: *Ghost-Stories of an Antiquary* (1904); *More Ghost Stories of an Antiquary* (1911); *A Thin Ghost and Others* (1919); and *A Warning to the Curious* (1925). This relatively slim body of work—which comprises less than 650 pages in the later omnibus, *The Collected Ghost Stories of M. R. James* (1931)—is nonetheless a landmark in weird literature. If nothing else, it represents the extreme refinement of the conventional ghost story, and James's perfection of this form seems to have led directly to the evolution of the psychological ghost story in the hands of Walter de la Mare, Oliver Onions, and L. P. Hartley. James was a master at short story construction; the structure of some of his lengthier tales is at times so complex that there is an extreme disjunction between the actual chronological sequence of the story and its sequence of narration. James also was one of the few who could write in a fairly chatty, whimsical, and bantering style without destroying the potency of his horrors; Lovecraft, while admiring this feature in James, took care to warn younger associates not to try to duplicate it. Like Lovecraft and Machen, James has attracted a somewhat fanatical cadre of devotees. But in all honesty, much of James's work is thin and insubstantial: he had no vision of the world to put across, as Machen, Dunsany, Blackwood, and Lovecraft did, and many of his tales seem like academic exercises in shudder-mongering. Lovecraft seems first to have read James at the New York Public Library in mid-December 1925.[114] By late January 1926 he had read the first three collections and was looking forward to reading *A Warning to the Curious,* then just out. Although his enthusiasm for him was high at the time—"James' mastery of horror is almost unsurpassable"[115]—it would later cool off. Although in "Supernatural Horror in Literature" he would rank James as a "modern master," by 1932 he declared that "he isn't really in the Machen, Blackwood, & Dunsany class. He is the earthiest member of the 'big four.'"[116]

The structure of "Supernatural Horror in Literature" is exceptionally elegant. The ten chapters break down as follows:

     I.   Introduction
     II.   The Dawn of the Horror-Tale
     III.   The Early Gothic Novel
     IV.   The Apex of Gothic Romance
     V.   The Aftermath of Gothic Fiction
     VI.   Spectral Literature on the Continent
     VII.   Edgar Allan Poe
     VIII.   The Weird Tradition in America
     IX.   The Weird Tradition in the British Isles
     X.   The Modern Masters

The introduction lays down the theory of the weird tale as Lovecraft saw it. The next four chapters discuss the weird tale from antiquity to the end of the Gothic school in the early nineteenth century, after which a chapter focuses on foreign weird fiction. Poe occupies a central place in the historical sequence, and his influence becomes evident in the final three chapters.

I have previously mentioned the relative paucity of criticism on weird fiction up to this time. Lovecraft read Edith Birkhead's *The Tale of Terror* (1921), a landmark study of Gothic fiction, in late November; and, in spite of August Derleth's statements to the contrary,[117] it is quite clear that Lovecraft borrowed heavily from this treatise in his chapters (II–V) on the Gothics, both in the structure of his analysis and in some points of evaluation. Lovecraft cites Birkhead by name, along with Saintsbury, at the end of chapter IV. Eino Railo's *The Haunted Castle* (1927) came out just about the time of Lovecraft's own essay; it is a very penetrating historical and thematic study that Lovecraft read with appreciation.

Conversely, the only exhaustive study of *modern* weird fiction was Dorothy Scarborough's *The Supernatural in Modern English Fiction* (1917), which Lovecraft would not read until 1932; but when he did so, he rightly criticised it as being overly schematic in its thematic analyses and hampered by an amusing squeamishness in the face of the explicit horrors of Stoker, Machen, and others. Lovecraft's essay, accordingly, gains its greatest originality as an historical study in its final six chapters. Even today very little work in English has been done on foreign weird writing, and Lovecraft's championing of such writers as Maupassant, Balzac, Erckmann-Chatrian, Gautier, Ewers, and others is pioneering. His lengthy chapter on Poe is, I think, one of the most perceptive short analyses ever written, in spite of a certain flamboyancy in its diction. Lovecraft could not summon up much enthusiasm for the later Victorians in England, but his lengthy discussions of Hawthorne and Bierce in chapter VIII are highly illuminating. And his greatest achievement, perhaps, was to designate Machen, Dunsany, Blackwood, and M. R. James as the four "modern masters" of the weird tale; a judgment that, in spite of the carpings of Edmund Wilson and others, has been justified by subsequent scholarship. Indeed, the only "master" lacking from this list is Lovecraft himself.

At this point it might be well to discuss in general how complete Lovecraft's treatise is. Critics have not been inclined to agree with Fred Lewis Pattee's dictum that it "has omitted nothing important":[118] Peter Penzoldt chided Lovecraft for not even mentioning Oliver Onions and Robert Hichens,[119] while Jack Sullivan has taken Lovecraft to task for his scanty mention of Le Fanu.[120] After my own recent rereading of Le Fanu's largely verbose and unimaginative work, I am by no means ready to admit that Lovecraft is seriously in error here. It is true that he had not even read Le Fanu when he wrote the first version of his essay; at this time he knew him only by reputation. He later read Le Fanu's mediocre novel, *The House by the Churchyard* (1863) and had a justifiably low opinion of it. What work by Le Fanu deserves any attention at all is his short stories and novelettes, and these had evidently become quite scarce by the early twentieth century. When, in 1932, Lovecraft read "Green Tea" (Le Fanu's one unqualified masterwork) in Dorothy L. Sayers's *Omnibus of Crime* (1928), he still did not feel the need to revise his estimate significantly: "I at last have the 'Omnibus', & have read 'Green Tea'. It is certainly better than anything else of Le Fanu's that I have ever seen, though I'd hardly put it in the Poe-Blackwood-Machen class."[121]

But beyond even its perceptive discussions of individual writers, beyond the sure grasp it displays of the historical progression of the field—and recall that this was the *first* time when such an historical survey was attempted (Scarborough's was a thematic study)—"Supernatural Horror in Literature" gains its greatest distinction in its introduction, which simultaneously presents a defence of the weird tale as a serious literary mode and elaborates upon such earlier writings as the *In Defence of Dagon* essays in its clarification of what actually constitutes a weird tale. In the former task, Lovecraft declares resoundingly in the opening sentence that "The oldest and strongest emotion of mankind is fear, and the oldest and strongest kind of fear is fear of the unknown," a "fact" that "must establish for all time the genuineness and dignity of the weirdly horrible tale as a literary form"; he goes on to refer, with tart sarcasm, to the weird tale's struggle against "a naively insipid idealism which deprecates the aesthetic motive and calls for a didactic literature to 'uplift' the reader toward a suitable degree of smirking optimism." All this leads, as it did in *In Defence of Dagon,* to a champion of the weird as appealing largely "to minds of the requisite sensitiveness"; or, as he states at the end, "It is a narrow though essential branch of human expression, and will chiefly appeal as always to a limited audience with keen special sensibilities."

In defining the weird tale, Lovecraft has made contributions of lasting importance. A critical passage in "Supernatural Horror in Literature" attempts to distinguish between the weird and the merely grisly: "This type of fear-literature must not be confounded with a type externally similar but psychologically widely different; the literature of mere physical fear and the mundanely gruesome." The mention of psychology is critical here, for it leads directly to Lovecraft's canonical definition of the weird tale:

> The true weird tale has something more than secret murder, bloody bones, or a sheeted form clanking chains according to rule. A certain atmosphere of breathless and unexplainable dread of outer, unknown forces must be present; and there must be a hint, expressed with a seriousness and portentousness becoming its subject, of that most terrible conception of the human brain—a malign and particular suspension or defeat of those fixed laws of Nature which are our only safeguard against the assaults of chaos and the daemons of unplumbed space.

It could well be said that this is nothing more than an after-the-fact justification of Lovecraft's own brand of cosmic horror; but I think it has a wider application than that. Essentially, Lovecraft is arguing that *supernaturalism* is central to the weird tale, because it is this that distinguishes weird fiction from all other types of literature, which deal strictly with what is possible and therefore have substantially different metaphysical, epistemological, and psychological overtones. Lovecraft does, in "Supernatural Horror in Literature," discuss a few instances of non-supernatural horror—Poe's "The Man of the Crowd," some of Bierce's grim tales of psychological suspense—but they are very few; and he explicitly segregates the *conte cruel*—defined as a story "in which the wrenching of the emotions is accomplished through dramatic tantalisations, frustrations, and gruesome physical horrors"—even though he himself admired many examples of it, such as the tales of Maurice Level, "whose very brief episodes have lent themselves so readily to theatrical adaptation in the 'thrillers' of the Grand Guignol."

In recent years a great deal of material published under the guise of weird fiction falls into the category of psychological suspense (or "dark suspense" or "dark mystery," to use once-fashionable if ill-defined terms). The springboard for much of this writing is Robert Bloch's *Psycho* (1959), certainly a very able piece of work; but more recent works—especially those that involve the already clichéd topos of the serial killer—do not seem to come to terms with either their generic or their ontological status. Are the writers of such works attempting to maintain that "gruesome physical horror" at times can become so extreme as to be emotionally or metaphysically equivalent to supernatural horror? How are their works different from mere suspense stories? These questions remain unanswered, and until they are answered, Lovecraft's definition of the weird tale must stand.

Lovecraft admitted that the writing of this essay produced two good effects; first: "It's good preparation for composing a new series of weird tales of my own";[122] and second: "This course of reading & writing I am going through for the Cook article is excellent mental discipline, & a fine gesture of demarcation betwixt my aimless, lost existence of the past year or two & the resumed Providence-like hermitage amidst which I hope to grind out some tales worth writing."[123] The second effect is one more in a succession of resolutions to cease his all-day and all-night gallivanting with the gang and get down to real work; how successful this was, it is difficult to say, in the absence of a diary for 1926. As for the first effect, it came to fruition in late February, when "Cool Air" was apparently written.

"Cool Air" is the last and perhaps the best of Lovecraft's New York stories. It is a compact exposition of pure physical loathsomeness. The unnamed narrator, having "secured some dreary and unprofitable magazine work" in the spring of 1923, finds himself in a run-down boarding-house whose landlady is a "slatternly, almost bearded Spanish woman named Herrero" and occupied generally by low-life except for one Dr Muñoz, a cultivated and intelligent retired medical man who is continually experimenting with chemicals and indulges in the eccentricity of keeping his room at a temperature of about 55° by means of an ammonia cooling system. The narrator is impressed by Muñoz:

The figure before me was short but exquisitely proportioned, and clad in somewhat formal dress of perfect cut and fit. A high-bred face of masterful though not arrogant expression was adorned by a short iron-grey full beard, and an old-fashioned pince-nez shielded the full, dark eyes and surmounted an aquiline nose which gave a Moorish touch to a physiognomy otherwise dominantly Celtiberian. Thick, well-trimmed hair that argued the punctual calls of a barber was parted gracefully above a high forehead; and the whole picture was one of striking intelligence and superior blood and breeding.

Muñoz, clearly, embodies Lovecraft's ideal type: a man who belongs both to the aristocracy of blood and the aristocracy of intellect; who is highly learned in his field but also dresses well. How can we not fail to recall Lovecraft's own lengthy tirades on the subject when he was deprived of his suits? We are, therefore, meant to sympathise wholly with Muñoz's plight, especially as he is clearly suffering from the effects of some horrible malady that struck him eighteen years ago. When, weeks later, his ammonia cooling system fails, the narrator undertakes a frantic effort to fix it, at the same time enlisting "a seedy-looking loafer" to keep the doctor supplied with the ice that he repeatedly demands in ever larger amounts. But it is to no avail: when the narrator finally returns from his quest to find air-conditioner repairmen, the boarding-house is in turmoil; and when he enters the room, he sees a "kind of dark, slimy trail [that] led from the open bathroom to the hall door" and that "ended unutterably." In fact, Muñoz died eighteen years before and had been attempting to keep himself functioning by artificial preservation.

There are no transcendent philosophical issues raised by "Cool Air," but some of the gruesome touches are uncommonly fine. When at one point Muñoz experiences a "spasm [that] caused him to clap his hands to his eyes and rush into the bathroom," we are clearly to understand that his excitement has caused his eyes nearly to pop out of his head. There is, to be sure, a perhaps deliberate undercurrent of the comic in the whole story, especially when Muñoz, now holed up in a bathtub full of ice, cries through his bathroom door, "More—more!"

Interestingly, Lovecraft later admitted that the chief inspiration for the tale was not Poe's "Facts in the Case of M. Valdemar" but Machen's "Novel of the White Powder,"[124] where a hapless student unwittingly takes a drug that reduces him to "a dark and putrid mass, seething with corruption and hideous rottenness, neither liquid nor solid, but melting and changing before our eyes, and bubbling with unctuous oily bubbles like boiling pitch."[125] And yet, one can hardly deny that M. Valdemar, the man who, after his presumed death, is kept alive after a fashion for months by hypnosis and who at the end collapses "in a nearly liquid mass of loathsome—of detestable putridity,"[126] was somewhere in the back of Lovecraft's mind in the writing of "Cool Air." This story, much more than "The

Horror at Red Hook," is Lovecraft's most successful evocation of the horror to be found in the teeming clangour of America's only true megalopolis.

The setting of the tale is the brownstone occupied by George Kirk both as a residence and as the site of his Chelsea Book Shop at 317 West 14th Street (between Eighth and Ninth Avenues) in Manhattan. Kirk had left 169 Clinton Street as early as June 1925, after less than five months there. He first moved in with Martin and Sara Kamin, his partner, at 617 West 115th Street in Manhattan, and then, after a brief return to Cleveland, settled at the 14th Street boarding-house in August. Even this did not last long, for by October Kirk moved both his residence and his shop to 365 West 15th Street. Here he remained until he married Lucile Dvorak on March 5, 1927, then opening the Chelsea Book Shop at 58 West 8th Street and remaining there for more than a decade.[127]

Lovecraft therefore had access to the 14th Street residence only for about two months, but it was ample time for him to become familiar with it. Very shortly after Kirk moved in, Lovecraft described the place:

> . . . Kirk has hired a pair of immense Victorian rooms as combined office & residence. . . . It is a typical Victorian home of New York's "Age of Innocence", with tiled hall, carved marble mantels, vast pier glasses & mantel mirrors with massive gilt frames, incredibly high ceilings covered with stucco ornamentation, round arched doorways with elaborate rococo pediments, & all the other earmarks of New York's age of vast wealth & impossible taste. Kirk's rooms are the great ground-floor parlours, connected by an open arch, & having windows only in the front room. These two windows open to the south on 14th St., & have the disadvantage of admitting all the babel & clangour of that great crosstown thoroughfare with its teeming traffick & ceaseless street-cars.[128]

That last sentence clearly led to the resounding utterance near the beginning of "Cool Air": "It is a mistake to fancy that horror is associated inextricably with darkness, silence, and solitude. I found it in the glare of mid-afternoon, in the clangour of a metropolis, and in the teeming midst of a shabby and commonplace rooming-house . . ."

Even the ammonia cooling system used in the story has an autobiographical source. In August 1925 Lillian had told Lovecraft of a visit to a theatre in Providence, to which he replied: "Glad you have kept up with the Albee Co., though surprised to hear that the theatre is *hot.* They have a fine ammonia cooling system installed, & if they do not use it it can only be through a niggardly sense of economy."[129]

Farnsworth Wright incredibly and inexplicably rejected "Cool Air," even though it is just the sort of safe, macabre tale he would have liked. Perhaps, as with "In the Vault," he was afraid of its grisly conclusion. In any event, Lovecraft was forced to sell the story for a very low price to the short-lived *Tales of Magic and Mystery,* where it appeared in the March 1928 issue.

Sonia's one stay in New York during the first three months of 1926 occurred between roughly February 15 and March 5. This was, evidently, the first extended period she could get off from Halle's; and Lovecraft reported upon her departure that, if things went well at the department store, she was not expected to return until June.[130] Meanwhile Lovecraft himself finally secured some employment, even if it was of a temporary and, frankly, ignominious sort. In September Loveman had secured work at the prestigious Dauber & Pine bookshop at Fifth Avenue and 12th Street, and he convinced his superiors to hire Lovecraft as an envelope-addresser for three weeks, probably beginning on March 7. Lovecraft had helped Kirk out at this task on several occasions in 1925, doing the work for nothing because of Kirk's many kindnesses to him; indeed, on occasion several of the Kalems would address envelopes en masse, talking, singing old songs, and generally making an amusing evening of it. The pay at the Dauber & Pine job would be $17.50 per week. Lovecraft spoke of the enterprise as a lark ("Moriturus te saluto! Before the final plunge into the abyss I am squaring all my indebtedness to mankind, & will reply briefly to your appreciated note . . ."[131]); but in a later letter to Loveman, Sonia wrote: "I knew that when I was in Cleveland you managed to get a couple of weeks' work for H.P.L. addressing envelopes for Dauber & Pine catalogues. He worked just 2 weeks at $17 a week, and *hated* it."[132] I think Sonia is wrong about the duration of the job, since there are no letters to Lillian between March 6 and March 27; but she is probably right about Lovecraft's reaction to the work, as he never relished repetitive, mechanical tasks of this sort.

Lovecraft himself did not say anything to Lillian about liking or disliking the job. Perhaps he did not wish to seem unwilling to earn a living; but perhaps, by March 27, he had other things on his mind. His letter to Lillian of that date began:

> Well!!! All your epistles arrived & received a grateful welcome, but the third one was the climax that relegates everything else to the distance!! Whoop! Bang! I had to go on a celebration forthwith, . . . & have now returned to gloat & reply. A E P G's letter came, too—riotous symposium!! . . .
>
> And now about your invitation. Hooray!! Long live the State of Rhode-Island & Providence-Plantations!!![133]

In other words, Lovecraft had at last been invited to return to Providence.

17. Paradise Regain'd (1926)

Writing to Arthur Harris in late July 1924, Lovecraft stated: "Though now in New York, I hope to return to Providence some day; for it has a quiet dignity I have never elsewhere observed save in some of the Massachusetts coast towns."[1] This is an anomalously early indication of his wish to come home, possibly belying the conventional wisdom that Lovecraft's "honeymoon" with New York lasted for at least half a year; and, in charity, we can assume that such a repatriation would also have included Sonia in some fashion or other. But the real saga of Lovecraft's efforts to return to Providence can be said to commence around April 1925, when he wrote to Lillian:

> As to trips— . . . I couldn't bear to see Providence again till I can be there for ever. When I do get home, I shall hesitate about going even to Pawtucket or East Providence, whilst the thought of crossing the line into Massachusetts at Hunt's Mills will fill me with positive horror! But a temporary glimpse would be like that of a distrest mariner swept by a storm within sight of his own harbour, then washed away again into the illimitable blackness of an alien sea.[2]

Lillian had clearly suggested that Lovecraft pay a visit, perhaps to relieve the tedium and even depression that his lack of work, his dismal Clinton Street apartment, and the rocky state of his marriage had engendered. Lovecraft's response is noteworthy: he does not say "if I get home," but "when I do get home," even though he surely knew that any immediate return was economically out of the question. The "alien sea" remark is also highly revealing: it can be nothing other than a reference to New York; and yet, for all his whining about the "aliens" in the city, it was Lovecraft who did not belong. In 1927 he wrote that "I was an unassimilated alien there,"[3] unaware that he has stumbled upon the heart of the matter.

When Lovecraft wrote in November 1925 that "My mental life is really at home"[4] in Providence, he was not exaggerating. For the entirety of his New York stay, he subscribed to the *Providence Evening Bulletin,* reading the *Providence Sunday Journal* (the *Bulletin* published no Sunday edition) along with the *New York Times* on Sunday. He went so far as to remark to Lillian that the *Bulletin* "is the only paper worth reading that I have ever seen."[5] He mentally attempted to stay in touch with Providence in other ways, specifically by reading as many books on Providence history as he could. In February 1925 he acquired *Providence: A Modern City* (1909), edited by William Kirk, as well as a replacement copy of Henry Mann's *Our Police: A History of the Providence Police Force from the*

First Watchman to the Latest Appointee (1889), an earlier copy of which he had let slip from his collection a little while before. Then, beginning in late July, he spent the better part of a month and a half making frequent trips to the genealogical reading room of the New York Public Library to read Gertrude Selwyn Kimball's *Providence in Colonial Times* (1912), an exhaustive history of the city in the seventeenth and eighteenth centuries written by an acquaintance of Annie Gamwell's who had died in 1910.

But reading books was clearly not enough. I have already quoted Sonia's testy remark that Lovecraft held on to his Providence furniture "with a morbid tenacity." This is the subject of one of the most remarkable passages in Lovecraft's letters to his aunts, and an accurate gauge of his temper during the worst of his New York period. Lillian had made the comment (perhaps as a consequence of Lovecraft's long-winded account of purchasing his best suit) that "possessions are a burden"; Lovecraft, in August 1925, flung this remark back in her face:

> Each individual's reason for living is different . . . i.e., to each individual there is some one thing or group of things which form the focus of all his interests & nucleus of all his emotions; & without which the mere process of survival not only means nothing whatsoever, but is often an intolerable load & anguish. Those to whom old associations & possessions do not form this single interest & life-necessity, may well sermonise on the folly of "slavery to worldly goods"—so long as they do not try to enforce their doctrines on others.

And where does Lovecraft stand on the issue?

> It so happens that I am unable to take pleasure or interest in anything but a mental re-creation of other & better days—for in sooth, I see no possibility of ever encountering a really congenial milieu or living among civilised people with old Yankee historic memories again—so in order to avoid the madness which leads to violence & suicide I must cling to the few shreds of old days & old ways which are left to me. Therefore no one need expect me to discard the ponderous furniture & paintings & clocks & books which help to keep 454 always in my dreams. When they go, I shall go, for they are all that make it possible for me to open my eyes in the morning or look forward to another day of consciousness without screaming in sheer desperation & pounding the walls & floor in a frenzied clamour to be waked up out of the nightmare of "reality" & my own room in Providence. Yes—such sensitivenesses of temperament are very inconvenient when one has no money—but it's easier to criticise than to cure them. When a poor fool possessing them allows himself to get exiled & sidetracked through temporarily false perspective & ignorance of the world, the only thing to do is to let him cling to his pathetic scraps as long as he can hold them. They are life for him.[6]

A treatise could be written on this inexpressibly poignant passage. No more do we find the confident "when I do get home"; now Lovecraft sees "no possibility" of ever returning. How Lillian reacted to her only nephew speaking with apparent seriousness—or, at least, with extreme bitterness—about suicide and screaming and pounding the walls, it is not possible to say; indeed, it is a little strange that there seems to be no follow-up to this discussion in subsequent letters.

One may as well at this point address a very curious sidelight on this entire matter. Winfield Townley Scott claimed that, according to Samuel Loveman, Lovecraft during the latter part of his New York period "carried a phial of poison with him" (Loveman's words) so as to be able to put an end to his existence if things became too unbearable.[7] In all honesty, I find this notion entirely preposterous. I flatly believe that Loveman has made up this story—whether to blacken Lovecraft's reputation or for some other reason, I cannot say. Loveman turned against Lovecraft's memory later in life, largely on the belief that Lovecraft's anti-Semitism (about which he learned from Sonia as early as 1948, and perhaps from other sources earlier) made him a hypocrite. It is also possible that Loveman simply misunderstood something that Lovecraft had said—perhaps something meant as a sardonic joke. There is certainly no independent confirmation of this anecdote, and no mention of it by any other friend or correspondent; and one suspects that Lovecraft would have confided in Long more than in Loveman on a matter of such delicacy. I think it is quite out of character for Lovecraft to have come so close to suicide even during this difficult period; indeed, the general tenor of his letters to his aunts, even taking into consideration such passages as I have quoted above, is by no means uniformly depressed or lugubrious. Lovecraft was making every effort within his power to adjust to his circumstances, and he was finding substantial relief from his miseries in antiquarian travels and in association with close friends.

But what about Sonia? The mention in the above letter of a "temporarily false perspective & ignorance of the world" can scarcely refer to anything other than Lovecraft's marriage, which he is now all but declaring a failure. It was at just about this time, or perhaps a little later, that George Kirk casually dropped this bombshell in a letter to his fiancée: "Don't dislike Mrs. L. She is, as I have said, at hospital. H more than intimated that they would separate."[8] This letter is undated, but it was probably written in the autumn of 1925. I do not know what the reference to Sonia's stay in the hospital could be. There is, of course, no allusion at all to such a thing in any of Lovecraft's letters to his aunts, not even toward the end of his New York stay. Indeed, when Lovecraft spoke either to his aunts or to others about a possible return to New England, he almost always spoke of a joint return. In June he writes to Moe: "The turmoil and throngs of N.Y. depress her, as they have begun to do me, and eventually we hope to clear out of this Babylonish burg for good. I . . . hope to get back to New England for the rest of my life . . ."[9]

The subject is not broached again in the surviving letters to Lillian until December:

As for the matter of permanent locations—bless my soul! but S H would only too gladly coöperate in establishing me wherever my mind would be most tranquil & effective! What I meant by 'a threat of having to return to N.Y.' was the matter of industrial opportunity, as exemplified in the Paterson possibility; for in my lean financial state almost any remunerative opening would constitute something which I could not with any degree of good sense or propriety refuse. Now if I were still in N.Y., I could perhaps bear such a thing with philosophical resignation; but if I were back home, I could not possibly contemplate the prospect of leaving again. Once in New England, I must be able to stick there—thenceforward scanning Boston or Providence or Salem or Portsmouth for openings, rather than having my eyes on Manhattan or Brooklyn or Paterson or such distant & unfamiliar realms.[10]

This passage makes it clear that the matter had been discussed previously, but the quoted phrase "a threat of having to return to N.Y." appears in no surviving letter. In any event, it appears that Lillian had made a suggestion to relocate to New England, but only temporarily; and this is something Lovecraft could not have endured. He goes on to say that "S H fully endorses my design of an ultimate return to New England, & herself intends to seek industrial openings in the Boston district after a time," then proceeds to sing Sonia's praises in a touching manner in spite of its almost bathetic tone:

S H's attitude on all such matters is so kindly & magnanimous that any design of permanent isolation on my part would seem little short of barbaric, & wholly contrary to the principles of taste which impel one to recognise & revere a devotion of the most unselfish quality & uncommon intensity. I have never beheld a more admirable attitude of disinterested & solicitous regard; in which each financial shortcoming of mine is accepted & condoned as soon as it is proved inevitable, & in which acquiescence is extended even to my statements . . . that the one *essential* ingredient of my life is a certain amount of quiet & freedom for creative literary composition . . . A devotion which can accept this combination of incompetence & aesthetic selfishness without a murmur, contrary tho' it must be to all expectations originally entertained; is assuredly a phenomenon so rare, & so akin to the historic quality of saintliness, that no one with the least sense of artistic proportion could possibly meet it with other than the keenest reciprocal esteem, respect, admiration, & affection . . .

What I believe has inspired this long-winded passage is a suggestion by Lillian that Lovecraft simply come home and forget about Sonia, leading Lovecraft to counter that he cannot countenance "any design of permanent isolation" from her given her boundlessly patient and understanding attitude. If this conjecture is correct, it lends further support to the belief that Lillian had opposed the marriage all along.

But after December, the issue of Lovecraft's return was evidently dropped, perhaps because all parties concerned were waiting to see whether his possible securing of employment at Morton's museum in Paterson might eventuate. Three more months passed with no prospect of work for Lovecraft except a temporary job as envelope-addresser; and so, on March 27, he finally received the invitation to come home.

What, or who, was behind the invitation? Was it merely Lillian's decision? Did Annie add her vote? Were there others involved? Winfield Townley Scott spoke to Frank Long on this matter, and he writes as follows:

> Mr. Long says "Howard became increasingly miserable and I feared that he might go off the deep end. . . . So I wrote," Long continues, "a long letter to Mrs. Gamwell, urging that arrangements be set in motion to restore him to Providence . . . he was so completely wretched in New York that I was tremendously relieved when he boarded a Providence-bound train a fortnight later."[11]

Long told Arthur Koki the same thing about fifteen years later.[12] But in his 1975 memoir Long tells a different story:

> My mother quickly realized that his sanity might indeed be imperiled if another month passed without a prospect of rescue and wrote a long letter to his aunts, describing the situation in detail. I doubt whether Sonia even knew about that letter. At least she never mentioned it in recalling that particular period. Two days later a letter from Mrs. Clark arrived at the Brooklyn rooming house in the morning mail, accompanied by a railway ticket and a small check.[13]

So who wrote the letter, Long or his mother? The latter theory is not at all improbable: during Lillian's month or so in New York during December 1924 and January 1925, she and Lovecraft visited the Longs frequently; and it seems that a bond was established between these two elderly women whose son and nephew, respectively, were such close friends. Still, Long's earlier mentions that he wrote the letter may perhaps be more reliable; or perhaps both Long and his mother did so.

Long is, however, clearly wrong in one detail in his later memoir: a railway ticket could not have been included with Lillian's March letter to Lovecraft, for it was another week or so before Providence was actually decided upon as his ultimate haven. After making the preliminary invitation, Lillian had evidently suggested Boston or Cambridge as a more likely place for Lovecraft to find literary work. Lovecraft grudgingly admitted the apparent good sense of this idea ("Naturally, since Providence is a commercial port whilst Cambridge is a cultural centre, the latter would be expected to fit a literarily inclined person much better"), but went on to maintain that "I am essentially a recluse who will have very little to do with people wherever he may be," and then, in words both poignant and a little sad, made a plea for residing in Providence:

> To all intents & purposes I am more naturally isolated from mankind than Nathaniel Hawthorne himself, who dwelt alone in the midst of crowds, & whom Sa-

lem knew only after he died. Therefore, it may be taken as axiomatic that the people of a place matter absolutely nothing to me except as components of the general landscape & scenery. . . . My life lies not among *people* but among *scenes*—my local affections are not personal, but topographical & architectural. . . . I am always an outsider—to all scenes & all people—but outsiders have their sentimental preferences in visual environment. I will be dogmatic only to the extent of saying that it is *New England* I *must* have—in some form or other. Providence is part of me—I *am* Providence . . . Providence is my home, & there I shall end my days if I can do so with any semblance of peace, dignity, or appropriateness. . . . Providence would always be at the back of my head as a goal to be worked toward—an ultimate Paradise to be regain'd at last.[14]

Whether this letter turned the trick or not, Lillian shortly afterward decided that her nephew should come back to Providence and not Boston or Cambridge. When the offer had first been made in late March, Lovecraft assumed that he might move into a room at Lillian's boarding-house at 115 Waterman Street; but now Lillian reported that she had found a place for both herself and Lovecraft at 10 Barnes Street, north of the Brown University campus, and asked Lovecraft whether she should take it. He responded with another near-hysterical letter:

> Whoopee!! Bang!! 'Rah!! For God's sake jump at that room without a second's delay!! I can't believe it—too good to be true! . . . Somebody wake me up before the dream becomes so poignant I can't bear to be waked up!!!
>
> Take it? Well, I should say so!! I can't write coherently, but I shall proceed at once to do what I can about packing. Barnes near Brown! What deep breaths I can take after this infernal squalor here!![15]

I have quoted these letters at such length—and several of them go on for pages in this vein—to display just how close to the end of his tether Lovecraft must have been. He had tried for two years to put the best face on things—had tried to convince Lillian, and perhaps himself, that his coming to New York was *not* a mistake—but when the prospect of going home was held out, he leaped at it with an alacrity that betrays his desperation.

The big question, of course, was where Sonia fit in—or, perhaps, whether she fit in. In his letter of April 1 he casually noted, "S H endorses the move most thoroughly—had a marvellously magnanimous letter from her yesterday"; and five days later he added briefly, "I hope she won't consider the move in too melancholy a light, or as anything to be criticised from the standpoint of loyalty & good taste."[16] I am not sure of the exact context or connotation of this remark. About a week later Lovecraft reported to Lillian that "S H has abandoned the immediate Boston plan, but will in all probability accompany me to Providence"[17]—although this means she will merely come back to Brooklyn to help him pack and accompany him home to get him ensconced in his new quarters; there was certainly no thought at this juncture of her actually living in Providence or working there.

And yet, such a course was clearly considered at some point—at least by Sonia, and perhaps by Lovecraft as well. She quotes the line from "He"—"I . . . still refrained from going home to my people lest I seem to crawl back ignobly in defeat"—which Cook had cited in his memoir, and adds tartly: "This is only part of the truth. He wanted more than anything else to go back to Providence but he also wanted *me* to come along, and this I could not do because there was no situation open there for me; that is, one fitting my ability and my need."[18] Perhaps the most dramatic passage in her entire memoir relates to this critical period:

> When he no longer could tolerate Brooklyn, I, myself, suggested that he return to Providence. Said he, "If we could but both return to live in Providence, the blessed city where I was born and reared, I am sure, there I could be happy." I agreed, "I'd love nothing better than to live in Providence if I could do my work there but Providence has no particular niche that I could fill." He returned to Providence himself. I came much later.
>
> H. P. lived in a large studio room at that time, where the kitchen was shared with two other occupants. His aunt, Mrs. Clark, had a room in the same house while Mrs. Gamwell, the younger aunt, lived elsewhere. Then we had a conference with the aunts. I suggested that I would take a large house, secure a good maid, pay all the expenses and have the two aunts live with us at no expense to them, or at least they would live better at no greater expense. H. P. and I actually negotiated the rental of such a house with the option to buy it if we found we liked it. H. P. was to use one side of it as his study and library, and I would use the other side as a business venture of my own. At this time the aunts gently but firmly informed me that neither they nor Howard could afford to have Howard's wife work for a living in Providence. That was that. I now knew where we all stood. Pride preferred to suffer in silence; both theirs and mine.[19]

This account is full of difficulties. First, it is clear that Sonia was not the one who "suggested that he return to Providence," otherwise Lovecraft would not have told Lillian repeatedly that she was merely "endorsing" the move. Second, it is not possible to ascertain exactly when this "conference" in Providence took place. Sonia goes on to say that she initially accepted a job in New York (having presumably given up the position at Halle's in Cleveland) so that she could be near Lovecraft and perhaps spend weekends in Providence, but that she received an offer of a job in Chicago that was too good to refuse. She therefore asked Lovecraft to come back to New York for a few days to see her off; and Lovecraft did indeed return to New York for a brief period in September, although Sonia claims she left for Chicago in July. It is possible, then, that the conference in Providence took place in early summer. Then again, Sonia's mention that she came to Providence "much later" may mean that she came only years later—perhaps as late as 1929, for it was only at this time that actual divorce proceedings, undertaken at Sonia's insistence, occurred.

The critical issue is the "pride" cited by Sonia. We here see the clash of cultures and generations at its clearest: on the one side the dynamic, perhaps domineering businesswoman striving to salvage her marriage by taking things into her own hands, and on the other side the Victorian shabby-genteel matrons who could not "afford" the social catastrophe of seeing their only nephew's wife set up a shop and support them in the very town where the name of Phillips still represented something akin to an aristocracy. The exact wording of Sonia's comment is of note: it carries the implication that the aunts might have countenanced her opening a shop somewhere other than Providence.

Are the aunts to be criticised for their attitude? Certainly, many of those today who believe that the acquisition of money is the highest moral good that human beings can attain will find it absurd, incomprehensible, and offensively class-conscious; but the 1920s in New England was a time when standards of propriety meant more than an income, and the aunts were simply adhering to the codes of behaviour by which they had led their entire lives. If anyone is to be criticised, it is Lovecraft; whether he agreed with his aunts on the issue or not (and, in spite of his Victorian upbringing, my feeling is that at this time he did not), he should have worked a little harder to express his own views and to act as an intermediary so that some compromise could have been worked out. Instead, he seems to have stood idly by and let his aunts make all the decisions for him. In all honesty, it is highly likely that he really wished the marriage to end at this point—or, at the very least, that he was perfectly content to see it continue only by correspondence, as indeed it did for the next several years. All he wanted was to come home; Sonia could shift for herself.

How are we to judge Lovecraft's two-year venture into matrimony? There is, certainly, enough blame to spread to all parties: to the aunts for being cool to the entire matter and for failing to provide either financial or emotional support to the struggling couple; to Sonia for feeling that she could mould Lovecraft to suit her wishes; and, of course, to Lovecraft himself for being generally thoughtless, spineless, emotionally remote, and financially incompetent. There is nothing but circumstantial evidence for this first point; but let us consider the last two more carefully.

Sonia's memoir makes it clear that she found in Lovecraft a sort of raw material which she wished to shape to her own desires. The fact that a great many women enter into marriage with such conceptions is no great mitigating factor. I have already noted the seriocomic episode of Sonia forcing Lovecraft to get a new suit because she disliked the old-fashioned cut of his old ones. Recall also how she wished to get rid of his lean and hungry look by beefing him up. In a broader way she also wanted to remake his entire personality—ostensibly to benefit him, but really to make him more satisfactory to herself. She bluntly declared that she initially wished Lovecraft and Loveman to meet in order to "cure" Lovecraft of his race prejudice; it would certainly have been a good thing if she had succeeded, but clearly that was beyond her powers. When discussing the nicknames Socrates and Xanthippe, she notes her belief in Lovecraft's "Socratic wisdom and genius" and goes on to say:

> It was *this* that I sensed in him and had hoped in time to humanize him further by encouraging him toward the wedded path of true love. I am afraid that my optimism and my excessive self-assurance misled me, and perhaps him, too. I had always admired great intellectuality perhaps more than anything else in the world (perhaps, too, because I lacked so much of it myself) and had hoped to lift H. P. out of his abysmal depths of loneliness and psychic complexes.[20]

This is the closest Sonia comes to admitting that she was partly to blame for the marriage's collapse. Whether her offhand psychoanalysis of Lovecraft has any merit, I shall not venture to say; probably she is right at least in noting his fundamental need for solitude and, perhaps, his inability (or unwillingness, if that does not amount to the same thing) to establish an intimate union with someone other than a close relative.

And yet, Sonia should have known what she was getting into. She states that, "early in the life of our romance,"[21] Lovecraft sent her a copy of George Gissing's *The Private Papers of Henry Ryecroft* (1903); she does not give Lovecraft's reason for doing so, but he must have been attempting to supply at least some hints about his own character and temperament. Lovecraft, strangely enough, does not mention this book to any other correspondents, as far as I know; but that it contains many suggestive passages is unquestionable.

Gissing's novel is the purported first-person account of a struggling writer who, late in life, receives an unexpected inheritance that allows him to retire to the country. He spends his time writing offhandedly in a diary, and Gissing as "editor" presents a carefully selected and organised series of excerpts from it, arranged generally by the course of the four seasons. It is, indeed, a very poignant work—but, I think, only if one agrees with the views being expressed by Ryecroft. I suspect that many modern readers would find these views in various ways repulsive or at least antiquated. Sonia herself claims that there is in the novel the same attitude toward minorities that she found in Lovecraft, but this is not one of its prominent features. What is more significant is Ryecroft's attitudes toward art and, by extension, society.

Ryecroft, although having spent much of his life writing articles for money, always hated such a life and now is in the position of scorning it. Writing is not, or ought not to be, a "profession": "Oh, you heavy-laden, who at this hour sit down to the cursed travail of the pen; writing, not because there is something in your mind, in your heart, which must needs be uttered, but because the pen is the only tool you can handle, your only means of earning bread!"[22] This leads more broadly to a scorn of the masses of humanity who read this lifeless work. "I am no friend of the people," he declares bluntly—a line that Sonia herself quotes in her memoir.[23] "Democracy," Ryecroft goes on in a passage that Lovecraft surely relished, "is full of menace to all the finer hopes of civilization . . ."[24]

In a more personal way, Ryecroft ruminates on himself and his capacity for emotion. Although he is himself a widower with a grown daughter, he declares: "Do I really believe that at any time of my life I have been the kind of man who merits affection? I think not. I have always been much too self-absorbed; too critical of all about me; too unreasonably proud."[25] Later on, in another passage that must have warmed Lovecraft's heart, Ryecroft defends prudishness:

> If by prude be meant a secretly vicious person who affects an excessive decorum, by all means let the prude disappear, even at the cost of some shamelessness. If, on the other hand, a prude is one who, living a decent life, cultivates, either by bent or by principle, a somewhat extreme delicacy of thought and speech with regard to elementary facts of human nature, then I say that this is most emphatically a fault in the right direction, and I have no desire to see its prevalence diminish.[26]

How can we not think of Lovecraft's letter to Sonia on the subject, in which sex is regarded as a momentary and irrational passion of youth which "mature middle age" should relinquish? How can we not recall Lovecraft's squeamishness at the mere mention of the word "sex"? Sonia rightly declared that the whole of *The Private Papers of Henry Ryecroft* should be read to understand Lovecraft; in his attachment to his home, his disdain for society, his devotion to books, and in so many other ways Ryecroft seems an uncanny echo of Lovecraft, and one can imagine the latter's sense of wonder at reading a book that seemed to be laying bare his own inmost thoughts.

The point is, of course, that Sonia read *Ryecroft* and knew of Lovecraft's general unsuitability as a husband; but, as she declares, she overestimated her "self-assurance" and believed she could relieve his "complexes" and make him, if not a conventional bourgeois breadwinner—she surely knew he could never be that—at least a somewhat more outgoing, loving husband and an even more gifted writer than he was. I do not doubt that Sonia genuinely loved Lovecraft and that she went into the marriage with the best of intentions, and with the idea of bringing out what she felt was the best in her husband; but she really ought to have known that Lovecraft was not so easily malleable.

It seems hardly profitable at this juncture to blame Lovecraft for his many failings as a husband—nothing can be accomplished now by such a schoolmasterly attitude—but much in his behaviour is inexcusable. The most inexcusable, of course, is the decision to marry at all, a decision he made with very little awareness of the difficulties involved (beyond any of the financial concerns that emerged unexpectedly at a later date) and without any sense of how unsuited he was to be a husband. Here was a man with an unusually low sex drive, with a deep-seated love of his native region, with severe prejudice against racial minorities, suddenly deciding to marry a woman who, although several years older than he, clearly wished both a physical as well as intellectual union, and deciding also to uproot himself from his place of birth to move into a bustling, cosmopolitan, racially heterogeneous megalopolis without a job and, it appears, entirely content to be supported by his wife until such time as he got one.

Once actually married, Lovecraft displayed singularly little consideration for his wife. He found it much more entertaining to spend most of his evenings, and even nights, with the boys, and quickly ceased bothering to get home early so that he could go to sleep together with Sonia. He did make a concerted effort to find work in 1924, however bunglingly he set about it, but virtually gave up the attempt in 1925–26. Once he came to the realisation that married life did not suit him, he seems to have become entirely content—when Sonia was forced to move to the Midwest in 1925—to conduct a marriage at long distance by correspondence.

And yet, mitigating factors must be brought to bear. Once the glamour of New York wore off, Lovecraft's state of mind rapidly deteriorated. At what point did he sense that he had made a mistake? Did he come to believe that Sonia was in some way responsible for his plight? Perhaps it is not surprising that he found more comfort in the presence of his friends than of his wife.

Three years after the débâcle Lovecraft pondered the whole matter, and to his words not much need be added. Although he later maintained the charade that the collapse of the marriage was "98% financial,"[27] he plainly admitted that a fundamental difference in character caused the breakup:

> I haven't a doubt but that matrimony can become a very helpful and pleasing permanent arrangement when both parties happen to harbour the potentialities of parallel mental and imaginative lives—similar or at least mutually comprehensible reactions to the same salient points in environment, reading, historic and philosophic reflection, and so on; and corresponding needs and aspirations in geographic, social, and intellectual milieu . . . With a wife of the same temperament as my mother and aunts, I would probably have been able to reconstruct a type of domestic life not unlike that of Angell St. days, even though I would have had a different status in the household hierarchy. But years brought out basic and essential diversities in reactions to the various landmarks of the time-stream, and antipodal ambitions and conceptions of value in planning a fixed joint milieu. It was the clash of the abstract-traditional-individual-retrospective-Apollonian aesthetic with the concrete-emotional-present-dwelling-social-ethical-Dionysian aesthetic; and amidst this, the originally fancied congeniality, based on a shared disillusion, philosophic bent, and sensitiveness to beauty, waged a losing struggle.[28]

Abstract as this sounds, it reveals a clear grasp of the fundamentals of the matter: he and Sonia were simply not temperamentally suited to each other. In theory Lovecraft conceded that some woman more similar to him, or to his mother and aunts, might make a suitable wife; but elsewhere in this same letter, while defending marriage as an institution, he virtually ruled it out for himself:

> . . . I've no fault to find with the institution, but think the chances of success for a strongly individualised, opinionated, and imaginative person are damn slender. It's a hundred to one shot that any four or five consecutive plunges he might make would turn out to be flivvers equally oppressive to himself and to his fellow-victim, so if he's a wise guy he "lays off" after the collapse of venture #1 . . . or if he's very wise he avoids even that! Matrimony may be more or less normal, and socially essential in the abstract, and all that—but nothing in heaven or earth is so important to the man of spirit and imagination as the inviolate integrity of his cerebral life—his sense of utter integration and defiant independence as a proud, lone entity face to face with the illimitable cosmos.

And that is about all that Lovecraft has to say on the matter.

As for Sonia herself, she is remarkably reticent—publicly, at least—on what she believed to be the causes of the marriage's failure. In her published memoir, she appears in some sense to lay the blame on Lillian and Annie for their unwillingness to allow her to set up a shop in Providence; but in an appendix to her memoir, titled "Re Samuel Loveman," she writes at length about the burgeoning of Lovecraft's racial prejudice while in New York and concludes, "If the truth be known, it was *this* attitude toward minorities and his desire to escape them that prompted him back to Providence."[29] This point is elaborated upon in a letter to Samuel Loveman, in which she disputes the belief (whether held by Loveman or not is unclear) that the marriage dissolved because of Lovecraft's inability to earn an income. "I did *not* leave him on account of non-providence, but chiefly on account of his harping hatred of J—s. This and this alone was the real reason."[30] This certainly seems unambiguous enough, and I think we are obliged to accept it as at least one reason—and perhaps the major one—for the collapse of the marriage. There were financial problems, there were temperamental differences; but overriding these, or exacerbating them, was, on the one side, Lovecraft's increasing hatred of New York and its denizens and, on the other side, Sonia's inability to relieve Lovecraft of his rooted prejudices.

What is more remarkable is that in later years Lovecraft would in many instances actually conceal the fact that he ever was married. When giving the essentials of his life to new correspondents, he would mention the New York episode but not Sonia or his marriage; and only if some correspondent bluntly and nosily asked him point-blank whether or not he was ever married would he admit that he was. A letter written to Donald Wandrei in February 1927 is typical: "A good nine-tenths of my best friends reside in New York from accident or necessity, & I thought three years ago that it was the logical place for me to settle—at least for several years. Accordingly I transferred my belongings thither in March 1924, & remained till April 1926, at the end of which time I found I absolutely could stand the beastly place no longer."[31] Now Lovecraft is claiming that he came to New York only to be in close contact with "friends"! If this reticence to new colleagues in private correspondence is perhaps excusable (Lovecraft was under no obligation to tell of his personal affairs to anyone if he chose not to do so), it is perhaps less so when it is manifested in the formal autobiographical essays of the last ten years of his life. It is as if his marriage, and his entire New York stay, had never happened.

One subject on which Lovecraft never tired of expatiating was both the wretched state of his existence in New York, especially at Clinton Street, and more generally his loathing of the metropolis and everything it stood for. As for the first:

> The keynote of the whole setting—house, neighbourhood, and shop, was that of loathsome and insidious decay; masked just enough by the reliques of former splendour and beauty to add terror and mystery and the fascination of crawling motion to a deadness and dinginess otherwise static and prosaic. I conceived the idea that the great brownstone house was a malignly sentient thing—a dead, vampire creature which sucked something out of those within it and implanted in them the seeds of some horrible and immaterial psychic growth. Every closed door seemed to hide some brooding crime—or blasphemy too deep to form a crime in the crude and superficial calendar of earth. I never quite learned the exact topography of that rambling and enormous house. How to get to my room, and to Kirk's room when he was there, and to the landlady's quarters to pay my rent or ask in vain for heat until I bought an oil stove of my own—these things I knew, but there were wings and stairways that I never saw opened. I know there were rooms above ground without windows, and was at liberty to guess what might lie below ground.[32]

If there is a certain amount of playful hyperbole here, his other remarks are anything but playful:

> ... in New York I could not live. Everything I saw became unreal & two-dimensional, & everything I thought & did became trivial & devoid of meaning through lack of any points of reference belonging to any fabric of which I could conceivably form a part. I was stifled—poisoned—imprisoned in a nightmare—& now not even the threat of damnation could induce me to dwell in the accursed place again.[33]

There is little here that is not found, for example, in the opening pages of "He"; but to read it in unvarnished form in letters, without even a thin veil of fictionalisation, is poignant. It is telling that Lovecraft never said anything like the above to

Lillian until right at the end of his New York stay: would such an admission make it too clear that he was "crawling back ignobly in defeat"?

Lovecraft was, of course, at liberty to hate New York; where he seemed to commit a lapse of logic was in maintaining that all "normal" or healthy individuals ought to find the place unendurable. The underlying theme of these rants is, of course, the "foreigners" who have presumably overrun the city, although I do not believe that Lovecraft's sentiments can be reduced to simple racism; instead, the foreigners are the most noticeable symbol of New York's departure from the norms he had known all his life:

> In a colourless or monotonous environment I should be hopelessly soul-starved—New York almost finished me, as it was! I find that I draw my prime contentment from beauty & mellowness as expressed in quaint town vistas & in the scenery of ancient farming & woodland regions. Continuous growth from the past is a sine qua non—in fact, I have long acknowledged *archaism* as the chief motivating force of my being.[34]

Even here—or, rather, in his application of this credo to his discussions of New York—Lovecraft falls into a fallacy; for he imagines that New York's immigrants have somehow caused the city to deviate from its "natural" development, evidently by their mere presence (his continual contrasts of New York with Boston or Philadelphia, then still dominantly Anglo-Saxon, are noteworthy). At times this view becomes comically absurd: "New York represents such a stupendous ruin & decay—such a hideous replacement of virile & sound-heritaged stock by whipped, cringing, furtive dregs & offscourings—that I don't see how anyone can live long in it without sickening."[35] How remarkable that these whipped dregs have managed to overwhelm the virile Aryans!

But these rants really served a largely psychological purpose: New York is now the "other," a symbol of everything that is wrong with modern American civilisation. It is not surprising that, although now once again ensconced in the comfortable and familiar haven of Providence, Lovecraft began in the late 1920s to develop his notions of the decline of the West—notions that his reading of Oswald Spengler's great work on the subject only helped to clarify and develop.

Meanwhile there was the actual move from Brooklyn to Providence to undertake. Lovecraft's letters to his aunts for the first half of April are full of mundane details on the matter—what moving company to hire, how to pack up his books and other belongings, when he will arrive, and the like. I have previously mentioned that Sonia was planning to come back to assist in the move; indeed, this whole issue led to another testy passage in her memoir. She quotes Cook's statement that the aunts "despatch[ed] a truck which brought Howard back to Providence lock, stock and barrel" and then says that she "came on a special trip from out of town to help him pack his things and saw to it that all was well before I left. And it was out of my funds that it was paid for, including his fare."[36] Sonia arrived on the morning of Sunday, April 11; that evening they went back to their old stamping-grounds in Flatbush, had ice cream, saw a movie, and came home late. The next day was similarly spent in frivolity, as the couple saw the film of *Cyrano de Bergerac* and dined at the Elysée on East 56th Street. Lovecraft admits that Sonia quite consciously wished "to remove to some extent my extreme disgust with N Y, & to substitute in my mind some more favourable parting impressions";[37] too little too late, but at least Lovecraft got a nice meal out of it (fruit cocktail, soup, lamb chop, french fries, peas, coffee, and a cherry tart).

The packing was all done by Tuesday the 13th, which left Lovecraft time to take in one final Kalem meeting at Long's on Wednesday. Morton, Loveman, Kirk, Kleiner, Orton, and Leeds came; Long's mother served dinner; and, as always, spirited conversation ensued. The meeting broke up at 11.30, and Lovecraft and Kirk decided to undertake one final all-night walking tour. They walked from Long's home (West End Avenue and 100th Street) to all the way down to the Battery. Lovecraft did not come home until 6 A.M., but got up at 10 A.M. to receive the movers.

Lovecraft's letter to Lillian of April 15 is the last letter we have prior to the move, so that the last two days are not entirely clear. He boarded a train (probably at Grand Central Station) in the morning of Saturday, April 17, and arrived early in the afternoon. He tells the story inimitably in a letter to Long:

> Well—the train sped on, & I experienced silent convulsions of joy in returning step by step to a waking & tri-dimensional life. New Haven—New London—& then quaint *Mystic,* with its colonial hillside & landlocked cove. Then at last a still subtler magick fill'd the air—nobler roofs & steeples, with the train rushing airily above them on its lofty viaduct—*Westerly*—in His Majesty's Province of RHODE-ISLAND & PROVIDENCE-PLANTATIONS! GOD SAVE THE KING!! Intoxication follow'd—Kingston—East Greenwich with its steep Georgian alleys climbing up from the railway—Apponaug & its ancient roofs—Auburn—just outside the city limits—I fumble with bags & wraps in a desperate effort to appear calm—THEN—a delirious marble dome outside the window—a hissing of air brakes—a slackening of speed—surges of ecstasy & dropping of clouds from my eyes & mind—HOME—UNION STATION— ***PROVIDENCE!!!!***[38]

The printed text cannot tell the whole story, for as Lovecraft approaches the triumphant conclusion his handwriting begins to grow larger and larger, until that final word is nearly an inch high. It is symmetrically balanced by four exclamation marks and four underscores. Maurice Lévy is right to say of this passage: "There is something moving in the account he gives of this mythical return to his home, something that betrays a vital, primordial experience."[39]

This entire letter to Long, written two weeks after his return, is full of astonishing insights. In effect, Lovecraft was attempting to maintain that the two years spent in New York simply did not happen—that they were a "dream" and he had now simply waken up. To be sure, this was said with tongue in cheek, but there was clearly an undercurrent of sincerity to it: ". . . 1923—1924—1925—1926—1925—1924—1923—crash! Two years to the bad, but who the hell gives a damn? 1923 ends—1926 begins! . . . What does a blind spot or two in one's existence matter?" Perhaps Lovecraft should be allowed his moment of wish-fulfilment; in no long time he came to understand that he would have to come to terms with those two New York years and reshape his life accordingly. Much as he might yearn to return to the carefree state he enjoyed prior to his marriage, he knew it was only a fantasy. The subsequent eleven years of his life will, I think, sustain the truth of W. Paul Cook's celebrated remark: "He came back to Providence a human being—and what a human being! He had been tried in the fire and came out pure gold."[40]

Did Sonia accompany Lovecraft back to Providence? His letter to Long is singularly ambiguous on the point: he never mentions her by name in the entire ten-page document, and the early pages of the account are entirely in the first-person singular; but perhaps Long knew the situation so well that Lovecraft did not feel the need to specify. From what I can ascertain, Sonia did not in fact come with him, but joined him a few days later to help him settle in; Lovecraft indirectly confirms this speculation by using the first-person plural in the latter stages of his letter to Long.[41] After spending a few days unpacking, Lovecraft and Sonia went to Boston on Thursday, April 22, and on the next day they explored Neutaconkanut Hill on the west side of Providence, where Lovecraft had gone in October 1923. It is not clear when Sonia returned to New York, but she probably did not stay for much more than a week.

Cook has another imperishable account of Lovecraft's settling in:

> I saw him in Providence on his return from New York and before he had his things all unpacked and his room settled, and he was without question the happiest man I ever saw—he could have posed for an "After Taking" picture for the medical ads. He *had* taken it and shown that he *could* take it. His touch was caressing as he put his things in place, a real love-light shone in his eyes as he glanced out of the window. He was so happy he hummed—if he had possessed the necessary apparatus he would have purred.[42]

In his letter to Long he supplies a detailed plan of the large one-bedroom apartment with kitchen alcove:

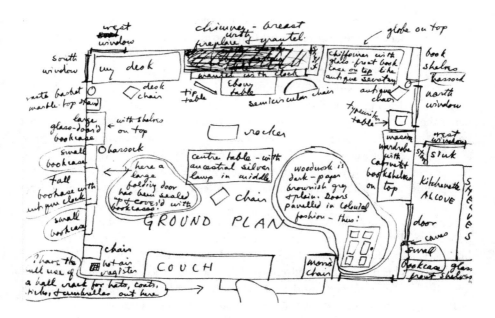

Further maps indicate what is on the walls, including a painting of a rose by his mother and other paintings (of a stag and a farmhouse), perhaps by Lillian, on the east wall (which also contains the door leading out of the apartment), the south wall entirely covered by bookshelves, and the west wall with its fireplace and mantelpiece. The house itself was built only around 1880, so it is by no means colonial; but it is a pleasing and spacious edifice. Like 598 Angell Street, it is a double house, the western half being 10 Barnes and the eastern half 12 Barnes. Lovecraft added further:

> The house is immaculately clean, & inhabited only by select persons of the good old families . . . The neighbourhood is perfect—all old Yankee Providence homes, with a good percentage of the houses colonial. . . . The vista from my pseudo-oriel desk corner is delectable—bits of antique houses, stately trees, urn-topp'd white Georgian fence, & an ecstatic old-fashion'd garden which will be breathlessly transporting in a couple of months.[43]

The view has not changed much since Lovecraft's day. The house, then as now, is a series of apartments.

We do not know much of what Lovecraft was doing during the first few months of his return to Providence. In April, May, and June he reported seeing several parts of the city he had never seen before, at least once in the company of Annie Gamwell, who at this time was residing at the Truman Beckwith house at College and Benefit Streets. He expressed the wish to do more reading and collecting of Rhode Island matter, and claimed that a special corner of the reference room of the Providence Public Library would now be among his principal haunts.

Providence enters into several of the tales he wrote in the year after his return; indeed, this period—from the summer of 1926 to the spring of 1927—represents the most remarkable outburst of fiction-writing in Lovecraft's entire career. Only a month after leaving New York he wrote to Morton: "It is astonishing how much better the old head works since its restoration to those native scenes amidst which it belongs. As my exile progressed, even reading and writing became relatively slow and formidable processes . . ."[44] Now things were very different: two short novels, two novelettes, and three short stories, totalling some 150,000 words, were written at this time, along with a handful of poems and essays. All the tales are set, at least in part, in New England.

First on the agenda is "The Call of Cthulhu," written probably in August or September. This story had, of course, been plotted a full year earlier, as recorded in his diary entry for August 12–13, 1925: "Write out story plot—'The Call of Cthulhu.'" The plot of this well-known tale does not need elaborate description. The subtitle, "(Found Among the Papers of the Late Francis Wayland Thurston, of Boston)," announces that the text is an account written by Thurston (who is otherwise not named in the text) of the strange facts he has assembled, both from the papers of his recently deceased grand-uncle, George Gammell Angell, and from personal investigation. Angell, a professor of Semitic languages at Brown University, had collected several peculiar pieces of data. First, he had taken extensive notes of the dreams and artwork of a young sculptor, Henry Anthony Wilcox, who had come to him with a bas-relief he had fashioned in his sleep on the night of March 1, 1925. The sculpture is of a hideous-looking alien entity, and Wilcox had reported that in the dream that had inspired it he had repeatedly heard the words *"Cthulhu fhtagn."* It was this that had piqued Angell's interest, for he had encountered these words or sounds years before, at a meeting of the American Archaeological Society, in which a New Orleans police inspector named John Raymond Legrasse had brought in a sculpture very much like Wilcox's and claimed that it had been worshipped by a degraded cult in the Louisiana bayou which had chanted the phrase *"Ph'nglui mglw'nafh Cthulhu R'lyeh wgah'nagl fhtagn."* One of the cult members had proffered a translation of this outlandish utterance: "In his house at R'lyeh dead Cthulhu waits dreaming." Legrasse had also interviewed one cultist, a mestizo named Castro, who had told them that Cthulhu was a vast being that had come from the stars when the earth was young, along with another set of entities named the Great Old Ones; he was buried in the sunken city of R'lyeh and would emerge when the "stars were ready" to reclaim control of the earth. The cult "would always be waiting to liberate him." Castro points out that these matters are spoken of in the *Necronomicon* of the mad Arab Abdul Alhazred.

Thurston scarcely knows what to make of this bizarre material, but then by accident he finds a newspaper clipping telling of strange events aboard a ship in the Pacific Ocean; accompanying the article is a picture of another bas-relief very similar to that fashioned by Wilcox and found by Legrasse. Thurston goes to Oslo to talk with the Norwegian sailor, Gustaf Johansen, who had been on board the ship, but finds that he is dead. Johansen has, however, left behind an account of his experience, and this shows that he had actually encountered the dreaded Cthulhu when the city of R'lyeh rose from the sea-bottom as the result of an earthquake; but, presumably because the stars are not "ready," the city sinks again, returning Cthulhu to the bottom of the ocean. But the mere existence of this titanic entity is an unending source of profound unease to Thurston because it shows how tenuous is mankind's vaunted supremacy upon this planet.

It is difficult to convey by this bald summary the rich texture of this substantial work: its implications of cosmic menace, its insidiously gradual climax, its complexity of structure and multitude of narrative voices, and the absolute perfection of its style—sober and clinical at the outset, but reaching at the end heights of prose-poetic horror that attain an almost epic grandeur. It is his best tale since "The Rats in the Walls"; and, like that tale, it has an *assurance* and *maturity* lacking in much of his early work, but which would be the hallmarks of much of the writing of his last decade.

And yet, the origin of the tale goes back even beyond the evidently detailed plot-synopsis of 1925. Its kernel is recorded in an entry in his commonplace book (#25) that must date to 1920:

> Man visits museum of antiquities—asks that it accept a bas-relief *he has* just made—*old* & learned curator laughs & says he cannot accept anything so modern. Man says that
>
> > 'dreams are older than brooding Egypt or the contemplative Sphinx or garden-girdled Babylonia'
>
> & that he had fashioned the sculpture in his dreams. Curator bids him shew his product, & when he does so curator shews horror, asks who the man may be. He tells modern name. "No—*before that*" says curator. Man does not remember except in dreams. Then curator offers high price, but man fears he means to destroy sculpture. Asks fabulous price—curator will consult directors. ¶ Add good development & describe nature of bas-relief.

This is, of course, the fairly literal encapsulation of a dream Lovecraft had in early 1920, which he describes at length in two letters of the period.[45] The entry has been quoted at length to give some idea of how tangential are the inspirational foci of some of Lovecraft's tales. Only a small portion of this plot-kernel has made its way into the finished story—indeed, nothing is left except the mere fashioning of a strange bas-relief by a modern sculptor under the influence of dreams. And although Wilcox actually says to Angell the words in the entry, this utterance is now (rightly) dismissed by the narrator as "of a fantastically poetic cast which must have typified his whole conversation."

The fact that Wilcox fashioned the bas-relief in his dreams is a tip of the hat to the dominant literary influence on the tale, Guy de Maupassant's "The Horla." It is not likely that Lovecraft had read this tale when he had the dream in 1920 inspiring the commonplace book entry, but he no doubt read it well before writing "The Call of Cthulhu": it is contained in both Joseph Lewis French's *Masterpieces of Mystery* (1920) and in Julian Hawthorne's *Lock and Key Library* (1909), the latter of which Lovecraft obtained on one of his New York trips of 1922. In "Supernatural Horror in Literature" he recognised that "The Horla" was Maupassant's masterpiece of horror and wrote of it: "Relating the advent to France of an invisible being who lives on water and milk, sways the minds of others, and seems to be the vanguard of a horde of extra-terrestrial organisms arrived on earth to subjugate and overwhelm mankind, this tense narrative is perhaps without a peer in its particular department ..." Cthulhu is not, of course, invisible, but the rest of the description tallies uncannily with the events of the story. Some of the reflections by Maupassant's narrator, especially after he reads a book that relates "the history and the manifestations of all the invisible beings which haunt mankind or appear in dreams," are potently cosmic:

> From reading this book I have the impression that man, ever since he has had the ability to think, has had the foreboding that a new creature would appear, someone stronger than himself, who would be his successor on earth. . . .
>
> . . . Who inhabits those far-away worlds? What forms of life, what kind of beings, what animals and plants live out there? And if there are thinking beings in those distant universes how much more do they know than we do? How much more can they do than we can? What things can they see which we do not even suspect? Just suppose that one of them were to travel through space one of these days and come to this earth to conquer it, rather like the Normans in the olden days crossing the sea to enslave weaker races!
>
> We are so feeble, so helpless, so ignorant, so tiny, we creatures on this whirling speck of mud and water . . .
>
> . . .
>
> Now I know. Now I can see the point. The rule of man has come to an end.[46]

No wonder Lovecraft was so taken with this tale. And yet, it must frankly be admitted that Lovecraft himself handles the theme with vastly greater subtlety and richness than Maupassant.

Robert M. Price points to another significant influence on the tale—theosophy.[47] The theosophical movement originated with Helena Petrovna Blavatsky, whose *Isis Unveiled* (1877) and *The Secret Doctrine* (1888–97) introduced this peculiar mélange of science, mysticism, and religion into the West. It would be cumbersome and profitless to give an elaborate account of theosophy; suffice it to say that its stories of such lost realms as Atlantis and Lemuria—derived from the supposedly ancient *Book of Dzyan,* of which *The Secret Doctrine* purports to be an immense commentary—fired Lovecraft's imagination. He read W. Scott-Elliot's *The Story of Atlantis and the Lost Lemuria* (1925; actually a compendium of two of Scott-Elliot's books, *The Story of Atlantis* [1896] and *The Lost Lemuria* [1904]) in the summer of 1926,[48] and actually mentions the book in his tale; the theosophists are themselves mentioned in the second paragraph. Castro's wild tale of the Great Old Ones makes allusions to cryptic secrets that "deathless China-men" told him—a nod to the theosophists' accounts of Shamballah, the Tibetan holy city (the prototype of Shangri-La) whence the doctrines of theosophy are sup-posed to have originated. Lovecraft, of course, did not believe this nonsense; in fact, he has a little fun with it when he says: "Old Castro remembered bits of hide-ous legend that paled the speculations of theosophists and made man and the world seem recent and transient indeed."

Still another influence is "The Moon Pool," a novelette by A. Merritt (1884–1943). Lovecraft frequently rhapsodised about this tale, which was first published in the *All-Story* for June 22, 1918, and which takes place on or near the island of Po-nape, in the Carolines. Merritt's mention of a "moon-door" that, when tilted, leads the characters into a lower region of wonder and horror seems similar to the huge door whose inadvertent opening by the sailors causes Cthulhu to emerge from R'lyeh.

It may be worth dwelling briefly on the autobiographical features in the story before discussing the larger issues it raises. Some of these are superficial, scarcely above the level of in-jokes: the name of the narrator, Francis Wayland Thurston, is clearly derived from Francis Wayland (1796–1865), president of Brown University from 1827 to 1855; Gammell is a legitimate variant of Gamwell, while Angell is at once the name of one of the principal thoroughfares and one of the most distin-guished families in the city; Wilcox is a name from Lovecraft's ancestry;[49] and when Thurston finds the clipping about Johansen while "visiting a learned friend in Pater-son, New Jersey; the curator of a local museum and a mineralogist of note," we scarcely need be told that James F. Morton is being alluded to. (One false autobio-graphical detail is the mestizo Castro, whose name was believed to derive from Ad-olphe Danziger de Castro, the friend of Bierce's who became Lovecraft's revision client; but Lovecraft did not come into contact with de Castro until late 1927.[50])

The residence of Wilcox at the Fleur-de-Lys building at 7 Thomas Street is a real structure, still standing; Lovecraft is correct in describing it scornfully as "a hideous Victorian imitation of seventeenth-century Breton architecture which flaunts its stuccoed front amidst the lovely colonial houses on the ancient hill, and under the very shadow of the finest Georgian steeple in America" (i.e., the First

Baptist Church). The fact of Wilcox's occupation of this structure would have an interesting sequel a few years later.

The earthquake cited in the story is also a real event. There is no extant letter to Lillian for the precise period in question, but Lovecraft's diary entry for February 28, 1925 tells the story: "G[eorge] K[irk] & S[amuel] L[oveman] call— . . . —house shakes 9:30 p m . . ." Steven J. Mariconda, who has written exhaustively on the genesis of the tale, notes: "In New York, lamps fell from tables and mirrors from walls; walls themselves cracked, and windows shattered; people fled into the street."[51] It is of some note that the celebrated underwater city of R'lyeh, brought up by this earthquake, was first coined by Lovecraft as L'yeh.[52]

"The Call of Cthulhu" is manifestly an exhaustive reworking of one of Lovecraft's earliest stories, "Dagon" (1917). In that tale we have many nuclei of the later work—an earthquake that causes an undersea land mass to emerge to the surface; the notion of a titanic monster dwelling under the sea; and—although this is barely hinted in "Dagon"—the fact that an entire civilisation, hostile or at best indifferent to mankind, is lurking on the underside of our world. The last notion is also at the heart of Arthur Machen's tales of the "little people," and there is indeed a general Machen influence upon "The Call of Cthulhu"; especially relevant is "Novel of the Black Seal" (an episode in *The Three Impostors*), where Professor Gregg, like Thurston, pieces together disparate bits of information that by themselves reveal little but, when taken together, suggest an appalling horror awaiting the human race.

"The Call of Cthulhu" presents the greatest structural complexity of any of Lovecraft's tales written up to this point. It is one of the first tales to make extensive use of the narrative-within-a-narrative device—a device that ordinarily requires the novel for proper execution, but which Lovecraft utilises effectively here because of the extreme compression of the text. Lovecraft was, as a critic, aware of the aesthetic problems entailed by an improper or bungling use of the narrative within a narrative, in particular the danger of allowing the subnarrative to overwhelm the principal narrative and thereby destroy the unity of the tale as a whole. Of Maturin's *Melmoth the Wanderer* he remarked in "Supernatural Horror in Literature" that the subnarrative of John and Monçada "takes up the bulk of Maturin's four-volume book; this disproportion being considered one of the chief technical faults of the composition." (Lovecraft expresses himself here in this rather tentative way because, as we have seen, he himself never read the entirety of *Melmoth* but only two anthology excepts of it.) The means to avoid structural awkwardness is to integrate the subsidiary narrative with the main narrative, specifically by allowing the protagonist of the main narrative to become intimately involved in the subsidiary one in some fashion or other. In "The Call of Cthulhu" we have a main narrator (Francis Wayland Thurston) paraphrasing the notes of a subsidiary narrator (George Gammell Angell) who himself paraphrases two accounts, that of the artist Wilcox and that of

Inspector Legrasse, who paraphrases yet another subsidiary account, the tale of Old Castro; Thurston then comes upon a newspaper article and the Johansen narrative, items that confirm the truth of Angell's accounts. This entire sequence can be depicted by the following chart of narrative voices:

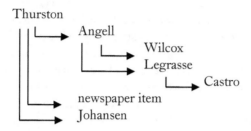

Thurston

Angell

Wilcox

Legrasse

Castro

newspaper item

Johansen

This structure never becomes clumsy because we are always aware of the presence of the principal narrator, who has both assembled the various other narratives and repeatedly comments upon them. It should be noted that the most "sensational" part of the story—Castro's wild tale of the Great Old Ones—is *three times* removed from the principal narrative: Thurston—Angell—Legrasse—Castro. This is narrative "distance" with a vengeance! When Lovecraft commented in later years that he felt the story was "cumbrous,"[53] he was perhaps referring to this structural complexity—a complexity, however, that is undeniably effective in conveying with power and verisimilitude what is to be conveyed.

But no analysis of "The Call of Cthulhu" can begin to convey the rich satisfaction one derives from reading it. From the celebratedly pensive opening (itself a radical refinement of the opening of "Facts concerning the Late Arthur Jermyn and His Family")—

> The most merciful thing in the world, I think, is the inability of the human mind to correlate all its contents. We live on a placid island of ignornace in the midst of black seas of infinity, and it was not meant that we should voyage far. The sciences, each straining in its own direction, have hitherto harmed us little; but some day the piecing together of dissociated knowledge will open up such terrifying vistas of reality, and of our frightful position therein, that we shall either go mad from the revelation or flee from the deadly light into the peace and safety of a new dark age.

—to Johansen's spectacular encounter with Cthulhu—

> There was a mighty eddying and foaming in the noisome brine, and as the steam mounted higher and higher the brave Norwegian drove his vessel head on against the pursuing jelly which rose above the unclean froth like the stern of a daemon galleon. The awful squid-head with writhing feelers came nearly up to the bowsprit of the sturdy yacht, but Johansen drove on relentlessly. There was a bursting

as of an exploding bladder, a slushy nastiness as of a cloven sunfish, a stench as of a thousand opened graves, and a sound that the chronicler would not put on paper.

—the tale is a masterstroke of narrative pacing and cumulative horror. In 12,000 words it has all the density and complexity of a novel.

The true importance of "The Call of Cthulhu," however, lies not in its incorporation of autobiographical details nor even in its intrinsic excellence, but in its being the first significant contribution to what came to be called the "Cthulhu Mythos." This tale certainly contains many of the elements that would be utilised in subsequent "Cthulhu Mythos" fiction by Lovecraft and others. There is, to be sure, something going on in many of the tales of Lovecraft's last decade of writing: they are frequently interrelated by a complex series of cross-references to a constantly evolving body of imagined myth, and many of them build upon features—superficial or profound as the case may be—in previous tales. But certain basic points can now be made, although even some of these are not without controversy: 1) Lovecraft himself did not coin the term "Cthulhu Mythos"; 2) Lovecraft felt that *all* his tales embodied his basic philosophical principles; 3) the mythos, if it can be said to be anything, is not the tales themselves nor even the philosophy behind the tales, but a series of *plot devices* utilised to convey that philosophy. Let us study each of these points further.

1) The term "Cthulhu Mythos" was invented by August Derleth after Lovecraft's death; of this there is no question. The closest Lovecraft ever came to giving his invented pantheon and related phenomena a name was when he made a casual reference to "Cthulhuism & Yog-Sothothery,"[54] and it is not at all clear what these terms really signify.

2) When Lovecraft claimed in a letter to Frank Belknap Long in 1931 that "'Yog-Sothoth' is a basically immature conception, & unfitted for really serious literature,"[55] he may perhaps have been unduly modest, whatever he may have meant by "Yog-Sothoth" here. But as the rest of this letter makes clear, Lovecraft was utilising his pseudomythology as one (among many) of the ways to convey his fundamental philosophical message, whose chief feature was cosmicism. This point is made clear in a letter written to Farnsworth Wright in July 1927 upon the resubmittal of "The Call of Cthulhu" to *Weird Tales* (it had been rejected upon initial submission):

> Now all my tales are based on the fundamental premise that common human laws and interests and emotions have no validity or significance in the vast cosmos-at-large. To me there is nothing but puerility in a tale in which the human form—and the local human passions and conditions and standards—are depicted as native to other worlds or other universes. To achieve the essence of real externality, whether of time or space or dimension, one must forget that such things as organic life, good and evil, love and hate, and all such local attributes of a negligible and temporary race called mankind, have any existence at all.[56]

This statement may perhaps not be capable of bearing quite the philosophical weight that some (including myself) have placed upon it: in spite of the very general nature of the first sentence, the bulk of the passage (and of the letter as a whole) deals with a fairly specific point of *technique* in regard to the weird or science fiction tale—the portrayal of extraterrestrials. What Lovecraft was combating was the already well-established convention (found in Edgar Rice Burroughs, Ray Cummings, and others) of depicting extraterrestrials as not merely humanoid in appearance but also in language, habits, and emotional or psychological makeup. This is why Lovecraft created such an outré name as "Cthulhu" to designate a creature that had come from the depths of space.

And yet, the passage quoted above maintains that *all* Lovecraft's tales emphasise cosmicism in some form or another. Whether this is actually the case is another matter, but at least Lovecraft felt it to be so. If, then, we segregate certain of his tales as employing the framework of his "artificial pantheon and myth-background" (as he writes in "Some Notes on a Nonentity"), it is purely for convenience, with a full knowledge that Lovecraft's work is not to be grouped arbitrarily, rigidly, or exclusively into discrete categories ("New England tales," "Dunsanian tales," and "Cthulhu Mythos tales," as Derleth decreed), since it is transparently clear that these (or any other) categories are not well-defined nor mutually exclusive.

3) It is careless and inaccurate to say that the Lovecraft Mythos *is* Lovecraft's philosophy: his philosophy is mechanistic materialism and all its ramifications, and if the Lovecraft Mythos is anything, it is a series of plot devices meant to facilitate the expression of this philosophy. These various plot devices need not concern us here except in their broadest features. They can perhaps be placed in three general groups: a) invented "gods" and the cults or worshippers that have grown up around them; b) an ever-increasing library of mythical books of occult lore; and c) a fictitious New England topography (Arkham, Dunwich, Innsmouth, etc.). It will readily be noted that the latter two were already present in nebulous form in much earlier tales; but the three features only came together in Lovecraft's later work. Indeed, the third feature does not appreciably foster Lovecraft's cosmic message, and it can be found in tales that are anything but cosmic (e.g., "The Picture in the House"); but it is a phenomenon that has exercised much fascination and can still be said to be an important component of the Lovecraft Mythos. It is an unfortunate fact, of course, that these surface features have frequently taken precedence with readers, writers, and even critics, rather than the philosophy of which they are symbols or representations.

It is at this point scarcely profitable to examine some of the misinterpretations foisted upon the Lovecraft Mythos by August Derleth; the only value in so doing is to serve as a prelude to examining what the mythos actually meant to Lovecraft. The errors can be summed up under three heads: 1) that Lovecraft's "gods" are elementals; 2) that the "gods" can be differentiated between "Elder Gods," who represent the forces of good, and the "Old Ones," who are the forces of evil; and 3) that the mythos as a whole is philosophically akin to Christianity.

It does not require much thought to deem all these points absurd and ridiculous. The notion that the "gods" are elementals seems largely derived from the fact that Cthulhu is imprisoned under water and that he resembles an octopus, and is therefore supposedly a water elemental; but the facts that he clearly came from *outer space,* and that he is *imprisoned* in sunken R'lyeh, must make it obvious both that his resemblance to an octopus is fortuitous and that water is not his natural element. Derleth's attempt to make elementals of the other "gods" is still more preposterous: Nyarlathotep is arbitrarily deemed an earth elemental and Hastur (a name that is only mentioned in passing once in "The Whisperer in Darkness") is claimed to be an air elemental. Not only does this leave out what are, by all accounts, the two chief deities in Lovecraft's pantheon—Azathoth and Yog-Sothoth—but Derleth is then forced to maintain that Lovecraft "failed" in some inexplicable fashion to provide a fire elemental, in spite of the fact that he was (in Derleth's view) working steadily on the "Cthulhu Mythos" for the last ten years of his life. (Derleth came to Lovecraft's rescue by supplying Cthugha, the purportedly missing fire elemental.)

Derleth, himself a practising Catholic, was unable to endure Lovecraft's bleak atheistic vision, and so he invented out of whole cloth the "Elder Gods" (led by the Britanno-Roman god Nodens) as a counterweight to the "evil" Old Ones, who had been "expelled" from the earth but are eternally preparing to reemerge and destroy humanity. Derleth seems to have taken a clue from *The Dream-Quest of Unknown Kadath* (which, paradoxically, he then refused to number among "tales of the Cthulhu Mythos") whereby Nodens seems to take Randolph Carter's side (although actually doing nothing for Carter) against the machinations of Nyarlathotep. In any case, this invention of "Elder Gods" allowed him to maintain that the "Cthulhu Mythos" is substantially akin to Christianity, therefore making it acceptable to people of his conventional temperament. An important piece of "evidence" that Derleth repeatedly cited to bolster his claims was the following "quotation," presumably from a letter by Lovecraft: "All my stories, unconnected as they may be, are based on the fundamental lore or legend that this world was inhabited at one time by another race who, in practising black magic, lost their foothold and were expelled, yet live on outside ever ready to take possession of this earth again." In spite of its superficial similarity with the "All my stories . . ." quotation previously cited (with which Derleth was familiar), this quotation does not sound at all like Lovecraft—at any rate, it is entirely in conflict with the thrust of his philosophy. When Derleth in later years was asked to produce the actual letter from which this quotation was purportedly taken, he could not do so, and for a very good reason: it does not in fact occur in any letter by Lovecraft. It comes from a letter to Derleth written by Harold S. Farnese, the composer who had corresponded briefly with

Lovecraft and who, evidently, severely misconstrued the direction of Lovecraft's work and thought very much as Derleth did.[57] But Derleth seized upon this "quotation" as a trump card for his erroneous views.

By now there is little need to rehash this entire matter: the work of such modern critics as Richard L. Tierney, Dirk W. Mosig, and others has been so conclusive that any attempt to overturn it can only seem reactionary. There is no cosmic "good vs. evil" struggle in Lovecraft's tales; there certainly are struggles between various extraterrestrial entities, but these have no moral overtones and are merely part of the history of the universe. There are no "Elder Gods" whose goal is to protect humanity from the "evil" Old Ones; the Old Ones were not "expelled" by anyone and are not (aside from Cthulhu) "trapped" in the earth or elsewhere. Lovecraft's vision is far less cheerful: humanity is *not* at centre stage in the cosmos, and there is no one to help us against the entities who have from time to time descended upon the earth and wreaked havoc; indeed, the "gods" of the Mythos are not really gods at all, but merely extraterrestrials who occasionally manipulate their human followers for their own advantage.

This last point is worth examining specifically in relation to "The Call of Cthulhu," to which we can now finally return. The outlandish story about the Great Old Ones told to Legrasse by Castro speaks of the intimate relation between the human cult of Cthulhu worshippers and the objects of their worship: "That cult would never die till the stars came right again, and the secret priests would take great Cthulhu from His tomb to revive His subjects and resume His rule of earth." The critical issue is this: Is Castro right or wrong? The tale when read as a whole seems emphatically to suggest that he is wrong; in other words, that the cult has nothing to do with the emergence of Cthulhu (it certainly did not do so in March 1925, since that was the product of an earthquake), and in fact is of no importance to Cthulhu and his ultimate plans, whatever they may be. This is where Lovecraft's remark about the avoidance of human emotions as applied to extraterrestrials comes into play: we scarcely know anything about the real motivations of Cthulhu, but his pathetic and ignorant human worshippers wish to flatter their sense of self-importance by believing that they are somehow integral to his ultimate resurrection, and that they will share in his domination of the earth (if, indeed, that is what he wishes to do).

And it is here that we finally approach the heart of the Lovecraft Mythos. Lovecraft's remark in "Some Notes on a Nonentity" that it was Lord Dunsany "from whom I got the idea of the artificial pantheon and myth-background represented by 'Cthulhu', 'Yog-Sothoth', 'Yuggoth', etc." has either been misunderstood or ignored; but it is central to the understanding of what the pseudomythology meant to Lovecraft. Dunsany had created his artificial pantheon in his first two books (and only there), *The Gods of Pegāna* (1905) and *Time and the Gods*

(1906). The mere act of creating an imaginary religion calls for some comment: it clearly denotes some dissatisfaction with the religion (Christianity) with which the author was raised. Dunsany was, by all accounts, an atheist, although not quite so vociferous a one as Lovecraft; and his gods were, like Lovecraft's, *symbols* for some of his most deeply held philosophical beliefs. In Dunsany's case, these were such things as the need for human reunification with the natural world and distaste for many features of modern civilisation (business, advertising, and in general the absence of beauty and poetry in contemporary life). Lovecraft, having his own philosophical message to convey, used his imaginary pantheon for analogous purposes. But the critical revision Lovecraft made was to transfer this pantheon from an imaginary never-never-land into the objectively real world; in the process he effected a transition from pure fantasy to supernatural horror, making his entities much more baleful than they would have been had they populated a realm like Pegāna.

What Lovecraft was really doing, in other words, was creating (as David E. Schultz has felicitously expressed it[58]) an *anti-mythology*. What is the purpose behind most religions and mythologies? It is to "justify the ways of God to men."[59] Human beings have always considered themselves at the centre of the universe; they have peopled the universe with gods of varying natures and capacities as a means of explaining natural phenomena, of accounting for their own existence, and of shielding themselves from the grim prospect of oblivion after death. Every religion and mythology has established some vital connexion between gods and human beings, and it is exactly this connexion that Lovecraft is seeking to subvert with his pseudomythology. And yet, he knew enough anthropology and psychology to realise that most human beings—either primitive or civilised—are incapable of accepting an atheistic view of existence, and so he peopled his tales with cults that in their own perverted way attempted to reestablish that bond between the gods and themselves; but these cults are incapable of understanding that what they deem "gods" are merely extraterrestrial entities who have no intimate relation with human beings or with anything on this planet, and who are doing no more than pursuing their own ends, whatever they may happen to be.

"The Call of Cthulhu" is a quantum leap for Lovecraft in more ways than one. It is, most emphatically, the first of his tales that can genuinely be termed cosmic. "Dagon," "Beyond the Wall of Sleep," and a few others had dimly hinted at cosmicism; but "The Call of Cthulhu" realises the notion fully and satisfyingly. The suggestion that various phenomena all around the world—bas-reliefs found in New Orleans, Greenland, and the South Pacific, and carved by a Providence artist; anomalously similar dreams had by a wide variety of individuals—may all be insidiously linked to Cthulhu makes Thurston realise that it is not he alone who is in danger, but all the inhabitants of the globe. And the mere fact that Cthulhu still lives at the bottom of the ocean, even though he may be quiescent for years, decades, centuries, or millennia, causes Thurston to reflect poignantly: "I have looked upon all that the universe has to hold of horror, and even the skies of spring and the flowers of summer must ever afterward be poison to me." It is a sentiment that many of Lovecraft's later narrators will echo.

A rather trivial point, but one that has consumed the interest of readers and scholars alike, is the actual pronunciation of the word *Cthulhu*. In various letters Lovecraft appears to give somewhat different pronunciations; his canonical utterance, however, occurs in 1934:

> . . . the word is supposed to represent a fumbling human attempt to catch the phonetics of an *absolutely non-human* word. The name of the hellish entity was invented by beings whose vocal organs were not like man's, hence it has no relation to the human speech equipment. The syllables were determined by a physiological equipment wholly unlike ours, *hence could never be uttered perfectly by human throats.* . . . The actual sound—as nearly as human organs could imitate it or human letters record it—may be taken as something like *Khlûl'-hloo,* with the first syllable pronounced gutturally and very thickly. The *u* is about like that in *full;* and the first syllable is not unlike *klul* in sound, hence the *h* represents the guttural thickness.[60]

In contrast to this, we have the (clearly inaccurate) reports of certain colleagues who claim to have heard Lovecraft pronounce the word. Donald Wandrei renders it as *K-Lütl-Lütl*,[61] R. H. Barlow supplies *Koot-u-lew.*[62] The one pronunciation we can definitively rule out—even though many continue unashamedly to use it—is *Ka-thul-hoo.* Wandrei states that he had initially pronounced it this way in Lovecraft's presence and received nothing but a blank stare in return.

From the cosmicism of "The Call of Cthulhu" to the apparent mundaneness of "Pickman's Model"—written, apparently, in early September—seems a long step backward; and while this tale cannot by any means be deemed one of Lovecraft's best, it contains some features of interest. The narrator, Thurber, writing in a colloquial style very unusual for Lovecraft, tells why he no longer associates with the painter Richard Upton Pickman of Boston, who has in fact recently disappeared. He had maintained relations with Pickman long after his other acquaintances dropped him because of the grotesqueness of his paintings, and so on one occasion he was taken to Pickman's secret cellar studio in the decaying North End of Boston, near the ancient Copp's Hill Burying Ground. Here were some of Pickman's most spectacularly daemonic paintings; one in particular depicts a "colossal and nameless blasphemy with glaring red eyes" nibbling at a man's head the way a child chews a stick of candy. A strange noise is heard, and Pickman harriedly maintains that it must be rats clambering through the underground tunnels honeycombing the area. Pickman, in another room, fires all six chambers of his revolver—a rather odd way to kill rats. After leaving, Thurston finds that he had inadvertently taken away a photograph affixed to the canvas; thinking it a mere shot of scenic background, he is horrified to find that it is a picture of the monster itself— *"it was a photograph from life."*

No reader is likely to have failed to predict this conclusion, but the tale is more interesting not for its actual plot but for its setting and its aesthetics. The North End setting is—or, rather, was—portrayed quite faithfully, right down to many of the street names; but, less than a year after writing the story, Lovecraft was disappointed to find that much of the area had been razed to make way for new development. But the tunnels he describes are real: they probably date from the colonial period and may have been used for smuggling.[64] Lovecraft captures the atmosphere of hoary decay vividly, and in so doing he enunciates (through Pickman) his own views on the need for a long-established cultural heritage:

> "God, man! Don't you realise that places like that [the North End] weren't merely *made,* but actually *grew?* Generation after generation lived and felt and died there, and in days when people weren't afraid to live and feel and die. . . . No, Thurber, these ancient places are dreaming gorgeously and overflowing with wonder and terror and escapes from the commonplace, and yet there's not a living soul to understand or profit by them."

But "Pickman's Model" states other views close to Lovecraft's heart. In effect, it expresses, in fictionalised form, many of the aesthetic principles on weird fiction that Lovecraft had just outlined in "Supernatural Horror in Literature." When Thurber declares that "any magazine-cover hack can splash paint around wildly and call it a nightmare or a Witches' Sabbath or a portrait of the devil," he is repeating the many censures found in letters about the need for artistic *sincerity* and a knowledge of the true foundations of fear in the production of weird art. Thurber continues: ". . . only the real artist knows the actual anatomy of the terrible or the physiology of fear—the exact sort of lines and proportions that connect up with latent instincts or hereditary memories of fright, and the proper colour contrasts and lighting effects to stir the dormant sense of strangeness." This statement, *mutatis mutandis,* is Lovecraft's ideal of weird literature as well. And when Thurber confesses that "Pickman was in every sense—in conception and in execution—a thorough, painstaking, and almost scientific *realist,*" it is as if Lovecraft is reiterating his own recent abandonment of the Dunsanian prose-poetic technique for the "prose realism" that would be the hallmark of his later work.

"Pickman's Model," however, suffers from several flaws aside from its rather obvious plot. Thurber, although supposedly a "tough" guy who had been through the world war, expresses implausible horror and shock at Pickman's paintings: his reactions seem strained and hysterical, and make the reader think that he is not at all as hardened as he repeatedly claims he is. And the colloquial style is—as is the case with "In the Vault"—simply not suited to Lovecraft, and it is well that he subsequently abandoned it except for his ventures into New England dialect.

I have remarked that "The Call of Cthulhu" was rejected by Farnsworth Wright of *Weird Tales;* Lovecraft gives little indication of Wright's reasons aside from reporting casually that Wright thought the tale "slow";[64] there is no suggestion that Wright felt it too bold or *outré* for his readership. It is, nevertheless, predictable that Wright would snap up the more conventional "Pickman's Model," publishing it in the October 1927 issue.

Interestingly enough, in late August 1926 Lovecraft submitted three tales to *Ghost Stories*—"In the Vault" and two others that he does not specify (they were probably "Cool Air" and "The Nameless City").[65] As with his submissions to *Detective Tales,* Lovecraft was attempting to secure another professional market aside from *Weird Tales;* perhaps the rejections of "The Shunned House" and "Cool Air" ("The Call of Cthulhu" was not rejected until October) were already beginning to rankle. *Ghost Stories* (1926–32) was, however, a very peculiar market for Lovecraft to approach: although it paid 2¢ a word,[66] it consisted largely of obviously fabricated "true-confession" accounts of encounters with ghostly phenomena, illustrated by equally contrived and doctored photographs. It did eventually publish random tales by Agatha Christie, Carl Jacobi, and a few other notables; Frank Long actually managed to sell a story to it ("The Man Who Died Twice" in the January 1927 issue), as did Lovecraft's later colleague Robert E. Howard. At this time it was not a pulp magazine, being issued in a large bedsheet format on slick paper. Lovecraft did in fact read a few issues; but he noted accurately: "It hasn't improved—& is about as poor as a magazine can be."[67] But it paid 2¢ a word! Alas, all three of Lovecraft's submissions not surprisingly came back.

Lovecraft was doing more than writing original fiction; he was no doubt continuing to make a meagre living by revision, and in the process was slowly attracting would-be weird writers who offered him stories for correction. He had done no work of this kind since revising four tales for C. M. Eddy, Jr, in 1923–24, but now in the summer of 1926 his new friend Wilfred B. Talman came to him with a story entitled "Two Black Bottles." Lovecraft found promise in the tale—Talman, let us recall, was only twenty-two at this time, and writing was by no means his principal creative outlet—but felt that changes were in order. By October the tale was finished, more or less to both writers' satisfaction. The end result is nothing to write home about, but it managed to land with *Weird Tales* and appeared in the August 1927 issue.

"Two Black Bottles" is the first-person account of a man named Hoffman who comes to examine the estate of his uncle, Dominie Johannes Vanderhoof, who has just died. Vanderhoof was the pastor of the small town of Daalbergen in the Ramapo Mountains (located in northern New Jersey and extending into New York State), and strange tales were told of him. He had fallen under the influence of an aged sexton, Abel Foster, and had taken to delivering fiery and daemoniac sermons to an ever-dwindling congregation. Hoffman, investigating the matter, finds Foster in the church, drunk but also frightened. Foster tells a strange tale of the first pastor of the church, Dominie Guilliam Slott, who in the early eighteenth century had amassed a collection of esoteric volumes and appeared to practise some form of daemonology. Foster reads these books himself and follows in Slott's footsteps—to the point that, when Vanderhoof dies, he takes his soul from his body and puts it in a little black bottle. But Vanderhoof, now caught between heaven and hell, rests uneasily in his grave, and there are indications that he is trying to emerge from it. Hoffman, scarcely knowing what to make of this wild story, now sees the cross on Vanderhoof's grave tilting perceptibly. Then seeing two black bottles on the table near Foster, he reaches for one of them, and in a scuffle with Foster one of them breaks. Foster shrieks: "I'm done fer! That one in there was mine! *Dominie Slott took it out two hundred years ago!*" Foster's body crumbles rapidly into dust.

This tale is not entirely ineffective, and it actually works up a convincing atmosphere of clutching horror toward the end, largely via the colloquial patois of Foster's account. What is in question is the exact degree of Lovecraft's role in the shaping and writing of the story. Judging from his letters to Talman, it seems clear that Lovecraft has not only written some of the tale—especially the portions in dialect—but also made significant suggestions regarding its structure. Talman had evidently sent Lovecraft both a draft and a synopsis—or, perhaps, a draft of only the beginning and a synopsis of the rest. Lovecraft recommended a simplification of the structure so that all the events are seen through the eyes of Hoffman. In terms of the diction, Lovecraft writes: "As for what I've done to the MS.—I am sure you'll find nothing to interfere with your sense of creation. My changes are in virtually every case merely verbal, and all in the interest of finish and fluency of style."[68]

In his 1973 memoir Talman reveals some irritation at Lovecraft's revisions: "He did some minor gratuitous editing, particularly of dialog . . . After re-reading it in print, I wish Lovecraft hadn't changed the dialog, for his use of dialect was stilted."[69] I think Talman's irritation has led him to downplay Lovecraft's role in the work, for there are many passages beyond the dialect portions that clearly reveal his hand. "Two Black Bottles"—like many of Lovecraft's later revisions—is just the sort of conventional horror tale that Farnsworth Wright liked, and it is not surprising that he readily accepted it while rejecting Lovecraft's own more challenging work.

A revision job of a very different sort on which Lovecraft worked in October was *The Cancer of Superstition*. Not much is known about this project, but it appears to have been a collaborative revision on which Lovecraft and C. M. Eddy worked at the instigation of Harry Houdini. Houdini performed in Providence in early October, at which time he asked Lovecraft to do a rush job—an article attacking astrology—for which he paid $75.00.[70] This article has not come to light; but perhaps it supplied the nucleus for what was apparently to be a full-length polemic against superstitions of all sorts. Houdini had, of course, himself written several works of this kind—including *A Magician among the Spirits* (1924), a copy of which he gave to Lovecraft with an inscription—but he now wished something with more scholarly rigour.

What survives of *The Cancer of Superstition* is an outline by Lovecraft and the opening pages of the book as written from the outline by Eddy. The outline predictably speaks of the origin of superstition in primitive times ("All superstitions & religious ideas due to primitive man's effort to assign causes for the natural phenomena around him"), drawing specifically upon Fiske's *Myths and Myth-Makers* and Frazer's *Golden Bough* as support. The surviving chapter is clearly by Eddy; I see little of Lovecraft's actual prose in it, although no doubt many of the facts cited in it were supplied by him.

But Houdini's sudden death on October 31 put an end to the endeavour, as Houdini's wife did not wish to pursue it. This may have been just as well, for the existing material is undistinguished and largely lacks the academic support a work of this kind needs. Lovecraft may have been well versed in anthropology for a layman, but neither he nor Eddy had the scholarly authority to bring this venture to a suitable conclusion.

Shortly after the writing of "Pickman's Model," something strange occurred—Lovecraft was back in New York. He arrived no later than Monday, September 13, for he spoke of seeing a cinema with Sonia that evening. I am not certain of the purpose of this visit—it was clearly only a visit, and I suspect the impetus came from Sonia. As I have mentioned earlier, she reports that she had given up the Cleveland position and returned to New York so as to be closer to Providence (she was hoping to spend weekends there, but this does not seem to have happened); but then she was offered a position in Chicago that was too good to refuse, so she went there. She states that she was in Chicago from July to Christmas of 1926 except for fortnightly shopping trips to New York.[71] Either she is mistaken about the exact time of her departure for Chicago (it may have been September rather than July), or this was one of her shopping trips, and she may have called Lovecraft back to be with her. I suspect it is the latter, for Lovecraft spoke not of residing with her at any apartment but of taking a room with her at the Astor Hotel at Broadway and 44th Street in Manhattan, and he also said that on Tuesday morning "S H had to attend early to business, & was to be rushed so crowdedly that she could not have a moment of the leisure she planned."[72] Lovecraft, although of course still married to Sonia, seems to have reverted to the guest status he occupied during his 1922 visits: he spent most of his time with the gang, particularly Long, Kirk, and Orton.

On Sunday the 19th Lovecraft left for Philadelphia—Sonia had insisted on treating him to this excursion,[73] presumably as recompense for returning to the "pest-zone"—and he stayed there till Monday evening, doing a more thorough exploration of the Wissahickon valley than he had been able to do in 1924 and also seeing Germantown and Fairmount Park. Returning to New York, he attended a gang meeting on the 23rd at Long's, during which two odd things occurred: he, along with the other Kalems, listened to the Dempsey-Tunney fight on the radio, and he met Howard Wolf, a friend of Kirk's who was a reporter for the *Akron Beacon Journal*. Lovecraft seems to have felt that this was nothing more than a social call, but later he was astounded to find that Wolf had written an article on the meeting, and specifically on him, for the column Wolf conducted, "Variety." This article is one of the first—indeed, perhaps the very first—article on Lovecraft outside of the amateur press or the weird fiction field; it is, accordingly, unfortunate that we do not know its exact date of appearance. I have had access only to a clipping of it; it seems to have appeared in the spring of 1927, as Lovecraft himself said that he did not secure the article until the spring of 1928, when Kirk, who had been carrying it around for a full year, gave it to him.

Wolf, referring to Lovecraft as a "still 'undiscovered' writer of horror stories whose work will stand comparison with any now being done in that field," noted that he and Lovecraft talked of weird fiction all evening long. He went on to say that over the next few months he read many back issues of *Weird Tales* and became more and more impressed with Lovecraft. "The Outsider" is "a genuine masterpiece"; "The Tomb" is "almost equally as good"; Wolf even had kind things to say about "The Unnamable" and "The Moon-Bog," although "The Temple" is "not so good." He concluded with a prophecy: "The man has never submitted his stories to a book publisher, I am told. Publisher's readers chancing on this are advised to induce him to collect his tales and offer them for publication. Any volume he might gather together would be a critical and probably a popular success." Neither Wolf nor Lovecraft could have known how long it would take for such an eventuality to occur.

Lovecraft stayed in New York until Saturday the 25th, when he came home by bus. Judging by his letters to his aunts, it was a pleasant enough fortnight, filled with the sightseeing and congregating with friends that had represented the one saving grace of his years in the metropolis. Both Lovecraft and Sonia must have been entirely aware that this was only to be a visit on his part.

With Annie Gamwell, Lovecraft made another excursion in late October, although this one was much closer to home. It was, in fact, nothing less than his first visit to his ancestral region of Foster since 1908. It is heartwarming to read Lovecraft's account of this journey, in which he not only absorbed the intrinsic loveliness of a rural New England he had always cherished but also reestablished bonds with family members who still revered the memory of Whipple Phillips: "Certainly, I was drawn back to the ancestral sources more vividly than at any other time I can recall; and have since thought about little else! I am infus'd and saturated with the vital forces of my inherited being, and rebaptis'd in the mood, atmosphere, and personality of sturdy New-England forbears."[74]

That Lovecraft had indeed "thought about little else" is evident in his next work of fiction, "The Silver Key," presumably written in early November. In this tale Randolph Carter—resurrected from "The Unnamable" (1923)—is now thirty; he has "lost the key of the gate of dreams" and therefore seeks to reconcile himself to the real world, which he now finds prosy and aesthetically unrewarding. He tries all manner of literary and physical novelties until one day he does find the key—or, at any rate, a key of silver in his attic. Driving out in his car along "the old remembered way," he goes back to the rural New England region of his childhood and, in some magical and wisely unexplained manner, finds himself transformed into a nine-year-old boy. Sitting down to dinner with his aunt Martha, Uncle Chris, and the hired man Benijah Corey, Carter finds perfect content as a boy who has sloughed off the tedious complications of adult life for the eternal wonder of childhood.

"The Silver Key" is generally considered a "Dunsanian" tale—on the sole ground that it is a work of dreamlike fantasy rather than a horror tale; but it has very little to do with Dunsany except perhaps in its use of fantasy for philosophical purposes, and even this may not derive directly from Dunsany. And yet, one further fascinating and subtle connexion may exist. Carter, having lost the dream-world, resumes the writing of books (recall that he was a writer of horror tales in "The Unnamable"); but it brings him no satisfaction:

> . . . for the touch of earth was upon his mind, and he could not think of lovely things as he had done of yore. Ironic humour dragged down all the twilight mina-rets he reared, and the earthy fear of improbability blasted all the delicate and amazing flowers in his faery gardens. The convention of assumed pity spilt mawk-ishness on his characters, while the myth of an important reality and significant human events and emotions debased all his high fantasy into thin-veiled allegory and cheap social satire. . . . They were very graceful novels, in which he urbanely laughed at the dreams he lightly sketched; but he saw that their sophistication had sapped all their life away.

This, I believe, is an encapsulation of Lovecraft's own attitude toward Dunsany's later work, which he believed to be lacking in the childlike wonder and high fantasy that characterised his early period. I have already cited an astute remark Lovecraft made in a 1936 letter, but it is worth quoting again:

> As he [Dunsany] gained in age and sophistication, he lost in freshness and sim-plicity. He was ashamed to be uncritically naive, and began to step aside from his tales and visibly smile at them even as they unfolded. Instead of remaining what the true fantaisiste must be—a child in a child's world of dream—he became anx-ious to show that he was really an adult good-naturedly pretending to be a child in a child's world.[75]

What "The Silver Key" really is, of course, is a very lightly fictionalised exposition of Lovecraft's own social, ethical, and aesthetic philosophy. It is not even so
much a story as a parable or philosophical diatribe. He attacks literary realism ("He
did not dissent when they told him that the animal pain of a stuck pig or dyspeptic
ploughman in real life is a greater thing than the peerless beauty of Narath with its
hundred carven gates and domes of chalcedony . . ."), conventional religion (". . . he
had turned to the gentle churchly faith endeared to him by the naive trust of his fathers . . . Only on closer view did he mark the starved fancy and beauty, the stale
and prosy triteness, and the owlish gravity and grotesque claims of solid truth which
reigned boresomely and overwhelmingly among most of its professors . . . It wearied
Carter to see how solemnly people tried to make earthly reality out of old myths
which every step of their boasted science confuted . . ."), and bohemianism (". . .
their lives were dragged malodorously out in pain, ugliness, and disproportion, yet
filled with a ludicrous pride at having escaped from something no more unsound
than that which still held them. They had traded the false gods of fear and blind
piety for those of licence and anarchy"). Each one of these passages, and others
throughout the story, has its exact corollary in his letters. It is rare that Lovecraft so
bluntly expressed his philosophy in a work of fiction; but "The Silver Key" can be
seen as his definitive repudiation both of Decadence as a literary theory and of cos-
mopolitanism as a way of life. Ironically enough, the structural framework of the
story at this point—Carter samples in succession a variety of aesthetic, religious, and
personal experiences in an attempt to lend meaning or interest to his life—may well
have been derived from that textbook of Decadence, Huysmans's *A Rebours,* in the
prologue to which Des Esseintes undertakes exactly such an intellectual journey.
Perhaps Lovecraft knowingly borrowed this aspect of Huysmans's work as another
means of repudiating the philosophy that supported it. Carter's return to childhood
may perhaps exemplify a much earlier statement of Lovecraft's—"Adulthood is
hell"[76]—but in reality his return is not so much to childhood as to ancestral ways,
the one means Lovecraft saw of warding off the sense of futility engendered by the
manifest truth of man's insignificance in the cosmos.

    For it should by now be obvious that, as Kenneth W. Faig, Jr, has exhaustively
pointed out, "The Silver Key" is in large part a fictionalised account of Lovecraft's
recent Foster visit.[77] Details of topography, character names (Benijah Corey is
probably an adaptation of two names: Benejah Place, the owner of the farm across
the road from the house where Lovecraft stayed, and Emma (Corey) Phillips, the
widow of Walter Herbert Phillips, whose grave Lovecraft must have seen in his
1926 visit), and other similarities make this conclusion unshakable. Just as Lovecraft felt the need, after two rootless years in New York, to restore connexions with
the places that had given him and his family birth, so in his fiction did he need to
announce that, henceforth, however far his imagination might stray, it would al-

ways return to New England and look upon it as a source of bedrock values and emotional sustenance.

The exact relation of "The Silver Key" to the other Randolph Carter tales has not been much studied. This story depicts Carter's entire lifetime from his childhood up to the age of fifty-four, at which point he doubles back on his own timeline and reverts to boyhood. In terms of this chronology, *The Dream-Quest of Unknown Kadath* is the "first" Randolph Carter tale, for Carter is presumably in his twenties at the time of its events. After he has lost the key of the gate of dreams at thirty, Carter undertakes his experiments in sampling literary realism, religion, bohemianism, and so on; finding all these things unsatisfying, he turns to darker mysteries, involving himself in occultism and more. It is at this time (his age is unspecified) that he encounters Harley Warren and has the experience described in "The Statement of Randolph Carter"; shortly thereafter, returning to Arkham, he appears to experience the events of "The Unnamable," although they are alluded to very obliquely. Even these dallyings into the weird Carter fails to find rewarding, until at age fifty-four he finds the silver key.

Not long after writing the story Lovecraft noted that it is "not in its final form; but will shortly undergo an extensive amputation of philosophical matter in the early part, which delays the development & kills the interest before the narrative is fairly begun."[78] Lovecraft never undertook such a revision, for he must have realised that an "amputation" of the philosophical matter would actually render the story meaningless: Carter's return to his childhood would carry no weight unless it were prefaced by his thorough awareness that modern adult life had little to offer him. Naturally, this results in a tale that is by no means oriented toward a popular audience, and it is no surprise that Farnsworth Wright rejected it for *Weird Tales*.[79] In the summer of 1928, however, Wright asked to see the tale again and this time accepted it for $70.00.[80] Predictably, however, when the tale appeared in the January 1929 issue, Wright reported to Lovecraft that readers "violently disliked" the story![81] Out of charity, however, Wright did not print any of these hostile letters in the magazine's letter column.

"The Strange High House in the Mist," written on November 9, is more concretely Dunsanian than "The Silver Key," and shows that the Dunsany influence had now been thoroughly internalised so as to allow for the expression of Lovecraft's own sentiments through Dunsany's idiom and general atmosphere. Indeed, the only genuine connexions to Dunsany's work may perhaps be in some details of the setting and in the manifestly philosophical, even satiric purpose which the fantasy is made to serve.

We are now again in Kingsport, a city to which Lovecraft had not returned since "The Festival" (1923), the tale that first embodied his impressions of Marblehead and its magical preservation of the tokens of the past. North of Kingsport "the crags climb lofty and curious, terrace on terrace, till the northernmost hangs in the sky like a grey frozen wind-cloud." On that cliff is an ancient house inhabited by some individual whom none of the townsfolk—not even the Terrible Old Man—have ever seen. One day a tourist, the "philosopher" Thomas Olney, decides to visit that house and its secret inhabitant; for he has always longed for the strange and the wondrous. He arduously scales the cliff, but upon reaching the house finds that there is no door on this side, only "a couple of small lattice windows with dingy bull's-eye panes leaded in seventeenth-century fashion"; the house's only door is on the *other* side, flush with the sheer cliff. Then Olney hears a soft voice, and a "great black-bearded face" protrudes from a window and invites him in. Olney climbs through the window and has a colloquy with the occupant:

> And the day wore on, and still Olney listened to rumours of old times and far places, and heard how the Kings of Atlantis fought with the slippery blasphemies that wriggled out of rifts in ocean's floor, and how the pillared and weedy temple of Poseidonis is still glimpsed at midnight by lost ships, who know by its sight that they are lost. Years of the Titans were recalled, but the host grew timid when he spoke of the dim first age of chaos before the gods or even the Elder Ones were born, and when only *the other gods* came to dance on the peak of Hatheg-Kla in the stony desert near Ulthar, beyond the river Skai.

Then a knock is heard at the door—the door that faces the cliff. Eventually the host opens the door, and he and Olney find the room occupied by all manner of wondrous presences—"Trident-bearing Neptune," "hoary Nodens," and others—and when Olney returns to Kingsport the next day, the Terrible Old Man vows that the man who went up that cliff is not the same one who came down. No longer does Olney's soul long for wonder and mystery; instead, he is content to lead his prosy bourgeois life with his wife and children. But people in Kingsport, looking up at the house on the cliff, say that "at evening the little low windows are brighter than formerly."

On various occasions Lovecraft admitted that he had no specific locale in mind when writing this tale: he stated that memories of the "titan cliffs of Magnolia"[82] in part prompted the setting, but that there is no house on the cliff as in the story; a headland near Gloucester which Lovecraft calls "Mother Ann,"[83] and which has not been precisely identified, also inspired the setting. There is a passage in Dunsany's *Chronicles of Rodriguez* about the home of a wizard on the top of a crag which Lovecraft may have had in mind.[84] What this means is that Lovecraft metamorphosed the New England landscape in this story more than he did in his "realistic" tales, and did so for the purpose of augmenting the fantastic element: "The Strange High House in the Mist" contains little in the way of specific topographical description, and we are clearly in a never-never land where—anomalously for Lovecraft—the focus is on human character.

For the strange transformation of Thomas Olney is at the heart of the tale. What is its meaning? How has he lost that sense of wonder which had guided his life up to his visit to Kingsport? The Terrible Old Man hints at the answer: "somewhere under that grey peaked roof, or amidst inconceivable reaches of that sinister white mist, there lingered still the lost spirit of him who was Thomas Olney." The body has returned to the normal round of things, but the spirit has remained with the occupant of the strange high house in the mist; the encounter with Neptune and Nodens has been an apotheosis, and Olney realises that it is in this realm of nebulous wonder that he truly belongs. His body is now an empty shell, without soul and without imagination: "His good wife waxes stouter and his children older and prosier and more useful, and he never fails to smile correctly with pride when the occasion calls for it." This tale could be read as a sort of mirror-image of "Celephaïs": whereas Kuranes had to die in the real world in order for his spirit to attain his fantasy realm, Olney's body survives intact but his spirit stays behind.

One other small item that can be noted here is the poem published in *Weird Tales* for December 1926 as "Yule Horror." This effective four-stanza poem, written in the same Swinburnian metre as "Nemesis," "The House," and "The City," is actually a Christmas poem sent to Farnsworth Wright under the title "Festival"; Wright was so taken with it that he omitted the last stanza, a reference to himself—

> And mayst thou to such deeds
> Be an abbot and priest,
> Singing cannibal greeds
> At each devil-wrought feast,
> And to all the incredulous world shewing dimly the sign of the beast.

—and, to Lovecraft's surprise and pleasure, published it. Lovecraft's only other poetic contributions during his first eight months in Providence are a plangent elegy (written in late June) on Oscar, a cat owned by a neighbour of George Kirk's who was killed by a car, and "The Return," a poem on C. W. Smith published in the *Tryout* for December 1926.

A significant prose item written on November 23 was the essay "Cats and Dogs" (later retitled by Derleth as "Something about Cats"). The Blue Pencil Club of Brooklyn was planning to have a discussion concerning the relative merits of cats and dogs. Lovecraft naturally would have liked to participate in person, especially since a majority of the members were dog-lovers; but since he could not go (or was unwilling to do so), he wrote a lengthy brief simultaneously outlining his affection for cats and—with tongue only partially in his cheek—supplying an elaborate philosophical defence of this affection. The result is one of the most delightful pieces Lovecraft ever wrote, even if some of the sentiments expressed in it are a little tart.

In essence, Lovecraft's argument is that the cat is the pet of the artist and thinker, while the dog is the pet of the stolid bourgeoisie. "The dog appeals to cheap and facile emotions; the cat to the deepest founts of imagination and cosmic perception in the human mind." This leads inevitably to a class distinction that is neatly summed up in the compact utterance: "The dog is a peasant and the cat is a gentleman."

It is merely the "cheap" emotions of sentimentality and the need for subservience that impel praise for the "faithfulness" and devotion of the dog while scorning the aloof independence of the cat. It is a fallacy that the dog's "pointless sociability and friendliness, or slavering devotion and obedience, constitute anything intrinsically admirable or exalted." Consider the respective behaviour of the two animals: "Throw a stick, and the servile dog wheezes and pants and shambles to bring it to you. Do the same before a cat, and he will eye you with coolly polite and somewhat bored amusement." And yet, do we not rate a human being as superior for having independence of thought and action? Why then do we withhold praise for the cat when it exhibits these qualities? One does not, in fact, *own* a cat (as one does a dog); one *entertains* a cat. It is a guest, not a servant.

There is much more, but this is sufficient to indicate the extraordinary elegance and dry humour of "Cats and Dogs"—a piece that delightfully unites philosophy, aesthetics, and personal sentiment in a triumphant evocation of that species that Lovecraft admired more than any others (including his own) on this planet. It is perhaps not surprising that, when R. H. Barlow came to publish this essay in the second issue of *Leaves* (1938), he felt obligated to tone down some of Lovecraft's more provocative (and only half-joking) political allusions. Toward the end of the essay Lovecraft remarks: "The star of the cat, I think, is just now in the ascendant, as we emerge little by little from the dreams of ethics and democracy which clouded the nineteenth century"; Barlow changed "democracy" to "conformity." A little later, Lovecraft says: "Whether a renaissance of monarchy and beauty will restore our western civilisation, or whether the forces of disintegration are already too powerful for even the fascist sentiment to check, none may yet say . . ." Barlow changed "monarchy" to "power" and "even the fascist sentiment" to "any hand." But in spite—or perhaps because—of these very politically incorrect utterances, "Cats and Dogs" is a virtuoso performance that Lovecraft rarely excelled.

But Lovecraft was by no means done with writing. In a departure from his normal habits, he wrote "The Silver Key" and "The Strange High House in the Mist" while simultaneously at work on a much longer work. Writing to August Derleth in early December, he notes: "I am now on page 72 of my dreamland fantasy . . ."[85] The result, finished in late January, would be the longest work of fiction he had written up to that time—*The Dream-Quest of Unknown Kadath*.

18. COSMIC OUTSIDENESS
(1927–1928)

T *he Dream-Quest of Unknown Kadath* was finished at 43,000 words on January 22, 1927.[1] Even while writing it, Lovecraft expressed doubts about its merits—

I . . . am very fearful that Randolph Carter's adventures may have reached the point of palling on the reader; or that the very plethora of weird imagery may have destroyed the power of any one image to produce the desired impression of strangeness.[2]

As for my novel . . . it is a picaresque chronicle of impossible adventures in dream-land, and is composed under no illusion of professional acceptance. There is cer-tainly nothing of popular or best-seller psychology in it—although, in consonance with the mood in which it was conceived, it contains more of the naive fairy-tale wonder-spirit than of actual Baudelairian decadence. Actually, it isn't much good; but forms useful practice for later and more authentic attempts in the novel form.[3]

This final remark is about as accurate a judgment as can be delivered on the work. More than any other of Lovecraft's major stories, it has elicited antipodally oppo-site reactions even from devotees: L. Sprague de Camp compared it to George MacDonald's *Lilith* and *Phantastes* and the *Alice* books,[4] while other Lovecraft scholars find it almost unreadable. For my part, I think it is an entirely charming but relatively insubstantial work: Carter's adventures through dreamland do indeed pall after a time, but the novel is saved by its extraordinarily poignant conclusion. Its chief feature may be its autobiographical significance: it is, in fact, Lovecraft's spiritual autobiography for this precise moment in his life.

It is scarcely worth while to pursue the rambling plot of this short novel, which in its continuous, chapterless meandering consciously resembles not only Dunsany (although Dunsany never wrote a long work exactly of this kind) but William Beckford's *Vathek* (1786); several points of plot and imagery also bring Beckford's Arabian fantasy to mind.[5] Lovecraft resurrects Randolph Carter, previously used in "The Statement of Randolph Carter" (1919) and "The Unnamable" (1923), in a quest through dreamland for his "sunset city," which is described as follows:

All golden and lovely it blazed in the sunset, with walls, temples, colonnades, and arched bridges of veined marble, silver-basined fountains of prismatic spray in broad squares and perfumed gardens, and wide streets marching between delicate trees and blossom-laden urns and ivory statues in gleaming rows; while on steep northward slopes climbed tiers of red roofs and old peaked gables harbouring little lanes of grassy cobbles.

This certainly sounds—except for some odd details at the end—like some Dunsanian realm of the imagination; but what does Carter discover as he leaves his hometown of Boston to make a laborious excursion through dreamland to the throne of the Great Ones who dwell in an onyx castle on unknown Kadath? Nyarlathotep, the messenger of the gods, tells him in a passage as moving as any in Lovecraft:

> "For know you, that your gold and marble city of wonder is only the sum of what you have seen and loved in youth. It is the glory of Boston's hillside roofs and western windows aflame with sunset; of the flower-fragrant Common and the great dome on the hill and the tangle of gables and chimneys in the violet valley where the many-bridged Charles flows drowsily. These things you saw, Randolph Carter, when your nurse first wheeled you out in the springtime, and they will be the last things you will ever see with eyes of memory and of love. . . .
>
> "These, Randolph Carter, are your city; for they are yourself. New-England bore you, and into your soul she poured a liquid loveliness which cannot die. This loveliness, moulded, crystallised, and polished by years of memory and dreaming, is your terraced wonder of elusive sunsets; and to find that marble parapet with curious urns and carven rail, and descend at last those endless balustraded steps to the city of broad squares and prismatic fountains, you need only to turn back to the thoughts and visions of your wistful boyhood."

We suddenly realise why that "sunset city" contained such otherwise curious features as gables and cobblestoned lanes. And we also realise why it is that the various fantastic creatures Carter meets along his journey—zoogs, gugs, ghasts, ghouls, moonbeasts—touch no chord in us: they are not meant to. They are all very charming, in that "Dresden-china" way Lovecraft mistook Dunsany to be; but they amount to nothing because they do not correspond to anything in our memories and dreams. So all that Carter has to do—and what he does in fact do at the end—is merely to wake up in his Boston room, leave dreamland behind, and realise the beauty to be found on his doorstep: "Birds sang in hidden gardens and the perfume of trellised vines came wistful from arbours his grandfather had reared. Beauty and light glowed from classic mantel and carven cornice and walls grotesquely figured, while a sleek black cat rose yawning from hearthside sleep that his master's start and shriek had disturbed."

Carter's revelation is brilliantly prefigured in an earlier episode in which he meets King Kuranes, the protagonist of "Celephaïs" (1920). In that story Kuranes, a London writer, had dreamt as a child of the realm of Celephaïs, which is indeed a land of otherworldly beauty; at the end of the tale his body dies but his spirit is somehow transported to the land of his dreams. Carter meets him in Celephaïs, but he finds that Kuranes is not quite as happy as he thought he would be:

It seems that he could no more find content in those places, but had formed a mighty longing for the English cliffs and downlands of his boyhood, where in little dreaming villages England's old songs hover at evening behind lattice windows, and where grey church towers peep lovely through the verdure of distant valleys. . . . For though Kuranes was a monarch in the land of dream, with all imagined pomps and marvels, splendours and beauties, ecstasies and delights, novelties and excitements at his command, he would gladly have resigned forever the whole of his power and luxury and freedom for one blessed day as a simple boy in that pure and quiet England, that ancient, beloved England which had moulded his being and of which he must always be immutably a part.

It has frequently been conjectured that *The Dream-Quest of Unknown Kadath* is the carrying out of Lovecraft's old novel idea "Azathoth" (1922); but while this may be true superficially in the sense that both works seem to centre around protagonists venturing on a quest for some wondrous land, in reality the novel of 1926 presents a thematic reversal of the novel idea of 1922. In the earlier work—written at the height of Lovecraft's Decadent phase—the unnamed narrator "travelled out of life on a quest into the spaces whither the world's dreams had fled"; but he does this because "age fell upon the world, and wonder went out of the minds of men." In other words, the narrator's only refuge from prosy reality is the world of dream. Carter thinks that that is the case for him, but at the end he finds more value and beauty in that reality—transmuted, of course, by his dreams and memories—than he believed.

Of course, *The Dream-Quest of Unknown Kadath* is full of delightful tableaux of wonder, fantasy, and even horror that make it a very engaging work; such scenes as Carter being wafted from the moon back to the earth on the bodies of legions of cats, his encounter with the dreaded high-priest not to be named on the plateau of Leng, and of course his climactic appearance in Kadath before Nyarlathotep are triumphs of fantastic imagination. A certain whimsy and even flippancy lend a distinctive tone to the novel, as in Carter's grotesque encounter with his old friend Richard Upton Pickman (whose first appearance, of course, was in "Pickman's Model," written a few months before the novel was finished), who has now become a full-fledged ghoul:

> There, on a tombstone of 1768 stolen from the Granary Burying Ground in Boston, sat the ghoul which was once the artist Richard Upton Pickman. It was naked and rubbery, and had acquired so much of the ghoulish physiognomy that its human origin was already obscured. But it still remembered a little English, and was able to converse with Carter in grunts and monosyllables, helped out now and then by the glibbering of ghouls.

The Dream-Quest of Unknown Kadath also seeks to unite most of Lovecraft's previous "Dunsanian" tales, making explicit references to features and characters in such tales as "Celephaïs," "The Cats of Ulthar," "The Other Gods," "The White Ship," and others; but in doing so it creates considerable confusion. In particular, it suddenly transfers the settings of these tales into the dreamworld, whereas those tales themselves had manifestly been set in the dim prehistory of the real world. Lovecraft, of course, is under no obligation to adhere to earlier conceptions in such matters, but it does not seem as if he has thought through the precise metaphysical status of the dreamworld, which is full of ambiguities and paradoxes.[6] It is not likely that Lovecraft would have done much to iron out these difficulties in a subsequent revision, given that he regarded the work merely as "useful practice" for novel-length fiction, writing it not only without thought of publication but without any real desire to tie up all the loose ends. In later years he repudiated it, refusing several colleagues' desires to prepare a typed copy of the manuscript until finally R. H. Barlow badgered him to pass along the text. Barlow typed less than half of the novel, but Lovecraft did nothing with this portion; the full text was not published until it was included in *Beyond the Wall of Sleep* (1943).

It is worth giving some thought to why Lovecraft revived Randolph Carter just at this time—for this novel must have been begun some time before "The Silver Key" was written, and indeed must have been fully conceived at the outset, since the events of "The Silver Key" manifestly take place after those of the *Dream-Quest.* Clearly Lovecraft was wishing a character that might serve as an alter ego, and it has been carelessly assumed that Carter is indeed such a character; but what has frequently not been observed is how *different* Carter is in each of the five tales in which he appears. In "The Statement of Randolph Carter" he is merely a passive and colourless witness to events; in "The Unnamable" he is a somewhat jaundiced author of weird fiction; in the *Dream-Quest* he is a wide-eyed explorer of dreams; in "The Silver Key" he is a jaded writer who has tried every intellectual and aesthetic stimulus to ward off a sense of cosmic futility; and in the later collaboration "Through the Gates of the Silver Key" he is a dynamic action-hero in the best (or worst) pulp tradition. It must frankly be admitted that Carter has no concrete or coherent personality, and that Lovecraft resurrected him—at least, in the three tales ("The Unnamable," "The Silver Key," and the *Dream-Quest*) where he has a personality at all—as a convenient mouthpiece for views that were indeed his at that moment.

In the *Dream-Quest,* then, Carter serves as a means for emphatically underscoring Lovecraft's New England heritage. In "The Unnamable" a New England origin was merely implied for Carter; in the novel he definitively becomes a resident of Boston—as Lovecraft would very likely have been had his father not taken ill in 1893. Carter's peregrinations in the dreamworld, whatever mythic significance they may have, function chiefly as mirrors of Lovecraft's own wanderings, particularly to that glittering Dunsanian realm that New York was for him during his visits of 1922 and the first few months of his residence there in 1924.

In an analogous way, the resurrection of the Dunsanian idiom—not used since "The Other Gods" (1921)—is meant not so much as an homage as a repudiation of Dunsany, at least of what Lovecraft at this moment took Dunsany to be. Just as, when he wrote "Lord Dunsany and His Work" in 1922, he felt that the only escape from modern disillusion would be to "worship afresh the music and colour of divine language, and take an Epicurean delight in those combinations of ideas and fancies which we know to be artificial," so in 1926—after two years spent away from the New England soil that he now realised was his one true anchor against chaos and meaninglessness—he felt the need to reject these decorative artificialities. By 1930—only seven years after claiming, in pitiable wish-fulfilment, that "Dunsany *is myself*"—he made a definitive break with his once-revered mentor:

> What I do *not* think I shall use much in future is the Dunsanian pseudo-poetic vein—not because I don't admire it, but because I don't think it is natural to me. The fact that I used it only sparingly before reading Dunsany, but immediately began to overwork it upon doing so, gives me a strong suspicion of its artificiality so far as I am concerned. That kind of thing takes a better poet than I.[7]

The curious thing is that Dunsany's own work was moving in exactly this direction, and Lovecraft was not merely unaware of it but actually resented Dunsany's departure from what he took to be the "Dresden-china" prettiness of *The Gods of Pegāna* and other early works. Dunsany himself had definitively abandoned his bejewelled style and the prodigal invention of imaginary worlds by 1919 and in his novels of the 1920s and 1930s—especially *The Blessing of Pan* (1927) and, preeminently, *The Curse of the Wise Woman* (1933)—drawn more and more deeply upon his own memories of life in England and Ireland; but Lovecraft, although dutifully reading each new work by Dunsany, continued to lament at the passing of his "old" manner.

One other possible influence on the *Dream-Quest* is John Uri Lloyd's curious novel of underworld adventure, *Etidorhpa* (1895), which Lovecraft read in 1918.[8] It must have left a powerful impression upon him, for he was recalling it as late as 1928, when, recounting his exploration of the Endless Caverns in Virginia, he writes: "I thought, above all else, of that strange old novel *Etidorhpa* once pass'd around our Kleicomolo circle and perus'd with such varying reactions" ("Observations on Several Parts of America"). This strange work, full of windy philosophy and science defending the idea of a hollow earth, nevertheless contains some spectacularly bizarre and cosmic imagery of the narrator's seemingly endless underworld adventures, although I cannot find any specific passage echoed in the *Dream-Quest.* Nevertheless, Lovecraft's dreamworld creates the impression of being somehow underground (as in Carter's descent of the 700 steps to the gate of deeper slumber), so perhaps he was thinking of how Lloyd's narrator purportedly plunges beneath the actual surface of the earth on his peregrinations.

*   *   *

It is remarkable that, almost immediately after completing *The Dream-Quest of Unknown Kadath* in late January 1927, Lovecraft plunged into another "young novel,"[9] *The Case of Charles Dexter Ward.* Actually, at the outset he did not regard it as anything more than a novelette: on January 29 he announced that "I am already at work on a new shorter tale";[10] by February 9 he was on page 56, with an estimated 25 pages more to go;[11] by February 20 he finally realised what he had got himself into, for he was on page 96 "with much still to be said";[12] the last page of the autograph manuscript (page 147) notes that the work was finished on March 1. At approximately 51,000 words, it is the longest piece of fiction Lovecraft would ever write. While it does betray a few signs of haste, and while he would no doubt have polished it had he made the effort to prepare it for publication, the fact is that he felt so discouraged as to its quality—as well as its marketability—that he never made such an effort, and the work remained unpublished until four years after his death.

Perhaps, however, it is not so odd that Lovecraft wrote *The Case of Charles Dexter Ward* in a blinding rush nine months after his return to Providence; for this novel—the second of his major tales (after "The Shunned House") to be set entirely in the city of his birth—had been gestating for at least a year or more. I have mentioned that in August 1925 he was contemplating a novel about Salem; but then, in September, he read Gertrude Selwyn Kimball's *Providence in Colonial Times* (1912) at the New York Public Library, and this rather dry historical work clearly fired his imagination. He was, however, still talking of the Salem idea just as he was finishing the *Dream-Quest:* ". . . sometime I wish to write a novel of more naturalistic setting, in which some hideous threads of witchcraft trail down the centuries against the sombre & memory-haunted background of ancient Salem."[13] But perhaps the Kimball book—as well, of course, as his return to Providence—led to a uniting of the Salem idea with a work about his hometown.

The plot of the novel is relatively simple, although full of subtle touches. Joseph Curwen, a learned scholar and man of affairs, leaves Salem for Providence in 1692, eventually building a succession of elegant homes in the oldest residential section of the city. Curwen attracts attention because he does not seem to age much, even after the passing of fifty or more years. He also acquires very peculiar substances from all around the world for apparent chemical—or, more specifically, alchemical—experiments; and his haunting of graveyards does nothing to salvage his reputation. When Dr John Merritt visits Curwen, he is both impressed and disturbed by the number of alchemical and cabbalistic books on his shelves; in particular, he sees a copy of Borellus with one key passage—concerning the use of the "essential Saltes" of humans or animals for purposes of resurrection—heavily underscored.

Things come to a head when Curwen, in an effort to restore his reputation, arranges a marriage for himself with the well-born Eliza Tillinghast, the daughter of a ship-captain under Curwen's control. This so enrages Ezra Weeden, who had hoped to marry Eliza himself, that he begins an exhaustive investigation of Curwen's affairs. After several more anomalous incidents, it is decided by the elders of the city—among them the four Brown brothers; Rev. James Manning, president of the recently established college (later to be known as Brown University); Stephen Hopkins, former governor of the colony; and others—that something must be done. A raid on Curwen's property in 1771, however, produces death, destruction, and psychological trauma amongst the participants well beyond what might have been expected of a venture of this sort. Curwen is evidently killed, and his body is returned to his wife for burial. He is never spoken of again, and as many records concerning him as can be found are destroyed.

A century and a half pass, and in 1918 Charles Dexter Ward—Curwen's direct descendant by way of his daughter Ann—accidentally discovers his relation to the old wizard and seeks to learn all he can about him. Although always fascinated by the past, Ward had previously exhibited no especial interest in the outré; but as he unearths more and more information about Curwen—whose exact physical double he proves to be—he strives more and more to duplicate his ancestor's cabbalistic and alchemical feats. He undertakes a long voyage overseas to visit the presumable descendants of individuals with whom Curwen had been in touch in the eighteenth century. He finds Curwen's remains and, by the proper manipulation of his "essential Saltes," resurrects him. But something begins to go astray. He writes a harried letter to Dr Marinus Bicknell Willett, the family doctor, with the following disturbing message:

> Instead of triumph I have found terror, and my talk with you will not be a boast of victory but a plea for help and advice in saving both myself and the world from a horror beyond all human conception or calculation. . . . Upon us depends more than can be put into words—all civilisation, all natural law, perhaps even the fate of the solar system and the universe. I have brought to light a monstrous abnormality, but I did it for the sake of knowledge. Now for the sake of all life and Nature you must help me thrust it back into the dark again.

But, perversely, Ward does not stay for the appointed meeting with Willett. Willett finally does track him down, but something astounding has occurred: although still of youthful appearance, his talk is very eccentric and old-fashioned, and his stock of memories of his own life seems to have been bizarrely depleted. Willett later undertakes a harrowing exploration of Curwen's old Pawtuxet bungalow, which Ward had restored for the conducting of experiments; he finds, among other anomalies, all manner of half-formed creatures at the bottom of deep pits. He confronts Ward—whom he now realises is no other than Curwen—in the madhouse in which he has been placed; Curwen attempts to summon up an incantation against him, but Willett counters with one of his own, reducing Curwen to a "thin coating of fine bluish-grey dust."

This skeletonic summary cannot begin to convey the textural and tonal richness of *The Case of Charles Dexter Ward,* which in spite of the speed of its composition remains among the most carefully wrought fictions in Lovecraft's entire corpus. The historical flashback—occupying the second of the five chapters—is as evocative a passage as any in his work.

The evolution of the work goes back even beyond August 1925. The quotation from Borellus—Pierre Borel (c. 1620–1689), the French physician and chemist—is a translation or paraphrase by Cotton Mather in the *Magnalia Christi Americana* (1702), which Lovecraft owned. Since the epigraph from Lactantius that heads "The Festival" (1923) also comes from the *Magnalia,* perhaps Lovecraft found the Borellus passage at that time also. It is copied down in his commonplace book as entry 87, which David E. Schultz dates conjecturally to April 1923.

In late August 1925 Lovecraft heard an interesting story from Lillian: "So the Halsey house is haunted! Ugh! That's where Wild Tom Halsey kept live terrapins in the cellar—maybe it's their ghosts. Anyway, it's a magnificent old mansion, & a credit to a magnificent old town!"[14] The Thomas Lloyd Halsey house at 140 Prospect Street is the model for Charles Dexter Ward's residence; in the story Lovecraft numbers it 100 Prospect Street, perhaps to disguise its identity (and the privacy of the occupants, in the event that curious readers might wish to look it up). Although now broken up into apartments, it is a superb late Georgian structure (c. 1800) fully deserving of Lovecraft's encomium: "His [Ward's] home was a great Georgian mansion atop the well-nigh precipitous hill that rises just east of the river; and from the rear windows of its rambling wings he could look dizzily out over all the clustered spires, domes, roofs, and skyscraper summits of the lower town to the purple hills of the countryside beyond." Lovecraft was presumably never in the Halsey mansion, but had a clear view of it from 10 Barnes Street; looking northwestward from his aunt's upstairs back window, he could see it distinctly.

As for the house's ghostly legendry, we read the following in the WPA guide to Rhode Island (1937):

> [Halsey] was a famous *bon vivant* in Colonial days, and there is a legend that he kept live terrapins in his cellar. For many years during which the mansion was empty, Negroes in the vicinity were convinced a piano-playing ghost haunted the property. They would not enter the house under any circumstances, and at night always gave it a wide berth. It is also said that a blood-stain on the floor has defied many years of scrubbing.[15]

No doubt these were the sorts of stories Lillian heard in 1925.

Lovecraft began reading *Providence in Colonial Times* at the very end of July 1925. Since he could not check the book out of the New York Public Library but had to read it in the genealogical reading room during library hours, his consumption of it was sporadic, and he only began making headway in it in mid-September. It was at this time that he read of John Merritt as well as of the Rev. John Checkley, "famous as a wit & man of the world,"[16] both of whom would later pay visits to Joseph Curwen. Lovecraft's letters for the rest of the month contain much other matter derived from reading the Kimball book, and there is no question but that it helped to solidify his knowledge of colonial Providence so that he could rework it in fiction a year and a half later. Lovecraft, of course, does much more than merely recycle odd bits of history—he mingles history and fiction in an inextricable union, breathing vivid life into the dry facts he had gathered over a lifetime of study of his native region and insidiously inserting the imaginary, the fantastic, and the weird into the known historical record.

One significant literary influence may be noted here: Walter de la Mare's novel *The Return* (1910). Lovecraft had first read de la Mare in the summer of 1926, and stated that the British author "can be exceedingly powerful when he chooses";[17] of *The Return* he remarked in "Supernatural Horror in Literature": "we see the soul of a dead man reach out of its grave of two centuries and fasten itself upon the flesh of the living, so that even the face of the victim becomes that which had long ago returned to dust." In de la Mare's novel, of course, there is actual psychic possession involved, as there is not in *Charles Dexter Ward;* and, although the focus in *The Return* is on the afflicted man's personal trauma—in particular his relations with his wife and daughter—rather than the unnaturalness of his condition, Lovecraft has manifestly adapted the general scenario in his own work. Another literary influence is that of M. R. James's "Count Magnus." Numerous parallels exist in the characters of the baleful sorcerer Count Magnus and Joseph Curwen—and, correspondingly, with the characters of their chosen victims, Mr. Wraxall and Charles Dexter Ward.[18]

Other, more minor sources can also be noted. Marinus Bicknell Willett's name surely derives from a book that Lillian sent him in November of that year:[19]

> Francis Read. *Westminster Street, Providence, as It Was about 1824.* From Drawings Made by Francis Read and Lately Presented by His Daughter, Mrs. Marinus Willett Gardner, to the Rhode Island Historical Society. Providence: Printed for the Society, 1917.

Bicknell is an old Providence name. Thomas William Bicknell, for example, was a well-known historian who wrote a five-volume *History of the State of Rhode Island* (1920). I am not entirely sure, however, where Lovecraft derived the name Charles Dexter Ward. Ward is a name from Providence colonial history, and in the novel Lovecraft refers to a political dispute between the party backing Samuel Ward and the one backing Stephen Hopkins around 1760. Lovecraft also owned two anthologies of English literature compiled by Charles Dexter Cleveland. Dexter, of course, is a prominent family in Providence.

If the source for Ward's name is unclear, the source for the character himself is not. Of course, there are many autobiographical touches in the portraiture of Ward, which I shall examine presently; but many surface details appear to be taken from a person actually living in the Halsey mansion at this time, William Lippitt Mauran (b. 1910). Lovecraft was probably not acquainted with Mauran, but it is highly likely that he observed Mauran on the street and knew of him. Mauran was a sickly child who spent much of his youth as an invalid, being wheeled through the streets in a carriage by a nurse. Indeed, a mention early in the novel that Ward as a young boy was "wheeled . . . in a carriage" in front of the "lovely classic porch of the double-bayed brick building" that was his home may reflect an actual glimpse Lovecraft had of Mauran in the early 1920s, before he ever went to New York. Moreover, the Mauran family also owned a farmhouse in Pawtuxet, exactly as Curwen is said to have done. Other details of Ward's character also fit Mauran more closely than Lovecraft. One other amusing in-joke is a mention of Manuel Arruda, captain of a Spanish vessel, the *Fortaleza,* which delivers a nameless cargo to Curwen in 1770. Manuel Arruda was actually a Portuguese door-to-door fruit merchant operating on College Hill in the later 1920s![20]

But what, beyond these obscure tips of the hat and in-jokes, is the fundamental message of *The Case of Charles Dexter Ward?* To answer this question, we must first ascertain exactly what Curwen and his cohorts around the world were attempting to do by gathering up these "essential Saltes." Lovecraft makes the matter a trifle too clear in a passage toward the end—a passage which, one hopes, he might have had the good sense to omit in a revised version: "What these horrible creatures—and Charles Ward as well—were doing or trying to do seemed fairly clear . . . They were robbing the tombs of all the ages, including those of the world's wisest and greatest men, in the hope of recovering from the bygone ashes some vestige of the consciousness and lore which had once animated and informed them." It is not, indeed, entirely clear how the tapping of human brains—even the "world's wisest and greatest"—would result in some scenario that might threaten "all civilisation, all natural law, perhaps even the fate of the solar system and the universe." Curwen occasionally speaks in notes and letters about calling up entities from "Outside ye Spheres"—including perhaps Yog-Sothoth, who is first mentioned in this novel—but these hints are so nebulous that not much can be made of them. There are further hints that Curwen in 1771 died not because of the raid by the citizenry but because he had raised some nameless entity and could not control it. Nevertheless, the basic conception of a Faustian quest for knowledge has led Barton L. St Armand, one of the acutest commentators on the work, to declare:

"The simple moral of *The Case of Charles Dexter Ward* is that it is dangerous to know too much, especially about one's own ancestors."[21]

Well, perhaps it is not so simple as that. By this interpretation, Ward himself becomes the villain of the piece; but surely it is Curwen who is the real villain, for it is he who conceived the idea of ransacking the world's brains for his own (rather unclear) purposes. Ward certainly does pursue knowledge ardently, and he certainly does resurrect Curwen's body; but it is false to say (as St Armand does) that Curwen "possesses" Ward. There is, as I have already remarked, no psychic possession—not, at least, of the obvious sort—here, as there is in "The Tomb" and as there will be again in "The Thing on the Doorstep" (1933). Curwen is physically resurrected, and when Ward proves unwilling to assist him in carrying out his plans, Curwen ruthlessly kills him and tries to pass himself off as Ward. And note Ward's defence of his actions in the letter to Willett, specifically the sentence: "I have brought to light a monstrous abnormality, but I did it for the sake of knowledge." This single utterance comprises Ward's (and Lovecraft's) justification: in the first part of the sentence Ward confesses to moral culpability; but the second part of the sentence is preceded by "but" because Ward (with Lovecraft) sees the pursuit of knowledge as intrinsically good. Sometimes, however, that pursuit simply leads to unfortunate and unforeseen consequences. Ward was perhaps naive in thinking that his resurrection of Curwen would lead to no harm; but, as Willett himself says at the end: ". . . he was never a fiend or even truly a madman, but only an eager, studious, and curious boy whose love of mystery and of the past was his undoing."

Psychic possession of a subtler sort may, nevertheless, be involved in the tale. Curwen marries not only because he wishes to repair his reputation, but because he needs a descendant. He seems to know that he will one day die and himself require resurrection by the recovery of his "essential Saltes," so he makes careful arrangements to this effect: he prepares a notebook for "One Who Shal Come After" and leaves sufficient clues toward the location of his remains. It may well be, then, that Curwen exercises psychic possession on Ward so that the latter finds first his effects, then his body, and bring him back to life. Perhaps it would be more accurate to say that the whole scenario embodies Lovecraft's notions of fate and determinism: Ward seems inevitably compelled to pursue the course he does, and this inevitability adds a measure of poignancy to the horror of the situation.

The Case of Charles Dexter Ward represents one of Lovecraft's few relative triumphs of characterisation. Both Curwen and Ward are vividly realised—the latter largely because Lovecraft drew unaffectedly upon his own deepest emotions in the portrayal. Willett is not so successful, and on occasion he reveals himself to be somewhat pompous and self-important. After solving the case he makes the following ludicrous speech: "I can answer no questions, but I will say that there are different kinds of magic. I have made a great purgation, and those in this house will sleep the better for it."

But St Armand is nonetheless right in seeing Providence itself as the principal "character" of the novel. It would require a lengthy commentary to specify not only all the historical data Lovecraft has unearthed, but the countless autobiographical details he has enmeshed into his narrative. The opening descriptions of Ward as a youth are filled with echoes of Lovecraft's own upbringing, although with provocative changes. For example, a description of "one of the child's first memories"—"the great westward sea of hazy roofs and domes and steeples and far hills which he saw one winter afternoon from that great railed embankment, all violet and mystic against a fevered, apocalyptic sunset of reds and golds and purples and curious greens"—is situated in Prospect Terrace, whereas in letters Lovecraft identifies this mystic vision as occurring on the railway embankment in Auburndale, Massachusetts, around 1892. Ward's ecstatic return to Providence after several years abroad can scarcely be anything but a transparent echo of Lovecraft's own return to Providence after two years in New York. The simple utterance that concludes this passage—"It was twilight, and Charles Dexter Ward had come home"—is one of the most quietly moving statements in all Lovecraft's work.

It is of interest to note how Willett's complete eradication of Curwen stands in such stark contrast to Malone's obvious failure to eliminate the age-old horror in Red Hook: New York may be the haven of all horror, but Providence must at the end emerge cleansed of any evil taint. We will observe this occurring in all Lovecraft's tales of Providence. In many ways, indeed, *The Case of Charles Dexter Ward* is a refinement of "The Horror at Red Hook." Several features of the plot are borrowed from that earlier story: Curwen's alchemy parallels Suydam's cabbalistic activities; Curwen's attempt to repair his standing in the community with an advantageous marriage echoes Suydam's marriage with Cornelia Gerritsen; Willett as the valiant counterweight to Curwen matches Malone as the adversary of Suydam. Lovecraft has once again reverted to his relatively small store of basic plot elements, and once again he has transformed a mediocre tale into a masterful one.

It is certainly a pity that Lovecraft made no efforts to prepare *The Case of Charles Dexter Ward* for publication, even when book publishers in the 1930s were specifically asking for a novel from his pen; but we are in no position to question Lovecraft's own judgment that the novel was an inferior piece of work, a "cumbrous, creaking bit of self-conscious antiquarianism."[22] It has certainly now been acknowledged as one of his finest works, and it emphasises the message of *The Dream-Quest of Unknown Kadath* all over again: Lovecraft is who he is because of his birth and upbringing as a New England Yankee. The need to root his work in his native soil became more and more clear to him as time went on, and it led to his gradual transformation of all New England as the locus of both wonder and terror.

* * *

The last tale of Lovecraft's great spate of fiction-writing of 1926–27 is "The Colour out of Space," written in March 1927. It is unquestionably one of his great tales, and it always remained Lovecraft's own favourite. Here again the plot is too well known to require lengthy description. A surveyor for the new reservoir to be built "west of Arkham" encounters a bleak terrain where nothing will grow; the locals call it the "blasted heath." The surveyor, seeking an explanation for the term and for the cause of the devastation, finally finds an old man, Ammi Pierce, living near the area, who tells him an unbelievable tale of events that occurred in 1882. A meteorite had landed on the property of Nahum Gardner and his family. Scientists from Miskatonic University who come to examine the object find that its properties are of the most bizarre sort: the substance refuses to grow cool, displays shining bands on a spectroscope that had never been seen before, and fails to react to conventional solvents applied to it. Within the meteorite is a "large coloured globule": "The colour . . . was almost impossible to describe; and it was only by analogy that they called it colour at all." When tapped with a hammer, it bursts. The meteorite itself, continuing to shrink anomalously, finally disappears altogether.

Henceforth increasingly odd things occur. Nahum's harvest of apples and pears, though unprecedentedly huge in size, proves unfit to eat; plants and animals with peculiar mutations are seen; Nahum's cows start giving bad milk. Then Nahum's wife Nabby goes mad, "screaming about things in the air which she could not describe"; she is locked in an upstairs room. Soon all the vegetation starts to crumble to a greyish powder. Nahum's son Thaddeus goes mad after a visit to the well, and his other sons Merwin and Zenas also break down. Then there is a period of days when Nahum is not seen or heard from. Ammi finally summons up the courage to visit his farm, and finds that the worst has happened: Nahum himself has snapped, and he can only utter confused fragments:

> "Nothin' . . . nothin' . . . the colour . . . it burns . . . cold an' wet, but it burns . . . it lived in the well . . . suckin' the life out of everything . . . in that stone . . . it must a' come in that stone . . . pizened the whole place . . . dun't know what it wants . . . it beats down your mind an' then gits ye . . . can't git away . . . draws ye . . . ye know summ'at's comin', but 'tain't no use . . ."

But that is all: "That which spoke could speak no more because it had completely caved in." Ammi brings policemen, a coroner, and other officials to the place, and after a series of bizarre events they see a column of the unknown colour shoot vertically into the sky from the well; but Ammi sees one small fragment of it return to earth. Now they say that the grey expanse of the "blasted heath" grows by an inch per year, and no one can say when it will end.

Lovecraft was correct in calling this tale an "atmospheric study,"[23] for he has rarely captured the atmosphere of inexplicable horror better than he has here. First let us consider the setting. The reservoir mentioned in the tale is a very real one: the Quabbin Reservoir, plans for which were announced in 1926, although it was not completed until 1939. And yet, Lovecraft declared in a late letter that it was not this reservoir but the Scituate Reservoir in Rhode Island (built in 1926) that caused him to use the reservoir element in the story.[24] He saw this reservoir when he passed through this area in the west-central part of the state on the way to Foster in late October.[25] I cannot, however, believe that Lovecraft was not also thinking of the Quabbin, which is located exactly in the area of central Massachusetts where the tale takes place, and which involved the abandonment and submersion of entire towns in the region. Whatever the case, the bleak rural terrain is portrayed with mastery, as its opening paragraph is sufficient to demonstrate:

> West of Arkham the hills rise wild, and there are valleys with deep woods that no axe has ever cut. There are dark narrow glens where the trees slope fantastic-ally, and where thin brooklets trickle without ever having caught the glint of sunlight. On the gentler slopes there are farms, ancient and rocky, with squat, moss-covered cottages brooding eternally over old New England secrets in the lee of great ledges; but these are all vacant now, the wide chimneys crumbling and the shingled sides bulging perilously beneath low gambrel roofs.

Donald R. Burleson has plausibly suggested a literary influence on this passage from Milton's "Il Penseroso" ("arched walks of twilight groves, / And shadows brown, that Sylvan loves, / Of pine, or monumental oak, / Where the rude axe with heaved stroke / Was never heard the nymphs to daunt"); but there may be an auto-biographical connexion also. Lovecraft seems to have seen a region very much like this one, although curiously enough it was not in New England. Consider his de-scription of the primal forest he traversed in the New Jersey Palisades along the way to Buttermilk Falls in August 1925:

> To reach this scenick Mecca we traversed some of the finest woodland country I have ever seen—unlimited acres of stately forest untouched by the woodman's axe; hill & dale, brooklet & glen, ravine & precipice, rock ledge & pinnacle, marsh & brake, glade & hidden meadow, landscape & prospect, spring & cleft, bower & berry-patch, bird-paradise & mineral treasury.[26]

This opening is also a refinement of the opening of "The Picture in the House" (1920), which might be thought to have piled on the horror—and the adjectives—a little too strongly; here greater restraint is shown, and the entire story could be regarded as one long but subdued prose-poem.

The key to the story, of course, is the anomalous meteorite. Is it—or the col-oured globules inside it—animate in any sense we can recognise? Does it house a single entity or many entities? What are their physical properties? More signifi-cantly, what are their aims, goals, and motives? The fact that we can answer none of these questions very clearly is by no means a failing; indeed, this is exactly the source of terror in the tale. As Lovecraft said of Machen's "The White People," "the *lack of anything concrete* is the *great asset* of the story."[27] In other words, it is precisely because we cannot define the nature—either physical or psychological—of the entities in "The Colour out of Space" (or even know whether they are entities or living creatures as we understand them) that produces the sense of nameless horror. Lovecraft later maintained (probably correctly) that his habit of writing—even if unconsciously—with a pulp audience in mind had corrupted his technique by making his work too obvious and explicit. We will indeed find this problem in some later tales, but here Lovecraft has exercised the most exquisite artistic restraint in not fully defining the nature of the phenomena at hand.

It is, therefore, in "The Colour out of Space" that Lovecraft has most closely achieved his goal of avoiding the depiction of "the human form—and the local human passions and conditions and standards— . . . as native to other worlds or other universes." For it is manifest that the meteorite in "The Colour out of Space" must have come from some dim corner of the universe where natural laws work very differently from the way they do here: "It was just a colour out of space—a frightful messenger from unformed realms of infinity beyond all nature as we know it; from realms whose mere existence stuns the brain and numbs us with the black extra-cosmic gulfs it throws open before our frenzied eyes." The chemical experiments performed on the object establish that it is *physically* unlike anything we know; and the utter absence of any sense of wilful viciousness, or conventionalised "evil" in the object or the entities it contains similarly results in a *psychological* distancing from human or earthly standards. To be sure, the meteorite causes great destruction, and because some remnants of it are still on the planet, it will continue to do so; but perhaps this is an inevitable product of the mingling of our world and its own. In order for an animate being to be morally culpable of "evil," it must be conscious that it is doing what is regarded as evil; but who can say whether the entities in "The Colour out of Space" are conscious at all? Nahum Gardner's poignant dying speech makes the matter clear: his simple utterance, "dun't know what it wants," puts the matter in a nutshell. We have no way of ascertaining the mental or emotional orientation of the anomalous entities, and as a result we cannot possibly apportion praise or blame to them by any conventional moral standard.

But Lovecraft has rendered the plight of the Gardner family inexpressibly poignant and tragic, so that although we cannot "blame" the meteorite for causing their deaths, we still experience a tremendous sense of sorrow mingled with horror at their fate. It is not merely that they have been physically destroyed; the meteorite has also beaten down their minds and wills, so that they are unable to escape its effects. When Ammi tells Nahum that the well water is bad, Nahum ignores him: "He and the boys continued to use the tainted supply, drinking it as listlessly and mechanically as they ate their meager and ill-cooked meals and did their thankless and monotonous chores through the aimless days." This single sentence is one of the most heart-rending and depressing moments in all Lovecraft.

"The Colour out of Space" is of course the first of Lovecraft's major tales to effect that union of horror and science fiction which would become the hallmark of his later work. It continues the pattern already established in "The Call of Cthulhu" of transferring "the focus of supernatural dread from man and his little world and his gods, to the stars and the black and unplumbed gulfs of intergalactic space," as Fritz Leiber ably termed it.[28] In a sense, of course, Lovecraft was taking the easy way out: by simply having his entities come from some remote corner of the universe, he could attribute nearly any physical properties to them and not be required to give a plausible explanation for them. But the abundance of chemical and biological verisimilitude Lovecraft provides makes these unknown properties highly convincing, as does the gradually enveloping atmosphere of the tale. If there is any flaw in "The Colour out of Space," it is that it is just a little too long: the scene with Ammi and the others in the Gardner farmhouse is dragged out well beyond the requirements for the tale and actually dilutes some of the tensity of atmosphere Lovecraft has so carefully fashioned. But beyond this slight and debatable flaw, "The Colour out of Space" is an achievement Lovecraft rarely, perhaps never, equalled.

In a sense the most controversial aspect of the tale is the mundane matter of its publication history. "The Colour out of Space" appeared in *Amazing Stories* for September 1927; but the critical question is whether the tale was ever submitted to *Weird Tales*. Apparently the only evidence for this occurs in Sam Moskowitz's article, "A Study in Horror: The Eerie Life of H. P. Lovecraft," first published in *Fantastic* for May 1960 and reprinted (as "The Lore of H. P. Lovecraft") in Moskowitz's *Explorers of the Infinite* (1963). There Moskowitz writes:

> So full of high hope for this story, Lovecraft was stunned when it was rejected by *Weird Tales*. In a letter to Frank Belknap Long, Lovecraft stormed at the shortsightedness of Farnsworth Wright. Though *Weird Tales* printed numerous science fiction stories, Wright preferred the romantic adventure so popular in *Argosy*, or even straight action stories. Lovecraft submitted the story to *Argosy*, which also rejected it as being a bit too "strong" for their readership.[29]

Here now are two remarkable assertions: that the tale was submitted both to *Argosy* and to *Weird Tales*. Moskowitz, however, told me[30] that his article was originally written at the request of Frank Belknap Long for *Satellite Science Fiction* (of which Long was an associate editor), and that Long had provided him with the information about the rejections of "The Colour out of Space." At this time (1959), however, Long no longer had his letters from Lovecraft: he had sold them to Samuel Loveman in the early 1940s. My feeling, therefore, is that Long has misremembered the entire episode, confusing it with the rejection of "The Call of Cthulhu." There is no mention of any rejection by *Weird Tales* in any of the letters to Long that I have read for this period, although there may be other letters to which I have not had access; but Lovecraft's total silence on this matter in letters to other colleagues—particularly August Derleth (to whom he mentions, in late April, merely the *intention* of submitting the tale to Wright[31]) and Donald Wandrei, with whom he was corresponding very frequently in 1927 and to whom he was making frequent mention of acceptances and rejections—is significant. Consider also Lovecraft's comment to Farnsworth Wright in his letter of July 5, 1927: ". . . this spring and summer I've been too busy with revisory and kindred activities to write more than one tale—which, oddly enough, was accepted at once by *Amazing Stories* . . ."[32] The wording of this letter suggests that this is Lovecraft's first mention of the story to Wright. There is equal silence concerning a possible *Argosy* rejection; Long may have confused this with the rejection of "The Rats in the Walls" in 1923. In 1930 Lovecraft wrote to Smith: "I must try the *Argosy* some day, though I gave up the Munsey group in disgust when the celebrated Robert H. Davis turned down my 'Rats in the Walls' as 'too horrible and improbable'—or something like that—some seven years ago."[33] Unless one assumes that Lovecraft is uncharacteristically lying, this certainly suggests that he had made no submission to *Argosy* since 1923.

It would not at all be unusual for Lovecraft at this time to be trying new markets. As early as April 1927 he was complaining of "Wright's increasing disinclination to accept my stuff,"[34] and we have already seen his attempt to land his work in *Ghost Stories* in 1926. In May 1927 the redoubtable Edwin Baird resurfaced with plans for a new magazine; in spite of his past troubles with Baird, Lovecraft submitted six stories to him.[35] The magazine of course never materialised. Also at this time Lovecraft submitted "The Call of Cthulhu" to *Mystery Stories,* edited by Robert Sampson, where it was rejected on the ground (as Lovecraft tartly termed it) "that it was 'too heavy' for his airy & popular publication."[36]

Amazing Stories was the first authentic science fiction magazine in English, and it continues to be published today. Lovecraft remarked wryly, "The magazine certainly lived up to its name so far as I am concerned, for I really hadn't the remotest idea the thing would 'land'. I guess the pseudo-scientific camouflage near the beginning was what turned the trick."[37] Scientific romance of a sort had been featured in the early decades of the century in *Argosy, All-Story,* the *Thrill Book,* and others, but *Amazing* was the first to make a coordinated effort to print material of this kind—material, too, that was fairly sound in its scientific premises. During its first year, when Lovecraft subscribed to it, it also attempted to draw upon what editor Hugo Gernsback perceived to be the literary origins of the field by reprinting Jules Verne, H. G. Wells, and other "classics." When these reprints ceased, Lovecraft found the new work not sufficiently interesting to warrant purchasing the magazine.

But if he was hoping that he had somehow found an alternative to *Weird Tales,* he was in for a rude awakening. Although his later work, as it turns out, contained a fairly significant scientific element, *Amazing* became a closed market to him when Gernsback paid him only $25.00 for the story—a mere 1/5¢ per word—and this only after three dunning letters. Gernsback paid incredibly poorly and also delayed payment for months or even years. The inevitable occurred: many potential writers abandoned the magazine, and others who—like Clark Ashton Smith—published in it or in Gernsback's later magazine, *Wonder Stories* (where the same financial practices prevailed), were compelled to file suit against him to receive payment. In the 1930s there was a lawyer who made a specialty of exacting payment from Gernsback. Although in later years Lovecraft briefly considered requests from Gernsback or from his associate editor, C. A. Brandt, for further submissions, he never again sent a tale to *Amazing.* He also took to calling Gernsback "Hugo the Rat."

One further work of fiction that may be considered here is the fragment titled (by R. H. Barlow) "The Descendant." This has customarily been dated, on no evidence that I can ascertain, to 1926; but it is conceivable that an early 1927 date is more probable. The clue may reside in a letter of April 1927:

> Just now I'm making a very careful study of *London* by means of maps, books, & pictures, in order to get background for tales involving richer antiquities than America can furnish. . . . If there's anything I hate, it's writing about a locality without an adequate knowledge of its history, topography, & general atmosphere; & I don't wish to make this blunder in anything I may concoct with an Old London setting.[38]

Lovecraft does not, of course, say in this letter or in any other I have read that he had actually written anything with a London setting; but "The Descendant" certainly has a London setting, as no other work of this period does. The only other clue to dating the fragment is the mention in it of Charles Fort; Lovecraft, although having previously heard of Fort, did not read any of his work until Donald Wandrei lent him *The Book of the Damned* in March 1927.[39]

I do not know that much more can be made of this piece; it is clearly a false start, and it is just as well that Lovecraft abandoned it after a few pages. It is written in that frenetic, overheated style of some of his earlier tales—a style that Lovecraft, with "The Call of Cthulhu" and "The Colour out of Space," was wisely starting to abandon. This tale, like "The Rats in the Walls," brings Roman Britain into play; and, as in that story, Lovecraft continues to make errors regarding which legion was in England (the second, not the third Augustan) and the location of its legionary fortress (Isca Silurum [Caerleon-on-Usk], not Lindum [Lincoln]). Again, these changes could perhaps be deliberate, but I fail to see their point if they are. There is also a focus on the *Necronomicon,* and the scene in which one character purchases the tome from a "Jew's shop in the squalid precincts of Clare Market" is surprisingly similar to the opening sonnet of the later *Fungi from Yuggoth* (1929–30) sequence. Some external features of another character, Lord Northam, bring Arthur Machen and Lord Dunsany to mind, although in a superficial way. Northam lives at Gray's Inn, where Machen lived for many years; and Northam is the "nineteenth Baron of a line whose beginnings went uncomfortably far back into the past," just as Dunsany was the eighteenth Baron in a line founded in the twelfth century. Northam, like Randolph Carter in "The Silver Key," undertakes a wide-ranging sampling of various religious and aesthetic ideals ("Northam in youth and young manhood drained in turn the founts of formal religion and occult mystery"), allowing us perhaps to believe that the fragment was written after "The Silver Key." Beyond these things, there does not seem to be much to say about "The Descendant."

Just before writing "The Colour out of Space," Lovecraft had to hurry up and type "Supernatural Horror in Literature," since Cook wished it immediately for the *Recluse*. When he had returned from New York, Lovecraft noted that "somebody [C. M. Eddy?] has put me on the track of a list of weird fiction at the public library which (if I can get access to it) may cause me to expand the text considerably."[40] He did read, in the summer and fall of 1926, some material new to him and made a few additions. Among them was the substantial work of Walter de la Mare, whose two collections, *The Riddle and Other Stories* (1926) and *The Connoisseur and Other Stories* (1926), as well as the novel *The Return,* are among the most subtle examples of atmospheric and psychologically acute weird fiction of its time; Lovecraft came to rank de la Mare only just below his four "modern masters," and in later years yearned to achieve the sort of indirection and allusiveness found in de la Mare's best work—"Seaton's Aunt," "All Hallows," "Mr. Kempe," and others. Other works he read at this time were Sax Rohmer's *Brood of the Witch Queen* (1924) and H. Rider Haggard's *She* (1887).[41] Cook's rush order, however, compelled Lovecraft to type up the essay without the more significant enlargements, whatever they may have been.[42] The typescript came to 72 pages. Cook must have done the typesetting incredibly rapidly, for he had already delivered the first set of page proofs to Lovecraft by the end of March, scarcely two weeks after he received the text.

Even this, however, was not quite the end. Late in the month Donald Wandrei lent F. Marion Crawford's superb posthumous collection of horror tales, *Wandering Ghosts* (1911), to Lovecraft,[43] while in April Lovecraft borrowed Robert W. Chambers's early collection *The King in Yellow* (1895) from Cook;[44] he was so taken with these works that he added paragraphs on both writers in the page proofs.

Neither Lovecraft's fondness for the weird work of Chambers (1865–1933) nor the amazement he expressed when he came upon it—". . . the forgotten early work of *Robert W. Chambers* (can you believe it?) who turned out some powerful bizarre stuff between 1895 & 1904"[45]—need be a surprise. *The King in Yellow,* he writes in "Supernatural Horror in Literature," "is a series of vaguely connected short stories having as a background a monstrous and suppressed book whose perusal brings fright, madness, and spectral tragedy"—in other words, rather uncannily like the *Necronomicon!* It is natural that some critics (such as Lin Carter), not knowing when Lovecraft first read Chambers, would think that *The King in Yellow* was the actual inspiration for the *Necronomicon.* Chambers's volume is a powerful collection and is now recognised as a landmark; indeed, Lovecraft himself is chiefly responsible for this recognition. Lovecraft went on to read some of Chambers's other weird work—*The Maker of Moons* (1896), *In Search of the Unknown* (1904), and the mediocre later novel, *The Slayer of Souls* (1920)—but never seems to have read *The Mystery of Choice* (1897), another early collection in some ways nearly equal to *The King in Yellow.* The "can you believe it?" remark relates to the fact that Chambers abandoned the weird around the turn of the century to write an endless series of shopgirl romances that were perennial best-sellers, making Chambers very wealthy but spelling his complete aesthetic ruination. Lovecraft correctly remarks, "Chambers is like Rupert Hughes & a few other fallen Titans—equipped with the right brains & education, but wholly out of the habit of using them."[46]

The *Recluse* appeared in August 1927; although initially planned as a quarterly, this was the only issue ever published. It is a landmark in more ways than one; but I think it an error to regard it as being strictly a publication devoted to the weird. It certainly was not conceived as such, and the issue—although containing a large proportion of weird material by Lovecraft and his friends—was simply another of Cook's long line of amateur ventures. The lead item, taking up the first fourteen (out of seventy-seven) pages, is a detailed study of Vermont poets and poetry by Walter J. Coates. Lovecraft's essay does indeed take up the bulk of the issue (pages 23–59); he was, in fact, not certain whether Cook would run it all in the first issue, and as it turns out it was fortunate that Cook did so. There is some fine weird writing by Clark Ashton Smith (the poem "After Armageddon"; "Brumes et Pluies," translated from Baudelaire), Donald Wandrei (the story "A Fragment of a Dream" and the poem "In the Grave" [later titled "The Corpse Speaks"]), and H. Warner Munn (the story "The Green Porcelain Dog"); Frank Long's poem "Ballad of St. Anthony" is an admirable romantic specimen, and Samuel Loveman's essay on Hubert Crackanthorpe is a sensitive analysis. One of the most striking pieces is Vrest Orton's superb line drawing for the cover—a picture of a bearded old man poring over ancient tomes in a mediaeval study, with iron-hasped books and beakers containing strange substances heaped about, and three flickering candles providing scanty illumination. All in all, it is a remarkable cover to a remarkable issue.

Cook expressed the wish to send the *Recluse* to certain "celebrities," in particular to all four of Lovecraft's "modern masters," Machen, Dunsany, Blackwood, and M. R. James. As it happened, the issue did find its way to some of these figures, and their responses to Lovecraft's essay are of interest. James somewhat unkindly declared in a letter that Lovecraft's style "is of the most offensive"; his criticism evidently focusing on the fact that "He uses the word cosmic about 24 times." A little more charitably he remarks: "But he has taken pains to search about & treat the subject from its beginning to MRJ, to whom he devotes several columns."[47] Machen's response can only be gauged from Donald Wandrei's comment to Lovecraft: "I received a letter to-day from Machen, in which he mentioned your article and its hold on him."[48] I do not know of any comment by Machen himself on Lovecraft's essay. Copies were also apparently sent to Blackwood, Dunsany, Rudyard Kipling, Charlotte Perkins Gilman, Mary E. Wilkins Freeman, and several others.

As early as April 1927 Lovecraft already had a "vague and nebulous idea"[49] of expanding "Supernatural Horror in Literature" for a putative second edition, and Cook occasionally mentioned the possibility of issuing such an edition separately as a monograph. Lovecraft set up a section in his commonplace book entitled "Books to mention in new edition of weird article," listing such things as Leonard Cline's superb novel of hereditary memory, *The Dark Chamber* (1927), Herbert Gorman's sinister novel of witchcraft in backwoods New England, *The Place Called Dagon* (1927), and other works he read in the subsequent months and years; but Cook's subsequent physical and financial collapse confounded, or at least delayed, the plans, and the second edition did not materialise until 1933, and in a form very different from what Lovecraft imagined.

Having by 1927 already published nearly a score of tales in *Weird Tales,* and finding that amateur work was at a virtual end with the demise of the UAPA, Lovecraft now began gathering colleagues specifically devoted to weird fiction. The last decade of his life would see him become a friend, correspondent, and mentor of more than a dozen writers who would follow in his footsteps and become well known in the fields of weird, mystery, and science fiction.

August Derleth (1909–1971) wrote to Lovecraft through *Weird Tales.* He must have written to Farnsworth Wright before Lovecraft's departure from New York in mid-April 1926, for Wright supplied Lovecraft's 169 Clinton Street address; Derleth wrote a direct letter to Lovecraft only in late July, and the latter responded at once in early August. From that time on, the two men kept up a steady correspondence—usually once a week—for the next ten and a half years.

Derleth had just finished high school in Sauk City, Wisconsin, and in the fall of 1926 would begin attendance at the University of Wisconsin at Madison, where in 1930 he would write as an honours thesis "The Weird Tale in English Since 1890"—a work embarrassingly dependent upon Lovecraft's "Supernatural Horror in Literature" and in part a plagiarism of some of its actual language. But Derleth was not a critic by nature; rather, his forte was fiction and, in lesser degree, poetry. As a fiction writer he would reveal astounding range and precocity. Although his first story in *Weird Tales* dates to his eighteenth year ("Bat's Belfry" in the May 1926 issue), his weird tales—whether written by himself or in collaboration with the young Mark Schorer—would be in many ways the least interesting aspect of his work; they are conventional, relatively unoriginal, and largely undistinguished, and he readily admitted to Lovecraft that they were written merely to supply cash. Derleth's more serious work—for which he would eventually gain considerable renown, and which today remains the most significant branch of his output—is a series of regional sagas drawing upon his native Wisconsin and written in a poignant, Proustian, reminiscent vein whose simple elegance allows for evocative character portrayal. The first of these works to be published was *Place of Hawks* (1935), a series of novellas, although Derleth was working as early as 1929 on a novel he initially titled *The Early Years,* eventually published in 1941 as *Evening in Spring.* Those who fail to read these two works, along with their many successors in Derleth's long and fertile career, will have no conception why Lovecraft, as early as 1930, wrote with such enthusiasm about his younger colleague and disciple:

> Derleth impressed me tremendously favourably from the moment I began to hear from him personally. I saw that he had a prodigious fund of activity & reserve mental energy, & that it would only be a question of time before he began to correlate it to real aesthetic advantage. There was a bit of callow egotism also—but that was only to be expected . . . And surely enough, as the years passed, I saw that the kid was truly growing. The delicate reminiscent sketches begun a couple of years ago were the final proof—for there, indeed, he had reached what was unmistakably sincere & serious self-expression of a high order. . . . There was no disputing that he *really had something to say* . . . & that he was trying to say it honestly & effectively, with a minimum of the jaunty hack devices & stylistic tricks which went into his printed pot-boiling material.[50]

In later years Lovecraft marvelled both at Derleth's tremendous fecundity in reading and writing and at his Janus-like ability to write cheap hackwork for the pulp magazines while writing poignant sketches of human life for the little magazines.

Derleth was also attracted to the mystery field. In the early 1930s he began writing novels involving Judge Peck. Lovecraft read the first three of them (there would eventually be ten, the last in 1953) and spoke charitably of them, but in all frankness they are dreadful potboilers. In 1929 Derleth began a series of short stories—pastiches of Conan Doyle's Sherlock Holmes—involving Solar Pons; these are much more successful and may be considered among the best imitations of the Holmes canon in existence. They would eventually fill six volumes of short stories and one short novel.

In the early years of their association, Lovecraft and Derleth would spend much time talking of weird fiction; Derleth, in his zeal to sell his work, would alert

Lovecraft to many new markets as they opened up, and he would later even take the initiative of submitting Lovecraft's stories to *Weird Tales* when Lovecraft himself felt reluctant to do so. Their discussions would also span modern literature, Derleth's own writing (Lovecraft would frequently offer advice for the revision of Derleth's tales, most of which Derleth ignored or rejected), spiritualism and paranormal phenomena (in which Derleth was a firm believer), and other matters. And yet, the correspondence never really develops an intimacy as those with Morton, Long, Smith, and others do. This may be because the two never met—Derleth once contemplated an eastern trip, but he never made it until after Lovecraft's death; Lovecraft, for his part, wistfully thought of going to Wisconsin, but never had the funds or, I suspect, the true inclination to do so—but it may also have something to do with Derleth's own personality. Lovecraft was right in thinking Derleth self-centred, and it is a trait that seemed only to increase as he became a "successful" writer with published books to his credit. Derleth had difficulty talking of anything aside from himself, and Lovecraft's replies, though always cordial, are limited by their subject-matter and seem reserved and formulaic. No doubt Lovecraft had great and sincere admiration for his young friend, who he frequently predicted would be the one writer of his circle to make a name for himself in general literature; but he never opened up to Derleth as he did to Long and Morton.

Donald Wandrei (1908–1987) got in touch with Lovecraft in late 1926 through Clark Ashton Smith. Smith was the first writer to whom Wandrei was devoted, and in some ways he remained Wandrei's model in both fiction and poetry. Through the influence of George Sterling, Wandrei's rhapsodic appreciation of Smith, "The Emperor of Dreams," appeared in the *Overland Monthly* for December 1926. Here is an extract:

> Some of his poems are like shadowed gold; some are like flame-encircled ebony; some are crystal-clear and pure; others are as unearthly starshine. One is coldly wrought in marble; another is curiously carved in jade; there are a few glittering diamonds; and there are many rubies and emeralds aflame, glowing with a secret fire. Here and there may be found a poppy-flower, an orchid from the hotbed of Hell, the whisper of an eldritch wind, a breath from the burning sands of region infernal.

And so on. Anyone who has fallen under the influence of Smith's poetry develops a fatal temptation to write about it like this. Wandrei certainly did better critical work, and his essay "Arthur Machen and *The Hill of Dreams*" (*Minnesota Quarterly,* Spring 1926) is a fine appreciation. But criticism was not his chief aesthetic outlet, although he did send Lovecraft the term papers on Gothic fiction he was writing at the University of Minnesota. Instead, Wandrei was initially attracted to poetry, and it should be no surprise that much of his early verse is heavily influenced by Smith. There is perhaps somewhat more horrific content in Wandrei's poetry than Smith's—as in the *Sonnets of the Midnight Hours,* to be considered a little later—but there is also a great deal of cosmic and love poetry, like Smith's. Some philosophical verse is tinged with the misanthropy and pessimism Wandrei felt in his youth, as in "Chaos Resolved":

> So few the days, so much that one could know,
> So little light, so many corridors,
> So dark whichever pathway one may go,
> So great the gap, and firmly barred the doors,
> That I am weary though I've gone not far,
> And find defeat ere I have much begun;
> Wherefor, solution distant as a star,
> And certainty, by doubt and change, undone,
> And conquest everlastingly beyond,
> Where no man walks, and shall not ever see,
> Nor ever have; and since this mortal bond
> Is too exacting for man's magistry,—
> Therefor am I, with what I have, content,
> But still assail the deeper firmament.[51]

Wandrei was also experimenting with prose fiction—in some cases prose-poems, many of them appearing in his college's student magazine, the *Minnesota Quarterly,* and also with longer tales. He had already written one story, "The Chuckler," that was a very loose sequel to Lovecraft's "The Statement of Randolph Carter," although it would not be published until 1934. Some of this early work is quite striking, especially "The Red Brain" (*Weird Tales,* October 1927), which Wandrei had originally entitled "The Twilight of Time." It, along with several other works such as the celebrated "Colossus" (*Astounding Stories,* January 1934), reveals a staggeringly cosmic imagination second only to Lovecraft's in intensity; it is not surprising that the two men found much to talk about in the first year or so of their association. Like Derleth, who spent nearly the whole of his life in and around Sauk City, Wisconsin, Wandrei lived almost his entire life in his family home in St Paul, Minnesota, save for various periods in New York in the 1920s and '30s; but unlike the cheerful Derleth, Wandrei had a brooding and misanthropic streak that often intrigued Lovecraft and may perhaps have helped to shape his own later philosophical views.

I wish I knew more about Bernard Austin Dwyer (1897–1943), but as he published relatively little and was more an appreciator than a creator, he remains a nebulous figure. He lived nearly the whole of his life in and around the tiny village of West Shokan, in upstate New York, near the towns of Hurley, New Paltz, and Kingston. Although attracted to weird fiction and the author of a short poem published in *Weird Tales* ("Ol' Black Sarah" in the October 1928 issue), his chief interest was weird art; and in this capacity he naturally became fast friends with Clark Ashton Smith. Lovecraft met him in 1928 and spoke of him warmly:

> Dwyer is quite a chap, beyond a doubt; with a lot more points in his favour than against him. He has an imagination of the utmost sensitiveness, delicacy, and picturesqueness; and the way he assimilates the many books I lend him (for he has no way of getting books himself in his absolute backwoods isolation) is a proof of his thorough intelligence, sound aesthetic sense, and deep-seated literary sincerity. . . . As Wandrei has probably told you, he is a handsome, youngish near-giant—a mighty woodcutter and athlete and a modest, well-bred, and generally unspoiled personality as a whole.[52]

One gains the impression that Dwyer was a kind of mute, inglorious Milton. He came in touch with Lovecraft through *Weird Tales* in the early part of 1927.

In the spring of 1927 Frank Belknap Long met Vincent Starrett as the latter was passing through New York and gave him some of Lovecraft's stories to read. In April a brief correspondence sprang up between the two—the first, and nearly the last, time that Lovecraft came into contact with a recognised literary figure.

Starrett (1886–1974) had already achieved renown for his bibliography of Ambrose Bierce (1920), his collection of essays, *Buried Caesars* (1923), containing fine appreciations of Bierce, Cabell, W. C. Morrow, and other writers, and especially for his championing of Arthur Machen. Starrett had done much to introduce Machen to American readers, writing the essay *Arthur Machen: A Novelist of Ecstasy and Sin* (1918) and compiling two volumes of Machen's miscellaneous works, *The Shining Pyramid* (1923) and *The Glorious Mystery* (1925). These volumes had, indeed, given rise to a contretemps between the Welsh author and his American disciple (now gathered in *Starrett vs. Machen,* 1978), as Machen felt that Starrett's publication of these books with the Chicago firm of Covici-McGee undermined Knopf's efforts to reprint his work in a standard American edition; but in a few years the feud was settled. Starrett was, as I have mentioned, one of the few established authors to contribute to the early issues of *Weird Tales,* and he either forgot, did not notice, or did not care about Lovecraft's tart comment on his story "Penelope" in the May 1923 issue: "'Penelope' is clever—but Holy Pete! If the illustrious Starrett's ignorance of astronomy is an artfully conceived attribute of his character's whimsical narrative, I'll say he's right there with the verisimilitude!" (letter to the editor, printed in the October 1923 issue).

The correspondence, which lasted nearly a year (April 1927–January 1928), was cordial but reserved. Lovecraft sent Starrett several more of his tales, as well as a copy of the *Recluse* with "Supernatural Horror in Literature"; but it appears that Starrett eventually grew weary of writing to Lovecraft. It is not clear if Lovecraft expected anything to come of the association; he wrote to Wandrei: ". . . if he likes my junk he could probably help a good deal with editors by speaking a good word for it; but I doubt if he will grow very enthusiastic."[53] Starrett does indeed seem to have liked Lovecraft's stories, but apparently not enough to do any active promotion of them at the time. After Lovecraft's death he would write favourable reviews of some of Lovecraft's posthumously published volumes in the *Chicago Tribune.*

One colleague who came to Lovecraft's attention at this time but who was not an enthusiast of the weird is Walter J. Coates (1880–1941). Coates had, as I have mentioned, written the lengthy essay on Vermont literature that opens the *Recluse.* I imagine he got in touch with Lovecraft through Cook, although I am not sure what reason he had for doing so; they clearly shared a fondness for backwoods New England, and very likely discussed this subject in their correspondence (most of which has not been made available to me). Coates had at about this time founded the regional magazine *Driftwind,* and in one of the early issues he published Lovecraft's essay "The Materialist Today" (October 1926). Lovecraft declared that this was part of a letter to Coates and prepared for publication at Coates's insistence.[54] Coates also issued it as a pamphlet in a print run of 15 copies, making it one of the rarest of Lovecraft's separate publications; indeed, for many years it was thought that no copies of it survived, but lately one or two copies have surfaced. Various of Lovecraft's remarks suggest that it actually predates the magazine appearance. The essay is a short, compact, and somewhat cynical enunciation of materialist principles. Coates would later publish several of Lovecraft's *Fungi from Yuggoth* sonnets in *Driftwind.*

In the summer of 1927 Lovecraft both played host to a succession of visitors to Providence and undertook several journeys of his own—something that would become a habit every spring and summer, as he roamed increasingly widely in quest of antiquarian oases. First on the agenda was his new friend Donald Wandrei, who undertook a trip from St Paul, Minnesota, to Providence entirely by hitchhiking. One would like to think that such an expedition was a little safer then than it would be now, and perhaps it was; Wandrei seemed to have no difficulty getting rides, even though on occasion he had to spend nights under the open sky, sometimes in the rain. He himself remarked in a postcard to Lovecraft: ". . . I think I am unusually fortunate in general because I don't look like a bum."[55] Indeed, Wandrei was a gaunt six-footer who, in some photographs of this period, seems to bear an uncanny resemblance to Boris Karloff's portrayal of Frankenstein's monster.

Arriving in Chicago on the 20th of June, where he confirmed all Lovecraft's impressions of the place ("Unimpressed. Going on. The city is filthy"[56]), Wandrei went to the *Weird Tales* office and met Farnsworth Wright. Lovecraft himself had spoken to Wright about Wandrei's work early in the year, and perhaps as a result of this Wandrei's "The Twilight of Time"—rejected a year earlier—was accepted in March, appearing under its better-known but less stimulating title "The Red Brain" in the October 1927 issue. Wandrei felt the need to return the favour, so he spoke to Wright about "The Call of Cthulhu." In a memoir he supplies an engaging account of what he said:

> I casually worked in a reference to a story, *The Call of Cthulhu,* that Lovecraft was revising and finishing and which I thought was a wonderful tale. But I added that for some reason or other, Lovecraft had talked about submitting it to other magazines. I said I just couldn't understand why he was apparently planning to by-pass *Weird Tales* unless he was seeking to broaden his markets or widen his reading public. None of this was true, but I could see that my fanciful account took effect, in the way Wright began to fidget and show signs of agitation . . .[57]

As we have seen, Wright indeed asked Lovecraft to resubmit the tale and then accepted it for $165.00; it appeared in the February 1928 issue. The amusing thing is that Lovecraft's letter to Wright accompanying the tale—the landmark letter of July 5, 1927, in which he enunciated his theory of extraterrestrialism—casually mentioned the acceptance of "The Colour out of Space" by *Amazing,* thereby unwittingly fostering Wandrei's charade! This did not, of course, prevent Wright from rejecting "The Strange High House in the Mist" (it was "not sufficiently clear for the acute minds of his highly intelligent readers"[58]) and "The Silver Key" later in the summer; but in both cases he asked to see them again. "The Silver Key" was accepted the next year for $70.00, but, although Wright specifically asked to see it in the summer of 1929, Lovecraft did not immediately resubmit "The Strange High House" because it had been promised for the second issue of Cook's *Recluse;*[59] by 1931, however, when it was clear that the *Recluse* was defunct, Lovecraft let Wright have it for $55.00. It appeared in October 1931.

Wandrei, meanwhile, continued on from Chicago through Fort Wayne, Indiana, Wooster, Ohio, Lancaster, Pennsylvania, and finally New York City. Initially, of course—in spite of Lovecraft's furious rants about the loathsomeness of the place—Wandrei was overwhelmed and captivated; and yet, in some ways his response was not dissimilar to Lovecraft's: "So far, I have been fascinated by the city, its immensity, and wealth, and speed. But, like you, I hate the people. I have been through good districts only as yet, but everywhere are mongrel anthropoid types, the scum of Europe and Asia. I can not imagine what the slums contain."[60] But there was always the gang: he met Long, Loveman, Kirk, and the rest, and did all the things that a tourist of his type would do—bookstore hunting, museum going, reading his fellow writers' works in progress, and the like. Lovecraft had sent him a long letter detailing some of the high spots (in his view) that he should see, including some of the unspoiled suburbs, particularly Flushing and Hempstead; but it does not appear as if Wandrei had much of an opportunity to follow Lovecraft's suggestions. Lovecraft also gave him detailed instructions on how to reach his home once he got to Providence, supplying also the telephone number of 10 Barnes (DExter 9617). (It was not his private line, but that of his landlady, Florence Reynolds.)

On July 12 Wandrei arrived in Providence, staying till the 29th. Lovecraft had arranged for him to stay in an upstairs room at 10 Barnes for $3.50 a week. Very shortly after his arrival Lovecraft began squiring him to what had by now become the customary sights in both Providence and the surrounding area. On the 13th the two went to Newport, where Wandrei could indulge his lifelong wish to look out over the open sea. The next few days were spent in Quinsnicket and Roger Williams Parks, where Wandrei relates an amusing occurrence:

> One afternoon he put the morning mail and writing supplies in a cardboard portmanteau, and we went to Roger Williams Park where he sat on a bench using the back of the portmanteau as a writing surface. I climbed up on a huge outcrop of rock nearby, and fell asleep in the warm sun. About two hours later I wakened, to find Lovecraft casting an anxious eye in my direction. I quite mistook his meaning, and when I clambered down assured him I was a light sleeper and in no danger of falling off the giant boulder. But he blandly and without malice informed me that he was not at all concerned about my safety; anyone able to nap on solid rock was unlikely to fracture so thick a hide by a mere tumble to lesser rocks below; the sun was westering, however, and since he had no topcoat he was anxious to return home before the evening chill set in.[61]

Wandrei goes on to note that Lovecraft had written a dozen or so letters and postcards during this period, as well as several pages of a "bulky reply" to Long. Even the advent of a guest could not allow Lovecraft an intermission from his customary "wrestling" with correspondence, lest he fall hopelessly behind.

On the 16th Lovecraft and Wandrei set out for Boston, staying over at the YMCA, and the next day went to Salem and Marblehead. The Boston excursion was somewhat of a disappointment, in spite of their taking in the superb Museum of Fine Arts and some of the colonial sites. Lovecraft had been especially keen on showing Wandrei the sinister, decaying North End where "Pickman's Model" was set, but was mortified to find that "the actual alley & house of the tale [had been] utterly demolished; a whole crooked line of buildings having been torn down."[62] (Copp's Hill, of course, being an historic cemetery, still flourishes in its spectral way.) This remark is of interest in indicating that Lovecraft had an actual house in mind for Pickman's North End studio.

On Tuesday, July 19, Frank Long and his parents drove up from New York City, while simultaneously James F. Morton came down from Green Acre, Maine, where he had been visiting. Morton stayed at the Crown Hotel downtown, but the Longs put up at 10 Barnes in rooms directly across from Lovecraft's on the first floor. There was the usual round of Providence sightseeing, and on the evening of the 20th C. M. Eddy joined the crowd for a gang meeting. The next day the entire crew went to Newport, where Morton, Wandrei, and Lovecraft went to the Hanging Rocks and wrote impromptu verses on Bishop George Berkeley, who had stayed briefly there and written his *Alciphron; or, The Minute Philosopher* (1732). (The verses are not extant.)

On the 22nd the Longs left, continuing their voyage up to Cape Cod, Maine, and elsewhere. Morton then dragged Lovecraft and Wandrei to the rock quarry on which Lovecraft still held the mortgage, and for which he was still receiving his pittance of a payment ($37.08) every six months. The owner, Mariano de Magistris, set his men to hunting up specimens, while his son drove them home in his car. "That's what I call real Latin courtesy!" Lovecraft remarked in a rare show of tolerance for non-Aryans.[63]

On Saturday the 23rd occurred an historic pilgrimage—to Julia A. Maxfield's in Warren, where Lovecraft, Morton, and Wandrei staged an ice-cream-eating contest. Maxfield's advertised twenty-eight flavours of ice cream, and the contestants sampled them all:

> Each would order a double portion—two kinds—and by dividing equally would ensure *six* flavours each round. *Five* rounds took us all through the twenty-eight and two to carry. Mortonius and I each consumed two and one-half quarts, but Wandrei fell down toward the last. Now James Ferdinand and I will have to stage an elimination match to determine the champion![64]

Wandrei notes that, even after "falling down," he managed to dip his spoon into the remaining flavours so that he could at least say he had tasted them all. The three of them wrote out a statement saying that they had tried all twenty-eight flavours and signed their names; on later visits they were delighted to find that the statement had been framed and posted on the wall of the store!

That afternoon a contingent from Athol, Massachusetts, arrived—W. Paul Cook and his protégé, H. Warner Munn (1903–1981). Lovecraft had no doubt heard something of Munn before. Munn's "The Werewolf of Ponkert" (*Weird Tales*, July 1925) was apparently inspired by a comment in Lovecraft's letter to Edwin Baird published in the March 1924 issue ("Take a werewolf story, for instance—who ever wrote a story from the point of view of the wolf, and sympathising strongly with the devil to whom he has sold himself?"). Although Munn failed to understand the thrust of Lovecraft's remark, making the wolf lament his anomalous condition, the story proved popular and Munn went on to write several sequels to it. He contributed extensively to the pulps and over his long career wrote many supernatural and adventure novels; but perhaps his most distinguished works were historical novels written late in his career, notably *Merlin's Ring* (1974) and *The Lost Legion* (1980). The latter, a long novel about a Roman legion that wanders to China, would have fired Lovecraft's imagination. Lovecraft took to Munn readily, finding him "a splendid young chap—blond and burly";[65] he would visit him frequently when passing through Athol.

At some point during his stay Wandrei badgered Lovecraft to let him read his short novels of 1926–27, *The Dream-Quest of Unknown Kadath* and *The Case of Charles Dexter Ward,* still untyped and destined to remain so to the end of Lovecraft's life. Wandrei thereby became the first person other than their creator to lay eyes on these texts; he gives no opinion of them in his subsequent letters or his later memoirs, but Lovecraft made a passing comment in a 1930 letter: "Wandrei read [the *Dream-Quest*] in manuscript & didn't think much of it."[66] And yet, Wandrei's interest may be gauged by the fact that a few years later he offered to type them. Lovecraft, horrified at the prospect of someone undertaking this backbreaking toil on works whose value he greatly questioned, scuttled the idea.

On the 29th Wandrei finally left, heading up to Athol via Worcester. After that he went to West Shokan, New York, where he stayed a day or two with Bernard Austin Dwyer. Then he began the long trek home, finally reaching St Paul on the 11th of August and writing Lovecraft a one-word postcard: "Home!!!"[67] Lovecraft clearly enjoyed Wandrei's visit: almost every one of his letters and postcards to Wandrei over the next few years expresses the wish that he return, but Wandrei did not have the opportunity to do so until 1932.

Lovecraft's own travels were, however, by no means over. On August 19 he went up to Worcester, where Cook picked him up and brought him back to Athol for a brief stay. The next day (his thirty-eighth birthday) Cook took Lovecraft to Amherst and Deerfield, the latter town of which Lovecraft found extraordinarily captivating. On Sunday the 21st they went to Lake Sunapee, New Hampshire, where Cook's sister lived. From here they made an unexpected detour into Vermont to visit the amateur poet Arthur Goodenough. A decade before, Goodenough had praised Lovecraft in a poem ("Lovecraft—an Appreciation") containing the grotesque image, "Laurels from thy very temples sprout." Lovecraft had thought Goodenough was spoofing him, and Cook had difficulty preventing Lovecraft from writing some devastating reply; instead, he wrote a poem in return, "To Arthur Goodenough, Esq." (*Tryout,* September 1918). Now, when meeting him, Lovecraft was captivated by Goodenough, and especially by the archaic and rustic charm of his dress and demeanour:

> Goodenough is a typical old-time rustic of a pattern almost extinct today. He has never seen a city of any size, & seldom goes even to the adjacent small town of Brattleboro. In speech, dress, & manner he reflects an admirable though vanished phase of American life ... His stately courtesy & hospitality are worthy of the 17th century to which he intellectually belongs ...[68]

He exclaimed to Cook, "Why, the man is genuine!" Cook replied, "Howard, you are yourself genuine, although different from Arthur."[69]

Lovecraft later wrote a rhapsodic essay on his entire Vermont visit, "Vermont—A First Impression," which appropriately enough appeared in Coates's

Driftwind for March 1928. I shall have more to say of this visit, and of the essay, farther on.

After a few more days in Athol, Lovecraft went on a lone tour first to Boston on the 24th and then, the next day, to Portland, Maine. He spent two days in Portland and enjoyed the town immensely: although it was not as rich in antiquities as Marblehead or Portsmouth, it was scenically lovely—it occupies a peninsula with hills at the eastern and western ends, and has many beautiful drives and promenades—and at least had things like the two Longfellow houses (birthplace and principal residence), which Lovecraft explored thoroughly. On the 26th he took a side-trip to Yarmouth, a colonial town thirteen miles northeast of Portland on the coast, and on the 27th he took a cheap excursion to the White Mountains in New Hampshire—the first time Lovecraft saw "real mountains"[70] (if one can so refer to eminences less than 6300 feet above sea level).

Sunday the 28th found Lovecraft in Portsmouth, New Hampshire, and the next day he returned to Newburyport, Massachusetts, which he had not seen since 1923. He stayed there until the 30th, at which time he went to Amesbury and Haverhill, stopping by at the home of his old amateur friend C. W. Smith. He would write up his travels in a very compressed and, frankly, not very interesting essay called "The Trip of Theobald," which Smith would publish in the *Tryout* for September 1927. Wednesday the 31st he returned to Newburyport, thence moving on to Ipswich and then to Gloucester. He had not been to the latter place since 1922 (when he went with Sonia), and found it much more stimulating this time:

> Pre-Revolutionary houses are more numerous than I expected, & there is a ghoulish hidden graveyard just off a side street. An 1805 belfry dominates the skyline. I climbed a high hill & had a stupendous view. Gloucester has an *active* maritime atmosphere not possessed by any other town I have seen. Its whole community life is unique & local, & the main street retains most of its Georgian brick buildings.[71]

He spent two days in Gloucester, after which he passed through Manchester, Marblehead, and Salem, finally coming home on September 2. This two-week trek through four states was entirely delightful; in "The Trip of Theobald" he wrote: "The trip, as a whole, exceeded all others I have taken in general pleasure and picturesqueness, and will surely be difficult to improve upon in future years." And yet, each spring and summer for the next eight years would see trips of increasing scope, so that he would be inclined to repeat that last statement after almost every one of them.

In September Wilfred B. Talman visited Lovecraft in Providence and hectored him to coordinate and expand his genealogical data. Talman was an indefatigable genealogist, and his enthusiasm infected Lovecraft at least to the degree of ascertaining his coat of arms (Arms: Vert, a Chevron engrailed, Or, between three Foxes' Heads, erased, Or; Crest: On a wreath, a Tower, Or; Motto: *Quae amamus tuemur*) and in hypothesising some frivolously recherché connexions to certain distinguished individuals. Through a Welsh ancestor, Rachel Morris, he found a link to David Jenkins of Machynlleth ("get that, Arthur?"); through the Fulford line he hooked up to the Moretons ("Shades of Edward John *Moreton* Drax Plunkett! I don't know what—if any—the relationship is, but I'm now calling Dunsany 'Cousin Ned'");[72] an even more remote connexion linked him to Owen Gwynedd, Prince of North Wales. "Now GWYNEDD is obviously the source of the modern name *Gwinnett* . . . and thus I am very clearly a second or third or three-thousandth cousin of my fellow-fantaisiste *Ambrose Gwinnett Bierce!* . . . No use talking—all us Machyns and Moretons and Gwynetts jes' nachelly take to imaginative writing. It's in the blood—ya can't stop us!"[73] All this is good fun; but, even though the Gwynedd/Gwinnett connexion is meant in fun, Lovecraft probably did not know that Bierce's father took the name Ambrose Gwinnett from a pseudonymously published pamphlet of 1770 entitled *The Life and Strange, Unparallel'd, and Unheard-of Voyages and Adventures of Ambrose Gwinet.*[74] Strangely enough, the pseudonym used for this publication was Isaac Bickerstaffe, which Lovecraft himself had used in 1914.

Meanwhile various prospects for the book publication of Lovecraft's stories were developing. As early as the summer of 1926, the redoubtable J. C. Henneberger reemerged on the scene with importunate requests to be allowed to market a collection of Lovecraft's stories; Lovecraft did so, "to keep him quiet,"[75] but clearly nothing came of this improbable venture.

A more serious possibility began taking shape late that year when Farnsworth Wright broached the idea of a collection. Lovecraft noted: ". . . one of the business backers of W.T. says he is going to show certain things of mine to publishers; but I don't really think anything will come of it."[76] This project would keep Lovecraft dangling for several years before finally collapsing. The reasons for this are perhaps not far to seek. Sometime in 1927 *Weird Tales* (under its official imprint, the Popular Fiction Publishing Company) issued *The Moon Terror* by A. G. Birch and others; it contained the title novelette, which was wildly popular when it appeared as a two-part serial in May and June 1923, along with other stories from early issues ("Ooze" by Anthony M. Rud, "Penelope" by Vincent Starrett, and "An Adventure in the Fourth Dimension" by Farnsworth Wright). For whatever reason, the book was a complete commercial disaster, remaining in print nearly as long as *Weird Tales* itself was in existence (1954). And, of course, the onset of the depression hit the magazine very hard, and for various periods in the 1930s it was forced to adopt a bimonthly schedule; at this time the issuance of a book was the last thing on the publishers' minds.

Nevertheless, in late December 1927 negotiations were still serious enough for Lovecraft to write a long letter giving his own preferences as to the contents. The collection was planned for about 45,000 words, and Lovecraft considered the "*in-dispensable* nucleus" to consist of the following stories: "The Outsider," "Arthur Jermyn," "The Rats in the Walls," "The Picture in the House," "Pickman's Model," "The Music of Erich Zann," "Dagon," "The Statement of Randolph Carter," and "The Cats of Ulthar." This, according to Lovecraft's count, would come to 32,400 words. He then wished one of the following three longer stories to be included—"The Colour out of Space," "The Call of Cthulhu" (not yet published), or "The Horror at Red Hook," with preference for "Colour"—and, as "fillers," some of his shorter tales, such as "The Festival," "The Unnamable," or "The Terrible Old Man."

On the whole, this would have made a very worthy collection—certainly it would have contained much of the best that Lovecraft had written up to this time. It would have been better, perhaps, to have included both "Colour" and "Cthulhu," but the volume still would have been substantial. One remark made in Lovecraft's long letter is worth quoting: "As for a *title*—my choice is *The Outsider and Other Stories.* This is because I consider the touch of cosmic *outsideness*—of dim, shadowy *non-terrestrial* hints—to be the characteristic feature of my writing."[77]

One story Lovecraft only grudgingly offered for the collection was "The Lurking Fear," which he dismissed as "thunderously melodramatic" but nevertheless one that "ought to please the followers of Nictzin Dyalhis and his congeners." (Dyalhis was a wretched writer of hack space operas.) Lovecraft sent the tale to Wright, who surprised him by wanting to print it in *Weird Tales* for $78.00. Lovecraft was for a time concerned about the possibility of a copyright problem with *Home Brew,* but, given that the magazine had folded years ago, he came to the conclusion that no conflict existed and permitted Wright to print the tale in spite of his aesthetic misgivings.

A story Lovecraft did not offer (probably just as well, as Wright had already rejected it for the magazine) was "The Shunned House," which W. Paul Cook wished to publish as a small book. Cook had initially conceived of including it in the *Recluse,*[78] but presumably held off because the magazine had already attained enormous size. Then, around February 1927, he first broached the idea of printing it as a chapbook.[79] Cook had issued Long's slim collection of poetry, *The Man from Genoa,* in early 1926 (the book had been financed by Long's wealthy aunt, Mrs William B. Symmes[80]), and later that year issued Loveman's *The Hermaphrodite;* "The Shunned House" would complete a trilogy of books uniform in format. The book was planned for 60 pages, which could be managed by printing the text with a large amount of white space on the borders. Later Cook asked Frank Long to write a preface, even though Lovecraft felt that a preface to a short story was ridiculous.

The issuance of the *Recluse* delayed work on this book project, but in the spring of 1928 things began to move. By late May Cook was importuning Lovecraft to read proofs quickly, and Lovecraft did so in early June even though he was then on another extensive series of travels.[81] By the end of June Lovecraft announced that *The Shunned House* was all printed but not bound.[82] About 300 copies were printed.

Unfortunately, things soured at this very moment. Both Cook's finances and his health were in a very shaky state. Already in February 1928 Lovecraft notified Wandrei—who had paid Cook to print his first volume of poems, *Ecstasy*—that Cook had suffered some sort of nervous breakdown, causing a delay in the book.[83] Cook managed to recover from this and get out *Ecstasy* in April; but *The Shunned House*—which Cook was financing, without any contribution by Lovecraft—had to be put on the back burner. In late July Cook and his wife moved to a 100-acre farm east of Athol, but found that it had no heat and that they could not install heating before the winter, so they had to move out. Then, in January 1930, Cook's wife died and Cook suffered another and severer nervous breakdown. Moreover, he was having trouble with his appendix: he knew he should have an operation to remove it, but had such a phobia of the surgeon's knife that he delayed for months or even years on the procedure. Somehow he managed to limp along feebly; but then the depression completed his devastation, and emergence of *The Shunned House* became increasingly remote. By the summer of 1930 Lovecraft heard that the sheets had been sent to a binder in Boston,[84] but the book still did not come out. The matter hung fire all the way to Lovecraft's death.

Another book project involved editing rather than writing. In February 1927 John Ravenor Bullen, Lovecraft's Canadian amateur associate, died. In the fall of that year a friend of his in Chicago named Archibald Freer decided to finance the issuance of Bullen's collected poetry as a tribute to the man and a gift to his family. Bullen's mother selected Lovecraft to edit the volume—during his lifetime Bullen had already talked with Lovecraft about assisting him in preparing just such a volume[85]—and Lovecraft chose Cook as the publisher. Lovecraft found only forty of Bullen's poems fit for the book, and he no doubt revised them to some small degree; he also refurbished his article, "The Poetry of John Ravenor Bullen" (from the *United Amateur,* September 1925), as an introduction. The volume was entitled *White Fire.* Freer was very free with money, at one point sending an extra $500 so that Cook could do a more lavish job in printing and binding. The end result—which Lovecraft, although complaining bitterly about the tedium of revising and proofreading, claimed was the one book he knew that was absolutely without typographical errors—really is a very fine product. The regular edition sold for $2.00, and there was also a special leather-bound edition, which I have never seen and whose price I do not know. Although dated on the title page to 1927, the book came out only in January 1928.[86] Lovecraft sent out a good many complimentary and review copies, but I have not seen any reviews. Lovecraft reported one appearing in the *Honolulu Star-Bulletin* written by Clifford Gessler, a poet who was a friend of Frank Long.[87]

Meanwhile there was some other encouraging news. Late in 1927 Derleth told Lovecraft of a new magazine, *Tales of Magic and Mystery,* which began publication with an issue dated December 1927. This magazine (it is debatable whether it should be considered a pulp) was to feature both fact and fiction of a mystical or occult variety. Lovecraft sent the editor, Walter B. Gibson, eight stories; one by one they were rejected, but Gibson at last accepted "Cool Air." It appeared in the March 1928 issue. In various letters of the period Lovecraft states that he received $17.50, $18.00, and $18.50 for the story (about ½¢ per word). No doubt this did not encourage him to submit any more stories to the magazine, which in any case folded after its fifth (April 1928) issue. "Cool Air" is now regarded as the only notable contribution in the entire run.

Late in 1927 Lovecraft received *You'll Need a Night Light,* a British anthology edited by Christine Campbell Thomson and published by Selwyn & Blount. It contained "The Horror at Red Hook," marking the first time that a story of Lovecraft's appeared in hardcover. The volume was part of a series of "Not at Night" books edited by Thomson; the stories for most of the volumes were culled from *Weird Tales,* and several of Lovecraft's tales and revisions would later be reprinted. Although pleased at its appearance, Lovecraft had no illusions as to the anthology's merits. "As for that 'Not at Night'—that's a mere lowbrow hash of absolutely no taste or significance. Aesthetically speaking, it doesn't exist."[88]

Rather more significant—and indeed, one of the most important items in the critical recognition of Lovecraft prior to his death—was the appearance of "The Colour out of Space" on the "Roll of Honor" of the 1928 volume of Edward J. O'Brien's *Best Short Stories.* When Lovecraft first heard from O'Brien, he was not sure whether the story was actually going to be reprinted in the volume or merely receive the highest (three-star) ranking and be listed in the "Roll of Honor"; when he learned it would be the latter, he downplayed the matter: "the 'biographical roll of honour' is so long as to lack all essential distinction."[89] This is not at all the case, and Lovecraft had eminent reason to be proud of the distinction (as, in fact, he clearly was). In the 1924 volume "The Picture in the House" had received a one-star ranking, and in the 1928 volume of the *O. Henry Memorial Award Prize Stories* (edited by Blanche Colton Williams and published by Doubleday, Doran) "Pickman's Model" was placed in a category of "Stories Ranking Third"; but Lovecraft properly had less regard for the *O. Henry* series, as its selections tended to cater more to popular taste than to abstract literary merit, as O'Brien's did. Lovecraft would receive rankings in several subsequent O'Brien and *O. Henry* volumes, but this first appearance always remained unique.

Lovecraft sent O'Brien a somewhat lengthy autobiographical paragraph; he expected O'Brien merely to select from it, but instead the latter printed it intact, and it occupied eighteen lines of text, longer than any other biography in the volume. It is worth quoting in full:

> LOVECRAFT, HOWARD PHILLIPS. Was born of old Yankee-English stock on August 20, 1890, in Providence, Rhode Island. Has always lived there except for very brief periods. Educated in local schools and privately; ill-health precluding university. Interested early in colour and mystery of things. More youthful products—verse and essays—voluminous, valueless, mostly privately printed. Contributed astronomical articles to press 1906–18. Serious literary efforts now confined to tales of dream-life, strange shadow, and cosmic "outsideness", notwithstanding sceptical rationalism of outlook and keen regard for the sciences. Lives quietly and eventlessly, with classical and antiquarian tastes. Especially fond of atmosphere of colonial New England. Favourite authors—in most intimate personal sense—Poe, Arthur Machen, Lord Dunsany, Walter de la Mare, Algernon Blackwood. Occupation—literary hack work including revision and special editorial jobs. Has contributed macabre fiction to *Weird Tales* regularly since 1923. Conservative in general perspective and method so far as compatible with phantasy in art and mechanistic materialism in philosophy. Lives in Providence, Rhode Island.

Again we may take note of some of the things Lovecraft does *not* say, especially his marriage to Sonia. But on the whole this is an exceptionally accurate and compact account of Lovecraft's life and beliefs, and all that is required to flesh out the picture is masses of detail.

In the autumn of 1927 Frank Belknap Long took it into his head to write a longish short story entitled "The Space-Eaters." This story can be said to have two distinctive qualities: it is the first work to involve Lovecraft as a character (if we exclude whimsies like Edith Miniter's "Falco Ossifracus," in which the central character, while modelled on Randolph Carter, shares some characteristics with Lovecraft), and—although this point is somewhat debatable—it is the first "addition" to Lovecraft's mythos.

The characters in the story are actually named Frank and Howard (no last names are provided). Long told Lovecraft about the story, and the latter in mocksternness warned Long about how he should be portrayed: ". . . look here, young man, you'd better be mighty careful how you treat your aged and dignified Grandpa as here! You mustn't make me do anything cheerful or wholesome, and remember that only the direst of damnations can befit so inveterate a daemon of the cosmic abysses. And, young man, *don't forget that I am prodigiously lean.* I am *lean*—LEAN, I tell you! *Lean!*"[90] The crash diet of 1925 was probably still fresh in his memory. On this point, however, he need not have worried. Long writes in the story: "He was a tall, slim man with a slight stoop and abnormally broad shoulders. In profile his face was impressive. He had an extremely broad forehead, long nose, and slightly protuberant chin—a strong, sensitive face which suggested a wildly imaginative nature held in restraint by a skeptical and truly extraordinary intellect."[91] And yet, to be perfectly honest, "The Space-Eaters" is a preposterous and ridiculous story. This wild, histrionic account of some entities who are apparently "eating their way through space," are attacking people's brains, but are in some mysterious manner prevented from overwhelming the earth, is frankly an embarrassment. In this sense, however, it is sadly prophetic of most of the "contributions" other writers would make to Lovecraft's conceptions.

Whether it is indeed an addition to or extrapolation from Lovecraft's mythos is a debatable question. The entities in question are never named, and there are no references to any of Lovecraft's "gods" (only Cthulhu and Yog-Sothoth had even been invented at this time, the latter in the unpublished *Case of Charles Dexter Ward*). What there is, however, is an epigraph (omitted from the first appearance—*Weird Tales,* July 1928—and many subsequent reprintings) from "John Dee's Necronomicon"—i.e., from a purported English translation of Olaus Wormius's Latin translation of the *Necronomicon.* Lovecraft did make frequent citations of this Dee translation in later stories. This phenomenon will recur throughout Lovecraft's lifetime: a writer—usually a colleague—would either devise an elaboration upon some myth-element in Lovecraft's stories or would create an entirely new element, which Lovecraft would then co-opt in some subsequent story of his own. This whole procedure was largely meant in fun—as a way of investing this growing body of myth with a sense of actuality by its citation in different texts, and also as a sort of tip of the hat to each writer's creations. What the phenomenon became after Lovecraft's death is worth separate treatment.

Lovecraft, meanwhile, was doing relatively little fiction writing of his own—he had written nothing since "The Colour out of Space." What he did do, however, on Hallowe'en was to have a spectacular dream that might well have been incorporated into a story but never was—not, at least, by Lovecraft. He maintained that his reading of James Rhoades's translation of the *Aeneid* (1921) exactly around the Hallowe'en period engendered the dream—the most vivid he had had in years. Rhoades's *Aeneid* really is a fine rendition, in smoothly flowing pentameter blank verse. Consider the passage Lovecraft found most stimulating—"Anchises' prophecy of future Roman glory"[92] at the end of Book VI:

> "Others the breathing brass shall softlier mould,
> I doubt not, draw the lineaments of life
> From marble, at the bar plead better, trace
> With rod the courses of the sky, or tell
> The rise of stars: remember, Roman, thou,

> To rule the nations as their master: these
> Thine arts shall be, to engraft the law of peace,
> Forbear the conquered, and war down the proud."[93]

Lovecraft's dream is a spectacular one in which he adopted a different persona—that of Lucius Caelius Rufus, a provincial quaestor in Hispania Citerior—and spent days in and around the towns of Calagurris (Calabarra) and Pompelo (Pamplona), Spain. He had argued with Cnaeus Balbutius, legatus of the XIIth Legion, about the need to extirpate a group of strange dark folk (*miri nigri*) who dwelt in the hills near Pompelo. These folk, who spoke a language not understood either by Romans or by locals, usually kidnapped a small number of Celtiberian citizens for nameless rites on the Kalends of May and November; but this year there had been a scuffle in the market in which some of these folk had been killed, and what was worrying Rufus was that so far no townspeople had been taken: "It was *not natural* for the Strange Dark Folk to spare them like that. *Something worse* must be brewing."[94] Balbutius, however, did not think it wise to rouse up possible resentment by moving against the dark folk—they seemed to have many sympathisers and followers in the colony. But Rufus persisted, calling in the proconsul, Publius Scribonius Libo. Libo, convinced by Rufus of the need to suppress the dark folk, ordered Balbutius to send a cohort to Pompelo to put down the menace; he himself went along, as did Rufus, Balbutius, and other prominent officials. As they approached the hills, the continual drumming of the dark folk became increasingly disturbing. Night had fallen, and after a time the cohort could scarcely stumble up the hill; the leaders, who had been on horseback, had to leave their horses at the foot of the hill. Then, suddenly, came a bizarre sound—the horses began *screaming* (not merely neighing), and simultaneously the cohort's local guide killed himself by plunging a short sword into his body. The cohort stampeded, many men being killed in the process.

> From the slopes and peaks above us a crackling chorus of daemoniac laughter burst, and winds of ice swept down to engulf us all. My spirit could endure the strain no longer, and I awaked—bounding down the centuries to Providence and the present. But still there ring in my ears those last calm words of the old proconsul— "*Malitia vetus—malitia vetus est—venit—tandem venit...*"[95]

This must indeed have been an extraordinary dream—full of realistic details (the tedium of the march to Pompelo; a manuscript of Lucretius which Rufus was reading at the beginning, with an actual line of text quoted from Book V of *De Rerum Natura;* a dream within the dream when Rufus goes to sleep the night before the march) and with a spectacularly horrific, if somewhat ill-defined, climax. It is no wonder that Lovecraft subsequently wrote a long account of the dream to several colleagues—Frank Belknap Long, Donald Wandrei, Bernard Austin Dwyer, and perhaps others.

These accounts, however, present some problems and make us wonder how much was actually in the dream and how much is subtle, perhaps unconscious, elaboration by Lovecraft for literary effect. Aside from various minor inconsistencies—the local guide in the letter to Wandrei is named Vercellius; in the letters to Long and Dwyer, he is called Accius—the three existing accounts are surprisingly different in their scope and focus. The letter to Long was apparently written first, perhaps on the 1st or 2nd of November; the letter to Wandrei is dated only "Thursday" (i.e., November 3); the letter to Dwyer—by far the longest and most detailed—is apparently undated, but probably was written on the 4th or 5th. This last letter is the main difficulty, for it is here that several details occur not found in the other two letters. One may charitably think that Lovecraft, as he continued to ponder the dream in writing it out, remembered more and more of it; but one may also wonder whether he was half-consciously fashioning it into a weird tale full of realistic historical details and sly hints of terror that did not actually exist in the dream itself. Certainty on the matter is of course impossible, and no matter which version of the dream one accepts, it must have been a potent imaginative influence.

One would have liked to see Lovecraft himself write up the dream into an actual story, as Dwyer and Wandrei urged him to do; but, although he told both Dwyer and Long of some possible elaborations of the dream and of how it might be incorporated into a narrative, he never did anything with it. In 1929 Long asked Lovecraft to be allowed to use his letter verbatim in a short novel he was writing, and Lovecraft acceded. The result was *The Horror from the Hills,* published in two parts in *Weird Tales* (January and February 1931) and later as a book.

Later in the month of November Lovecraft had another peculiar dream, involving a street-car conductor whose head suddenly turns into "a mere white cone tapering to one blood-red tentacle."[96] The account of this dream appears in a letter to Wandrei of November 24, 1927. This letter is of interest because it has proved the source of a hoax whereby a work entitled "The Thing in the Moonlight" was spuriously attributed to Lovecraft. After Lovecraft's death Wandrei had passed along the texts of both the Roman dream and this shorter dream to J. Chapman Miske, editor of *Scienti-Snaps.* The Roman dream appeared in *Scienti-Snaps* (under the title "The Very Old Folk") in the Summer 1940 issue. When Miske renamed *Scienti-Snaps* as *Bizarre,* he printed the other dream-account, adding opening and closing paragraphs of his own and calling the whole farrago "The Thing in the Moonlight by H. P. Lovecraft." August Derleth, not aware that this item was not entirely Lovecraft's, reprinted it in *Marginalia* (1944). When Miske saw the volume, he wrote to Derleth informing him of the true nature of the text; but Derleth must have forgotten the matter, for he reprinted the piece again as a "fragment" in *Dagon and Other Macabre Tales* (1965). Only recently has this matter been clarified by David E. Schultz.[97]

Around this time Lovecraft also wrote a history of his mythical book, the *Ne-cronomicon,* although largely for the purpose of keeping references clear in his own mind. He noted in a letter to Clark Ashton Smith of November 27, 1927, that he had "drawn up some data on the celebrated & unmentionable *Necronomicon* of the mad Arab Abdul Alhazred";[98] this item bears the title "History of the Ne-cronomicon." The autograph manuscript is written on the back and front of a letter to Lovecraft by William L. Bryant, director of the museum at Roger Williams Park, dating to April 27, 1927, pertaining to Morton's visit in quest of mineral samples. On this draft the following sentence is added as an apparent afterthought: "An English translation made by Dr. Dee was never printed, & exists only in fragments recovered from the original MS." This leads one to believe that Love-craft wrote the bulk of the text prior to seeing Long's "The Space-Eaters." He noted that he had "just received" that story in a letter to Wandrei in late Septem-ber,[99] so perhaps "History of the Necronomicon" was written just before this time.

One datum in this text is of interest. Lovecraft noted that the Greek text was suppressed by the patriarch Michael in 1050. "After this it is only heard of furtively, but (1228) Olaus Wormius made a Latin translation later in the Middle Ages . . ." Those readers and critics who know anything about Olaus Wormius may wonder why Lovecraft dated him to the thirteenth century when he (1588–1654) is so clearly a Danish historian and philologist of the seventeenth century. So far as I can tell, this is a plain error; but Lovecraft came by the error in a peculiar way.

In 1914 Lovecraft wrote a poem entitled "Regner Lodbrog's Epicedium." He wrote to Moe late in the year:

> I recently tried the "Hiawatha" type of blank verse in translating a curious bit of primitive Teutonic martial poetry which Dr. Blair quotes in his "Critical Disserta-tion on the Poems of Ossian". This fragment is a funeral song composed in Runes by the old Danish monarch Regner Lodbrok (eighth century A.D.). In the Mid-dle Ages Olaus Wormius made the rather incoherent Latin version which Blair uses. It is in stanzas, each headed by the words "Pugnavimus ensibus". In translat-ing, I end each stanza with a rhyming couplet.[100]

This tells us all we need to know. Hugh Blair's *A Critical Dissertation on the Po-ems of Ossian, the Son of Fingal* (1763), the celebrated defence of the authenticity of the poems of "Ossian" (James Macpherson), is frequently included in editions of Macpherson. Lovecraft had such an edition, but it is not certain which one; in any event, he clearly consulted Blair's *Dissertation* somehow. His knowledge of Olaus Wormius seems not to extend beyond what Blair writes. In discussing "the ancient poetical remains . . . of the northern nations," Blair first mentions that "Saxo Grammaticus, a Danish historian of considerable note, who flourished in the thirteenth century," said that such songs were engraved in Runic characters; Blair then goes on to quote one such example as translated into Latin by Olaus Wormius. This twenty-nine-stanza item is Regner Lodbrog's epicedium; Lovecraft has translated only the first seven stanzas, and at that he has been aided by an English prose translation of the second through seventh stanzas that Blair supplies. In any event, my feeling is that Lovecraft either confused the *floruit* of Olaus Wormius (which Blair never gives) with that of Saxo Grammaticus, or else assumed that both scholars lived at the same time.[101]

Lovecraft's poetic output for 1927 was meagre. Most of his five poems relate to amateur matters. In February he wrote his usual birthday greeting to Jonathan E. Hoag, who had now achieved the age of ninety-six; but Hoag died on October 17, and Lovecraft wrote a no doubt heartfelt but lamentably wooden elegy, "Ave atque Vale" (*Tryout,* December 1927). Another elegy is "The Absent Leader," a poem written for *In Memoriam: Hazel Pratt Adams* (1927), a volume evidently prepared by the Blue Pencil Club in Brooklyn. Adams (1888–1927) was one of the founders of this club; I do not know the reason for her early death. This poem of Lovecraft's is a little more effective, at least in its evocations of some of the landscape around both Brooklyn and the New Jersey Palisades, based as they are on first-hand experience. Then there is a curious poem, "To Miss Beryl Hoyt, Upon Her First Birthday—February 21, 1927," a delightful and delicate two-stanza ditty on a person about whom I know nothing.

Probably the best poem of the year is "Hedone" (Greek for "pleasure"), written on January 3. This piece, in ten quatrains, contrasts the life of Catullus and Virgil in emphasising the superiority of mental tranquillity over sexual pleasure—rather like a versified version of his "Lovecraft on Love" letter to Sonia, but more effective. I have no idea why Lovecraft wrote this poem; but it displays a moderately successful use of the classical learning he had accumulated over a lifetime.

In late 1927 Lovecraft declared that he had never yet advertised for his revisory services[102] (he had evidently forgotten about the "Crafton Service Bureau" ad in *L'Alouette* in 1924), so that new revision clients would have come to him only by referral. Two such clients made their appearance about this time—Adolphe de Castro and Zealia Brown Reed Bishop.

De Castro (1859–1959), formerly Gustav Adolphe Danziger (he adopted his mother's name shortly after World War I because of anti-German prejudice), was an odd case. He met Ambrose Bierce in 1886 and become an enthusiastic devotee and colleague. A few years later he translated Richard Voss's short novel, *Der Mönch des Berchtesgaden* (1890–91), and had Bierce revise it; it was published serially (as by Bierce and Danziger—Voss having been forgotten) as *The Monk and the Hangman's Daughter* in the *San Francisco Examiner* in September 1891 and then as a book in 1892. With Bierce (and some help from Joaquin Miller and W. C. Morrow), Danziger formed the Western Authors Publishing Association, which issued Bierce's poetry collection *Black Beetles in Amber* (1892) and Danziger's own short story collection, *In the Confessional and the Following* (1893). Shortly thereafter, however, Bierce and Danziger had a falling out—mostly over financial wrangling over the profits from the *Monk* and over Danziger's management of the publishing company—and although Danziger occasionally met up with Bierce on random subsequent occasions, the two did no further work together.

Bierce went down to Mexico in late 1913, evidently to observe or to participate in the Mexican Civil War between Pancho Villa and Venustiano Carranza. Danziger (now de Castro) lived in Mexico between 1922 and 1925 editing a weekly newspaper. In 1923 he managed to talk with Villa, who maintained that he threw Bierce out of his camp when Bierce began praising Carranza. Later, it appears, his body and that of a peon were found by the side of a road. (This account of Bierce's death is almost certainly false.) De Castro wrote an article in the *American Parade* for October 1926 entitled "Ambrose Bierce as He Really Was," going on at length about his collaboration on the *Monk* and discussing his search for Bierce in Mexico. The matter was elaborated in an article by Bob Davis—the old *All-Story* editor—in the *New York Sun* for November 17, 1927.[103]

It was at this point that de Castro came in touch with Lovecraft. With the publicity he was now receiving, he felt the time was right to capitalise on his association with Bierce. He knew Samuel Loveman, and the latter recommended that de Castro write to Lovecraft and seek his help "in bringing out one or the other of my labors which sadly need revision."[104] This referred to two projects: a book-length memoir of Bierce, specifically discussing the collaboration on the *Monk* and de Castro's subsequent efforts to find information on Bierce in Mexico; and a revision of the story collection, *In the Confessional.*

Lovecraft, in a non-extant reply, appears to have quoted some rates regarding his work, the fees dependent on the nature of the work involved (ranging from mere reading and comment to light revision to wholesale rewriting). It is not clear that these rates are the same as those he was offering at a later period (a complete list is included in a letter to Richard F. Searight dated August 31, 1933). On de Castro's letter of December 5, 1927, accompanying one story he sent to Lovecraft, there are the following pen notations by Lovecraft:

> 0.50 per p. untyped
> 0.65 typed
> This story 16.00 untyped
>   20.00 typed
>
> (higher) Reconsidered rate
> 1.00 per page untyped
> 1.15 "   "   typed[105]

I do not know what the difference between the first quoted rate and the "Reconsidered" rate is. Whether the story in question is the one Lovecraft actually revised at this time—titled "A Sacrifice to Science" in de Castro's book, retitled "Clarendon's Last Test" by Lovecraft, and published as "The Last Test" in *Weird Tales* for November 1928—is not clear; Lovecraft indeed received $16.00 for this work[106] (de Castro received $175.00 from *Weird Tales*), but the story is not—at least in its initial printed version—32 pages, as Lovecraft's rate would suggest it to be. In any event, Lovecraft complained bitterly about the "measly cheque"[107] he received for this work, but perhaps it was his own fault: he may have quoted a fee of $16.00 to de Castro and then felt obliged to adhere to it even though the story ended up being a full 20,000 words long.

"The Last Test" is one of the poorest of Lovecraft's revisions. It tells the melodramatic story of a doctor, Alfred Clarendon, who is apparently developing an antitoxin for black fever while in charge of the California State Penitentiary at San Quentin but who in reality has fallen under the influence of an evil Atlantean magus, Surama, who has developed a disease that "isn't of this earth" to overwhelm mankind. All this is narrated in the most stiff and pompous manner conceivable, and the story is further crippled by the fact that it is entirely lacking in vibrant and distinctive characters (assuming, of course, that such a hackneyed plot could ever have such), since characterisation was far and away the weakest point in Lovecraft's literary arsenal. In particular, a romance element between Clarendon's sister Georgina and the governor of California, James Dalton, is handled very badly. (De Castro's handling of it, of course, is infinitely worse.)

It should be pointed out that de Castro's original tale is not at all supernatural. It is merely a long drawn-out melodrama or adventure story in which a scientist seeks a cure for a new type of fever (never described at all in detail) and, having run out of patients because of the bad reputation he has gained as a man who cares only for science and not for human life, seeks to convince his own sister to be a "sacrifice to science" in the furtherance of his quest. Lovecraft has turned the whole scenario into a supernatural tale while yet preserving the basic framework—the California setting, the characters (although the names of some have been changed), the search for a cure to a new type of fever, and (although this now becomes only a minor part of the climax) Clarendon's attempt to persuade his sister to sacrifice herself. But— aside from replacing the nebulously depicted assistant of Dr Clarendon ("Dr Clinton" in de Castro) named Mort with the much more redoubtable Surama—he has added much better motivation for the characters and the story as a whole. This, if anything, was Lovecraft's strong point. He has made the tale about half again as long as de Castro's original; and although he remarked of the latter that "I nearly exploded over the dragging monotony of [the] silly thing,"[108] Lovecraft's own version is not without monotony and prolixity of its own.

To liven things up, if only for himself, Lovecraft has thrown in quite irrelevant references to his own developing myth-cycle. Consider this confrontation between Clarendon and Surama:

> "Be careful, you ————! There are powers against your powers—I didn't go to China for nothing, and there are things in Alhazred's *Azif* which weren't known in Atlantis! We've both meddled in dangerous things, but you needn't think you know all my resources. How about the Nemesis of Flame? I talked in Yemen with an old man who had come back alive from the Crimson Desert—he had seen Irem, the City of Pillars, and had worshipped at the underground shrines of Nug and Yeb—Iä! Shub-Niggurath!"

This passage represents, curiously enough, the only time in a story (as opposed to the "History of the Necronomicon") that the Arabic title of the *Necronomicon* (*Al Azif*) is cited, the first time that the mysterious entities Nug and Yeb (later deemed twin offspring of Yog-Sothoth and Shub-Niggurath) are mentioned, and the first time the oath "Iä! Shub-Niggurath!" appears in a story. But these moments of fun cannot relieve the tedium of the tale.

De Castro was not satisfied with "Clarendon's Last Test" and sent it back to Lovecraft for extensive further revisions—based, according to Lovecraft, solely on the new ideas he himself had inserted. Losing patience, Lovecraft hurled the whole thing back to him along with the $16.00 cheque; but de Castro, chastened, accepted the version as it stood. He himself typed it, making very minor changes in diction,[109] and sent it to *Weird Tales,* where, as I have remarked, it was accepted. If it seems unjust that Lovecraft got less than one-tenth of what de Castro was paid, these were the conditions under which Lovecraft operated his revision service: he was at least assured of his fee whether the end result sold or not. (Occasionally, of course, he had difficulty collecting on this fee, but that is a separate matter.) In many cases the revised or ghostwritten tale did not in fact sell. Lovecraft would, in any case, never have wanted to acknowledge such a piece of drivel as "The Last Test," and it is in some ways unfortunate that his posthumous celebrity has resulted in the unearthing of such items and their republication under his name—the very thing he was trying to avoid.

Even before Lovecraft finished "The Last Test," de Castro was pleading with him to help him with his memoirs of Bierce. This was a much more difficult proposition, and Lovecraft was properly reluctant to undertake the task without advance payment. De Castro, being hard up for cash, could not assent to this; so Lovecraft turned him over to Frank Long, who was getting into the revision business himself. Long offered to do the revision for no advance pay if he could write a signed preface to the volume (Lovecraft at one point wrote that de Castro ought to affix Long's name as coauthor,[110] but Long apparently made no such stipulation). De Castro agreed to this, and Long did what appears to have been a very light revision—he finished the work in two days. This version, however (in spite of de Castro's earlier boast that "Bob Davis assures me that he will get me a publisher at once"[111]), was rejected by three publishers, so that de Castro came back to Lovecraft and pleaded with him to take over the project. Lovecraft again demanded that de Castro pay him $150.00 in advance,[112] and once again de Castro declined. He appears then to have gone back to Long.

The book did in fact come out—with how much more revision by Long, or anyone else, is unclear—as *Portrait of Ambrose Bierce,* published by the Century Company in the spring of 1929 and with a preface by "Belknap Long." Lovecraft claimed to take a sardonic satisfaction in the bad reviews the book received (Lewis Mumford wrote that "his portrait is beslobbered with irrelevant emotions and confessions, is full of pretentious judgments and in general has an authentic air of unreliability";[113] Napier Wilt wrote that "Such a naively uncritical picture can hardly be called a biography"[114]), but Carey McWilliams—author of a landmark biography of Bierce that came out later in 1929—was surprisingly charitable: "Dr. Danziger's book remains an interesting memoir . . . He succeeds best when he merely records remarks that Bierce made at various times. Some of these have about them the unmistakable imprint of Bierce's thought."[115] And yet, the book really is a confused farrago of mediocre biography, memoir, and not so subtle self-promotion on de Castro's part. Long's preface, a sensitive analysis of Bierce's work, may be the best thing in the volume.

Lovecraft had very mixed feelings about de Castro. He felt that both Bierce and de Castro had overstated their own role in the creation of *The Monk and the Hangman's Daughter,* the real virtues of the tale—its capturing of the wild topography of the Bavarian mountains—being in Lovecraft's impression clearly the work of Voss. De Castro does seem to have been trying to magnify his own contribution to the work and minimise that of Bierce, who was no longer around to defend himself. Moreover, de Castro comes off as both wheedling and sly, trying to get Lovecraft and Long to do work for him for little or no pay and for the mythical prospect of vast revenues at a later date (he thought he could rake in $50,000 for his Bierce reminiscence). At one point Lovecraft wrote: "This especial old bird, according to an anecdote recorded by George Sterling, parted from Bierce under the dramatic circumstance of having a cane broken over his head!" (The anecdote is found in Sterling's introduction to the Modern Library edition of Bierce's *In the Midst of Life* [1927].) Lovecraft then adds charitably: "When I saw his fiction I wondered why Ambrosius didn't use a crowbar."[116]

And yet, de Castro was not a complete charlatan. He had published a number of distinguished books of scholarship, especially in the realm of religious studies, with major publishers (e.g., *Jewish Forerunners of Christianity* [E. P. Dutton, 1903]), and also published (in some cases, admittedly, self-published) novels and poetry. The Western Authors Publishing Association issued a book of his as late as 1950.[117] De

Castro also seemed to know many languages and had served as a minor functionary in the U.S. government for many years. If there is a certain ghoulishness in his attempt to cash in on his friendship with Bierce, he was certainly not alone in this.

Another revision client that came into Lovecraft's horizon at this time was Zealia Brown Reed Bishop (1897–1968). Bishop, by her own statement,[118] was studying journalism at Columbia and also writing articles and stories to support herself and her young son. I take it that she was divorced at this point, although she never says so. One day while in Cleveland (she dates this to 1928, but this is clearly an error), she wandered into a bookstore managed by Samuel Loveman, who told her about Lovecraft's revisory service. She wrote to him in what must have been late spring of 1927, for this is when the first of Lovecraft's letters to her appears. Indeed, there may be an allusion to her in a letter of May 1927, when he speaks of "the most deodamnate piece of unending Bushwork I've ever tackled since the apogee of the immortal Davidius himself—the sappy, half-baked *Woman's Home Companion* stuff of a female whose pencil has hopelessly outdistanc'd her imagination."[119]

Bishop was in fact interested in writing *Woman's Home Companion* stuff, and—although she expresses great admiration for Lovecraft's intellect and literary skill—in her memoir she also admits rather petulantly that Lovecraft tried to steer her in directions contrary to her natural inclination: "Being young and romantic, I wanted to follow my own impulse for fresh, youthful stories. Lovecraft was not convinced that [t]his course was best. I was his protégé[e] and he meant to bend my career to his direction." There are some very odd statements in her memoir at this point—such as Lovecraft's supposed admonition to read Somerset Maugham's *Of Human Bondage* three times—but in the absence of the many letters he must have written her, we may perhaps accept as authentic some of the criticisms he levelled against the romantic fiction she sent him: "No gentleman would dare kiss a girl in that fashion"; "No gentleman would think of knocking on a lady's bedroom door even at a houseparty."

Bishop complains that "The stories I sent him always came back so revised from their basic idea that I felt I was a complete failure as a writer." It is difficult to know which stories are referred to here; they may not survive. Bishop goes on to say that at this point she returned to her sister's ranch in Oklahoma, where she heard some tales by Grandma Compton, her sister's mother-in-law, about a pioneer couple in Oklahoma not far away. Bishop concludes: "I wrote a tale called *The Curse of Yig,* in which snakes figured, wove it around some of my Aztec knowledge instilled in me by Lovecraft, and sent it off to him. He was delighted with this trend toward realism and horror, and fairly showered me with letters and instructions."

There is, clearly, a large amount of prevarication here. It can hardly be doubted that the story as we have it is almost entirely the work of Lovecraft except for the bare nucleus of the plot. "The Curse of Yig" is quite an effective piece of work, telling of a couple, Walker and Audrey Davis, who settle in the Oklahoma Territory in 1889. Walker has an exceptional fear of snakes, and has heard tales of Yig ("the snake-god of the central plains tribes—presumably the primal source of the more southerly Quetzalcoatl or Kukulcan . . . an odd, half-anthropomorphic devil of highly arbitrary and capricious nature") and of how the god avenges any harm that may come to snakes; so he is particularly horrified when his wife kills a brood of rattlers near their home. Late one night, the couple sees the entire floor of their bedroom covered with snakes; Walker gets up to stamp them out but falls down, extinguishing the lantern he is carrying. Audrey, now petrified with terror, soon hears a hideous popping noise—it must be Walker's body, so puffed with snake-venom that the skin has burst. Then she sees an anthropoid shape silhouetted in the window. It must be Yig—so when it enters the room she takes an axe and hacks it to pieces. In the morning the truth is known: the body that burst was their old dog, while the figure that has been hacked to pieces is Walker. In a final twist, it is learned that a loathsome half-snake, half-human entity kept in a nearby asylum is not Audrey herself but the entity to which she gave birth three-quarters of a year later.

Lovecraft wrote of his contribution to the story in a letter to Derleth:

> By the way—if you want to see a new story which is practically mine, read "The Curse of Yig" in the current W.T. Mrs. Reed is a client for whom Long & I have done oceans of work, & this story is about 75% mine. All I had to work on was a synopsis describing a couple of pioneers in a cabin with a nest of rattlesnakes beneath, the killing of the husband by snakes, the bursting of the corpse, & the madness of the wife, who was an eye-witness to the horror. There was no plot or motivation—no prologue or aftermath to the incident—so that one might say the story, as a story, is wholly my own. I invented the snake-god & the curse, the tragic wielding of the axe by the wife, the matter of the snake-victim's identity, & the asylum epilogue. Also, I worked up the geographic & other incidental colour—getting some data from the alleged authoress, who knows Oklahoma, but more from books.[120]

Lovecraft sent the completed tale to Bishop in early March 1928, making it clear in his letter to her that even the title is his. He adds: "I took a great deal of care with this tale, and was especially anxious to get the beginning smoothly adjusted. . . . For geographical atmosphere and colour I had of course to rely wholly on your answers to my questionnaire, plus such printed descriptions of Oklahoma as I could find." Of Yig he states: "The deity in question is entirely a product of my own imaginative theogony . . ."[121] Yig becomes a minor deity in the evolving Lovecraft pantheon, although cited only once in an original work of fiction ("The Whisperer in Darkness," and there only in passing) as opposed to revisions, where it appears with some frequency.

Lovecraft charged Bishop $17.50 for the tale; she already owed him $25.00 for unspecified earlier work, bringing the total to $42.50. It is not clear whether she ever entirely paid off this debt. She managed to sell the story to *Weird Tales,* where it appeared in the November 1929 issue; she received $45.00 for it.

Lovecraft's early correspondence with Zealia Bishop was very cordial and revelatory, and it seems to go well beyond the courtesy Lovecraft felt was due to a woman correspondent. He gives her quite sound advice on the nature of writing; it may not be the kind of advice she wanted—how to write salable fiction—but it was advice that anyone wishing to write sincere work should ponder. He summarises his long discussions in a letter of 1929:

> This, then, is the writer's fivefold problem:
> 1. To get the facts of life.
> 2. To think straight and tell the truth.
> 3. To cut out maudlin and extravagant emotion.
> 4. To cultivate an ear for strong, direct, harmonious, simple, and graphic language.
> 5. To write what one really sees and feels.[122]

At a later stage I shall examine how Lovecraft himself had come to embrace and, in large measure, to practise these principles.

But the correspondence with Bishop extends far beyond mere literary tutoring. He tells her much about his personal life, his philosophical beliefs, and the details of his daily existence. Perhaps Bishop was merely curious about these things—it is clear that she was writing to him frequently during 1927–29—but whatever the case, Lovecraft was unusually forthcoming about himself in these letters. However, Bishop's persistent failure to pay up her debt caused the association to cool considerably on Lovecraft's side, so that by the mid-1930s he was regarding her more as a pest than as a colleague.

One letter Lovecraft wrote to Bishop in late spring of 1928 is of interest:

> When you perceive the foregoing temporary address, and correlate it with what I have quite frequently expressed as my unvarnished sentiments toward the New York region, you will probably appreciate the extent of the combined burdens and nerve-taxes which have, through malign coincidence, utterly disrupted my programme this spring, and brought me to the verge of what would be a complete breakdown if I did not have a staunch and brilliant colleague—my young "adopted grandchild" Frank B. Long—to whom to lean for coöperation and assistance in getting my tasks in shape.[123]

What could be the meaning of this? The address at the head of this letter—395 East 16th Street, Brooklyn, New York—tells part of the story; the other part—which Lovecraft told almost none of his colleagues (those, at any rate, who did not already know the situation)—is that Sonia had called him back to New York.

Lovecraft's apartment
at 169 Clinton Street, Brooklyn

Lovecraft's home from 1926 to 1933
at 10 Barnes Street, Providence

Fleur-de-Lys Studios
at 7 Thomas Street, Providence
(featured in "The Call of Cthulhu")

August Derleth

The Thomas Lloyd Halsey house at 140 Prospect Street, Providence
(featured in The Case of Charles Dexter Ward)

Arthur Goodenough and Lovecraft
in West Guilford, Vermont

Robert E. Howard

19. FANLIGHTS AND GEORGIAN STEEPLES (1928–1930)

Lovecraft must have arrived in New York in late April, for a long letter to Lillian is dated April 29–30 and refers to incidents occurring on Tuesday the 24th. Sonia writes in her memoir: "Late that spring (1928) I invited Howard to come on a visit once more. He gladly accepted but as a visit, only. To me, even that crumb of his nearness was better than nothing."[1] Clearly Sonia still felt considerable affection for Lovecraft; but she knew that he could not be persuaded to spend more than a few weeks in a city he loathed, and in a situation—married life—with which he was clearly uncomfortable after two full years of resumed bachelorhood.

How "gladly" Lovecraft accepted this invitation we have already seen in the letter to Zealia Bishop; to other new correspondents (to most of whom he had not even mentioned the fact of his marriage) he was more circumspect. To Derleth he writes: ". . . I am on alien soil just now—circumstances having forced me to be in the N.Y. region for quite a spell. I don't welcome this sojourn, since I hate N.Y. like poison . . ."[2] To Wandrei: "Necessity has forced me to be in the N.Y. region for a month or so, & I am making the best of it by sojourning in the oasis of Flatbush . . ."[3] To his old friend Morton he was a little more expansive: "The wife had to camp out here for quite a spell on account of business, and thought it only fair that I drop around for a while. Not having any snappy comeback, and wishing to avoid any domestick civil war, I played the pacifist . . . and here I am."[4]

The "business" referred to is Sonia's attempt to set up a hat shop in Brooklyn—368 East 17th Street, in the very next block from where she was living. This structure does not survive, and there is no longer even any address with this number, unless a small garage neighbouring the present 370 East 17th Street is the place. The apartment house, however, still survives, and Lovecraft found Sonia's flat (on the third floor, numbered 9) relatively comfortable: "The dining or sitting room is panelled in squares of dark oak, whilst the woodwork elsewhere is white or oak of varying degrees of richness. Papers on the walls & rugs on the floors are uniformly in good taste. The dining-sitting room has a great central indirect-lighting fixture, whilst the library has a group of chain-hung lamps precisely like those in my room."[5] Sonia's cooking had not suffered any lapse either in quality or in abundance ("Spaghetti with S H's inimitable sauce, meat prepared in magical ways beyond the divining of the layman, waffles with maple syrup, popovers with honey—such are the challenges to leanness wherewith my pathway is beset!").

Sonia had invested $1000 of her own money to set up the shop, which formally opened on Saturday the 28th. She worked hard securing hatboxes and materials and fixing up the shop to appeal to customers. Lovecraft helped Sonia on "sundry errands" on several occasions, including one stint of addressing envelopes from 11.30 P.M. to 3.30 A.M. one night. On Sunday the 29th he and Sonia went on a "delightfully circuitous walk" that led back to their old neighbourhood—the Prospect Park area—and they noticed that it was already starting that decline in spruceness and social status which has continued to the present day.

But let us not be deceived; Lovecraft was by no means resuming his marriage any more than was necessary. Sonia writes with considerable tartness: "But while visiting me, all I saw of Howard was during the few early morning hours when he would return from his jaunts with either Morton, Loveman, Long, Kleiner, or with some or all of them. This lasted through the summer."[6] Indeed it did; and his gallivanting began almost as soon as he came to town. On April 24th he did some shopping with Sonia, but then went off on a lone walk to Prospect Park, then headed to Frank Long's new residence at 230 West 97th Street (823 West End Avenue having been torn down to make way for a new building, now numbered 825). He returned to Brooklyn only to have dinner with Sonia, then left immediately to visit Samuel Loveman, first at his bookshop in 59th Street, Manhattan, then to his residence in Columbia Heights. He did not return home till 4 A.M.

April 27th was Long's birthday, so his parents took him on a drive along the Hudson River to Lake Mahopac; Lovecraft accompanied them and found the wild, hilly scenery stimulating. Later trips with the Longs in May reached as far north as Peekskill and as far east as Stamford and Ridgefield in Connecticut. On one occasion they visited West Point and witnessed an impressive dress-parade.

Lovecraft also did much solo exploration in the area. He mentioned going to some region called Gravesend, "south of Flatbush on the road to Coney-Island";[7] this appears to be a district now designated by the community of Bensonhurst. Lovecraft found "near on a dozen cottages in plain sight [that] date from before 1700." Other expeditions took him to Flatlands and New Utrecht (to the east and west of Bensonhurst, respectively).

Naturally, there were also gang meetings—although Lovecraft noted with some surprise and even dismay that the gang had "almost dissolved."[8] Plainly, he had been its guiding force during 1924–26. After one of them (on May 2), George Kirk invited Lovecraft and Everett McNeil to accompany him back to his apartment, where his new wife Lucile—half expecting such a continuation of the meeting—had tea, crackers, and cheese ready. Lovecraft again did not return home till 4 A.M.

On May 12 Lovecraft visited James F. Morton in Paterson, finding the scenery along the bus ride very poor—"oil tanks & factories . . . ugly & depressing factory towns & monotonous flatlands."[9] New Jersey's reputation for scenic dismalness, based upon the New Jersey Turnpike, was already in evidence! But Morton's museum building was very prepossessing, the entire upstairs floor being given over to his hall of minerals. Although Lovecraft got home late that evening, he still got up early enough the next day to go with Sonia to Bryn Mawr Park, the area in Yonkers where they had purchased a home lot in 1924. Sonia still owned this property—or, rather, one of the two lots, the other one having been sold. Sonia could not decide whether to build a small house on the property or to sell it.

On Thursday, May 24, Lovecraft rose at the unheard-of hour of 4 A.M. in order to meet Talman in Hoboken to catch a 6.15 train to Spring Valley, in Rockland County just above the New Jersey border. Talman lived in an estate outside the city, built in 1905 by his father. Lovecraft found both the rural countryside and the ancient farmhouses (built between 1690 and 1800) very charming, and took care to note the differences in their architectural details from corresponding structures in New England. He was, both through reading and through personal examination, becoming a formidable expert in colonial American architecture. That afternoon Talman and Lovecraft went to the town of Tappan, where Major John André—the young British officer who conspired with Benedict Arnold to effect the surrender of West Point—was tried and hanged in 1780.

Talman drove Lovecraft to Nyack, on the western shore of the Hudson, where Lovecraft caught a ferry for Tarrytown, on the eastern shore. Here, naturally, he took a bus to Sleepy Hollow, whose 1685 church and the wooded ravine nearby he appreciated. He walked back to Tarrytown and made his way to the Washington Irving estate, but it was in private hands and not open to visitors. A ferry at Hastings-on-Hudson took him back to New York.

On the 25th Lovecraft got up early again—6.30—in order to get to Long's house by 8.30. The Long family went on a long motor drive through some of the area Lovecraft had just explored the previous day. It was an all-day expedition, and Lovecraft did not reach home until midnight. On the 29th Lovecraft met his new revision client Zealia Bishop, for whom Long was also doing some work. Subsequent days were taken up with solitary exploration closer to home—Astoria and Elmhurst (in Queens), Flushing (then still a separate community), and elsewhere. With Sonia he went to several towns in Staten Island on June 3, and he did the same with Long on June 6. The very next day, however, he unexpectedly received an invitation from Vrest Orton that changed his travel plans significantly. He had been planning to visit Bernard Austin Dwyer in West Shokan, then head south for perhaps a week to Philadelphia or Washington, D.C.; but Orton—although living in the pleasant Riverdale section of the Bronx—was disgusted with New York and wished to move out to a farm near Brattleboro, Vermont, which he had just purchased. He insisted that Lovecraft come along, and it took little persuasion for him to accede.

Lovecraft's New York stay was not entirely occupied with frivolity. Aside from his daily wrestling with mountainous correspondence, there was revision work—or, at least, the prospect of it. Long and Lovecraft had decided to team up, and they prepared the following ad that appeared in the August 1928 issue of *Weird Tales:*

FRANK BELKNAP LONG, Jr.	H. P. LOVECRAFT
Critical and advisory service for writers of prose and verse; literary revision in all degrees of extensiveness. Address: Frank B. Long, Jr., 230 West 97th St., New York, New York City.[10]	

Toward the end of the year, however, Lovecraft reported lugubriously that "Belknap & I didn't net many returns from our revision advt."[11] In fact, I cannot see that a single new client emerged from the ad, which presumably sought to bring in more would-be weird writers like Zealia Bishop.

Adolphe de Castro was being an annoyance, asking Lovecraft and Long to see him at his apartment uptown and also pestering Lovecraft both at Sonia's apartment and even at the hat shop. He was full of big plans both for his Bierce memoirs and for his other works; but Lovecraft resolutely stood by his demand of receiving $150.00 in advance for work on the Bierce book, although he charitably prepared a "critical synopsis"[12] that Long, who did the actual revision on the book, may or may not have followed. At one point de Castro became so irritating that Lovecraft fumed: "I hope he goes down to Mexico & gets shot or imprisoned!"[13]

One odd piece of writing that Lovecraft did around this time is a preface to a book of travel impressions, *Old World Footprints,* by Frank Long's wealthy aunt. The book was published later in 1928 by W. Paul Cook (surely at Mrs Symmes's expense), but the preface—signed "Frank Belknap Long, Jr., June, 1928"—is the work of Lovecraft, who noted that Long was under the pressure of other work and could not write it in time for Cook's deadline.[14]

Old World Footprints may well be the last book publication to emerge from the Recluse Press. Although Lovecraft read proofs of *The Shunned House* toward the end of his New York stay, we have already seen how that project became mired in delays at this very time. Lovecraft and Cook also worked on a second printing of Bullen's *White Fire,* since an unexpected sale of the volume in Canada had exhausted the supply; but although unbound sheets were produced, this item was also never bound or distributed.

What are we to make of the six weeks Lovecraft spent in New York? His accounts make it clear that he fell back into the old habit of congregating with friends—and avoiding his wife—that he had adopted almost immediately after his marriage. For all his loathing of the city, he seemed to have a good enough time, but he jumped at the chance to return to New England shores. There is no indication of how long Lovecraft had promised Sonia he would stay with her; his letters to Lillian suggest that the hat shop was getting off the ground pretty well (at one point Sonia hired a part-time assistant to help with orders), but Sonia says little about the matter in her memoir and I do not know how long it stayed in business. Her irritation at Lovecraft's failure to spend any significant time with her comes out in her memoir, and in all likelihood was expressed to him in person; but it probably made little impression, since he had virtually taken the attitude that he was really no more than a guest, as he was in 1922 (he did, however, offer to pay his share of the food bills). If Sonia somehow expected this trip to jump-start the marriage, she was in for a disappointment; it is no wonder that she forced Lovecraft to pursue divorce proceedings the next year.

Lovecraft's faint taste of Vermont in 1927 had only whetted his appetite; now he would spend a full two weeks in quaint rusticity, and he made the most of it. Orton was, of course, not coming alone, but brought his whole family—wife, infant son, parents, and maternal grandmother, Mrs Teachout, an eighty-year-old woman whose recollections of the past Lovecraft found fascinating. The entire party arrived around June 10, and Lovecraft stayed till the 24th.

It is charming to read of the simple chores Lovecraft performed ("I have learned how to build a wood fire, & have helped the neighbours' boys round up a straying cow"[15])—no doubt he could momentarily indulge in the fantasy of being a grizzled farmer. Orton's farm, indeed, had few modern amenities—no plumbing except for a lead pipe to lead in the spring water, and no illumination except with oil lamps and candles.

Most of the time, however, Lovecraft struck out on lone trips of exploration. On the 13th he climbed Governor's Mountain (1823 feet above sea level), but was disappointed to find that the summit was wooded, thereby failing to provide any vista of the surrounding area. The next day he called on his old amateur friend Arthur Goodenough and then went across the Connecticut River into New Hampshire to climb Mt. Wantastiquet. On the 18th he went to Deerfield and Greenfield in Massachusetts by bus.

On the 16th Walter J. Coates came down from Montpelier, driving nearly a hundred miles just to see Lovecraft. They discussed literature and philosophy till 3 A.M., after which Orton and Lovecraft went to a neighbouring hill to build a fire and watch the sun rise. A more significant meeting occurred on the next day, when Lovecraft, Orton, and Coates went to Goodenough's home in Brattleboro for a literary conclave with several other local writers. Lovecraft reported that this gathering was written up in the *Brattleboro Reformer,* and indeed it was, as Donovan K. Loucks has discovered.[16]

Another item has, however, also appeared in the same paper: an article on Lovecraft by Vrest Orton entitled "A Weird Writer Is In Our Midst," published on June 16. Lovecraft modestly describes it as a "puff," and it certainly is that; but

in other ways it is a remarkably astute and even prophetic document. Although Orton himself had little actual interest in the weird (he said that after reading some of
Lovecraft's tales he was "struck with such unmitigated horror that I shall undoubtedly never read any more"), he told of Lovecraft's popularity with *Weird Tales*
("The readers of this magazine . . . are kept in a state of unsatisfied hunger for his
stuff"), explained his philosophy of the weird (shamelessly pillaging "Supernatural
Horror in Literature" for the purpose), and concluded by comparing him with Poe:

> . . . like Poe, he will, I haven't the slightest doubt, set a mark for writers to shoot at
> for a long time. Some say he is greater than Poe as a writer of the weird . . . I don't
> know, but I do know that his stories strike me as having been written by a man far
> more profoundly interested in the subject of the weird than was Poe. . . . I do not
> say he is a greater writer than Poe, for in some departments he is not. But I do say
> that as a scholar and research worker in the one subject of the weird from his point
> of view, and a writer on that subject exclusively, H. P. Lovecraft is the greatest
> this country has ever seen or maybe will ever see.[17]

This article appeared in a column called "The Pendrifter," conducted by Charles
Crane. Lovecraft met Crane on the 21st, finding him a delightful and typical Vermont Yankee.

Other locals Lovecraft met were the Lee boys, Charley, Bill, and Henry, the
neighbours whom he helped round up a stray cow. On the afternoon of the 21st
Charley took Lovecraft to meet an eccentric farmer named Bert G. Akley, a self-
taught painter and photographer of much native skill. Lovecraft was captivated:

> His paintings—covering every field, but specialising in the local scenery, are of a
> remarkable degree of excellence; yet he has never taken a lesson in his life. He is
> Talman's equal or superior in heraldic painting, & is likewise a landscape & still-
> life photographer of the highest skill & taste. In other fields, too, he is a veritable
> jack-of-all-trades. Through it all he retains the primitiveness of the agrestic yeo-
> man, & lives in unbelievable heaps & piles of disorder.[18]

Vermont was a tremendous imaginative stimulus for Lovecraft. He felt himself
close to the old New England spirit that had departed from the more populated and
modernised southern states, and in this way he effected that *defeat of time* which was
simultaneously the source of his antiquarianism and his sense of the weird:

> Here life has gone on in the same way since before the Revolution—the same
> landscape, buildings, families, occupations, & modes of thought & speech. The
> eternal cycle of sowing & reaping, feeding & milking, planting & haying, here
> constitute the very backbone of existence; & old traditions of New England sim-
> plicity govern all things from dairying to fox-hunting. That Arcadian world which
> we see faintly reflected in the Farmer's Almanack is here a vital & vivid actual-
> ity—in all truth, the people of Vermont are our contemporary ancestors! Hills &

brooks & ancient elms—farmhouse gables peeping over bends of the road at the crest of hills—white steeples in distant valleys at twilight—all these lovely reliques of the old days flourish in undiminished strength, & bid fair to transmit themselves for many generations into the future. To dwell amidst this concentrated old-fashionedness for two weeks, seeing about one every day the low-ceiled, antique-furnished rooms of a venerable farmhouse, & the limitless green reaches of planted fields, steep, stone-walled meadows, & mystical hanging woods & brook-murmurous valleys, is to acquire such a hold on the very fundamentals of authentic Novanglianism that no account of urban existence can counteract or dilute it.[19]

On the 23rd W. Paul Cook, who had already paid two visits to the Orton farm during Lovecraft's stay there, arrived with his wife and spent the night; the next day he drove Lovecraft down to Athol for a stay of about a week. Lovecraft did nothing of great note there except for buying a new suit for $17.50, meeting with H. Warner Munn, writing letters in Phillips Park whenever it wasn't raining, and seeing *The Shunned House* being printed at the *Athol Transcript* office. Perhaps the only notable event of his Athol trip occurred on the 28th, when Munn took Lovecraft to a remarkable forest gorge southwest of the city called the Bear's Den.

But on Friday, June 29, Lovecraft moved on to another leg of his journey as distinctive as his Vermont stay; for Edith Miniter, the old-time amateur, almost demanded that Lovecraft pay her a visit in Wilbraham, Massachusetts, where she was residing with her cousin, Evanore Beebe. Accordingly, Lovecraft rose at 6.30 to catch an 8 o'clock train to North Wilbraham. He stayed for eight days, being charmed by the vast array of antiques collected by Beebe, the seven cats and two dogs who had the run of the place, and especially by the spectral local folklore Miniter told him. In "Mrs. Miniter—Estimates and Recollections" (1934) Lovecraft wrote:

> I saw the ruinous, deserted old Randolph Beebe house where the whippoor-wills cluster abnormally, and learned that these birds are feared by the rustics as evil psychopomps. It is whispered that they linger and flutter around houses where death is approaching, hoping to catch the soul of the departed as it leaves. If the soul eludes them, they disperse in quiet disappointment; but sometimes they set up a chorused clamour of excited, triumphant chattering which makes the watchers turn pale and mutter—with that air of hushed, awestruck portentousness which only a backwoods Yankee can assume—"They got 'im!"

There was also a spectacular firefly display one night: "They leaped in the meadows, & under the spectral old oaks at the bend of the road. They danced tumultuously in the swampy hollow, & held witches' sabbaths beneath the gnarled, ancient trees of the orchard."[20] This trip certainly combined the archaic, the rustic, and the weird!

Finally, on July 7, Lovecraft prepared for his southern jaunt. He first took a bus to Springfield (the largest town near Wilbraham), then on up to Greenfield, where he stayed in a hotel overnight before taking the bus to Albany (over the Mohawk Trail) the next day. Lovecraft found Albany dismally Victorian, but it was meant only as a way station. The next day he took a boat down the Hudson, stopping in New York to change valises (he had borrowed Sonia's $35 suitcase for his Vermont-Massachusetts trip, but now reclaimed his own 99¢ papier-mâché bag). Strangely enough, he remarked that because Sonia was "without commodious living quarters at present," he spent the night at the Bossart Hotel in Montague Street, Brooklyn.[21] I wonder why, in the month between his departure for Vermont and his return to New York, Sonia's quarters had suddenly become unavailable to him. In any case, on the 10th he met Long and Wandrei and had dinner with Sonia at the Milan restaurant, then saw a movie with her before boarding the 1.30 A.M. train for Philadephia.

Lovecraft spent only the afternoon in Philadelphia, which he had of course seen several times before; he then took the bus to Baltimore, reaching there around sunset. Although the bulk of the town was unmistakably Victorian, he found some compensating features: the Catholic cathedral (1808), a column erected in 1815, and various country seats dating from as early as 1754. There was, however, one more landmark: "But to me the culminating thing in Baltimore was a dingy monument in a corner of Westminster Presbyterian Churchyard, which the slums have long overtaken. It is near a high wall, and a willow weeps over it. Melancholy broods around it, and black wings brush it in the night—for it is the grave of Edgar Allan Poe." Things have not changed much since. It is a pity that Lovecraft does not seem to have entered the church itself, for in the cellar are some of the most charnelly hideous catacombs in the nation.

Lovecraft was going to go directly from Baltimore to Washington, but the colonial relics of Annapolis proved a fatal temptation; and they were no disappointment. He spent only one day (July 12) there, but saw much of the place—the naval academy, the old state house (1772–74), St John's College, and the abundance of colonial residences, which "make Annapolis the Marblehead of the south."[22]

That evening Lovecraft left for Washington, spending the next three days there. He revisited Alexandria (which he had seen briefly in 1925), saw Mt. Vernon (George Washington's home) and archaic Georgetown, and took a trip to Falls Church, a small town in Virginia. He tried to look up Edward Lloyd Sechrist, but found that he was away on business in Wyoming.

At this point yet another temptation proved fatally alluring—an excursion to the Endless Caverns in New Market, Virginia. This was a good four hours by bus from Washington, but the rate was so cheap ($2.50) that Lovecraft could ill resist. Having written about caves from boyhood, he found that the chance actually to visit one was not to be denied. As with his entire trip, this was no disappointment:

> As deep gave place to deep, gallery to gallery, and chamber to chamber, I felt transported to the strangest regions of nocturnal fancy. Grotesque formations

leer'd on every hand, and the ever-sinking level appris'd me of the stupendous depth I was attaining. Glimpses of far black vistas beyond the radius of the lights—sheer drops of incalculable depth to unknown chasms, or arcades beckoning laterally to mysteries yet untasted by human eye—brought my soul close to the frightful and obscure frontiers of the material world, and conjured up suspicions of vague and unhallowed dimensions whose formless beings lurk ever close to the visible world of man's five senses. Buried aeras—submerged civilisations—subterraneous universes and unsuspected orders of beings and influences that haunt the sightless depths—all these flitted thro' an imagination confronted by the actual presence of soundless and eternal night.[23]

The rest of the trip was anticlimax. A bus ride to Philadelphia, then another to New York. Lovecraft was hoping for a leisurely journey home, but in New York he found a letter from Annie Gamwell reporting that Lillian had fallen ill with lumbago, so he immediately boarded a train for home. He had been away almost exactly three months.

Shortly after returning to Providence Lovecraft wrote a lengthy account of his spring travels, "Observations on Several Parts of America." It is the first of several lengthy travelogues—some of the others are "Travels in the Provinces of America" (1929), "An Account of *Charleston*" (1930), and "A Description of the Town of Quebeck" (1930–31), the single longest work Lovecraft ever wrote—and it is among the best. Its flawless capturing of eighteenth-century diction ("a compleat record of my late wanderings must embrace near three months of time, and a territory of extream bigness") is matched by the deftness with which it weaves travel impressions, history, and personal asides into a smoothly flowing narrative.

Certain practical souls have shed bitter tears at Lovecraft's "wasting" his time writing these lengthy accounts, which were manifestly produced with no idea of publication and—in the cases of the latter two documents mentioned above—with not even the prospect of meeting any other eye than their author's. Here is one of many occasions in which later commentators have tried to live Lovecraft's life for him. The only "purpose" of these items is to afford pleasure to Lovecraft and to some of his friends, and that is enough. The "Observations" and the "Travels" are single-spaced typescripts, and in effect are open letters, the first written to Maurice W. Moe ("Dost recall it, O Sage?" Lovecraft interjects at one point) although surely circulated to other close associates. No doubt he drew upon his diaries for the periods in question, and perhaps also upon his letters to Lillian, for the details of his travels; and the historical digressions must have been derived from guidebooks and formal histories of the regions as well as personal investigation.

One small part of the "Observations" did in fact achieve print in Lovecraft's lifetime. Maurice W. Moe was assisting Sterling Leonard and Harold Y. Moffett in editing a series of literature textbooks for young adults, and was so captivated by

Lovecraft's description of visiting Sleepy Hollow that he included it as an one-paragraph extract, titled "Sleepy Hollow To-day," in *Junior Literature: Book Two,* published by Macmillan in 1930. The text was printed fairly faithfully, although eliminating Lovecraft's archaisms. Only one substantive change was made: Lovecraft spoke of the river gorge "forming a place of convocation for the numerous ghouls attendant upon the subterraneous population," but Moe substituted "ghosts" for "ghouls," rendering the passage a trifle obscure. Lovecraft professed delight at the inclusion of his piece: "Wright may reject my stuff, but at least, my name will achieve a mild & grudging kind of immortality on the reluctant lips of the young."[24] Well, not exactly: although the book was reprinted in 1935, it thereafter lapsed out of print and has become one of the rarest of Lovecraft's publications.

Lovecraft did manage to do some writing aside from letters and his travelogue; in early August he wrote "The Dunwich Horror." This is, certainly, one of his most popular tales, but I cannot help finding serious flaws of conception, execution, and style in it. Its plot is well known. In the seedy area of Dunwich in "north central Massachusetts" live a small handful of backwoods farmers. One of these, the Whateleys, have been the source of particular suspicion ever since the birth, on Candlemas 1913, of Wilbur Whateley, the offspring of his albino mother and an unknown father. Lavinia's father, Old Whateley, shortly after the birth makes an ominous prediction: *"some day yew folks'll hear a child o' Lavinny's a-callin' its father's name on the top o' Sentinel Hill!"*

Wilbur grows up anomalously fast, and by age thirteen is already nearly seven feet tall. He is intellectually precocious also, having been educated by the old books in Old Whateley's shabby library. In 1924 Old Whateley dies, but manages to wheeze instructions to his grandson to consult "page 751 *of the complete edition*" of some book so that he can "open up the gates to Yog-Sothoth." Two years later Lavinia disappears and is never seen again. In the winter of 1927 Whateley makes his first trip out of Dunwich, to consult the Latin edition of the *Necronomicon* at the Miskatonic University Library; but when he asks to borrow the volume over-night, he is denied by the old librarian Henry Armitage. He tries to do the same at Harvard but is similarly rebuffed. Then, in the late spring of 1928, Wilbur breaks into the library to steal the volume, but is killed by the vicious guard-dog. His death is very repulsive:

> . . . it is permissible to say that, aside from the external appearance of face and hands, the really human element in Wilbur Whateley must have been very small. When the medical examiner came, there was only a sticky whitish mass on the painted boards, and the monstrous odour had nearly disappeared. Apparently Whateley had no skull or bony skeleton; at least, in any true or stable sense. He had taken somewhat after his unknown father.

Meanwhile bizarre things are happening elsewhere. Some monstrous entity whom the Whateleys had evidently been raising in their home now bursts forth, having no one to feed or tend to it. It creates havoc throughout the town, crushing houses as if they were matchsticks. Worst of all, it is completely invisible, leaving only huge footprints to indicate its presence. It descends into a ravine called the Bear's Den, then later comes up again and causes hideous devastation. Armitage has in the meantime been decoding the diary in cipher that Wilbur had kept, and finally learns what the true state of affairs is:

> His wilder wanderings were very startling indeed, including . . . fantastic references to some plan for the extirpation of the entire human race and all animal and vegetable life from the earth by some terrible elder race of beings from another dimension. He would shout that the world was in danger, since the Elder Things wished to strip it and drag it away from the solar system and cosmos of matter into some other plane or phase of entity from which it had once fallen, vigintillions of years ago.

But he knows how to stop it, and he and two colleagues go to the top of a small hill facing Sentinel Hill, where the monster appears to be heading. They are armed with an incantation to send the creature back to the other dimension it came from, as well as a sprayer containing a powder that will make it visible for an instant. Sure enough, both the incantation and the powder work, and the entity is seen to be a huge, ropy, tentacled monstrosity that shouts, "HELP! HELP! . . . *ff—ff—ff—* FATHER! FATHER! YOG-SOTHOTH!" and is completely obliterated. It was Wilbur Whateley's twin brother.

It should be evident even from this narration that many points of plotting and characterisation in the story are painfully inept. Let us first contrast the *moral* implications of "The Dunwich Horror" with those of "The Colour out of Space." We have seen that it is nearly impossible to deem the entities in the earlier story "evil" by any conventional standard; but the Whateleys—especially Wilbur and his twin—are clearly meant to be perceived as evil because of their plans to destroy the human race. And yet, was it not Lovecraft himself who, five years earlier, had whimsically written the following to Edwin Baird of *Weird Tales?*

> Popular authors do not and apparently cannot appreciate the fact that true art is obtainable only by rejecting normality and conventionality in toto, and approaching a theme purged utterly of any usual or preconceived point of view. Wild and "different" as they may consider their quasi-weird products, it remains a fact that the bizarrerie is on the surface alone; and that basically they reiterate the same old conventional values and motives and perspectives. Good and evil, teleological illusion, sugary sentiment, anthropocentric psychology—the usual superficial stock in trade, all shot through with the eternal and inescapable commonplace. . . . Who

ever wrote a story from the point of view that man is a blemish on the cosmos, who ought to be eradicated?[25]

This criticism applies perfectly to "The Dunwich Horror." What we have here is an elementary "good vs. evil" struggle between Armitage and the Whateleys. The only way around this conclusion is to assume that "The Dunwich Horror" is a parody of some sort; this is, indeed, exactly what Donald R. Burleson has done in an interesting essay,[26] pointing out that it is the Whateley twins (regarded as a single entity) who, in mythic terms, fulfil the traditional role of the "hero" much more than Armitage does (e.g., the mythic hero's descent to the underworld is paralleled by the twin's descent into the Bear's Den), and pointing out also that the passage from the *Necronomicon* cited in the tale—"Man rules now where They [the Old Ones] ruled once; They shall soon rule where man rules now"—makes Armitage's "defeat" of the Whateleys a mere temporary staving off of the inevitable. These points are well taken, but there is no evidence in Lovecraft's letters that "The Dunwich Horror" was meant parodically (i.e., as a satire on immature readers of the pulp magazines) or that the figure of Armitage is meant anything but seriously. Indeed, Lovecraft clearly suggests the reverse when he says in a letter to Derleth that "[I] found myself psychologically identifying with one of the characters (an aged scholar who finally combats the menace) toward the end."[27]

Armitage is, indeed, clearly modelled upon Willett of *The Case of Charles Dexter Ward:* he defeats the "villains" by incantations, and he is susceptible to the same flaws—pomposity, arrogance, self-importance—that can be seen in Willett. Armitage is, indeed, the prize buffoon in all Lovecraft, and some of his statements—such as the melodramatic *"But what, in God's name, can we do?"*—make painful reading, as does the silly lecture he delivers to the Dunwich folk at the end: "We have no business calling in such things from outside, and only very wicked people and very wicked cults ever try to."

There are problems of plot, also. What, exactly, is the *purpose* of the "powder" Armitage uses to make the creature visible for an instant? What is to be gained by this procedure? It seems to be used simply to allow Lovecraft to write luridly about ropy tentacles and the like. The spectacle of three small human figures—Armitage and his stalwart cohorts—waving their arms about and shouting incantations on the top of a hill is so comical that it seems incredible that Lovecraft could have missed the humour in it; but he seems to have done so, for this is presumably the climactic scene in the story.

What "The Dunwich Horror" did was, in effect, to make possible the rest of the "Cthulhu Mythos" (i.e., the contributions by other and less skilful hands). Its luridness, melodrama, and naive moral dichotomy were picked up by later writers (it was, not surprisingly, one of Derleth's favourite tales) rather than the subtler work embodied in "The Call of Cthulhu," "The Colour out of Space," and others.

In a sense, then, Lovecraft bears some responsibility for bringing the "Cthulhu Mythos" and some of its unfortunate results upon his own head.

In an important sense, indeed, "The Dunwich Horror" itself turns out to be not much more than a pastiche. The central premise—the sexual union of a "god" or monster with a human woman—is taken directly from Machen's "The Great God Pan"; Lovecraft makes no secret of the borrowing, having Armitage say of the Dunwich people at one point, "Great God, what simpletons! Shew them Arthur Machen's Great God Pan and they'll think it a common Dunwich scandal!" The use of bizarre footsteps to indicate the presence of an otherwise undetectable entity is borrowed from Blackwood's "The Wendigo." Lovecraft was clearly aware of the number of tales featuring invisible monsters—Maupassant's "The Horla" (certain features of which, as we have seen, had already been adapted for "The Call of Cthulhu"); Fitz-James O'Brien's "What Was it?"; Bierce's "The Damned Thing"— and derived hints from each of them in his own creation. The fact that Lovecraft on occasion borrowed from previous sources need not be a source of criticism, for he ordinarily made exhaustive alterations in what he borrowed; but in this case the borrowings go beyond mere surface details of imagery to the very core of the plot.

"The Dunwich Horror" is, of course, not a complete failure. Its portrayal of the decaying backwoods Massachusetts terrain is vivid and memorable, even if a little more hyperbolic than that of "The Colour out of Space"; and it is, as should now be evident, largely the result of personal experience. Lovecraft later admitted that Dunwich was located in the Wilbraham area, and it is clear that both the topography and some of the folklore (whippoorwills as psychopomps of the dead) are in large part derived from his two weeks with Edith Miniter. But, if Wilbraham is roughly the setting for Dunwich, why does Lovecraft in the very first sentence of the story declare that the town is located in "*north* central Massachusetts"? Some parts of the locale are indeed taken from that region, specifically the Bear's Den, which Lovecraft describes vividly in a letter to Lillian:

> There is a deep forest gorge there; approached dramatically from a rising path ending in a cleft boulder, & containing a magnificent terraced waterfall over the sheer bed-rock. Above the tumbling stream rise high rock precipices crusted with strange lichens & honeycombed with alluring caves. Of the latter several extend far into the hillside, though too narrowly to admit a human being beyond a few yards.[28]

The site is very much the same today. And just as H. Warner Munn took Lovecraft there in 1928, so about fifty years later he helped to lead Donald R. Burleson to the place.[29] The name Sentinel Hill is taken from a Sentinel Elm Farm in Athol.[30] Lovecraft has, in other words, *mingled* topographical impressions from various sites and coalesced them into a single imagined locale.

For those interested in following the surface details of the "Cthulhu Mythos," "The Dunwich Horror" offers much fodder for argument. That it builds in part upon "The Call of Cthulhu" and other tales is clear from the mentions of Cthulhu, Kadath, and other terms in the lengthy quotation from the *Necronomicon* in the story; but the term "Old Ones" is ambiguous, and it does not appear to refer to the "Great Old Ones" of "The Call of Cthulhu," nor is it clear whether Yog-Sothoth—who never recurs as a major figure in any subsequent Lovecraft tale—is one of the Old Ones or not. Probably Lovecraft did not expect his casually coined terms to be sifted and analysed by later critics as if they were biblical texts, and he threw them off largely for the sake of resonance and atmosphere. As will become manifestly evident, Lovecraft not only did not plan out all (or any) of the details of his pseudomythology in advance, but also had no compunction whatever in altering its details when it suited him, never being bound by previous usage—something that later critics have also found infuriating, as if it were some violation of the sanctity or unity of a mythos that never had any sanctity or unity to begin with. It should also be pointed out that this is the only story that contains a lengthy extract from the *Necronomicon;* later writers have not been so reticent, but their bungling quotations—written with a lamentable lack of subtlety and (in Derleth's case especially) a pitiable ignorance of archaic diction—have resulted in the watering down of the potentially powerful conception of a book of "forbidden" knowledge.

Lovecraft's most interesting comment in this regard is his casual remark, just after finishing the story, that it "belongs to the Arkham cycle."[31] He does not explain this expression here, nor does he ever use it again. It at least suggests that Lovecraft was by now aware that some of his tales (he doesn't say which) form some sort of pattern or sequence. The term is clearly topographical in connotation, as if Lovecraft believed that all the tales of his fictitious New England geography (including such things as "The Picture in the House," which no later critic includes within the scope of the "Cthulhu Mythos") are linked; or perhaps it refers to the fact that Arkham is the defining point for the other mythical towns. One simply does not know.

A brief note as to the name Dunwich may be in order. It has been pointed out that there is a real town in England with this name—or, rather, that there *was* such a town on the southeast coast of the island, a town that suffered inexorable desertion as the sea washed away more and more of the coastal terrain on which it stood. It was the subject of Swinburne's memorable poem "By the North Sea" (although it is never mentioned by name there), and is cited in Arthur Machen's *The Terror* (1917). The curious thing, however, is that the English Dunwich is more similar to Lovecraft's decaying seaport of Innsmouth than it is to the inland town of Dunwich; nevertheless, it is likely enough that the name alone was indeed derived from this English counterpart. There are, of course, any number of towns in New England with the *-wich* ending (e.g., Greenwich, one of the Massachusetts towns evacuated to make way for the Quabbin Reservoir).

It is not at all surprising either that "The Dunwich Horror" was snapped up by *Weird Tales* (Lovecraft received $240.00 for it, the largest single cheque for original fiction he had ever received) or that, when it appeared in the April 1929 issue, its praises were sung by the readership. A. V. Pershing, boasting that he has read "some 'real' authors" like Shakespeare and Poe, wrote: "I say that Lovecraft has an uncanny, nearly superhuman power of transporting one bodily to scenes of his unparalleled 'horrors' and forcing upon his the exquisite pleasure of 'living the story . . .'" Lovecraft's friend Bernard Austin Dwyer, praising Clark Ashton Smith and Wandrei in passing, stated: "I can not find words sufficiently to declare my admiration of his virginity [*sic*] of conception—the weird, the outré, unhackneyed, fully satisfying depth of colorful imagery and fantasy—as strange, as terrible, and as alien to the land of our everyday experiences as a fever-dream." These two letters appeared in the June 1929 issue; in the August issue E. L. Mengshoel anticipated the queries of many by remarking: "I would like to ask [Lovecraft] if there has not really existed an old work of writing named the *Necronomicon,* which is mentioned in 'The Dunwich Horror.'" These and other comments are a sad verification of the low esteem in which Lovecraft held what he would later call the "'Eyrie'-bombarding proletariat."[32]

The rest of 1928 was quiescent. Lovecraft wrote a poem toward the end of the year; it survives under two titles. The autograph manuscript gives the title as "To a Sophisticated Young Gentleman, Presented by His Grandfather with a Volume of Contemporary Literature"; in a letter to Maurice Moe we find the title "An Epistle to Francis, Ld. Belknap, With a Volume of Proust, Presented to Him by His Aged Grandsire, Lewis Theobald, Jun." In other words, Lovecraft was giving Frank Long a copy of *Swann's Way,* the first volume of *Remembrance of Things Past.* In the process he reveals considerable familiarity with contemporary phenomena, both popular ("Devoid of Pomp as *Woolworth's* or *McCrory's,* / And cerebral as *Vogue* and *Snappy-Stories*") and elevated ("Cubist and Futurist combine to shew / Sublimer Heights in *Kreymborg* and *Cocteau*"); and yet, these references are encased in a delectable pastiche—or parody—of the eighteenth-century idiom. It is a delightful piece of work.

One other piece of fiction appears to have been written around this time, "Ibid." In a letter of 1931 Lovecraft dated this piece to 1927,[33] but several comments by Maurice W. Moe seem to date it to 1928. The first we hear of it is in a letter by Moe dated August 3, 1928, when he mentions "that delightful Spectator paper on the marvellous history of old man Ibid."[34] It is, I suppose, still possible the piece was written considerably before this mention, so a date of 1927 is conceivable.

"Ibid" was either included in a letter to Moe or was a separate enclosure in a letter to him; whether its epigraph ("'. . . As Ibid says in his famous *Lives of the*

Poets.'—From a student theme") refers to some actual statement found in a paper by one of Moe's students, I do not know; I think it quite likely. In any event, Lovecraft uses this real or fabricated piece of fatuity as the springboard for an exquisite tongue-in-cheek "biography" of the celebrated Ibidus, whose masterpiece was not the *Lives of the Poets* but in fact the famous "*Op. Cit.* wherein all the significant undercurrents of Graeco-Roman expression were crystallised once for all."

But the real target of the satire in "Ibid"—the third of Lovecraft's comic tales, along with "A Reminiscence of Dr. Samuel Johnson" and "Sweet Ermengarde"— is not so much the follies of grammar-school students as the pomposity of academic scholarship. In this sense "Ibid" is more timely today than when it was first written. Full of learned but preposterous footnotes, the piece traces the life of Ibid to his death in 587, then the fortunes of his skull—which proved, among other things, to be the vessel with which Pope Leo administered the royal unction to Charlemagne—from antiquity to the twentieth century. Its deadpan tone is flawless:

> It was captured by the private soldier Read-'em-and-Weep Hopkins, who not long after traded it to Rest-in-Jehovah Stubbs for a quid of new Virginia weed. Stubbs, upon sending forth his son Zerubbabel to seek his fortune in New England in 1661 (for he thought ill of the Restoration atmosphere for a pious young yeoman), gave him St. Ibid's—or rather Brother Ibid's, for he abhorred all that was Popish—skull as a talisman. Upon landing in Salem Zerubbabel set it up in his cupboard beside the chimney, he having built a modest house near the town pump. However, he had not been wholly unaffected by the Restoration influence; and having become addicted to gaming, lost the skull to one Epenetus Dexter, a visiting freeman of Providence.

Moe was considering submitting the sketch to the *American Mercury* or some such journal, and apparently asked Lovecraft to revise it slightly; but nothing seems to have been done, and in late January Moe (who had typed the piece and sent it to Lovecraft) agreed that revision for a commercial magazine was not possible, and that the work "would have to be content with private circulation."[35] That publication did not occur until 1938, when it appeared in the amateur journal, the *O-Wash-Ta-Nong,* edited by Lovecraft's old friend George W. Macauley.

Toward the end of the year Lovecraft heard from an anthologist, T. Everett Harré, who wished to reprint "The Call of Cthulhu" for a volume entitled *Beware After Dark!* Lovecraft felt obligated to bring the matter up with Farnsworth Wright, since "Cthulhu" was evidently being considered as a centrepiece to his proposed collection of tales. We have seen that Lovecraft had recommended "The Colour out of Space" over "Cthulhu" as the main novelette to be used; but Wright presumably chose the latter, perhaps because it had actually been published in *Weird Tales* whereas "Colour" had not been. In any event, Wright allowed the release of the story; perhaps, as Lovecraft was coming to suspect, he had already come to think it very unlikely that the Popular Fiction Publishing Company would ever issue a volume of Lovecraft's stories.

Harré bought the story for $15.00[36]—apparently not a bad deal for second rights. Wandrei lent considerable assistance to Harré in the selection of contents, and Lovecraft expressed disappointment that Harré did not see fit to acknowledge this help. The volume appeared from the Macaulay Co. in the fall of 1929; it is a notable volume. Lovecraft is in very good company—with Ellen Glasgow, Hawthorne, Machen, Stevenson, and Lafcadio Hearn—and "The Call of Cthulhu" is one of only five stories from *Weird Tales* to be included. Harré remarks in his introduction: "H. P. Lovecraft, one of the newer fantasy writers, has done some of the best things in such fiction; only limited editions of his tales have been published. His 'Call of Cthulhu,' in its cumulative awesomeness and building of effect to its appalling finale, is reminiscent of Poe."[37] Lovecraft later met Harré in New York.

Another anthology appearance—"The Horror at Red Hook" in Herbert Asbury's *Not at Night!* (Macy-Masius, 1928)—was less happy. This matter is somewhat confused, but it appears that Asbury—a noted journalist and editor, author of the celebrated *Gangs of New York* (1928)—had pirated the contents of several of the Christine Campbell Thomson "Not at Night" anthologies published by Selwyn & Blount and illegally published an American edition. "The Horror at Red Hook" had already appeared in Thomson's *You'll Need a Night Light* (1927). In an early 1929 letter to Wright, Lovecraft gave grudging permission to lend his name in a list of plaintiffs in a lawsuit, "so long as there is positively no obligation for expense on my part in case of defeat. My financial stress is such that I am absolutely unable to incur any possible outgo or assessment beyond the barest necessities . . ."[38] Lovecraft certainly did not lose any money on the matter, but he did not gain any either; he later mentioned that Macy-Masius withdrew the book rather than pay any royalties or damages to *Weird Tales.*[39]

In the fall of 1928 Lovecraft heard from an elderly poet named Elizabeth Toldridge (1861–1940), who five years earlier had been involved in some poetry contest of which Lovecraft was a judge. I do not know what this contest was, but presumably it was either part or an outgrowth of his amateur critical work. Toldridge was a disabled person who lived a drab life in various hotels in Washington, D.C. She had published—no doubt at her own expense—two slim volumes earlier in the century, *The Soul of Love* (1910), a book of prose-poems, and *Mother's Love Songs* (1911), a poetry collection. Lovecraft wrote to her cordially and promptly, since he felt it gentlemanly to do so; and because Toldridge herself wrote with unfailing regularity, the correspondence flourished to the end of Lovecraft's life. Toldridge was, indeed, one of the few later correspondents of Lovecraft not involved in weird fiction.

The correspondence naturally focused on the nature of poetry and its the philosophical underpinnings. Toldridge was clearly a Victorian holdover both in her poetry and in her outlook on life; and Lovecraft, while treating her views with nothing but studied respect, made it clear that he did not share them at all. It was just at this time that he was beginning a revaluation of poetic style; and the barrage of old-fashioned poetry Toldridge sent to him helped to refine his views. In response to one such poem he wrote:

> It would be an excellent thing if you could gradually work out of the idea that this kind of stilted & artificial language is "poetical" in any way; for truly, it is *not*. It is a drag & hindrance on real poetic feeling & expression, because *real* poetry means spontaneous expression in the simplest & most poignantly vital *living* language. The great object of the poet is to get rid of the cumbrous & the emptily quaint, & buckle down to *the plain, the direct, & the vital*—the pure, precious stuff of actual life & human daily speech.[40]

Lovecraft knew he was not yet ready to practice what he preached; but the mere fact that he had written very little poetry since about 1922 meant both that prose fiction had become his chief aesthetic outlet and that he had come to be profoundly disappointed in his earlier poetic work. It was in an early 1929 letter to Toldridge that he heaped abuse upon himself for being "a chronic & inveterate mimic"; although he even extended this condemnation to his prose work: "There are my 'Poe' pieces & my 'Dunsany' pieces—but alas—where are any *Lovecraft* pieces?"[41]

But if Lovecraft could not yet exemplify his new poetic theories, he could at least help to inculcate them in others. Maurice Moe was preparing a volume entitled *Doorways to Poetry,* which Lovecraft in late 1928 announced as provisionally accepted (on the basis of an outline) by Macmillan.[42] As the book developed, he came to have more and more regard for it; by the fall of 1929 he was calling it

> without exception the best & clearest exposition of the inner essence of poetry that I've ever seen—& virtually the *only* work which comes anywhere near the miracle of making novices able to distinguish good verse from cheap & specious hokum. The method is absolutely original with Moe, & involves the insertion of many columns of parallel specimens of verse of varying badness & excellence, together with a key containing critical & elucidative comment. The answers in the key will be largely my work, since Moe thinks I can express subtle differences between degrees of merit better than he can. I am also preparing specimen bits of verse for illustrative use in the body of the text—unusual metres, stanzaic forms, Italian & Shakespearian sonnets, & so on.[43]

This gives us some idea of the nature of Lovecraft's work on the book, for which he refused to accept any payment.[44] It is, as a result, unfortunate that the manuscript of the volume does not seem to survive; for, as with so many projects by Lovecraft and his friends, *Doorways to Poetry* was never published—neither by Macmillan, nor by The American Book Company, to which Moe had then marketed it, nor even with the Kenyon Press of Wauwatosa, Wisconsin, a small pedagogical firm that did issue a very slim pamphlet by Moe, *Imagery Aids* (1931), which may be the final pathetic remnant of *Doorways*. The specimens of verse to which Lovecraft alluded do survive in an immense letter to Moe of late summer 1927 on which he must have worked for days, and in which he collects all manner of peculiar metres and rhyme-schemes from the standard poets.[45]

Another bit survives as a typescript (probably prepared by Moe) entitled "Sonnet Study." This contains two sonnets, written by Lovecraft, one in the Italian form, the other in the Shakespearean form, with brief commentary by Moe. Neither of the poems amounts to much, but at least they begin to exemplify Lovecraft's new views on the use of living language in poetry.

In late summer 1927 Wilfred B. Talman, in gratitude for Lovecraft's assistance on his fiction, offered to design a bookplate for a nominal fee. Lovecraft was enraptured by the idea: he had never had a bookplate, and I know of none possessed by any member of his family; up to this point he had merely signed his name in his books. Some of the volumes in his library also bear a cryptic code or numbering sequence—perhaps a shelf arrangement scheme of some kind. Talman was an accomplished draughtsman and, as we have seen, an ardent genealogist. He made two suggestions for a design: a vista of colonial Providence or Lovecraft's coat-of-arms. In a long series of letters back and forth the two men debated these choices, but finally Lovecraft opted for the former. What was actually produced, around the summer of 1929, was certainly worth waiting for: a sketch of a Providence doorway with fanlight, and the simple words "EX LIBRIS / HOWARD PHILLIPS LOVECRAFT" in the lower left-hand corner. Lovecraft waxed rhapsodic when he saw the proofs: "Mynheer, I am knock'd out . . . I grow absolutely maudlin & lyrical . . . the thing is *splendid,* beyond even those high expectations which I form'd from a survey of your pencil design! You have caught perfectly the spirit that I wished to see reproduced, & I can't find anything to criticise in any detail of the workmanship."[46] Lovecraft initially ordered only 500 to be printed, since that was the number of books he felt were in decent enough condition to merit a bookplate. He justifiably showed the thing off wherever he went.

At the very beginning of 1929 Sam Loveman came to Providence, and the two went to Boston, Salem, and Marblehead for a few days before Loveman took the boat back to New York. But before Lovecraft could undertake the southern tour he was planning for the spring, he had one small matter to take care of—his divorce from Sonia.

Around the end of 1928 Sonia must have begun pressing for a divorce. Interestingly enough, Lovecraft was opposed to the move: ". . . during this period of time he tried every method he could devise to persuade me how much he appreciated me and that divorce would cause him great unhappiness; and that a gentleman does not divorce his wife unless he has a cause, and that he has no cause for doing so."[47] It is not, certainly, that Lovecraft was contemplating any return to cohabitation, either in New York or in Providence; it is simply that the *fact* of divorce disturbed him, upsetting his notions of what a gentleman ought to do. He was perfectly willing to carry on a marriage by correspondence, and actually put forth the case of someone he knew who was ill and lived apart from his wife, only writing letters. Sonia did not welcome such a plan: "My reply was that neither of us was really sick and that I did not wish to be a long-distance wife 'enjoying' the company of a long-distance husband by letter-writing only."

What subsequently happened is still not entirely clear. According to Arthur S. Koki, who consulted various documents in Providence, on January 24 a subpoena was issued by the Providence Superior Court for Sonia to appear on March 1. On February 6 Lovecraft, Annie Gamwell, and C. M. Eddy went to the office of a lawyer, Ralph M. Greenlaw, at 76 Westminster Street (the Turk's Head Building), and presented the following testimony:

1Q: Your full name?

A: Howard Phillips Lovecraft.

2Q: You have resided in Providence for more than two years prior to the 24th day of January, 1929?

A: Since April 17, 1926.

3Q: And you are now a domiciled inhabitant of the City of Providence, State of Rhode Island?

A: Yes.

4Q: And you were married to Sonia H. Lovecraft?

A: Yes.

5Q: When?

A: March 3, 1924.

6Q: Have you a certified copy of your marriage certificate?

A: I have.

(Same received in evidence and marked by the Magistrate Petitioner as Exhibit A.)

7Q: Now have you demeaned yourself as a faithful husband since your marriage?

A: Yes.

8Q: And performed all the obligations of the marriage covenant?

A: Yes.

9Q: Now, has the respondent, Sonia H. Lovecraft, deserted you?

A: Since the 31st of December, 1924.

10Q: You gave her no cause for deserting you?

A: None whatever.

11Q: There were no children born of this marriage?

A: No.

Koki adds: "The testimony of Mrs. Gamwell and Mr. Eddy corroborated Lovecraft's assertion that his wife had deserted him, and that he was not to blame."[48]

All this was, of course, a charade; but it was necessary because of the reactionary divorce laws prevailing in the State of New York, where until 1933 the only grounds for divorce were adultery or if one of the parties was sentenced to life imprisonment. The only other option in New York was to have a marriage annulled if it had been entered into "by reason of force, duress, or fraud" (the last term being interpreted at a judge's discretion) or if one party was declared legally insane for five years.[49] Obviously these options did not exist for Lovecraft and Sonia; and so the fiction that she "deserted" him was soberly perpetrated, surely with the knowledge of all parties in question. Lovecraft acknowledged the legal difficulties in a letter to Moe later that year:

> . . . in most enlightened states like Rhode Island the divorce laws are such as to allow rational readjustments when no other solution is wholly adequate. If other kinds of states—such as New York or South Carolina, with their mediaeval lack of liberal statutes—were equally intelligent in their solicitude for the half-moribund institution of monogamy, they would hasten to follow suit in legislation . . .[50]

The overriding question, however, is this: Was the divorce ever finalised? The answer is clearly no. The final decree was never signed. Sonia may or may not have come to Providence on March 1, in accordance with the subpoena; if she did not, it would only emphasise her "desertion." The decree was probably signed at a later date, and Sonia must have signed it, as she was the one pressing for the divorce. But how could she have allowed Lovecraft not to sign it himself? In any case, this seems to be the state of affairs. One can only believe that Lovecraft's refusal to sign was deliberate—he simply could not bear the thought of divorcing Sonia, not because he really wanted to be married to her, but because a "gentleman does not divorce his wife without cause." This purely abstract consideration, based upon social values Lovecraft was already increasingly coming to reject, is highly puzzling. But the matter had at least one unfortunate sequel. It is certain that Sonia's subsequent marriage to Dr Nathaniel Davis of Los Angeles was legally bigamous—a fact that disturbed her considerably when she was told of it late in life. It was a fittingly botched ending to the whole affair.

Lovecraft's spring travels commenced on April 4. On that day he reached New York early in the morning, spent most of the day with Frank Long and his parents, then met his host, Vrest Orton, who drove him up to a home in Yonkers which he was occupying with his wife, child, and grandmother. (I am not sure whether or why the farm in Vermont was abandoned.) The place, built around 1830 and set in an idyllic rural area, charmed Lovecraft: "Flagstone walks, old white gate, low ceilings, small-paned windows, wide-boarded floors, white-mantled fireplaces, cobwebbed attic, rag carpets & hooked rugs, old furniture, centuried Connecticut clock with wooden works, pictures & decorations of the 'God-bless-our-home' type—in short, everything that bespeaks an ancient New England hearthside."[51] One need hardly remark the fact that Lovecraft is staying with Orton rather than Sonia; now that they were (at least in their own minds) divorced, it would hardly have been suitable for him to stay with her. Indeed, I cannot find any evidence that he even saw her during his three weeks in New York, although he may well have done so and not informed anyone (even—or especially—his aunt Lillian, to whom he was writing frequently) of the fact.

Lovecraft spent his time visiting the gang, going to various literary gatherings arranged by Orton, and generally enjoying his freedom from responsibility and work. On April 11 Lovecraft and Long looked up old Everett McNeil, now finally out of Hell's Kitchen and dwelling in a comfortable flat in Astoria. McNeil was working on a new novel, about Cortez, but he would never finish it. Not long afterward he had to go to the hospital, and Lovecraft and Long visited him there several times. On the 24th Lovecraft visited Morton in Paterson. On the 25th was a large gang meeting at the Longs', with Loveman, Wandrei, Talman, Morton, and others showing up. The next day the Longs took Lovecraft on a motor trip north of the city and over into Connecticut.

As before, Lovecraft played the outdoorsman by helping Orton about the farm: "We cleared the grounds of leaves, changed the course of a brook, built 2 stone foot bridges, pruned the numerous peach trees, (whose blossoms are exquisite) & trained the climbing rose vines on a new home-made trellis."[52]

Random business propositions of a nebulous sort emerged, but none of them amounted to anything. Talman spent the wee hours following the gang meeting discussing the possibility of Lovecraft's working for a newspaper. Orton declared that he could get Lovecraft a job with a Manhattan publisher at any time, as he appears to have done for Wandrei, who was working in the advertising department of E. P. Dutton; but Lovecraft made a typical response: "a job *in New York* is a very dubious substitute for a peaceful berth at the poorhouse in Cranston, or the Dexter Asylum!"[53] T. Everett Harré had given Lovecraft a letter of introduction to Arthur McKeogh, editor of the *Red Book,* and Lovecraft went to see him toward the end of the month; but he rightly concluded that "I don't think McKeogh of the

Red Book can use any of my stuff, for the tone of his magazine is very different from mine."[54] Lovecraft was right: although *Red Book* (founded in 1903 and later to become metamorphosed into the women's magazine we know) was at this time largely a fiction magazine, the material it published was of the usual cheap adventure or romance sort with very little emphasis on the weird and much emphasis on conventionality of outlook.

On May 1 Lovecraft's travels began in earnest. He went right down to Washington, stayed overnight at a cheap hotel (he got a room for $1.00), then caught the 6.45 A.M. bus the next morning to Richmond, Virginia. He stayed in Virginia for only four days but took in an astonishing number of sites—Richmond, Williamsburg, Jamestown, Yorktown, Fredericksburg, and Falmouth. All were delightful. Richmond, although it had no one colonial section, nevertheless revealed substantial traces of antiquity to the diligent searcher; of course, it had suffered terrible damage during the Civil War, but was rapidly rebuilt shortly thereafter, and Lovecraft—sympathetic as he always was to the Confederate cause—found the frequent monuments to the Confederate heroes heartwarming. But it was the colonial remains that most pleased him: the State Capitol (1785–92), the John Marshall house, and especially the many old churches throughout the city.

He did not forego seeing the Valentine Museum, which contained the then recently discovered letters by Poe to his guardian, John Allan, used by Hervey Allen in his biography (really a sort of biographical novel) *Israfel* (1926). He also saw the farmhouse—built either in 1685 or 1737, and probably the oldest surviving structure in Richmond—that formed the Poe Shrine (now the Edgar Allan Poe Museum), which had also opened only recently. Aside from actual furniture owned by Poe, this place had a delightful model of the entire city of Richmond as it was around 1820; this made it much easier for Lovecraft to orient himself and to locate the surviving antiquities. "I never set eyes on the place till yesterday—yet today I know it like an old resident."[55] He saw the churchyard of St. John's Church, where Poe's mother is buried. Inside he noted the pew where, in 1775, Patrick Henry "uttered those cheaply melodramatic words which have become such a favourite saw of schoolboys—'Give me liberty or give me death!'"; but "as a loyal subject of the King I refused to enter it."[56]

On May 3 Lovecraft saw Williamsburg (then only in the early stages of its restoration as a colonial village), Jamestown, and Yorktown all in a single day. Jamestown in particular—"birthplace of the British civilisation in America"—he found particularly moving, even though only the foundations of the original settlement (dating to 1607) remain, as the town was abandoned after 1700. Yorktown, in spite of its dubious fame as the place where Lord Cornwallis surrendered in 1781, struck Lovecraft as "a kind of southern Marblehead."[57]

Fredericksburg, fifty miles north of Richmond, was explored on the 5th. Again, Lovecraft was more interested in the colonial than in the Civil War town, but he saw both aspects in the five hours he had. Early in his explorations Lovecraft encountered a "kindly, talkative, well-bred & scholarly old man"[58] named Mr Alexander who observed that he was a tourist and guided him through many of the antiquities of the place. This seems rather uncannily like the situation in "He," but Lovecraft does not seem to have perceived the resemblance; in any case, Mr Alexander no doubt wished to exhibit some of that hospitality and courtesy on which the South prided itself. Lovecraft did not fail to take in Kenmore, the mansion occupied by George Washington's sister, as well as Falmouth, the quaint town across the Rappahannock from Fredericksburg.

On May 6 Lovecraft was back in Washington. This time his amateur friend Edward Lloyd Sechrist was in town, and Lovecraft had a cordial meeting with him. He also looked up his new correspondent Elizabeth Toldridge, whom he found less boring and tiresome than he had expected. But it was the museums that most interested him. He saw interesting exhibits at the Library of Congress, went through the Corcoran and Freer Galleries, and—best of all—canvassed the Smithsonian several times, seeing the spectacular stone idols from Easter Island ("last mute and terrible survivors of an unknown elder age when the towers of weird Lemurian cities clawed at the sky where now only the trackless waters roll"[59]) that had haunted his imagination for decades. These are the only actual specimens in the country, the American Museum of Natural History in New York having only a reproduction.

Lovecraft went to Philadelphia on May 8, seeing the usual sites but this time also taking in the new art museum situated at the end of Benjamin Franklin Parkway. Lovecraft concluded that this structure

> is absolutely the most magnificent museum building in the world—the most exquisite, impressive, and imagination-stirring piece of contemporary architecture I have ever lay'd eyes on—the most gorgeously perfected and crystallised dream of beauty which the modern world hath to give. It is a vast Grecian temple group atop a high elevation (a former reservoir) which terminates the Parkway vista toward the Schuylkill; reacht by broad, spacious flights of steps, flankt by waterfalls, and with a gigantick fountain playing in the centre of the great tessellated courtyard. A veritable Acropolis . . .[60]

Lovecraft had seen it before but had never approached or entered it; and the interior proved no disappointment, either, with its fine array of period rooms and paintings by such eighteenth-century British artists as Gainsborough and Gilbert Stuart.

Returning to New York on the 9th, Lovecraft found that the Longs were planning a fishing trip upstate, so that they could conveniently take him right to the doorstep of Bernard Austin Dwyer, who, although residing chiefly in the town of

West Shokan, was at this time occupying a house at 177 Green Street in nearby Kingston. (This house no longer survives.) They left the next morning, reaching Kingston in the early afternoon; Dwyer was not available until 6 P.M., so Lovecraft explored the town briefly in the interim. When he finally met Dwyer, he found him as congenial as he expected: "He is an absolutely delightful chap—6 ft 3 in tall, heavily built, & with an extremely handsome, open, & winning face which frequently breaks out into an infectious smile. A pleasant, deep voice, & a refreshingly pure diction & apt choice of words—& a phenomenally sensitive imagination. A true artist if ever there was one."[61] For the next several evenings they sat up discussing literature and philosophy till far into the night. On the 14th Lovecraft visited the neighbouring towns of Hurley and New Paltz, both of them full of Dutch colonial remains. Hurley is nothing more than an array of houses along a central road; perhaps its most notable structure is the Van Deusen house (1723), which was then open as an antique shop and which Lovecraft explored thoroughly. New Paltz is a larger town, but its colonial section is some distance from the modern business district, so that its antiquity has been well preserved. Huguenot Street, which Lovecraft examined with rapture, is lined with stone houses of the early eighteenth century; one of them—the Jean Hasbrouck house (1712)—was open as a museum, and he canvassed the place thoroughly.[62]

Just before seeing these towns, Lovecraft was the victim of a robbery—nothing quite so spectacular as the Clinton Street raid of 1925, but one that resulted in the loss of his customary black enamel-cloth bag "containing my stationery & diary, two copies of Weird Tales, my pocket telescope, & some postcards & printed matter of Kingston."[63] The important thing to note here is the existence of a diary. Lovecraft went on to say that it contained "the record of all my spring travels & all my addresses," but that the former could be reconstructed "from the letters & cards I have written home." It seems likely that similar diaries for each of his spring-summer travels for the next seven years existed, but only a quite different diary for a small portion of 1936 has come to light.

Lovecraft was hoping to take the Mohawk Trail by bus from Albany, but found to his great irritation that the service would not start until May 30, even though it continued to be advertised in travel brochures; so he was forced to take the more expensive and less scenically stimulating train to Athol. Nevertheless, he was thrilled to return home to New England after an interval of five weeks: "Then the hills grew wilder & greener & more beautiful—yet less luxuriant in folige as we receded from the warmth of the south. Finally I saw a station-name which made my heart leap—*North-Pownal, in His Majesty's New-Hampshire Grants, latterly call'd Vermont, in New-England!* God Save the King!! ... Home at last ..."[64] The return was perhaps not quite as transporting as the homecoming from New York in 1926, for Lovecraft knew he would come home sooner or later; but the sentiments are distinctly analogous. Lovecraft met both Cook and Munn in Athol, and on the 17th they all made a brief excursion to Brattleboro, Vermont, where they looked up Arthur Goodenough. The next day Munn drove Lovecraft and Cook to Westminster, which had not changed in the thirty years since Lovecraft saw it last (as a boy in the company of his mother), then continued on to Providence via Petersham and Barre.

It had been a great trip, with ten states plus the District of Columbia traversed; and it had given Lovecraft his first fleeting taste of the South, although in later years he would see far more of it. As with his previous year's travels, he wrote up his 1929 jaunt in a tremendous 18,000-word travelogue entitled "Travels in the Provinces of America," which, however, was not published until 1995. It surely made the rounds of Lovecraft's friends and correspondents; and if they were pleased and informed—as they could hardly fail to have been—then the essay's purpose would have been fulfilled.

And yet, Lovecraft's travels were not quite at an end. On August 5 he took a bus trip to the Fairbanks house (1636) in Dedham, Massachusetts, the oldest surviving building of English origin in New England. Actually, the bus (run by a Mr A. Johnson) was going to the Red Horse Tavern in Sudbury (site of Longfellow's *Tales of a Wayside Inn*), and it was Lovecraft who suggested the detour to Johnson. Aside from wings added in 1641 and 1648, the Fairbanks house had undergone no alterations whatever since its first construction; and it so struck Lovecraft (who wrote a short, charming essay about his journey, "An Account of a Trip to the Antient Fairbanks House, in Dedham, and to the Red Horse Tavern in Sudbury, in the Province of the Massachusetts-Bay") that

> For once I forgot my periwigg'd membership in the rational eighteenth century, and allow'd my self to be ingulph'd by the sinister sorcery of the dark seventeenth. Verily, this was the most poignantly imagination-stirring house I had ever seen. . . . I cou'd hear the sound of the builder's axe in the nighted woods three hundred years ago, when King Charles the First, still unmartyr'd by Roundhead treason, sate on the throne, and the lone, questing canoe of Roger Williams and his companions dug its prow into the sand of Moshassuck's pathless shoar, not four squares downhill from the spot where I am now seated.

Again I must emphasise the keenness of perception and imagination that allows Lovecraft to drink in such sites and weave such striking fancies around them. Is it any wonder that so many details of his travels found their way into his later fiction? The Red Horse Tavern (1683 et seq.) was also pleasing (it was then owned by Henry Ford, "a very respectable coach-maker"), but not nearly as stimulating as the hoary Fairbanks house.

On August 13 the Longs drove through Providence on their way to Cape Cod and picked up Lovecraft to accompany them. New Bedford was explored that day, and Lovecraft found the Whaling Museum—housed on the bark *Lagoda*—tremendously stirring. The next day they reached Onset, on the Cape, where they presumably stayed in a hotel or lodge; later that day they explored other towns in the vicinity—Chatham, Orleans, Hyannis, Sandwich. Lovecraft did not find the Cape very rich in colonial antiquities or even as "picturesque as its popular reputation would argue,"[65] but it was pleasing enough, especially in light of the fact that he was getting free room and board with the Longs. The next day's explorations included Wood's Hole, Sagamore, and Falmouth.

But the best part of the journey for Lovecraft was on the 17th, when he took his first ride in an airplane. It was only $3.00, and would fly passengers all over Buzzard's Bay. It proved no disappointment: "The landscape effect was that of a bird's eye view map—& the scene was such as to lend itself to this inspection with maximum advantage. . . . This aeroplane ride (which attained a pretty good height at its maximum) adds a finishing touch to the perfection of the present outing."[66] For someone with so cosmic an imagination as Lovecraft, it is scarcely to be wondered that a ride in an airplane—the only time he was actually off the surface of the earth—would be a powerful imaginative stimulus; and only poverty prevented his ever repeating the experience.

One more trip occurred on August 29. Lovecraft and Annie Gamwell took yet another sojourn to the ancestral Foster region, renewing their acquaintances of three years earlier and extending their explorations still further. This time they investigated the area called Howard Hill, where Asaph Phillips had built his homestead in 1790. They met several people who recalled Whipple Phillips and Robie Place, saw old Phillips gravestones, and consulted genealogical records that helped Lovecraft fill in details of his ancestry. Later they returned to Moosup Valley, the site of their 1926 trip, and again Lovecraft was charmed at the unchanged nature of the region: "Here, indeed, was a small and glorious world of the past *completely* sever'd from the sullying tides of time; a world *exactly* the same as before the revolution, with *absolutely nothing* changed in the way of ritual details, currents of folk-feeling, identity of families, or social and economick order."[67] How unfortunate that such places are now so few!

This was the extent of Lovecraft's 1929 travels; but if the mountain would not come to Mohammad, Mohammad would come to the mountain. Several of his friends dropped by in Providence for brief visits—Morton in mid-June, Cook and Munn in late June, and George Kirk and his wife in early September.[68] Lovecraft himself had become a Mecca for the many friends and correspondents—in amateurdom, weird fiction, and other realms—he had developed over a lifetime.

In early July Lovecraft was forced to wrestle with the revision of another story by Adolphe de Castro, since, incredibly, de Castro had paid for it in advance.[69] This tale, which in de Castro's 1893 collection was called "The Automatic Executioner," was retitled "The Electric Executioner" by Lovecraft. In the course of rewriting it, Lovecraft transformed it into a *comic* weird tale—not a parody, but a story that actually mingles humour and horror. He repeatedly asserted that these two modes did not mix, and in general I believe he is right; but humour was at least one way of relieving the drudgery of working on a tale that had little enough potential to start with.

An unnamed narrator is asked by the president of his company to track down a man named Feldon who has disappeared with some papers in Mexico. Boarding a train, the man later finds that he is alone in a car with one other occupant, who proves to be a dangerous maniac. This person has apparently devised an hoodlike instrument for performing executions and wishes the narrator to be the first experimental victim. Realising that he cannot overwhelm the man by force, the narrator seeks to delay the experiment until the train reaches the next station, Mexico City. He first asks to be allowed to write a letter disposing of his effects; then he asserts that he has newspaper friends in Sacramento who would be interested in publicising the invention; and finally he says that he would like to make a sketch of the thing in operation—why doesn't the man put it on his own head so that it can be drawn? The madman does so; but then the narrator, having earlier perceived that the madman has an attraction for Aztec mythology, pretends to be possessed by religious fervour and begins shouting Aztec and other names at random as a further stalling tactic. The madman does so also, and in the process his device pulls taut over his neck and executes him; the narrator faints. When revived, the narrator finds that the madman is no longer in the car, although a crowd of people is there; he is informed that in fact no one was ever in the car. Later Feldon is discovered dead in a remote cave—with certain objects unquestionably belonging to the narrator.

In de Castro's stilted and lifeless prose, this tale comes off as *unintentionally* funny; Lovecraft makes it consciously so. In so doing, he makes several in-jokes. Part of the characterisation of the madman is drawn from a rather more harmless person Lovecraft met on the train ride from New York to Washington on his recent journey—a German who kept repeating "Efferythingk iss luffly!," "I vass shoost leddingk my light shine!" and other random utterances.[70] The madman in "The Electric Executioner" does in fact say at one point, "I shall let my light shine, as it were." Later, in the course of uttering the names of various Aztec gods, the narrator cries out: "Ya-R'lyeh! Ya-R'lyeh! . . . Cthulhutl fhtaghn! Niguratl-Yig! Yog-Sototl—" The spelling variants are intentional, as Lovecraft wished to give an Aztec cast to the names so as to suggest they were part of that culture's theology. Otherwise, Lovecraft has followed de Castro's plot far more faithfully than in "The Last Test"—retaining character names, the basic sequence of incidents, and even the final supernatural twist (although sensibly suggesting that it was Feldon's astral body, not the narrator's, that was in the car). He has, of course, fleshed out the plot considerably, adding better motivation and livelier descriptive and narrative touches. The tale is not an entire failure.

I do not know how much Lovecraft got paid for "The Electric Executioner," but it landed with *Weird Tales* and appeared in the August 1930 issue. Predictably, readers began noticing the dropping of invented names in both this and the earlier de Castro revision; N. J. O'Neail queried in the March 1930 issue about the origin of Yog-Sothoth, saying that "Mr. Lovecraft links the latter with Cthulhu in 'The Dunwich Horror' and Adolphe de Castro also refers to Yog-Sothoth in 'The Last Test.'" Lovecraft, both tickled and mortified at the deception, wrote to Robert E. Howard: "I ought, though, to write Mr. O'Neail and disabuse him of the idea that there is a large blind spot in his mythological erudition!"[71]

At some subsequent period Lovecraft revised a third tale for de Castro. He remarked in late 1930: ". . . I did accidentally land . . . three tales of Old Dolph's,"[72] and later declared: "I've also put Yog-Sothoth and Tsathoggua in yarns ghost-written for Adolphe de Castro . . ."[73] As Robert M. Price has noted,[74] these statements imply two things: 1) that Lovecraft actually *sold* (not merely revised) three stories, and that the third story makes at least passing mention of Tsathoggua, since the two known stories do not. A consultation of periodical indexes in both the general and weird/fantasy/science fiction fields has not turned up any other published tale by de Castro in this period, leading one to believe that the story may have been sold to some periodical (not *Weird Tales,* clearly) that folded before the tale could be printed. I do not believe we have lost any masterwork of literature as a result.

In the fall of 1929 Lovecraft and Derleth engaged in a debate over the best weird stories ever written. This may have been part of the honours thesis Derleth was writing ("The Weird Tale in English Since 1890," completed in 1930 and published in W. Paul Cook's late amateur journal, the *Ghost,* for May 1945), but whatever the case, the discussion ended up having an unexpectedly wider audience. In a letter of October 6 Lovecraft evaluated the ten or twelve stories Derleth had selected as his list of "bests," agreeing with some and disagreeing with others (Derleth had already by this time gained his idolatrous fondness for "The Outsider"). Shortly thereafter Frank Long insinuated himself in the controversy. In the middle of November Lovecraft wrote to Derleth:

> The other day the literary editor of the local *Journal* had a discussion in his daily column about the weirdest story ever written—& his choices were so commonplace that I couldn't resist writing him myself & enclosing transcripts (with my own tales omitted) of your & Belknap's lists of best horror tales. He wrote back asking permission to discuss the matter publicly in his column, mentioning you, Belknap, & myself by name—& I have told him he may do so.[75]

This refers to Bertrand Kelton Hart, who signed himself B. K. Hart and wrote a column called "The Sideshow" that ran daily (except for Sundays) in the *Providence Journal,* devoted largely but not exclusively to literary matters. In the course of several columns Hart transcribed lists of best weird tales by all three participants; Lovecraft's (published in the issue for November 23) is as follows:

"The Willows" by Algernon Blackwood
"[Novel of] The White Powder" by Arthur Machen
"The White People" by Arthur Machen
"[Novel of] The Black Seal" by Arthur Machen
"The Fall of the House of Usher" by Edgar Allan Poe
"The House of Sounds" by M. P. Shiel
"The Yellow Sign" by Robert W. Chambers

A group of second choices includes:

"Count Magnus" by M. R. James
"The Death of Halpin Frayser" by Ambrose Bierce
"The Suitable Surroundings" by Ambrose Bierce
"Seaton's Aunt" by Walter de la Mare

This is very similar to a list published as "Favorite Weird Stories of H. P. Lovecraft" (*Fantasy Fan,* October 1934), and would make an excellent anthology in spite of the number of Machen items listed.

Lovecraft was tickled by his appearance in the paper. He did not ordinarily like to obtrude himself as a persistent bombarder of letters to the editorial page, feeling it callow and self-promotional; but around this time another matter far more pressing to him than an academic discussion of weird fiction forced him once again into a vigorous letter-writing campaign. In spring it had been announced that the old warehouses along South Water Street would be torn down to make way for what was announced as a new hall of records (adjacent to the fine neo-Georgian court house, built in 1928–33, at the corner of College and North Main Streets). Lovecraft had already written a letter three years earlier in which, amidst a general paean to the archaic wonders of Providence, he had specifically praised these structures ("the incomparable colorful row of 1816 warehouses in South Water street"[76]); this letter, written on October 5, 1926, appeared in the *Sunday Journal* for October 10. Now, appalled at the threatened destruction, he wrote a long letter on March 20, 1929 (titled by Lovecraft "The Old Brick Row," published in the *Providence Sunday Journal* for March 24 in abridged form as "Retain Historic 'Old Brick Row'"), appealing almost frantically to the city government not to destroy the buildings. In his letter Lovecraft chided those who declared them "shabby, ramshackle old rookeries"; but the fact of the matter is that these utilitarian structures really had reached a state of decrepitude, and—since it was decades before the restoration of colonial sites in the city would begin—there was little option but to tear them down. On September 24 the City Council approved a measure to condemn the buildings.[77] Lovecraft tried to keep up a brave front, urging Morton to write to the *Journal* also. Morton did so on December 17 (it was published in the *Sunday Journal* for December 22); but Lovecraft must have known that the fate of the warehouses was sealed.

As a final ploy Lovecraft resurrected his rusty poetic skills and wrote the poignant twelve-stanza poem, "The East India Brick Row," on December 12:

> They are the sills that hold the lights of home;
>> The links that join us to the years before;
> The haven of old questing wraiths that roam
>> Down long, dim aisles to a familiar shore.
>
> They store the charm that years build, cell by cell,
>> Like coral, from our lives, our past, our land;
> Beauty that dreamers know and cherish well,
>> But hard eyes slight, too dulled to understand.

But Lovecraft knew the end was coming, and so he concluded:

> So if at last a callous age must tear
>> These jewels from the old town's quiet dress,
> I think the harbour streets will always wear
>> A puzzled look of wistful emptiness.

This poem appeared in the *Providence Journal* as "Brick Row" on January 8, 1930. It received such a favourable response that the editor wrote a cordial letter to Lovecraft about it;[78] but it was too late. The Brick Row must have come down about this time, although ironically the hall of records was never built; instead, the land became a park dedicated to the memory of Henry B. Gardner, Jr, a Providence lawyer.

"The East India Brick Row" was written in the midst of an unexpected burst of poetry at the end of 1929. At the very beginning of the year, or perhaps in late 1928, Lovecraft had written the powerful weird poem "The Wood" (*Tryout*, January 1929), telling of the cutting down of an ancient wood and the building of a lavish city on its site:

> Forests may fall, but not the dusk they shield;
>> So on the spot where that proud city stood,
> The shuddering dawn no single stone reveal'd,
>> But fled the blackness of a primal wood.

This may be nothing more than a refined version of the shudder-mongering of earlier poems such as "The Rutted Road" or "Nemesis," but at least it is artfully done—and, what is more, it is finally beginning to exemplify those principles of poetry as a living language that Lovecraft had now embraced and was inculcating to Elizabeth Toldridge and others.

One other poem, written apparently in the summer,[79] prefaced the flood of verse at the end of the year—a 212-line mock-epic entitled "An Epistle to the Rt. Hon[ble] Maurice Winter Moe, Esq. of Zythopolis, in the Northwest Territory of His Majesty's American Dominions," written both as a sort of versified letter to Moe (Zythopolis is a neo-Greek compound meaning "Beer-City," i.e., Milwaukee) and as a celebration of the year 1904. It was evidently designed for inclusion in a memorial booklet for the twenty-fifth reunion of the Class of 1904 at the University of Wisconsin; this item has not turned up, so I am not sure whether the poem actually appeared there. What the poem shows, if anything, is how completely Lovecraft had come to use his once-beloved heroic couplets for the purpose of self-parody.

"The Outpost," written on November 26, inaugurates the poetic outburst. It is not a great success and was rejected by Farnsworth Wright as being too long (it is in thirteen quatrains).[80] It speaks of the "great King who fears to dream" in a palace in Zimbabwe. The poem seems clearly inspired by various anecdotes told to Lovecraft by Edward Lloyd Sechrist, who had actually been to the ruins of Zimbabwe in Africa. One evening when Lovecraft met Sechrist in Washington in May 1929

> he shewed me many rare curiosities such as rare woods, rhinoceras-hide, &c. &c.—& especially a prehistoric bird-idol of strangely crude design found near the cryptical & mysterious ruins of Zimbabwe (remnants of a vanished & unknown race & civilisation) in the jungle, & resembling the colossal bird-idols found on the walls of that baffling & fancy-provoking town. I made a sketch of this, for it at once suggested a multiplicity of ideas for weird fictional development.[81]

No bird or bird-idol actually figures in the poem, but I have no doubt that at least some of the imagery derives from Lovecraft's talks with Sechrist.

At this point B. K. Hart reenters the scene. The discussion of weird fiction had about died down when Hart stumbled upon a copy of Harré's *Beware After Dark!* containing "The Call of Cthulhu." While enjoying the tale, he was startled to note that Wilcox's residence at 7 Thomas Street was one he himself had once occupied. Hart, in a column published in the *Journal* for November 30, pretended to take umbrage ("I won't have it. My own little ghost shadows, slinking home to the sun in the healthy dawn, are quite enough for Thomas street, and I reject these sinister brutes from the other side of the beyond, cluttering up the traffic with their gargantuan bulk") and made a dire threat: ". . . I shall not be happy until, joining league with wraiths and ghouls, I have plumped down at least one large and abiding ghost by way of reprisal upon his own doorstep in Barnes street. . . . I think I shall teach it to moan in a minor dissonance every morning at 3 o'clock sharp, with a clinking of chains."[82] What else could Lovecraft do but, that night at 3 A.M., write "The Messenger"?

> The thing, he said, would come that night at three
> From the old churchyard on the hill below;
> But crouching by an oak fire's wholesome glow,
> I tried to tell myself it could not be.
> Surely, I mused, it was a pleasantry
> Devised by one who did not truly know
> The Elder Sign, bequeathed from long ago,
> That sets the fumbling forms of darkness free.
>
> He had not meant it—no—but still I lit
> Another lamp as starry Leo climbed
> Out of the Seekonk, and a steeple chimed
> Three—and the firelight faded, bit by bit.
> Then at the door that cautious rattling came—
> And the mad truth devoured me like a flame!

Winfield Townley Scott—he who had referred to the bulk of Lovecraft's verse as "eighteenth-century rubbish"—calls this "perhaps as wholly satisfactory as any poem he ever wrote."[83] I am not entirely certain of this—the poem seems again simply an extraordinarily skilled shudder, but with no depth of thought behind it—but somehow Lovecraft had suddenly come to master a poetic idiom beyond that of the stilted heroic couplet. Both the remarkable simplicity and naturalness of the language and the unusually frequent enjambement (lack of end-stopping) are to be noted. B. K. Hart must have been pleased with the piece, for he printed it in his column for December 3, 1929.

"The East India Brick Row" followed in early December, after which Lovecraft wrote what *I* might regard as his single most successful poem, "The Ancient Track." "There was no hand to hold me back / That night I found the ancient track," begins—and ends—this brooding, pensive lyric, written in Poe-esque iambic trimeter. The narrator seems to remember the area in which he has entered ("There was a milestone that I knew— / 'Two miles to Dunwich' . . ."—the only other reference to Dunwich in all Lovecraft's fiction and poetry), but once he reaches the crest he sees nothing but "A valley of the lost and dead" and a fog

> Whose curling talons mocked the thought
> That I had ever known this spot.

Too well I saw from the mad scene
That my loved past had never been—

But nevertheless, "There was no hand to hold me back / That night I found the ancient track." This poem readily sold to *Weird Tales,* where it appeared in the March 1930 issue and for which Lovecraft received $11.00.[84]

Then, in the remarkable week between December 27 and January 4, Lovecraft wrote *Fungi from Yuggoth.* The thirty-six sonnets that make up this sequence are generally regarded as his most sustained weird poetic work, and the cycle has accordingly generated a considerable body of criticism. Before studying the text itself, it may be well to consider some of the factors that may have led to this tremendous outburst of weird verse.

The most general influence, perhaps, is Clark Ashton Smith. While it is true that fiction had, by around 1921, already come at least to equal poetry as Lovecraft's major aesthetic outlet, it can also be no accident that the virtual surcease of his poetic output from 1922 to 1928 commenced at the very time he came in touch with Smith. Here was a poet who was writing dense, vigorous weird and cosmic poetry in a vibrant, vital manner as far removed as possible from the eighteenth century or even from the poetry of Poe. Lovecraft, who had long realised, in an abstract way, the deficiencies of his own poetry but had rarely encountered a *living* poet doing work he could admire and even envy, now came upon just such a poet. Lovecraft's verse during this period accordingly descends to harmless birthday odes or other occasional verse, with rare exceptions such as the powerful "The Cats," "Primavera," or "Festival" ("Yule Horror").

Then, around 1928, Lovecraft began work on Moe's *Doorways to Poetry.* After a long period of quiescence, he was forced to turn his attention again to the theory of poetry, and—at least in a small way (as in the "Sonnet Study")—to its practice. It was at this time that he began voicing his new theory of poetry as simple, straightforward diction that uses the language of its own day to convey its message. A random comment made just after writing "The Outpost" suggests that Lovecraft had at least a nebulous idea that these two factors (Clark Ashton Smith and the *Doorways*) had had their effect: "Meanwhile some malign influence—prob'ly revising that Moe text book on poetick appreciation—has got me invadin' one of Klarkash-Ton's provinces . . ."[85]

The immediate influence on the *Fungi,* however, clearly seems to be Wandrei's *Sonnets of the Midnight Hours,* which Lovecraft read no later than November 1927.[86] It is difficult to know which or how many of these Lovecraft read: there are at least twenty-eight of them, but only twenty-six appear in their final (and presumably definitive) appearance in Wandrei's *Poems for Midnight* (1964); Wandrei excluded two that had earlier appeared in *Weird Tales,* perhaps because he was not satisfied with their quality. In any event, this cycle—in which all the poems are written in the first person and all are inspired by actual dreams by Wandrei—is certainly very powerful, but does not seem to me quite as polished or as cumulatively affecting as Lovecraft's. Nevertheless, Lovecraft clearly derived the basic idea of a sonnet cycle from this work, even though his differs considerably from it in actual execution.

Winfield Townley Scott and Edmund Wilson independently believed that the *Fungi* may have been influenced by Edwin Arlington Robinson, but I cannot verify that Lovecraft had read Robinson by this time, or in fact ever read him. He is not mentioned in any correspondence I have seen prior to 1935. The parallels in diction adduced by Scott seem to be of a very general sort and do not establish a sound case for any such influence.

We now come to the vexed question of what *Fungi from Yuggoth* actually is. Is it a strictly unified poem that reveals some sort of continuity, or is it merely a random collection of sonnets flitting from topic to topic with little order or sequence? I remain inclined toward the latter view. No one can possibly believe that there is any actual *plot* to this work, in spite of various critics' laboured attempts to find such a thing; and other critics' claims for a kind of "unity" based on structure or theme or imagery are similarly unconvincing because the "unity" so discovered does not seem at all systematic or coherent. My conclusion remains that the *Fungi* sonnets provided Lovecraft with an opportunity to crystallise various conceptions, types of imagery, and fragments of dreams that could not have found creative expression in fiction—a sort of imaginative housecleaning. The fact that he so exhaustively used ideas from his commonplace book for the sonnets supports this conclusion.

Certainly, the number of autobiographical features—relating both to specific details of imagery and to the overall philosophical thrust—in the *Fungi* is very large. The very first sonnet, "The Book," speaks of a man who enters a bookstore with books piled to the ceiling ("crumbling elder lore at little cost") but with evidently no "seller old in craft" tending the place. This immediately recalls Lovecraft's stream-of-consciousness recollection of various bookstalls he visited in New York ("the mystic bookstalls with their hellish bearded guardians . . . monstrous books from nightmare lands for sale at a song if one might chance to pick the right one from mouldering, ceiling-high piles"[87]). "The Pigeon-Flyers" (X) is a literal account of a strange custom in the "'Hell's Kitchen' slum of New York, where bonfire-building & pigeon-flying are the two leading recreations of youth."[88] Such examples could be multiplied almost indefinitely.

Some of the sonnets seem to be reworkings of some of the dominant conceptions of previous stories. "Nyarlathotep" (XXI) is a close retelling of the prose poem of 1920; "The Elder Pharos" (XXVII) speaks of a figure who "wears a silken mask," whom we first saw in *The Dream-Quest of Unknown Kadath;* "Alienation" (XXXII) seems roughly based upon "The Strange High House in the Mist." More significantly, some poems seem to be anticipations of stories Lovecraft would write in later years, making the *Fungi* a sort of recapitulation of what he had written before and a presage of his subsequent work.

It may be true that many of the sonnets, like so much of Lovecraft's weird verse, have no purpose but sending a chill up one's spine; but toward the middle and end of the sequence some very different poems begin to appear, which have either beauty as their keynote or pensive autobiography. "Hesperia" (XIII) is the first such item, speaking of a "land where beauty's meaning flowers," but concluding bitterly that "human tread has never soiled these streets." "The Gardens of Yin" (XVIII) attempts to depict what was for Lovecraft the quintessence of beauty ("There would be terraced gardens, rich with flowers, / And flutter of bird and butterfly and bee. / There would be walks, and bridges arching over / Warm lotos-pools reflecting temple eaves"); some of this imagery seems to derive from Robert W. Chambers's novelette "The Maker of Moons" (in the 1896 collection of that title). The best of this type is "Background" (XXX):

> I never can be tied to raw, new things,
> For I first saw the light in an old town,
> Where from my window huddled roofs sloped down
> To a quaint harbour rich with visionings.
> Streets with carved doorways where the sunset beams
> Flooded old fanlights and small window-panes,
> And Georgian steeples topped with gilded vanes—
> These were the sights that shaped my childhood dreams.

These lines are now embossed on the H. P. Lovecraft memorial plaque at the John Hay Library in Providence, R.I.

The cycle is fittingly concluded with "Continuity" (XXXVI), which attempts to account for Lovecraft's cosmic orientation:

> There is in some ancient things a trace
> Of some dim essence—more than form or weight;
> A tenuous aether, indeterminate,
> Yet linked with all the laws of time and space.
> A faint, veiled sign of continuities
> That outward eyes can never quite descry;
> Of locked dimensions harbouring years gone by,
> And out of reach except for hidden keys.
>
> It moves me most when slanting sunbeams glow
> On old farm buildings set against a hill,
> And paint with life the shapes which linger still

From centuries less a dream than this we know.
In that strange light I feel I am not far
From the fixt mass whose sides the ages are.

In one compact poem Lovecraft's antiquarianism, cosmicism, love of the weird, and his attachment to his native land are all fused into a unity. It is his most condensed, and most poignant, autobiographical statement.

Those who argue for the "unity" of the *Fungi* must take account of the somewhat odd manner in which it achieved its present state. "Recapture" (now sonnet XXXIV) was written in late November, presumably as a separate poem. For years after it was written, the *Fungi* comprised only thirty-five sonnets. When R. H. Barlow considered publishing it as a booklet, he suggested that "Recpature" be added to the cycle; but when he rather casually tacked it on at the end of a type-script he was preparing, Lovecraft felt that it should be placed third from the end: "'Recapture' seems somehow more *specific* & *localised* in spirit than either of the others named, hence would go better before them—allowing the *Fungi* to come to a close with more diffusive ideas."[89] To my mind, this suggests no more than that Lovecraft had some rough idea that the cycle ought to be read in sequence and ought to end with a more general utterance. And yet, shortly after finishing the series he was still mentioning casually the possibility of "grind[ing] out a dozen or so more before I consider the sequence concluded."[90]

Certainly, Lovecraft had no compunction in allowing the individual sonnets of the *Fungi* to appear quite randomly in the widest array of publications. Eleven sonnets (IX, XIII, XIV, XV, XIX, XXI, XXII, XXIII, XXVII, XXXII, XXXIV) appeared in *Weird Tales* in 1930–31 (only ten appeared under the specific heading *Fungi from Yuggoth,* since "Recapture" had been accepted earlier and appeared separately); five more (XI, XX, XXIX, XXX, XXXI) appeared in the *Providence Journal* in the early months of 1930; nine (IV, VI, VII, VIII, XII, XVI, XVIII, XXIV, XXVI) appeared in Walter J. Coates's *Driftwind* from 1930 to 1932; the remainder appeared later in amateur journals or fan magazines, and after Lovecraft's death many more were printed in *Weird Tales.* "Expectancy" (XXVIII) was the only poem never to be periodically published in or just after Lovecraft's lifetime; and the cycle as a unit was not published until 1943.

As a whole, the *Fungi from Yuggoth* constitutes the summit of Lovecraft's weird verse. It is a compressed transcription of many of the themes, images, and conceptions that most frequently and obsessively haunted his imagination, and their expression in a relatively simple, non-archaic, but highly condensed and piquant diction (with such novel and stirring compounds as "dream-transient," "storm-crazed," and "dream-plagued") represent Lovecraft's triumphant if belated declaration of independence from the deadening influence of eighteenth-century verse. They perhaps do not precisely conform either to the Italian or Shakespearean sonnet form (which may account for Lovecraft's frequent reference to them as "pseudo-sonnets"); but they are orthodox enough in metre to be an implied rebuke to those poets who had too readily given up standard metre for the supposed liberation of free verse. It is a shame that none of his illustrious contemporaries ever saw them.

Shortly after finishing the *Fungi* Lovecraft was jolted to hear of the death of Everett McNeil, which had occurred on December 14, 1929 but news of which did not get out until well into the next month. Lovecraft wrote a paean to him in various letters—a paean that brought back all the memories of his own New York experience:

> When Sonny [Frank Long] and I first met him, in 1922, his affairs were at their lowest ebb, and he dwelt in the frightful slum of Hell's Kitchen . . . High in a squalid tenement house amidst this welter lived good old Mac—his little flat an oasis of neatness and wholesomeness with its quaint, homely pictures, rows of simple books, and curious mechanical devices which his ingenuity concocted to aid his work—lap boards, files, etc., etc. He lived on meagre rations of canned soup and crackers, and did not whimper at his lot. . . . He had suffered a lot in his day—and at one time had nothing to eat but the sugar which he could pick up free at lunch rooms and dissolve in water for the sake of its nourishment. . . . I shall always associate him with the great grey glamorous stretches of sedgy flat lands in Southern Brooklyn—salt marshes with inlets, like the Holland coast, and dotted with lonely Dutch cottages with curving roof-lines. All gone now—like Mac . . .[91]

Perhaps, Lovecraft felt, he had been all too close to being reduced to Mac's state before he fled for the peace and safety of Providence.

Somewhat more positive news had emerged at the very beginning of January: the critic William Bolitho had casually worked in a favourable mention of Lovecraft in his column in the New York *World* for January 4, 1930. The title of this instalment, "Pulp Magazines," tells the whole story: Bolitho was asserting that these humble organs of literature can provide not merely greater pleasure but sometimes even greater literary substance than more prestigious literary venues. Bolitho concludes:

> In this world there are chiefs, evidently. I am inclined to think they must be pretty good. There is Otis Adelbert Kline and H. P. Lovecraft, whom I am sure I would rather read than many fashionable lady novelists they give teas to; and poets too. Meditate on that, you who are tired of the strained prettiness of the verse in the great periodicals, that there are still poets here of the pure Poe school who sell and are printed for a vast public.[92]

Lovecraft was aware of this remark—he could hardly fail to be, as Bolitho's entire column was reprinted in *Weird Tales* for April 1930—and on one occasion expressed mortification at the linkage to Kline: "Another recent thing which rather tickled me was a favourable mention of my tales in William Bolitho's column in the *N. Y. World*—although it was spoiled by the coupling of my name with that of the amiable hack Otis Adelbert Kline!"[93]

It had been more than a year since Lovecraft had written any original fiction; and that tale—"The Dunwich Horror"—was itself written after more than a year's interval since its predecessor, "The Colour out of Space." Revision, travel, and inevitably correspondence ate up all the time Lovecraft might have had for fiction, for he stated repeatedly that he required a completely free schedule to achieve the mental clarity needed for writing stories. Now, however, at the end of 1929, a revision job came up that allowed him to exercise his fictional pen far beyond what he expected—and, frankly, beyond what was required by the job in question. But however prodigal Lovecraft may have been in the task, the result—"The Mound," ghostwritten for Zealia Bishop—was well worth the effort.

Of this story it is difficult to speak in small compass. It is itself, at 25,000 words, the lengthiest of Lovecraft's revisions of a weird tale and is comparable in length to "The Whisperer in Darkness." That it is entirely the work of Lovecraft can be gauged by Bishop's original plot-germ, as recorded by R. H. Barlow: "There is an Indian mound near here, which is haunted by a headless ghost. Sometimes it is a woman."[94] Lovecraft found this idea "insufferably tame & flat"[95] and fabricated an entire novelette of underground horror, incorporating many conceptions of his evolving myth-cycle, including Cthulhu (under the variant form Tulu).

"The Mound" concerns a member of Coronado's expedition of 1541, Panfilo de Zamacona y Nuñez, who leaves the main group and conducts a solitary expedition to the mound region of what is now Oklahoma. There he hears tales of an underground realm of fabulous antiquity and (more to his interest) great wealth, and finds an Indian who will lead him to one of the few remaining entrances to this realm, although the Indian refuses to accompany him on the actual journey. Zamacona comes upon the civilisation of Xinaian (which he pronounces "K'n-yan"), established by quasi-human creatures who (implausibly) came from outer space. These inhabitants have developed remarkable mental abilities, including telepathy and the power of dematerialisation—the process of dissolving themselves and selected objects around them to their component atoms and recombining them at some other location. Zamacona initially expresses wonder at this civilisation, but gradually finds that it has declined both intellectually and morally from a much higher level and has now become corrupt and decadent. He attempts to escape, but suffers a horrible fate. A manuscript that he had written of his adventures is unearthed in modern times by an archaeologist, who paraphrases his incredible tale.

This skeletonic plot outline cannot begin to convey the textural richness of the story, which—although perhaps not as carefully written as many of Lovecraft's original works—is successful in depicting vast gulfs of time and in vivifying with a great abundance of detail the underground world of K'n-yan. What should also be evident is that "The Mound" is the first, but by no means the last, of Lovecraft's tales to utilise an alien civilisation as a transparent metaphor for certain phases of human (and, more specifically, Western) civilisation. Initially, K'n-yan seems a Lovecraftian utopia: the people have conquered old age, have no poverty because of their relatively few numbers and their thorough mastery of technology, use religion only as an aesthetic ornament, practise selective breeding to ensure the vigour of the "ruling type," and pass the day largely in aesthetic and intellectual activity. Lovecraft makes no secret of the parallels he is drawing to contemporary Western civilisation:

> The nation [had] gone through a period of idealistic industrial democracy which gave equal opportunities to all, and thus, by raising the naturally intelligent to power, drained the masses of all their brains and stamina. . . . Physical comfort was ensured by an urban mechanisation of standardised and easily maintained pattern. . . . Literature was all highly individual and analytical. . . . The modern tendency was to feel rather than to think. . . .

Lovecraft even notes that in "bygone eras . . . K'n-yan had held ideas much like those of the classic and renaissance outer world, and had possessed a natural character and art full of what Europeans regard as dignity, kindness, and nobility." But as Zamacona continues to observe the people, he begins to notice disturbing signs of decadence. Consider the state of literature and art at the time of his arrival:

> The dominance of machinery had at one time broken up the growth of normal aesthetics, introducing a lifelessly geometrical tradition fatal to sound expression. This had soon been outgrown, but had left its mark upon all pictorial and decorative attempts; so that except for conventionalised religious designs, there was little depth or feeling in any later work. Archaistic reproductions of earlier work had been found much preferable for general enjoyment.

The similarity of these remarks to those on modern art and architecture as found in "Heritage or Modernism: Common Sense in Art Forms" (1935) is manifest:

> They [the modernists] launch new decorative designs of cones and cubes and triangles and segments—wheels and belts, smokestacks and stream-lined sausage moulders—problems in Euclid and nightmares from alcoholic orgies—and tell us that these things are the only authentic symbols of the age in which we live. . . . When a given age has no new *natural* impulses toward change, is it not better to continue building on the established forms than to concoct grotesque and meaningless novelties out of thin academic theory? Indeed, under certain conditions is not a policy of frank and virile antiquarianism—a healthy, vigorous revival of old forms still justified by their relation to life—infinitely sounder than a feverish mania for the destruction of familiar things and the laboured, freakish, uninspired search for strange shapes which nobody wants and which really mean nothing?

But the problems of K'n-yan spread beyond aesthetics. Science was "falling into decay"; history was "more and more neglected"; and gradually religion was becoming less a matter of aesthetic ritual and more a sort of degraded superstition: "Rationalism degenerated more and more into fanatical and orgiastic superstition . . . and tolerance steadily dissolved into a series of frenzied hatreds, especially toward the outer world." The narrator concludes: "It is evident that K'n-yan was far along in its decadence—reacting with mixed apathy and hysteria against the standardised and time-tabled life of stultifying regularity which machinery had brought it during its middle period." How can one fail to recall Lovecraft's condemnation of the "machine-culture" dominating his own age and its probable outcome?

> We shall hear of all sorts of futile reforms and reformers—standardised culture-outlines, synthetic sports and spectacles, professional play-leaders and study-guides, and kindred examples of machine-made uplift and brotherly spirit. And it will amount to just about as much as most reforms do! Meanwhile the tension of boredom and unsatisfied imagination will increase—breaking out with increasing frequency in crimes of morbid perversity and explosive violence.[96]

These dour and sadly accurate reflections point to the fundamental difference between "The Mound" and such later tales as *At the Mountains of Madness* and "The Shadow out of Time": Lovecraft has not yet developed his later political theory of "fascistic socialism" whereby the spreading of economic wealth among the many and the restricting of political power to the few will (to his mind) produce a genuine utopia of useful citizens who work only a few hours a week and spend the rest of their time engaging in wholesome intellectual and aesthetic activity. That pipe-dream only emerged around 1931, as the depression became increasingly severe and forced Lovecraft wholly to renounce both democracy (in which he had never believed) and laissez-faire capitalism. The civilisation of K'n-yan is, perhaps a little surprisingly, said to be "a kind of communistic or semi-anarchical state"; but we have already seen that there is a "ruling type" which had "become highly superior through selective breeding and social evolution," so that in reality K'n-yan is an aristocracy of intellect where "habit rather than law determin[ed] the daily order of things." There is no mention of socialism, and the notion that a "period of idealistic industrial democracy" had been "passed through" bespeaks Lovecraft's hope against hope that mechanisation could somehow be overcome or tamed in order to leave traditional aesthetics and modes of behaviour relatively unscathed. The fact that in the story this proves not to be the case makes one aware that Lovecraft, for a variety of reasons that I shall explore in the next chapter, had become very pessimistic about the ultimate fate of Western culture.

Rich in intellectual substance as "The Mound" is, it is far longer a work than Lovecraft needed to write for this purpose; and this length bode ill for its publication prospects. *Weird Tales* was on increasingly shaky ground, and Farnsworth

Wright had to be careful what he accepted. It is not at all surprising to hear Love-craft lament in early 1930: "The damned fool has just turned down the story I 'ghost-wrote' for my Kansas City client, on the ground that it was too long for sin-gle publication, yet structurally unadapted to division. I'm not worrying, because I've got my cash; but it does sicken me to watch the caprices of that editorial jack-ass!"[97] Lovecraft does not say how much he got from Bishop for the work; there may be a certain wish-fulfilment here, for as late as 1934 she still owed him a fair amount of money.

The lingering belief that Frank Belknap Long had some hand in the writing of the story—derived from Zealia Bishop's declaration that "Long . . . advised and worked with me on that short novel"[98]—has presumably been squelched by Long's own declaration in 1975 that "I had nothing whatever to do with the writing of *The Mound*. That brooding, somber, and magnificently atmospheric story is Love-craftian from the first page to the last."[99] But since Long does not explain how or why Bishop attributed the work to him (perhaps because he had already forgotten), it may be well to clear up the matter here.

Long was at this time acting as Bishop's agent. He shared Lovecraft's disgust over the tale's rejection: "It was incredibly asinine of him [Wright] to reject The Mound—and on such a flimsy pretext."[100] Long's involvement up to this point had, so far as I can tell, extended only to the degree of typing Lovecraft's handwrit-ten manuscript of the tale, for the typescript seems to come from Long's typewriter (and there are portions of the text that are garbled or incoherent—the presumable result of his inability to read Lovecraft's handwriting in these places). It was now evidently decided (probably by Bishop) to abridge the text in order to make it more salable. Long did this by reducing the initial typescript's 82 pages to 69—not by retyping, but by merely omitting some sheets and scratching out portions of others with a pen. The carbon was kept intact. Long must have made some attempt to market this shortened version (he in fact said so to me), but Lovecraft later ex-pressed scepticism on the point, writing in 1934: "I assumed that Sonny Belknap . . . *had* done so [i.e., tried to market the story]; & am astonished to find that any stone was left unturned."[101] Whatever the case, the story obviously failed to land anywhere, and it was finally first published only in *Weird Tales* for November 1940, and then in a severely abridged form.

In addition to enjoyable revision work like "The Mound," Lovecraft was perform-ing what is likely to have been less congenial revision for his old amateur associate Anne Tillery Renshaw (still teaching at either the high school or college level) and for a new client, Woodburn Harris. Harris (1888–1988) came from Vermont,[102] so may have been referred to Lovecraft by Walter J. Coates; amusingly enough (given Lovecraft's strict teetotallism), among the work Harris was dumping on Lovecraft was the revision of various broadsides urging the repeal of the 18th Amendment![103] But Harris had clearly gone well beyond the client stage. Lovecraft seemed to warm to this rather poorly educated but earnest rustic, for around this time he wrote to him some of the longest letters of his lifetime—including one in late 1929 that begins with the sensible caveat: "*WARNING!* Don't try to read this all at once! I've been gradually writing it for a week, & it comes to just *70 pages*—being, so far as I recall, the longest letter I have written in a lifetime now numbering 39 years, 2 months, & 26 days. *Pax vobiscum!*"[104] (The 70 pages refer to 35 sheets written on both sides.) Only three letters to Harris survive, although there were probably more; one dates to as late as 1935. Very little is known about Woodburn Harris, but if nothing else he inspired some of the most intellectually challenging of Lovecraft's epistles.

One of the things Lovecraft may have done for Anne Tillery Renshaw is an essay entitled "Notes on 'Alias Peter Marchall' by A. F. Lorenz." This undated essay dissects some beginner's story (a melodrama involving the difficulties of two people in achieving true love) and subjects it to searching analysis. In particular, Lovecraft is keen on the would-be author's eliminating elements of "artificiality and stereotyped convention" in his work (an entire litany follows: typical "society" atmosphere; typical adolescent romance; etc.); Lovecraft then concludes:

> The way to get rid of them all is to cast aside the idea of drawing material from one's light fictional reading, and to subject every incident in the tale to the acid test of *what ordinarily happens in actual life.* No author can be ignorant of the prosaic daily life around him. . . . It is from this kind of knowledge, and not from one's recollection of novels and magazine tales, that the material for sound fiction must be drawn.

Much of this sounds like a refinement of Lovecraft's old "Department of Public Criticism" screeds; but now, having himself become a practising fiction writer, he can speak from experience. How he justified his brand of weird fiction when, by necessity, some or much of it cannot be said to constitute "what ordinarily happens in actual life," can be reserved for a later discussion.

Lovecraft's travels for the spring–summer of 1930 began in late April. Charleston, South Carolina, was his goal, and he seems to have shot down to the South with scarcely a stop along the route—not even in New York, if the absence of postcards or letters from there is any indication. He reported being in Richmond on the afternoon of April 27 and spending a night in Winston-Salem, North Carolina. April 28 found him in Columbia, South Carolina, sitting in Capitol Park and, in spite of the fact that the town was "*not colonial* but rather *ante-bellum*," being utterly charmed by the southern atmosphere—even the countryside he saw along the way, which in spite of being "weirdly ugly & repellent" featured villages that were "*inef-*

fably quaint & backward."[105] Of course, he saw these things merely from the window of the bus.

But this was only a foretaste of the real pleasures to come. Later on the 28th Lovecraft caught another bus that took him directly to Charleston. Strangely enough, there are no extant letters to Lillian until May 6; but a postcard written to Derleth on April 29 may give some inkling of Lovecraft's sentiments:

> Revelling in the most marvellously fascinating environment—scenically, architecturally, historically, & climatically—that I've ever encountered in my life! I can't begin to convey any idea of it except by exclamation points—I'd move here in a second if my sentimental attachment to New England were less strong. . . . Will stay here as long as my cash holds out, even if I have to cut all the rest of my contemplated trip.[106]

Lovecraft remained in Charleston until May 9, seeing everything there was to see; and there certainly was much to see. Charleston remains today one of the most well-preserved colonial oases on the eastern seaboard—thanks, of course, to a vigorous restoration and preservation movement that makes it today even more attractive than it was in Lovecraft's day, when some of the colonial remains were in a state of dilapidation. Nearly everything that Lovecraft describes in his lengthy travelogue, "An Account of *Charleston*" (1930), survives, with rare exceptions. As with Providence's "Brick Row," a series of old warehouses along East Bay Street are gone, replaced with a series of children's playgrounds; the Charleston Orphan House (1792) on Calhoun Street has been torn down, the site now occupied by the administration building of the College of Charleston; the site of the Old Quaker Meeting House on King Street (burned in the fire of 1861) is now occupied by the Charleston County Parking Garage (!); and so on. Of more recent sites, the YMCA on George Street, where Lovecraft no doubt stayed, is gone, as is the Timrod Inn on Meeting Street; the Francis Marion Hotel on Marion Square, opened in 1924, was renovated in the 1990s and is now a choice and expensive establishment.

In his travelogue Lovecraft, aside from supplying a detailed history of the town (including digressions on Charleston architecture, gardens, wrought-iron work, and the piquant cries of street vendors, mostly black), lays down a systematic walking tour—which he optimistically states can be covered in a single day (I did so, although it took me about seven hours and several rest-stops)—which covers all the prominent antiquities of Charleston (i.e., houses and structures up to the Civil War) with a minimum of backtracking. The tour leaves out some fairly picturesque sections that are not colonial (the western end of South Battery, for example), as well as outlying areas such as Fort Sumter, Fort Moultrie on Sullivan's Island, the Citadel, and the like, although Lovecraft probably explored these himself. He recognised that the heart of colonial Charleston is the relatively small area south of Broad Street between Legare and East Bay, including such exquisite thoroughfares as Tradd, Church, Water, and the like; the alleys in this section—Bedon's Alley, Stolls Alley, Longitude Lane, St. Michael's Alley—are worth a study all their own. Progressing northward, the section between Broad and Calhoun becomes increasingly post-Revolutionary and antebellum in architecture, although the town's centre of government and business still remains the critical intersection of Broad and Meeting. North of Calhoun there is scarcely anything of antiquarian interest. Needless to say, even in the colonial or semi-colonial areas there have been some invasions of modernity: King Street between Hasell and Broad is now almost entirely made up of antique shops and various yuppie emporia; Meeting Street north of Broad has any number of hotels and inns catering to the tourist trade; and the northern stretches of East Bay are also drearily yuppified. But even the recent Charleston structures are in relative harmony with the colonial atmosphere, and I saw few freakishly modern specimens.

Some of the dates Lovecraft gives in his travelogue for the construction of houses, buildings, and churches are considerably in error, although perhaps this is due to more thorough antiquarian research in the past sixty years. Lovecraft's main guidebook, as mentioned in his travelogue, is *Street Strolls around Charleston, South Carolina* by Miriam Bellangee Wilson (1930), which does not seem an especially authoritative source. Many of the structures cherished by Lovecraft are actually older than he believed, a fact he would certainly have welcomed.

Charleston is very much a southern Providence: the streets may be lined with palmettos, but the houses themselves are almost exactly of the sort to be found on College Hill, and in many places are even more opulent. This fact alone perhaps accounts for part of Lovecraft's fascination with the place—it was new to him, and yet its architecture and general ambiance were of the kind he had known all his life. But there is more to it than that. In Charleston (so Lovecraft, at any rate, liked to believe) there is a *continuity* from the past: the city is not merely a fossilised museum, like Salem or even Newport, but a thriving, bustling centre of commerce and society. Lovecraft stresses this point over and over again in his travelogue:

> . . . Charleston is still Charleston, and the culture we know and respect is not dead there. . . . The original families still hold sway—Rhetts, Izards, Pringles, Bulls, Hugers, Ravenels, Manigaults, Draytons, Stoneys, Rutledges, and so on—and still uphold the basic truths and values of a civilisation which is genuine because it represents a settled adjustment betwixt people and landscape . . . Business is not dehumanised by speed and time-tabling, or denuded of courtesy and leisureliness. Quality, not quantity, is the standard, and there is as yet scant use for the modern fetish of "maximum returns" to be obtain'd even at the sacrifice of everything which makes those returns worth having, or life itself worth preserving. . . . The more one observes of Charleston, the more impress'd is he that he is looking upon the only thoroughly civilised city now remaining in the United States.

If that last sentence seems surprising to one whose fondness for his native city was so ardent, it cannot be attributed merely to Lovecraft's initial enthusiasm of the discovery of so charming a place; he would continue to repeat it in later years, and on every trip to the South he would make sure to spend at least a few days in Charleston, however slim his purse. He wanted to move there, and might have done so if his attachment to the scenes of his childhood were not so great.

On May 9 Lovecraft reluctantly left Charleston and proceeded to Richmond, where he remained for about ten days. In a library he had managed to find Mary C. Phillips's *Edgar Allan Poe, the Man* (1926), which, though overshadowed by Hervey Allen's *Israfel,* had a considerable amount of background information on Poe sites in Richmond. Lovecraft thereupon systematically tracked these down, as well as revisiting the Poe Shrine he had seen the year before.

On the 13th he took an excursion to Petersburg, a town about fifteen miles south of Richmond full of colonial antiquities. Although finding it very provoking that the town was so indifferent to its historic landmarks that it had no guidebook or even a city map, he managed to do much pedestrian exploration, aided by two old men "of considerable information & loquacious bent."[107] He also went on a tour of the site of the Battle of Petersburg (the culmination, on April 2, 1865, of the siege of Petersburg that had begun in mid-June 1864 and which made inevitable the Confederacy's surrender a week later), guided by an eighty-year-old Confederate veteran who had enlisted at the age of fourteen. Returning late in the afternoon to Richmond, he took in a performance of Sheridan's *The Rivals* at the Lyric Theatre. He knew the play so well from memory that he could detect the two cuts made in the original text.

Lovecraft was learning to cut expenses on the road. Wandrei tells us how he saved on cleaning bills away from home: "He neatly laid out his trousers between the mattresses of his bed in order to renew the crease and press overnight. He detached the collar from his shirt, washed it, smoothed it between the folds of a hand towel, and weighted it with the Gideon Bible, thus preparing a fresh collar for the morning."[108] So the Gideon Bible had some use for Lovecraft after all! He was now becoming an amateur self-barber, using a "patent hair-cutter"[109] he had picked up—no doubt a sort of trimmer.

On May 15 Lovecraft stumbled upon Maymont Park in Richmond, which sent him into rhapsodies. Declaring it to be superior even to the exquisite Japanese garden in the Brooklyn Botanical Gardens, and saying that it is "Poe's 'Domain of Arnheim' and 'Island of the Fay' all rolled into one . . . with mine own 'Gardens of Yin' [sonnet XVIII of *Fungi from Yuggoth*] added for good measure,"[110] Lovecraft went on:

> You are no doubt sensible . . . that to me the quality of *utter, perfect beauty* assumes *two* supreme incarnations or adumbrations: one, the sight of mystical city

towers and roofs outlined against a sunset and glimps'd from a fairly distant balus-traded terrace; and the other, the experience of walking (or, as in most of my dreams, aerially floating) thro' aetherial and enchanted gardens of exotick delicacy and opulence, with carved stone bridges, labyrinthine walks, marble fountains, ter-races and staircases, strange pagodas, hillside grottos, curious statues, termini, sun-dials, benches, basins, and lanthorns, lily'd pools of swans and streams with tiers of waterfalls, spreading gingko-trees and drooping feathery willows, and sun-touched flowers of a bizarre, Klarkash-Tonic pattern never beheld on sea or land. . . .

Well, by god, Sir, call me an aged liar or not—I vow *I have actually found the garden of my earliest dreams*—and in no other city than Richmond, home of my beloved Poe!

This makes one think of what Lovecraft had said a few years ago to Donald Wan-drei in justification of his constant and tireless antiquarian travels:

Sometimes I stumble accidentally on rare combinations of slope, curved street-line, roofs & gables & chimneys, & accessory details of verdure & background, which in the magic of late afternoon assume a mystic majesty & exotic significance beyond the power of words to describe. Absolutely nothing else in life now has the power to move me so much; for in these momentary vistas there seem to open before me be-wildering avenues to all the wonders & lovelinesses I have ever sought, & to all those gardens of eld whose memory trembles just beyond the rim of conscious recollection, yet close enough to lend to life all the significance it possesses. All that I live for is to recapture some fragment of this hidden & just unreachable beauty . . .[111]

For a few moments, at least, in Maymont Park Lovecraft had found the garden of his dreams.

In Richmond he did most of the work on another ghost job for Zealia Bishop, although it seems not to have been finished until August.[112] She surely contributed as much (or as little) to this one as to the previous two; but in this case one is more regretful of the fact, for it means that the many flaws and absurdities in the tale must be placed solely or largely at Lovecraft's door. "Medusa's Coil" is as con-fused, bombastic, and just plain silly a work as anything in Lovecraft's entire cor-pus. Like some of his early tales, it is ruined by a woeful excess of supernaturalism that produces complete chaos at the end, as well as a lack of subtlety in characteri-sation that (as in "The Last Test") cripples a tale based fundamentally on a conflict of characters.

The story tells of a young man, Denis de Russy, who falls in love with a myste-rious Frenchwoman, Marceline Bedard, marries her, and brings her back to his family estate in Missouri. It transpires that Marceline is some sort of ancient entity whose hair is animate, and she ultimately brings death and destruction upon all persons concerned—Denis, his father (the narrator of the bulk of the story), the painter Frank Marsh (who tries to warn Denis of the true horror of his wife), and herself. But for Lovecraft, the real climax—the horror that surpasses all the other horrors of the tale—is the revelation that Marceline was, "though in deceitfully slight proportion . . . a negress." As if this fatuous racism were not a bad enough ending, this proves not in fact to be the end—for it is later found that the mansion was destroyed many years ago, forcing the narrator (and the reader) to believe that it had somehow supernaturally reappeared solely to torment the hapless traveller.

The overriding problem with this tale—beyond the luridly pulpish plot—is that the characters are so wooden and stereotyped that they never come to life. Lovecraft well knew that he had both a limited understanding of and limited interest in human beings. He contrived his own fiction such that the human figures were by no means the focus of action; but in a revision—where, presumably, he had to follow at least the skeleton of the plot provided by his client—he was not always able to evade the need for vivid characterisation, and it is precisely those revisions where such characterisation is absent that rank the poorest. Notes for the story survive, which include both a plot outline and a "Manner of Narration" (a synopsis of events in order of narration); and here too it is made clear that the final racist revelation—"woman revealed as vampire, lamia, &c. &c.—& unmistakably (surprise to reader as in original tale) a negress"[113]—is meant to be the culminating horror of the tale. The mention here of an "original tale" may suggest that there was a preexisting draft of some kind by Bishop; but if so, it does not survive.

It is, certainly, not the tale's lack of quality that prevented its publication in a pulp market, for much worse stories were published with great regularity; but for whatever reason (and excessive length may again have had something to do with it), "Medusa's Coil" was rejected by *Weird Tales*. Later in the year Lovecraft discussed with Long the possibility of sending it to *Ghost Stories*,[114] but if it was sent there, it was also rejected. It finally appeared in *Weird Tales* for January 1939. Both "The Mound" and "Medusa's Coil" were heavily altered and rewritten by Derleth for their magazine appearances, and he continued to reprint the adulterated texts in book form up to his death. The corrected texts did not see print until 1989.

Back in New York on May 20, Lovecraft was excited to read one interesting piece of forwarded mail—a letter from Clifton P. Fadiman of Simon & Schuster encouraging Lovecraft to submit a novel.[115] Lovecraft immediately responded by saying that, although he might write a novel later (clearly *The Case of Charles Dexter Ward* was not even considered as a submission), he would like to submit a collection of short stories. A few days later Lovecraft's enthusiasm waned considerably: he discovered that the letter was merely a mimeographed form-letter sent to everyone who had appeared on the "Honor Roll" of the O'Brien short story annuals; moreover, Fadiman had responded by saying: "I am afraid that you are right in that our interest in a collection of short stories would not be very vivid. I hope, however, that you will buckle down & do that novel you speak of. If it is good, its subject matter will be a help rather than a hindrance."[116]

It is interesting to note that mainstream publishers' now inveterate reluctance to publish weird short story collections was already evident in 1930. Very few American weird writers issued collections at this time, and those that were published were usually reprints of British editions by already established authors like Machen, Dunsany, and Blackwood. The weird novel was, however, flourishing after a fashion in the mainstream press: such things as Francis Brett Young's *Cold Harbour* (A. L. Burt, 1925 [British edition 1924]), E. R. Eddison's *The Worm Ouroboros* (Albert & Charles Boni, 1926 [British edition 1922]), Leonard Cline's *Dark Chamber* (Viking, 1927), Herbert Gorman's *The Place Called Dagon* (George H. Doran, 1927), H. B. Drake's *The Shadowy Thing* (Macy-Masius, 1928 [British edition 1925]), and several others were all relished by Lovecraft and most were cited in either the original or the revised version of "Supernatural Horror in Literature." But Lovecraft never did "buckle down" to a novel of this exact kind, and events that occurred about a year later may clarify why.

In New York Lovecraft also saw the newly opened Nicholas Roerich Museum, then located at 103rd Street and Riverside Drive (now at 317 West 107th Street). Roerich (1874–1947) was a Russian painter who had spent several years in Tibet and become a Buddhist. His paintings of the Himalayas are spectacularly cosmic both in their suggestions of the vast bulk of the mountains and in the vivid and distinctive colours used. His work seems largely unrelated to any of the Western art movements of the period, and its closest analogue is perhaps to Russian folk art. Lovecraft, who went with Long to the museum, was transported: "Neither Belknap nor I had ever been in it before; & when we did see the outré & esoteric nature of its contents, we went virtually wild over the imaginative vistas presented. Surely Roerich is one of those rare fantastic souls who have glimpsed the grotesque, terrible secrets outside space & beyond time, & who have retained some ability to hint at the marvels they have seen."[117] Roerich was perhaps not a consciously fantastic artist, but in Lovecraft's mind he took his place with Goya, Gustave Doré, Aubrey Beardsley, S. H. Sime, John Martin (the Romantic painter and illustrator), and (the only questionable selection) Clark Ashton Smith in the gallery of weird art.

Otherwise the two weeks spent in New York included additional museum-going (Metropolitan and Brooklyn) as well as the usual round of catching up on old friendships. One unexpected acquaintance whom Lovecraft met was Hart Crane, who came to Loveman's apartment on the evening of May 24 when Lovecraft was there. *The Bridge* had been published that spring, making him "one of the most celebrated & talked-of figures of contemporary American letters." Lovecraft's portrait of him is simultaneously admiring and pitying:

When he entered, his discourse was of alcoholics in various phases—& of the correct amount of whiskey one ought to drink in order to speak well in public—but as soon as a bit of poetic & philosophic discussion sprang up, this sordid side of his strange dual personality slipped off like a cloak, & left him as a man of great scholarship, intelligence, & aesthetic taste, who can argue as interestingly & profoundly as anyone I have ever seen. Poor devil—he has "arrived" at last as a standard American poet seriously regarded by all reviewers & critics; yet at the very crest of his fame he is on the verge of psychological, physical, & financial disintegration, & with no certainty of ever having the inspiration to write a major work of literature again. After about three hours of acute & intelligent argument poor Crane left—to hunt up a new supply of whiskey & banish reality for the rest of the night![118]

Lovecraft was sadly correct in his prediction, for Crane would commit suicide two years later. Lovecraft goes on to say that "'The Bridge' really is a thing of astonishing merit"; but I find it difficult to imagine him actually enjoying this extraordinarily opaque if imagistically scintillating epic, even with his "new" views on the nature of poetry. He may well have relished those poignant lines about Poe's final days:

> And when they dragged your retching flesh,
> Your trembling hands that night through Baltimore—
> That last night on the ballot rounds, did you,
> Shaking, did you deny the ticket, Poe?[119]

Around June 2 Lovecraft moved up to Kingston to see Bernard Austin Dwyer for a few days; both host and guest spent much time in the open country, which for Lovecraft must surely have presented a welcome contrast to the metropolitan zone. From here Lovecraft proceeded via the Mohawk Trail (where the bus service was now operating) to Athol for a visit with W. Paul Cook and H. Warner Munn. Because of Cook's recent breakdown, Lovecraft stayed with Munn in a five-room apartment at 451 Main Street. They made sure to revisit the Bear's Den as well as some spectral graveyards nearby. A new site was Doane's Falls, a spectacular waterfall northeast of Athol. Lovecraft reported that another issue of the *Recluse* "was partly on the press, though it may not appear for another year";[120] this issue no doubt contained "The Strange High House in the Mist," and of course it never appeared at all.

Lovecraft's return home on June 13 or 14 ended another record-breaking sojourn, but it was by no means the end of his year's travels. In early July he decided to take in the NAPA convention in Boston—only the second national amateur convention he had ever attended, the other being the NAPA convention of 1921. Lovecraft was slowly being drawn back to amateurdom, although it would never be the consuming interest it was in 1914–21. Somehow he managed to persuade himself that the apathy that had killed his UAPA in 1926 was, among the NAPA members, slowly giving way to renewed interest; in his effusive convention report ("The Convention," *Tryout,* July 1930) he wrote: "Not a delegate failed to express his keen enjoyment; everyone carried away a sense of stimulus and renewed activity which can, with proper encouragement and coöperation, be made to accomplish much in amateurdom."

The convention took place on July 3, 4, and 5 at the Hotel Statler, but Lovecraft stayed at the (no doubt cheaper) Technology Chambers near the Back Bay station. Many of his old-time colleagues were there—James F. Morton (who was presiding officer at the business sessions), Edward H. Cole, Albert A. Sandusky, Laurie A. Sawyer, and others. Victor E. Bacon (the last UAPA president) was elected President, and Helm C. Spink, a young man of whom Lovecraft thought highly, was elected Official Editor. Lovecraft did not give any speeches, as he had nine years before, but did participate in a leisurely boat ride up the Charles River on the final day of the convention. A large gathering at Laurie A. Sawyer's house in Allston allowed him to reminisce about old times—perhaps he remembered when he had been there ten years ago, then still a shy, withdrawn recluse scarcely comfortable outside the confines of his own home. How far he had come since then! The next day he took Spink and Edward H. Suhre to Salem and Marblehead, and a little later Spink visited Lovecraft in Providence and went with him on a boat ride to Newport.[121]

In mid-August the Longs invited Lovecraft to stay with them again at Onset on Cape Cod. This time he took the bus to New Bedford, where the Longs picked him up in their car. They had secured a cottage across the street from the one they had occupied the year before; Lovecraft stayed there from the 15th to the 17th before returning home, while the Longs remained for at least two more weeks.

Even this was not the end of Lovecraft's travels. On August 30 we find him boarding a train north—to Quebec. It would be his first and last time out of the United States, aside from two further visits there in later years. Lovecraft had come upon a remarkably cheap $12.00 excursion fare to Quebec, and he could not pass up the chance to see a place of whose antiquarian marvels he had so long heard. The sight of the Canadian countryside—with its quaint old farmhouses built in the French manner and small rustic villages with picturesque church steeples—was pleasing enough, but as he approached the goal on the train he knew he was about to experience something remarkable. And he did:

> Never have I seen another place like it! All my former standards of urban beauty must be abandoned after my sight of Quebec! It hardly belongs to the world of prosaic reality at all—it is a dream of city walls, fortress-crowned cliffs, silver spires, narrow, winding, perpendicular streets, magnificent vistas, & the mellow, leisurely civilisation of an elder world. . . . Horse vehicles still abound, & the atmosphere is altogether of the past. It is a perfectly preserved bit of old royalist France, transplanted to the New World with very little loss of atmosphere.[122]

He stayed only three days, but by keeping constantly on the move saw almost every-thing there was to see—City Hall Square, Montmorency Park, Notre Dame des Victoires, Chateau Frontenac, the Ursuline Convent, and much more. A side trip to the falls of the Montmorency River capped the visit. Returning to Boston, he took an all-day boat trip to Provincetown and back; that Cape Cod town did not impress him, but the fact of being completely out of the sight of land at one point stirred his fancy.

The travels of 1930 had again surpassed their predecessors and were high-lighted by two transcendent sites—Charleston and Quebec. In later years Love-craft returned to both these havens of antiquity as often as his meagre funds would allow. In the meantime he could at least write about them, both in rapturous letters and postcards to his friends and in formal travelogues; and he did just that. "An Account of *Charleston,* in His Maj^ty's Province of *South-Carolina,*" which I have already discussed, is undated, but was probably written in the fall; and this 20,000-word sketch of the history, architecture, and topography of the old town remains one of the best of his travelogues. This essay is not to be confused with the bro-chure mimeographed by H. C. Koenig in 1936 as *Charleston;* for that is nothing more than a long letter to Koenig in which Lovecraft paraphrased and condensed his earlier account, writing it in modern English and leaving out some of the more charmingly idiosyncratic portions. (There is also a four-page manuscript, only re-cently published, entitled "Account of a Visit to Charleston, S.C.," giving Love-craft's first impressions of the city.) "An Account of *Charleston*" was not, evidently, even typed by Lovecraft, and it is unlikely that it ever met any other eye.

But Quebec impelled an even more heroic work. In late October Lovecraft wrote to Morton: ". . . I'm *trying* to devise a *Quebeck* travelogue of some sort, which you shall behold upon its completion";[123] by late December he reports being on page 65, and by mid-January he tells Morton: "Well, Sir, I have the honour to state, that I last Wednesday [January 14] compleated the following work, design'd solely for my own perusal and for the crystallisation of my recollections, in *136* pages of this crabbed cacography . . ."[124] The work in question was:

A DESCRIPTION OF THE
TOWN OF
QUEBECK, IN *New-France,*
Lately added to His *Britannick* Majesty's Dominions.

It was the longest single work he would ever write. After a very comprehensive history of the region, there is a study of Quebec architecture (with appropriate drawings of distinctive features of roofs, windows, and the like), a detailed hand-drawn map of the principal sites, and a detailed walking tour of both the town itself and "suburban pilgrimages." That Lovecraft could have absorbed enough of the town in three days to have written even the travelogue portion (the historical section was clearly learned later through much reading) is a sufficient indication of what those three crowded days must have been like.

The Quebec travelogue also lay in manuscript until long after Lovecraft's death. In spite of Lovecraft's comment to Morton, it is pretty clear that no one other than its author ever saw it during his lifetime, and it was published only in 1976.

But beginning early in the year and continuing all through the spring, summer, and early autumn, Lovecraft was at work on a document that was actually was designed to be read by the general public: "The Whisperer in Darkness." Although this would be among the most difficult in its composition of any of his major stories, this 25,000-word novelette—the longest of his fictions up to that time aside from his two "practice" novels—conjures up the hoary grandeur of the New England countryside even more poignantly than any of his previous works, even if it suffers from some flaws of conception and motivation.

The Vermont floods of November 3, 1927, cause great destruction in the rural parts of the state and also engender reports of strange bodies—not recognisably human or animal—floating down the flood-choked rivers. Albert N. Wilmarth, a professor of literature at Miskatonic University with a side interest in folklore, dismisses these accounts as standard myth-making; but then he hears from a reclusive but evidently learned individual in Vermont, Henry Wentworth Akeley, who not only confirms the reports but maintains that there is an entire colony of extraterrestrials dwelling in the region, whose purpose is to mine a metal they cannot find on their own planet (which may be the recently discovered ninth planet of the solar system, called Yuggoth in various occult writings) and also, by means of a complicated mechanical device, to remove the brains of human beings from their bodies and to take them on fantastic cosmic voyagings. Wilmarth is naturally sceptical of Akeley's tale, but the latter sends him photographs of a hideous black stone with inexplicable hieroglyphs on it along with a phonograph recording he made of some sort of ritual in the woods near his home—a ritual in which both humans and (judging from the highly anomalous buzzing voice) some utterly non-human creatures participated. As their correspondence continues, Wilmarth slowly becomes convinced of the truth of Akeley's claims—and is both wholly convinced and increasingly alarmed as some of their letters go unaccountably astray and Akeley finds himself embroiled in a battle with guns and dogs as the aliens besiege his house. Then, in a startling reversal, Akeley sends him a reassuring letter stating that he has come to terms with the aliens: he had misinterpreted their motives and now believes that they are merely trying to establish a workable rapport with human beings for mutual benefit. He is reconciled to the prospect of his brain being removed and taken to Yuggoth and beyond, for he will thereby acquire cosmic knowledge made available only to a handful of human beings since the beginning of civilisation. He urges Wilmarth to visit him to discuss the matter, reminding him to bring all the papers and other materials he had sent so that they can be consulted if necessary. Wilmarth agrees, taking a spectral journey into the heart of the Vermont backwoods and meeting with Akeley, who has suffered some inexplicable malady: he can only speak in a whisper, and he is wrapped from head to foot with a blanket except for his face and hands. He tells Wilmarth wondrous tales of travelling faster than the speed of light and of the strange machines in the room used to transport brains through the cosmos. Numbed with astonishment, Wilmarth retires to bed, but hears a disturbing colloquy in Akeley's room with several of the buzzing voices and other, human voices. But what makes him flee from the place is a very simple thing he sees as he sneaks down to Akeley's room late at night: "For the things in the chair, perfect to the last, subtle detail of microscopic resemblance—or identity—were the face and hands of Henry Wentworth Akeley."

Without the necessity of stating it, Lovecraft makes clear the true state of affairs: the last, reassuring letter by "Akeley" was in fact a forgery by the alien entities, written as a means of getting Wilmarth to come up to Vermont with all the evidence of his relations with Akeley; the speaker in the chair was not Akeley— whose brain had already been removed from his body and placed in one of the machines—but one of the aliens, perhaps Nyarlathotep himself, whom they worship. The attempted "rapport" which the aliens claim to desire with human beings is a sham, and they in fact wish to enslave the human race; hence Wilmarth must write his account to warn the world of this lurking menace.

The genesis of the tale is nearly as interesting as the tale itself; Steven J. Mariconda has studied the matter in detail, and in large part I am echoing his conclusions.[125] Lovecraft of course knew of the Vermont floods of 1927, as they were extensively reported in newspapers across the East Coast; he wrote to Derleth: "I shall ask Cook to lend me 'Uncanny Tales' if the floods haven't washed it . . . or him . . . away. The current cataclysm centres quite near him, & I haven't had any word in over a week."[126] More generally, the Vermont background of the tale is clearly derived from Lovecraft's visits of 1927 and 1928; indeed, whole passages of "Vermont—A First Impression" have been bodily inserted into the text, but they have been subtly altered in such a way as to emphasise both the terror and the fascination of the rustic landscape. To choose only one example, consider first a passage from the essay and then the corresponding passage from the story:

> The nearness and intimacy of the little domed hills have become almost breathtaking. Their steepness and abruptness hold nothing in common with the humdrum, standardised world we know, and we cannot help feeling that their outlines have some strange and almost-forgotten meaning, like vast hieroglyphs left by a rumoured titan race whose glories live only in rare, deep dreams.

The nearness and intimacy of the dwarfed, domed hills now became veritably breath-taking. Their steepness and abruptness were even greater than I had imagined from hearsay, and suggested nothing in common with the prosaic objective world we know. The dense, unvisited woods on those inaccessible slopes seemed to harbour alien and incredible things, and I felt that the very outline of the hills themselves held some strange and aeon-forgotten meaning, as if they were the vast hieroglyphs left by a rumoured titan race whose glories live only in rare, deep dreams.

Indeed, this very ride into Vermont in a Ford car duplicates the ride Lovecraft took to Orton's farm in 1928: "We were met [in Brattleboro] with a Ford, owned by a neighbour, & hurried out of all earthly reality amongst the vivid hills & mystic winding roads of a land unchanged for a century."[127] It should by now by evident that Henry Wentworth Akeley is based in part on the rustic Bert G. Akley whom Lovecraft met on this trip. In fact, the first time Lovecraft heard of this person, he misspelled his name (in a letter to Lillian) as "Akeley"; in the story Lovecraft echoes this error by having the aliens misspell a forged telegram as "Akely." Akeley's secluded farmhouse seems to be a commingling of the Orton residence in Brattleboro and Goodenough's home farther to the north. There is a mention of "The Pendrifter" (the columnist for the *Brattleboro Reformer*) early in the story, and the later mention of "Lee's Swamp" is a tip of the hat to the Lee boys who were Vrest Orton's neighbours. This tale represents, then, one of the most remarkable fusions of fact and fiction in Lovecraft's entire corpus.

And yet, the actual writing of the tale was very difficult and unusually prolonged. The last page of the autograph manuscript reads: "Begun Providence, R.I., Feby. 24, 1930 / Provisionally finished Charleston, S.C., May 7, 1930 / Polishing completed Providence, R.I., Sept. 26, 1930." What is remarkable about this is that Lovecraft actually took the text with him on his lengthy travels of the spring and summer—something he had, as far as I know, never done before with a work of fiction. On March 14, before his travels began, he wrote to Long: "I am still stall'd on p. 26 of my new Vermont horror."[128] But in a postscript to a letter to Morton written the very next day, Lovecraft writes: "Whatcha thinka the NEW PLANET? HOT STUFF!!! It is probably Yuggoth."[129] This of course refers to Pluto, which C. W. Tombaugh had discovered on January 23 but which was first announced on the front page of the *New York Times* only on March 14. Lovecraft was tremendously captivated by the discovery: ". . . you have no doubt read reports of the discovery of the new trans-Neptunian planet . . . a thing which excites me more than any other happening of recent times. . . . I have always wished I could live to see such a thing come to light—& here it is! The first real planet to be discovered since 1846, & only the *third* in the history of the human race!"[130] (What Lovecraft presumably meant by that last remark is that, aside from Uranus, Neptune, and Pluto, all the planets in the solar system have been known since the dawn of civilisation.) It is evident that the Yuggoth-element could not have been part of the story's initial conception, but was only inserted—quite deftly—at an early stage of composition. Yuggoth, of course, had first been coined by Lovecraft in the *Fungi from Yuggoth;* but the citations there do not absolutely make it clear that it was actually conceived as a planet ("Recognition" [IV]: "But Yuggoth, past the starry voids"; "Star-Winds" [XIV]: "This is the hour when moonstruck poets know / What fungi sprout on Yuggoth"). But Lovecraft's comment in the letter to Morton ("It is probably Yuggoth") perhaps suggests that Yuggoth had already been conceived as the solar system's ninth planet.

But the story underwent significant revisions after it was "provisionally finished" in Charleston. Lovecraft first took it to New York, where he read it to Frank Long. In a 1944 memoir, Long speaks of the matter; although some parts of his account are clearly erroneous, there is perhaps a kernel of truth in his recollection of one point: "Howard's voice becoming suddenly sepulchral: 'And from the box a tortured voice spoke: "Go while there is still time—"'"[131] But then he went up to Kingston to visit Dwyer, and read the story to him as well. Lovecraft thereafter writes to Derleth:

> My "Whisperer in Darkness" has retrogressed to the constructional stage as a result of some extremely sound & penetrating criticism on Dwyer's part. I shall not try to tinker with it during the residue of this trip, but shall make it the first item of work on my programme after I get home—which will no doubt be in less than a week now. There will be considerable condensation throughout, & a great deal of subtilisation at the end.[132]

Lovecraft, of course, did not finish the revision until after his trips to Boston (the NAPA convention), Onset, and Quebec. Nevertheless, it now becomes clear that at least one point on which Dwyer suggested revision is this warning to Akeley (presumably by Akeley's brain from one of the canisters), which is so obvious that it would dilute the purported "surprise" ending of the story (if indeed the story in this version ended as it did). It also appears that Dwyer recommended that Wilmarth be made a rather less gullible figure, but on this point Lovecraft did not make much headway: although random details were apparently inserted to heighten Wilmarth's scepticism, especially in regard to the obviously forged final letter by "Akeley," he still seems very naive in proceeding blithely up to Vermont with all the documentary evidence he has received from Akeley. And yet, Wilmarth exhibits in extreme form something we have seen in many of Lovecraft's characters: the difficulty in believing that a supernatural or supernormal event has occurred. As a professor of literature he immediately detects the alteration in style and tone in "Akeley's" last letter: "Word-choice, spelling—all were subtly different. And with my academic sensitiveness to prose style, I could trace profound divergences in his commonest reactions and rhythm-responses." But he attributes this—not entirely implausibly—to the spectacular alteration in Akeley's consciousness that has resulted from his "rapport" with the aliens.

But "The Whisperer in Darkness" suffers from a somewhat more severe flaw, one that we have already seen in "The Dunwich Horror." Once again, in violation of Lovecraft's stated wish to discard conventional morality in regard to his extraterrestrials, he has endowed his aliens with common—and rather petty—human flaws and motivations. They are guilty of cheap forgery on two occasions—both in that last letter and in an earlier telegram they had sent under Akeley's name to prevent Wilmarth from coming prematurely to Vermont; and on that occasion the aliens were so inept as to misspell Akeley's name, in spite of the fact that, as they themselves maintain, "Their brain-capacity exceeds that of any other surviving lifeform." Their gun-battle with Akeley takes on unintentionally comic overtones, reminiscent of shoot-outs in cheap western movies. When Wilmarth comes to the Akeley farmhouse, they drug his coffee to make him sleep; but he, disliking the taste, does not drink it, hence overhears parts of a colloquy not meant for his ears.

But whereas such flaws of conception and execution cripple "The Dunwich Horror," here they are only minor blemishes in an otherwise magnificent tale. "The Whisperer in Darkness" remains a monument in Lovecraft's work for its throbbingly vital evocation of New England landscape, its air of documentary verisimilitude, its insidiously subtle atmosphere of cumulative horror, and its breathtaking intimations of the cosmic.

The story occupies a sort of middle ground in terms of Lovecraft's portrayal of extraterrestrials. So far we have seen aliens regarded as violent but "beyond good and evil" ("The Call of Cthulhu"), as utterly incomprehensible ("The Colour out of Space"), and as conventionally "evil" ("The Dunwich Horror"); "The Whisperer in Darkness" falls somewhere in between, asking us to express great horror at the aliens' physically outré form and properties (they cannot be photographed by regular cameras), their deceit and trickery, and, preeminently, their plans to remove human brains and take them off the earth in canisters. And yet, on this last point Lovecraft begins to waver a little. Wilmarth, after receiving the forged letter, ruminates: "To shake off the maddening and wearying limitations of time and space and natural law—to be linked with the vast *outside*—to come close to the nighted and abysmal secrets of the infinite and the ultimate—surely such a thing was worth the risk of one's life, soul, and sanity!" Such a thing actually sounds rather appealing; and the utterance exactly parallels Lovecraft's own views as to the function of weird fiction, as expressed in the later essay "Notes on Writing Weird Fiction" (1933): "I choose weird stories because . . . one of my strongest and most persistent wishes [is] to achieve, momentarily, the illusion of some strange suspension or violation of the galling limitations of time, space, and natural law." But Wilmarth cannot sustain his enthusiasm for long. One of the encased brains in Akeley's room (a human being) tells him: "Do you realise what it means when I say I have been on thirty-seven different celestial bodies—planets, dark stars, and less definable objects—including eight outside our galaxy and two outside the curved cosmos of space and time?" This is a powerfully cosmic conception, and again a rather attractive one; but Wilmarth ultimately backs away in horror: "My scientific zeal had vanished amidst fear and loathing . . ."

"The Whisperer in Darkness" resembles "The Colour out of Space" more than "The Dunwich Horror" in its tantalising *hints* of wonders and horrors beyond our ken, especially in such things as the fragmentary transcript of the ritual recorded by Akeley, the almost self-parodic dropping of countless "Mythos" names and terms as contained in one of Akeley's letters, the muffled colloquy heard at the end by Wilmarth (of which he himself remarks that "even their frightful effect on me was one of *suggestion* rather than *revelation*"), and, especially, what the false Akeley tells him about the hidden nature of the cosmos. "Never was a sane man more dangerously close to the arcana of basic entity," Wilmarth states, but then refuses to do more than tease the reader with some of what he learnt:

> I learned whence Cthulhu *first* came, and why half the great temporary stars of history had flared forth. I guessed—from hints which made even my informant pause timidly—the secret behind the Magellanic Clouds and globular nebulae, and the black truth veiled by the immemorial allegory of Tao. . . . I started with loathing when told of the monstrous nuclear chaos beyond angled space which the *Necronomicon* had mercifully cloaked under the name of Azathoth.

If Lovecraft's later followers had exercised such restraint, the "Cthulhu Mythos" would not be quite the travesty it became.

One of the "hints" that Lovecraft never clarified is the possibility that the false Akeley is not merely one of the fungi but is in fact Nyarlathotep himself, whom the aliens worship. The evidence we have comes chiefly from the phonograph recording of the ritual in the woods made by Akeley, in which one of the fungi at one point declares, "To Nyarlathotep, Mighty Messenger, must all things be told. And He shall put on the semblance of men, the waxen mask and the robe that hides, and come down from the world of Seven Suns to mock . . ." This seems a clear allusion to Nyarlathotep disguised with Akeley's face and hands; but if so, it means that at this time actually *is,* in bodily form, one of the fungi—especially if, as seems likely, Nyarlathotep is one of the two buzzing voices Wilmarth overhears at the end (the one who "held an unmistakable note of authority").

And yet, there are problems with this identification. Nyarlathotep has been regarded by some critics as a shapeshifter, but only because he appears in various stories in widely different forms—as an Egyptian pharaoh in the prose-poem of 1920 and *The Dream-Quest of Unknown Kadath,* here as an extraterrestrial entity, as the "Black Man" in "The Dreams in the Witch House" (1932), and so on; his "avatar" appears as a winged entity in "The Haunter of the Dark" (1935). But if Nyarlathotep was a true shapeshifter, why would he have to don the face and hands of Akeley instead of merely reshaping himself as Akeley? It does not appear as if Lovecraft has entirely thought through the role of Nyarlathotep in this story; and, to my mind, Nyarlathotep never gains a coherent personality in the whole of Lovecraft's work. This is not entirely a flaw—certainly Lovecraft wished this figure to retain a certain nebulousness and mystery—but it makes life difficult for those who wish to tidy up after him.

"The Whisperer in Darkness," being the longest story Lovecraft actually bothered to type and submit to a publisher, brought corresponding proceeds. It was readily accepted by Farnsworth Wright, who paid Lovecraft $350.00 for it—the largest check he had ever received and, indeed, ever would receive for a single work of fiction. Wright planned to run it as a two-part serial; but early in 1931 *Weird Tales* was forced into bimonthly publication for about half a year, so that the story appeared complete in the August 1931 issue. The initial plan was to alternate *Weird Tales* with *Oriental Stories,* but by the summer of 1931 *Oriental* had already lapsed into a quarterly (it would change its name to *Magic Carpet* in 1933 and be published for another year) and *Weird Tales* had resumed monthly publication.

This three-year period saw Lovecraft write only two original weird tales (the severely flawed "The Dunwich Horror" and the somewhat flawed but otherwise monumental "The Whisperer in Darkness") along with three revisions for Zealia Bishop: one highly significant ("The Mound"), another fair to middling ("The Curse of Yig"), and one totally forgettable ("Medusa's Coil"). But to measure Lovecraft solely on his weird output would be an injustice both to the man and the writer. His travels to Vermont, Virginia, Charleston, Quebec, and other antiquarian oases provided much imaginative nourishment, and his accounts of his journeys, both in letters and in travel essays, are among his most heartwarming pieces. His correspondence continued to increase as he gained new acquaintances, and their differing views—as well as his constant absorption of new information and new perspectives through books and through observation of the world around him—allowed him considerably to refine his philosophical thought. By 1930 he had resolved many issues to his satisfaction, and in later years only his political and economic views would undergo extensive revision. It is, then, appropriate to examine his thought before proceeding to the examination of the subsequent literary work based upon it.

20. Non-Supernatural Cosmic Art
(1930–1931)

By the early 1930s Lovecraft had resolved many of the philosophical issues that had concerned him in prior years; in particular, he had come to terms with the Einstein theory and managed to incorporate it into what was still a dominantly materialistic system. In so doing, he evolved a system of thought not unlike that of his later philosophical mentors, Bertrand Russell and George Santayana.

It appears that Lovecraft first read both these thinkers between 1927 and 1929. My suspicion is that he discovered Russell through reading the Modern Library edition of the *Selected Papers of Bertrand Russell* (1927), since the first mention I have found of Russell in Lovecraft's letters ("China of the old tradition was probably as great a civilisation as ours—perhaps greater, as Bertrand Russell thinks"[1]) seems to allude to a chapter in the *Selected Papers* entitled "Chinese and Western Civilization Contrasted" (from Russell's *The Problem of China* [1922]). Lovecraft clearly found Russell's reliance on science and his secular ethics to his liking, although Russell was far from being an atheist. In 1927 Russell encapsulated his philosophical outlook in terms Lovecraft would have welcomed: "I still believe that the major processes of the universe proceed according to the laws of physics; that they have no reference to our wishes, and are likely to involve the extinction of life on this planet; that there is no good reason for expecting life after death; and that good and evil are ideas which throw no light upon the nonhuman world."[2]

Santayana is a more difficult problem. Lovecraft advised Elizabeth Toldridge: "Begin with his *Scepticism and Animal Faith,* and then proceed to the five-volume *Life of Reason.*"[3] Did Lovecraft actually read these works? It is probable enough; he must surely have been tickled by Santayana's charming admission in the preface to the former title: "Now in actual philosophy I am a decided materialist— apparently the only one living."[4] But what Lovecraft does not seem to have realised—at least in suggesting that one read *Scepticism and Animal Faith* (1923) prior to *The Life of Reason* (1905–06)—is that the former work is meant as an introduction to a philosophy (embodied in a series of books called *The Realms of Being* [1927–40]) that is designed to supplant, or at least radically to qualify, the latter. In any case, Santayana is a notoriously difficult philosopher—not through any use of the prodigiously technical vocabulary and conceptions of logic and epistemology, as with Wittgenstein, but on account of a cloudy and "poetical" use of philosophical—and even ordinary—language that baffles many readers. As John Passmore remarks: "From volumes with such titles as *The Realm of Essence* and

The Realm of Matter the philosopher is entitled to demand a degree of precision appropriate to the subject matter. This he does not get: 'both in the realm of essence and that of matter,' Santayana confesses, 'I give only some initial hints.' And the hints are certainly dark ones."[5] Still, I think that Lovecraft either borrowed some central aspects of his later thought from Santayana or (and this is entirely conceivable) arrived independently at views strikingly similar to Santayana's.

What Lovecraft had come to realise about the Einstein theory—in particular, its bearing on the three principles of materialism emphasised by Hugh Elliot (the uniformity of law, the denial of teleology, and the denial of substances not envisaged by physics and chemistry)—is that Newtonian laws of physics still work entirely adequately in the immediate universe around us: "The given area *isn't big enough* to let relativity get in its major effects—*hence we can rely on the never-failing laws of earth to give absolutely reliable results in the nearer heavens.*"[6] This allowed Lovecraft to preserve at least the first and third of Elliot's principles. As for the second:

> The actual cosmos of pattern'd energy, including what we know as matter, is of a contour and nature absolutely impossible of realisation by the human brain; and the more we learn of it the more we perceive this circumstance. All we can say of it, is that it contains no visible central principle so like the physical brains of terrestrial mammals that we may reasonably attribute to it the purely terrestrial and biological phaenomenon call'd *conscious purpose;* and that we form, even allowing for the most radical conceptions of the relativist, so insignificant and temporary a part of it (whether all space be infinite or curved, and transgalactic distances constant or variable, we know that within the bounds of our stellar system no relativistic circumstance can banish the approximate dimensions we recognise. The relative place of our solar system among the stars is as much a proximate reality as the relative positions of Providence, N.Y., and Chicago) that all notions of special relationships and names and destinies expressed in human conduct must necessarily be vestigial myths.[7]

This passage reveals how intimately the denial of teleology is, for Lovecraft, connected with the idea of human insignificance: each really entails the other. If human beings are insignificant, there is no reason why some cosmic force (whether we identify it with God or not) should be leading the universe in any given direction for the benefit of humanity; conversely, the evident absence of conscious purpose in the universe at large is one more—and perhaps the most important—indication of the triviality and evanescence of the human species.

Lovecraft was still more emphatic on the third point (denial of spirit):

> The truth is, that the discovery of matter's identity with energy—and of its consequent lack of vital intrinsic difference from empty space—is *an absolute coup de grace to the primitive and irresponsible myth of "spirit". For matter, it appears, really is exactly what "spirit" was always supposed to be.* Thus it is proved *that*

wandering energy always has a detectable form—that if it doesn't take the form of waves or electron-streams, *it becomes matter itself;* and that the absence of matter or any other detectable energy-form indicates *not the presence of spirit, but the absence of anything whatever.*[8]

This entire letter must be read to appreciate Lovecraft's really admirable reconcilation of Einstein and materialism here. I have no doubt that Lovecraft derived much of his data from contemporary literature on the subject—perhaps in the form of magazine or newspaper articles—but the vigour of his writing argues for a reasoned synthesis that is surely his own.

Lovecraft had a little more difficulty with quantum theory, which affects Elliot's first principle, and which Lovecraft seems to have absorbed around this time. Quantum theory asserts that the action of certain sub-atomic particles is inherently random, so that we can only establish statistical averages of how a given reaction will transpire. Lovecraft addresses quantum theory significantly, to my knowledge, only once in his correspondence—in a letter to Long in late 1930: "What most physicists take the quantum theory, at present, to mean, is *not that any cosmic uncertainty exists* as to which of several courses a given reaction will take; but that in certain instances *no conceivable channel of information can ever tell human beings which courses will be taken,* or by what exact course a certain observed result came about."[9] It is clear from this that Lovecraft is merely repeating the views of experts; in fact, he follows the above remark with the statement: "There is room for much discussion on this point, and I can cite some very pertinent articles on the subject if necessary." The point Lovecraft is trying to establish is that the "uncertainty" of quantum theory is not *ontological,* but *epistemological;* that it is only our inability (an inherent inability, not merely some deficiency in our sense-perception or general reasoning capacity) to predict the behaviour of sub-atomic particles that results in uncertainty. Even this admission must have been a difficult one for Lovecraft to make, for it shatters the theoretical possibility—in which most of the nineteenth-century scientists and positivist philosophers had believed—that the human mind can someday absolutely predict the course of Nature if it has enough evidence at its disposal. Nevertheless, this conclusion—although accepted by Einstein in his celebrated dictum "God does not play dice with the cosmos"—appears to be wrong. Bertrand Russell has declared that the "absence of complete determinism is not due to any incompleteness in the theory, but is a genuine characteristic of small-scale occurrences";[10] although he goes on to say that atomic and molecular reactions are still largely deterministic.

And yet, in the late twenties and early thirties quantum theory was hailed as shattering the first of Elliot's materialistic principles—the uniformity of law—just as relativity was thought to have shattered, or at least qualified, the second and third. We now know—insofar as we really know the ultimate ramifications of quantum theory—that the uniformity of law is itself only qualified, and perhaps not even in a way that has any philosophical significance. The relation between quantum theory and, say, the possibility of free will is anything but clear, and there is as yet no reason to carry the effects of quantum theory into the behaviour of macrocosmic phenomena.

Some of the most bracing pages in Lovecraft's letters of this period deal with his emphatic assertion of atheism against those of his colleagues (especially Frank Long) who felt that the "uncertainty" revealed by modern astrophysics left room for the recrudescence of conventional religious belief. Lovecraft was well aware that he was living in a time of both social and intellectual ferment; but he had nothing but contempt for those thinkers who were using the relativity and quantum theories to resurrect old-time belief:

> Although these new turns of science don't really mean a thing in relation to the myth of cosmic consciousness and teleology, a new brood of despairing and horrified moderns is seizing on the doubt of all positive knowledge which they imply; and is deducing therefrom that, *since nothing is true,* therefore *anything can be true* . . . whence one may invent or revive any sort of mythology that fancy or nostalgia or desperation may dictate, and defy anyone to prove that it isn't "emotionally" true—whatever that means. This sickly, decadent neomysticism—a protest not only against machine materialism but against pure science with its destruction of the mystery and dignity of human emotion and experience—will be the dominant creed of middle twentieth centuries aesthetes . . . Little Belknap is already falling for it.[11]

He went on to note the various "plans of escape" that various thinkers have evolved: "[Ralph Adams] Cram favours mediaevalism and the ivory tower, [Joseph Wood] Krutch the grim and gritted bicuspids, [Henry] Adams the resigned superiority of contemplation, [John Crowe] Ransom the return to the older spirit where it *can* be saved, Eliot the wholesale readoption of tradition—blindly, desperately undertaken in a mad escape from the Waste Land he so terribly depicted," and the like. But "still more tragic are the ostrich-heads who shut off their reason altogether at a certain point—beyond which they prattle in the artificial twilight of a pretended mental infancy . . . G. K. Chesterton with his synthetic popery, Prof. [Arthur] Eddington with his observation-contradicting slush, Dr. Henri Bergson with his popular metaphysical pap, and so on, and so on."

And in order that "Little Belknap" not fall for this—Long was apparently toying with some sort of aesthetic belief in Catholicism at the time—Lovecraft writes him a devastating response in late 1930. "Get this straight—*for there is no other road to probability*," begins his screed.[12] All that the new uncertainties of science have produced, philosophically, is a situation wherein any religious explanation of the universe "has an *equal theoretical chance* with any other orthodoxy or with any theory of science of being true"; but "*it most positively has no greater chance* than has ANY RANDOM SYSTEM OF FICTION, DEVISED CAPRICIOUS-LY BY IGNORANCE, DISEASE, WHIM, ACCIDENT, EMOTION, GREED, OR ANY OTHER AGENCY INCLUDING CONSCIOUS MENDACITY, HALLUCINATION, POLITICAL OR SOCIAL INTER-EST, AND ULTERIOR CONSIDERATIONS IN GENERAL." What we must do is to assemble

> *all the tentative data of 1930, and forming a fresh chain of partial indications based exclusively on that data and on no conceptions derived from earlier arrays of data;* meanwhile testing, by the psychological knowledge of 1930, the workings and in-clinations of our minds in accepting, correlating, and making deductions from data, *and most particularly weeding out all tendencies to give more than equal con-sideration to conceptions which would never have occurred to us had we not for-merly harboured ideas of the universe now conclusively known to be false.*

What result does this yield? We now see that "the actual visual and mathematical evidence of 1930 does not suggest anything very strikingly different in its general probabilities . . . from the automatick and impersonal cosmos envisaged at an ear-lier period, which was as a negligible, purposeless, accidental, and ephemeral atom fortuitously occurring amidst the kaleidoscopic pattern-seething . . ."

The critical question then becomes: Why do religious beliefs remain even among highly intelligent individuals, even when the evidence of 1930 renders them overwhelmingly unlikely?

> Chief of all is the fact that the generation of men now in the saddle is old enough to have been mentally crippled by early pro-mythological bias in conventional homes. Their emotions are permanently distorted—trained to think the unreal real, and ea-ger to grasp at any excuse for belief. They resent the cold probabilities of the cos-mos because they have been taught to expect fairy-tale values and adjustments—hence as soon as any uncertainty appears in positive knowledge, they catch avidly at the loophole as an excuse to revive their comfortingly familiar superstitions. Sec-ond—many persons attribute the present bewildering changes in the social and cul-tural order to the decline of theistic belief, hence snatch at any chance to bolster up a placid and stabilising mythology—whether or not they inwardly believe it. Third—some persons think habitually in terms of vague, grandiose, and superficial emo-tions, hence find it difficult to envisage the impersonal cosmos as it is. Any system seems actually improbable to them which does not satisfy their false sense of impor-tance, their artificial set of purpose-values, and their pseudo-wonder springing from an arbitrary and unreal standard of norms and causations.

This analysis seems to me entirely accurate, and much of it is of relevance to the present day. Lovecraft still believed that conventional religion was doomed, once a new generation of individuals not mentally crippled by youthful indoctrination into religion arises. He came to see this indoctrination as one of the greatest evils that religion produces:

> We all know that *any* emotional bias—irrespective of truth or falsity—can be implanted by suggestion in the emotions of the young, hence the inherited traditions of an orthodox community are absolutely without evidential value regarding the real "is-or-isn'tness" of things. . . . If religion were true, its followers would not try to bludgeon their young into an artificial conformity; but would merely insist on their unbending quest for *truth,* irrespective of artificial backgrounds or practical consequences. With such an honest and inflexible *openness to evidence,* they could not fail to receive any *real truth* which might be manifesting itself around them. The fact that religionists do *not* follow this honourable course, but cheat at their game by invoking juvenile quasi-hypnosis, is enough to destroy their pretentions in my eyes even if their absurdity were not manifest in every other direction.[13]

This last diatribe was directed at Maurice W. Moe, who could not have been very pleased with it; his orthodoxy had caused Lovecraft to unearth such barbs since at least 1918. Neither individual apparently affected the other's views much, nor was their friendship in any way affected by their differing stances.

Lovecraft's later ethics is in many ways a direct outgrowth of his metaphysics, and it is also intimately connected with his evolving social and political views. The question for Lovecraft was: how to conduct oneself with the realisation that the human race was an insignificant atom in the vast realms of the cosmos? One solution was to adopt the perspective of a sort of bland cosmic spectator upon the human race. As he writes to Morton in late 1929:

> Contrary to what you may assume, I am *not a pessimist* but an *indifferentist*—that is, I don't make the mistake of thinking that the resultant of the natural forces surrounding and governing organic life will have any connexion with the wishes or tastes of any part of that organic life-process. Pessimists are just as illogical as optimists; insomuch as both envisage the aims of mankind as unified, and as having a direct relationship (either of frustration or of fulfilment) to the inevitable flow of terrestrial motivation and events. That is—both schools retain in a vestigial way the primitive concept of a conscious teleology—of a cosmos which gives a damn one way or the other about the especial wants and ultimate welfare of mosquitoes, rats, lice, dogs, men, horses, pterodactyls, trees, fungi, dodos, or other forms of biological energy.[14]

This is very piquant and even true to a point: cosmicism as a metaphysical principle could plausibly be said to entail indifferentism as an abstract ethical corollary. But this is not a very useful yardstick for actual behaviour, and Lovecraft had to devise some system of conduct, at least for himself, that might be consistent with cosmicism. It is only at this time that he came to espouse an aesthetic retention of *tradi-*

tion as a bulwark against the potential nihilism of his metaphysics. This view had no doubt been evolving unconsciously for many years, but it becomes explicit only now; but in so doing, Lovecraft left himself open to criticism at several points.

Throughout his life Lovecraft wavered between (validly) recommending tradition *for himself* and (invalidly) recommending it *for everyone.* In 1928 he had properly asserted the relativity of values (the only thing possible in a universe that has no governing deity): "Value is wholly relative, and the very idea of such a thing as meaning postulates a symmetrical relation to something else. No one thing, cosmically speaking, can be either good or evil, beautiful or unbeautiful; for entity is simply entity."[15] To Derleth in 1930 he wrote: "Each person lives in his own world of values, and can obviously (except for a few generalities based on essential similarities in human nature) speak only for himself when he calls this thing 'silly and irrelevant' and that thing 'vital and significant', as the case may be. We are all meaningless atoms adrift in the void."[16]

All this is unexceptionable, and yet it gradually gives way to a much less defensible view: that, given the relativity of values, the only true anchor of fixity is tradition—specifically the racial and cultural tradition out of which each person grows. The matter crops up in a discussion with Morton, who appears to have questioned why Lovecraft was so passionately concerned about the preservation of Western civilisation when he believed in a purposeless cosmos:

> It is *because* the cosmos is meaningless that we must secure our individual illusions of values, direction, and interest by upholding the artificial streams which gave us such worlds of salutary illusion. That is—since nothing means anything in itself, we must preserve the proximate and arbitrary background which makes things around us seem as if they did mean something. In other words, we are either Englishmen or nothing whatever.[17]

That "we" is very ominous. Lovecraft seems unaware that it is only in those, like himself, in whom the sense of tradition has been strongly ingrained who will clutch at tradition—racial, cultural, political, and aesthetic—as the only bulwark against nihilism. Occasionally Lovecraft does realise that it is only he and people like him are who are affected: "I follow this acceptance [of traditional folkways] purely for my own personal pleasure—because I would feel lost in a limitless and impersonal cosmos if I had no way of thinking of myself but as a dissociated and independent point."[18] But this view is not consistent in Lovecraft, and he often lapsed into the paradox of offering an absolutist ethic of his own while at the same time scorning others for so doing:

> In a cosmos without absolute values we have to rely on the relative values affecting our daily sense of comfort, pleasure, & emotional satisfaction. What gives us relative painlessness & contentment we may arbitrarily call "good", & vice versa. This local nomenclature is necessary to give us that benign illusion of placement, direc-

tion, & stable background on which the still more important illusions of "worth-whileness", dramatic significance in events, & interest in life depend. Now what gives one person or race or age relative painlessness & contentment often disagrees sharply on the psychological side from what gives these same boons to another person or race or age. Therefore "good" is a relative & variable quality, depending on ancestry, chronology, geography, nationality, & individual temperament. Amidst this variability there is *only one anchor of fixity* which we can seize upon as the working pseudo-standard of "values" which we need in order to feel settled & contented—& that anchor is *tradition,* the potent emotional legacy bequeathed to us by the massed experience of our ancestors, individual or national or biological or cultural. Tradition means nothing cosmically, but it means everything locally & pragmatically because we have nothing else to shield us from a devastating sense of "lostness" in endless time & space.[19]

The curious thing, also, is that Lovecraft was aware of the degree to which he had departed intellectually from many of the prevailing beliefs of his tradition-stream by his atheism, his moral relativism, his scorn of democracy, and perhaps even in his taste for weird fiction, none of which were at all common to the Anglo-American culture to which he wished to associate himself: "One does not have to take these traditions seriously, in an intellectual way, and one may even laugh at their points of naiveté and delusion—as indeed I laugh at the piety, narrowness, and conventionality of the New England background which I love so well and find so necessary to contentment."[20]

It should now be clear why Lovecraft not only clung to tradition so firmly but why he so ardently sought to preserve his civilisation against onslaughts from all sides—from foreigners, from the rising tide of mechanisation, and even from radical aesthetic movements. In 1931 he was still arguing for the biological inferiority of blacks ("The black *is* vastly inferior. There can be no question of this among contemporary and unsentimental biologists—eminent Europeans for whom the prejudice-problem does not exist"[21]); but gradually his views were shifting toward a belief in the radical *cultural* incompatibility of various races, ethnic or cultural groups, and even nationalities. He actually admitted in 1929 that "the French have a profounder culture than we have,"[22] and later admired the tenacity with which the citizens of Quebec retained their French folkways; but he nevertheless believed that the French and the English should be kept apart in order that each could preserve its own proper heritage. I do not wish to discuss Lovecraft's racial views at this juncture save to indicate that he still believed that even a small amount of mingling between different groups would weaken those bonds of tradition which he felt to be our only bulwark against cosmic meaninglessness.

But as the 1920s progressed, Lovecraft began to sense a much greater foe to tradition: the machine culture. His views on the subject are by no means original to him and can be found in many thinkers of the period; but his remarks are both incisive and compelling. What Lovecraft was coming to believe was that the present age no longer represented a continuation of "American civilisation" in any sense:

> It is "American" only in a geographic sense, & is not a "civilisation" at all except according to the Spenglerian definition of the word. It is a wholly alien & wholly puerile barbarism; based on physical comfort instead of mental excellence, & having no claim to the consideration of real colonial Americans. Of course, like other barbarisms, it may some day give birth to a culture—but that culture will not be ours, & it is natural for us to fight its incursions over territory which we wish to preserve for our own culture.[23]

Later in the same letter Lovecraft painted a picture of the future:

> The social-political future of the United States is one of domination by vast economic interests devoted to ideals of material gain, aimless activity, & physical comfort—interests controlled by shrewd, insensitive, & not often well-bred leaders recruited from the standardised herd through a competition of hard wit & practical craftiness—a struggle for place & power which will eliminate the true & the beautiful as goals, & substitute the strong, the huge, & the mechanically effective.

We have already seen views like this espoused in "The Mound"; and later works of fiction will also ruminate on the idea.

Two books powerfully affected Lovecraft's thinking on these matters, although he could say with justice that he had arrived at least nebulously at the same fundamental conceptions prior to reading them. They were Oswald Spengler's *The Decline of the West* (*Der Untergang des Abendlandes* [1918–22]; translated in two volumes in 1926 and 1928) and Joseph Wood Krutch's *The Modern Temper* (1929). Lovecraft read the first volume of Spengler (he never read the second, so far as I can tell) in the spring of 1927,[24] and seems to have read Krutch no later than the fall of 1929.[25]

Lovecraft had long been inclined to accept Spengler's basic thesis of the successive rise and fall of civilisations as each passes through a period of youth, adulthood, and old age. He later expressed reservations, as many others did, on the degree to which this biological analogy could be pressed; but as early as 1921, in the *In Defence of Dagon* essays, he was saying: "No civilisation has lasted for ever, and perhaps our own is perishing of natural old age. If so, the end cannot well be deferred." Here he went on to hold out a possibility that "we may be merely passing from youth to maturity—a period of more realistic and sophisticated life may lie ahead of us," but even this frail optimism disappears by the later 1920s. In early 1929 Lovecraft gave his dissection of the causes for America's decline:

> Real America had the start of a splendid civilisation—the British stream, enriched by a geographical setting well-calculated to develop a vital, adventurous, and imaginatively fertile existence. . . . What destroyed it as the dominant culture of

this continent? Well—first came the poison of social democracy, which gradually introduced the notion of diffused rather than intensive development. Idealists wanted to raise the level of the ground by tearing down all the towers and strewing them over the surface—and when it was done they wondered why the ground didn't seem much higher, after all. And they had lost their towers! Then came the premature shifting of the economic centre of gravity to the relatively immature west; which brought western crudeness, "push", and quantity-feeling to the fore, and accelerated the evils of democracy. Sudden financial overturns and the rise of a loathsome parvenu class—natural things in a rapidly expanding nation—helped on the disaster, whilst worst of all was the rashly and idealistically admitted flood of alien, degenerate, and unassimilable immigrants—the supreme calamity of the western world. On this dangerous and unstable cultural chaos finally fell the curse of the machine age—a condition peculiarly adapted to favour the crude and imaginationless and to operate against the sensitive and the civilised. Its first re-sults we behold today, though the depths of its cultural darkness are reserved for the torture of later generations.[26]

Democracy, quantity and money over quality, foreigners, and mechanisation—these are the causes of America's ruination. In all honesty, I am not at all inclined to dis-pute Lovecraft on the first, second, or fourth of these. In this same letter he elabo-rated upon his precise complaints about democracy, especially the mass democracy of his day. What he found offensive in it was its hostility to excellence. Given that *"the maintenance of [a] high cultural standard is the only social or political enthusi-asm I possess."* the answer to him seemed (at least in principle) simple: establish, or recognise, an aristocracy of culture that will foster artistic excellence:

Nobody really gives a hang about existing aristocratic families *as such.* All that is desired is *to maintain the existing standards of thought, aesthetics, and manners,* and not to allow them to sink to low levels through the dominance of coarsely-organised, sordid-minded, and aesthetically insensitive people who are satisfied with less and who would establish a national atmosphere intolerable to those civi-lised persons who require more.

It would only be a few years later that Lovecraft would see the full extent of the prob-lem—the conspiracy of democracy and capitalism that produced "mass culture" and made artistic excellence less and less economically feasible—and it would also take him some years to evolve at least a theoretical model for the reversal of this situation.

Lovecraft's political concerns were at this time still in the realm of theory rather than in the politics of the moment. As late as 1928 he was still admitting that "my real *interest* in politics is virtually nil."[27] To Aunt Lillian he had expressed congratulations on the election of Coolidge in 1924,[28] then never mentioned him or any political event for the next four years. He admitted to supporting Hoover in 1928,[29] although I suspect this may have been largely because the Democratic candidate, Alfred E. Smith, vehemently opposed Prohibition (which Lovecraft still generally supported, although he was clearly aware of the difficulties in its enforcement) and also advocated modifying the restrictive alien immigration laws passed earlier in the decade.

Lovecraft has been criticised for not taking any notice of the stock market crash of October 1929, but the full effects of the depression were not manifest for several years; Lovecraft's own revision service did not seem to suffer significantly as a result of the crash (not that it was ever a flourishing business), and in any case he had seen at first hand the hardships of unemployment in New York during the supposedly booming 1920s. And yet, the inclusion of extensive, and rather gloomy, political reflections in "The Mound" in late 1929 can hardly be accidental.

In terms of aesthetics, Lovecraft's abandonment of Decadence and his nearly wholesale rejection of Modernism allowed him to revert to a sort of refined eighteenth-century view of art as an elegant amusement. Indeed, he had casually used exactly that phrase in a letter to Elizabeth Toldridge, and in her Victorian way she had expressed surprise and disagreement; so that Lovecraft was forced to add some nuance to this stance:

> I wished to make it clear that the fun and function of poetry are all comprised within the process of creating it, and that it is needless and unwise to worry about what happens to it once it is written. Its importance resides in the pleasure it gives you during the writing—the mental and emotional satisfaction of self-expression. Once it has given you this, it has fully and adequately performed its function; and there is no need to bother about who else sees it . . .[30]

This is similar to the views anent "self-expression" found in the *In Defence of Dagon* papers; now Lovecraft develops the argument by bringing in modern developments in biology, and in this way hopes to fashion a means for distinguishing true art from hackwork:

> In stern fact, the relentless demands prompted by our glandular and nervous reactions are exceedingly complex, contradictory, and imperious in their nature; and subject to rigid and intricate laws of psychology, physiology, biochemistry, and physics which must be realistically studied and familiarly known before they can be adequately dealt with. . . . False or insincere amusement is the sort of activity which does not meet the real psychological demands of the human glandular-nervous system, but merely affects to do so. Real amusement is the sort which is based on a knowledge of real needs, and which therefore hits the spot. *This latter kind of amusement is what art is*—and there is nothing more important in the universe.

The crux of this passage rests upon the then-recent discovery of the importance of glands in affecting human behaviour. In making this discovery, however, many biologists and philosophers vastly overstated the case. Louis Berman's *The Glands Regulating Personality* (1921)—a book recommended by Lovecraft in "Suggestions for a Reading Guide" (1936)—is typical: focusing on the endocrine glands (chiefly the adrenal, thyroid, and pituitary), Berman maintained that they control, and perhaps even cause, all the emotions as well as the imagination and intellect:

> The internal secretions constitute and determine much of the inherited powers of the individual and their development. They control physical and mental growth and all the metabolic processes of fundamental importance. They dominate all the vital functions during the three cycles of life. They coöperate in an intimate relationship which may be compared to an interlocking directorate. A derangement of their function, causing an insufficiency of them, an excess, or an abnormality, upsets the entire equilibrium of the body, with transforming effects upon the mind and the organs. In short, they control human nature, and whoever controls them, controls human nature.[31]

Let it pass that Berman's argument is in part eugenicist and even racist (he claims that the Caucasian has a greater number of internal gland secretions and is therefore superior to the Mongoloid or the Negro); even in less extreme form his views were highly representative. Modern endocrinologists are much more reserved in their views: glandular secretions (hormones) are clearly of great importance to growth and sexual development, but the interrelation between glands, the central nervous system, and the mind and emotions is still much debated.

This emphasis on glandular "control" of emotion and intellect was, however, very useful to Lovecraft, in that it emphasised his long-standing belief in man as a "machine" who is at the mercy of forces beyond his control; his cautious embracing of Freud pointed in much the same direction. In his aesthetics Lovecraft then used this conception as a sort of objective way of distinguishing good art from bad; but what is left unclear is how anyone is to know except by some sort of introspection whether a given work of art has "hit the spot" (satisfied the "demands prompted by our glandular and nervous reactions") or merely affected to do so.

Another phase of Lovecraft's theory of art grew out of his notions of sense-perception. Being forcefully made aware from modern psychology that each person's comprehension of the external world is at least slightly, and in some cases significantly, different from every other person's (the differences depending upon heredity, upbringing, education, and all the other biological and cultural factors that distinguish each of us as human beings), Lovecraft came to believe that

> good art means the ability of any one man to pin down in some permanent and intelligible medium a sort of idea of what he sees in Nature that nobody else sees. In other words, to make the other fellow grasp, through skilled selective care in interpretative reproduction or symbolism, some inkling of what only the artist himself could possibly see in the actual objective scene itself.[32]

The end result—and this is a dim reflection of Oscar Wilde's clever paradox that we see "more" of Nature in a painting of Turner's than in the natural scene itself—

is that *"We see and feel more in Nature from having assimilated works of authentic art";* and so, "The constant discovery of different peoples' subjective impressions of things, as contained in genuine art, forms a slow, gradual approach, or faint approximation of an approach, to *the mystic substance of absolute reality itself*—the stark, cosmic reality which lurks behind our varying subjective perceptions." All this sounds a trifle abstract, and we have already seen an adumbration of it in the story "Hypnos" (1922).

Lovecraft's reading of Krutch's *The Modern Temper* brought him down from these abstractions and made him face the situation of art and culture in the modern world. Krutch's book is a lugubrious but chillingly compelling work that particularly addresses itself to the question of what intellectual and aesthetic possibilities remain in an age in which so many illusions—in particular the illusions of our importance in the cosmos and of the "sanctity" or even validity of our emotional life—have been shattered by science. This is a theme on which Lovecraft had been expatiating since at least 1922, with "Lord Dunsany and His Work." Indeed, I believe Krutch's work was instrumental in helping Lovecraft to evolve his aesthetics to a new level. He had already passed from classicism to Decadence to a sort of antiquarian regionalism. But he was no ostrich: he knew that the past—that is, prior modes of behaviour, thought, and aesthetic expression—could be preserved only up to a point. The new realities revealed by modern science had to be faced. Around this time he began some further ruminations on art and its place in society, in particular weird art; and in so doing he produced a radical change in his theory of weird fiction that would affect much of what he would subsequently write.

Frank Long was again, somehow, the catalyst for the expression of these views. Evidently Long was lamenting the rapid rate of cultural change and was advocating a return to "splendid and traditional ways of life"—a view Lovecraft rightly regarded as somewhat sophomoric in someone who did not know much about what these traditional ways actually were. In an immense letter written in late February 1931, Lovecraft began by repeating Krutch's argument that much of prior literature had ceased to be vital to us because we could no longer share, and in some cases could only remotely understand, the values that produced it; he then wrote: "Some former art attitudes—like sentimental romance, loud heroics, ethical didacticism, &c.—are so patently hollow as to be visibly absurd & non-usable from the start." Some attitudes, however, may still be viable:

> Fantastic literature cannot be treated as a single unit, because it is a composite resting on widely divergent bases. I really agree that "Yog-Sothoth" is a basically immature conception, & unfitted for really serious literature. The fact is, I have never approached serious literature as yet. . . . The only permanently artistic use of Yog-Sothothery, I think, is in symbolic or assocative phantasy of the frankly poetic type; in which fixed dream-patterns of the natural organism are given an embodiment &

crystallisation. The reasonable permanence of this phase of poetic phantasy as a *possible* art form (whether or not favoured by current fashion) seems to me a highly strong probability.

I do not know what exactly Lovecraft means by "Yog-Sothothery" here. My feeling is that it may refer to Dunsany's prodigal invention of gods in *The Gods of Pegāna,* which we have already seen Lovecraft to have repudiated as far as his own creative expression is concerned; indeed, he said here of this type of material that "I hardly expect to produce anything even remotely approaching it myself." He continued:

> But there is another phase of cosmic phantasy (which may or may not include frank Yog-Sothothery) whose foundations appear to me as better grounded than those of ordinary oneiroscopy; personal limitation regarding the *sense of outsideness.* I refer to the aesthetic crystallisation of that burning & inextinguishable feeling of mixed wonder & oppression which the sensitive imagination experiences upon scaling itself & its restrictions against the vast & provocative abyss of the unknown. This has always been the chief emotion in my psychology; & whilst it obviously figures less in the psychology of the majority, it is clearly a well-defined & permanent factor from which very few sensitive persons are wholly free.

That last remark may be a little sanguine, but let it pass. We are now getting more to the crux of the matter: Lovecraft was beginning to provide a rationale for the type of weird fiction he had been writing for the past few years, which was a fundamentally realistic approach to the "sense of outsideness" by the suggestion of the vast gulfs of space and time—in short, cosmicism. At this moment there was nothing here that was different from prior utterances of this idea, but Lovecraft was now keen on establishing that the relativity theory had no bearing on the matter:

> Reason as we may, we cannot destroy a normal perception of the highly limited & fragmentary nature of our visible world of perception & experience as scaled against the outside abyss of unthinkable galaxies & unplumbed dimensions—an abyss wherein our solar system is the merest dot (by the same *local* principle that makes a sand-grain a dot as compared with the whole planet earth) *no matter what relativistic system we may use in conceiving the cosmos as a whole . . .*

Lovecraft went on to say that "A great part of religion is merely a childish & diluted pseudo-gratification of this perpetual gnawing toward the ultimate illimitable void"; but sensible people can no longer use religion for this purpose, so what is left?

> The time has come when the normal revolt against time, space, & matter must assume a form not overtly incompatible with what is known of reality—when it must be gratified by images forming *supplements* rather than *contradictions* of the visible & mensurable universe. And what, if not a form of *non-supernatural cosmic art,* is to pacify this sense of revolt—as well as gratify the cognate sense of curiosity?[33]

This may be the most important theoretical utterance Lovecraft ever made: the renunciation of the supernatural, as well as the need to offer supplements rather than contradictions to known phenomena, make it clear that Lovecraft was now consciously moving toward a union of weird fiction and science fiction (although perhaps not the science fiction largely published in the pulp magazines of this time). Indeed, in formal terms nearly all his work subsequent to "The Call of Cthulhu" *is* science fiction, if by that we mean that it supplies a *scientific justification* (although in some cases a justification based upon some hypothetical advance of science) for the purportedly "supernatural" events; it is only in his manifest wish to *terrify* that his work remains on the borderline of science fiction rather than being wholly within its domain.

Lovecraft's work had been inexorably moving in this direction since at least the writing of "The Shunned House." Even in much earlier tales—"Dagon" (1917), "Beyond the Wall of Sleep" (1919), "The Temple" (1920), "Arthur Jermyn" (1920), "From Beyond" (1920), "The Nameless City" (1921), and even perhaps "Herbert West—Reanimator" (1921–22)—he had already provided pseudo-scientific rationales for weird events, and such things as *At the Mountains of Madness* (1931) and "The Shadow out of Time" (1934–35) are only the pinnacles in this development. Pure supernaturalism had, in fact—aside from such minor works as "The Moon-Bog" (1921)—*never* been much utilised by Lovecraft.

What, then, do we make of a statement uttered less than a year after the one I have quoted above? ". . . the crux of a *weird* tale is something which *could not possibly happen*."[34] Here, certainly, "something which could not possibly happen" must be regarded as supernatural. But the context of this utterance must be examined with care. It was made in the course of a discussion with August Derleth regarding William Faulkner's "A Rose for Emily," that masterful story of necrophilia; it was included in Dashiell Hammett's *Creeps by Night* (1931), a very diverse anthology that also contained "The Music of Erich Zann." Lovecraft, while admiring Faulkner's tale, was maintaining that it was not "weird" because necrophilia is a mundane horror that does not involve the contravention of natural law *as we know it.* The letter continues:

> If any unexpected advance of physics, chemistry, or biology were to indicate the *possibility* of any phenomena related by the weird tale, that particular set of phenomena would cease to be *weird* in the ultimate sense because it would become surrounded by a different set of emotions. It would no longer represent imaginative liberation, because it would no longer indicate a suspension or violation of the natural laws against whose universal dominance our fancies rebel.

Lovecraft is carving out a very special position for his type of weird tale: it can neither be a mere *conte cruel* or a tale of physical gruesomeness (what is now termed "psychological suspense"), nor can it plainly violate *currently known* natural laws, as in standard supernatural fiction. Only the intermediate ground—"non-supernatural cosmic art," art that presents accounts of phenomena not currently explainable by science—can offer possibilities for creative expression in this field, at least for Lovecraft.

At the Mountains of Madness, written in early 1931 (the autograph manuscript declares it to have been begun on February 24 and completed on March 22), is Lovecraft's most ambitious attempt at "non-supernatural cosmic art"; it is a triumph in every way. At 40,000 words it is his longest work of fiction save *The Case of Charles Dexter Ward;* and just as his other two novels represent apotheoses of earlier phases of his career—*The Dream-Quest of Unknown Kadath* the culmination of Dunsanianism, *Ward* the pinnacle of pure supernaturalism—so is *At the Mountains of Madness* the greatest of his attempts to fuse weird fiction and science fiction.

The Miskatonic Antarctic Expedition of 1930–31, led by William Dyer (his full name is never supplied here but is given in "The Shadow out of Time"), begins very promisingly but ends in tragedy and horror. Spurred by a new boring device invented by engineer Frank H. Pabodie, the expedition makes great progress at sites on the shore of McMurdo Sound (on the opposite side of the Ross Ice Shelf from where Byrd's expedition had only recently camped). But the biologist Lake, struck by some peculiar markings on soapstone fragments he has found, feels the need to conduct a sub-expedition far to the northwest. There he makes a spectacular discovery: not only the world's tallest mountains ("Everest out of the running," he laconically radios back to the camp), but then the frozen remains—some damaged, some intact—of monstrous barrel-shaped creatures that cannot be reconciled with the known evolution of this planet. They seem half-animal and half-vegetable, with tremendous brain-capacity and, apparently, with more senses than we have. Lake, who has read the *Necronomicon,* jocosely thinks they may be the Elder Things or Old Ones spoken of in that book and elsewhere, who are "supposed to have created all earth-life as jest or mistake."

Later Lake's sub-expedition loses radio contact with the main party, apparently because of the high winds in that region. After a day or so passes, Dyer feels he must come to Lake's aid and takes a small group of men in some airplanes to see what has gone amiss. To their horror, they find the camp devastated—either by winds or by the sled dogs or by some other nameless forces—but discover no trace of the intact specimens of the Old Ones; they do come upon the damaged specimens "insanely" buried in the snow, and are forced to conclude that it is the work of the one missing human, Gedney. Dyer and the graduate student Danforth decide to take a trip by themselves beyond the titanic mountain plateau to see if they can find any explanation for the tragedy.

As they scale the immense plateau, they find to their amazement an enormous stone city, fifty to one hundred miles in extent, clearly built millions of years ago, long before there could have been any humans on the planet. Exploring some of the interiors, they are eventually forced to conclude that the city was built by the Old Ones. Because the buildings contain, as wall decorations, many bas-reliefs supplying the history of the Old Ones' civilisation, they are able to learn that the Old Ones came from space some fifty million years ago, settling in the Antarctic and eventually branching out to other areas of the earth. They built their huge cities with the aid of shoggoths—amorphous, fifteen-foot masses of protoplasm which they controlled by hypnotic suggestion. Unfortunately, over time these shoggoths gained a semi-stable brain and began to develop a will of their own, forcing the Old Ones to conduct several campaigns of resubjugation. Later other extraterrestrial races—including the fungi from Yuggoth and the Cthulhu spawn—came to the earth and engaged in battles over territory with the Old Ones, and eventually the latter were forced back to their original Antarctic settlement. They had also lost the ability to fly through space. The reasons for their abandonment of this city, and for their extinction, are unfathomable.

Dyer and Danforth then stumble upon traces that someone dragging a sled had passed by, and they follow it, finding first some huge albino penguins, then the sled with the remains of Gedney and a dog, then a group of decapitated Old Ones, who had obviously come to life by being thawed in Lake's camp. Then they hear an anomalous sound—a musical piping over a wide range. Could it be some other Old Ones? Not stopping to investigate, they flee madly; but they simultaneously turn their flashlights upon the thing for an instant, and find that it is nothing but a loathsome shoggoth:

> It was a terrible, indescribable thing vaster than any subway train—a shapeless con-
> geries of protoplasmic bubbles, faintly self-luminous, and with myriads of temporary
> eyes forming and unforming as pustules of greenish light all over the tunnel-filling
> front that bore down upon us, crushing the frantic penguins and slithering over the
> glistening floor that it and its kind had swept so evilly free of all litter.

As they fly back to camp, Danforth shrieks out in horror: he has seen some further sight that unhinges his mind, but he refuses to tell Dyer what it is. All he can do is make the eldritch cry, *"Tekeli-li! Tekeli-li!"*

Once again the utter inadequacy of a synopsis of this short novel will be evident to every reader. In the first place, it cannot begin to convey the rich, detailed, and utterly convincing scientific erudition that creates the sense of verisimilitude so neces-sary in a tale so otherwise *outré*. We have already seen how Lovecraft was, since at least the age of twelve, an ardent student of the Antarctic: he had written small trea-tises on "Wilkes's Explorations" and "The Voyages of Capt. Ross, R.N." as a boy, and had followed with avidity reports of the explorations of Borchgrevink, Scott,

Amundsen, and others in the early decades of the century. Indeed, as Jason C. Eckhardt has demonstrated,[35] the early parts of Lovecraft's tale clearly show the influence of Admiral Byrd's expedition of 1928–30, as well as other contemporary expeditions. I believe he also found a few hints on points of style and imagery in the early pages of M. P. Shiel's great novel *The Purple Cloud* (1901; reissued 1930), which relates an expedition to the Arctic. But it is also Lovecraft's thorough knowledge of geology, biology, chemistry, physics, and natural history that lead to a passage like this:

> This was my first word of the discovery, and it told of the identification of early shells, bones of ganoids and placoderms, remnants of labyrinthodonts and thecodonts, great mososaur skull fragments, dinosaur vertebrae and armour-plates, pterodactyl teeth and wing-bones, archaeopteryx debris, Miocene sharks' teeth, primitive bird-skulls, and skulls, vertebrae, and other bones of archaic mammals such as palaeotheres, xiphodons, dinoceras, eohippi, oreodons, and titanotheres.

Lovecraft's science in this novel is absolutely sound for its period, although subsequent discoveries have made a few points obsolete. In fact, he was so concerned about the scientific authenticity of the work that, prior to its first publication in *Astounding Stories* (February, March, and April 1936), he inserted some revisions eliminating an hypothesis he had made that the Antarctic continent had originally been two land masses separated by a frozen channel between the Ross and Weddell Seas—an hypothesis that had been proven false by the first airplane flight across the continent, by Lincoln Ellsworth and Herbert Hollick-Kenyon in late 1935.

One must wonder, however, what compelled Lovecraft to write the novel at this very time. He never provides any explicit statement on this matter, but one conjecture made by David E. Schultz is suggestive. The lead story in the November 1930 issue of *Weird Tales* was a poorly written and unimaginative tale by Katharine Metcalf Roof, "A Million Years After," that dealt with the hatching of ancient dinosaur eggs. Lovecraft fumed when he saw this tale, not only because it won the cover design but because he had been badgering Frank Long to write a story on this idea for years; Long had held off because he felt that H. G. Wells's "Æpyornis Island" had anticipated the idea. In mid-October Lovecraft wrote of the Roof tale:

> Rotten—cheap—puerile—yet winning prime distinction *because of the subject matter.* Now didn't Grandpa tell a bright young man just eight years ago this month to write a story like that? . . . Fie, Sir! Somebody else wasn't so afraid of the subject—and now a wretched mess of hash, just on the strength of its theme, gets the place of honour that Young Genoa might have had! . . . Why, damn it, boy, I've half a mind to write an egg story myself right now—though I fancy my primal ovoid would hatch out something infinitely more palaeogean and unrecognisable than the relatively commonplace dinosaur.[36]

Sure enough, Lovecraft seems to have done just that. But he may have felt that the actual use of a dinosaur egg was itself ruled out, so that the only other solution would be the freezing of alien bodies in the Arctic or Antarctic regions. All this is, of course, conjecture, but it seems to me a highly plausible one.

And, of course, it can scarcely be denied that Lovecraft's sight of the spectacular paintings of the Himalayas by Nicholas Roerich—seen only the previous year in New York—played a factor in the genesis of the work. Roerich is mentioned a total of six times throughout the course of the novel, as if Lovecraft is going out of his way to signal the influence. Indeed, the Roerich connexion may help to explain one anomaly in the text. Lovecraft here equates the vast superplateau discovered by Dyer and Danforth with the Plateau of Leng; but when he had first invented this locale (in "The Hound") he had placed it in Asia. Lovecraft may have been so struck by Roerich's paintings—which seemed to embody his own conception of the Plateau of Leng—that he bodily transferred both the mountains they depicted (recall that the "mountains of madness" are explicitly declared to be taller than Everest) and the plateau to the ice-bound south. He probably did not set the tale in the Himalayas themselves both because they were already becoming well known and because he wanted to create the sense of awe implicit in mountains taller than any yet discovered on the planet. Only the relatively uncharted antarctic continent could fulfil both these functions.

Some impatient readers have found the scientific passages—especially at the beginning—excessive, but they are essential for establishing the atmosphere of realism (and also of the protagonists' rationality) that make the latter parts of the novel insidiously convincing. *At the Mountains of Madness,* which avowedly presents itself as a scientific report, is the greatest instance of Lovecraft's dictum that "no weird story can truly produce terror unless it is devised with all the care & verisimilitude of an actual *hoax.*"[37] Indeed, the narrator claims that even this account is a less formal version of a treatise that will appear "in an official bulletin of Miskatonic University."

The real focus of *At the Mountains of Madness* is the Old Ones. Indeed, although initially portrayed as objects of terror, they ultimately yield to the shoggoths in this regard; as Fritz Leiber remarked, "the author shows us horrors and then pulls back the curtain a little farther, letting us glimpse the horrors of which even the horrors are afraid!"[38] There is, however, even more to it than this. It is not merely that the Old Ones become the secondary "horrors" in the tale; it is that they cease, toward the end, to be horrors at all. Dyer, studying the history of the Old Ones—their colonisation of the earth; their building of titanic cities on the Antarctic and elsewhere; their pursuit of knowledge—gradually comes to realise the profound bonds human beings share with them, and which neither share with the loathsome, primitive, virtually mindless shoggoths. The canonical passage occurs near the end, as he sees the group of dead Old Ones decapitated by the shoggoth:

Poor devils! After all, they were not evil things of their kind. They were the men of another age and another order of being. Nature had played a hellish jest on them . . . and this was their tragic homecoming.

> . . . Scientists to the last—what had they done that we would not have done in their place? God, what intelligence and persistence! What a facing of the incredible, just as those carven kinsmen and forbears had faced things only a little less incredible! Radiates, vegetables, monstrosities, star-spawn—whatever they had been, they were men!

This triumphant conclusion is, however, prefigured in a number of ways. When Lake's decimated camp is discovered, it is evident to every reader (although Dyer cannot bring himself to admit it) that the destruction has been the work of the Old Ones. But are they morally culpable here? It is later ascertained that the immediate cause of the violence was a vicious attack upon them by the dogs of Lake's party (Dyer, trying to look at matters from the Old Ones' perspective, alludes to "an attack by the furry, frantically barking quadrupeds, and a dazed defence against them and the equally frantic white simians with the queer wrappings and paraphernalia"). Some of Lake's men have been "incised and subtracted from in the most curious, cold-blooded, and inhuman fashion" by the Old Ones; but how is this different from the crude dissection Lake himself had attempted on one of the damaged specimens? Later, when Dyer and Danforth discover the sled containing the body of Gedney (a specimen which the Old Ones had taken with them), Dyer notes that it was "wrapped with patent care to prevent further damage."

The most significant way in which the Old Ones are identified with human beings is in the historical digression Dyer provides, specifically in regard to the Old Ones' social and economic organisation. In many ways they represent a utopia toward which Lovecraft clearly hopes humanity itself will one day move. The single sentence "Government was evidently complex and probably socialistic" establishes that Lovecraft had himself by this time converted to moderate socialism. Of course, the Old Ones' civilisation is founded upon slavery of a sort; and one wonders whether the shoggoths might be, in part, a metaphor for blacks. There is one tantalising hint to this effect. Late in the novel the protagonists stumble upon an area that, as they learn later, has been decorated with bas-reliefs by the shoggoths themselves. Dyer reports that there is a vast difference between this work and that of the Old Ones—

> a difference in basic nature as well as in mere quality, and involving so profound and calamitous a degradation of skill that nothing in the hitherto observed rate of decline could have led one to expect it.
>
> This new and degenerate work was coarse, bold, and wholly lacking in delicacy of detail. . . .

Recall Lovecraft's remark in "An Account of *Charleston*" (written less than a year earlier) on the decline of architecture in Charleston in the nineteenth century: "Architectural details became heavy and almost crude as negro craftsmen replaced skill'd white carvers, though the good models of the eighteenth century were never wholly lost sight of." But the identification of shoggoths and blacks is perhaps too nebulous and imprecise to be worth pressing.

The Old Ones, of course, are not human beings, and Lovecraft never makes us forget that in many ways—intellectual capacity, sensory development, aesthetic skill—they are vastly our superiors. Even this point may be capable of a sociocultural interpretation, for the Old Ones—who created all earth life—can perhaps be seen as analogous to the Greeks and Romans who, in Lovecraft's view, created the best phases of our own civilisation. There are a number of similarities between the Old Ones and the ancients, slavery being only one of them. At one point an explicit parallel is drawn between the Old Ones in their decline and the Romans under Constantine. One thinks of *In Defence of Dagon:* "Modern civilisation is the direct heir of Hellenic culture—all that we have is Greek"; and elsewhere in the same essay: "perhaps one should not wonder at *anything* Greek; the race was a super-race." The Old Ones, too, are a super-race.

The exhaustive history of the Old Ones on this planet is of consuming interest, not only for its imaginative power but for its exemplification of a belief that Lovecraft had long held and which was emphasised by his reading of Spengler's *The Decline of the West:* the inexorable rise and fall of successive civilisations. Although the Old Ones are vastly superior to human beings, they are no less subject to the forces of "decadence" than other races. As Dyer and Danforth examine the bas-reliefs and piece together the history of their civilisation, they can detect clear instances of decline from even greater heights of physical, intellectual, and aesthetic mastery. No simplistic moral is drawn from this decline—there is, for example, no suggestion whatever that the Old Ones are morally blameworthy for their creation of shoggoths as slaves, only regret that they were not able to exercise greater control over these entities and thereby subdue their rebelliousness—and it seems as if Lovecraft sees their decadence as an inevitable result of complex historical forces.

Not only have the Old Ones created all earth-life, including human beings; they have done more: "It interested us to see in some of the very last and most decadent sculptures a shambling primitive mammal, used sometimes for food and sometimes as an amusing buffoon by the land dwellers, whose vaguely simian and human foreshadowings were unmistakable." This must be one of the most misanthropic utterances ever made—the degradation of humanity can go no further. The Old Ones had created all earth-life as "jest or mistake"; and yet, "Nature had played a hellish jest" on those very Old Ones—first, perhaps, because they were annihilated by the shoggoths, and then because the few remnants of their species who had fortuitously survived to our age were revivified and suffered further horrors at the hands of the loathsome protoplasmic entities they have created. Human beings, accordingly, become merely the dupes of dupes, and Nature has the last laugh.

In terms of the Lovecraft mythos, *At the Mountains of Madness* makes explicit what has been evident all along—that most of the "gods" of the mythos are mere extraterrestrials, and that their followers (including the authors of the books of occult lore to which reference is so frequently made by Lovecraft and others) are mistaken as to their true nature. Robert M. Price, who first noted this "demythologising" feature in Lovecraft,[39] has in later articles gone on to point out that *At the Mountains of Madness* does not make any radical break in this pattern, but it does emphasise the point more clearly than elsewhere. The critical passage occurs in the middle of the novel, when Dyer finally acknowledges that the titanic city in which he has been wandering must have been built by the Old Ones: "They were the makers and enslavers of [earth] life, and above all doubt the originals of the fiendish elder myths which things like the Pnakotic Manuscripts and the *Necronomicon* affrightedly hint about." The content of the *Necronomicon* has now been reduced to "myth." As for the various wars waged by the Old Ones against such creatures as the fungi from Yuggoth (from "The Whisperer in Darkness") and the Cthulhu spawn (from "The Call of Cthulhu"), it has been pointed out that Lovecraft has not consistently followed his earlier tales in his accounts of their arrival on the earth; but, as I have mentioned earlier, Lovecraft was not concerned with this sort of pedantic accuracy in his mythos, and there are even more flagrant instances of "inconsistency" in later works.

The casually made claim that the novel is a "sequel" to Poe's *Narrative of Arthur Gordon Pym* deserves some analysis. In my view, the novel is not a true sequel at all—it picks up on very little of Poe's enigmatic work except for the cry "Tekeli-li!," as unexplained in Poe as in Lovecraft—and the various references to *Pym* throughout the story end up being more in the manner of in-jokes. It is not clear that *Pym* even influenced the work in any significant way. Lovecraft was, of course, fascinated with *Pym,* in particular its enigmatic conclusion, in which the protagonists sail deep into the southern hemisphere and near the Antarctic continent; and perhaps *At the Mountains of Madness* could be regarded as a sort of tongue-in-cheek extrapolation as to what Poe left so tantalisingly unexplained. When Clark Ashton Smith heard from Lovecraft about his plans to write the novel, he replied: "I think your idea for an Antarctic story would be excellent, in spite of 'Pym' and subsequent tales."[40] Jules Zanger has aptly noted that *At the Mountains of Madness* "is, of course, no completion [of *Pym*] at all: it might be better described as a parallel text, the two tales coexisting in a shared context of allusion."[41]

At the Mountains of Madness is not without a few flaws. The wealth of information Dyer and Danforth manage to decipher from bas-reliefs strains credulity, as does the revival of the frozen Old Ones after millennia spent in some sort of cryogenic suspended animation. But the impressive scientific erudition in the novel, its breathtakingly cosmic sweep as it portrays millions of years of this planet's prehistory, and the harrowingly gripping conclusion with the emergence of the shoggoth—perhaps the most frightening moment in all Lovecraft, if not in all horror literature—cause this work to stand at the very pinnacle of Lovecraft's fictional achievement, even higher than "The Colour out of Space."

The fate of *At the Mountains of Madness* in print was very unfortunate. Lovecraft declared that the short novel was "capable of a major serial division in the exact middle"[42] (meaning, presumably, after Chapter VI), leading one to think that he could envision the work as a two-part serial in *Weird Tales*—which is not to say that he composed the work with that eventuality in mind. But, although he delayed his spring travels till early May while undertaking what was for him the herculean task of typing the text (it came to 115 pages), he was shattered to learn in mid-June of the rejection of the tale by Farnsworth Wright. Lovecraft wrote bitterly in early August:

> Yes—Wright "explained" his rejection of the "Mountains of Madness" in almost the same language as that with which he "explained" other recent rejections to Long & Derleth. It was "too long", "not easily divisible into parts", "not convincing"—& so on. Just what he has said of other things of mine (except for length)—some of which he has ultimately accepted after many hesitations.[43]

It was not only Wright's adverse reaction that affected Lovecraft; several colleagues to whom he had circulated the text also seemed less than enthusiastic. One of the unkindest cuts of all may have come from W. Paul Cook, the very man who had chiefly been responsible for Lovecraft's resumption of weird fiction in 1917. In 1932 Lovecraft made a passing comment on the several factors that had caused him to be severely discouraged about his work, one of which was "Cook's poor opinion of my recent things";[44] and Cook, both in his memoir and in later articles, made it very clear that he did not care at all for Lovecraft's later pseudo-scientific narratives, so that *At the Mountains of Madness* must clearly have been in Lovecraft's mind here.

There are several questions to be dealt with in this whole matter. First, let us consider whether Wright was justified in rejecting the tale. In later years Lovecraft frequently complained that Wright would accept long and mediocre serials by Otis Adelbert Kline, Edmond Hamilton, and other clearly inferior writers while rejecting his own lengthy work; but some defence of Wright might perhaps be made. The serials in *Weird Tales* may indeed have been, from an abstract literary perspective, mediocre; but Wright knew that they were critical in compelling readers to continue buying the magazine. As a result, they were by and large geared toward the lowest level of the readership, full of sensationalised action, readily identifiable human characters, and a simple (if not simple-minded) prose style. *At the Mountains of Madness* could not be said to have any of these characteristics: it was slow-moving, atmospheric, densely written, and with characters who were by design bland and colourless so as to serve as conduits for the reader's perception of the bleak Antarctic waste and the horrors that lay within it. Some of Wright's cavils, as recorded by Lovecraft, were indeed unjust; in particular, the comment "not convincing" cannot possibly be said to apply to this work. But Lovecraft himself knew that Wright had come to use this phrase as a sort of rubber-stamp whenever he was looking for an excuse to reject a work.

The strange thing is Lovecraft knew well that Wright was merely a business-man who, especially at the onset of the depression, could not allow purely literary judgments to guide his choice of material. As early as 1927 he had written to Donald Wandrei:

> Wright . . . isn't such an ass as you'd think from his editorial dicta. He knows—at least, I assume that he knows—what junk he prints, but chooses it on the basis of its proved appeal to the brachycephalic longshoremen & coal-heavers who form his clientele & scrawl "fan letters" to the Eyrie with their stubby pencils & ruled five-cent pads. I think he works intelligently—as a sound business man—doing what he's paid to do, & steadily building up the magazine as a paying proposition . . .[45]

There was, then, no abstractly logical reason why Lovecraft should have been so shattered merely because Wright had rejected it.

It is possible, however, that the rejection affected Lovecraft so badly because it coincided with yet another rejection—that of a collection of his tales by G. P. Put-nam's Sons. In the spring of 1931 Winfield Shiras, an editor at Putnam's, had asked to see some of Lovecraft's stories for possible book publication. Lovecraft sent thirty stories[46]—nearly all the manuscripts or tearsheets he had in the house at the time—and, in spite of his characteristic predictions that nothing would come of it, he may well have held out a hope that he might see his name on a hardcover book. Putnam's had, after all, come to him, and not as a matter of form as Simon & Schuster had done the year before. But by mid-July the dismal news came: the collection was rejected, and even though "Shiras . . . hems & haws & talks of changes he would like to see & plans he would like to make after the lapse of a few months,"[47] Lovecraft knew a polite letdown when he saw one.

The Putnam's rejection may in fact have been more staggering than that of *At the Mountains of Madness:*

> The grounds for rejection were twofold—first, that some of the tales are not subtle enough . . . too obvious & well-explained—(admitted! That ass Wright got me into the habit of obvious writing with his never-ending complaints against the in-definiteness of my early stuff.) & secondly, that all the tales are uniformly macabre in mood to stand collected publication. This second reason is sheer bull—for as a matter of fact unity of mood is a positive asset in a fictional collection. But I suppose the herd must have their comic relief![48]

I think Lovecraft is right on both points here. His later tales do not, perhaps, leave enough to the imagination, and in part this may indeed be a result of subconsciously writing with *Weird Tales'* market demands in mind; but in part this is precisely because of the tendency of this work to gravitate more toward science fiction. Lovecraft was in the position of being a pioneer in the fusion of weird and science fiction, but the short-term result was that his work was found unsatisfactory both to pulp magazines and to commercial publishers that were locked in their stereotypical conventions.

A third rejection occurred at the hands of Harry Bates. Bates had been appointed editor of *Strange Tales,* a magazine launched in 1931 by the William Clayton Company. Word about the magazine must have gone out by spring (although the first issue was dated September), for in April Lovecraft sent along four old stories (all rejected by Wright), "The Doom That Came to Sarnath," "The Nameless City," "Beyond the Wall of Sleep," and "Polaris."[49] They were all rejected. The next month Bates rejected "In the Vault."[50] Lovecraft should not have been much surprised at this: not only were these on the whole inferior stories, but the Clayton firm was long known as preferring fast-paced action to atmosphere. "In the Vault" seems to have come closest to acceptance, for Lovecraft reports Bates's belief that "a better story of that kind would be rather in his line."

Strange Tales seemed at first to be a serious rival to *Weird Tales:* it paid 2¢ per word on acceptance, and it formed a significant market for such writers as Clark Ashton Smith, Henry S. Whitehead, August Derleth, and Hugh B. Cave who could mould their styles to suit Bates's requirements. Wright must have been greatly alarmed at the emergence of this magazine, for it meant that some of his best writers would submit their tales to it first and only send material to *Weird Tales* that had been rejected by *Strange Tales.* But the magazine only lasted for seven issues, folding in January 1933.

The whole issue of Lovecraft's sensitivity to rejection, or to bad opinions of his work generally, deserves consideration. Did not Lovecraft say, in the *In Defence of Dagon* essays of 1921, that he scorned the idea of writing about "ordinary people" in order to increase his audience, and that "There are probably seven persons, in all, who really like my work; and they are enough. I should write even if I were the only patient reader, for my aim is merely self-expression"? Granted that this statement was made well before his work had become more widely available in the pulp magazines; but "self-expression" remained the cornerstone of his aesthetic to the end. Lovecraft was aware of the apparent contradiction, for the issue came up in discussions with Derleth. Lovecraft had already told Derleth that "I have a sort of dislike of sending in anything which has been once rejected,"[51] an attitude that Derleth— who in his hard-boiled way sometimes submitted a single story to *Weird Tales* up to a dozen times before it was finally accepted by Wright—must have found nearly incomprehensible. Now, in early 1932, Lovecraft expanded on the idea:

I can see why you consider my anti-rejection policy a stubbornly foolish & needlessly short-sighted one, & am not prepared to offer any defence other than the mere fact that repeated rejections *do* work in a certain way on my psychology—rationally or not—& that their effect is to cause in me a certain literary lockjaw which absolutely prevents further fictional composition despite my most arduous efforts. I would be the last to say that they *ought* to produce such an effect, or that they would—even in a slight degree—upon a psychology of 100% toughness & balance. But unfortunately my nervous equilibrium has always been a rather uncertain quantity, & it is now in one of its more ragged phases . . .[52]

Lovecraft had always been modest about his own achievements—excessively so, as we look back upon it; now, rejections by Wright, Bates, and Putnam's, and the cool reactions of colleagues to whom he had sent stories in manuscript, nearly shattered whatever confidence he may have had in his own work. He spent the few remaining years of his life trying to regain that confidence, and he never seems to have done so except in fleeting moments. We can see the effect of this state of mind in his very next story.

"The Shadow over Innsmouth" was written in November and December of 1931. Lovecraft reported that his revisiting of the decaying seaport of Newburyport, Massachusetts (which he had first seen in 1923), had led him to conduct a sort of "laboratory experimentation"[53] to see which style or manner was best suited to the theme. Four drafts (whether complete or not is not clear) were written and discarded,[54] and finally Lovecraft simply wrote the story in his accustomed manner, producing a 25,000-word novelette whose extraordinary richness of atmosphere scarcely betrays the almost agonising difficulty he experienced in its writing.

In "The Shadow over Innsmouth" the narrator, Robert Olmstead (never mentioned by name in the story, but identified in the surviving notes), a native of Ohio, celebrates his coming of age by undertaking a tour of New England—"sightseeing, antiquarian, and genealogical"—and, finding that the train fare from Newburyport to Arkham (whence his family derives) is higher than he would like, is grudgingly told by a ticket agent of a bus that makes the trip by way of a seedy coastal town called Innsmouth. The place does not seem to appear on most maps, and many odd rumours are whispered about it. Innsmouth was a flourishing seaport up to 1846, when an epidemic of some sort killed over half the citizens; people believe it may have had something to do with the voyages of Captain Obed Marsh, who sailed extensively in China and the South Seas and somehow acquired vast sums in gold and jewels. Now the Marsh refinery is just about the only business of importance in Innsmouth aside from fishing off the shore near Devil's Reef, where fish are always unusually abundant. All the townspeople seem to have repulsive deformities or traits—which are collectively termed "the Innsmouth look"—and are studiously avoided by the neighbouring communities.

This account piques Olmstead's interest as an antiquarian, and he decides to spend at least a day in Innsmouth, planning to catch a bus in the morning and leaving for Arkham in the evening. He goes to the Newburyport Historical Society and sees a tiara that came from Innsmouth; it fascinates him more and more: "It clearly belonged to some settled technique of infinite maturity and perfection, yet that technique was utterly remote from any—Eastern or Western, ancient or modern—which I had ever heard of or seen exemplified. It was as if the workmanship were that of another planet." Going to Innsmouth on a seedy bus run by Joe Sargent, whose hairlessness, fishy odour, and never-blinking eyes inspire his loathing, Olmstead begins exploration, aided by directions and a map supplied by a normal-looking young man who works in a grocery chain. All around he sees signs of both physical and moral decay from a once distinguished level. The atmosphere begins to oppress him, and he thinks about leaving the town early; but then he catches sight of a nonagenarian named Zadok Allen who, he has been told, is a fount of knowledge about the history of Innsmouth. Olmstead has a chat with Zadok, loosening his tongue with bootleg whiskey.

Zadok tells him a wild story about alien creatures, half fish and half frog, whom Obed Marsh had encountered in the South Seas. Zadok maintains that Obed struck up an agreement with these creatures: they would provide him with bountiful gold and fish in exchange for human sacrifices. This arrangement worked for a while, but then the fish-frogs sought to mate with humans. It was this that provoked a violent uproar in the town in 1846: many citizens died and the remainder were forced to take the Oath of Dagon, professing loyalty to the hybrid entities. There is, however, a compensating benefit of a sort. As humans continue to mate with the fish-frogs, they acquire a type of immortality: they undergo a physical change, gaining many of the properties of the aliens, and then they take to the sea and live in vast underwater cities for millennia.

Scarcely knowing what to make of this bizarre tale and alarmed at Zadok's maniacal plea that he leave the town at once because they have been seen talking, Olmsted makes efforts to catch the evening bus out of Innsmouth. But he is in bad luck: it has suffered inexplicable engine trouble and cannot be repaired until the next day; he will have to put up in the seedy Gilman House, the one hotel in the town. Reluctantly checking into the place, he feels ever-growing intimations of horror and menace as he hears anomalous voices outside his room and other strange noises. Finally he knows he is in peril: his doorknob is tried from the outside. He begins a frenetic series of attempts to leave the hotel and escape the town, but at one point is almost overwhelmed at both the number and the loathsomeness of his pursuers:

> And yet I saw them in a limitless stream—flopping, hopping, croaking, bleating—surging inhumanly through the spectral moonlight in a grotesque, malignant saraband of fantastic nightmare. And some of them had tall tiaras of that nameless

whitish-gold metal . . . and some were strangely robed . . . and one, who led the way, was clad in a ghoulishly humped black coat and striped trousers, and had a man's felt hat perched on the shapeless thing that answered for a head. . . .

Olmstead escapes, but his tale is not over. After a much-needed rest, he continues to pursue genealogical research, and finds appalling evidence that he may himself be related to the Marsh family in a fairly direct way. He learns of a cousin locked in a madhouse in Canton, and an uncle who committed suicide because he learned something nameless about himself. Strange dreams of swimming underwater begin to afflict him, and gradually he breaks down. Then one morning he awakes to learn that he has acquired "the Innsmouth look." He thinks of shooting himself, but "certain dreams deterred me." Later he comes to his decision: "I shall plan my cousin's escape from that Canton madhouse, and together we shall go to marvel-shadowed Innsmouth. We shall swim out to that brooding reef in the sea and dive down through black abysses to Cyclopean and many-columned Y'ha-nthlei, and in that lair of the Deep Ones we shall dwell amidst wonder and glory for ever."

This masterful tale of insidious regional horror requires volumes of commentary, but we can only touch upon a few notable features here. To begin most mundanely, let us specify the location of Innsmouth. The name had been invented in so early a tale as "Celephaïs" (1920), but was clearly located in England; Lovecraft resurrected the name for the eighth sonnet ("The Port") of the *Fungi from Yuggoth* (1929–30), where the setting is not entirely clear, although a New England locale is likely. In any event, it is plain that Newburyport is the basic setting for Innsmouth, even if today it has been substantially renovated into a yuppie resort town and is no longer the decaying backwater that Lovecraft saw. Robert D. Marten has soundly refuted Will Murray's contention that some aspects of the topography of Innsmouth derive from other towns, such as Gloucester.[55]

"The Shadow over Innsmouth" is Lovecraft's greatest tale of degeneration; but the causes for that degeneration here are quite different from what we have seen earlier. In such tales as "The Lurking Fear" and "The Dunwich Horror," unwholesome inbreeding within a homogeneous community has caused a descent upon the evolutionary scale; in "The Horror at Red Hook" it is merely said that "modern people under lawless conditions tend uncannily to repeat the darkest instinctive patterns of primitive half-ape savagery," and all we can perhaps infer is that the breeding of foreigners amongst themselves has resulted in the wholesale squalor we now see in Red Hook. "The Shadow over Innsmouth" is, however, clearly a cautionary tale on the ill effects of *miscegenation,* or the sexual union of different races, and as such may well be considered a vast expansion and subtilisation of the plot of "Facts concerning the Late Arthur Jermyn and His Family" (1920). It is, accordingly, difficult to deny a suggestion of racism running all through the story. By means of his protagonist, Lovecraft occasionally betrays his own paranoia: during his escape from Innsmouth, Olmstead hears "horrible croaking voices exchanging low cries in what was certainly not English," as if a foreign language were in itself a sign of aberration. All through the tale the narrator expresses—and expects us to share—his revulsion at the physical grotesqueness of the Innsmouth people, just as in his own life Lovecraft frequently comments on the "peculiar" appearance of all races but his own.

This racist interpretation is not refuted by the suggestion made by Zadok Allen that human beings are ultimately related to the fish-frogs; for this has an entirely different implication. Zadok declares: "Seems that human folks has got a kind o' relation to sech water-beasts—that everything alive come aout o' the water onct, an' only needs a little change to go back agin." Forget for the nonce that Lovecraft had, in *At the Mountains of Madness,* supplied an entirely different account of the emergence of humanity: the intent here and in that story is the same—the denigration of human importance by the suggestion of a contemptible and degrading origin of our species.

An examination of the literary influences upon the story can clarify how Lovecraft has vastly enriched a conception that was by no means his own invention. There is little doubt that the use of hybrid fishlike entities was derived from at least two prior works for which Lovecraft always retained a fondness: Irvin S. Cobb's "Fishhead" (which Lovecraft read in the *Cavalier* in 1913 and praised in a letter to the editor, and which was also reprinted in Harré's *Beware After Dark!,* where Lovecraft surely reread it) and Robert W. Chambers's "The Harbor-Master," a short story later included as the first five chapters of the episodic novel *In Search of the Unknown* (1904). (Derleth had given a copy of this book to Lovecraft in the fall of 1930.[56]) But in both these stories we are dealing with a *single* case of hybridism, not an entire community or civilisation; this latter feature is, however, found in Algernon Blackwood's masterful novelette "Ancient Sorceries" (in *John Silence—Physician Extraordinary* [1908]), where the inhabitants of a small French town appear, through witchcraft, to transform themselves at night into cats. Lovecraft vastly expands on this conception to create the sense of worldwide menace that we find in "The Shadow over Innsmouth." What is more, there is no guarantee that human beings will prevail in any future conflict with the fish-frogs; for, loathsome as they are, they nevertheless possess—as do the fungi from Yuggoth and the Old Ones—qualities that raise them in many ways above our species. Aside from their near-immortality (Olmstead in a dream meets his great-great-grandmother, who has lived for 80,000 years), they clearly possess aesthetic skills of a high order (that tiara "belonged to some settled technique of infinite maturity and perfection"), and in fact are allowing human beings to dwell on the earth on *their* sufferance: as Zadok says, "they cud wipe aout the hull brood o' humans ef they was willin' to bother." And, although they are damaged by the destruction of the town in 1927–28 when Olmstead calls in Federal authorities after his experience, they are by no means extirpated; Olmstead ponders ominously at the very end: "For the present they would rest; but some day, if they remembered, they would rise again for the tribute Great Cthulhu craved. It would be a city greater than Innsmouth next time."

The lengthy chase scene that occupies the fourth chapter of the story is certainly engaging enough reading, if only because we witness the customarily staid and mild-mannered Lovecraftian protagonist battering through doors, leaping out windows, and fleeing along streets or railway tracks. It is, of course, typical that he does not engage in any actual fisticuffs (he is far outnumbered by his enemies), and he reverts to the Lovecraftian norm by fainting as he cowers in a railway cut and watches the loathsome phalanx of hybrids rush by him. More seriously, this notion of *seeing* horrors go by is of some significance in augmenting the atmosphere of nightmarish terror Lovecraft is clearly wishing to achieve; as he wrote in a letter: "I believe that—because of the foundation of most weird concepts in dream-phenomena—the best weird tales are those in which the narrator or central figure remains (as in actual dreams) largely passive, & witnesses or experiences a stream of bizarre events which—as the case may be—flows past him, just touches him, or engulfs him utterly."[57]

As for Zadok Allen's monologue—which occupies nearly the entirety of the third chapter—it has been criticised for excessive length, but Lovecraft was writing at a time when the use of dialect for long stretches was much commoner than now. The dialogue portions of John Buchan's enormously long novel *Witch Wood* (1927) are almost entirely in Scots dialect, as is the whole of Robert Louis Stevenson's "Thrawn Janet." Zadok's speech is undeniably effective in both supplying the necessary historical backdrop of the tale and in creating a sense of insidious horror. Zadok occupies a structurally important place in the narrative: because he has witnessed, at first hand, the successive generations of Innsmouth folk become increasingly corrupted by the Deep Ones, his account carries irrefutable weight, in spite of Olmstead's harried attempt to dismiss it as the ravings of a senile toper. Olmstead could not possibly have come by this information in any other way, even by some laborious course of historical research. And some of Zadok's words are both hideous and poignant:

> "Hey, yew, why dun't ye say somethin'? Haow'd ye like to be livin' in a town like this, with everything a-rottin' an' a-dyin', an' boarded-up monsters crawlin' an' bleatin' an' barkin' an' hoppin' araoun' black cellars an' attics every way ye turn? Hey? Haow'd ye like to hear the haowlin' night arter night from the churches an' Order o' Dagon Hall, *an' know what's doin' part o' the haowlin'?* Haow'd ye like to hear what comes from that awful reef every May-Eve an' Hallowmass? Hey? Think the old man's crazy, eh? Wal, Sir, *let me tell ye that ain't the wust!*"

There seem to be two dominant influences upon the creation of Zadok Allen, one real and the other fictional. The life dates of Lovecraft's aged amateur friend, Jonathan E. Hoag (1831–1927), coincide exactly with those of Zadok. More substantially, Zadok seems loosely based upon the figure of Humphrey Lathrop, an elderly doctor in Herbert Gorman's *The Place Called Dagon* (1927), which Lovecraft read in March 1928.[58] Like Zadok, Lathrop is the repository for the secret history of the Massachusetts town in which he resides (Leominster, in the north-central part of Massachusetts); and, like Zadok, he is partial to spirits—in this case apple-jack!

But it is Olmstead around whom the entire story revolves—unusually so for the cosmically oriented Lovecraft; and yet, in this tale Lovecraft succeeds brilliantly both in making Olmstead's plight inexpressibly tragic and also in hinting at the awesome horrors that threaten the entire planet. It is his greatest union of internal and external horror. The many mundane details that lend substance and reality to Olmstead's character are in large part derived from Lovecraft's own temperament and, especially, from his habits as a frugal antiquarian traveller. Olmstead always "seek[s] the cheapest possible route," and this is usually—for Olmstead as for Lovecraft—by bus. His reading up on Innsmouth in the library, and his systematic exploration of the town by way of the map and instructions given him by the grocery youth, parallel Lovecraft's own thorough researches into the history and topography of the places he wished to visit and his frequent trips to libraries, chambers of commerce, and elsewhere for maps, guidebooks, and historical background.

Even the ascetic meal Olmstead eats at a restaurant—"A bowl of vegetable soup with crackers was enough for me"—echoes Lovecraft's parsimonious diet both at home and on his travels. But it does more than that. Lovecraft's characters have frequently but inanely been criticised for their failure to eat, go to the bathroom, or indulge in long-winded conversation; but it should be evident by now that this type of mundane realism was not to his purpose. Even in his novelettes and short novels, Lovecraft's prime concern—beyond even verisimilitude and topographical realism—was a rigid adherence to Poe's theory of unity of effect; that is, the elimination of any words, sentences, or whole incidents that do not have a direct bearing on the story. Accordingly, a character's eating habits are wholly dispensed with because they are inessential to the denouement of a tale and will only dilute that air of tensity and inevitability which Lovecraft is seeking to establish. It is significant that virtually the only two characters in Lovecraft who do eat—Olmstead and Wilmarth (in "The Whisperer in Darkness")—do so for reasons that are critical to the development of the plot: Wilmarth because Lovecraft wishes to hint at the unsuccessful attempt to drug him with coffee, and Olmstead because he is forced to spend the evening in Innsmouth and this frugal meal contributes to the psychological portrait of a tourist increasingly agitated by his sinister surroundings.

But it is Olmstead's spectacular conversion at the end—where he not merely becomes reconciled to his fate as a nameless hybrid but actually embraces it—that is the most controversial point of the tale. Does this mean that Lovecraft, as in *At the Mountains of Madness,* wishes to transform the Deep Ones from objects of horror to objects of sympathy or identification? Or rather, are we to imagine Olmstead's change of heart as an augmentation of the horror? I can only believe that the latter is intended. There is no gradual "reformation" of the Deep Ones as there is of the Old Ones in the earlier novel: our revulsion at their physical hideousness is not mollified or tempered by any subsequent appreciation of their intelligence, courage, or nobility. Olmstead's transformation is the climax of the story and the pinnacle of its horrific scenario: it shows that not merely his physical body but also his mind has been ineluctably corrupted.

This transformation is achieved in many ways, subtle and obvious; one of the most subtle is in the simple use of descriptives. The title, "The Shadow over Innsmouth," is not chosen by accident; for throughout the tale it is used with provocative variations. We first encounter it when Olmstead, after hearing the account of the ticket agent, states: "That was the first I ever heard of shadowed Innsmouth." This mildly ominous usage then successively becomes "rumour-shadowed Innsmouth," "evil-shadowed Innsmouth," and other coinages that bespeak Olmstead's increasing sense of loathing at the town and its inhabitants; but then, as he undergoes his "conversion," we read at the very end of "marvel-shadowed Innsmouth" and the even greater marvels of Y'ha-nthlei, where he shall "dwell amidst wonder and glory for ever"—an utterance that, in its hideous parody of the 23rd Psalm ("Surely goodness and mercy shall follow me all the days of my life: and I will dwell in the house of the Lord for ever"), ineffably unites Olmstead's sense of triumph and the reader's sense of utter horror.

In the end, "The Shadow over Innsmouth" is about the inexorable call of heredity; it is one more meditation on that poignant utterance, "The past is *real*—it is *all there is.*"[59] For Lovecraft, the future was essentially unknown in its unpredictability; the present, conversely, was nothing but the inevitable result of all antecedent and circumjacent events of the past, whether we are aware of them or not. Throughout the story Olmstead is secretly guided by his heredity, but is entirely oblivious of the fact. His ambivalent utterance when he sees Zadok Allen and decides to question him—"It must have been some imp of the perverse—or some sardonic pull from dark, hidden sources"—neatly conveys this point, for that "sardonic pull" is nothing other than the past, embodied by his own heredity, that is ineluctably leading him to Innsmouth and causing him to undergo what he believes to be a merely fortuitous series of unrelated events.

Lovecraft never achieved a greater atmosphere of insidious decay than in "The Shadow over Innsmouth": one can almost smell the overwhelming stench of fish,

see the physical anomalies of the inhabitants, and perceive the century-long dilapidation of an entire town in the story's evocative prose. And once again he has produced a narrative that progresses from first word to last without a false note to a
cataclysmic conclusion—a conclusion, as noted before, that simultaneously focuses
on the pitiable fate of a single human being and hints tantalisingly of the future
destruction of the entire race. The cosmic and the local, the past and the present,
the internal and the external, and self and the other are all fused into an inextricable
unity. It is something that Lovecraft had never achieved before and would never
achieve again save—in a very different way—in his last major story, "The Shadow
out of Time."

And yet, Lovecraft was profoundly dissatisfied with the story. A week after finishing it on December 3, he wrote lugubriously to Derleth:

> I don't think the experimenting came to very much. The result, 68 pages
> long, has all the defects I deplore—especially in point of style, where hackneyed
> phrases & rhythms have crept in despite all precautions. Use of any other style was
> like working in a foreign language—hence I was left high & dry. Possibly I shall
> try experimenting with another plot—of as widely different nature as I can think
> of—but I think an hiatus like that of 1908 is the best thing. I have been paying too
> much attention to the demands of markets & the opinions of others—hence if I
> am ever to write again I must begin afresh; writing only for myself & getting into
> the old habit of non-self-conscious storytelling without any technical thoughts.
> No—I don't intend to offer "The Shadow over Innsmouth" for publication, for it
> would stand no chance of acceptance.[60]

Given this statement, is it nevertheless possible that Lovecraft was, even subconsciously, thinking of a specific market in mind when writing the story? Will
Murray, largely on the strength of the chase scene in the fourth chapter, has conjectured that Lovecraft may have had *Strange Tales* in mind;[61] but the theory must
remain unproven in the entire absence of any documentary evidence to this effect.
We have seen that *Strange Tales* not only paid better than *Weird Tales,* but that
Harry Bates wished "action" stories, and the chase scene is otherwise uncharacteristic of Lovecraft; but if *Strange Tales* was the contemplated market, it is odd that
Lovecraft did not actually submit the tale there (or anywhere), forcing Murray to
conclude that Lovecraft was so dissatisfied with the story when he finished it that
he did not wish to submit it to a professional market. This makes Murray's theory
incapable either of proof or refutation—barring, of course, the unlikely emergence
of a statement by Lovecraft in a letter during the writing of the tale that *Strange
Tales* was the market he had in mind.

August Derleth had, in the meantime, developed a sort of frantic interest in the
story—or, more specifically, in its sale to a pulp market. After hearing of Lovecraft's discouragement about the tale, Derleth offered to type it himself;[62] this at

least prodded Lovecraft to prepare a typescript, which he completed around the middle of January 1932.[63] Derleth read and evidently liked the story, for by late January he was already asking his new artist protégé Frank Utpatel to prepare some illustrations for it, even though it had not been accepted or even submitted anywhere.[64] Derleth had, however, suggested some changes—specifically, he felt that the narrator's "taint" had not been sufficiently prepared for in the early part of the story (Clark Ashton Smith echoed this view[65]) and thought Lovecraft should drop a few more hints at the beginning. Lovecraft was, however, "so thoroughly sick of the tale from repeated re-revisions that it would be out of the question to touch it for years."[66] At this point Derleth himself offered to make the revisions![67] Lovecraft naturally rejected this idea, but did allow Derleth to keep a permanent copy of one of the two carbons.

Meanwhile, evidently in response to Wright's request to send in new work (perhaps he had heard of "The Shadow over Innsmouth" from Lovecraft's colleagues), Lovecraft wrote an extraordinarily snide letter in mid-February 1932:

> Sorry to say I haven't anything new which you would be likely to care for. Lately my tales have run to studies in geographical atmosphere requiring greater length than the popular editorial fancy relishes—my new "Shadow over Innsmouth" is three typed pages longer than "Whisperer in Darkness", and conventional magazine standards would undoubtedly rate it "intolerably slow", "not conveniently divisible", or something of the sort.[68]

Lovecraft has deliberately thrown back into Wright's face the remarks Wright had made about *At the Mountains of Madness*.

But if Lovecraft himself refused to submit "The Shadow over Innsmouth" to *Weird Tales*, Derleth was not so reticent. Without Lovecraft's permission or knowledge, he sent to Wright the carbon of the story in early 1933; but Wright's verdict was perhaps to be expected:

> I have read Lovecraft's story, THE SHADOW OVER INNSMOUTH, and must confess that it fascinates me. But I don't know just what I can do with it. It is hard to break a story of this kind into two parts, and it is too long to run complete in one part.
>
> I will keep this story in mind, and if some time in the near future I can figure out how to use it, I will write to Lovecraft and ask him to send me the manuscript.[69]

Lovecraft must have eventually found out about this surreptitious submission, for by 1934 he was speaking of its rejection by Wright.[70] Lovecraft himself, it should be pointed out, did not—with one exception—personally submit a story to Wright for five and a half years after the rejection of *At the Mountains of Madness*.

Shortly after writing "The Rats in the Walls" in the fall of 1923, Lovecraft discussed with Long one possible drawback about using some Celtic words (lifted directly from Fiona Macleod's "The Sin-Eater") at the end of the story: "The only objection to the phrase is that it's *Gaelic* instead of *Cymric* as the south-of-England locale demands. But as with anthropology—details don't count. Nobody will ever stop to note the difference."[71]

Lovecraft was wrong on two counts. First, the notion that the Gaels arrived first in Britain and were driven north by the Cymri is now seriously doubted by historians and anthropologists; second, someone did note the difference. When "The Rats in the Walls" was reprinted in *Weird Tales* for June 1930, a young writer wrote Farnsworth Wright asking whether Lovecraft was adhering to an alternate theory about the settling of Britain. Wright felt that the letter was interesting enough to pass on to Lovecraft. It was in this way that Lovecraft came into contact with Robert E. Howard.

Robert Ervin Howard (1906–1936) is a writer about whom it is difficult to be impartial. Like Lovecraft, he has attracted a fanatical cadre of supporters who both claim significant literary status for at least some of his work and take great offence at those who do not acknowledge its merits. My own opinion, however, is that, although individual stories are exceptional (but none equal to the best of Lovecraft's), the bulk of Howard's work is simply above-average pulp writing.

Howard himself is in many ways more interesting than his stories. Born in the small town of Peaster, Texas, about twenty miles west of Fort Worth, he spent the bulk of his short life in Cross Plains. His ancestors were among the earliest settlers of this "post oaks" region of central Texas, and his father, Dr I. M. Howard, was one of the pioneer physicians in the area. Howard was more hampered by his lack of formal education than Lovecraft—he briefly attended Howard Payne College in Brownwood, but only to take bookkeeping courses—because of the lack of libraries in his town; his learning was, accordingly, very uneven, and he was quick to take very strong and dogmatic opinions on subjects about which he knew little.

As an adolescent Howard was introverted and bookish; as a result, he was bullied by his peers, and to protect himself he undertook a vigorous course of bodybuilding that made him, as an adult of 5' 11" and 200 pounds, a formidable physical specimen. He took to writing early, however, and it became his only career aside from the odd jobs at which he occasionally worked. A taste for adventure, fantasy, and horror—he was an ardent devotee of Jack London—and a talent for writing allowed him to break into *Weird Tales* in July 1925 with "Spear and Fang." Although Howard later published in a wide variety of other pulp magazines, from *Cowboy Stories* to *Argosy*, *Weird Tales* remained his chief market and published his most representative work.

That work runs the gamut from westerns to sports stories to "Orientales" to weird fiction. Many of his tales fall into loose cycles revolving around recurring characters, including Bran Mak Morn (a Celtic chieftain in Roman Britain), King Kull (a warrior-king of the mythical prehistoric realm of Valusia, in central Europe), Solomon Kane (an English Puritan of the seventeenth century), and, most famously, Conan, a barbarian chieftain of the mythical land of Cimmeria. Howard was keenly drawn to the period of the prehistoric barbarians—whether because that age dimly reflected the conditions of pioneer Texas that he learnt and admired from his elders, or from early readings, or from some other cause. Howard himself was not entirely clear on the sources for this attraction:

> ... I have lived in the Southwest all my life, yet most of my dreams are laid in cold, giant lands of icy wastes and gloomy skies, and of wild, windswept fens and wilderness over which sweep great sea-winds, and which are inhabited by shock-headed savages with light fierce eyes. With the exception of one dream, I am never, in these dreams of ancient times, a civilized man. Always I am the barbarian, the skin-clad, tousle-haired, light-eyed wild man, armed with a rude axe or sword, fighting the elements and wild beasts, or grappling with armored hosts marching with the tread of civilized discipline, from fallow fruitful lands and walled cities. This is reflected in my writings, too, for when I begin a tale of old times, I always find myself instinctively arrayed on the side of the barbarian, against the powers of organized civilization.[72]

One does not, of course, wish to deny all literary value to Howard's work. He is certainly to be credited with the founding of the subgenre of "sword-and-sorcery," although Fritz Leiber would later vastly refine the form; and, although many of Howard's stories were written purely for the sake of cash, his own views do emerge clearly from them. The simple fact is, however, that these views are not of any great substance or profundity and that Howard's style is on the whole crude, slipshod, and unwieldy. Several of Howard's tales are, in addition, appallingly racist—more barefacedly so than anything Lovecraft ever wrote.

Howard's letters, as Lovecraft rightly maintained, deserve to be classed as literature far more than does his fiction. It might well be imagined that the letters of two writers so antipodally different in temperament as Lovecraft and Howard might at the very least be provocative, and sure enough their six-year correspondence not only ranges widely in subject-matter—from somewhat pedantic and now very antiquated discussions of racial origins and types ("The truly Semitic Jew is doubtless superior to the Mongoloid Jew in moral and cultural aspects," Howard once opined[73]) to long disquisitions on each writer's upbringing to arguments about the relative merits of civilisation and barbarism to contemporary political matters (Howard would probably be classified today as a libertarian in his violent objection to any sort of authority)—but also becomes, at times, somewhat testy as each man expresses his views with vigour and determination. I shall have more to say about the substance of some of these disputes later, but one interesting fact can be noted now. Actual rough drafts of some of Howard's letters to Lovecraft have recently been discovered, making it plain that Howard wished to present himself as cogently as he could in his arguments. Howard was clearly intimidated by Lovecraft's learning and felt hopelessly inferior academically; but perhaps he also felt that he had a better grasp of the realities of life than the sheltered Lovecraft, so that he was not about to back down on some of his cherished beliefs. In some instances, as in his frequent descriptions of the violent conditions of the frontier with fights, shootouts, and the like, one almost feels as if Howard is subtly teasing Lovecraft or attempting to shock him; some of Howard's accounts of these matters may, in fact, have been invented.

And yet, Lovecraft is entirely right in his assessment of Howard the man:

> There's a bird whose *basic mentality* seems to me just about the good respectable citizen's (bank cashier, medium shopkeeper, ordinary lawyer, stockbroker, high school teacher, prosperous farmer, pulp fictionist, skilled mechanic, successful salesman, responsible government clerk, routine army or navy officer up to a colonel, &c.) average—bright & keen, accurate & retentive, but not profound or analytical—yet who is at the same time one of the most eminently interesting beings I know. Two-Gun is interesting because he has refused to let his thoughts & feelings be standardised. He remains himself. He couldn't—today—solve a quadratic equation, & probably thinks that Santayana is a brand of coffee—but he has a set of emotions which he has moulded & directed in uniquely harmonious patterns, & from which proceed his marvellous outbursts of historic retrospection & geographical description (in letters), & his vivid, energised & spontaneous pictures of a prehistoric world of battle in fiction . . . pictures which insist on remaining distinctive & self-expressive despite all outward concessions to the stultifying pulp ideal.[74]

Lovecraft habitually overpraised his friends' writings, but on the whole this assessment is quite accurate.

One of Howard's earliest enquiries to Lovecraft was information regarding Cthulhu, Yog-Sothoth, and the like, which Howard took to be genuine mythic lore; the issue was of particular interest in that one reader of *Weird Tales,* N. J. O'Neail, had thought that Howard's Kathulos (a preternatural Egyptian entity featured in "Skull-Face" [*Weird Tales,* October–December 1929]) was somehow related to or derived from Cthulhu. Naturally, Lovecraft told Howard the true state of affairs. As a result, Howard decided to start dropping references to Lovecraft's pseudomythology in his own work; and he did so in exactly the spirit Lovecraft intended—as fleeting background allusions to create a sense of unholy presences behind the surface of life. Very few of Howard's stories seem to me to owe much to Lovecraft's own tales or conceptions, and there are almost no actual pastiches. The *Necronomicon* is cited any number of times; Cthulhu, R'lyeh, and

Yog-Sothoth come in for mention on occasion; but that is all.

Howard's "contribution" to the "Cthulhu Mythos" was a new mythical book, Von Junzt's *Nameless Cults,* frequently referred to by the variant title "Black Book" and apparently first cited in "The Children of the Night" (*Weird Tales,* April–May 1931). In 1932 Lovecraft thought to devise a German title for this work, coming up with the rather ungainly *Ungenennte Heidenthume.* August Derleth vetoed this title, replacing it with *Unaussprechlichen Kulten.* At this point a pedantic argument developed among Lovecraft's colleagues, and also with Farnsworth Wright, who felt that *unaussprechlich* could only mean "unpronounceable" and not "unspeakable" or "nameless"; he wished to substitute the rather colourless *Unnenbaren Kulten,* but the *Weird Tales* artist C. C. Senf, a native German, approved of *Unaussprechlichen Kulten,* and so it has come down to us.[75] To add to the absurdity, this title itself is flawed German, and should either be *Die Unaussprechlichen Kulten* or *Unaussprechliche Kulten.* Even more preposterously, Lovecraft was under the impression that he had, in a ghostwritten story, devised a first name—Friedrich—for von Junzt, which Howard himself had neglected to do, when in fact Lovecraft did so only in a letter.[76] Such are the complexities of "Cthulhu Mythos" scholarship.

Meanwhile Clark Ashton Smith was getting into the act. In the spring of 1925 he had written "The Abominations of Yondo"—the first short story he had written since the early teens. It was not, however, until the fall of 1929, with "The Last Incantation," that he began writing stories in earnest; over the next five years he wrote more than a hundred tales, surpassing in quantity Lovecraft's entire fictional output. Like much of Howard's work, a large proportion of Smith's fiction is routine pulp hackwork, although very different in subject-matter; and because Smith was writing primarily to make money (chiefly to support himself and his increasingly ailing parents), he felt little compunction in altering his tales radically to suit the various pulp markets he cultivated. *Weird Tales* was by no means his only venue; he also wrote for *Strange Tales* and wrote many science fiction tales for *Wonder Stories.* Like Howard's, Smith's tales divide into loose cycles, although they focus not on a character but on a setting: Hyperborea (a prehistoric continent), Atlantis, Averoigne (a region in mediaeval France; the name clearly derived from the actual French province of Auvergne), Zothique (a continent of the far future, when the sun is dying), a conventionalised Mars, and several others.

Smith's stories also exact widely differing responses. They are overcoloured almost beyond belief—and, to some, beyond tolerance; but while Smith unleashes his wide and esoteric vocabulary without restraint, his plots tend to be simple, even simple-minded. My belief is that Smith's fiction is largely an outgrowth of his poetry—or, at least, has many of the same functions as his poetry—in the sense that what he was chiefly trying to achieve was a kind of sensory overload, in which the exotic and the outré are presented merely as such, as a foil to prosy mundanity. There is, therefore, by design little depth or profundity to his fiction; its chief value resides in its glittering surface.

Naturally, some facets of Smith's work are better than others. The Zothique cycle may perhaps be his most successful, and some of the tales—"Xeethra" (*Weird Tales,* February–March 1934), "The Dark Eidolon" (*Weird Tales,* January 1935)—meld beauty and horror in a highly distinctive way. Smith was, in fact, not very successful at pure horror, as for example in his Averoigne tales, which lapse into conventionality in their exhibition of routine vampires and lamias. His science fiction tales have dated lamentably, although "The City of the Singing Flame" (*Wonder Stories,* January 1931) is intoxicatingly exotic, while the horror/science fiction tale "The Vaults of Yoh-Vombis" (*Weird Tales,* May 1932) may be his single finest prose work.

Smith's allusions to Lovecraft's pseudomythology are, like Howard's, very fleeting; indeed, it is highly misleading to think that Smith was somehow "contributing" to Lovecraft's mythos, since from the beginning he felt that he was devising his own parallel mythology. Smith's chief invention is the god Tsathoggua, first created in "The Tale of Satampra Zeiros." Written in the fall of 1929, this story evoked raptures from Lovecraft:

> I must not delay in expressing my well-nigh delirious delight at "The Tale of Satampra Zeiros"—which has veritably given me the one arch-kick of 1929! ... I can see & feel & smell the jungle around immemorial Commoriom, which I am sure must lie buried today in glacial ice near Olathoë, in the land of Lomar! It is of this crux of elder horror, I am certain, that the mad Arab Abdul Alhazred was thinking when he—even he—left something unmention'd & signified by a row of stars in the surviving codex of his accursed & forbidden "Necronomicon"![77]

And so on. Lovecraft is again being very charitable, for the story is rather reminiscent of some of Dunsany's flippant tales of thieves who come to a bad end when they attempt to steal from the gods. Here we have two burglars who seek to rob the temple of Tsathoggua; their end is entirely predictable. But the description of Tsathoggua is of interest: "He was very squat and pot-bellied, his head was more like that of a monstrous toad than a deity, and his whole body was covered with an imitation of short fur, giving somehow a vague suggestion of both the bat and the sloth. His sleep lids were half-lowered over his globular eyes; and the tip of a queer tongue issued from his fat mouth."[78] Lovecraft generally followed this description in most of his citations of the god. Indeed, he was so taken with the invention that he cited it immediately in "The Mound" (1929–30) and "The Whisperer in Darkness"; and since the latter tale was printed in *Weird Tales* for August 1931, three months before "The Tale of Satampra Zeiros," Lovecraft beat Smith into print with the mention of the god. Smith also invented the *Book of Eibon,* which Love-

craft cited frequently. It might well be said that Smith would perhaps not have created the god or the book without Lovecraft's example; indeed, it could well be that
Lovecraft's diligent work as a fiction writer (which Smith had seen develop from
1922 onward) encouraged Smith in the writing of tales, although Lovecraft's actual
work does not seem to have influenced Smith's appreciably.

Nevertheless, Lovecraft was fully aware that he was borrowing from Smith. In
disabusing Robert E. Howard about the reality of the myth-cycle, he remarks:
"Clark Ashton Smith is launching another mock mythology revolving around the
black, furry toad-god 'Tsathoggua' . . ."[79] Smith himself, noting a few years later
how many other writers had borrowed the elements he had invented, remarked to
Derleth: "It would seem that I am starting a mythology."[80]

Smith of course returned the favour and cited Lovecraft's inventions in later
tales—the *Necronomicon,* Yog-Sothoth (under the variant forms Yok-Sothoth and
Iog-Sotôt), Cthulhu (also under variant forms). Just as Robert E. Howard mentioned Lovecraft's "The Call of Cthulhu" by name in "The Children of the Night,"
Smith cited Lovecraft in "The Hunters from Beyond" (*Strange Tales,* October
1932), a story that, in its account of a mad painter, may have been inspired by
"Pickman's Model." (Lovecraft had already cited Smith in *At the Mountains of
Madness* as "Klarkash-Ton.") Most of Smith's borrowings from Lovecraft appear
in the tales of his Hyperborea cycle.

August Derleth was also active. As early as 1931 he felt that this developing
pseudomythology should be given a name; and he suggested, of all things, the
"Mythology of Hastur." Hastur had been alluded to in only a single passage in
"The Whisperer in Darkness" (and it is not even clear there whether Hastur is an
entity—as it is in the work of Ambrose Bierce, who invented the term—or a place,
as in the work of Robert W. Chambers, who borrowed it from Bierce); but Derleth
became fascinated with this term, as later events will show. Lovecraft—who had
never given his pseudomythology a name except when referring to it somewhat
flippantly as the "Arkham cycle" or "Yog-Sothothery"—gently deflected the idea:

> It's not a bad idea to call this Cthulhuism & Yog-Sothothery of mine "The Mythol-
> ogy of Hastur"—although it was really from Machen & Dunsany & others, rather
> than through the Bierce-Chambers line, that I picked up my gradually developing
> hash of theogony—or daimonogony. Come to think of it, I guess I sling this stuff
> more as Chambers does than as Machen & Dunsany do—though I had written a
> good deal of it before I ever suspected that Chambers ever wrote a weird story![81]

It would, certainly, have been better for Lovecraft's subsequent reputation had
the "Cthulhu Mythos" not been exploited as it later was; but that exploitation—
under the aegis of Derleth—occurred in a very different manner from the way it
did in Lovecraft's lifetime, and Lovecraft cannot be held responsible for it. It is a
phenomenon we shall have to study at length later.

Some other new colleagues were coming into Lovecraft's horizon at this time. One was Henry George Weiss (1898–1946), who published under the name "Francis Flagg." Weiss was a poet of some note but published a small amount of weird and science fiction in the pulps, beginning with "The Machine Man of Ardathia" in *Amazing Stories* for November 1927. His "The Chemical Brain" appeared in the January 1929 issue of *Weird Tales,* and he went on to publish several other stories there and in *Amazing* and *Astounding.*

Weiss came in touch with Lovecraft in early 1929 by means of their mutual friend Walter J. Coates.[82] Weiss was a full-fledged communist, and he and Lovecraft must have argued vigorously on the issue; unfortunately, little of Lovecraft's side of the correspondence has turned up. Weiss, at any rate, seems to have been one of the few who could match Lovecraft in epistolary verbosity: in August 1930 he sent Lovecraft a forty-page single-spaced typed letter. Weiss may have had something to do with waking Lovecraft up to the importance of economic issues for an understanding of society.

Toward the end of 1930 Lovecraft heard from Henry St Clair Whitehead (1882–1932), an established pulp writer who published voluminously in *Adventure, Weird Tales, Strange Tales,* and elsewhere. In "In Memoriam: Henry St Clair Whitehead" (1933) Lovecraft states that Whitehead was a native of New Jersey who attended Harvard in the same class as Franklin Delano Roosevelt, and that he later gained a Ph.D. from Harvard, studying for a time under Santayana. Whether he was told this by Whitehead is unclear (the correspondence on both sides seems to have perished), but A. Langley Searles has ascertained that several of these details are either false or unverified.[83] In fact, Whitehead attended both Harvard and Columbia, but did not receive even a B.A., much less a Ph.D., from either institution. In 1912 he was ordained as a deacon of the Episcopal Church, later serving as rector in parishes in Connecticut and New York City. In the late 1920s he was archdeacon in the Virgin Islands, where he gained the local colour for many of his weird tales. By 1930 he was established in a rectory in Dunedin, Florida.

Whitehead's urbane, erudite weird fiction is one of the few literary high spots of *Weird Tales,* although its lack of intensity and the relative conventionality of its supernaturalism have not won it many followers in recent years. Still, his two collections, *Jumbee and Other Uncanny Tales* (1944) and *West India Lights* (1946), contain some fine work. There is some little mystery as to what has become of Lovecraft's correspondence with Whitehead; it appears to have been inadvertently destroyed.[84] In any case, the two men became fast friends and had great respect for each other, both as writers and as human beings. Whitehead's early death was one of a succession of tragedies that would darken Lovecraft's later years.

Another significant correspondent was Joseph Vernon Shea (1912–1981).

Lovecraft may have been momentarily amused to read a letter by Shea in the letter column of *Weird Tales* for October 1926: "I am just a boy of thirteen, but I am in the opinion that *Weird Tales* is the best magazine ever published." Shea went on to praise "The Outsider" as "the weirdest, most thrilling and most eery tale I have ever had the good fortune to read." But Shea did not feel courageous enough to write to Lovecraft himself until 1931; but when he did so (sending a letter to *Weird Tales* for forwarding), there rapidly developed a warm and extensive correspondence—in many senses one of the most interesting of Lovecraft's later letter-cycles, even if some of the material is embarrassingly racist and militarist in content. Shea was blunt and, in youth, a trifle cocksure in the expression of his opinions, and he inspired Lovecraft to some vivid and piquant rebuttals.

Shea was born in Kentucky but spent most of his youth in Pittsburgh. He attended the University of Pittsburgh for only a year before being forced to withdraw because of his parents' impoverishment from the depression. As a result, he too was largely self-taught, and in the process became a considerable authority on music and film. He attempted to write both weird and mainstream fiction in youth, but he did not pursue writing vigorously, even though he later published some weird and science fiction tales in magazines. He edited two anthologies, *Strange Desires* (1954), concerning sexual aberrations, and *Strange Barriers* (1955), about interracial relationships. Some of his essays on Lovecraft—especially "H. P. Lovecraft: The House and the Shadows" (1966)—are quite notable.

Another young colleague that came into Lovecraft's horizon in 1931 was Robert Hayward Barlow (1918–1951). It is certain that Lovecraft had no knowledge, when first receiving a letter from Barlow, that his new correspondent was thirteen years old; for Barlow was then already a surprisingly mature individual whose chief hobby was, indeed, the somewhat juvenile one of collecting pulp fiction, but who was quite well read in weird fiction and enthusiastically embraced a myriad of other interests, from playing the piano to painting to printing to raising rabbits. Barlow was born in Kansas City, Missouri, and spent much of his youth at Fort Benning, Georgia, where his father, Col. E. D. Barlow, was stationed; around 1932 Col. Barlow received a medical discharge and settled his family in the small town of DeLand, in central Florida. Family difficulties later forced Barlow to move to Washington, D.C., and Kansas.

Lovecraft was taken with Barlow, although their correspondence was rather perfunctory for the first year or so. He recognised the youth's zeal and incipient brilliance, and nurtured his youthful attempts at writing weird fiction. Barlow was more interested in pure fantasy than in supernatural horror, and the models for his early work are Lord Dunsany and Clark Ashton Smith; he was so fond of Smith that he bestowed upon the closet where he stored his choicest collectibles the name "The Vaults of Yoh-Vombis." This collecting mania—which extended to manuscripts as well as published material—would prove a godsend in later years. As early as 1932 he was offering to type Lovecraft's old stories in exchange for the autograph or the (by then tattered) original typed manuscripts; Lovecraft, whose horror of the typewriter was by this time reaching phobic proportions, welcomed the offer, and in fact felt a little sheepish in trading clean typescripts for what he regarded as the worthless scrawls of a literary nonentity. Barlow even pestered Lovecraft into letting him attempt to type *The Dream-Quest of Unknown Kadath* and *The Case of Charles Dexter Ward,* but he did not get very far with these.

By the time he got to know Barlow well, Lovecraft regarded him as a child prodigy on the order of Alfred Galpin; and in this he may not have been far wrong. It is true that Barlow sometimes spread himself too thin and had difficulty focusing on any single project, with the result that his actual accomplishments prior to Lovecraft's death seem somewhat meagre; but in his later years he distinguished himself in an entirely different field—Mexican anthropology—and his early death deprived the world of a fine poet and scholar. Lovecraft did not err in appointing Barlow his literary executor.

One may as well give some consideration now to Lovecraft's correspondence, for it would only grow in later years as he became the focal point of the fantasy fandom movement of the 1930s. He himself addresses the issue with Long in late 1930:

> As for Grandpa's correspondence list—well, Sir, I concede it stands badly in need of abridgment . . . yet where, after all, is one to begin? A few figures of older years have indeed disappeared as frequent bombarders, but the increase seems to exceed the elimination a trifle. In the last five years the permanent additions have been Derleth, Wandrei, Talman, Dwyer, [Woodburn] Harris, Weiss, Howard, and (if permanent) Whitehead; of whom Derleth is frequent but not voluminous, Wandrei sparse of late, Talman medium, Dwyer ample but infrequent, Howard heavy and moderate, Weiss encyclopaedic but very infrequent, and Harris voluminous and frequent. Orton, Munn, and Coates are not heavy enough to be counted in. As a palliative measure I can think of nothing at the moment save cutting down Harris a bit.[85]

This list, of course, does not include his old-time amateur colleagues—Moe, Edward H. Cole, Galpin (probably infrequent by this time), Morton, Kleiner (probably very infrequent), and Long himself. Routine amateur correspondence was, of course, at an end, but Lovecraft is probably understating the matter when he says that the "increase seems to exceed the elimination a trifle". In late 1931 he estimated that his regular correspondents numbered between fifty and seventy-five.[86] But numbers do not tell the entire story. It certainly does seem as if Lovecraft—perhaps under the incentive of his own developing philosophical thought—was engaging in increasingly lengthy arguments with a variety of colleagues. I have already mentioned the seventy-page letter he wrote to Woodburn Harris in early 1929; a letter to Long in early 1931 may have been nearly as long (it occupies fifty-two pages in *Selected Letters* and is clearly abridged). His letters are always of consuming interest, but on occasion one feels as if Lovecraft is having some difficulty shutting up.

Many have complained about the amount of time Lovecraft spent (or, as some have termed it, "wasted") on his correspondence, whining that he could have written more fiction instead. Certainly, his array of original fiction (exclusive of revisions) over the last several years was not numerically large: one story in 1928, none in 1929, one in 1930, and two in 1931. Numbers again, however, are deceiving. Almost any one of these five stories would be in itself sufficient to give Lovecraft a place in weird fiction, for most of them are novelettes or short novels of a richness and substance rarely seen outside the work of Poe, Machen, Blackwood, and Dunsany. Moreover, it is by no means certain that Lovecraft would have written more fiction even had he the leisure, for his fiction-writing was always dependent upon the proper mood and the proper gestation of a fictional conception; sometimes such a conception took years to develop.

But the overriding injustice in this whole matter is the belief that Lovecraft should have lived his life for us and not for himself. If he had written no stories but only letters, it would have been our loss but his prerogative. Lovecraft did indeed justify his letter-writing in the same letter to Long:

> . . . an isolated person requires correspondence as a means of seeing his ideas as others see them, and thus guarding against the dogmatisms and extravagances of solitary and uncorrected speculation. No man can learn to reason and appraise from a mere perusal of the writing of others. If he live not in the world, where he can observe the publick at first-hand and be directed toward solid reality by the force of conversation and spoken debate, then he must sharpen his discrimination and regulate his perceptive balance by an equivalent exchange of ideas in epistolary form.

There is certainly much truth in this, and anyone can tell the difference between the cocksure Lovecraft of 1914 and the mature Lovecraft of 1930. What he does not say here, however, is that one of the chief motivations for his correspondence was simple courtesy. Lovecraft answered almost every letter he ever received, and he usually answered it within a few days. He felt it was his obligation as a gentleman to do so. His first letter to J. Vernon Shea is fourteen pages (seven large sheets written on both sides), although in part this is because Shea's first letter to him was a sort of rapid-fire questionnaire probing nosily into both his writing habits and his private life. But this is the sort of thing Lovecraft did habitually, and this is how he established strong bonds of friendship with far-flung associates, many of whom never met him; it is why he became, both during and after his lifetime, a revered figure in the little worlds of amateur journalism and weird fiction.

21. MENTAL GREED
(1931—1933)

The year 1931 was, of course, not an entire disaster for Lovecraft, even though the rejections of some of his best work stung him. In fact, his now customary late spring and summer travels reached the widest extent they would ever achieve in his lifetime, and he returned home with a fund of new impressions that well offset his literary misfortunes.

Lovecraft began his travels on Saturday, May 2, the day after finishing the back-breaking work of typing *At the Mountains of Madness.* His customary stop in New York was very brief: he merely went to the Longs' apartment for dinner, then caught the 12.40 A.M. bus for Charleston via Washington, D.C., Richmond, Winston-Salem and Charlotte, North Carolina, and Columbia, South Carolina. The total time of this bus ride was thirty-six hours. The ride through Virginia was enlivened by music from a blind guitar player and a cross-eyed tenor who regaled their captive audience with "the traditional folk airs of ancient Virginia."[1] They sang purely for the fun of it, and tried to refuse a collection taken up for them, saying, "We don' expeck any money, folks! We're having jes' as good a tahm as you all!"

Lovecraft found Charleston pretty much the same as the year before, aside from the fact that one old Charleston house had been demolished to make way for a filling station—but even this station was (somehow) of Old Charleston architecture! Tuesday the 5th was chilly and cloudy, so Lovecraft devoted himself to interiors, including the Old Exchange with its spectral basement dungeon, the Charleston Museum, and elsewhere. On the 6th Lovecraft took a bus for Savannah, and from there caught another bus for Jacksonville (saving a night's hotel or YMCA bill), arriving at 6 A.M. on the 7th. Jacksonville was a modern town and hence had no appeal for Lovecraft; it was only a way station to a more archaic place—nothing less than the oldest continuously inhabited city in the United States, St Augustine, Florida.

In the two weeks Lovecraft spent in St Augustine he absorbed all the antiquities the town had to offer. The mere fact of being in such an ancient place delighted him, although the town, with its predominantly Hispanic background, did not strike so deep a chord as a town of British origin such as Charleston did. Nevertheless, he was marvellously invigorated by St Augustine—both spiritually and physically, since the genuine tropicality of the town endowed him with reserves of strength unknown in the chilly North. He stayed at the Rio Vista Hotel on Bay Street for $4.00 a week, and during much of his stay he was accompanied by Dudley Newton (1864–1954)—an elderly acquaintance about whom we know virtually nothing.

Lovecraft canvassed the entire town—including the Post Office (housed in a 1591 mansion), Fort San Marcos, the Fountain of Youth, the Bridge of Lions, the Franciscan monastery, and what is presumed to be the oldest house in the United States, built in 1565—as well as nearby Anastasia Island, which offers a spectacular view of the archaic skyline. Lovecraft rhapsodised about the place in letters and postcards sent to friends:

> Around me are the narrow lanes & ancient buildings of the old Spanish capital, the formidable bulk of ancient Fort San Marcos, on whose turreted, sun-drenched parapet I love to sit, the sleepy old market (now a benched loafing-place) in the Plaza de la Constitución, & the whole languorous atmosphere (the tourist season being over) of an elder, sounder, & more leisurely civilisation. Here is a city founded in 1565, 42 years before the first Jamestown colonist landed, & 55 years before the first Pilgrim set foot on Plymouth Rock. Here, too, is the region where Ponce de Leon fared on his vain quest of 1513. . . . It will be like pulling a tooth to break away from here . . .[2]

Lovecraft finally did break away around May 21, as his new correspondent Henry S. Whitehead insisted that he come and visit for an extended period in Dunedin, a small town on a peninsula north of St Petersburg and Clearwater. Letters to Lillian during this three-week stay are in curiously short supply, so that we do not know much about this visit; but Lovecraft found both the environment and his host delightful. He also met several of Whitehead's friends and neighbours, including a young man named Allan Grayson, for whom he wrote a poem in two quatrains entitled "To a Young Poet in Dunedin," the first bit of verse he had written since *Fungi from Yuggoth* a year and a half before. On one occasion Lovecraft recited a sort of synopsis of "The Cats of Ulthar" (he presumably did not have the actual text with him) to a group of young boys from a nearby boys' club. Lovecraft and Whitehead were of almost exactly the same build, and the latter lent Lovecraft a white tropical suit to wear during especially hot days, later making a present of it.

Lovecraft made an excursion to Tampa, the nearest large city, but he found it "sprawling & squalid & without any buildings or traditions of great age."[3] Dunedin itself was not especially ancient, but it was a pleasing small town with well-landscaped gardens, and the Gulf of Mexico was only a few feet from Whitehead's front steps. The natural scenery was magnificent, and in a postcard to Derleth written jointly by Lovecraft and Whitehead, the former waxed eloquent: "Last night we saw the white tropic moon making a magical path on the westward-stretching gulf that lapped at a gleaming, deserted beach on a remote key. Boy! What a sight! It took one's breath away!"[4] The birds were also remarkable—herons, cranes, flamingoes, and others who fluttered very near to where Lovecraft sat reading or writing postcards on the shore. The whippoorwills had a curiously different type of cry than those in New England. Toward the end of his stay Whitehead caught a mottled snake, pickled it, and presented it to Lovecraft.

Either while at Dunedin or when he returned home a month or two later, Lovecraft assisted Whitehead on the writing of a story, "The Trap." He noted in one letter that he "revised & totally recast"[5] the tale, and in another letter said that he "suppl[ied] the central part myself."[6] My feeling is that the latter three-fourths of the story is Lovecraft's. "The Trap" is an entertaining if insubstantial account of an anomalous mirror that sucks hapless individuals into a strange realm where colours are altered and where objects, both animate and inanimate, have a sort of intangible, dreamlike existence. The mirror had been devised by a seventeenth-century Danish glassblower named Axel Holm who yearned for immortality and found it, after a fashion, in his mirror-world, since "'life' in the sense of form and consciousness would go on virtually forever" so long as the mirror itself was not destroyed. A boy, Robert Grandison, one of the pupils at the Connecticut academy where Gerald Canevin teaches, gets drawn into this world, and the tale—narrated in the first person by Canevin—tells of the ultimately successful effort to extricate him.

Because this was a tale that would appear under Whitehead's name—Lovecraft, in his gentlemanly way, refused a collaborative byline—Lovecraft did not drag in references (whimsical or otherwise) to his pseudomythology as he had done in the tales ghostwritten for Zealia Bishop or Adolphe de Castro. (Whitehead is, indeed, one of the few literary associates of Lovecraft's who did not draw upon this body of invented myth or create new elements of his own as "additions" to it.) Whitehead's and Lovecraft's styles do not seem to me to meld very well, and the urbanely conversational style of Whitehead's beginning abruptly gives way to Lovecraft's long paragraphs of dense exposition. The tale was published in the March 1932 issue of *Strange Tales*—Lovecraft's only "appearance" (if it can be called that) in the magazine.

By early June Lovecraft was ready to return north, although he wished to spend at least another week each in St Augustine and Charleston; but two timely revision checks allowed him to prolong the trip unexpectedly. Instead of heading north, on June 10 he went south to Miami—whose vegetation he found strikingly tropical, and which he generally found more prepossessing than Tampa or Jacksonville—and the next day he arrived at his ultimate destination, Key West. This was the farthest south Lovecraft would ever reach, although on this and several other occasions he yearned to hop on a boat and get to Havana, but never had quite enough money to make the plunge.

Key West, the most remote of the Florida Keys, was reached by a succession of ferries and bus rides, since the depression had not allowed the state to construct the continuous series of causeways that now connects all the Keys. Lovecraft wished to explore this place not only because of its remoteness but because of its genuine antiquity: it had been settled in the early nineteenth century by Spaniards, who called it Cayo Hueso (Bone Key); later the name was corrupted by Americans to Key West. Its naval base was of great importance in the Spanish-American War of 1898. Because of its relative isolation, it had not yet been invaded by tourists, so that its archaic charm was preserved: "the town is absolutely natural & unspoiled; a perfect bit of old-time simplicity which is truly quaint because it does not know that it is quaint."[7] Lovecraft spent only a few days in Key West, but he canvassed the place thoroughly.

Lovecraft then returned, apparently, to Miami, as he described making a side-trip to a Seminole village and also a trip over a coral reef on a glass-bottomed boat;[8] it is possible, however, that these Miami excursions had occurred earlier, on his way down. In any event, by June 16 he was back in St Augustine, soaking up the antiquity and spending more time with Dudley Newton. It was at this time that Lovecraft learned that the "accursed cheap skate"[9] Wright had turned down *At the Mountains of Madness.* The manuscript had of course been sent back to Providence, and Lillian had told him of a large parcel that had come from *Weird Tales;* Lovecraft, suspecting the worst, asked her to open it, remove any letter Wright may have enclosed, and send it on to Frank Long, where he would read the bad news as he passed through New York. But the charm of St Augustine took his mind off things for a while. It is interesting to note, however, that Lovecraft remarks having done "quite a bit on a new story yesterday"[10] (June 21), but he ceased abruptly once he heard the news of the rejection. This story fragment does not, apparently, survive.

On the evening of June 22 Lovecraft took a bus back to Jacksonville, then a midnight bus to Savannah. In two hours he looked up all the old parts of the town (he apparently had had no time to do so on his trip down), finding considerable charm in the ancient district: "The town in general is marvellously attractive, having a drowsy & beautiful atmosphere all its own, & being utterly different from CHARLESTON. . . . The whole effect of Savannah is that of one vast sleepy park."[11] He especially liked some of the burying-grounds, including the vast cemetery outside the compact part of the town called Colonial Park with its above-ground wall graves. This is where the Rhode Island colonial general Nathanael Greene is buried, and Lovecraft made sure to seek out this reminder of home.

At 7.30 A.M. on the 23rd Lovecraft took a bus to Charleston, where he stayed a mere two days. Late afternoon on the 25th he left for Richmond, reaching there at noon the next day. He spent less than a day there, exploring some of the Poe sites, and the next morning (the 27th) he made his way to Fredericksburg. The day after found him passing through Philadelphia on his way to New York, which he reached that evening. After a week of looking up his old friends, visiting museums (including the Roerich), and a weekend with the Longs at the seaside resort of Asbury Park, New Jersey, Lovecraft accepted Wilfred B. Talman's offer to spend a week in his large Flatbush apartment. Like Whitehead, Talman also gave Lovecraft one of his suits, as he had become too stout for it. (Throughout his trip Lovecraft worked hard to keep to his "ideal" weight of 140 pounds.) On July 6 a gang meeting at Talman's featured, as a special guest, Seabury Quinn, the *Weird Tales* hack. Lovecraft, although taking a dim view of his endless array of clichéd stories (most revolving around the psychic detective Jules de Grandin), found him "exceedingly tasteful & intelligent,"[12] although more a businessman than an aesthete. Another curious encounter was with a friend of Loveman's named Leonard Gaynor, connected with Paramount. He had become interested in possible film adaptations of Lovecraft's work from Loveman's descriptions of it, but clearly nothing came of this meeting. On Friday the 10th Lovecraft accompanied the Longs on their usual motor trip, this time to the Croton Dam in Westchester County. The scenery was spectacular: "Vivid green slopes, fantastic clusters of trees, blue threads & patches of water, & great lines of outspread hills from the green eminences close at hand to the faint, half-fabulous purple peaks on the far horizon."[13] After another ten days of dawdling in the metropolitan area (including hearing the bad news on the 14th of the rejection by Putnam's of his story collection), Lovecraft finally returned home on July 20. It had been another record-breaking trip, but aside from the letters to Lillian—some of which have clearly been lost—and to other correspondents, he produced no connected travelogue of the journey.

The rest of the year was taken up with lesser trips or with visits to Providence by friends. The day after Lovecraft came home, James F. Morton visited for three days.[14] August 24 found Lovecraft spending the day in Plymouth because of the cheap ($1.75) bus fares. At the beginning of September a journey of a somewhat shorter distance ensued: steam heat was being installed at 10 Barnes, and the resulting racket and disruption forced Lovecraft to spend most of the days at aunt Annie's flat, at 61 Slater Avenue on the East Side. It was at this time that Lovecraft, passing by 454 Angell Street, discovered to his dismay that the old barn of the place had been torn down a month before. Annie also was heartbroken:

> . . . she had seen it built—it being newer than the house. Last month she recovered from the shattered walls the baking-powder tin with "historical data"—tintype, newspaper sheet, & "to whom it may concern" letter—which she had put in in 1881, for the benefit of future archaeologists. How melancholy—& how illustrative of the emptiness of human designs—that she should have to reclaim herself that which was intended for a remote posterity! Eheu, fugaces . . . sic transit gloria mundi![15]

In early October Lovecraft took a trip with Cook to Boston, Newburyport, and Haverhill, looking up the Old Ship Church (1681) in Hingham and visiting with Tryout Smith. Around this time Lovecraft organised an informal fund to purchase a new set of typesetting equipment for Tryout, calling on all his amateur friends to contribute and himself adding a dollar.[16] The fund was completed early the next year and the equipment purchased shortly thereafter; but it did not seem to make much difference in the accuracy of the *Tryout*, which was as error-riddled as before.

In early November, Indian summer lingering unusually late, Lovecraft and Cook took another excursion to Boston, Salem, Marblehead, Newburyport, and Portsmouth.[17] No doubt these visits were the immediate inspiration for "The Shadow over Innsmouth," begun later in the month and finished in early December. At this point, however, the cold curtailed any further outings that required extensive outdoor travel.

New Year's Day 1932, a Friday, was exceptionally mild, so Lovecraft took occasion to spend the weekend with Cook in Boston. They saw five museums in Cambridge on the 2nd (Germanic, Semitic, Peabody, Agassiz, and Fogg) and two more in Boston (Fine Arts and Gardner) the next day. More destruction was occurring in the "Pickman's Model" district in the North End, but of course much of the area had already been razed in 1927.[18]

Lovecraft's financial situation was not getting any better, although for the moment it was not getting any worse. The publication of "The Whisperer in Darkness" in the August 1931 *Weird Tales* enriched him by $350.00—a sum that, given his boast that he had now reduced his expenses to $15.00 per week, could have lasted him for more than five months. Here is how he did it:

> $15.00 per week will float any man of sense in a very tolerable way—lodging him in a cultivated neighbourhood if he knows how to look for rooms, (this one rule, though, breaks down in really megalopolitan centres like New York—but it will work in Providence, Richmond, or Charleston, & would probably work in most of the moderate-sized cities of the northwest) keeping him dressed in soberly conservative neatness if he knows how to choose quiet designs & durable fabrics among cheap suits, & feeding him amply & palatably if he is not an epicurean crank, & if he does not attempt to depend upon restaurants. One must have a kitchen-alcove & obtain provisions at grocery & delicatessen prices rather than pay cafes & cafeterias the additional price they demand for mere service.[19]

Of course, this is predicated on Lovecraft's habit of eating only two (very frugal) meals a day. He actually maintained that "my digestion raises hell if I try to eat oftener than once in 7 hours."[20]

But original fiction—especially now that he was writing work that was not meeting the plebeian criteria of pulp editors—was not going to help much in making ends meet. Reprints brought in very little: he received $12.25 from Selwyn &

Blount in mid-1931[21] (probably for "The Rats in the Walls" in Christine Campbell Thomson's *Switch On the Light* [1931]), and another $25.00 for "The Music of Erich Zann" in Dashiell Hammett's *Creeps by Night* (1931);[22] but, aside from "The Whisperer in Darkness" and $55.00 for "The Strange High House in the Mist" from *Weird Tales,* that may have been all for original fiction sold for the year. Of course, after his double rejections of the summer, Lovecraft was in no mood to hawk his work about. In the fall he sent Derleth several stories the latter had asked to see, including "In the Vault." On his own initiative Derleth retyped the story (Lovecraft's typescript was becoming tattered to the point of disintegration), and then badgered Lovecraft into resubmitting it to Wright; Lovecraft did so, and the tale was accepted in early 1932 for $55.00.[23]

The *Creeps by Night* anthology is worth pausing over, since it evolved into a kind of literary meeting-place for Lovecraft's associates and also represented one of those fleeting occasions in which he—or, in this case, his work—came to the attention of an established literary figure. Dashiell Hammett, who had attained celebrity initially by writing hard-boiled detective stories in the magazine—*Black Mask*—that years earlier had rejected Lovecraft, had already published his first two novels, *Red Harvest* (1929) and *The Maltese Falcon* (1930). Now he was commissioned by the John Day Co. to compile an anthology of weird, horror, and suspense tales. Hammett assembled the volume, however, in a peculiar way: he solicited suggestions from readers and offered them $10 if a story they recommended was selected for the book. In this way August Derleth pocketed $10 for suggesting "The Music of Erich Zann." Of the twenty stories in the volume, six come from *Weird Tales;* aside from Lovecraft's, the others are S. Fowler Wright's "The Rat," Donald Wandrei's "The Red Brain," W. Elwyn Backus's "The Phantom Bus," Paul Suter's "Beyond the Door" (an early favourite of Lovecraft's), and Frank Belknap Long's "A Visitor from Egypt." Something of Derleth's was considered but did not make the final cut.

Lovecraft professed to be somewhat disappointed with *Creeps by Night,* because (understandably in light of Hammett's own work) it tended to feature *contes cruels* rather than tales of the supernatural. And yet, the volume would be notable solely for being the first book appearance (following its publication in the *Forum* for April 1930) of William Faulkner's "A Rose for Emily"; such other superb tales as Hanns Heins Ewers's "The Spider" and Conrad Aiken's "Mr. Arcularis" are also included. Lovecraft violently disliked John Collier's "Green Thoughts," but he never cared for the mingling of humour and horror, even the dark, sardonic humour of Collier. Hammett's very brief introduction makes no mention of Lovecraft's story or any other in the volume. Largely on the basis of his name, *Creeps by Night* proved notably successful, being reprinted by Victor Gollancz in England in 1932 under the title *Modern Tales of Horror,* by Blue Ribbon Books in 1936, by the World Publishing Co. in 1944, and in sundry abridged paperback editions. It was the British edition that surely led to the reprinting of "The Music of Erich Zann" in the London *Evening Standard* on October 24, 1932, netting Lovecraft another $21.61.[24]

In early 1932 a potential new magazine market emerged, only to fizzle. A Carl Swanson of Washburn, North Dakota, had come up with the idea of a semi-professional magazine, *Galaxy,* that would use both original stories and reprints from *Weird Tales.* At this stage Swanson had not determined how much he would pay, but he promised to pay something. Lovecraft heard about the magazine from Henry George Weiss and was about to write to Swanson when Swanson himself wrote. Lovecraft sent him "The Nameless City" and "Beyond the Wall of Sleep" (both *Weird Tales* rejects), and Swanson accepted them with alacrity.[25] Lovecraft was also keen on sending Swanson some *Weird Tales* stories for which he owned second serial rights; and because he evidently did not know for which stories he owned such rights, he asked Farnsworth Wright about the matter. Lovecraft told Talman what Wright's response was:

> Wright replied that it was nix on the ones he owned, and that—since Swanson was likely to prove a rival of his—he did not favour the second sale of those tales in which I hold later rights. In other words, this bozo who has exploited his authors for his own profit—cabbaging all their rights until they learned to reserve them, rejecting their best tales, reprinting others without added remuneration, and backing out of book-publishing promises while he pushes the work of his pal [Otis Adelbert] Kline—this hard egg who actually boasted to a friend of Belknap's that he has his authors at his mercy financially because for the most part there's nowhere else they can place their work—expects his lamb-like contributors to forfeit their legitimate rights as a personal favour to him in exchange for his unnumbered kindnesses! Gents, I like that! Well—what I did was to give him the civilised Rhodinsular equivalent of that curt injunction so popular in his own tempest-swept cosmopolis—"go jump in the lake"![26]

Lovecraft's relations with Wright had certainly reached rock-bottom. Wright was clearly using strong-arm tactics to dissuade his authors from submitting to Swanson, suggesting that he would be disinclined to accept stories of theirs if they published in *Galaxy.* Frank Long was so intimidated by this threat that he had nothing to do with Swanson. Lovecraft, who at this juncture was not much inclined to send anything to Wright anyway, felt no such compunction.

Unfortunately, the Swanson venture never materialised: by late March it had collapsed, as Swanson was unable to arrange for the financing and printing of the magazine. He had vague ideas of issuing a mimeographed magazine or a series of booklets, but Lovecraft rightly concluded that this did not sound very promising, and in fact it never came about. Swanson disappeared and was never heard of again.

It was certainly unfortunate that Lovecraft, in the course of his entire life, was never able to secure a reliable second market for his work aside from *Weird Tales.* His one sale to *Amazing Stories* was his last, as the pay was outrageously low and late in coming. *Tales of Magic and Mystery* also paid poorly and folded after five issues. Lovecraft's submissions to *Strange Tales* were all rejected (it died after seven issues anyway), and his two sales to *Astounding Stories* came only in the mid-1930s and were essentially luck-shots. If such a second market had emerged, Lovecraft could have used it as leverage to persuade Wright to accept items that he might otherwise have been hesitant to take, in order to retain Lovecraft's presence in *Weird Tales.*

Of course, a book would have been a real venue to both financial gain and literary recognition. In March 1932 such a prospect emerged for the third time, but once again it collapsed. Arthur Leeds had spoken to a friend of his who was an editor at Vanguard (formerly Macy-Masius, which had been involved in the Asbury *Not at Night* imbroglio) about Lovecraft, who accordingly received a letter of enquiry. Vanguard wanted a novel, but Lovecraft (having already repudiated *The Dream-Quest of Unknown Kadath* and *The Case of Charles Dexter Ward* and evidently not considering *At the Mountains of Madness* a true novel) said he had none at hand. Nevertheless, the firm did ask to see some of his short stories, so Lovecraft sent them "Pickman's Model," "The Dunwich Horror," "The Rats in the Walls," and "The Call of Cthulhu."[27] The stories eventually came back.

How was revision faring? Not especially well. After the work done for Zealia Bishop and Adolphe de Castro, no new would-be weird writers were appearing on the horizon. Of course, the revision of weird fiction was a relatively small facet of his revisory work, which centred on more mundane matter—textbooks, poetry, and the like. But the departure of David Van Bush as a regular client, along with Lovecraft's unwillingness or lack of success in advertising his services, made this work very irregular.

It was around this time that Lovecraft prepared a definitive chart of his revisory rates, giving full particulars of the type of activity he would undertake (from mere reading to full-fledged ghostwriting) and the rates he would charge. These rates, although perhaps a little higher than what he was charging earlier, still seem criminally low; and yet, Lovecraft appears to have been lucky to get the clients he did even with these rates. The chart reads as follows:

H. P. Lovecraft—Prose Revision Rates

Reading Only—rough general remarks

1000 words or less	0.50
1000–2000	0.65
2000–4000	1.00
4000–5000	1.25

20¢ for each 1000 wds over 5000

Criticism Only—analytical estimate in detail
without revision

1000 words or less	1.50
1000–2000	2.00
2000–4000	3.00
4000–5000	3.75

60¢ for each 1000 wds over 5000

Revision & Copying (Per page of 330 words)

(a) Copying on typewriter—double space, 1 carbon. No revision except spelling, punctuation, & grammar _____ 0.25

(b) Light revision, no copying (prose improved locally—no new ideas) _____ 0.25

(c) Light revision typed, double-space with 1 carbon _____ 0.50

(d) Extensive revision, no copying (through improvement, including structural change, transposition, addition, or excision—possible introduction of new ideas or plot elements. Requires new text or separate MS.) In rough draught longhand _____ 0.75

(e) Extensive revision as above, typed, double space, 1 carbon ____ 1.00

(f) Rewriting from old MS., synopsis, plot-notes, idea-germ, or mere suggestion—i.e., "ghost-writing". Text in full by reviser—both language & development. Rough draught, longhand _____ 2.25

(g) Rewriting as above, typed, double space, 1 carbon _____ 2.50

Special flat rates quoted for special jobs, depending on estimated consumption of time & energy.[28]

The prospect of a regular position apparently emerged sometime in 1931, but Lovecraft was unable to accept it. Early in the year he speaks of a "reading & revisory post" that was offered to him, but it was in Vermont, which "made it physically out of the question as a year-round matter."[29] I am not sure whether this is the same or similar to the offer that he talked about later in the year, when the Stephen Daye Press of Brattleboro, Vermont (managed by Vrest Orton), gave him the job of revising and proofreading Leon Burr Richardson's *History of Dartmouth College* (1932). Lovecraft mentioned this in September,[30] and stated that he might have to go to Vermont to work on it; but that does not seem to have occurred. A month later, however, in early October, a telegram summoned him to Hartford, Connecticut, for a "personal conference" of some kind connected with the project. Although Lovecraft received only $50.00 plus expenses for his work on the book, he thought that it "may prove the opening wedge for a good deal of work from the Stephen Daye";[31] but, again, this did not happen. Lovecraft's revision on the Dartmouth College history really amounted to mere copyediting, for I cannot detect much actual Lovecraft prose in the treatise.

Lovecraft also occasionally had problems collecting on the revision work he did. I have already mentioned that Zealia Bishop was quite remiss in paying her bill: she still owed Lovecraft money till the day he died, and long after he had ceased to do any work for her. One amusing incident occurred in the fall of 1930, when one Lee Alexander Stone inexplicably failed to pay $7.50 for an article, "Is Chicago a Crime-Ridden City?," that Lovecraft had revised a year and a half before. Wearying of dunning Stone for the amount, Lovecraft finally wrote it off as a loss, but sent a tart letter to Stone as a parting shot:

> In the matter of your persistently unpaid revision bill—concerning which you so persistently withhold all explanations despite repeated inquiries—I have decided, at the risk of encouraging sharp practices, to forego the use of a collecting agency and make you a present of the amount involved.
>
> This is my first encounter with such a hopelessly bad bill, and I believe I may consider the sum ($7.50) as not ill spent in acquiring practical experience. I needed to be taught caution in accepting unknown clients without ample references—especially clients from a strident region which cultivates ostentatious commercial expansion rather than the honour customary among gentlemen.
>
> Meanwhile I am grateful for so concrete an answer to the popular question, "Is Chicago a Crime-Ridden City?"[32]

Quite a zinger. But Lovecraft later learned from Farnsworth Wright—who had recommended Stone—that Stone was bankrupt and ill. Lovecraft was a little abashed, although he still wrote petulantly, ". . . the fellow *might* have written me instead of ignoring all my polite early reminders!"[33]

Lovecraft did occasionally make other attempts to bring in cash. Wilfred Blanch Talman had left his position at the *New York Times* and begun work for Texaco; part of his responsibilities involved the editorship of several trade papers, including the *Texaco Star*. In late 1930 Lovecraft said to Talman that he could write a whole series of "descriptive travel-treatises" with the series title "On the Trail of the Past."[34] This offer seems to have been made somewhat whimsically, and of course nothing came of it. Talman did, however, urge Lovecraft to try to market his travelogue material, but Lovecraft was sceptical:

> I have my doubts about the commercial availability of such material, since my style—as well as my basic principles of selection in assembling material—would seem to me to be one to which the modern world of trade is antipodally alien & even actively hostile. I have seen some of the publications of coach companies— which are stacked for distribution in waiting rooms—& have so far found their travel material altogether different in tone, atmosphere, & content from mine. Possibly I might artificially turn out something to suit their needs if I studied those needs more exactly . . . Marketing, though, is easier said than done. Various persons have thought my stuff might fit the Christian Science Monitor, which has rather a bias toward travel; but upon examination it appears that Monitor stuff always concerns more exotic & unusual places than I visit.[35]

Lovecraft is probably right in his assessment. For his travelogues to become marketable would have required not merely the elimination of his archaisms of style but a radical recasting and reemphasis, and the suppression of his piquant personal opinions. The travelogues as they stand are so delightful to read precisely because they are the product of a person who is both keenly observant and delightfully idiosyncratic; and, given Lovecraft's temperament, the attempt to water them down to suit a commercial market would have been as difficult and repugnant as the production of hack fiction.

One very curious job Lovecraft had around this time was that of a ticket-seller in a movie theatre. A professor at Brown University, Robert Kenny (1902–1983), maintained that he saw Lovecraft go downtown in the evening (he worked the night shift) and sit in a booth in one of the theatres, reading a book whenever he was not actually dispensing tickets. Harry K. Brobst confirms the story, stating that Lovecraft admitted to him that he had held such a job, saying that he actually liked it at the start, but that it did not last very long. Brobst does not know when Lovecraft held the position, but he believes it to have been in the early days of the depression, perhaps 1929–30.

Somehow or other, in spite of rejections and the precarious status of his revision work, Lovecraft managed to write another tale in February 1932, "The Dreams in the Witch House." Its working title—"The Dreams of Walter Gilman"—tells the whole story. A mathematics student at Miskatonic University named Walter Gilman who lives in a peculiarly angled room in the old Witch House in Arkham begins experiencing bizarre dreams filled with sights, sounds, and shapes of an utterly indescribable cast; other dreams, much more realistic in nature, reveal a huge rat with human hands named Brown Jenkin, who appears to be the familiar of the witch Keziah Mason, who once dwelt in the Witch House. Meanwhile Gilman, in his classwork, begins to display a remarkable intuitive grasp of hyperspace, or the fourth dimension. But then his dreams take an even weirder turn, and there are indications that he is sleepwalking. Keziah seems to be urging him on in some nameless errand ("He must meet the Black Man, and go with them all to the throne of Azathoth at the centre of ultimate Chaos"). Then in one very clear dream he sees himself "half lying on a high, fantastically balustraded terrace above a boundless jungle of outlandish, incredible peaks, balanced planes, domes, minarets, horizontal discs poisoned on pinnacles, and numberless forms of still greater wildness." The balustrade is decorated with curious designs representing ridged, barrel-shaped entities (i.e., the Old Ones from *At the Mountains of Madness*); but Gilman wakes screaming when he sees the living barrel-shaped entities coming toward him. The next morning the barrel-shaped ornament—which he had broken off the balustrade *in the dream*—is found in his bed.

Things seem rapidly to be reaching some hideous culmination. A baby is kidnapped and cannot be found. Then, in a dream, Gilman finds himself in some strangely angled room with Keziah, Brown Jenkin, and the baby. Keziah is going to sacrifice the child, but Gilman knocks the knife out of her hand and sends it clattering down some nearby abyss. He and Keziah engage in a fight, and he manages to frighten her momentarily by displaying a crucifix given to him by a fellow tenant; when Brown Jenkin comes to her aid, he kicks the familiar down the abyss, but not before it has made some sort of sacrificial offering with the baby's blood. The next night Gilman's friend Frank Elwood witnesses a nameless horror: he sees some ratlike creature literally eat its way through Gilman's body to his heart. The Witch House is rented no more, and years later, when it is torn down, an enormous pile of human bones going back centuries is discovered, along with the bones of some huge ratlike entity.

One can agree wholeheartedly with Steven J. Mariconda's labelling this story "Lovecraft's Magnificent Failure."[36] In a sense, "The Dreams in the Witch House" is the most cosmic story Lovecraft ever wrote: he has made a genuine, and very provocative, attempt actually to visualise the fourth dimension:

> All the objects—organic and inorganic alike—were totally beyond description or even comprehension. Gilman sometimes compared the inorganic masses to prisms, labyrinths, clusters of cubes and planes, and Cyclopean buildings; and the

organic things struck him variously as groups of bubbles, octopi, centipedes, living Hindoo idols, and intricate Arabesques roused into a kind of ophidian animation.

The imaginative scope of the novelette is almost unthinkably vast; but it is utterly confounded by slipshod writing and a complete confusion as to where the story is going. Lovecraft here lapses into hackneyed and overblown purple prose that sounds almost like a parody of his own style: "Everything he saw was unspeakably menacing and horrible; . . . he felt a stark, hideous fright." There are countless unresolved elements in the tale. What is the significance of the sudden appearance of the Old Ones in the story? To what purpose is the baby kidnapped and sacrificed? How can Lovecraft the atheist allow Keziah to be frightened off by the sight of a crucifix? In the final confrontation with Keziah, what is the purpose of the abyss aside from providing a convenient place down which to kick Brown Jenkin? How does Brown Jenkin subsequently emerge from the abyss to eat out Gilman's heart? Lovecraft does not seem to have thought out any of these issues; it is as if he were aiming merely for a succession of startling images without bothering to think through their logical sequence or coherence.

Nevertheless, the "cosmic" portions of "The Dreams in the Witch House" almost redeem the many flaws in the tale. "Dreams" is really the critical term here; for this story brings to a culmination all Lovecraft's previous ruminations on the "occasionally titanic significance of dreams," as he commented in "Beyond the Wall of Sleep." Gilman's are not, indeed, ordinary dreams—"faint and fantastic reflections of our waking experiences"—but avenues toward other realms of entity normally inaccessible to human beings. This point is made perhaps a little too obviously by the appearance of the balustrade-ornament from hyperspace into our world.

"The Dreams in the Witch House" is also Lovecraft's ultimate modernisation of a conventional myth (witchcraft) by means of modern science. Fritz Leiber, who has written the most perspicacious essay on the tale, notes that it is "Lovecraft's most carefully worked out story of hyperspace-travel. Here (1) a rational foundation for such travel is set up; (2) hyperspace is visualized; and (3) a trigger for such travel is devised."[37] Leiber elaborates keenly on these points, noting that the absence of any mechanical device for such travel is vital to the tale, for otherwise it would be impossible to imagine how a "witch" of the seventeenth century could have managed the trick; in effect, Keziah simply applied advanced mathematics and "thought" herself into hyperspace.

Lovecraft's hints that Keziah's hyperspace-travel is a secret type of knowledge that is only now coming to light in the work of advanced astrophysicists (Planck, Heisenberg, Einstein, and Willem de Sitter are mentioned by name) make for one more "updating" of an older Lovecraftian conception. When Gilman boldly maintains that "Time could not exist in certain belts of space" and goes on to justify this view, we are cast back to the early story "The White Ship" (1919), in which the narrator remarks: "In the Land of Sona-Nyl there is neither time nor space, neither suffering nor death; and there I dwelt for many aeons." Granting the difference between a Dunsanian fantasy and a quasi-science fiction tale, the greater intellectual rigour now underlying Lovecraft's fiction is manifest.

Nevertheless, "The Dreams in the Witch House" overall is indeed a failure, and is one of the most disappointing of his later tales. Lovecraft seems to have known that it was perhaps a step backward in his fictional development, and he never ranked it high among his works.

Lovecraft remarked that the story was typed by a revision client as payment for revisory work.[38] I do not know who this is; perhaps it is Zealia Bishop. The type-script is remarkably accurate, and the typist seems to have had a fair ability to read Lovecraft's handwriting. Lovecraft was, however, still in such a state of uncertainty about the merits of his own work that he felt the need to elicit his colleagues' opin-ion on the story before he submitted it anywhere, and so he sent both the original and the carbon on a series of rounds among his correspondents. Several seemed to like the story, but August Derleth's reaction was very much the contrary. One can gauge the severity of Derleth's criticism by Lovecraft's response: ". . . your reaction to my poor 'Dreams in the Witch House' is, in kind, about what I expected—although I hardly thought the miserable mess was *quite* as bad as you found it. . . . The whole incident shews me that my fictional days are probably over."[39] This is not exactly what Lovecraft needed to hear at this point, even if Derleth was (in this instance) correct in his analysis. Elsewhere he elaborated on Derleth's verdict: ". . . Derleth didn't say it was *unsalable;* in fact, he rather thought it *would* sell. He said it was a *poor story,* which is an entirely different and much more lamentably impor-tant thing."[40] In other words, in Derleth's opinion the story was just like most of the junk appearing in *Weird Tales,* on which Lovecraft regularly heaped abuse. It is not surprising that Lovecraft refused to submit the tale to any magazine and merely let it gather dust.

A year or so later Derleth redeemed himself by asking to see the story again and surreptitiously submitting it to Farnsworth Wright, who accepted it readily and paid Lovecraft $140.00 for it. It appeared in the July 1933 issue of *Weird Tales.*

Around this time still more fans, colleagues, and writers were coming into Love-craft's horizon. One was a very strange individual named William Lumley. Love-craft writes of him to Derleth in 1931:

> Did I tell you of the amusing freak who has looked me up through W.T.? A chap named William Lumley of Buffalo N.Y., who *believes in magic* & has seri-ously read all such half-fabulous tomes as Paracelsus, Delrio, &c. &c.—despite an

illiteracy which makes him virtually unable to spell. He wanted to know the real facts about the Cthulhu & Yog-Sothoth cults—& when I disillusioned him he made me a gift of a splendid illustrated copy of "Vathek"![41]

To Clark Ashton Smith he wrote:

[Lumley] says he has witnessed monstrous rites in deserted cities, has slept in pre-human ruins and awaked 20 years older, has seen strange elemental spirits in all lands (including Buffalo, N.Y.—where he frequently visits a haunted valley and sees a white, misty Presence), has written and collaborated on powerful dramas, has conversed with incredibly wise and monstrously ancient wizards in remote Asiatic fastnesses . . ., and not long ago had sent him from India for perusal a pa-laeogean and terrible book in an unknown tongue . . . which he could not open without certain ceremonies of purification, including the donning of a white robe![42]

Lumley (1880–1960) was one of several individuals who had become intrigued with Lovecraft's evolving pseudomythology (in 1929 Lovecraft had heard from a woman in Boston who was descended from the Salem witches[43] and from a "gro-tesque Maine person"[44] who sought information on diabolism from Lovecraft, promising not to put it to malign use); most of these correspondents drifted away after a few weeks or months, but Lumley persisted. As with several modern occult-ists, he was convinced of the literal truth of Lovecraft's mythos, and it did not mat-ter that Lovecraft and his colleagues claimed it all to be an invention: "We may *think* we're writing fiction, and may even (absurd thought!) disbelieve what we write, but at bottom we are telling the truth in spite of ourselves—serving unwit-tingly as mouthpieces of Tsathoggua, Crom, Cthulhu, and other pleasant Outside gentry."[45]

A rather more level-headed person was Harry Kern Brobst (1909–2010), who was born in Wilmington, Delaware, and moved to Allentown, Pennsylvania, in 1921. He had become interested in weird and science fiction as a youth, being es-pecially fond of the work of Poe, Verne, Dunsany, Clark Ashton Smith, and Love-craft. Writing to Farnsworth Wright of *Weird Tales,* he acquired Lovecraft's ad-dress and began a correspondence, probably in the autumn of 1931. Not long thereafter, however, a fortunate circumstance brought him into much closer touch with his new colleague.

After graduating from high school, Brobst decided to enter the field of psychi-atric nursing. A friend of his recommended that he apply to the medical program at Butler Hospital in Providence, and he was accepted. Telling Lovecraft of this turn of events, Brobst received a long letter detailing all the antiquarian glories of Providence and making Brobst feel, as it were, at home in the city even before he got there.

Brobst arrived in Providence in February 1932. A few weeks later he came to visit Lovecraft, and his impressions both of the man and his humble residence at 10 Barnes Street are affecting:

> He was a tall man, of sallow complexion, very animated . . ., with dark, sparkling eyes. I don't know if this description makes much sense, but that was the impression he made—a very *vital* person. We were friends immediately. . . .
>
> Now at 10 Barnes Street I believe he was on the ground floor. . . . when you went into the room that he occupied there were no windows—it was completely cut off, and he just lived by artificial light. I remember going in there one time and it was in the colder time of the year . . . The room was stuffy, very dusty (he wouldn't allow anybody to dust it, especially the books); his bedding was quite (I hate to say this) dirty. . . . And he had nothing to eat excepting a piece of cheese.[46]

How will Lovecraft ever live down the ignominy of dirty sheets! He who was so meticulous about his personal tidiness appears to have been less scrupulous about his surroundings. Brobst goes on to say that Lovecraft somewhat theatrically took a book from his shelves and blew off the dust that had accumulated upon it: evidently he felt it quaint for an old fossil like himself to have shelves full of dusty old books.

Brobst would be in very close contact with Lovecraft for the next five years, visiting him several times a week, going with him to museums, having meals with him in restaurants, and welcoming Lovecraft's out-of-town visitors as they came to visit him. Few knew Lovecraft better at this period, on a personal level, than Harry Brobst. He would later gain a B.A. from Brown in psychology and an M.A. and Ph.D. from the University of Pennsylvania. He spent many years teaching at Oklahoma State University, and later resided in Stillwater, Oklahoma.

Carl Ferdinand Strauch (1908–1989) was a friend of Brobst's who first wrote to Lovecraft in the autumn of 1931. Born in Lehighton, Pennsylvania, Strauch spent most of his life in Allentown, graduating from Muhlenberg College and later receiving a M.A. from Lehigh (1934) and a Ph.D. from Yale (1946). He worked at the Muhlenberg College library from 1930 to 1933, then began a long teaching career at Lehigh, retiring in 1974 as a full professor. Strauch had published a slim book of poetry, *Twenty-nine Poems,* in 1932. He later became a distinguished scholar of American literature, publishing studies of Emerson and serving on the editorial board of the Harvard University Press edition of Emerson's *Collected Works* (1971f.).

Strauch wrote to Lovecraft quite regularly for a period of about two years; but the correspondence broke off abruptly in the summer of 1933. Strauch had sent Lovecraft a story to assess, and during an all-night session Lovecraft, E. Hoffmann Price, and Brobst evidently tore the thing to shreds, although not maliciously. Brobst believes that Strauch was so crushed by this criticism that he became discouraged and ceased writing to Lovecraft.

In the summer of 1932 Lovecraft came in touch with Ernest A. Edkins. Edkins (1867–1946) was a renowned amateur from the "halcyon days" of amateurdom in the 1890s; Lovecraft much admired this early work, some of which was powerfully weird, although later Edkins repudiated it and claimed to have a great disdain for weird fiction. Lovecraft managed to lure him back into amateurdom in the mid-1930s, and Edkins issued several fine issues of the amateur journal *Causerie* in 1936. Incredibly, Lovecraft kept all of Edkins's letters to him, something he rarely did because of his chronic lack of space; and these letters suggest that their correspondence must have been of exceptional interest. But Edkins has written that he somehow lost most or all of Lovecraft's letters.[47]

Richard Ely Morse (1909–1986) was another associate whom Samuel Loveman introduced to Lovecraft. The two met in person in May 1932, when Lovecraft passed through New York on his way south, and after Lovecraft's return a brisk correspondence ensued. Morse, a graduate of Amherst College with family ties to Princeton University, had published a book of poetry, *Winter Garden* (1931), at Amherst, although he did not do much writing thereafter. He worked for a time at the Princeton University Library, then in 1933 was hired by his uncle to do research at the Library of Congress in Washington.

Lovecraft's feelings about Morse were mixed. While admiring Morse's sensitivity to poetry, art, and the weird, he saw some drawbacks in his character: "He is a very lean, hatchet-faced dark chap with horn-rimmed glasses. Just a trifle dandified—immaculate, & inclined toward walking-sticks. A suspicion of languid affectation in his voice—which the passing years will doubtless dispel. . . . Decidedly pleasant, on the whole."[48] Later he was still harsher: "Didn't see Morse after all— for which I'm rather glad. He has many gifts, and much taste in many fields, but affected, sissified poseurs give me a pain in the neck."[49]

The Minnesota pulp writer Carl Jacobi (1908–1997) came into personal communication with Lovecraft in late February 1932. Lovecraft spoke warmly of his enjoyment of Jacobi's fine tale of undersea horror, "Mive" (*Weird Tales*, January 1932), which might have been influenced by Lovecraft. He read other of Jacobi's works in the weird, science fiction, and "weird menace" pulps with somewhat less enthusiasm. Jacobi does not seem to have become a regular correspondent of Lovecraft's, and only one letter (February 27, 1932) has come to light. August Derleth would publish three collections of Jacobi's weird fiction with Arkham House.

When Harry Brobst arrived in Providence in February 1932, Lovecraft gave him the now customary tour of the city's antiquarian delights. On this occasion Lovecraft and Brobst saw at the Athenaeum an issue of the *American Review* for December 1847 containing an unsigned appearance of Poe's "Ulalume," with the copy signed in pencil by Poe himself.[50] On April 21 Lovecraft went to Boston, where he met with W. Paul Cook and H. Warner Munn.[51] But the real travels for the year began on May 18.

On that day Lovecraft left for New York, intending to stop only briefly before proceeding farther south; but Frank Long persuaded him to stay a week, since his family's apartment would be undergoing renovation in June and it would therefore be awkward for Lovecraft to stay there on his return trip. Lovecraft underwent the usual flurry of social calls on the New York gang—Morton, Leeds, Loveman, Kirk, Kleiner, Talman, and others—but finally managed to pull away on May 25, taking the night bus to Washington and from there a succession of buses to Knoxville, Chattanooga (where he went up Lookout Mountain and also into a cave in the mountain), and Memphis (where he saw the Mississippi River for the first time), then down to Vicksburg (whose quaint streets he appreciated) and finally to Natchez.

In Natchez Lovecraft was stimulated both by the spectacular natural landscape (200-foot bluffs above the Mississippi, invigorating tropical climate and vegetation) and the antiquities of the town itself. It had been founded by the French in 1716, transferred to Great Britain in 1763, overrun by the Spanish in 1779, and ceded to the United States in 1798. Many stately mansions still remain, and—rather like Charleston and Newport—the very fact that it gave way in commercial importance to another town (Vicksburg) has allowed its antiquities to be preserved in a sort of museum effect. Lovecraft spent only two days there, but averred that "It takes rank with Charleston, Quebec, Salem, Marblehead, & Newburyport as one of my favourite early-American backwaters."[52]

Lovecraft then proceeded still farther south to his ultimate destination—New Orleans. It did not take long for him to feel the charm of this distinctive city: having arrived in late May, he was ready to declare by June 6 that the three towns of Charleston, Quebec, and New Orleans "stand out as the most thoroughly ancient & exotic urban centres of North America."[53] Naturally the French Quarter—the Vieux Carré—with its unique conjoining of French and Spanish architectural styles appealed to him most, although he found even the newer parts with their long shady streets and stately homes appealing. Such things as above-ground cemeteries, inner courtyards of both public and private buildings, the great 1794 cathedral in Jackson Square, and other sites were absorbed; and on June 11 Lovecraft took a ferry across the river to the suburb of Algiers, thus representing the only time in his life that he would set foot on land west of the Mississippi.

An interesting social call occurred toward the end of Lovecraft's New Orleans stay. He had written of his trip to Robert E. Howard, who bitterly regretted his inability to travel there himself and meet his much-admired correspondent; but Howard did the next best thing and telegraphed his friend E. Hoffmann Price, who had a room in the French Quarter, and told him of Lovecraft's presence. Price accordingly met Lovecraft on Sunday, June 12, conducting a call that lasted 25½ hours, till midnight on Monday.

Edgar Hoffmann Price (1898–1988) was certainly an unusual individual. A man of many talents ranging from Arabic to fencing, he wrote some fine stories for *Weird Tales* and other pulps in the early 1920s, including the superb "Stranger from Kurdistan" (*Weird Tales,* July 1925), which I have already noted as being a possible influence on "The Horror at Red Hook." Price was a good friend of Farnsworth Wright and may have been acquainted with him even before he became editor of *Weird Tales.* Lovecraft makes the odd remark in 1927 that "after due deliberation & grave consultation with E. Hoffman [*sic*] Price, Wright has very properly rejected my 'Strange High House in the Mist,' as not sufficiently clear for the acute minds of his highly intelligent readers,"[54] suggesting that Price was acting as a sort of informal consultant to Wright. In 1931 Lovecraft heard from Robert E. Howard that Price and his fellow-writer W. Kirk Mashburn were planning an anthology that would include "Pickman's Model," but this came to nothing and Lovecraft evidently did not hear from Price directly on the matter.[55] The next year Price and an agent named August Lenniger conceived of another anthology that would include "The Picture in the House," but this too came to nothing.

The depression hurt Price in more than one way: in May 1932 he was laid off from the well-paying job he had held with the Prestolite Company, and he decided to try his hand at making a living by writing. He felt he could do so only by writing exactly what the editors wanted, so he began catering quite coldbloodedly to market requirements in many different realms of pulp fiction—weird, "Oriental," "weird menace," and the like. The result was that throughout the 1930s and '40s Price landed a flood of very slick but literarily valueless material in such magazines as *Weird Tales, Strange Detective Stories, Spicy-Adventure Stories, Argosy, Strange Stories, Terror Tales,* and the like, spelling his aesthetic damnation and relegating the vast majority of his work to the oblivion it deserves.

And yet, Lovecraft was very taken with Price as a person:

> Price is a remarkable chap—a West-Pointer, war veteran, Arabic student, connoisseur of Oriental rugs, amateur fencing-master, mathematician, dilettante coppersmith & iron worker, chess-champion, pianist, & what not! He is dark & trim of figure, not very tall, & with a small black moustache. He talks fluently & incessantly, & might be thought a bore by some—although I like to hear him rattling on.[56]

Price, in turn, has an affecting account of his first meeting with Lovecraft:

> . . . he carried himself with enough of a slouch to make me underestimate his height as well as the breadth of his shoulders. His face was thin and narrow, longish, with long chin and jaw. He walked with a quick stride. His speech was quick

and inclined to jerkiness. It was as though his body was hard put to it to keep up with the agility of his mind. . . .

He was not pompous, and he was not pretentious—quite the contrary. He merely had a knack of using formal and academic diction for the most casual remark. We had not walked a block before I realized that no other way of speech could be truly natural for HPL. Had he used locutions less stilted, and taken to speaking as others did, *that* would have been an affectation. . . .

Twenty-eight hours we gabbled, swapping ideas, kicking fancies back and forth, topping each other's whimsies. He had an enormous enthusiasm for new experience: of sight, of sound, of word pattern, of idea pattern. I have met in all my time only one or two others who approached him in what I call "mental greed." A glutton for words, ideas, thoughts. He elaborated, combined, distilled, and at a machine gun tempo.[57]

As if it were not evident in so many other ways, this first encounter with Price goes far in showing how Lovecraft had matured as a human being over the past fifteen years. In 1917 his meeting with Rheinhart Kleiner—a man with whom he had been corresponding for two years—was stiff and formal to the point of eccentricity. Now, meeting a man with whom he was not previously acquainted at all, he acted with the informality and cordiality of a friend of many years' standing. It is scarcely to be wondered that a lively correspondence sprung up between the two men upon Lovecraft's return—a correspondence that Lovecraft himself valued so much, in spite of his antipodal opposition to many of Price's aesthetic views, that he saved every scrap of it. Aside from Price's, the only letters to Lovecraft we have in any abundance are those from Donald Wandrei, Robert E. Howard, Clark Ashton Smith, C. L. Moore, and Ernest A. Edkins.

One curious myth that has somehow developed from Lovecraft's New Orleans trip is the belief that Price took Lovecraft to a whorehouse where the girls proved to be avid readers of *Weird Tales* and were especially fond of Lovecraft's stories. In fact, this story applies to Seabury Quinn (assuming it is not entirely apocryphal); the story goes that the girls offered Quinn "one on the house" in honour of his illustrious status. Price explicitly and rather dryly remarks is his memoir that, out of deference to Lovecraft's sensibilities, "I skipped concubines entirely."

From New Orleans Lovecraft finally moved on to Mobile, Alabama, then to Montgomery and Atlanta, although the latter city was modern and had no attractions for him. He then proceeded up the Carolinas to Richmond, which he reached toward the end of June. After canvassing the usual sites relating to Poe and the Confederacy, Lovecraft stopped briefly at Fredericksburg, Annapolis, and Philadelphia, finally ending up back in New York around June 25. This time he stayed in an apartment a few doors away from Loveman in Brooklyn Heights. He expected to linger in the city for more than a week, but a telegram from Annie on July 1 called him suddenly home.

Lillian was critically ill and not expected to survive. Lovecraft caught the first train to Providence, arriving late on the 1st. He found Lillian in a semi-coma; she died on the 3rd without, apparently, regaining consciousness. She was seventy-six years old. The cause of death was given on her death certificate as atrophic arthritis. Lovecraft had spoken over the years of her various ailments—chiefly neuritis and lumbago—the general effect of which was to limit her mobility severely and render her largely housebound. These various maladies now finally caught up with her.

Lovecraft was not given to expressing extreme emotions in his correspondence, and that was his right; but his remarks to friends about Lillian's passing scarcely mask the deep grief he felt:

> The suddenness of the event is both bewildering and merciful—the latter because we cannot yet realise, *subjectively,* that it has actually occurred at all. It would, for example, seem incredibly unnatural to disturb the pillows now arranged for my aunt in the rocker beside my centre-table—her accustomed reading-place each evening.[58]

> The vacuum created in this household is easy to imagine, since my aunt was its presiding genius and animating spirit. It will be impossible for me to get concentrated on any project of moment for some time to come—and meanwhile there intervenes the painful task of distributing my aunt's effects . . . whose familiar arrangement, so expressive of her tastes and personality, I dread to disturb.[59]

That last remark is a dim echo of the turbulence Lovecraft felt at his mother's death eleven years before—dim because few would feel as much grief at the loss of an aunt as of a mother, and because in that decade's interval Lovecraft had matured to the point of being able to handle personal loss in a way that did not entail excessive melancholy or wild thoughts of suicide.

What, then, did Lillian mean to Lovecraft? It is unusually difficult to say, not only because of the absence of even a single document from her hand but because Lovecraft almost never spoke about her to correspondents. This does not mean that he cared little for her; rather, since 1926 she had become such an expected fixture at 10 Barnes, such a critical part of the normality of his world, that her absence would have been unthinkable. Any friction that may have been caused by her objections to his marriage (something that still remains only a conjecture) must long ago have passed; indeed, Lovecraft would not have poured his heart out to Lillian in letters during his New York stay if they were in any way estranged. Lillian was not only an important link to his mother, but also to his beloved uncle Franklin Chase Clark, who with Whipple Phillips had filled the role of father that Winfield Lovecraft had not had the opportunity to do.

In the short term, after the funeral—an Anglican service conducted at the Knowles Funeral Chapel on Benefit Street on July 6, with the Rev. Alfred Johnson, an old friend of both the Phillips and Clark families, presiding (he had also presided over Susie's funeral in 1921)—Lovecraft attempted to dispel his grief by travel. The local ferries were conducting fare wars, and Lovecraft found that he could get a round-trip fare to Newport for only 50¢. He took advantage of this bargain on several occasions in late July, writing on the cliffs overlooking the Atlantic. In early August Morton came by from New York, and the two of them went to Newport on the 5th.

In August Lovecraft received two small augmentations to his self-esteem. The July 1932 issue of the *American Author,* a writers' journal, contained an article by J. Randle Luten entitled "What Makes a Story Click?" It cited Lovecraft, Clark Ashton Smith, and Edmond Hamilton (!) as models of narrative prose. In fact, the article is an atrocious piece of work by a writer completely insensitive to any loftier narrative values than "glamor" and suspense. After quoting the first paragraph of "In the Vault," Luten remarks: "There you are, isn't that a good opening? Mr. Lovecraft gives his readers a nice morsel to chew on, and prepares you for a nice horror tale." Although Luten claims to have an admiration for Edgar Allan Poe, he repeatedly misspells his name as well as the title of Smith's story "The Gorgon." The article was clearly based on a reading of the April 1932 *Weird Tales,* which contained both "In the Vault" and "The Gorgon."

A somewhat more significant piece of recognition came from Harold S. Farnese (1885–1945), a composer who had won the 1911 composition prize at the Paris Conservatory and was then assistant director of the Institute of Musical Art at Los Angeles. Farnese wished to set two of Lovecraft's *Fungi from Yuggoth* sonnets, "Mirage" and "The Elder Pharos" (both in *Weird Tales* for February–March 1931) to music. Having done so shortly thereafter, Farnese then proposed that Lovecraft write the libretto of an entire opera or music drama based generally on his work, to be titled (rather outlandishly) *Yurregarth and Yannimaid* or *The Swamp City;*[60] but Lovecraft declined the offer, citing his complete lack of experience in dramatic composition (evidently his 1918 squib *Alfredo* did not qualify). It is difficult to imagine what such a work would have been like. As for the music for the two sonnets: from the single page of "The Elder Pharos" (presumably for alto and piano) that I have been able to examine,[61] the work seems like a typical modernist composition of the period, with wildly fluctuating modulations (the key signature gives one sharp, but the melody rarely resolves into either G major or E minor) and a florid and dissonant piano part. I have never heard either work performed.

One other datum of some moment has emerged from Lovecraft's brief association with Farnese. In several letters Lovecraft explained his theory of weird fiction at length, but Farnese did not seem quite to grasp its essence. After Lovecraft's death, Farnese, asked by August Derleth whether he had any letters from Lovecraft, said that he had two long letters and a postcard; but in relating to Derleth the basic thrust of the correspondence, Farnese wrote:

Upon congratulating HPL upon his work, he answered: *"You will, of course, realize that all my stories, unconnected as they may be, are based on one funda-mental lore or legend: that this world was inhabited at one time by another race, who in practicing black magic, lost their foothold and were expelled, yet live on outside, ever ready to take possession of this earth again"* [emphasis Farnese's]. "The Elders," as he called them.[62]

Incredible as it may seem, Farnese was not quoting any actual letter by Lovecraft but paraphrasing—erroneously—some passages from a letter of September 22, 1932. Consider the following:

> In my own efforts to crystallise this spaceward outreaching, I try to utilise as many as possible of the elements which have, under earlier mental and emotional conditions, given man a symbolic feeling of the unreal, the ethereal, & the mystical . . . I have tried to weave them into a kind of shadowy phantasmagoria which may have the same sort of vague coherence as a cycle of traditional myth or legend— with nebulous backgrounds of elder forces & trans-galactic entities which lurk about this infinitesimal planet, (& of course about others as well), establishing outposts thereon, & occasionally brushing aside other accidental forms of life (like human beings) in order to take up full habitation. . . . Having formed a cosmic pantheon, it remains for the fantaisiste to link this "outside" element to the earth in a suitably dramatic & convincing fashion. This, I have thought, is best done through glancing allusions to immemorially ancient cults & idols & documents at-testing the recognition of the "outside" forces by men—or by those terrestrial forces which preceded man. The actual climaxes of tales based on such elements naturally have to do with sudden latter-day intrusions of forgotten elder forces on the placid surface of the known . . .[63]

The result of Farnese's botched remembrance is vaguely similar to Lovecraft's let-ter to Farnsworth Wright of July 5, 1927 (when he resubmitted "The Call of Cthulhu"), but the real thrust of the spurious passage is very different. Neverthe-less, August Derleth seized upon it and circulated it (in slightly altered form) as an utterance by Lovecraft as early as "H. P. Lovecraft, Outsider" (*River,* June 1937), and it became the most notorious piece of "evidence" supporting Derleth's own misconception of the "Cthulhu Mythos" as a battle of good and evil fundamentally similar to Christianity. Until recently, this "quotation" has been the single most frequently cited sentence attributed to Lovecraft.

Farnese and Derleth share the blame pretty equally for circulating this apocry-phal utterance. Derleth at first had no reason to doubt that the sentence indeed came from a Lovecraft letter, since Farnese had enclosed it within quotation-marks; but he should have known better, for shortly thereafter Farnese sent Love-craft's actual letters to Derleth for transcription in the *Selected Letters* project, and they appear to have been transcribed in their entirety (although not ultimately published in their entirety), and no such quotation appears in these transcripts. But the passage seemed to Derleth so overwhelming a confirmation of his misguided view of Lovecraft—even though it contradicted everything else Lovecraft ever wrote on the subject—that he was unwilling to give it up. Toward the end of his life, when suspicion began to emerge as to the source of the quotation, Derleth became angry when asked to supply its provenance, since he was unable to find it in an actual Lovecraft letter; this led some scholars to believe that Derleth himself had fabricated the quotation—a plausible enough belief until David E. Schultz discovered the letters by Farnese that finally cleared up the whole sorry matter.[64]

Lovecraft's travels for 1932 were by no means over. On August 30 he went to Boston to spend time with Cook. The next day the two of them went to Newburyport to see the total solar eclipse, and were rewarded with a fine sight: "The landscape did not change in tone until the solar crescent was rather small, & then a kind of sunset vividness became apparent. When the crescent waned to extreme thinness, the scene grew strange & spectral—an almost deathlike quality inhering in the sickly yellowish light."[65] From there Lovecraft proceeded to Montreal and Quebec, spending four full days in the two towns (September 2–6). Lovecraft tried to persuade Cook to come along, but Cook did not relish the very ascetic manner in which his friend travelled (sleeping on trains or buses, scant meals, nonstop sightseeing, etc.). Cook did, however, see Lovecraft on his return, and his portrait is as vivid a reflexion of Lovecraft's manic travelling habits as one could ask for:

> Early the following Tuesday morning, before I had gone to work, Howard arrived back from Quebec. I have never before nor since seen such a sight. Folds of skin hanging from a skeleton. Eyes sunk in sockets like burnt holes in a blanket. Those delicate, sensitive artist's hands and fingers nothing but claws. The man was dead except for his nerves, on which he was functioning. . . . I was scared. Because I was scared I was angry. Possibly my anger was largely at myself for letting him go alone on that trip. But whatever its real cause, it was genuine anger that I took out on him. He needed a brake; well, he'd have the brake applied right now.[66]

Cook immediately took Lovecraft to a Waldorf restaurant and made him have a plentiful meal, then took him back to his rooming house so that he could rest. Cook, returning from work at five, forced Lovecraft to have another meal before letting him go. How Lovecraft could actually derive enjoyment from the places he visited, functioning on pure nervous energy and with so little food and rest, it is difficult to imagine; and yet, he did so again and again.

Almost immediately upon his return Lovecraft welcomed visitors to Providence. One of them, arriving on the 8th, was his new friend Carl Ferdinand Strauch. He evidently stayed a few days, and surely his old friend Harry Brobst joined in on the proceedings; but he could not stay long enough to meet Lovecraft's other visitor, Donald Wandrei, who returned to Providence after a five-year absence and arrived around the 13th. All this socialising threw Lovecraft's work schedule all out of whack—correspondence alone must have piled up prodigiously—but Lovecraft still managed to sneak in another trip to Boston, Salem, and Marblehead in early October.

Sometime in the spring or summer of 1932 a promising new revision client emerged—promising not because she showed any talent or inclination to become a writer in her own right but because she gave Lovecraft regular work. She was Hazel Heald (1896–1961), a woman about whom I know almost nothing. She was born and apparently spent most of her life in Somerville, Massachusetts, and so far as I know published nothing aside from the five stories Lovecraft revised or ghostwrote for her. Unlike Zealia Bishop, she wrote no memoir of Lovecraft, so that it is not clear how she came in touch with him and what their professional or personal relations were like. Muriel Eddy (if we can trust her on this point) reports that Heald had joined a writers' club established by the Eddys, and that the latter steered her to Lovecraft when the tenor of her work became evident. Eddy goes on to say that Heald confided to her a vague romantic interest in Lovecraft: she managed to persuade Lovecraft to come to her home in Somerville on one occasion, when she arranged a candlelight dinner with him.[67] I am not at all certain of the veracity of this entire account, given Muriel Eddy's apparent unreliability on other matters; indeed, the only thing in Lovecraft's own correspondence to suggest any sort of romantic involvement with Heald (even—as would surely have been the case—a one-sided one) is an amusing mention in a letter to Duane W. Rimel in late 1934, in which he comments on the disappearance of Mrs Heald's cat, "who ate some Paris green in the cellar, was seized with a sort of frenzy, and dashed out of the house, never to be seen again."[68] This suggests that their correspondence was not purely on business matters; but neither are his letters to Zealia Bishop, whom nobody suspects of carrying a torch for Lovecraft. Cook reports that Lovecraft was scheduled to meet Heald in Somerville upon his return from Quebec in early September, but this may have been a harmless half-business half-social call. The fact that Lovecraft refers to her as "Mrs Heald" must mean that she was either divorced or widowed.

There is good reason to believe that several, if not all five, of the stories Lovecraft revised for Heald were written in 1932 or 1933, even though the last of them did not appear in print until 1937. The first of them seems to have been "The Man of Stone" (*Wonder Stories,* October 1932). Heald wrote to Derleth about the tale: "Lovecraft helped me on this story as much as on the others, and did actually rewrite paragraphs. He would criticize paragraph after paragraph and pencil remarks beside them, and then make me rewrite them until they pleased him."[69] I think that nearly the entirety of this utterance is false or suspect. Judging from Lovecraft's comments on Heald's stories, it is unlikely that Lovecraft merely touched them up or recommended revisions that Heald herself then carried out; instead, most or all of the stories were based on mere synopses and were written by Lovecraft almost entirely on his own. Of all his revisions, along with those written for Zealia Bishop, they come the closest to original composition. None of them is as good as "The Mound," but several are very fine.

Lovecraft does not mention "The Man of Stone" in any correspondence I have seen, but he must have worked on it by the summer of 1932 at the latest in order for it to have appeared in the October *Wonder Stories*. It is in the end a conventional story about Daniel "Mad Dan" Morris, who finds in his ancestral copy of the *Book of Eibon* a formula to turn any living creature into a stone statue. Morris admits that the formula "depends more on plain chemistry than on the Outer Powers" and that "What it amounts to is a kind of petrification infinitely speeded up"—a pseudo-scientific explanation that evidently was sufficient to pass muster with Hugo Gernsback. Morris successfully turns the trick on Arthur Wheeler, a sculptor who he believes had been making overtures to his wife Rose, but when he attempts it on Rose herself, she tricks him and turns him into stone. Here again, aside from the implausible nature of the supernatural or pseudo-scientific mechanism, Lovecraft's inability at characterisation betrays him: his depiction of the love triangle is hackneyed and conventional, and Mad Dan's diary is written in an entirely unconvincing colloquialism. Of course, Lovecraft is hampered by the nature of the basic plot he was given to revise: he himself would never have chosen this scenario for a tale of his own.

The flaws in "Winged Death," however, seem largely of Lovecraft's own making. This preposterous story tells of a scientist, Thomas Slauenwite, who has discovered a rare insect in South Africa whose bite is fatal unless treated with a certain drug; the natives call this insect the "devil-fly" because after killing its victim it purportedly takes over the deceased's soul or personality. Slauenwite kills a rival scientist, Henry Moore, with this insect, but is later haunted by an insect that seems uncannily to bear tokens of Moore's personality. The tale ends ridiculously: Slauenwite himself is killed, his soul enters the body of the insect, and he writes a message on the ceiling of his room by dipping his insect body in ink and walking across the ceiling. This grotesque and unintentionally comical conclusion—which Lovecraft admitted was his own invention—is clearly intended to be the acme of horror, but ends up being merely bathetic.

Lovecraft discussed the story in a letter to Derleth that probably dates to August 1932:

> Sorry your new story parallelled [*sic*] an earlier author's work. Something odd befell a client of mine the other day—involving a story-element which *I* had intended & introduced under the impression that it was strictly original with me.

The tale was sent to Handsome Harry [Bates], & he rejected it on the ground that the element in question (the act of an insect dipping itself in ink & writing on a white surface with its own body) formed the crux of another tale which he *had* accepted. Hell's bells!—& I thought I'd hit on an idea of absolute novelty & uniqueness![70]

I do not know what immortal masterwork of literature beat Lovecraft to the punch in this insect-writing idea; but the note about the tale's submission to *Strange Tales* is of some interest. Although I have expressed my doubts about Will Murray's theory that "The Shadow over Innsmouth" was written with *Strange Tales* in mind, I think it quite plausible that the earlier Heald tales were written with that better-paying market in view; for here we have an actual submission made to Bates. There is no evidence that the other tales were submitted there; they could well have been, assuming that they were written prior to the magazine's folding at the end of the year. Lovecraft submitted "Winged Death" to Farnsworth Wright, but the latter must have delayed in accepting the tale, for it was published only in *Weird Tales* for March 1934. When it appeared, Lovecraft wrote: "'Winged Death' is nothing to run a temperature over . . . My share in it is something like 90 to 95%."[71]

I fervently hope that "The Horror in the Museum" is a conscious parody—in this case, a parody of Lovecraft's own myth-cycle. Here we are introduced to a new "god," Rhan-Tegoth, which the curator of a waxworks museum, George Rogers, claims to have found on an expedition to Alaska. Rogers's sceptical friend Stephen Jones looks at a photograph of the entity: "To say that such a thing could have an *expression* seems paradoxical; yet Jones felt that that triangle of bulging fish-eyes and that obliquely poised proboscis all bespoke a blend of hate, greed, and sheer cruelty incomprehensible to mankind because mixed with other emotions not of the world or this solar system." The extravagance of this utterance points clearly to parody. Indeed, "The Horror in the Museum" could be read as a parody of both "Pickman's Model" and "The Call of Cthulhu," Consider the absurdity of the scenario: it is not a mere representation of a god that is secreted in a crate in the cellar of the museum, but *the actual god itself!* The utterances of the raving Rogers as he madly seeks to sacrifice Jones to Rhan-Tegoth are grotesque:

> "Iä! Iä!" it [Rogers] was howling. "I am coming, O Rhan-Tegoth, coming with the nourishment. You have waited long and fed ill, but now you shall have what was promised. . . . You shall crush and drain him, with all his doubts, and grow strong thereby. And ever after among men he shall be shewn as a monument to your glory. Rhan-Tegoth, infinite and invincible, I am your slave and high-priest. You are hungry, and I provide. I read the sign and have led you forth. I shall feed you with blood, and you shall feed me with power. Iä! Shub-Niggurath! The Goat with a Thousand Young!"

Later Rogers spouts such oaths as "Spawn of Noth-Yidik and effluvium of K'thun! Son of the dogs that howl in the maelstrom of Azathoth!" Long before his talentless disciples and followers unwittingly reduced the "Cthulhu Mythos" to absurdity, Lovecraft himself consciously did so.

The story is mentioned in a letter of October 1932: "My latest revisory job comes so near to pure fictional ghost-writing that I am up against all the plot-devising problems of my bygone auctorial days";[72] he goes on to recite the plot of the story in a lurid manner that I hope indicates his awareness of its parodic nature. Elsewhere he said: "'The Horror in the Museum'—a piece which I 'ghost-wrote' for a client from a synopsis so poor that I well-nigh discarded it—is virtually my own work."[73] This story seems to have been readily accepted by Wright, for it appeared in *Weird Tales* for July 1933, in the same issue as "The Dreams in the Witch House." Lovecraft must have been wryly amused when a letter by Bernard J. Kenton (the pseudonym of Jerry Siegel, later the co-creator of *Superman*) appeared in "The Eyrie" for May 1934 in praise of the work: "Even Lovecraft—as powerful and artistic as he is with macabre suggestiveness—could hardly, I suspect, have surpassed the grotesque scene in which the other-dimensional shambler leaps out upon the hero."

"Out of the Aeons"—which Lovecraft was working on in early August 1933[74]—is perhaps the only genuinely successful Heald revision, although it too contains elements of extravagance that border on self-parody. This tale concerns an ancient mummy housed in the Cabot Museum of Archaeology in Boston and an accompanying scroll in indecipherable characters. The mummy and scroll remind the narrator—the curator of the museum—of a wild tale found in the *Black Book* or *Nameless Cults* of von Junzt, which tells of the god Ghatanothoa, "whom no living thing could behold . . . without suffering a change more horrible than death itself. Sight of the god, or its image . . . meant paralysis and petrification of a singularly shocking sort, in which the victim was turned to stone and leather on the outside, while the brain within remained perpetually alive . . ." This idea is, of course, suspiciously like the drug utilised in "The Man of Stone." Von Junzt goes on to speak of an individual named T'yog who, 175,000 years ago, attempted to scale Mount Yaddith-Gho on the lost continent of Mu, where Ghatanothoa resided, and to "deliver mankind from its brooding menace"; he was protected from Ghatanothoa's glance by a magic formula, but at the last minute the priests of Ghatanothoa stole the parchment on which the formula was written and substituted another one for it. The antediluvian mummy in the museum, therefore, is T'yog, petrified for millennia by Ghatanothoa.

It is manifestly obvious that Heald's sole contribution to this tale is the core notion of a mummy with a living brain; all the rest—Ghatanothoa, T'yog, the setting on Mu, and, of course, all the prose of the tale—are Lovecraft's. He admits as much when he says: "Regarding the scheduled 'Out of the Æons'—I should say *I did* have a hand in it . . . I *wrote* the damn thing!"[75] The tale is substantial, but it too is written with a certain flamboyance and lack of polish that bar it from taking its place with Lovecraft's own best tales. It is, however, of interest in uniting the atmosphere of his early "Dunsanian" tales with that of his later "Mythos" tales: T'yog's ascent of Yaddith-Gho bears thematic and stylistic similarities with Barzai the Wise's scaling of Ngranek in "The Other Gods," and the entire subnarrative about Mu is narrated in a style analogous to that of Dunsany's tales and plays of gods and men. The story appeared in *Weird Tales* for April 1935.

"The Horror in the Burying-Ground," on the other hand, returns us to earth very emphatically. Here we are in some unspecified rustic locale where the village undertaker, Henry Thorndike, has devised a peculiar chemical compound that, when injected into a living person, will simulate death even though the person is alive and conscious. Thorndike attempts to dispose of an enemy in this fashion, but in so doing is himself injected with the substance. The inevitable occurs: although the undertaker pleads not to be entombed, he is pronounced dead and buried alive.

Much of the story is narrated in a backwoods patois reminiscent—and perhaps a parody—of that used in "The Dunwich Horror." Other in-jokes—such as the use of the character names Akeley (from "The Whisperer in Darkness"), Zenas (from "The Colour out of Space"), Atwood (from *At the Mountains of Madness*), and Goodenough (referring to Lovecraft's amateur colleague Arthur Goodenough)—suggest that the story is meant, if not as an actual parody, at least as an instance of graveyard humour; and as such it is relatively successful. Lovecraft never mentions this revision in any correspondence I have seen, so I do not know when it was written; it did not appear in *Weird Tales* until May 1937.

It is clear from the synopses of these stories that several of them feature the same fundamental plot element: the idea of a living brain encased in a dead or immobilised body. This encompasses "Out of the Aeons" and "The Horror in the Burying-Ground"; in "The Horror in the Museum" the effect of Rhan-Tegoth's depradations is to leave the victim looking like a wax statue, a fate somewhat similar to that of "The Man of Stone"; while "Winged Death" presents a human brain or personality in an alien form. One wonders how much beyond this nucleus was provided by Heald, if indeed she even supplied this much.

Lovecraft no doubt was paid regularly by Heald, even though it took years for her stories to be published; at least, he makes no complaints about dilatory payments as he did for Zealia Bishop. Although Lovecraft was still speaking of her in the present tense as a revision client as late as the summer of 1935, it does not seem as if he did much work for her after the summer of 1933.

Another revision or collaboration in which Lovecraft became unwillingly involved in the fall of 1932 was "Through the Gates of the Silver Key." E. Hoffmann Price had become so enamoured of "The Silver Key" that, during Lovecraft's visit with him in New Orleans in June, he "suggested a sequel to account for Randolph Carter's doings after his disappearance."[76] There is no recorded response on Lovecraft's part to this suggestion, although it cannot have been very enthusiastic. On his own initiative, therefore, Price wrote his own sequel, "The Lord of Illusion." Sending it to Lovecraft in late August, he expressed the hope that Lovecraft might agree to revise it and allow it to be published as an acknowledged collaboration. Lovecraft took his time replying to Price's letter, but when he did so he stated that extensive changes would be needed to bring the sequel in line with the original story. In a charitable response of October 10, Price agreed with nearly all Lovecraft's suggestions. He went on to hope that Lovecraft could perform the revision in a few days—after all, he had written his own version in only two days.[77] Instead, Lovecraft did not finish the job until April 1933.

"The Lord of Illusion"[78] is an appallingly awful piece of work. It tells the ridiculous story of how Randolph Carter, after finding the silver key, enters a strange cavern in the hills behind his family home in Massachusetts and encounters a strange man who announces himself as "'Umr at-Tawil, your guide," who leads Carter to some other-dimensional realm where he meets the Ancient Ones. These entities explain the nature of the universe to Carter: just as a circle is produced from the intersection of a cone with a plane, so our three-dimensional world is produced from the intersection of a plane with a figure of a higher dimension; analogously, time is an illusion, being merely the result of this sort of "cutting" of infinity. It transpires that all Carters who have ever lived are part of a single archetype, so that if Carter could manipulate his "section-plane" (the plane that determines his situation in time), he could be any Carter he wished to be, from antiquity to the distant future. In a purported surprise ending, Carter reveals himself as an old man amongst a group of individuals who had assembled to divide up Carter's estate.

It would be difficult to imagine a story more lame than this, and yet Lovecraft felt some sort of obligation to try to make something of it. In the letter in which he evaluates Price's work, he specified several faults that must be rectified: 1) the style must be made more similar to that of "The Silver Key" (Price's version, although by no means full of his usual frenetic action and swordplay, is lamentably flat, stilted, and pompous); 2) various points of the plot must be reconciled with that of "The Silver Key"; 3) the transition from the mundane world to the hyperspace realm (if that is what it is) must be vastly subtilised; and 4) the atmosphere of lecture-room didacticism in the Ancient Ones' discussions with Carter must be eliminated. Lovecraft rightly concluded: "Hell, but it'll be a tough nut to crack!"[79] The rush of other work prevented him from working on it for months; by March 1933 he managed to grind out 7½ pages,[80] but more revision work delayed him until he finally finished the job in early April.[81]

The result cannot by any means be considered satisfactory. Whereas "The Silver Key" is a poignant reflection of some of Lovecraft's innermost sentiments and beliefs, "Through the Gates of the Silver Key" is nothing more than a fantastic adventure story with awkward and laboured mathematical and philosophical interludes. Lovecraft has made extensive revisions to the plot, although preserving as much of Price's ideas as he could. The story opens in New Orleans, where several individuals—Etienne Laurent de Marigny (a stand-in for Price himself), Ward Phillips (whose identity is no mystery), the lawyer Ernest B. Aspinwall, and a strange individual named the Swami Chandraputra—are gathered to discuss the disposition of Carter's estate. The Swami opposes any such action, since he maintains that Carter is still alive. He proceeds to tell a fabulous story of what happened to Carter after his return to boyhood (as noted in "The Silver Key"):

Carter passed through a succession of "Gates" into some realm "outside time and the dimensions we know," led by a "Guide," 'Umr at-Tawil, the Prolonged of Life. This guide eventually led Carter to the thrones of the Ancient Ones, from whom he learned that there are "archetypes" for every entity in the universe, and that each person's entire ancestry is nothing more than a facet of the single archetype; Carter learned that he himself is a facet of the "SUPREME ARCHETYPE," whatever that means. Then, in some mysterious fashion, Carter found himself in the body of a fantastically alien being, Zkauba the Wizard, on the planet Yaddith. He managed to return to earth, but must go about in concealment because of his alien form.

When the hard-nosed lawyer Aspinwall scoffs at this story by Swami Chandraputra, a final revelation—which can scarcely be a surprise to any reader—is made: the Swami is himself Randolph Carter, still in the monstrous shape of Zkauba. Aspinwall, having pulled off the mask Carter is wearing, dies immediately of apoplexy. Carter then disappears through a large clock in the room.

Price has remarked that "I estimated that [Lovecraft] had left unchanged fewer than fifty of my original words,"[82] a comment that has led many to believe that the finished version of "Through the Gates of the Silver Key" is radically different from Price's original; but, as we have seen, Lovecraft adhered to the basic framework of Price's tale as best he could. The quotations from the *Necronomicon* are largely Price's, although somewhat amended by Lovecraft; and a striking passage later on—"[Carter] wondered at the vast conceit of those who had babbled of the *malignant* Ancient Ones, as if They could pause from their everlasting dreams to wreak a wrath upon mankind"—is so strikingly similar to Lovecraft's own evolving conceptions of his pseudomythology that it is no wonder he left it in nearly intact.

Lovecraft sent his handwritten scrawl to Price for typing, adding typically—although in this case justifiably—deprecatory remarks ("I'm a rotten hand at collaboration—but at least I've done my poor best"[83]). Price, however, was enthusiastic, although expressing quibbles here and there; in particular, he did not care for Lovecraft's use of some terms from the theosophic mythology Price himself had earlier supplied him (Shalmali, Shamballah, Lords of Venus, and the like), and either changed some of these references himself or asked Lovecraft to do so. Another typescript must have been prepared, since the existing one contains numerous errors and several handwritten marginal notations by both Price and Lovecraft.

Price submitted the story to *Weird Tales* on June 19, both praising the story and minimising his own role in it: "It is so much a Lovecraft story, and so little mine that it seems of all things the most natural to sit here and tell you . . . this is one of the most self consistent, carefully worked out pictures of the cosmos and hyperspace that I have ever read."[84] Farnsworth Wright's response, in a letter to Lovecraft on August 17, is perhaps what one might have expected:

> I have carefully read THROUGH THE GATES OF THE SILVER KEY and am almost overwhelmed by the colossal scope of the story. It is cyclopean in its daring and titanic in its execution. . . .
>
> But I am afraid to offer it to our readers. Many there would be . . . who would go into raptures of esthetic delight while reading the story; just as certainly there would be a great many—probably a clear majority—of our readers who would be unable to wade through it. These would find the descriptions and discussions of polydimensional space poison to their enjoyment of the tale. . . .
>
> . . . I assure you that never have I turned down a story with more regret than in this case.[85]

That last comment is not likely to have appeased Lovecraft much, even though he had not placed much emotional stock in the selling of the story. Both Price and Lovecraft let the text sit, apparently disinclined to submit it elsewhere. It is a little peculiar that no thought was given to trying the tale on the science fiction pulps; perhaps it was felt that since "The Silver Key" had appeared in *Weird Tales,* no other market would have been appropriate or feasible. But, true to his contrary ways, by mid-November 1933 Wright was asking to see the story again,[86] and he accepted it a week later. It appeared in the issue for July 1934, where it did indeed receive a somewhat mixed reader response, although not quite of the sort that Wright had feared. An amusing letter by a very young Henry Kuttner in the September 1934 issue criticises the tale for being overexplanatory and for a contrived ending: "Lovecraft at one time could supply a good ending, but now he is getting trite as hell. It is a bad example of a forced surprize [*sic*] ending that he has on that story." Lovecraft evidently did not remember or had forgiven Kuttner for this remark when he came in touch with the youth two years later.

Slowly but inexorably Lovecraft was being drawn back into amateur activity, although this time in the National Amateur Press Association, since his United was defunct. Sometime in late 1931 he was persuaded to take a place on the Bureau of Critics, the NAPA's version of the Department of Public Criticism. On April 18 he produced an untitled essay-review for the *National Amateur,* but it proved to be so lengthy that it could not be fit into the issue, so Helm C. Spink, the Official Editor, arranged for the Official Printer, George G. Fetter of Lexington, Kentucky, to publish it as a separate pamphlet later in the year under the title *Further Criticism of Poetry.* It is one of Lovecraft's rarest publications. A typescript of the piece prepared by R. H. Barlow bears a title, "Notes on Verse Technique"; I am not entirely sure that this title is Lovecraft's, but I think it likely.

"Notes on Verse Technique" is a sensible disquisition on what constitutes "real poetry, as distinguished from mere rhyming prose," embodying Lovecraft's later views on the subject. Interestingly, he does not condemn free verse uniformly, remarking only that "the indiscriminate use of this medium is not to be highly recommended to the novice" because it is difficult for the novice to develop a natural sense of rhythm outside of the recognised metres. He quotes two poems—which B. K. Hart had published in his "Sideshow" column some years before—one of which is in standard quatrains, the other in free verse; and Lovecraft declares rightly that the latter is much more vital and genuinely poetic because of its distinctive, unhackneyed diction. This long theoretical discussion is only a somewhat topheavy preface to the actual evaluation of amateur verse that concludes the essay.

Lovecraft would in subsequent years be repeatedly drawn into serving on the Bureau of Critics, in spite of his pleas that he be called upon only if no other "victims" could be found (they never could). He usually handled poetry and usually managed to talk Edward H. Cole into contributing a criticism of prose contributions. Early in 1932 he also wrote a brief foreword to a slim book of poetry, *Thoughts and Pictures,* by the Rev. Eugene B. Kuntz, an old-time amateur whom Lovecraft always regarded fondly. The pamphlet was typically misprinted by "Tryout" Smith; the title page in fact declares that it was "Cooperatively published by H. P. Loveracft and C. W. Smith."

Another book project that would presumably have emerged out of the amateur community was a plan by Earl C. Kelley to issue the complete *Fungi from Yuggoth*—the first of several instances in Lovecraft's lifetime in which this sonnet series was to have been published, all of which would come to nothing. Kelley was editor of an amateur journal entitled *Ripples from Lake Champlain,* to which Lovecraft had earmarked a few of the *Fungi* sonnets; only one of them, "The Pigeon-Flyers," actually appeared there, in the Spring 1932 issue. In late February 1932 Kelley made his request to Lovecraft to print the cycle.[87] But his project never came to fruition. Kelley had been elected president of the NAPA in 1931 and presided over the 1932 convention in Montpelier, Vermont, in July, then proceeded to blow his brains out with a revolver.[88] He was twenty-seven years old.

Late in 1932 Lovecraft was pained by the death on November 23 of Henry S. Whitehead, who finally succumbed to the gastric ailment that had enfeebled him for years. Lovecraft's tribute to him is unaffected as he recalls his visit of the year before:

> It is doubtful if any other host ever reached quite his level of cordiality, thought-fulness, & generosity over a period exceeding a fortnight. I really had, for his sake, to be careful what books or other possessions of his I openly admired; for like some open-handed Eastern prince he would insist on presenting me with whatever seemed to arouse my enthusiasm. He compelled me to consider his wardrobe my own (for his physique was almost identical with mine), & there still hangs in my clothespress one of the white tropical suits he lent me—& finally insisted that I retain permanently as a souvenir. As I glance at my curio shelf I see a long mottled snake in a jar, & reflect how good old Canevin caught & killed it with his own hands—thinking I might like a sample of Dunedin's lurking horrors. He was not afraid of the devil himself, & the seizure of that noxious wriggler was highly typical of him. The astonishing versatility & multi-plicity of attractive qualities which he possessed sound almost fabulous to one who did not know him in person.[89]

In assessing Whitehead's fiction, Lovecraft made note of a series of three tales set in a New England town called Chadbourne—which Whitehead evidently con-ceived as a parallel to Lovecraft's own Arkham. One of these ("The Chadbourne Episode") had been accepted by *Weird Tales* and would appear in the issue for February 1933; the other two—which Lovecraft does not name—have not been identified and may not survive. One was accepted by Harry Bates for *Astounding* but returned when that magazine folded; the other had apparently not been submit-ted anywhere.

I have already mentioned Lovecraft's revision of Whitehead's "The Trap." There are two other stories on which he gave some assistance, although my belief is that he contributed no actual prose to either of them. One is "Cassius," which is clearly based upon entry 133 of Lovecraft's commonplace book: "Man has minia-ture shapeless Siamese twin—exhib. in circus—twin surgically detached—disappears—does hideous things with malign life of its own." Whitehead has fol-lowed the details of this entry exactly in his tale, with the exception of the circus element; instead, he transfers it to his customary West Indian locale, where a black servant of Gerald Canevin's named Brutus Hellman removes the diminutive twin that was attached to its groin, thereby releasing its malevolent instincts and causing it to attack Hellman repeatedly until it is finally killed.

"Cassius" (*Strange Tales,* November 1931) is an able and suspenseful story, although its middle section gets bogged down with a laborious pseudo-scientific discussion of the case, and it ends with unintentional comedy when Canevin—reluctant to kill the homunculus because it had been baptised and was therefore a Christian—tries to capture the creature with a net but is anticipated by its cat, which dispatches it with brutal efficiency. Whitehead, when first learning of the plot, wished Lovecraft to collaborate with him, but Lovecraft declined and made a present of the idea.

Lovecraft, however, later admitted that his own development of the idea would have been very different from Whitehead's:

> Th[e] idea was to have the connexion of the man and his miniature twin *much more complex and obscure* than any doctor had suspected. The operation of separation is performed—but lo! An unforeseen horror and tragedy results. For it seems *that the brain of the twin-burdened man lay in the minature twin alone . . .* so that the operation has produced *a hideous monster only a foot tall, with the keen brain of a man, and a handsome man-like shell with the undeveloped brain of a total idiot.* From this situation I planned to develop an appropriate plot, although—from the magnitude of the task—I had not progressed very far.[90]

What a shame that Lovecraft never wrote this story out! He went on to state that the plot was derived from witnessing a freak show at Hubert's Museum in New York in 1925, when he saw a man named Jean Libbera (Lovecraft misspells it Libera) had an anomalous little anthropoid excrescence growing out of his abdomen. It later transpired that Libbera (a friend of Arthur Leeds) was a fan of weird fiction and liked Lovecraft's own work in *Weird Tales!*

The other story on which Lovecraft had been assisting Whitehead was called "The Bruise," but he was uncertain whether it had ever been completed. This matter first comes up in April 1932, when Lovecraft noted that "I'm now helping Whitehead prepare a new ending and background for a story Bates had rejected." The story involves a man who suffers a bruise to the head and—in Lovecraft's version—"excite[s] cells of hereditary memory causing the man to hear the destruction and sinking of fabulous Mu 20,000 years ago!"[91] Some have believed that Lovecraft may have actually written or revised this story, but from internal evidence it seems to me that none of the writing is Lovecraft's.

There is, in fact, a distinct possibility that none of the writing is Whitehead's, either. The story was published (as "Bothon") in *Amazing Stories* for August 1946 and, nearly simultaneously, in Whitehead's second Arkham House volume, *West India Lights* (1946). The anomalously late publication of the story—clearly arranged by August Derleth—is to be noted. A. Langley Searles believes that Derleth himself may have written the story, having found Lovecraft's synopsis for it among Whitehead's papers. Searles claims that the story sounds radically different from anything else Whitehead ever wrote; and it must be kept in mind that Derleth was not above passing off his own work as that of others, as when he published a story of his entitled "The Churchyard Yew" in *Night's Yawning Peal* (1952) and attributed it to J. Sheridan Le Fanu. No external evidence for this theory has emerged, but it is worth keeping in mind.

Lovecraft wrote a two-page obituary of Whitehead and sent it to Farnsworth Wright, urging that it be used as a quarry for an announcement in *Weird Tales.* Wright ran the piece as a separate unsigned article—"In Memoriam: Henry St. Clair Whitehead"—in the March 1933 issue, but used only about a quarter of what Lovecraft had sent him,[92] and since Lovecraft kept no copy of his original, the full text has now been lost. Very likely, however, it was similar to the long tribute to Whitehead found in Lovecraft's letter to E. Hoffmann Price of December 7, 1932.

One strange piece of writing Lovecraft did at this time was "European Glimpses," dated on the manuscript to December 19. This is a very conventional-ised travelogue of the principal tourist sites in western Europe (chiefly in Germany, France, and England), and is nothing less than a ghostwriting job for his ex-wife Sonia, although Lovecraft—on the few occasions when he spoke of the assignment to correspondents—went out of his way to conceal the fact. Consider a remark made to Alfred Galpin in late 1933:

> For the past year I have had such a knowledge of Paris that I've felt tempted to advertise my services as a guide without ever having seen the damn place—this erudition coming from a ghost-writing job for a goof who wanted to be publicly eloquent about a trip from which he was apparently unable to extract any concrete first-hand impressions. I based my study on maps, guide-books, travel folders, de-scriptive volumes, & (above all) pictures . . .[93]

Lovecraft goes on in this letter to cite exactly the places—Paris, Chartres, Rheims, Versailles, Barbizon, Fontainebleau, and various locales in London—described in "European Glimpses." Consider now Sonia's remark in her memoir: ". . . In 1932 I went to Europe. I was almost tempted to invite him along but I knew that since I was no longer his wife he would not have accepted. However, I wrote to him from England, Germany and France, sending him books and pictures of every conceiv-able scene that I thought might interest him. . . . I sent a travelogue to H. P. which he revised for me."[94] Sonia also mentions in detail the sites described in the trave-logue. Why then did Lovecraft carry out this deception? Perhaps he felt embar-rassed to admit that he was still in touch with Sonia and was doing work for her—for which, I imagine, he did not charge her. Galpin was one of his oldest friends, and he had also known Sonia for more than a decade. Lovecraft does not, to my knowledge, even mention "European Glimpses" to any other correspondent except Galpin—who was a longtime resident of Paris, so that the passing citation would have been natural. Just as Lovecraft almost never mentioned the fact of his marriage to younger correspondents, so he here failed to acknowledge his continued association with his ex-wife.

"European Glimpses" itself is by far the least interesting of Lovecraft's travelogues—if, indeed, it can even be called such—because of its hackneyed descriptions of hackneyed tourist sites that no bourgeois traveller ever fails to visit. Perhaps its only interesting feature is its record of Sonia's glimpse of Hitler in the flesh in Wiesbaden:

> During my stay of five days in Wiesbaden I had opportunities to observe the disturbed political state of Germany, and the constant squabbles between various dismally uniformed factions of would-be patriots. Of all the self-appointed leaders, Hitler alone seems to retain a cohesive and enthusiastic following; his sheer magnetism and force of will serving—in spite of its deficiencies in true social insight—to charm, drug, or hypnotise the hordes of youthful "Nazis" who blindly revere and obey him. Without possessing any clear-cut or well-founded programme for Germany's economic reconstruction, he plays theatrically on the younger generation's military emotions and sense of national pride; urging them to overthrow the restrictive provisions of the Versailles treaty and reassert the strength and supremacy of the German people. . . .
>
> Hitler's lack of clear, concrete objectives seems to lose him nothing with the crowd; and when—during my stay—he was scheduled to speak of Wiesbaden, the Kurpark was crowded fully two hours before the event by a throng whose quiet seriousness was almost funereal. The contrast with America's jocose and apathetic election crowds was striking. When the leader finally appeared—his right hand lifted in an approved Fascist salute—the crowd shouted *"Heil!"* three times, and then subsided into an attentive silence devoid alike of applause, heckling, or hissing. The general spirit of the address was that of Cato's *"Delenda est Carthago"*— though one could not feel quite sure what particular Carthage, material or psychological, "Handsome Adolf" was trying to single out for anathema.

Some of this clearly represents Sonia's own impressions, and some of it is Lovecraft's overlay of opinion—for it was he who, as we shall see, passed so cavalierly over Hitler's "deficiencies in true social insight" in his grudging approval of him.

At the very end of 1932 Lovecraft instituted what would become another travelling ritual, as he spent the week or so after Christmas in New York with the Longs. Naturally, he spent Christmas with Annie in Providence, but the very next day he caught a bus for New York and arrived at 230 West 97th Street for a visit of seven or eight days. Loveman and Kirk were dumbfounded to see Lovecraft in the city, but Morton proved to be away from his museum for more than a week, so that no meeting could be arranged. On the 27th Lovecraft and Long saw the "modernistic junk"[95] at the Whitney Museum of American Art, then returned for a colossal turkey dinner prepared by Mrs Long. Lovecraft then went alone to look up Loveman in his new apartment at 17 Middagh Street in Brooklyn; he played with Loveman's radio (evidently the latter had replaced the one stolen from Lovecraft's Brooklyn flat in 1925), and was delighted to find a station in Mexico City speaking in suave Spanish.

On Friday, December 30, a gang meeting was held at the Longs', although only Wandrei, Leeds, Loveman, and Loveman's friend Patrick McGrath showed up. The next day Lovecraft apparently met Loveman and Richard Ely Morse, and on January 2 he and Long saw "Whistler's Mother"—a "splendid piece of quietly effective art"[96]—at the Museum of Modern Art. He returned home the next day.

Early in 1933 Lovecraft performed some revision work of a somewhat more con-genial variety than usual. Robert H. Barlow had begun to write fiction and, al-though scarcely fifteen years old at the time, was showing considerable promise. In February Lovecraft evaluated three items sent by Barlow, one of which was "The Slaying of the Monster" (the title, as is plain from the manuscript, was supplied by Lovecraft):

> I read your stories with a great deal of interest, & really think that they display a gratifying degree of merit & promise. You have a good idea of what a dramatic situation is, & seem to be distinctly sensitive to the nuances of style. Of course, there are at present many marks of the beginner's work—but these are only to be expected. Emphatically, I think you are headed in the right direction. . . . In "The Slaying of the Monster" I have taken the liberty of changing many words in order to carry out fully the Dunsanian prose-poetic effect which you are obviously seek-ing. . . . In changing parts of your text I have sought to give it some of the smoothness or rhythm which this kind of writing demands.[97]

Lovecraft urged Barlow to send the revised tales to some NAPA journal, but this was apparently not done. Barlow's first tale, however, appeared in the amateur press about this time: "Eyes of the God" was published in the *Sea Gull* for May 1933 and won the NAPA story laureateship for that year.

By March 1933 Barlow was showing Lovecraft some of his early "Annals of the Jinns" sketches, although Lovecraft does not seem to have revised them very much. A market for them did not open up until the *Fantasy Fan* was founded that fall. The "Annals" appeared fitfully throughout the entirety of that fan magazine's eighteen-month tenure: nine numbered episodes appeared in the issues for October 1933, November 1933, December 1933, January 1934, February 1934, May 1934, June 1934, August 1934, and February 1935. A tenth episode has been discovered in an issue of the *Phantagraph,* and there could conceivably have been others.

One of the "Annals"—the fourth, "The Sacred Bird"—is of importance in providing the background for "The Hoard of the Wizard-Beast," a story on which Lovecraft lent considerable assistance. This tale seems to be a loose sequel to "The Sacred Bird," for it picks up on that story's mention of a Sacred Bird and is also set in the land of Ullathia (spelled "Ulathia" in "The Sacred Bird"). It seems, therefore, very likely that "The Hoard of the Wizard-Beast" was meant as one of the "Annals of the Jinns," which for some reason Barlow did not send to the *Fantasy Fan*. That he sent it to some publisher (probably a fan magazine) is clear from the note he has written at the top of the manuscript ("only copy except at pub[lisher]"); but, if it was published, the appearance has not come to light.

Barlow has dated the manuscript to September 1933, but Lovecraft first saw it in a letter dating to December. He discusses the story at length:

> Your new tale is highly colourful & interesting, & I have taken the liberty to make a few changes in wording, rhythm, & transitional modulation, which may perhaps bring it a bit closer to the Dunsanian ideal evidently animating it. . . . If there is any defect, it is possibly a certain lack of compactness & unity—that is, the tale is not a closely-knit account of a *single episode,* but is rather a loosely-constructed record with which early space given to a description of the *occasion* for Yalden's journey, while the latter parts involve the *journey itself* in a way essentially dissociated from the *occasion.* An ideal short story would concentrate on a *single thing* like the *journey itself,* disposing of the *journey's reason* in as brief an explanatory paragraph as possible. The kind of vehicle for composite & diffuse narratives of this sort is the novel or picaresque romance. Still—it is to be admitted that Dunsany often creates similarly non-unified sketches of short story length, hence this specimen must not be criticised too severely. I'm letting it alone so far as this point goes. . . . As for your new tale—my changes largely concern certain niceties of language, & certain handlings of emotional stress at important turns of the action. A study of the altered text itself will be more instructive than any comment I can make here. What you need is simply more practice—which the years will readily supply.[98]

It is perhaps worth pausing to ponder the literary influences on both "The Slaying of the Monster" and "The Hoard of the Wizard-Beast." Lovecraft assumed that Dunsany is Barlow's model, and indeed he had lent Barlow several of his Dunsany volumes some years earlier; and while the ironically elementary moralism of the two stories does indeed bring Dunsany's *The Book of Wonder* (1912) and other early fantastic tales to mind, perhaps an equally strong influence is the fiction of Clark Ashton Smith, whom Barlow revered. Whatever the case, in his own fiction Barlow remained more drawn to the realm of pure fantasy than to the realistic supernaturalism of Lovecraft's later work.

The story as it stands is probably about 60% Lovecraft, although the end result is still a pretty mediocre piece of work, with a predictable and contrived comeuppance befalling a man who attempts to steal the vast treasure of the "wizard-beast." The revised version of the very short "Slaying of the Monster" is about 30% Lovecraft; it too amounts to little. Barlow's "Annals of the Jinns" do not bear many revisory touches by Lovecraft, and in many cases Lovecraft does not appear to have seen these items until after they were published. It would, however, not be long before Lovecraft was aiding Barlow on more significant items—and, indeed, it would not be long before Barlow himself was writing highly meritorious fiction of his own that could have given him a place in the field had he chosen to pursue this facet of his career.

Lovecraft's own writing career was, as noted, not progressing very well: only a single story ("The Dreams in the Witch House") in 1932, and none in the first half of 1933 (excluding the collaboration "Through the Gates of the Silver Key"). How much income the new revision client, Hazel Heald, along with other revision jobs, brought in is unclear; but some suggestion is offered by Lovecraft's remark to Donald Wandrei that in mid-February 1933 "my aunt & I had a desperate collo-quy on family finances,"[99] with the result that Lovecraft would move from 10 Bar-nes Street and Annie would move from 61 Slater Avenue and unite to form a single household. That Lovecraft and Annie could not afford even the meagre rent they were no doubt paying (Lovecraft's was $10 per week, Annie's probably similar) speaks volumes for the utter penury in which both of them existed—Annie eking by solely on Whipple Phillips's bequest, Lovecraft on whatever share of that be-quest remained ($5000 to his mother, $2500 to himself) along with his paltry revi-sion work and even paltrier sales of original fiction.

But luck was, on this occasion, with them. After looking at several apartments on the East Side and the college district, Lovecraft and Annie found a delightful house at 66 College Street, on the very crest of the hill, directly behind the John Hay Library and in the midst of Brown's fraternity row. The house was actually owned by the university and was leased out as two large apartments, one on each of the two floors. The top floor—five rooms plus two attic storerooms—had suddenly become vacant, and Lovecraft and Annie seized on it once they heard of its rent—$10 per week total, presumably half the combined rent for their two separate apartments. Best of all, from Lovecraft's perspective, was that the house was built in the colonial style. He thought that the house was actually colonial or post-colonial, built around 1800; but current research dates it to about 1825. He would have two rooms—a bedroom and a study—along with an attic storeroom for him-self. The place fell vacant on May 1, and Lovecraft moved in on May 15; Annie moved in two weeks later. Lovecraft was unable to believe his good fortune, and hoped only to be able to keep the place for a significant length of time. As it hap-pened, he would remain there for the four years remaining in his life.

22. IN MY OWN HANDWRITING (1933–1935)

The house is a square wooden edifice of the 1800 period . . . The fine colonial doorway is like my bookplate come to life, though of a slightly later period with side lights & fan carving instead of a fanlight. In the rear is a picturesque, village-like garden at a higher level than the front of the house. The upper flat we have taken contains 5 rooms besides bath & kitchenette nook on the main (2nd) floor, plus 2 attic storerooms—one of which is so attractive that I wish I could have it for an extra den! My quarters—a large study & a small adjoining bedroom—are on the south side, with my working desk under a west window affording a splendid view of the lower town's outspread roofs & of the mystical sunsets that flame behind them. The interior is as fascinating as the exterior—with colonial fireplaces, mantels, & chimney cupboards, curving Georgian staircase, wide floor-boards, old-fashioned latches, small-paned windows, six-panel doors, rear wing with floor at a different level (3 steps down), quaint attic stairs, &c.—just like the old houses open as museums. After admiring such all my life, I find something magical & dreamlike in the experience of actually *living in one* . . . I keep half-expecting a museum guard to come around & kick me out at 5 o'clock closing time![1]

A passage like this can be found in nearly every letter Lovecraft wrote during this period, and it testifies to the miraculous stroke of luck whereby a move made for purely economic reasons—and after Lovecraft had come to feel so at home at 10 Barnes after seven years' residence there—resulted in his landing in a colonial-style house he had always longed for. Even his birthplace, 454 Angell Street, was not colonial, although of course it remained dear to his heart for other reasons.

Lovecraft also provides a plan of the entire place.[2]

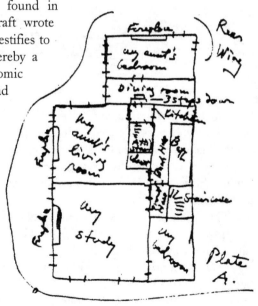

The space seems to have been pretty evenly divided between Lovecraft and Annie, since one imagines both had use of the kitchen and dining room. There certainly seemed to be an abundance of space; indeed, the two of them were able to rescue from storage several pieces of furniture and other items that had not been in use since 454 Angell Street days—a slat-back chair from the eighteenth century, a bust of Clytië on a pedestal, and an immense painting by Lillian.[3] Lovecraft goes on to provide a plan of his own two rooms:[4]

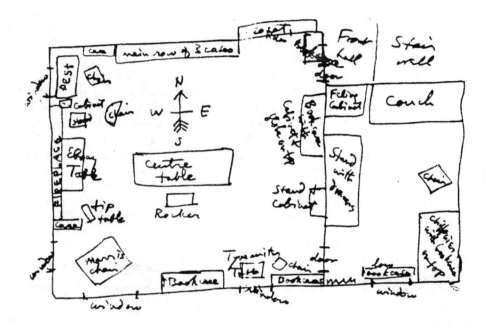

Examining this plan in conjunction with two photographs taken by R. H. Barlow[5] shortly after Lovecraft's death gives us a very good picture of Lovecraft's final home—the study at any rate, as no photographs of the bedroom survive. The study may seem a trifle congested, but Lovecraft always preferred to have as many of his familiar furnishings around him as possible, even if they violated abstract rules of interior decoration.

    The house itself was somewhat oddly positioned. Although the address was 66 College Street, it was set far back from the street, at the end of a narrow alley once called Ely's Lane; the house itself was perhaps closer to Waterman Street than College. Across the back garden was a boarding-house, at which Annie customarily ate both her meals; Lovecraft would eat there occasionally, but he preferred either going downtown to some cheaper eatery or making his own humble meals out of cans or from groceries purchased at delicatessens or grocery stores such as the Weybosset Food Basket (still in operation). The boarding-house occasionally served as a lodging for Lovecraft's out-of-town guests, although those who felt inclined to rough it used a mattressless camp cot that Lovecraft purchased.

One of the most engaging features of the place was a shed next to the boarding-house, whose flat roof supplied an excellent sunning place for the several cats in the area. It was not long before Lovecraft began to make friends with these cats, luring some to his study with catnip and allowing them to sleep in the morris chair or even play on his desk (they were fond of swatting at his rapidly moving pen as he wrote letters). Since he was living on what was then Brown University's fraternity row, Lovecraft christened this group of felines the Kappa Alpha Tau (K.A.T.), which he claimed stood for Κομπων 'Αιλουρων Τάξισ (Band of Elegant Cats). Their comings and goings would provide Lovecraft much pleasure, and some heartache, over the years.

A few months before he moved to 66 College, around March 11, Lovecraft had taken a trip to Hartford, Connecticut—on what he tells one correspondent as "a job of research which a client was conducting at the library there."[6] Again Lovecraft has prevaricated, and again the reason is connected with his ex-wife; for this was the last time he and Sonia saw each other face to face. After she returned from her European tour, Sonia took a trip to the Hartford suburbs of Farmington and Wethersfield; she was so captivated with the colonial antiquities in these towns that she wrote to Lovecraft and asked him to join her. He did so, spending a day and a night there.

That evening, before they parted for the night, Sonia said, "Howard, won't you kiss me goodnight?" Lovecraft replied, "No, it is better not to." The next morning they explored Hartford itself, and that evening, as they bade each other adieu, Sonia did not ask for a kiss.[7] They never saw each other again nor, so far as I can tell, corresponded.

The new household at 66 College got off, literally, on the wrong foot when, on June 14, Annie fell down the stairs in answering the doorbell and broke her ankle. She remained in Rhode Island Hospital for four weeks in a cast and returned home on July 5, essentially bedridden and with a nurse in attendance; the cast was removed on August 3, but Annie had to continue using crutches until well into the fall. She did not seem fully recovered from the injury until the next spring. Lovecraft dutifully visited the patient every day while she was in the hospital, and when she came back to 66 he had to stay home during afternoons while the nurse got a few hours off. Slight relief was provided by the installation of an automatic door-answerer in mid-September, shortly after the nurse was dismissed. All this could not have helped the finances of the household, and in an unguarded moment Lovecraft makes note of the "financial strain utterly ruinous to us at the present juncture!"[8] His plan to attend the NAPA convention in New York with W. Paul Cook in early July was abruptly cancelled.

There was some relief, however. On June 30 the peripatetic E. Hoffmann Price paid Lovecraft a four-day call in Providence in the course of an automobile tour across the country in a 1928 Ford that Lovecraft deemed the Juggernaut. This handy vehicle allowed Lovecraft to see parts of his own state that he had never visited before, in particular the so-called Narragansett Country or South County—the stretch of countryside on the western and southern side of Narragansett Bay, where in the colonial period actual plantations resembling those in the South had existed.

Harry Brobst joined in some of the festivities. It was at this time, apparently, that the three of them engaged in the all-night dissection of a story by Carl Strauch. There was also a midnight session in St John's Churchyard, and a feast of Indian curry prepared by Price—the first time Lovecraft had eaten this delicacy. The two had been discussing the exact ingredients to be used in this dish for months in their correspondence, and when it came time actually to make it, they behaved like mad scientists cooking up some nameless and sinister brew. As Price tells it:

> "More chemicals and acids?" I'd ask him.
>
> "Mmm . . . this is savory, and by no means lacking in fire, but it could be more vigorous."
>
> When he agreed that it was about right, I admitted that while I had eaten hotter curry in my time, this was certainly strong enough.[9]

Brobst, however, made the faux pas of bringing a six-pack of beer. Price in his memoir states that beer was now legal, but it would not become so until the end of the year; but repeal of the 18th Amendment was imminent, and no one had any fear from the police. Lovecraft, however, had apparently never seen such a quantity of alcoholic beverages before. Let Price again tell the story:

> "And what," he asked, out of scientific curiosity, "are you going to do with so *much* of it?"
>
> "Drink it," said Brobst. "Only three bottles a-piece."
>
> I'll never forget HPL's look of utter incredulity. . . . And he watched us with unconcealed curiosity, and with a touch of apprehension, as we drank three bottles a-piece. I'm sure he made a detailed entry in his journal to record this, to him, unusual feat.

Still another entertaining episode occurred when Lovecraft, responding to Price's relentless insistence, took his guest to a celebrated seafood restaurant in Pawtuxet for a clam dinner. Price knew of Lovecraft's detestation of seafood and should have predicted the response: "While you are devouring that *God-damned* stuff, I shall cross the street and eat a sandwich. Please excuse me." Price goes on to say that profanity of this sort was saved for "state occasions"; this seems to be the case both in speech and in correspondence, where the worst I have found is "goddamned bull-shit."[10]

Frank Long and his parents took Lovecraft again to Onset for a weekend in late July, and James F. Morton visited Lovecraft from July 31 to August 2. Among a flurry of activities were long rural walks and a boat trip to Newport, where the two of them sat on the sea-cliffs where, two centuries before, George Berkeley had dwelt for a few years.

Lovecraft's third and last trip to Quebec occurred in early September, when Annie gave Lovecraft a belated birthday present of a week's vacation from nursing. He prefaced the trip by visiting Cook in Boston on September 2, then crammed as much into the next four days as possible, seeing all the sights he had seen on his two previous visits. Lovecraft also managed one day in Montreal, which he found appealing if entirely modern. Annie tended to laugh at Lovecraft for wanting to visit the same spots over and over again (especially Charleston and Quebec);[11] but in reality Lovecraft in the last decade of his life did cover a pretty fair ground up and down the eastern seaboard. It is, however, no surprise that he kept being drawn to certain especial concentrations of antiquity and charm—they seemed to have the power to evoke endless chains of associations that allowed him to merge his consciousness into the historic time-stream of this continent and of its European founders.

In somewhat the same vein, Lovecraft in the fall did something he had been always been meaning to do: he spent Thanksgiving at Plymouth, where the ceremony had begun 312 years before. It was, in part, the incredibly warm temperature—68° in the afternoon—that permitted him to make such a trip so close to winter, and he had a delightful time: "The old town was fascinating ... I put in most of the time exploring, & saw an exquisite sunset from the top of Burial Hill. In the evening the moonlight on the harbour was fascinating."[12]

In late summer 1933 Samuel Loveman spoke with an editor at Alfred A. Knopf, Allen G. Ullman, about Lovecraft's stories, showing him "The Dreams in the Witch House." On the 1st of August Ullman wrote to Lovecraft asking to see a few more tales, and on the 3rd Lovecraft sent Ullman seven stories: "The Picture in the House," "The Music of Erich Zann," "The Rats in the Walls," "The Strange High House in the Mist," "Pickman's Model," "The Colour out of Space," and "The Dunwich Horror." Ullman seemed reasonably impressed with this batch and (apparently through Loveman) conveyed the desire to see still more—"everything which I or others have thought good in the past."[13] The result was that Lovecraft now sent Ullman eighteen more stories—nearly all the work he had not repudiated.

Sympathetic as I generally am to Lovecraft's relentlessly uncommercial stance, I have difficulty refraining from a strong inclination to kick him in the seat of the pants for the letter he wrote to Ullman accompanying these eighteen stories. Throughout the letter Lovecraft denigrates his own work out of what he fancies to be gentlemanly humility but which Ullman probably took to be lack of confidence in his own work. It is irrelevant that Lovecraft is probably correct in some of his evaluations; if he was serious in trying to sell a collection of his tales to one of the most prestigious of New York publishing houses, he ought not to have commented that "The Tomb" is "stiff in diction"; that "The Temple" is "nothing remarkable"; that "The Outsider" is "rather bombastic in style & mechanical in climax"; that "The Call of Cthulhu" is "not so bad"; and on and on. For some unexplained reason, perhaps because they were not published, Lovecraft did not send *At the Mountains of Madness* or "The Shadow over Innsmouth," two of his strongest works.

It is scarcely a surprise that Ullman ultimately rejected the collection, sending Lovecraft on another round of self-recrimination. And yet, in this case the rejection was not entirely the fault of Lovecraft's lack of salesmanship. Ullman had asked Farnsworth Wright of *Weird Tales* whether he could dispose of 1000 copies of a proposed collection of Lovecraft's stories through the magazine; Wright said he could not guarantee such a sale, and Ullman promptly turned down the stories.[14] Wright certainly seems to have been excessively cautious on the issue, although perhaps *Weird Tales'* own dubious fortunes in the depression had something to do with it. Wright compounded the problem by stating tantalisingly in the December 1933 issue of *Weird Tales* that "We hope to have an important announcement to make soon about Lovecraft's stories"[15]—a remark Lovecraft was forced to explain away to his many correspondents who saw it.

The Knopf deal is probably the closest Lovecraft ever came to having a book published in his lifetime by a mainstream publisher. If he had done so, the rest of his career—and, it is not too much to say, the entire subsequent history of American weird fiction—may have been very different. But, after this fourth failure at book publication (following *Weird Tales,* Putnam's, and Vanguard), the last four years of Lovecraft's life were increasingly filled with doubt, diffidence, and depression about his work, until toward the end he came to believe that he had entirely failed as a fictionist. Lovecraft's sensitivity to rejection was a regrettable flaw in his character, and it has perhaps robbed us of more stories from his pen.

In September 1933 *The Fantasy Fan* began publication. This is, canonically, the first "fan" magazine in the domain of weird/fantastic fiction, and it inaugurated a rich, complex, and somewhat unruly tradition—still flourishing today—of fan activity in this realm. The word "fan"—short for *fanatic*—began gaining currency in late nineteenth-century America as a term denoting followers of sporting teams, later being extended to devoted followers of any hobby or activity. From the beginning it connoted uncritical adulation, immaturity, and, perhaps, unworthiness of the object of devotion. These connotations, in some senses unjust, are perhaps not entirely to be dismissed. There may be fantasy fans, but there are no Beethoven fans.

It is an anomaly beyond my powers of explanation that the fields of fantasy, horror, and science fiction have attracted legions of fans who are not content to read and collect the literature but must write about it and its authors, and publish—often at considerable expense—small magazines or books devoted to the subject. There is no analogous fan network in the fields of detective fiction or the Western, even though the first of these fields certainly attracts a far larger body of fans than does weird fiction. Nor is this fan activity entirely to be despised: many of today's leading critics of weird fiction emerged from the realm of fandom and still retain connexions with it. Fandom is perhaps most charitably seen as a training ground that permits young writers and critics (most individuals become fans as teenagers) to hone their nascent abilities; but the field has gained well-deserved contempt because so many of its participants never seem to advance beyond its essentially juvenile level.

The *Fantasy Fan* was edited by Charles D. Hornig (1916–1999) of Elizabeth, New Jersey, who was scarcely seventeen when the magazine was launched. Celebrated as it is, it operated at a loss during its entire run: it had a pitifully small circulation in its day—only 60 subscribers[16] and a print run probably not exceeding 300—and, in spite of the fact that it was typeset (the printer was the young Conrad Ruppert), looks very crude and amateurish today, especially since it was printed on poor paper that has turned a dark brown over the years. But it attracted immediate attention throughout the world of weird fiction, not only among fans but among its leading authors. Lovecraft saw in it a chance to land (without pay, of course) his oft-rejected tales, so that in this way he could gain a modicum of lending copies in printed form and save wear and tear on his manuscripts. He urged Clark Ashton Smith, Robert E. Howard, and even the relentlessly professional August Derleth to send original stories to it, and the appearance of works by these and other writers has made *The Fantasy Fan* a choice collectible commanding high prices. It is rare to find a complete set of the eighteen monthly issues.

But *The Fantasy Fan* was not chiefly made up of contributions by the "big names" of the weird fiction field; instead, it offered ready access for novices to express their opinions in letters to the editor and brief articles and tales. R. H. Barlow published nine of his "Annals of the Jinns" sketches throughout the magazine's run; such fans as Duane W. Rimel, F. Lee Baldwin, and others who would later come into direct contact with Lovecraft had articles or columns in early issues.

Hornig did, however, make one mistake in judgment by instituting, in the very first issue, a write-in column called "The Boiling Point" in which controversial and polemical opinions were deliberately sought out. The first column featured a gauntlet thrown down by the redoubtable Forrest J Ackerman (1916–2008; the J stands for James, but Ackerman affected the policy of placing no period after it), then already a well-known fan. He criticised the publication of Clark Ashton Smith's "Dweller in Martian Depths" in *Wonder Stories* for March 1933: *Wonder Stories* was a prototypical "scientifiction" pulp, and in Ackerman's view Smith's tale was a pure horror story that had no place in the magazine. Had Ackerman restricted his criticism to this point, he would not have left himself so open to attack; but he went on actually to deny merit to the tale ("Frankly, I could not find one redeeming feature about the story"), going on to proclaim: "May the ink dry up in the pen from which [it] flow[s]!"

This was too much for Lovecraft and other supporters of Smith. Firstly, Smith's title for the story was "The Dweller in the Gulf"; and secondly, the ending had been wilfully changed, and not for the better, by the *Wonder Stories* staff. "The Dweller in the Gulf" may not be an immortal masterwork of literature, but purely as a story it was leagues better than much else that appeared in the magazine.

The next several issues of the *Fantasy Fan* included hot-tempered letters by Lovecraft, Barlow, and many others heaping abuse on Ackerman, Smith guardedly defending himself, Ackerman fighting back, and on and on. No one comes off very well in the debate, if it can be called that; Robert Nelson perhaps put it best when he said in the November 1933 issue, "The Ackerman-Smith controversy assumes all the aspects of a mad comedy." By February 1934 Hornig decided that "The Boiling Point" had served its purpose and had in fact aroused too much ill-feeling to be productive. And yet, bitter, vituperative controversies of this sort have remained common in fandom and continue to this day.

Hornig made a wiser decision when he accepted Lovecraft's offer of preparing a new edition of "Supernatural Horror in Literature" for serialisation in the magazine.[17] Since writing the essay seven years before, Lovecraft had continued to take notes for additions to it for some future republication. In letters Lovecraft frequently made note of the worthiness—or lack of it—of this or that weird writer for inclusion in his treatise. Finally, the humble *Fantasy Fan* offered him the chance for revision.

Lovecraft evidently revised the essay all at once, not piecemeal over the course of the serialisation (October 1933–February 1935); indeed, he seems simply to have sent Hornig an annotated copy of the *Recluse,* with separate typed (or even handwritten) sheets for the major additions.[18] This is borne out by the nature of the revisions: aside from random revisions in phraseology ("the modern writer D. H. Lawrence" becomes "the late D. H. Lawrence," since he had died in 1930), there is almost no change in the text save the following additions:

> Chapter VI: the small paragraph on H. H. Ewers and part of the concluding paragraph (on Meyrink's *The Golem*);
> Chapter VIII: the section beginning with the discussion of Cram's "The Dead

Valley" up to that discussing the tales of Edward Lucas White; the last paragraph, on Clark Ashton Smith, is augmented;

Chapter IX: the paragraph on Buchan, much of the long paragraph discussing "the weird short story", and the long section on Hodgson.

Of these, the section on Hodgson was added separately in August 1934, while the section on *The Golem* was revised after April 1935, when Lovecraft (who had based his note on the film version) read the actual novel and disconcertedly observed its enormous difference from the film.

The serialisation in the *Fantasy Fan* progressed very slowly, as the magazine could only accommodate a small portion of text in each issue; when the magazine folded in February 1935, it had only published the text up to the middle of Chapter VIII. For the rest of the two years of his life Lovecraft sought in vain to find some fan publisher to continue the serialisation. The complete, revised text of "Supernatural Horror in Literature" did not appear until *The Outsider and Others* (1939).

Another individual who established—or attempted to establish—various journals wavering uncertainly between the fan and semi-professional levels was William L. Crawford (1911–1984), with whom Lovecraft came in touch in the fall of 1933. Lovecraft would, with a certain good-natured maliciousness, poke fun at Crawford's lack of culture by referring to him as Hill-Billy, presumably alluding both to Crawford's residence in Everett, Pennsylvania (in the Alleghenies), and to his stolid insensitivity to highbrow literature. In a letter to Barlow he presented an annotated version of an actual letter he received from Crawford:

"I probably will never be able to appreciate literature. I can 'get it' [oh, yeah?], but I just can't appreciate it. When I want to read something deep, I think of a textbook [like Greenleaf's Primary-School Arithmetic or the First Reader, no doubt!]; when I want to be amused or entertained, I think of 'pulp' or light reading. The stories I get in Literature & Life practically put me to sleep—& I don't think—conceitedly maybe—that it's because I'm entirely a light-thinker, either, as I spend all my spare time, you might say, speculating on this or that." [Atta boy, Billy, but be careful not to wear out the ol' cerebrum!] [19]

Probably Lovecraft didn't need to add the annotations after all.

But Crawford meant well. Initially he proposed a non-paying weird magazine titled *Unusual Stories* but almost immediately ran into difficulties, even though he accepted Lovecraft's "Celephaïs" and "The Doom That Came to Sarnath" for the magazine. [20] By early 1934 he had proposed a second journal, *Marvel Tales,* either as a companion to *Unusual* or a replacement for it. "Celephaïs" appeared in the first issue (May 1934) of *Marvel,* while "The Doom That Came to Sarnath" finally appeared in the March–April 1935 issue. Two issues of *Unusual Stories* did emerge in 1935 (prefaced by a queer "advance issue" in the spring of 1934), but contained no work by Lovecraft.

But Crawford's bumbling attempts deserve commendation for at least one good result. In the fall of 1933 he asked Lovecraft for a 900-word autobiography for *Unusual,* evidently the first of a series. Lovecraft had great difficulty condensing his life and opinions into 900 words, so on November 23 he wrote a longer version of about 2300 words and somehow managed to trim this down to the requisite size. The shortened version, now lost, never appeared; but providentially Lovecraft sent the longer version to Barlow for preservation, and this is how we have the piece entitled "Some Notes on a Nonentity."

There is not much in this essay that Lovecraft had not said somewhere before, at least in letters; but it is a singularly felicitous and compact account of his life and, toward the end, of his views on the nature and purpose of weird fiction. Some anomalies—such as the omission of any mention of his marriage—have already been noted; but beyond such things, "Some Notes on a Nonentity" is a wonderfully illuminating document—not so much for facts (which we can secure in abundance elsewhere) but for Lovecraft's own impressions of his character and development. It is, moreover, an elegantly written essay in its own right—perhaps the best single essay Lovecraft ever wrote, with the possible exception of "Cats and Dogs":

> Nature . . . keenly touched my sense of the fantastic. My home was not far from what was then the edge of the settled residence district, so that I was just as used to the rolling fields, stone walls, giant elms, squat farmhouses, and deep woods of rural New England as to the ancient urban scene. This brooding, primitive landscape seemed to me to hold some vast but unknown significance, and certain dark wooded hollows near the Seekonk River took on an aura of strangeness not unmixed with vague horror. They figured in my dreams . . .

But the essay did not appear until 1943, and then in a corrupt text.[21]

Lovecraft was, inexorably, being drawn back into purely amateur as well as fannish activity. One such venture was the essay "Some Dutch Footprints in New England," which he wrote sometime in the summer or fall of 1933. The date is difficult to specify because the piece—less than 1500 words long—was the source of months of picayune wrangling between Lovecraft and Wilfred B. Talman, who commissioned it for the Holland Society's journal, *De Halve Maen,* which he edited. Talman reports in his memoir that "the quibbling in correspondence over spelling, punctuation, and historical facts before the script suited us both approached book-length proportions,"[22] and was—on Talman's part—inspired by Lovecraft's high-handed revision suggestions for "Two Black Bottles" seven years earlier. This is a remarkable admission by Talman, and one that does not redound to his credit: was he waiting nearly a decade to pay Lovecraft back in coin for work that actually launched Talman's (fleeting and undistinguished) career in the pulps?

Let it pass: Lovecraft was tickled at appearing in *De Halve Maen,* one of the few occasions in which he was published in other than an amateur, fan, or pulp magazine. The article itself—on Dutch colonial traces in various obscure corners of Rhode Island—is no more than competent.

The revision of "Supernatural Horror in Literature" coincided with an extensive course of rereading and analysing the weird classics in an attempt to revive what Lovecraft believed to be his flagging creative powers. Rejections were still affecting him keenly, and he was beginning to feel written out. Perhaps he needed a break from fiction as he had had in 1908–17; or perhaps a renewed critical reading of the landmarks in the field might rejuvenate him. Whatever the case, Lovecraft produced several interesting documents as a result of this work.

One can gain an exact knowledge of what Lovecraft read by consulting a notebook of jottings, similar to the commonplace book, titled "Weird Story Plots." Here we find analytical plot descriptions of works by Poe, Machen, Blackwood, de la Mare, M. R. James, Dunsany, E. F. Benson, Robert W. Chambers, John Buchan, Leonard Cline (*The Dark Chamber*), and a number of lesser items.[23] Rather more interesting, from an academic perspective, are such things as "Notes on Writing Weird Fiction," "Types of Weird Story," and "A List of Certain Basic Underlying Horrors Effectively Used in Weird Fiction" (this item matching the plot descriptions in "Weird Story Plots" fairly precisely), which represent in their rough and humble way some of the most suggestive theoretical work on the horror tale ever set down. "Notes on Writing Weird Fiction" (which exists in several different versions, all slightly different; the soundest text seems to be the one published posthumously in *Amateur Correspondent* for May–June 1937) is Lovecraft's canonical statement of his own goals for weird writing, as well as a schematic outline of how he himself wrote his own stories. The centrepiece of this latter section is the idea of preparing *two* synopses, one giving the scenario of a tale in order of its *chronological occurrence,* the second in order of its *narration in the story.* Naturally, the two could be quite different; indeed the degree of their difference is an index to the structural complexity of the tale.

And yet, this research does not seem to have helped Lovecraft much in the short term, for the first actual story he wrote at this time—"The Thing on the Doorstep," scribbled frenetically in pencil from August 21 to 24, 1933—is, like "The Dreams in the Witch House," one of his poorest later efforts.

The tale, narrated in the first person by Daniel Upton, tells of Upton's young friend Edward Derby, who since boyhood has displayed a remarkable aesthetic sensitivity toward the weird, in spite of the overprotective coddling he receives from his parents. Derby frequently visits Upton, using a characteristic knock—three raps followed by two more after an interval—to announce himself. Derby attends Miskatonic University and becomes a moderately recognised fantaisiste and poet. When he is thirty-eight he meets Asenath Waite, a young woman at Miskatonic, about whom strange things are whispered: she has anomalous hypnotic powers, creating the momentary impression in her subjects that they are in her body looking across at themselves. Even stranger things are whispered of her father, Ephraim Waite, who died under very peculiar circumstances. Over his father's opposition, Derby marries Asenath—who is one of the Innsmouth Waites—and settles in a home in Arkham. They seem to undertake very recondite and perhaps dangerous occult experiments. Moreover, people observe curious changes in both of them: whereas Asenath is extremely strong-willed and determined, Edward is flabby and weak-willed; but on occasion he is seen driving Asenath's car (even though he did not previously know how to drive) with a resolute and almost daemonic expression, and conversely Asenath is seen from a window looking unwontedly meek and defeated. One day Upton receives a call from Maine: Derby is there in a crazed state, and Upton has to fetch him because Derby has suddenly lost the ability to drive. On the trip back Derby tells Upton a wild tale of Asenath forcing him out of his body, and going on to suggest that Asenath is really Ephraim, who forced out the mind of his daughter and placed it in his own dying body. Abruptly Derby's ramblings come to an end, as if "shut off with an almost mechanical click": Derby takes the wheel away from Upton and tells him to pay no attention to what he may just have said.

Some months later Derby visits Upton again. He is in a tremendously excited state, claiming that Asenath has gone away and that he will seek a divorce. Around Christmas of that year Derby breaks down entirely. He cries out: "My brain! My brain! God, Dan—it's tugging—from beyond—knocking—clawing—that she-devil—even now—Ephraim . . ." He is placed in a mental hospital, and shows no signs of recovery until one day he suddenly seems to be better; but, to Upton's disappointment and even latent horror, Derby is now in that curiously "energised" state such as he had been during the ride back from Maine. Upton is in an utter turmoil of confusion when one evening he receives a phone call. He cannot make out what the caller is saying—it sounds like "glub . . . glub"—but a little later someone knocks at his door, using Derby's familiar three-and-two signal. This creature—a "foul, stunted parody" of a human being—is wearing one of Derby's old coats, which is clearly too big for it. It hands Upton a sheet of paper which explains the whole story: Derby had killed Asenath as a means of escaping her influence and her plans to switch bodies with him altogether; but death did not put an end to Asenath/Ephraim's mind, for it emerged from the body, thrust itself into the body of Derby, and hurled his mind into the decaying corpse of Asenath, buried in the cellar of their home. Now, with a final burst of determination, Derby (in the body of Asenath) has climbed out of the shallow grave and is now delivering this message to Upton, since he was unable to communicate with him on the phone.

Upton promptly goes to the madhouse and shoots the thing that is in Edward Derby's body; this account is his confession and attempt at exculpation.

"The Thing on the Doorstep" has many flaws: first, the obviousness of the basic scenario and the utter lack of subtlety in its execution; second, poor writing, laden (as with "The Dreams in the Witch House") with hyperbole, stale idioms, and dragging verbosity; and third, a complete absence of cosmicism in spite of the frequent dropping of the *word* "cosmic" throughout the tale ("some damnable, utterly accursed focus of unknown and malign cosmic forces"). The story was clearly influenced by H. B. Drake's *The Shadowy Thing* (1928), a poorly written but strangely compelling novel about a man who displays anomalous powers of hypnosis and mind-transference. An entry in the commonplace book (#158) records the plot-germ: "Man has terrible wizard friend who gains influence over him. Kills him in defence of his soul—walls body up in ancient cellar—BUT—the dead wizard (who has said strange things about soul lingering in body) *changes bodies with him* . . . leaving him a conscious corpse in cellar." This is not exactly a description of the plot of *The Shadowy Thing,* but rather an imaginative extrapolation based upon it. In Drake's novel, a man, Avery Booth, does indeed exhibit powers that seem akin to hypnosis, to such a degree that he can oust the mind or personality from another person's body and occupy it. Booth does so on several occasions throughout the novel, and in the final episode he appears to have come back from the dead (he had been killed in a battle in World War I) and occupied the body of a friend and soldier who had himself been horribly mangled in battle. Lovecraft has amended this plot by introducing the notion of *mind-exchange:* whereas Drake does not clarify what happens to the ousted mind when it is taken over by the mind of Booth, Lovecraft envisages an exact transference whereby the ousted mind occupies the body of its possessor. Lovecraft then adds a further twist by envisioning what might happen if the occupier's body were killed and a dispossessed mind was thrust into it. It turns out, then, that in "The Thing on the Doorstep" there are *two* supernatural phenomena at work: first, the mind-exchange practised by Ephraim/Asenath Waite; and second, the ability of Edward Derby to lend a sort of hideous animation to the dead body of Asenath purely by the strength of his own mind. (It is not at all surprising that the sexually reserved Lovecraft has nothing at all to say about the potentially intriguing gender-switching implied by this mind-exchange.)

The significant difference between the story and the plot-germ as recorded in the commonplace book is that the "wizard friend" has become the man's wife. This leads me to suspect the influence of another relatively obscure novel, Barry Pain's *An Exchange of Souls* (1911), a book Lovecraft had in his library, which tells the compelling tale of a man who invents a device that will effect the transfer of his "soul" or personality with that of his wife; the man is successful in the enterprise, but in the process his own body dies, leaving him stranded in that alien body of his wife. I have no doubt that Lovecraft picked up hints from this novel for his own tale; but at the same time, this husband-wife interchange allows the story to gain some interest, if only from a biographical perspective. I have earlier noted that some features of Edward Derby's life supply a masked version of Lovecraft's own marriage, as well as of certain aspects of his childhood. But there are some anomalies in the portrayal of the youthful Edward Derby that need to be addressed. Derby was "the most phenomenal child scholar I have ever known": would Lovecraft write something like this about a character who was modelled upon himself? It seems unlikely, given his characteristic modesty; and this makes me think that Derby is an amalgam of several individuals. Consider this remark on Alfred Galpin: "He is intellectually *exactly like me* save in degree. In degree he is immensely my superior";[24] elsewhere he refers to Galpin—who was only seventeen when Lovecraft first came in touch with him in 1918—as "the most brilliant, accurate, steel-cold intellect I have ever encountered."[25] However, Galpin never wrote "verse of a sombre, fantastic, almost morbid cast" as Derby did as a boy; nor did he publish a volume, *Azathoth and Other Horrors,* when he was eighteen. But did not Clark Ashton Smith create a sensation as a boy prodigy when he published *The Star-Treader and Other Poems* in 1912, when he was nineteen? And was Smith not a close colleague of George Sterling, who—like Justin Geoffrey in the tale—died in 1926 (Sterling by suicide, Geoffrey of unknown causes)? (Justin Geoffrey was invented by Robert E. Howard in "The Black Stone" [*Weird Tales,* November 1931], but the date of his death has here been invented by Lovecraft.) On a more whimsical note, Lovecraft's mention that Derby's "attempts to grow a moustache were discernible only with difficulty" recalls his frequent censures of the thin moustache Frank Belknap Long attempted for years to cultivate in the 1920s.

But if Derby's youth and young manhood are an amalgam of Lovecraft and some of his closest associates, his marriage to Asenath Waite brings certain aspects of Lovecraft's marriage to Sonia manifestly to mind. In the first place there is the fact that Sonia was clearly the more strong-willed member of the couple; it was certainly from her initiative that the marriage took place at all and that Lovecraft uprooted himself from Providence to come to live in New York. The objections of Derby's father to Asenath—and specifically to Derby's wish to marry her—may dimly echo the apparently unspoken objections of Lovecraft's aunts to his marriage to Sonia.

Aside from these points of biographical interest, however, "The Thing on the Doorstep" is crude, obvious, lacking in subtlety of execution or depth of conception, and histrionically written. One of its few memorable features is the hideous and grisly conclusion, where Edward—who, trapped in Asenath's decaying body, displays more will and determination than he ever had in his own body—resolutely attempts to call Upton over the phone and, finding that his decomposing body is incapable of enunciating words, writes a note to Upton and brings it to him before dissolving on his doorstep in "mostly liquescent horror." In a sense this story is a reprise of *The Case of Charles Dexter Ward,* although actual mind-exchange does not occur there as it does here; but the attempt by Asenath (in Derby's body) to pass herself off as Edward in the madhouse is precisely analogous to Joseph Curwen's attempts to maintain that he is Charles Dexter Ward. In this case, however, it cannot be said that Lovecraft has improved on the original.

One glancing note in the story that has caused considerable misunderstanding is Upton's remark about Asenath: "Her crowning rage . . . was that she was not a man; since she believed a male brain had certain unique and far-reaching cosmic powers." This sentiment is clearly expressed as Asenath's (who, let us recall, is only Ephraim in another body), and need not be attributed to Lovecraft. A decade earlier he had indeed uttered some silly remarks on women's intelligence: "Females are in Truth much given to affected Baby Lisping . . . They are by Nature literal, prosaic, and commonplace, given to dull realistick Details and practical Things, and incapable alike of vigorous artistick Creation and genuine, first-hand appreciation."[26] One wonders on what evidence this could have been based, since Lovecraft had known almost no women except members of his own family up to this time. But by the 1930s he had come to a more sensible position: "I do not regard the rise of woman as a bad sign. Rather do I fancy that her traditional subordination was itself an artificial and undesirable condition based on Oriental influences. . . . The feminine mind does not cover the same territory as the masculine, but is probably little if any inferior in total quality."[27] I am not sure what the exact import of that remark is, but at least his attitude is a little more rational than before—indeed, more rational than that of many of his generation.

The year 1933 seems to have been an especially difficult one for Lovecraft as a writer. He was clearly attempting to capture on paper various ideas clamouring for expression, but seemed unable to do so. At least two other works of fiction may have been written at this time; one of them is the fragment entitled (by R. H. Barlow) "The Book." The exact date of this item is not known, but in a letter of October 1933 Lovecraft wrote as follows: "I am at a sort of standstill in writing— disgusted at much of my older work, & uncertain as to avenues of improvement. In recent weeks I have done a tremendous amount of experimenting in different styles & perspectives, but have destroyed *most* [my italics] of the results."[28] If "The Book" was one of the things Lovecraft was writing at this time, it could well qualify as a piece of experimentation; for it appears to be nothing more than an attempt to write out *Fungi from Yuggoth* in *prose.* The first three sonnets of the cycle do indeed form a connected narrative; and the fact that the story fragment peters out into inconclusive vagueness after this point may further suggest that there is no "continuity"—certainly not on the level of plot—in the sonnet sequence. And the very fact that he undertook such a task suggests that Lovecraft, despairing of finding new ideas for fiction (in spite of the dozens of unused entries in his commonplace book), was desperately seeking to cannibalise from his own work in a vain attempt to revive his flagging inspiration.

The other item that was probably written in 1933 is "The Evil Clergyman." This is nothing more than an account of a dream written up in a letter to Bernard Austin Dwyer. The excerpt was made and a title ("The Wicked Clergyman") supplied by Dwyer; it was first published in *Weird Tales* (April 1939) and retitled "The Evil Clergyman" by Derleth. Lovecraft remarked in a letter to Clark Ashton Smith on October 22, 1933, that "Some months ago I had a dream of an evil clergyman in a garret full of forbidden books,"[29] and it is likely that the account of the dream was written up in a letter to Dwyer at this time or earlier; Derleth's dating of the item to 1937 is entirely unfounded.

It is hardly worth discussing "The Evil Clergyman" as a story, since it was never meant to stand as a discrete and self-contained narrative. Some of the imagery and atmosphere are reminiscent of "The Festival," although the dream takes place in England. Unlike "The Thing on the Doorstep" and other tales, this dream-fragment does not involve *mind*-transference but transference of a very physical sort: because the protagonist has unwisely handled a small box that he was specifically told not to touch, he has summoned the "evil clergyman" and somehow effected an exchange of external features with him, while yet retaining his mind and personality. It is difficult to say how Lovecraft would have developed this curiously conventional supernatural scenario in light of his later quasi-science fictional work.

Lovecraft was becoming the hub of an increasingly complex network of fans and writers in the field of weird and science fiction; and in the last four years of his life he attracted a substantial number of young people (mostly boys) who looked upon him as a living legend. I have already noted that R. H. Barlow first came in touch with Lovecraft at the age of thirteen in 1931; now other teenagers came to the fore.

The most promising of them—or, rather, the one who in the end amounted to the most—was Robert Bloch (1917–1994), who first wrote to Lovecraft in the spring of 1933. Bloch, born in Chicago but at this time a resident of Milwaukee, had just turned sixteen and had been reading *Weird Tales* since 1927. To the end of his life Bloch remained grateful to Lovecraft for his lengthy reply to his fan letter and for continuing to write to him over the next four years.

In that very first letter, Lovecraft asked his young correspondent whether he had written any weird work and, if so, whether he might see samples of it. Bloch took up Lovecraft's offer in late April, sending him two short items. Lovecraft's response to these pieces of juvenilia (which, along with a good many others Bloch sent to Lovecraft, do not survive) is typical: while praising them, he also gave helpful advice derived from his many years as both a critic and a practitioner of the weird tale:

> It was with the keenest interest & pleasure that I read your two brief horror-sketches; whose rhythm & atmospheric colouring convey a very genuine air of unholy immanence & nameless menace, & which strike me as promising in the very highest degree. I think you have managed to create a dark tension & apprehension of a sort all too seldom encountered in weird fiction, & believe that your gift for this atmosphere-weaving will serve you in good stead when you attempt longer & more intricately plotted pieces. . . . Of course, these productions are not free from the earmarks of youth. A critic might complain that the colouring is laid on too thickly—too much *overt inculcation* of horror as opposed to the *subtle, gradual suggestion of concealed horror* which actually raises fear to its highest pitch. In later work you will probably be less disposed to pile on great numbers of horrific words (an early & scarcely-conquered habit of my own), but will seek rather to select a *few* words—whose precise position in the text, & whose deep associative power, will make them in effect more terrible than any barrage of monstrous adjectives, malign nouns, & unhallowed verbs.[30]

This is a litany that Lovecraft would repeat for at least another year. The advice paid off more expeditiously than either correspondent could have imagined, for in just over a year, in July 1934, Bloch landed his first story in *Weird Tales.* The tale—"The Secret in the Tomb" (*Weird Tales,* May 1935)—appeared after his second accepted story, "The Feast in the Abbey" (*Weird Tales,* January 1935); but from this point on Bloch rapidly became a regular in the magazine, and—although this occurred chiefly after Lovecraft's death—branched out into the mystery and science fiction fields as well.

F. Lee Baldwin (1913–1987) came in touch with Lovecraft in the fall of 1933, as he wished to reissue "The Colour out of Space" as a booklet, in an edition of 200 copies that would sell for 25¢.[31] Although Lovecraft prepared a slightly revised text of the story for Baldwin, this venture was yet another of the many book prospects for Lovecraft's work that never came off. The correspondence continued, however, for another two years, until Baldwin lost interest in the field of weird fiction. Lovecraft found Baldwin interesting because he was a native of Lewiston, Idaho, and was familiar with the Snake River area where Lovecraft's grandfather Whipple Phillips had worked in the 1890s. In 1933 Baldwin was in Asotin, in the western part of Washington State.[32]

Strangely enough, Lovecraft independently came into contact with another individual in Asotin, Duane W. Rimel, in early 1934; he put Baldwin in touch with Rimel shortly thereafter. Rimel (1915–1996) continued his correspondence with Lovecraft until the latter's death and would become as close a colleague and informal revision client as their situation on opposite sides of the country allowed. Rimel

was, like Bloch, a budding writer of weird fiction, but even under Lovecraft's tute-
lage he did not develop into a full-fledged professional; he did manage to have a
few stories published in professional magazines (two in *Weird Tales*) and several
more in fan and semi-pro magazines, but that was all. After Lovecraft's death he
wrote Westerns and other hackwork (including soft-core pornography) under a
variety of pseudonyms.[33]

Richard F. Searight (1902–1975) was not exactly a teenage fan when he began
corresponding with Lovecraft in late summer of 1933; indeed, he had had one collaborative story in an early issue of *Weird Tales* ("The Brain in the Jar" in November 1924). A native of Michigan, Searight worked as a telegraph operator for many
years. By the early 1930s he decided to return to literature, writing a series of tales
and poems that he wished Lovecraft to revise and help him to place professionally.
Lovecraft felt that he could not help Searight in a revisory capacity (his stories' "occasional shortcomings are matters of subject-matter rather than of technique"[34]) but
encouraged him to reconceive his work along less conventional lines. Searight attempted to follow Lovecraft's advice and did manage to land some tales in *Wonder
Stories* and other science fiction pulps, although many remained unpublished.

One story that landed in *Weird Tales* for March 1935, "The Sealed Casket," is
worth some consideration—not intrinsically, for it is at best a mediocre item, but for
Lovecraft's tangential involvement in it. Lovecraft read the tale in January 1934,
remarking of it: "I . . . believe it is unqualifiedly the best thing you have done so
far."[35] There is no evidence that Lovecraft revised any portion of the text proper.
Some have believed that the epigraph—not published in *Weird Tales*—is Lovecraft's, but there is no evidence for this assertion, either. The epigraph and its purported source (the Eltdown Shards) are clearly the work of Searight: Lovecraft admitted only to altering a single word in the epigraph's text.[36] Lovecraft, of course,
later cited the Eltdown Shards as another of the many cryptic documents of occult
lore in his mythos, but the Shards themselves are clearly the invention of Searight.

Herman C. Koenig (1893–1959) was, like Searight, well beyond his teen years
when he wrote to Lovecraft in the fall of 1933. An employee of the Electrical Testing Laboratories in New York City, Koenig had an impressive private collection of
rare books, and he had asked Lovecraft about the *Necronomicon* and how it could
be procured. Lovecraft, disillusioning Koenig about the reality of the volume, nevertheless continued to stay in touch with him, and Koenig would lend him a significant number of weird books that would affect Lovecraft strongly over the next several years.

Helen V. Sully (1905–1997) met Lovecraft in person before corresponding
with him. The daughter of Genevieve K. Sully, a married woman in Auburn, California, with whom Clark Ashton Smith apparently carried on a longtime affair,
Sully decided to explore the eastern seaboard in the summer of 1933, and Smith

urged her to look up Lovecraft in Providence. She did so, arriving in the city in early July and being shown all the sites in Providence as well as Newport, New-buryport, and elsewhere. Lovecraft paid for all Sully's expenses—meals, trips, lodging at the boarding house across the street from 66 College—while he was her host; she could not have known what a severe burden this must have placed upon his own perilous financial condition. One evening Lovecraft took her to one of his favourite haunts, the hidden churchyard of St John's Episcopal Church:

> It was dark, and he began to tell me strange, weird stories in a sepulchral tone and, despite the fact that I am a very matter-of-fact person, something about his man-ner, the darkness, and a sort of eerie light that seemed to hover over the grave-stones got me so wrought up that I began to run out of the cemetery with him close at my heels, with the one thought that I must get up to the street before he, or whatever it was, grabbed me. I reached a street lamp, trembling, panting, and al-most in tears, and he had the strangest look on his face, almost of triumph. Noth-ing was said.[37]

What a ladies' man. It should be noted that Sully was indeed an exceptionally at-tractive woman. When she went to New York after visiting Lovecraft, she bowled over the entire weird fiction crowd there: Lovecraft dryly reports having to keep Frank Long and Donald Wandrei from fighting a duel over her.[38]

Lovecraft, for his part, regarded Sully with avuncular benignance, writing her long letters about his travels and about the morality of the younger generation; but he so irritated her with his formality of address that she demanded that he refer to her as Helen and not as Miss Sully, to which he replied sheepishly: "Certainly, I am no surname-addict!"[39] I shall have more to say about the content of these letters presently.

Meanwhile some of Lovecraft's older colleagues were achieving literary or commer-cial success in the pulp field at the very time that his own work was faring poorly because of its failure to conform to pulp conventions. Frank Belknap Long had made the transition from weird fiction to science fiction with ease, and by the early 1930s was grinding out hackwork for *Astounding* and other pulps. Earlier he had incorporated Lovecraft's "Roman dream" of 1927 into the novel *The Horror from the Hills,* serialised in *Weird Tales* in 1931 (it did not achieve separate book publi-cation until 1963). Long continued to publish short stories in *Weird Tales,* but he realised that he needed to expand his markets, so turned to "scientifiction." Love-craft was amused to note that Long, although flirting with communism, was enough of a businessman to make a suitable amount of spending money in pulp fiction.

Clark Ashton Smith—who, as I have mentioned earlier, voluminously took to fiction writing in early 1930—also came to realise that the field of science fiction or science fantasy offered more, and more lucrative, markets than the very narrow realm of weird fiction, where *Weird Tales* was basically alone aside from fleeting and sporadic competitors. Accordingly, Smith—whose work in some senses fitted naturally into the science fantasy mode in any event—managed to break into many markets that Lovecraft was unable or unwilling to attempt: Hugo Gernsback's *Wonder Stories,* the revived Street & Smith *Astounding Stories,* even now-obscure pulps such as *Amazing Detective Tales* (also edited by Gernsback). *Wonder Stories* proved to be Smith's most regular market, and its editors frequently asked him for series of interplanetary tales written more or less according to formula; Smith complied, attempting as best he could to infuse some of his own personality in them. The only problem with *Wonder Stories* was a mundane but highly irritating one: in true Gernsbackian fashion, it paid very poorly and very late. In the mid-1930s Smith actually had to hire a lawyer to collect on a debt of nearly $1000 owed him for many stories and novelettes.

But Smith continued to be rejected nearly as often as he was accepted by the weird and science fiction pulps. Six of his *Weird Tales* rejects—no worse, and in some cases much better, than the stories he published in the magazine—were self-published in the summer of 1933 as *The Double Shadow and Other Fantasies.* This oddly dimensioned booklet—8½ × 11½", in two columns, and consisting of only 30 pages—sold for 25¢; and at that, it took Smith several years to recoup his printing costs (the book was printed at the office of the *Auburn Journal*). Lovecraft frequently noted what a bargain Smith was offering: six stories for a quarter as opposed to his own stillborn *Shunned House,* a single story for which W. Paul Cook had planned to charge a dollar. Smith somehow managed to eke out a living for himself and his parents through the early 1930s. His mother died in September 1935 and his father in December 1937; but by then Smith had virtually ceased to write fiction, turning his attention to sculpture.

Donald Wandrei had published a second collection of poetry, *Dark Odyssey,* at his own expense in 1931, but he too then turned to the pulps to establish a name for himself as a weird and science fiction author. In the course of the 1930s Wandrei published in *Weird Tales, Astounding, Wonder Stories, Argosy,* and even the newly founded men's magazine *Esquire;* he also wrote a series of potboiler mysteries for *Clues Detective Stories.* A more serious work was a weird novel initially titled *Dead Titans, Waken!,* which Lovecraft read in manuscript in early 1932.[40] Lovecraft thought it a powerful work—especially the climactic scene of underground horror—but felt that earlier portions needed revision. Wandrei, however, could not bear the thought of retyping the novel so soon after finishing it; instead, he sent it on the rounds of publishers, who rejected it. Finally it was published, in a slightly different form, as *The Web of Easter Island* in 1948.

August Derleth had, since the mid-1920s, established himself as a fixture of sorts in *Weird Tales* with very short macabre tales. In 1929 he turned to what would, in effect, become his trademark: pastiche. A year before the death of Sir Arthur Conan Doyle, Derleth invented a Sherlock Holmes imitation named Solar Pons; the first story in which Pons figured, "The Adventure of the Black Narcissus," appeared in *Dragnet* for February 1929. Derleth asked Lovecraft to write a letter of commendation to the editor of *Dragnet* so that more of his stories might be considered; Lovecraft genially complied, writing in a letter to the editor (published in the April 1929 issue) that "'Solar Pons' seems eminently qualified to take rank with the standard detectives of fiction." Derleth published only one more Solar Pons story in *Dragnet,* but Pons's career was launched, and his adventures would eventually fill six collections of short stories, one short novel, and assorted addenda. In the early 1930s Derleth created another detective hero, Judge Peck. He wrote three novels in quick succession: *The Man on All Fours* (1934); *Three Who Died* (1935); and *The Sign of Fear* (1935). Lovecraft guessed the solutions to the murders on pp. 32, 145, and 259, respectively.

But Derleth had, Janus-like, been writing these potboilers with his left hand and sensitive regional and personality sketches with his right hand for non-paying little magazines since at least 1929. It was this work—beginning with a novel initially titled *The Early Years* that was later metamorphosed, after many revisions, into *Evening in Spring* (1941)—upon which Derleth hoped to build his mainstream reputation; for a time, just before and just after Lovecraft's death, he was doing exactly that.

Derleth's first serious work to be published in book form was *Place of Hawks* (1935), a series of four interconnected novelettes about individuals and families in the Sac Prairie region of Wisconsin, narrated by a young boy, Stephen Grendon (one of Derleth's pseudonyms), who observes his surroundings in the company of his doctor grandfather. *Place of Hawks* is a poignant volume and a credit to any writer intent on staking a claim in the mainstream literary world. One passage, placed in the mouth of a character, perhaps describes Derleth's own motives in writing:

> "Every spring to watch the earth grow green, to see the birds come back again, to feel the sky become a softer blue, to breathe new life with every breath; every summer to see the grain green and ripen, to mow and stack sweet-smelling hay, to drowse in the season's somnolence; every fall to gather fruit from laden branches, to see the leaves turn red and brown and fall, carpeting the earth, to watch the birds take flight; every winter to look out upon the fields and rolling hills, soothed by the soft white snow, to mark the drear, grey days with trivial details of living here—sweet, sweet living. That's my life. I want nothing more. I write. How could I keep from writing? How the wind crests the hills in April, how the violets purple the earth in May, how the spring night soothes with a thousand kindly hands. These things enrich my life."[41]

Affecting as this is, it is nevertheless an incomplete account of Derleth's serious work; for throughout *Place of Hawks* and other writings of this period Derleth reveals a remarkable skill at character portrayal and at the interplay of emotional tensions in close-knit rural families. As early as 1932 Lovecraft remarked to E. Hoffmann Price:

> Look how Derleth does it—he, a husky young egotist of 23, can for a time *actually be,* in a psychological sense, a wistful, faded old lady of 85, with all the natural thoughts, prejudices, feelings, perspectives, fears, prides, mental mannerisms, and speech-tricks of such a lady. Or he can be an elderly doctor—or a small boy—or a half-demented young mother—in every case understanding and entering into the type so fully that, for the moment, his interests and outlooks and difficulties and idioms are *those of the character,* with the corresponding qualities of August William Derleth quite forgotten.[42]

No doubt Lovecraft envied Derleth his skill in character portrayal, since this was one of his most significant deficiencies. He had read the novelettes comprising *Place of Hawks* as early as 1932 and had made comments on small points of language and motivation—points that Derleth resolutely ignored (as he ignored similar suggestions by Lovecraft for his weird and detective fiction), even though Lovecraft was clearly right on some issues.

Lovecraft had been reading *The Early Years* since 1929, but it is unclear how close is the final published book, *Evening in Spring,* to the several drafts Derleth successively wrote. Lovecraft's comments suggest that this work was a reminiscent novel in the manner of Proust, but *Evening in Spring* is merely a tale of young love with few if any of the extended, pseudo-stream-of-consciousness passages Lovecraft appears to have read. In its final form it is, to my mind, inferior to *Place of Hawks.* Nevertheless, upon its publication it was hailed as a significant contribution to American literature and Derleth a noteworthy young novelist (he was only thirty-two when it appeared); but, in the eyes of most readers and critics, Derleth failed to deliver on this early promise and after World War II his reputation declined inexorably.

Lovecraft's colleagues were not merely getting widely published in the pulps; they were writing work clearly influenced by Lovecraft and were laying the groundwork for the proliferation of what came to be called the "Cthulhu Mythos." After Lovecraft's death it was August Derleth who would spearhead this movement; but at this juncture the lead was perhaps taken by Smith, Howard, Wandrei, and Bloch.

It would be tedious to record the various name-droppings and other cross-references that Lovecraft and his colleagues made in their tales—a procedure that, as early as 1930, led some readers of *Weird Tales* to suspect that a real body of myth was being drawn upon. What was really happening was that some of Lovecraft's associates were evolving their own pseudo-mythological cycles that merged into Lovecraft's own cycle through mutual citation and allusion. It is, certainly, unlikely that this would have occurred had not Lovecraft's own work provided the model and impetus; but it is still somewhat problematical to meld his associates' creations into his own without considering their separate origin. Hence, Clark Ashton Smith invented the sorcerer Eibon (who wrote the *Book of Eibon*), the city of Commoriom, the god Tsathoggua, and the like; Howard, von Junzt's *Nameless Cults* (= *Unaussprechlichen Kulten*); Bloch, Ludvig Prinn's *Mysteries of the Worm* (*De Vermis Mysteriis*); and so on.

In terms of actual imitation of Lovecraft's style and manner, it was Wandrei who at this period led the way, but without appreciably "adding" to the overall mythology. Hence, "The Tree-Men of M'Bwa" (*Weird Tales,* February 1932) is considered a tale of the "Cthulhu Mythos" but makes no reference to any books, places, or entities of the cycle; it does, however, allude to a "master in the Whirling Flux" who is "of a different universe, a different dimension,"[43] bringing "The Dunwich Horror" to mind. "The Witch-Makers" (*Argosy,* May 2, 1936) is a story of mind-exchange, perhaps drawing upon "The Thing on the Doorstep" or "The Shadow out of Time." "The Crystal Bullet" (*Weird Tales,* March 1941) is clearly influenced by "The Colour out of Space" in its account of a large bulletlike object that falls from the sky upon a farm.

Howard attempted on occasion to imitate Lovecraft's cosmicism, but was not very successful at it. Consider this bombastic passage from "The Fire of Asshurbanipal" (*Weird Tales,* December 1936):

> "Mankind isn't the first owner of the earth; there were Beings here before his coming—and now, survivals of hideously ancient epochs. Maybe spheres of alien dimensions press unseen on this material universe today. Sorcerers have called up speeling devils before now and controlled them with magic. It is not unreasonable to suppose an Assyrian magician could invoke an elemental demon out of the earth to avenge him and guard something that must have come out of Hell in the first place."[44]

This is an unwitting travesty of Lovecraft, very much like what Derleth would write later.

Bloch is perhaps the most interesting case. In many of his tales of the mid-1930s he seems so saturated with the Lovecraftian influence that certain recollections of his mentor may be unconscious; hence, something so slight as one character's observation in "The Grinning Ghoul" (*Weird Tales,* June 1936) that there is no dust on the stairs of a crypt may be an echo of the similarly dust-free corridors of the ancient city in *At the Mountains of Madness,* swept clean by the passing of a shoggoth. "The Creeper in the Crypt" (*Weird Tales,* July 1937) is set in Arkham and makes clear allusion to Lovecraft's "The Dreams in the Witch House"; but it may also betray the influence of "The Shadow over Innsmouth" (the narrator, after his experiences, seeks aid from the federal government to suppress the horror), and also perhaps of "The Terrible Old Man," as the tale involves a Polish and an Italian criminal who kidnap a man only to meet a loathsome fate in the cellar of an old house, just as in Lovecraft's story a Pole, a Portuguese, and an Italian seek to rob the Terrible Old Man but meet death at his hands instead.

For all Lovecraft's assistance to Bloch (the former tirelessly read story after story by the latter in the 1933–35 period, making painstaking comments on each one), he seems to have done little actual revision of Bloch's work. In June 1933 Lovecraft remarked that "I added corrections here & there"[45] to a story entitled "The Madness of Lucian Grey," which was accepted for publication by *Marvel Tales* but was never published and does not now survive. A blurb in *Marvel Tales* described it as "a weird-fantasy story of an artist who was forced to paint a picture . . . and the frightful thing that came from it," which makes one immediately think of "Pickman's Model." Lovecraft seems to have done much more extensive work in November 1933 on a story called "The Merman":

> I have read "The Merman" with the keenest interest & pleasure, & am returning it with a few annotations & emendations. . . . My changes—the congested script of which I hope you can read—are of two sorts; simplifications of diffuse language in the interest of more direct & powerful expression, & attempts to make the *emotional modulations* more vivid, lifelike, & convincing at certain points where the narrative takes definite turns.[46]

But unfortunately this tale also does not survive.

If any extant work of Bloch's can be called a Lovecraft revision, it is "Satan's Servants," written in February 1935. Bloch has commented that the story came back from Lovecraft "copiously annotated and corrected, together with a lengthy and exhaustive list of suggestions for revision," and goes on to say that many of Lovecraft's additions are now undetectable, since they fused so well with his own style:

> From the purely personal standpoint, I was often fascinated during the process of revision by the way in which certain interpolated sentences or phrases of Lovecraft's seemed to dovetail with my own work—for in 1935 I was quite consciously a disciple of what has since come to be known as the "Lovecraft school" of weird fiction. I doubt greatly if even the self-professed "Lovecraft scholar" can pick out his actual verbal contributions to the finished tale; most of the passages which would be identified as "pure Lovecraft" are my work; all of the sentences and bridges he added are of an incidental nature and merely supplement the text.[47]

And yet, it is not surprising that the original version of the story was rejected by Farnsworth Wright of *Weird Tales;* his comment as noted by Bloch—"that the plot-structure was too flimsy for the extended length of the narrative"[48]—is an entirely accurate assessment of this overly long and unconvincing story.

"Satan's Servants" had initially been dedicated to Lovecraft, and after its rejection Bloch urged Lovecraft to collaborate on its revision; but, aside from whatever additions and corrections he made, Lovecraft bowed out of full-fledged collaboration. He did, however, have much to say on the need for historical accuracy in this tale of seventeenth-century New England, and he had other suggestions as to the pacing of the story. Bloch apparently did some revisions in 1949 for its publication in *Something about Cats,* but the story still labours under its excess verbiage and its rather comical ending: a pious Puritan, facing a mob of hundreds of devil-worshippers in a small Maine town, defeats them all by literally pounding them with a Bible! It is just as well that "Satan's Servants" lay in Bloch's files until resurrected purely as a literary curiosity.

Lovecraft's response to the rapid success (if publication in the pulps can be called success) of his colleagues is interesting. In early 1934 he offered a prediction on how his associates would fare in the broader literary world: "Of all the *W. T.* contributors, only a few are likely to break into real literature. Derleth will—though not through his weird work. Smith may. Wandrei & Long very possibly may. Howard has a chance—though he'd do better with traditional Texas material. Price *could,* but I don't think he will because commercial writing is 'getting' him."[49] That last comment is significant, for it was with the prototypical pulp hack Price that Lovecraft had some of his most searching debates about the value (if any) of pulp fiction and its relation to genuine literature. In reading both sides of this correspondence, one rapidly gains the impression that each writer is talking at cross-purposes with the other: each has so much difficulty comprehending the other's position sympathetically that the same views are repeated over and over again.

It would perhaps be unfair to present only Lovecraft's side, for Price does manage to argue his position cogently from the premises he has adopted: that writing is a business in which he has engaged in order to feed himself now that the depression has made it very difficult for him to find any other source of income; and that it may still be possible to infuse some actual literary substance—or, at least, some personality and sincerity—into work that is nevertheless basically formulaic. This position—given Lovecraft's entire philosophical and aesthetic upbringing, from the eighteenth-century ideal of literature as an elegant amusement through his Decadent phase and into his final "cosmic regionalism" period—was anathema to Lovecraft, not on highbrow grounds but because it was deeply and personally offensive and contradictory to his own purpose as a writer: "My attitude . . . is based upon a frank dislike of professional writing as a pursuit for persons anxious to approach actual literary expression. I think that literary aspirants ought to follow paying jobs outside literature and its fake penumbra, and keep their writing free from commercial objects." Lovecraft's sense of outrage is very clear; but as a sop to Price he adds somewhat more moderately, although with perhaps unconscious sarcasm: "As for the business of supplying artificial formula-writing to the various commercial media catering to herd tastes—that is an honest enough trade, but in my opinion more proper for clever craftsmen having no real urge toward self-expression than for persons who really have something definite to say."[50]

There is, of course, scarcely a doubt that Lovecraft is right. No one from the weird pulp magazines except Lovecraft himself has emerged as a serious figure in literature. "You don't call us clumsy *W.T.* hacks 'real authors' do you?" Lovecraft writes acidly to J. Vernon Shea in 1931:

> . . . the popular magazine world is essentially an *underworld* or caricature-imitation-world so far as serious writing is concerned. Absolutely nothing about it is worthy of mature consideration or permanent preservation. That is why I am so absolutely unwilling to make any 'concessions' to its standards, & so much disposed to repudiate it entirely in an effort to achieve real aesthetic expression even on the humblest plane.[51]

It is a litany Lovecraft would continue to repeat, with interesting modifications, throughout his career.

Lovecraft did not have much more enthusiasm for the art in the pulps, especially *Weird Tales;* in fact, to him it was even worse, on the whole, than the fiction, if that were possible. "All the alleged 'art' work is indescribably vile, & I feel lucky whenever Wright is merciful enough to leave the beastly stuff off my effusions," Lovecraft wrote as early as 1926.[52] Lovecraft did have kind words for a few of the earlier *Weird Tales* artists, such as J. Allen St John and especially Hugh Rankin (even though Rankin gave away the ending of "The Whisperer in Darkness" by depicting the face and hands of Akeley on a chair on the second page of the story). Later, when Margaret Brundage began her celebrated paintings of nude women (their more sensitive parts always concealed by curling smoke or other convenient stratagems), his disgust turned to mere resigned weariness. And yet, he was by no means as prudish as some of his own correspondents, who vehemently objected to such covers on moral grounds:

> About *WT* covers—they are really too trivial to get angry about. If they weren't totally irrelevant and unrepresentative nudes, they'd probably be something equally awkward and trivial, even though less irrelevant. . . . I have no objection to the nude in art—in fact, the human figure is as worthy a type of subject-matter as any other object of beauty in the visible world. But I don't see what the hell Mrs. Brundage's undressed ladies have to do with weird fiction![53]

A quotation like this should help to dispel the silly rumour that Lovecraft habitually tore off the covers of *Weird Tales* because he was either outraged or embarrassed by the nude covers; although the real proof of the falsity of this rumour comes from a consultation of his own complete file of the magazine, sitting perfectly intact at the John Hay Library of Brown University.

The curious thing, in light of his scorn of pulp fiction, is that Lovecraft's view of "real" weird writing—what in this letter to Shea he termed "the Blackwood-Dunsany-Machen-James type"—was not as high as one might imagine. Throughout the 1930s he found each of these once-revered figures wanting in various ways. On Machen: "People whose minds are—like Machen's—steeped in the orthodox myths of religion, naturally find a poignant fascination in the conception of things which religion brands with outlawry and horror. Such people take the artificial and obsolete conception of 'sin' seriously, and find it full of dark allurement."[54] On M. R. James: "I'll concede he isn't really in the Machen, Blackwood, & Dunsany class. He is the earthiest member of the 'big four.'"[55] Lovecraft's estimation of Blackwood remained generally high, but even this writer was not immune from criticism: "It's safe to say that Blackwood is the greatest living weirdist despite vast unevenness and a poor prose style."[56]

All his former mentors came in for qualified censure at one point: "What I miss in Machen, James, Dunsany, de la Mare, Shiel, and even Blackwood and Poe, is a sense of the *cosmic.* Dunsany—though he seldom adopts the darker and more serious approach—is the most cosmic of them all, but he gets only a little way."[57] This remark is significant because it was exactly cosmicism that Lovecraft himself elsewhere vaunted as the distinguishing feature of his own work. Is this whole procedure an attempt to escape, in part, from the influence of these titans? Without in any way raising himself to their level ("Some of my stuff . . . may be as good as the *poorer* work of Blackwood and the other big-timers"[58]), Lovecraft was perhaps unconsciously carving out a small corner of the field in which he could stand preeminent.

But Lovecraft never stopped seeking new works of weird fiction to relish. He continued reading the stories in *Weird Tales* with a kind of grim determination to find some worthy specimens, although he commented with increasing impatience about their shortcomings. "Someone ought to go over the cheap magazines and pick out story-germs which have been ruined by popular treatment; then getting the authors' permission and *actually writing the stories.*"[59] But it was thanks to a new colleague—H. C. Koenig—that he received one of the greatest surprises of his later years: the discovery, in the summer of 1934, of the forgotten work of William Hope Hodgson.

Hodgson (1877–1918) had published four novels and many short stories before dying in Belgium in a battle of the Great War. Lovecraft had previously been familiar with a collection of linked short stories, *Carnacki, the Ghost-Finder* (1913), a tepid imitation of Algernon Blackwood's "psychic detective" John Silence, so he was entirely unprepared for the radically superior if also flawed excellence of *The Boats of the "Glen Carrig"* (1907), *The House on the Borderland* (1908), *The Ghost Pirates* (1909), and *The Night Land* (1912). The first and third of these novels are powerful tales of sea horror; the second is probably Hodgson's most finished work, an almost unendurably potent compendium of regional and cosmic horror; and the last is a stupendous epic fantasy of the far future after the sun has died. Lovecraft immediately prepared a note on Hodgson to be inserted into the ninth chapter of the *Fantasy Fan* serialisation of "Supernatural Horror in Literature"; but the insert first appeared only as a separate article, "The Weird Work of William Hope Hodgson" (*Phantagraph,* February 1937), then in "Supernatural Horror in Literature" in *The Outsider and Others* (1939). Lovecraft and Koenig seem jointly responsible for the subsequent resurrection of Hodgson's work, perhaps a little more of the credit going to Koenig, who later teamed with August Derleth to republish the novels and tales.

Koenig later passed on to Lovecraft the novels of Charles Williams, the English colleague of J. R. R. Tolkien and C. S. Lewis; but Lovecraft's evaluation of these mystical, heavily religious works is very much on target:

> Essentially, they are not horror literature at all, but philosophic allegory in fictional form. Direct reproduction of the texture of life & the substance of moods is not the author's object. He is trying to illustrate human nature through symbols & turns of idea which possess significance for those taking a traditional or orthodox view of man's cosmic bearings. There is no true attempt to express the indefinable feelings experienced by man in confronting the unknown. . . . To get a full-sized kick from this stuff one must take seriously the orthodox view of cosmic organisation—which is rather impossible today.[60]

In other words, one must be a Christian, which Lovecraft emphatically was not.

The post-Christmas season of 1933–34 again found Lovecraft in New York, and this time he ended up meeting an unusual number of colleagues old and new. Leaving Providence Christmas night, he arrived at the Longs' residence (230 West 97th Street, Manhattan) at 9.30 A.M. on the 26th. That afternoon Samuel Loveman overwhelmed Lovecraft with a gift of an authentic Egyptian *ushabti* (a funerary ornament) nearly a foot long. Loveman had given Lovecraft two museum pieces the previous year.

From this point on the socialising began. On the 27th Lovecraft met Desmond Hall, the associate editor of *Astounding Stories* as revived by Street & Smith. (When Lovecraft first heard of the revival of *Astounding,* in August 1933, he was somehow led to believe that it would be a primarily weird magazine, or at least very receptive to weird fiction; but the early issues disillusioned him by being fairly conventional "scientifiction," so that he did not submit any of his stories to it.) Later in the day he went to Donald Wandrei's flat on Horatio Street, where he met both Donald and his younger brother Howard (1909–1956), whose magnificent weird drawings took his breath away. Lovecraft may or may not have noticed Howard Wandrei's illustrations in Donald's *Dark Odyssey* (1931); but seeing his work in the original was, understandably, an overwhelming experience. Lovecraft was bold enough to say of Howard: "he certainly has a vastly greater talent than anyone else in the gang. I was astonished at [the paintings'] sheer genius & maturity. When the name Wandrei first becomes known, it will probably be through this brother instead of Donald."[61] Frank Long declared hyperbolically that Howard Wandrei was a greater artist than Dürer. He may not have been that good, but he really is one of the premier fantastic artists of the century, and his work deserves to be much better known. He also went on to write a small number of weird, science fiction, and detective tales—some of which is as good as, or perhaps even a bit better than, the work of his brother.

On the 31st Lovecraft saw the old year out at Samuel Loveman's flat in Brooklyn Heights, where he renewed his acquaintance with Hart Crane's mother, whom he had met in Cleveland in 1922.[62] Crane, of course, had committed suicide in 1932. It was on this occasion, evidently—if Loveman's word can be trusted— that Loveman's roommate Patrick McGrath spiked Lovecraft's drink, causing him to talk even more animatedly than he usually did.[63] Lovecraft gave no indication of any such thing, and one would imagine that someone so sensitive to alcohol (its mere smell was nearly an emetic) would have detected the ruse. I am half inclined to doubt this anecdote, engaging as it is. On January 3 Lovecraft had dinner with the anthologist T. Everett Harré, who was somewhat of a lush but who had a delightful cat named William. Returning to Long's apartment, Lovecraft met his new correspondent H. C. Koenig, "a blond, boyish looking German of absolutely delightful qualities."[64]

But the culmination occurred on the 8th, when Lovecraft had dinner with A. Merritt at the Players Club near Gramercy Park. Merritt surely picked up the tab. Lovecraft reports: "He is genial & delightful—a fat, sandy, middle-aged chap, & a real genius in the weird. He knows all about my work, & praises it encouragingly."[65] Lovecraft, of course, had revered Merritt ever since he read "The Moon Pool" in the *All-Story* for June 22, 1918; and his correspondence shows that he was abundantly familiar with the whole of Merritt's published work up to that time. His final assessment of Merritt was mixed but fundamentally sound:

> Abe Merritt—who could have been a Machen or Blackwood or Dunsany or de la Mare or M. R. James . . . if he had but chosen—is so badly sunk that he's lost the critical faculty to realise it. . . . Every magazine trick & mannerism must be rigidly unlearned & banished even from one's subconsciousness before one can write seriously for educated mental adults. That's why Merritt lost—he learned the trained-dog tricks too well, & now he can't think & feel fictionally except in terms

of the meaningless & artificial clichés of 2¢-a-word romance. Machen & Dunsany & James *would not learn* the tricks—& they have a record of genuine creative achievement beside which a whole library-full of cheap *Ships of Ishtar* & *Creep, Shadows* remains essentially negligible.[66]

The remark about Merritt's admiration for Lovecraft's own work is interesting in that Merritt had just paid homage to Lovecraft in what is clearly a pastiche of sorts—the novel *Dwellers in the Mirage,* serialised in the *Argosy* from January 23 to February 25, 1932, and published as a book later in 1932. The use of Khalk'ru the Kraken, an octopuslike creature dwelling in the Gobi desert, is a clear nod to Lovecraft's Cthulhu, although otherwise the novel is full of conventional romance of the kind that Lovecraft would not have cared for. R. H. Barlow had lent Lovecraft at least some instalments of the *Dwellers in the Mirage* serial as early as March 1932,[67] but Lovecraft does not appear to have noticed the borrowing from himself.

Nor did he do so in the case of another, much more obscure author named Mearle Prout, who published a story in *Weird Tales* for October 1933 entitled "The House of the Worm." In the first place, it is a little odd that the title duplicates Lovecraft's unwritten novel idea of 1924; but the story is more interesting in being, in part, a clear plagiarism of "The Call of Cthulhu." Consider the following from "The House of the Worm":

> I think that the limitation of the human mind, far from being a curse, is the most merciful thing in the world. We live on a quiet, sheltered island of ignorance, and from the single current flowing by our shores we visualize the vastness of the black seas around us, and see—simplicity and safety. And yet, if only a portion of the cross-currents and whirling vortexes of mystery and chaos could be revealed to our consciousness, we should immediately go insane.

This is nothing but a watered-down version of the first paragraph of Lovecraft's story. Lovecraft actually took note of the author, remarking charitably: "This latter is a newcomer, but to me his story seems to have a singularly authentic quality despite certain touches of naiveté. It has a certain atmosphere and sense of brooding evil—things which most pulp contributors lack."[68] Lovecraft is quite right about the story: it gains a sense of cumulative power and sense of the cosmic that make it a notable early pastiche. Prout went on to publish three more stories in *Weird Tales* before vanishing into oblivion.

Lovecraft returned home to Providence to experience one of the bitterest winters of his life: in February the temperature descended to -17°, the lowest figure ever recorded up to that time by the weather bureau. Sometime in the beginning of the year he heard from a woman named Dorothy C. Walter (1889–1967), a Vermont native who was spending the winter in Providence. Her friend W. Paul Cook urged her to look up Lovecraft, but she felt diffident about marching up to his doorstep at 66 College Street and announcing herself, so she wrote a rather teasing letter to him asking him to visit her; she concluded the letter, "I think I shall take the princess's prerogative of anger if you do not wish to come."[69]

The gentlemanly Lovecraft could scarcely refuse an invitation of this sort, especially by a woman. But when the day for the visit came, he was compelled to beg off because of the bitter cold. On the phone he apologised profusely to Walter and begged to be allowed to come another day: "Do be kind and say I still may come—please don't be angry—but it's just too cold for me to come out!" Walter magnanimously agreed, and Lovecraft came a few days later. Their meeting—in the company of Walter's aunt and a rather pert housekeeper, Marguerite—was pretty innocuous: the topics were Vermont, the colonial antiquities of Providence, and the weather. Lovecraft tried in vain to interest the ladies in the weird. Walter does not appear to have had even the remotest romantic interest in Lovecraft and never met him in person again, but she found the three hours spent in his company sufficiently piquant to write a memoir of the occasion twenty-five years later. She also went on to write a fine essay, "Lovecraft and Benefit Street," shortly after Lovecraft's death.

Another woman with whom Lovecraft came in touch was Margaret Sylvester. Actually, Sylvester (b. 1918) was not quite sixteen years old at this time; she had written to Lovecraft care of *Weird Tales,* asking him to explain the origin and meaning of the term *Walpurgisnacht* (which she may have encountered in "The Dreams in the Witch House"). Only a few of his letters to her have turned up, but the correspondence continued right up to his death. Sylvester, for her part, remembered her association with Lovecraft; after marrying and becoming Margaret Ronan, she wrote the introduction to a school edition of Lovecraft's stories (*The Shadow over Innsmouth and Other Stories of Horror* [1971]).

The rest of the winter and early spring of 1934 passed uneventfully, until in mid-March R. H. Barlow made a momentous announcement: he invited Lovecraft for an indefinite visit to his family's home in DeLand, Florida. Lovecraft, whose last trip to Florida and its energising heat was in 1931, was exceptionally eager to accept the invitation, and the only obstacle was money. He remarked pointedly: "It all depends on whether I can collect certain amounts due me before starting-time—for I wouldn't dare dig into any sums reserved for household expenses. If I did that my aunt would—quite deservedly—give me hell!"[70] The "collect certain amounts" remark seems to refer to revision-checks, but it is not clear what these are. In March 1933 he had spoken of having to revise an 80,000-word novel,[71] and one would certainly like to know what this was and whether it was ever published.

In any case, the money does indeed seem to have come in, for by mid-April Lovecraft was making definite plans to head south. Still, he remarked ominously that "I never before planned so long a trip on so little cash":[72] the round trip bus fare from Providence to DeLand was $36.00, and Lovecraft would have only

$30.00 or so for all other expenses along the way. Of course, he would have to come to New York for at least a week (where he would stay with Frank Long), and he could not bear to go to Florida without first spending a little time in Charleston.

The trip began around April 17, when Lovecraft boarded the bus to New York. It is unclear what exactly he did in the five days he was there, but no doubt it was the usual round of looking up old friends. Lovecraft again met Howard Wandrei and was impressed afresh with the magnificence of his artwork. By the early morning of the 24th, after a day and a half on the bus, he was in Charleston, and he spent almost a week there, finally boarding a bus to DeLand via Savannah and Jacksonville. He stepped off the bus at DeLand just after noon on May 2.

Although Barlow's mailing address was DeLand, he and his family actually lived a good thirteen miles southwest of that city along what Barlow calls the "Eustis-DeLand highway"[73] (state road 44); the residence was probably closer to the small town of Cassia than to DeLand. There was a lake on the property, and the nearest neighbour was three miles away. Recently, Stephen J. Jordan, following clues in Lovecraft's letters and other sources, has located the residence, which is still standing. He writes:

> The imposing two-story log house and the adjoining lake, just visible through a thick growth of pines, appeared with startling suddenness on my left. The house next to the lake matched Lovecraft's description perfectly, which possibly accounted for my having the strange feeling I was viewing a time capsule of sorts. . . . The home, a sizeable two-story log house buttressed by two chimneys, is surrounded by woods.[74]

Barlow reports picking up some furniture for the guest room in his pickup truck on the morning before Lovecraft arrived, and then going to meet Lovecraft at the bus station. His first impression of Lovecraft is interesting: "He spoke interminably in a pleasant but somewhat harsh voice, and proved to be a smooth-skinned man of face not unlike Dante. His hair was short and thinningly grey."[75]

We do not know a great deal about what Lovecraft actually did in the more than six weeks he spent with Barlow. Barlow had by this time himself become perhaps his closest, and certainly one of his most voluminous and intimate, correspondents, far more so than Derleth or Wandrei or Howard (to whom Lovecraft's letters were lengthy but infrequent and not full of personal details); in the sudden absence of letters to Barlow we are left to reconstruct the particulars of the visit from correspondence to a wide variety of other associates, from Barlow's later memoir, "The Wind That Is in the Grass" (1944), and also from a unique document—Barlow's contemporaneous notes of the visit, first published in an adulterated form in 1959 as "The Barlow Journal" and in complete form in 1992.

It should be borne in mind that Barlow was at this time scarcely sixteen years old. Lovecraft does not seem to have been aware of the fact until he actually met

Barlow in the flesh, at which time he realised that he had begun correspondence with Barlow when the latter was thirteen. "The little imp!"[76] Barlow's notes, accordingly, are somewhat haphazard and not always insightful. There are, of course, all sorts of amusingly disparaging comments that Lovecraft made on his own tales ("I'm afraid 'The Hound' is a dead dog"; "'The White Ship' is sunk"), along with some more pertinent remarks on the genesis of some of his stories. There are some unusually catty criticisms of his colleagues ("He remarked also [that] Long is a Bolshevist, *poseur,* and has been even so mercenary as to sell letters of famous men to him; and his grandfather's cane"; "Adolphe de Castro Danziger . . . he pronounced a charlatan, though clever"), things Lovecraft would presumably allow himself to say in person but never in correspondence. Then, of course, there is Barlow's priceless account of going with Lovecraft and the hired hand Charles B. Johnston to pick berries beyond a shallow creek. As they were returning, Lovecraft lagged behind but claimed to know where Barlow had positioned a makeshift bridge over the creek. But clearly something went amiss, and Lovecraft returned to the Barlow home soaking wet, and with most of the berries gone. He then apologised to Barlow's mother for losing the berries!

In his later memoir Barlow gives an impressionistic account of the visit:

> We rowed on the lake, and played with the cats, or walked on the highway with these cats as the unbelievable sun went down among pines and cypresses . . . Above all, we talked, chiefly of the fantastic tales which he wrote and which I was trying to write. At breakfast he told us his dreams . . .
>
> . . . Our talk was full of off-hand references to ghouls and vaults of terror on the surfaces of strange stars, and Lovecraft wove an atmosphere of ominous illusion about any chance sound by the roadside as we walked with my three cats, one of whom he had named Alfred A. Knopf. At other times he could be prevailed upon to read his own stories aloud, always with sinister tones and silences in the proper spots. Especially he liked to read with an eighteenth century pronunciation, *sarvant* for "servant" and *mi* for "my."[77]

Antiquity was not in very great supply in this region of Florida, but Lovecraft and Barlow did manage to get to a Spanish sugar-mill at De Leon Springs constructed before 1763, and other sites at nearby New Smyrna, including a Franciscan mission built in 1696. In early June Lovecraft was taken to Silver Springs, about 45 miles northwest of DeLand: "There is a placid pool at the head of the Silver River whose floor is pitted with huge abysses—visible clearly through a glass-bottomed boat—while the Silver River itself is a tropical jungle stream like the Congo or Amazon. The cinema of Tarzan was taken on it. I rode 5 miles down stream & back in a launch, & saw alligators &c in their native habitat."[78] Lovecraft desperately hoped to get to Havana, but simply did not have the cash. Of course, the Barlows fed and housed him at their expense, and were so abundantly hospitable that they continually vetoed any suggestion that he move on. No doubt Barlow's parents perceived that their son and Lovecraft, in spite of the almost thirty-year difference in their ages, had become fast friends. Perhaps Barlow had a lonely existence, with his much older brother Wayne (born in 1908) in the army and not around to aid in his maturation. Barlow, of course, kept himself busy with all manner of literary, artistic, and publishing projects. One of the things he conceived at this time was to issue large 11 × 14" reproductions of Howard Wandrei's artwork, but Donald peremptorily rejected the plan, perhaps because he had his own notions (never realised, as it happened) of issuing his brother's work. Another photographic project that did succeed was the taking of a formal studio photograph of Lovecraft by Lucius B. Truesdell—an image that has helped to make Lovecraft's face an icon. For the rest of his life, Lovecraft continued to order duplicate prints of the Truesdell shot to circulate to friends and colleagues.

Another project by Barlow, more directly pertinent to Lovecraft, also ended in frustration. Since 1928 the sheets of W. Paul Cook's edition of *The Shunned House* had been knocking about from pillar to post in the wake of Cook's nervous and financial breakdown. Barlow first learnt of this stillborn enterprise in early 1933, and in February he proposed taking the unbound sheets and distributing them. Lovecraft was initially receptive to the idea and broached it to Cook, who agreed to it in principle; but then, in April, Cook was sheepishly obliged to back out because he had forgotten that he had promised to let Walter J. Coates (the editor of *Driftwind*) handle the distribution of the sheets. There the matter stood for nearly a year. When it became evident that Coates was going to do nothing on the matter, Lovecraft approached Barlow again to see if he was still interested in the idea. Barlow was.

Sometime in the late winter of 1933 or early spring of 1934 Barlow received 115 out of the 300 copies Cook had printed. For a time it was thought that these were all that survived, but in May 1935 Cook discovered another 150 more sheets and sent these to Barlow. (This leaves only 35 sheets unaccounted for, and these may have been distributed in 1928, lost, or damaged.) But Barlow himself—in the whirlwind of activities in which he was involved at this time—did little in terms of actual distribution. Although having by then become a skilled amateur binder, he bound only about eight copies in 1934–35: one in natural leather for Lovecraft, the other seven in boards. Some copies actually bear a printed label on the copyright page, "Copyright 1935 by R. H. Barlow"! Barlow may have distributed perhaps 40 more copies as unbound sheets, mostly to Lovecraft's colleagues. In late 1935 Samuel Loveman proposed assisting Barlow distribute the sheets through his bookstore, but Barlow for some reason failed to communicate with Loveman on the matter. Lovecraft expressed considerable irritation at Barlow's dilatoriness in the whole affair, finally resigning himself to the prospect that his first "book" was a total loss.[79]

Barlow has remarked in his memoir that he and Lovecraft were busy with various writing projects; but relatively little survives of this material. There are two poems bearing the respective titles "Beyond Zimbabwe" and "The White Elephant" and collectively titled "Bouts Rimés," in which Barlow has invented the rhymes and Lovecraft written the verses to match them. Barlow also reports Lovecraft correcting Barlow's partial typescripts of *The Dream-Quest of Unknown Kadath* and *The Case of Charles Dexter Ward,* which he had been badgering Lovecraft for years to send down to him for transcription; but Lovecraft's letters indicate that he sent these to Barlow only in October 1934,[80] so that this typing and correcting must have occurred during Lovecraft's 1935 visit.

One literary project actually did materialise—the spoof known as "The Battle That Ended the Century." Barlow was clearly the originator of this squib, as typescripts prepared by him survive, one with extensive revisions in pen by Lovecraft. The idea was to make joking mention of as many of the authors' mutual colleagues as possible in the course of the document, which purported to report the heavyweight fight between Two-Gun Bob, the Terror of the Plains (Robert E. Howard) and Knockout Bernie, the Wild Wolf of West Shokan (Bernard Austin Dwyer). More than thirty individuals are mentioned. Barlow had initially cited them by their actual names, but Lovecraft felt that this was not very interesting, so he devised parodic or punning names for them: instead of Frank Belknap Long, one reads of Frank Chimesleep Short. Lovecraft himself becomes Horse-Power Hateart. Some of the parodic names have only recently been correctly identified. All this is good if harmless fun, the only real maliciousness being the note about the pestiferous Forrest J Ackerman: "Meanwhile a potentate from a neighbouring kingdom, the Effjay of Akkamin (also known to himself as an amateur critic), expressed his frenzied disgust at the technique of the combatants, at the same time peddling photographs of the fighters (with himself in the foreground) at five cents each." (Ackerman really was offering photographs of himself at this time.)

Naturally, the thing to do was to circulate the whimsy, but in such a way that its authorship would not be immediately evident. The plan, so far as I can reconstruct it, was this: Barlow would mimeograph the item (copies exist in two long 8½ × 14" sheets, each with text on one side only) and then have the copies mailed from some other location, so that they could not be traced to either Lovecraft or Barlow. It appears that the 50 duplicated copies were prepared toward the middle of June and were sent to Washington, D.C., where they would be mailed (possibly by Elizabeth Toldridge, a colleague of both Lovecraft's and Barlow's but not associated with the weird fiction circle). This seems to have been done just before Lovecraft himself left DeLand and began heading north, so that the items would already be in the hands of associates by the time Lovecraft reached Washington.

But there is of course no question of Lovecraft's and Barlow's involvement in

"The Battle That Ended the Century," even though both of them—especially Lovecraft—never admitted authorship. The two of them talk in amusingly conspiratorial tones about its reception by colleagues: "Note the signature—Chimesleep Short—which indicates that our spoof has gone out & that he [Long] at least thinks I've seen the thing. Remember that if you didn't know anything about it, you'd consider it merely a whimsical trick of his own—& that if you'd merely seen the circular, you wouldn't think it worth commenting on. I'm ignoring the matter in my reply."[81] Long was clearly tickled, but others were less so. Lovecraft noted: "Wandrei wasn't exactly in a rage, but (according to Belknap) sent the folder on to Desmond Hall with the languid comment, 'Here's something that may interest you—it doesn't interest me.'"[82] Wandrei doesn't seem to have been a very good sport about the thing, and one wonders whether this incident (along with the earlier minor contretemps about the reproduction of Howard Wandrei's artwork) had anything to do with the bad blood between Wandrei and Barlow in later years.

Lovecraft pushed on to St Augustine on June 21, remaining there till the 28th. He then spent two days in Charleston, one in Richmond, one in Fredericksburg, two in Washington (where he looked up Elizabeth Toldridge), and one in Philadelphia. When he reached New York he found that the Longs were about to leave for the beach resorts of Asbury Park and Ocean Grove, in New Jersey, and he tagged along for the weekend. He finally returned home on July 10, nearly three months after he had set out.

But travel was by no means over for the year. August 4 found Lovecraft and James F. Morton at Buttonwoods, Rhode Island (a locality in the town of Warwick), as part of a three-day visit by the latter in quest of genealogical research. On August 23 Lovecraft met Cook and Cole in Boston; the next day he and Cook went to Salem and later met up with Tryout Smith in Lawrence; the next day Edward H. Cole took Lovecraft to Marblehead.

But all this proved merely the preliminary for a trip of relatively short distance but powerful imaginative stimulus. The island of Nantucket lay only 90 miles from Lovecraft's doorstep (six hours by combined bus and ferry), but he never visited it until the very end of August 1934. What a world of antiquity he stumbled upon:

> Whole networks of cobblestoned streets with nothing but colonial houses on either side—narrow, garden-bordered lanes—ancient belfries—picturesque waterfront—*everything* that the antiquarian could ask! . . . I've explored old houses, the 1746 windmill, the Hist. Soc. Museum, the whaling museum, etc.—and am doing every inch of the quaint streets and alleys on foot.[83]

But during Lovecraft's week-long stay (August 31–September 6) he did more than explore on foot: for the first time since boyhood he mounted a bicycle to cover the districts outside the actual town of Nantucket. "It was highly exhilarating after all these years—the whole thing brought back my youth so vividly that I felt as if I

ought to hurry home for the opening of Hope St. High School!"[84] Lovecraft ruefully regretted the social convention that frowned upon adults riding bicycles in
respectable cities like Providence.

Lovecraft's brief description of Nantucket, "The Unknown City in the
Ocean," must have been written around this time, it appeared in Chester P. Brad-
ley's amateur journal *Perspective Review* for Winter 1934. It is not one of his distinguished travelogues, and several letters of the period speak of his journey far
more piquantly.

Returning home, Lovecraft found the legion of cats called the Kappa Alpha Tau
flourishing in customary state. In August he had even devised a kind of anthem or
fight song for the band, the first stanza of which (all I can endure to quote) goes
like this:

> Here we are,
> The Kappa Alpha Tau boys;
> We'll give a great meow, boys,
> For Bast, & Sekhmet too.
> Near and far,
> We gather here as fellows,
> And none may e'er excel
> The Kappa Alpha Tau![85]

But tragedy was in the offing. A cat Lovecraft had named Sam Perkins, born
only in June of 1934, was found dead in the shrubbery on September 10. Lovecraft
immediately wrote the following elegy, now titled "Little Sam Perkins":

> The ancient garden seems tonight
>   A deeper gloom to bear,
> As if some silent shadow's blight
>   Were hov'ring in the air.
>
> With hidden griefs the grasses sway,
>   Unable quite to word them—
> Remembering from yesterday
>   The little paws that stirr'd them.

There were, of course, other cats still surviving: Peter Randall, president of the
fraternity; Vice-President Osterberg; Little Johnny Perkins, Sam's brother; and
others. And, of course, Lovecraft was always happy to be regaled by the antics of
his various colleagues' cats: Clark Ashton Smith's ancient matriarch Simaetha;
R. H. Barlow's legions of cats, including Doodlebug, High, Low, Cyrus and

Darius (two Persians, of course), Alfred A. Knopf, etc.; Duane W. Rimel's snow-white Crom; and, most engagingly, Nimrod, the ferocious cat who one day in early 1935 showed up on E. Hoffmann Price's doorstep and took up residence, wolfing down beans and raw meat, fighting with the dogs of the area, hunting out and devouring gophers, and disappearing on at least two occasions before finally vanishing for good sometime in 1936. Ailurophily ran high in the Lovecraft circle.

R. H. Barlow and Robert Bloch were not the only young boys who showered Lovecraft with their halting if promising works of fiction; another one who did so, almost from the beginning of his association with Lovecraft, was Duane W. Rimel. Rimel first needed to bone up on the classics of weird fiction, and to that end Lovecraft lent him key volumes from his library that Rimel could not get in his small and remote Washington town. From the first Lovecraft warned Rimel not to take the fiction in the pulp magazines as models:

> You can easily see that fully ¾ of the yarns in these pulp rags are "formula stories"—that is, mechanical concoctions designed to tickle simple & uncritical readers, & having cut-&-dried stock characters (brave young hero, beauteous heroine, mad scientist, &c. &c.) & absurdly artificial "action" plots. Only a very small minority of the tales have any serious merit or literary intent.[86]

Rimel attempted to follow Lovecraft's lofty advice as best he could. As early as February 1934, a month after he had begun correspondence with Lovecraft, Rimel sent him a story entitled "The Spell of the Blue Stone" (later, evidently, simply "The Blue Stone"), which Lovecraft praised as "very remarkable for a beginner's work."[87] This story does not seem to survive. By March there was mention of a story entitled "The Tree on the Hill," and Lovecraft saw it in May while in Florida with Barlow. He wrote: "I read your 'Tree on the Hill' with great interest, & believe it truly captures the essence of the weird. I like it exceedingly despite a certain cumbrousness & tendency toward anticlimax in the later parts. I've made a few emendations which you may find helpful, & have tried a bit of strengthening toward the end. Hope you'll like what I've done."[88] Whether Rimel liked what Lovecraft had done or not is not recorded, nor whether Rimel prepared a text of the story including Lovecraft's revisions to send to a publisher. For some reason the story did not see print until it appeared in the fan magazine *Polaris* for September 1940.

"The Tree on the Hill"—a rather confused tale in which a character stumbles upon a strange landscape (possibly from another planet), is unable to find it again, but then finally manages to photograph it—is clearly a Lovecraft revision, even if a minor one; of the three sections of the story, the final one—as well as the citation from a mythical volume, the *Chronicle of Nath* by Rudolf Yergler—is certainly by Lovecraft. Some have believed that much of the actual prose of the second section is also Lovecraft's, but this is an open question that must be decided merely from internal evidence, since no manuscript survives. Rimel has made it clear that both the title *Chronicle of Nath* and the extract from it are Lovecraft's invention.[89]

In July Lovecraft read a story which Rimel had entitled "The Sorcery of Alfred." Finding the use of a common English given name in what purported to be a Dunsanian fantasy unconvincing, Lovecraft changed the title to "The Sorcery of Aphlar" and also made a "few changes"[90] in the text itself. The tale appeared in the *Fantasy Fan* for December 1934 and then in the *Tri-State Times* (a small local newspaper published in upstate New York) for Spring 1937; in one copy of the latter publication someone (R. H. Barlow?) has written next to the story: "revised by HPL." On the basis of this note I reprinted the work as a Lovecraft revision, but I now do not believe that Lovecraft's changes (which again must be inferred only by internal evidence) are significant enough to warrant such a designation.

Rimel was also attempting to write poetry. In the summer of 1934 he sent Lovecraft the first sonnet in what would prove to be a cycle titled "Dreams of Yid"; evidently, Rimel was unaware that "Yid" was an opprobrious term for a Jew, so Lovecraft altered the title to "Dreams of Yith." There is manuscript evidence that Lovecraft and perhaps also Clark Ashton Smith[91] revised this cycle, the ten sonnets of which appeared in two parts in the *Fantasy Fan* (July and September 1934). Around this time Lovecraft confidently declared that "Rimel is gradually learning for himself";[92] but, with one remarkable exception, his later fictional work does not amount to much.

Rimel falls into one of two classes of revision clients for whom Lovecraft was willing to work for no charge:

> First—I help all genuine *beginners* who need a start. I tell them at the outset that I shan't keep it up for long, but that I'm willing to help them get an idea of some of the methods needed. If they have real stuff in them, they soon outgrow the need for such help. In either event, no one of them has my assistance for more than a year or so. Second—I help certain *old or handicapped people* who are pathetically in need of some cheering influence—these, even when I recognise them as incapable of improvement. In my opinion, the good accomplished by giving these poor souls a little more to live for, vastly overbalances any harm which could be wrought through their popular overestimation. Old Bill Lumley & old Doc Kuntz are typical cases of this sort. The good old fellows need a few rays of light in their last years, & anybody would be a damned prig not to let 'em have such if possible—irrespective of hyper-ethical minutiae.[93]

Even in his professional revision work, Lovecraft adopted a weird sort of altruism:

> When I revised the kindergarten pap and idiot-asylum slop of other fishes, I was, in a microscopic way, putting just the faintest bit of order, coherence, direction, and comprehensible language into something whose Neanderthaloid ineptitude was already mapped out. My work, ignominious as it was, was at least in the

right direction—making that which was utterly amorphous and drooling just the minutest trifle less close to the protozoan stage.[94]

More free work was being dumped on Lovecraft's shoulders at this time. The Bureau of the Critics of the NAPA was chronically understaffed, and by the mid-1930s Lovecraft was gradually allowing himself to be dragged back into his long-abandoned but never-forgotten role as public critic of amateurdom. For the 1933–34 term he had the chairmanship of the bureau shoved on him and immediately asked old-time amateur Edward H. Cole for assistance: Lovecraft would write the criticism of poetry contributions, Cole of prose. This pattern was repeated for the 1934–35 term, although Lovecraft eventually got the ancient amateur Truman J. Spencer (whose *Cyclopaedia of the Literature of Amateur Journalism* appeared so long ago as 1891) to relieve him as chairman.

Lovecraft ended up writing at least part of the Bureau of Critics columns in the *National Amateur* for the following issues: December 1931; December 1932; March, June, and December 1933; June, September, and December 1934; March, June, and December 1935. These articles are in essence similar to the old "Department of Public Criticism" columns for the *United Amateur* of 1914–19, but much briefer and incorporating the radical shifts in Lovecraft's aesthetic sensibility that had clearly occurred in the interval. The column for December 1931 enunciates his new conception of poetry:

> A real poem is always a mood or picture about which the writer feels very strongly, and is always couched in illustrative hints, concrete bits of appropriate pictorial imagery, or indirect symbolic allusions—never in the bald declarative language of prose. It may or may not have metre or rhyme or both. These are generally desirable, but they are not essential and in themselves most certainly do not make poetry.

Nevertheless, Lovecraft knew that few amateurs could ever exemplify these tenets. He was aware that most of the poetry coming under his review was (as he declared in the column for June 1934) "on the level of hit-or-miss doggerel" and that "The chief complaint against this type of writing is not that it is not poetry, but that it is not forcible or effective expression of any kind."

One other amateur task unexpectedly falling on Lovecraft's lap was caused by the death on June 8, 1934, of the amateur Edith Miniter. Although Lovecraft had not met Miniter since 1928, he always retained respect for her and did not wish her role as amateur, novelist, and folklore authority to be forgotten. On September 10 he wrote an uninspired poetic elegy, "Edith Miniter" (published in *Tryout* in an issue—seriously delayed, clearly—dated August 1934), then, on October 16, wrote the much more significant prose memoir, "Edith Miniter—Estimates and Recollections." Like "Some Notes on a Nonentity," it is one of his finest later essays and includes as much valuable information on himself as it does on its purported sub-

ject. It is here that we learn of Miniter's early parody of Lovecraft, "Falco Ossifracus, by Mr. Goodguile"; here, too, of her accounts of whippoorwills and other legends in the Wilbraham area, which Lovecraft worked into "The Dunwich Horror." It is a warm, heartfelt memoir, revealing the full breadth of the humanity that
flowered in his later years:

> It is difficult to realise that Mrs. Miniter is no longer a living presence; for
> the sharp insight, subtle wit, rich scholarship, and vivid literary force so fresh in
> one's memory are things savouring of the eternal and the indestructible. Of her
> charm and kindliness many will write reminiscently and at length. Of her genius,
> skill, courage, and determination, her work and career eloquently speak.

The essay, however, appeared only posthumously in Hyman Bradofsky's amateur
journal, the *Californian,* in Spring 1938.

Not long after Miniter's death, Lovecraft became embroiled in a dispute over
the disposition of her papers. The townspeople of Wilbraham may have destroyed
some of her fictional work because it showed them in what they took to be a bad
light. It is not clear what happened to her effects, although Lovecraft had previously obtained—from Miniter herself, I imagine—several manuscripts of her
work, including some lengthy pieces of fiction. These are now in the John Hay
Library. Lovecraft was also designated the editor of a proposed memorial volume
devoted to Miniter, to be issued by W. Paul Cook (who was apparently making an
attempt—vain, as it happened—to return to publishing). Although Lovecraft
gathered memoirs and other pieces desultorily for the next year or so and also accompanied Cook to see many Miniter associates in Boston in November 1934,[95]
the volume was never published.

Around July Lovecraft wrote an essay, "Homes and Shrines of Poe," for
Hyman Bradofsky's *Californian.* Bradofsky (1906–2002) quickly became one of
the significant figures in the NAPA during the mid-1930s; for although he was
himself an undistinguished writer, his *Californian* offered unprecedented space for
writers of articles and prose fiction. During the next several years he repeatedly
asked Lovecraft for pieces of substantial length; in this case Bradofsky wanted a
2000-word article for the Winter 1934 issue. Lovecraft decided to write an account
of all known Poe residences in America, but the resulting article is a little too mechanical and condensed to be effective.

A somewhat more significant amateur piece—perhaps an offshoot of his renewed work as public critic—is "What Belongs in Verse," published in the Spring
1935 issue of the *Perspective Review.* Here again Lovecraft, reflecting his new
views on the function of poetry, admonishes budding poets to ascertain what exactly is the domain of poetry before writing anything:

> It would be well if every metrical aspirant would pause and reflect on the
> question of just what, out of the various things he wants to utter, ought indeed to

be expressed in verse. The experiences of the ages have pretty well taught us that the heightened rhythms and unified patterns of verse are primarily adapted to *po-etry*—which consists of strong feelings sharply, simply, and non-intellectually presented through indirect, figurative, and pictorial images. Therefore it is scarcely wise to choose these rhythms and patterns when we wish merely to tell something or claim something or preach something.

Another essay that appeared in Bradofsky's *Californian* (in the Winter 1935 issue) is "Some Notes on Interplanetary Fiction"; but this piece had been composed around July 1934 for one of William L. Crawford's magazines[96] although, like "Some Notes on a Nonentity," it never appeared there. In this essay Lovecraft copied whole passages from "Notes on Writing Weird Fiction," and in the end he did not see a very promising future for science fiction unless certain significant changes in outlook were made by its writers: "Insincerity, conventionality, triteness, artificiality, false emotion, and puerile extravagance reign triumphant throughout this overcrowded genre, so that none but its rarest products can possibly claim a truly adult status. And the spectacle of such persistent hollowness has led many to ask whether, indeed, any fabric of real literature can ever grow out of the given subject-matter." Although his low opinion of the field was clearly derived from a sporadic reading of the science fiction pulps, Lovecraft did not think that "the idea of space-travel and other worlds is inherently unsuited to literary use"; such ideas must, however, be presented with much more seriousness and emotional preparation than had been done heretofore. What was cryingly essential, to Lovecraft's mind, is "an adequate sense of wonder, adequate emotions in the characters, realism in the setting and supplementary incidents, care in the choice of significant detail, and a studious avoidance of . . . hackneyed artificial characters and stupid conventional events and situations"—a mighty tall order for pulp writers, and one that most of them could not fill. Lovecraft of course singled out H. G. Wells as one of the few shining lights in the field (he did not place Verne in the rank of serious science fiction authors, his early fondness for him notwithstanding), and toward the end he cited some other random works that meet his approval: Olaf Stapledon's *Last and First Men,* G. MacLeod Winsor's *Station X* (1919; reprinted in *Amazing Stories* in July, August, and September 1926, where Lovecraft undoubtedly read it), Donald Wandrei's "The Red Brain," and "Clark Ashton Smith's best work." Lovecraft had not read the Stapledon novel by this time, as we shall see shortly, but must have heard reports of its literary substance.

It is difficult to gauge the influence of Lovecraft's essay on the subsequent development of the field, especially since it did not originally appear in a science fiction or even weird magazine and hence did not immediately reach the market for which it was written. Science fiction certainly did become a more aesthetically serious genre beginning around 1939, when John W. Campbell took over the editorship of *As-*

tounding; but whether Lovecraft had any direct influence on the leading writers of that period—Isaac Asimov, Robert A. Heinlein, A. E. Van Vogt, and others—is highly questionable. Nevertheless, it will become evident that he himself utilised the principles he had spelled out in this essay in his own later interplanetary work.

Late in the year Lovecraft wrote another essay for amateur publication, but it too did not appear in any amateur journal; indeed, until recently it was believed to be lost. Maurice W. Moe had asked Lovecraft to contribute an article of his choice for an amateur magazine being produced by his students. Lovecraft felt tempted to write on the subject of Roman architecture—or, more specifically, the influence of Roman architecture in the United States. The essay was finished on December 11,[97] and Lovecraft sent the autograph manuscript off to Moe without bothering to type it—a task he could not contemplate without horror and loathing. He later believed that Moe lost the essay, for it was indeed never published; but the text of it survives in a transcript made by Arkham House. It is not an especially distinguished piece of work, being a somewhat schematic account of Roman architecture and its influence on Romanesque, Renaissance, and classic revival architecture in Europe, England, and America. Lovecraft did, apparently, manage to preserve the introductory section of it, in which he vigorously attacked modernistic (and particularly functionalist) architecture; this was published in 1935 under the title "Heritage or Modernism: Common Sense in Art Forms."

The Christmas season of 1934 was an unusually festive one at 66 College Street. Lovecraft and Annie had a tree for the first time in a quarter-century, and Lovecraft took naive delight in describing its decoration: "All my old-time ornaments were of course long dispersed, but I laid in a new & inexpensive stock at my old friend Frank Winfield Woolworth's. The finished product—with tinsel star, baubles, & tinsel draped from the boughs like Spanish moss—is certainly something to take the eye!"[98]

The New Year's season of 1934–35 once more found Lovecraft in the New York area. He left Providence very late in the evening of December 30–31, barely getting to the station alive because of the cold: "Kept my handkerchief to my nose & mouth all the time, so avoided acute lung pain & stomach sickness. But the cold got at my heart action rather badly, so that I was forced to pant for some time."[99] Reaching Pennsylvania Station at 7 A.M. on the 31st, he cooled his heels for a bit before reaching the Longs' residence at 8 A.M. R. H. Barlow was in town, and he came over in the afternoon. On January 2 occurred an unprecedentedly large gang meeting, with fifteen present—Barlow, Kleiner, Leeds, Talman, Morton, Kirk, Loveman (with a friend named Gordon), Koenig, Donald and Howard Wandrei, Long, and someone named Phillips (probably not a relative) and his friend Harry, along with Lovecraft. Talman took pictures of the various guests, catching them in odd expressions: Lovecraft felt that his picture made him look as if he were about to whistle a tune or expectorate. On the 3rd Lovecraft, Barlow, and Long visited Koenig's Electrical Testing Laboratories, a rather bizarre, futuristic place where electrical appliances of various sorts were tested for durability. Lovecraft came home early in the morning of January 8.

On New Year's night Lovecraft had stayed up till 3 A.M. with Barlow revising a story of his—"'Till A' the Seas'" (*Californian,* Summer 1935). This fairly conventional "last man" story is of interest only because Barlow's typescript, with Lovecraft's revisions in pen, survives, so that the exact degree of the latter's authorship can be ascertained. Lovecraft has made no significant structural changes, merely making a number of cosmetic changes in style and diction; but he has written the bulk of the concluding section, especially the purportedly cosmic reflexions when the last man on earth finally meets his ironic death:

> And now at last the Earth was dead. The final, pitiful survivor had perished. All the teeming billions; the slow aeons; the empires and civilisations of mankind were summed up in this poor twisted form—and how titanically meaningless it all had been! Now indeed had come an end and climax to all the efforts of humanity—how monstrous and incredible a climax in the eyes of those poor complacent fools of the prosperous days! Not ever again would the planet know the thunderous tramping of human millions—or even the crawling of lizards and the buzz of insects, for they, too, had gone. Now was come the reign of sapless branches and endless fields of tough grasses. Earth, like its cold, imperturbable moon, was given over to silence and blackness forever.

Pretty routine stuff—but Lovecraft was at this very time in the midst of writing something on somewhat the same theme but in a much more compelling way.

By the fall of 1934 Lovecraft had not written a work of original fiction for more than a year. His confidence in his own powers as a fiction writer was clearly at a low ebb. In December 1933 he wrote to Clark Ashton Smith:

> In everything I do there is a certain concreteness, extravagance, or general crudeness which defeats the vague but insistent object I have in mind. I start out trying to find symbols expressive of a certain mood induced by a certain visual conception . . . , but when I come to put anything on paper the chosen symbols seem forced, awkward, childish, exaggerated, & essentially inexpressive. I have staged a cheap, melodramatic puppet-show without saying what I wanted to say in the first place.[100]

In March 1934 he fleetingly mentioned a plot idea:

> I'm not working on the actual text of any story just now, but am planning a novelette of the Arkham cycle—about what happened when somebody inherited a queer old house on the top of Frenchman's Hill & obeyed an irresistible urge to

dig in a certain queer, abandoned graveyard on Hangman's Hill at the other edge of the town. This story will probably not involve the actual supernatural—being more of the "Colour Out of Space" type . . . greatly-stretched "scientifiction".[101]

Nothing more is heard of this story, which was clearly not completed and perhaps not even begun. As a preliminary for the writing of this tale, however, Lovecraft did prepare a map of Arkham—one of perhaps three he prepared in his life. As the months dragged on, Lovecraft's colleagues began to wonder whether any new story would ever emerge from his pen. In October E. Hoffmann Price urged Lovecraft to write another story about Randolph Carter, but Lovecraft declined.

Given all the difficulties Lovecraft was experiencing in capturing his ideas in fiction, it is not surprising that the writing of his next tale, "The Shadow out of Time," took more than three months (November 10, 1934, to February 22, 1935, as dated on the autograph manuscript) and went through two or perhaps three entire drafts. Moreover, the genesis of the story can be traced back at least four years before its actual composition. Before examining the painful birth of the story, let us gain some idea of its basic plot.

Nathaniel Wingate Peaslee, a professor of political economy at Miskatonic University, suddenly experiences some sort of nervous breakdown on May 14, 1908, while teaching a class. Awaking in the hospital after a collapse, he appears to have suffered an amnesia so severe that it has affected even his vocal and motor faculties. Gradually he relearns the use of his body, and indeed develops tremendous mental capacity, seemingly far beyond that of a normal human being. His wife, sensing that something is gravely wrong, obtains a divorce, and only one of his three children, Wingate, continues to have anything to do with him. Peaslee spends the next five years conducting prodigious but anomalous research at various libraries around the world, and also undertakes expeditions to various mysterious realms. Finally, on September 27, 1913, he suddenly snaps back into his old life: when he awakes after a spell of unconsciousness, he believes he is still teaching the economics course in 1908.

From this point on Peaslee is plagued with dreams of increasing bizarrerie. He thinks that his mind has been placed in the body of an alien entity shaped like a ten-foot-high rugose cone, while this entity's mind occupies his own body. These creatures are called the Great Race "because it alone had conquered the secret of time": they have perfected a technique of mind-exchange with almost any other life-form throughout the universe and at any point in time—past, present, or future. The Great Race had established a colony on this planet in Australia 150,000,000 years ago; their minds had previously occupied the bodies of another race, but had left them because of some impending cataclysm; later they would migrate to other bodies after the cone-shaped beings were destroyed. They had compiled a voluminous library consisting of the accounts of all the other captive minds throughout the universe, and Peaslee himself writes an account of his own time for the Great Race's archives.

Peaslee believes that his dreams of the Great Race are merely the product of his esoteric study during his amnesia; but then an Australian explorer, having read some of Peaslee's articles on his dreams in psychological journals, writes to him to let him know that some archaeological remains very similar to the ones he has described as the city of the Great Race appear to have been recently discovered. Peaslee accompanies this explorer, Robert B. F. Mackenzie, on an expedition to the Great Sandy Desert, and is horrified to find that what he took to be dreams may have a real source. One night he leaves the camp to conduct a solitary exploration. He winds his way through the now underground corridors of the Great Race's city, increasingly unnerved at the *familiarity* of all the sites he has traversing. He knows that the only way to confirm whether his dreams are only dreams or some monstrous reality is to find that account he had written for the Great Race's archives. After a laborious descent he comes to the place, finds his own record, and opens it:

> No eye had seen, no hand had touched that book since the advent of man to this planet. And yet, when I flashed my torch upon it in that frightful megalithic abyss, I saw that the queerly pigmented letters on the brittle, aeon-browned cellulose pages were not indeed any nameless hieroglyphs of earth's youth. They were, instead, the letters of our familiar alphabet, spelling out the words of the English language in my own handwriting.

But because he loses this record on his maniacal ascent to the surface, he can still maintain, with harried rationalisation: "There is reason to hope that my experience was wholly or partly an hallucination."

The cosmic scope of this work—second only to *At the Mountains of Madness* in this regard—allows "The Shadow out of Time" to attain a very high place in Lovecraft's fictional work; and the wealth of circumstantial detail in the history, biology, and civilisation of the Great Race is as convincing as in *At the Mountains of Madness* and perhaps still better integrated into the story. Once again, it is cosmicism of both space and time that is at work here; this is made especially clear in a piquant passage in which Peaslee meets other captive minds of the Great Race:

> There was a mind from the planet we know as Venus, which would live incalculable epochs to come; and one from an outer moon of Jupiter six million years in the past. Of earthly minds there were some from the winged, star-headed, half-vegetable race of palaeogean Antarctica; one from the reptile people of fabled Valusia; three from the furry pre-human Hyperborean worshippers of Tsathoggua; one from the wholly abominable Tcho-Tchos; two from the arachnid denizens of earth's last age; five from the hardy coleopterous species immediately following mankind, to which the Great Race was some day to transfer its keenest minds en masse in the face of horrible peril; and several from different branches of humanity.

That mention of the "hardy coleopterous species" (i.e., beetles) again points to an undercurrent that we have already seen in other tales—the denigration of human self-importance. Lovecraft is, of course, on solid ground scientifically in believing that insects will in all likelihood survive humanity on this planet (he had appended a note to this effect to Barlow's "'Till A' the Seas,'" since Barlow had postulated that mankind would be the last species on the earth); but he adds a further dryly cynical twist by maintaining that beetles will not only outlast us but also become the dominant *intellectual* species on the planet, so much that the Great Race will deign to occupy their bodies when the cone-shaped bodies face peril. Shortly afterwards Peaslee adds a harrowing note: "I shivered at the mysteries the past may conceal, and trembled at the menaces the future may bring forth. What was hinted in the speech of the post-human entities of the fate of mankind produced such an effect on me that I will not set it down here."

Of course, it is the Great Race that become the centrepiece of the story, in such a way that they—like the Old Ones of *At the Mountains of Madness*—come to seem like the "heroes" of the tale. Much is told of their history and civilisation; but, unlike the Old Ones, they have suffered scarcely any decline from the prodigious intellectual and aesthetic heights they have achieved, perhaps because their goal is not so much the acquisition of territory and the establishment of colonies as the pure exercise of thought. I shall study the political and utopian speculations in this story a little later.

One of the few flaws in the tale, perhaps, is Lovecraft's imprecision—indeed, his complete silence—on the matter of exactly *how* the Great Race effect their mind-exchanges, especially across gulfs of time. When the mind of one of the Great Race is about to vacate Peaslee's body, it sets up a device made up of "a queer mixture of rods, wheels, and mirrors, though only about two feet tall, one foot wide, and one foot thick"; in some fashion this device effects the exchange, although there is absolutely no indication of how it does so. There is a later reference to "suitable mechanical aid" that somehow permits a mind to go forward in time and displace the mind of some entity, but this is again the only clue we ever receive of this procedure; and the mention of "mind-casting outside the recognised senses" and "extra-sensory" methods used by the Great Race stretches Lovecraft's mechanistic materialism to the very limit.

But this is a small blemish in a tale that opens up tremendous cosmic vistas and, as with *At the Mountains of Madness,* succeeds triumphantly in displacing humanity from centre stage and enthroning fabulously alien entities there instead. The spectacular concluding tableau—a man finding a document he must have written 150,000,000 years ago—must be one of the most outré moments in all literature. As Peaslee himself reflects, "If that abyss and what it held were real, there is no hope. Then, all too truly, there lies upon this world of man a mocking and incredible shadow out of time."

The basic mind-exchange scenario of the tale has been taken from at least three sources. First, of course, is H. B. Drake's *The Shadowy Thing,* which we have already seen as an influence on "The Thing on the Doorstep." Second, there is Henri Béraud's obscure novel *Lazarus* (1925), which Lovecraft had in his library and which he read in 1928.[102] This novel presents a man, Jean Mourin, who remains in a hospital for sixteen years (for the period 1906–22) while suffering a long amnesia; during this time he develops a personality (named Gervais by the hospital staff) very different from that of his usual self. Every now and then this alternate personality returns; once Jean thinks he sees Gervais when he looks in the mirror, and later he thinks Gervais is stalking him. Jean even undertakes a study of split personalities, as Peaslee does, in an attempt to come to grips with the situation. (Parenthetically, the amnesia motif in "The Shadow out of Time" makes for a very provocative autobiographical connexion. Peaslee's amnesia dates from 1908 to 1913, the exact time when Lovecraft himself, having had to withdraw from high school, descended into hermitry. Perhaps he had himself come to believe that another personality had taken over during this time.)

A third dominant influence is not a literary work but a film: *Berkeley Square* (1933), which enraptured Lovecraft by its portrayal of a man whose mind somehow drifts back into the body of his ancestor in the eighteenth century. This source in particular may have been critical, for it seems to have supplied Lovecraft with suggestions on how he might embody his long-held belief (expressed in "Notes on Writing Weird Fiction") that "*Conflict with time* seems to me the most potent and fruitful theme in all human expression."

Lovecraft first saw *Berkeley Square* in November 1933, on the recommendation of J. Vernon Shea, who even then was an ardent film enthusiast and would remain one for the rest of his life. Lovecraft was initially much taken with the fidelity with which the eighteenth-century atmosphere was captured;[103] but later, having seen the film again (he saw it a total of four times[104]), he began to detect some flaws in conception. *Berkeley Square* is based on a play of that title by John L. Balderston (1929), and is a very faithful adaptation of the play, since Balderston himself cowrote the screenplay. It tells the story of Peter Standish, a man in the early twentieth century who is so fascinated with the eighteenth century—and in particular his own ancestor and namesake—that he somehow transports himself literally into the past and into the body of his ancestor. Lovecraft detected two problems with the execution of the idea: 1) Where was the mind or personality of the eighteenth-century Peter Standish when the twentieth-century Peter was occupying his body? 2) How could the eighteenth-century Peter's diary, written in part while the twentieth-century Peter was occupying his body, not take cognisance of the fact?[105] These sorts of difficulties seem to adhere in any sort of time-travel story, but "The Shadow out of Time" seems to have obviated them as well as could be imagined.

Berkeley Square is a striking production, with Leslie Howard superbly playing the role of Peter Standish. In some ways it is more similar to Lovecraft's *The Case of Charles Dexter Ward,* which is perhaps why Lovecraft was so initially struck with it. I cannot tell whether Lovecraft ever read the play; certainly he had not before he saw the film. At one point in the play (but not in the film), Peter even compares himself to a shadow.[106] But both the play and the film are worth studying for their possible influence on this last of Lovecraft's major tales.

Other, smaller features in "The Shadow out of Time" may also have literary sources. Peaslee's alienation from his family may echo Walter de la Mare's novel *The Return* (1910), in which again an eighteenth-century personality seems to fasten itself upon the body of a twentieth-century individual, causing his wife to cease all relations with him. And Leonard Cline's *The Dark Chamber* (1927), in which a man attempts to recapture his entire past, is perhaps the source for the vast archives of the Great Race: Cline's protagonist, Richard Pride, keeps an immense warehouse full of documents about his own life, and toward the end of the novel the narrator frantically traverses this warehouse before finding Pride killed by his own dog.

Two other literary influences can be noted if only to be dismissed. It has frequently been assumed that "The Shadow out of Time" is simply an extrapolation upon Wells's *The Time Machine;* but there is really very little resemblance between the two works. Lovecraft did, as noted earlier, read Wells's novel in 1925, but there is little in it that might be thought to have a direct bearing on his story. Olaf Stapledon's *Last and First Men* (1930) has been suggested as an influence on the enormous stretches of time reflected in the story, but Lovecraft did not read this work until August 1935, months after the tale's completion.[107]

It is, indeed, highly misleading to imagine that "The Shadow out of Time" is merely a stitching-together of previous works of literature and film. Lovecraft would not have been struck by these works if he had not for many years had ideas running roughly parallel with them. At best, these various works gave suggestions as to how Lovecraft could execute his conception; and in the end he executed it in a manner far more intellectually compelling and imaginatively stimulating than any of his predecessors.

Lovecraft had, to be sure, suggested the vast gulfs of time in *At the Mountains of Madness,* but he does so here in a particularly *intimate* way that effects a powerful fusion between internal and external horror. Although Peaslee is emphatic (and correct) in believing that "What came, came from *somewhere else,*" the moment when, in his dream, he sees himself to be in the body of one of the alien entities is as chilling an instance of existential horror as one is likely to find. Peaslee comments poignantly, "it is not wholesome to watch monstrous objects doing what one had known only human beings to do." In a sense, it could be thought that this notion of "possession" by an extraterrestrial being harks back all the way to "Beyond the

Wall of Sleep" (1919); but the monumentally expanded and subtilised expression of the idea in "The Shadow out of Time" makes one realise the enormous strides Lovecraft had made as a writer in a mere fifteen years.

It is now time to return to the difficulties Lovecraft experienced in capturing the essence of this story on paper. The core of the plot had already been conceived as early as 1930, emerging out of a discussion between Lovecraft and Clark Ashton Smith regarding the plausibility of stories involving time-travel. Lovecraft properly noted: "The weakness of most tales with this theme is that they do not provide for the recording, in history, of those inexplicable events in the past which were caused by the backward time-voyagings of persons of the present & future."[108] He had already mapped out the cataclysmic ending at this time: "One baffling thing that could be introduced is to have a modern man discover, among documents exhumed from some prehistoric buried city, a mouldering papyrus or parchment *written in English, & in his own handwriting.*"

By March 1932 Lovecraft had already devised the basic idea of mind-exchange over time, as outlined in another letter to Smith:

> I have a sort of time idea of very simple nature floating around in the back of my head, but don't know when I shall ever get around to using it. The notion is that of a race in primal Lomar perhaps even before the founding of Olathoë & in the heyday of Hyperborean Commoriom—who gained a knowledge of all arts & sciences by sending thought-streams ahead to drain the minds of men in future ages—angling in time, as it were. Now & then they get hold of a really competent man of learning, & annex all his thoughts. Usually they only keep their victims tranced for a short time, but once in a while, when they need some special piece of continuous information, one of their number sacrifices himself for the race & actually changes bodies with the first thoroughly satisfactory victim he finds. The victim's brain then goes back to 100,000 B.C.—into the hypnotist's body to live in Lomar for the rest of his life, while hypnotist from dead aeons animates the modern clay of his victims.[109]

It is important to quote this passage at length to see both the significant alterations made in the finished story—where the mind of the Great Race rarely remains in a captive body for the rest of its life, but only for a period of years, after which a return switch is effected—and to show that the conception of mind-exchange over time had been devised *before* Lovecraft saw *Berkeley Square,* the only other work that may conceivably have influenced this point.

Lovecraft began the actual writing of "The Shadow out of Time" in late 1934. He announced in November: "I developed that story *mistily and allusively* in 16 pages, but it was no go. Thin and unconvincing, with the climactic revelation wholly unjustified by the hash of visions preceding it."[110] What this sixteen-page version could possibly have been like is almost beyond conjecture. The disquisition about the Great Race must have been radically compressed (Lovecraft suggested as much when he noted "an occasional plethora of *visibly explanatory* matter" in his tales and the possibility of replacing it with *"brief implication or suggestion"*[111]), and this is what clearly dissatisfied Lovecraft about this version; for he came to realise that this passage, far from being an irrelevant digression, was actually the heart of the story. What then occurred is a little unclear: Is the second draft the version we now have? In late December he spoke of a "second version" that "fails to satisfy me"[112] and was uncertain whether to finish it as it was or to destroy it and start afresh. He may have done the latter, for long after finishing the story he declared that the final version was "itself the 3d complete version of the same story."[113] Whether there were two or three entire versions must remain uncertain; but clearly this tale, scribbled harriedly in pencil in a small notebook later given to R. H. Barlow, was one of the most difficult in genesis of any of Lovecraft's tales. And yet, in many ways it is the culmination of his fictional career and by no means an unfitting capstone to a twenty-year attempt to capture the sense of wonder and awe he felt at the boundless reaches of space and time. Although Lovecraft would write one more original tale and work on several additional revisions and collaborations with colleagues, his life as a fiction writer ends, and ends fittingly, with "The Shadow out of Time."[114]

23. CARING ABOUT THE CIVILISATION
(1929–1937)

I n the summer of 1936 Lovecraft made an interesting admission:

> I used to be a hide-bound Tory simply for traditional and antiquarian rea-
> sons—and because I had never done any real *thinking* on civics and industry and
> the future. The depression—and its concomitant publicisation of industrial, finan-
> cial, and governmental problems—jolted me out of my lethargy and led me to reëx-
> amine the facts of history in the light of unsentimental scientific analysis; and it was
> not long before I realised what an ass I had been. The liberals at whom I used to
> laugh were the ones who were right—for they were living in the present while I had
> been living in the past. They had been using science while I had been using roman-
> tic antiquarianism. At last I began to recognise something of the way in which capi-
> talism works—always piling up concentrated wealth and impoverishing the bulk of
> the population until the strain becomes so intolerable as to force artificial reform.[1]

This is, oddly enough, one of the few times Lovecraft explicitly mentioned the depression as signalling a radical change in his beliefs on politics, economics, and
society; but perhaps he need not have made such an admission, for his letters from
1930 onward return again and again to these subjects.

The stock market crash of October 1929 would not have affected Lovecraft
very significantly, or at least directly, since of course the chief victims were those
who had invested in stocks, and Lovecraft was so poor that he had little money to
invest. Nor did he have any fears of immediate unemployment, since he was working freelance as a revisionist and very occasional contributor to the pulps. It is certainly true that many pulp magazines did not fare well in the depression—*Strange
Tales* (1931–33) folded after seven issues, *Astounding* temporarily ceased publication in 1933 and did not resume until it was sold to another publisher, and even
Weird Tales went temporarily to a bimonthly schedule in 1931—but Lovecraft
was not writing much original fiction at this time, so that he had no great concern
about the shrinkage in markets. The vast bulk of his revision work did not involve
selling stories to the pulps, but rather the revising or copyediting of general fiction,
essays, poetry, or treatises, and all through the 1930s he seems to have managed to
eke along in no worse a situation than he was before.

It is essential to emphasise all this, for it means that there was little in Lovecraft's
personal circumstances that led him to the adoption of a moderate socialism; he did
not—as many impoverished individuals did—become attracted to political or economic radicalism merely because he found himself destitute. Firstly, he was never
truly destitute—at least, not in comparison with many others in the depression (in-

cluding some of his own friends), who lost all their money and belongings and had no job and no roof over their heads; secondly, he scorned communism as unworkable and culturally devastating, recommending an economic system considerably to the left of what this country actually adopted under Roosevelt but nevertheless supporting the New Deal as the only plan of action that had any chance of being carried out.

And yet, Lovecraft's conversion to socialism was not entirely surprising, first because socialism as a political theory and a concrete alternative to capitalism was experiencing a resurgence during the 1930s, and second because Lovecraft's brand of socialism still retained many of the aristocratic features that had shaped his earlier political thought. The latter point I shall take up presently; the former is worth elaborating briefly.

The United States has never been an especially fertile soil for socialism or communism, but there have been occasions when they have been a little less unpopular than usual. Socialism had done reasonably well in the first two decades of the century: the I.W.W. (Industrial Workers of the World), founded in 1905, was gaining influence in its support of strikes by a variety of labour unions, and Eugene V. Debs won nearly a million votes in 1912 as a third-party candidate. But in the period immediately after World War I, with its "Red Scare" and virulent suppression of all radical groups, socialism was forced underground for nearly a decade.

The depression led to a resurgence in which socialists teamed with labour to demand reforms in working conditions. The socialist presidential candidate Norman Thomas polled a little less than 900,000 votes in 1932—not a very large figure, but a larger one than he achieved during any of his other campaigns (he was a candidate in every presidential election from 1928 to 1948). Intellectuals were also in support of socialism (either of a moderate or Marxist variety) or outright communism, as Lovecraft himself notes on one occasion:

> Virtually *all* the reputable authors & critics in the United States are political radicals—Dreiser, Sherwood Anderson, Hemingway, Dos Passos, Eastman, O'Neill, Lewis, Maxwell Anderson, MacLeish, Edmund Wilson, Fadiman—but the list is endless. . . . The cream of human brains—the sort of brains not wrapped up in personal luxury & immediate advantage is slowly drifting away from the blind class-loyalty toward a better-balanced position in which the symmetrical structure & permanent stability of the whole social organism is a paramount consideration.[2]

The degree to which Lovecraft's own thought underwent a radical shift in just over a decade is strikingly illustrated by contrasting his snide reference to the "lawless I.W.W." in "Bolshevism" (*Conservative*, July 1919) with his echo of the I.W.W. song "Hallelujah, I'm a bum!" in a 1936 letter.[3]

And yet, that shift was in many ways very slow, even grudging at the outset. It seems jointly to have been the result of observation of the increasingly desperate state of affairs engendered by the depression and by more searching thought on what could be done about it. President Hoover's staunch belief in voluntarism had made him unwilling to permit the government to give direct relief to the unemployed. In later years Lovecraft flayed the man he had supported in 1928 with the vicious and commonly used soubriquet "Let-'em-Starve Hoover"; Hoover was, however, not an evil man but merely a basically timid politician who did not realise the extraordinary difficulties into which the country had fallen and did not have the flexibility of imagination to propose radical solutions for them. Even Roosevelt was only just radical enough to advocate policies that kept the country from total economic collapse, and everyone knows that it was really World War II that pulled the United States and the world out of the depression.

It is in January 1931 that we first find an inkling of a change. Lovecraft wrote:

> Ethical idealism demands socialism on poetical cosmic grounds involving some mythical linkage of individuals to one another and to the universe—while hard-fact realism is gradually yielding to socialism because it is the only mechanical adjustment of forces which will save our culture-fostering stratified society in the face of a growing revolutionary pressure from increasingly desperate under-men whom mechanisation is gradually forcing into unemployment and starvation.[4]

But it can be seen from the tone of this passage—and of the whole letter in which it is embedded—that Lovecraft was advocating the second motive for socialism, and that what really concerned him was not the welfare of "the rabble" but the civilisation-ending revolution this rabble could cause if it was not appeased. For after all, "All that I care about is *the civilisation*".[5] "*The maintenance of [a] high cultural standard is the only social or political enthusiasm I possess* . . . In effect, I venerate the principle of aristocracy without being especially interested in aristocrats as persons. I don't care who has the dominance, so long as that dominance remains a *certain kind* of dominance, intellectually and aesthetically considered."[6] In other words, Lovecraft sought a state of culture that allowed for the free exercise of thought and imagination, the production of vital works of art, and a general ambiance of "civilised" values and modes of behaviour. Up to the last few years of his life, Lovecraft believed that only a socially recognised aristocracy could ensure such a condition—either through actual patronage of the arts or through a general climate of refined civilisation that would axiomatically be regarded as a condition toward which all society would aspire. Revolution of any kind was the last thing he wanted, and this is why he loathed Bolshevik Russia to the end of his days—because it had fostered a *cultural* destruction that was in no way necessary to the *economic* reform that its leaders were claiming as their paramount goals. It would take some years for Lovecraft to modify his position on aristocracy, but I may as well note here how that modification was finally articulated in 1936:

> . . . what I used to respect was not really aristocracy, but a set of personal qualities which aristocracy then developed better than any other system . . . a set of qualities,

however, whose merit lay only in a psychology of non-calculative, non-competitive disinterestedness, truthfulness, courage, and generosity fostered by good education, minimum economic stress, and assumed position, AND JUST AS ACHIEVABLE THROUGH SOCIALISM AS THROUGH ARISTO-CRACY.[7]

Lovecraft's debate with Robert E. Howard on the relative merits of civilisation and barbarism clarifies his political concerns while at the same time linking them with his general metaphysics and ethics. The debate was an offshoot of a number of polarities discussed by these two very different individuals—the physical vs. the intellectual, the frontier vs. the city, and the like. Neither man's position is as simple as these dichotomies suggest, and I don't think it is possible to assert (as many Howard supporters have done) that the debate—which became quite testy at times and even led to a certain hostility and resentment, although each always claimed to respect the other's position—was somehow "won" by Howard. As with Lovecraft's dispute with E. Hoffmann Price as to the relative merits of pulp fiction and literature, the matter really is one of temperamental preference rather than truth or falsity.

Lovecraft began the debate—and at the same time justified his advocacy of a political system that encourages what he felt to be the highest fruits of civilisation, aesthetic and intellectual development—by saying:

> We cannot, in view of what the cultural capacity of mankind has been shown to be, afford to base a civilisation on the low cultural standards of an undeveloped majority. Such a civilisation of mere working, eating, drinking, breeding, and vacantly loafing or childishly playing isn't worth maintaining. None of the members of it are really better off than as if they didn't exist at all. . . . No settled, civilised group has any reason to exist unless it can develop a decently high degree of intellectual and artistic cultivation. The more who can share in this cultivation the better, but we must not invidiously hinder its growth merely because the number of sharers has to be relatively small at first, and because it can perhaps never . . . include every individual in the whole group.[8]

Howard—although he admitted (perhaps disingenuously) that the physical side of human beings was "admittedly inferior to the mental side"—objected to what he believed to be Lovecraft's exaltation of the artist or intellectual as the summit of humanity; but in doing so he seriously distorted Lovecraft's point: "Of all snobberies, the assumption that intellectual endeavors, attainments and accomplishments are the only worth-while and important things in life, is the least justifiable."[9] Lovecraft countered:

> No one has ever claimed that the artist is more important in the maintenance of some sort of civilisation than is the farmer, mechanic, engineer, or statesman. . . . However, when we consider the vast enlargement of life made possible by the expansion of the personality under the influence of art; and realise how infinitely

more worth living is a life enriched by such an expansion; we are certainly justified in censuring any civilisation which does not favour this process. It is not that we regard art or any other thing in life as "sacred", but that we recognise the importance of something which naturally forms the chief life-interest of the most highly evolved types. Art certainly *is* more intrinsically removed from the unevolved protoplasmic stage of organic reaction than any other human manifestation except pure reason—hence our grouping of it as one of the "highest" things in life. By "highest" we do not mean "most important to survival", but simply "most advanced in intrinsic development".[10]

At this point Howard became angry, feeling insulted because of Lovecraft's suggestion (very implicit, but probably real in some sense) that Howard was somehow "inferior" for not being able to appreciate the "highest" fruits of culture; and the debate lost steam thereafter, as both sides apparently decided it would be politic to suspend it to preserve amity. Nevertheless, Lovecraft's conception of his ideal society is etched strongly in these and other letters of this period.

During the early years of the depression Lovecraft actually fancied that the plutocracy—now about the only thing equivalent to an aristocracy in this country—might itself take over the role as patron of the arts: "The chances are that our future plutocrats will try to cultivate all the aristocratic arts, and succeed at a fair number of them. The new culture will of course lack certain emotional overtones of the old culture which depended on obsolete views and feelings—but . . . there's no need of mourning about that too deeply."[11] My feeling is that this view was derived from observation of Samuel Insull, the Chicago electricity magnate who—at least before the spectacular collapse of his utilities empire in 1932 and his later indictment on embezzlement and larceny charges—was a leading patron of the arts (he had, among other things, been the chief financial backer of the new Chicago Civic Opera Building). Lovecraft also believed that the plutocrats would willingly make concessions to the masses simply in order to stave off revolution:

Being men of sense at bottom despite their present confused myopia, they will probably see the need of some new division of the fruits of industry, and will at last call in the perfectly disinterested sociological planners—the men of broad culture and historic perspective whom they have previously despised as mere academic theorists—who have some chance of devising workable middle courses. Rather than let an infuriated mob set up a communist state or drag society into complete anarchical chaos, the industrialists will probably consent to the enforcement of a fascistic regime under which will be ensured a tolerable minimum of subsistence in exchange for orderly conduct and a willingness to labour when labouring opportunities exist. They will accept their overwhelmingly reduced profits as an alternative preferable to complete collapse and business-social annihilation.[12]

These views may strike us as quite naive, but perhaps we have become too cynical from the rebirth of an appallingly consumeristic capitalism following World War II, in which the "captains of industry" are anything but cultivated in their artistic tastes or interested in anything but personal aggrandisement. In any case, in the course of time Lovecraft saw the error of his ways and discarded this approach to the solution of the problem.

There were probably no specific events that led Lovecraft to the shift, but rather an accumulation of many. He was well aware of the furore caused by the Bonus Army in the summer of 1932. The Bonus Army was a pathetic group of desperately poor unemployed World War I veterans who marched across the country to Washington in late May to demand the early distribution of a bonus that was not scheduled for payment until 1945. They hung about in makeshift tents for months; eventually their numbers swelled to about 20,000. On July 28 the police provoked a confrontation with the veterans, and in the ensuing riots two veterans were killed. In the end they disbanded without achieving their aim.

Lovecraft, commenting in August, believed that the government had no choice but to act with vigour ("The idea of marching on a capital with the idea of influencing legislation is at best a crazy one and at worst a dangerously revolutionary one"), but he nevertheless sympathised with the marchers and felt that the issue of the bonus itself was not easily resolved: "I find myself sometimes on one side and sometimes on the other."[13]

More significant, perhaps, was the so-called Technocracy survey of 1932. The term technocracy was coined by an inventor, William H. Smith, to mean rule by technologists. Elaborated by Howard Scott, an economist and intellectual, the notion led to what is perhaps Lovecraft's most important conclusion about the economic state of the nation: that technology had made full employment impossible even in principle because machines that required only a few workers to tend them were now doing the work previously done by many individuals, and this tendency would only increase as more and more sophisticated machines were developed:

> Do you attempt to account for the magnitude of the present depression? In surveying the effects of mechanis'd industry upon society, I have been led to a certain change of political views. . . . With the universal use and improvement of machinery, all the needed labour of the world can be perform'd by a relatively few persons, leaving vast numbers permanently unemployable, depression or no depression. If these people are not fed and amused, they will dangerously revolt; hence we must either institute a programme of steady pensioning—panem et circenses—or else subject industry to a governmental supervision which will lessen its profits but spread its jobs amongst more men working less hours. For many reasons the latter course seems to me most reasonable . . .[14]

Here again, of course, the danger of revolt seems uppermost in Lovecraft's mind. Although the Technocracy movement fizzled by early 1933, its influence on this aspect of Lovecraft's thought was permanent; and its real significance was in bringing emphatically home to Lovecraft the brutal truth—one that he had tried to prevent himself from acknowledging at least through 1930—that the machine age was here to stay. Any sensible and realistic economic and political system must then be based on this premise.

The election of 1932 was of course a landmark. Lovecraft actually declared just before the election that he didn't think there was much to choose between Hoover and Roosevelt,[15] since he claimed to believe that neither the Republicans nor the Democrats were bold enough to propose sufficiently radical measures to solve the long-term problem of capitalism; but he also knew that the election was a foregone conclusion. Roosevelt won in one of the largest landslides in American history; but his inauguration would not occur until March 4, 1933, and on February 22 Lovecraft wrote one of his most concentrated and impassioned pleas for political and economic reform—the essay "Some Repetitions on the Times."

The timing of the piece is no accident. The few weeks preceding Roosevelt's inauguration could well be said to have been the closest this country ever came to an actual revolt by the dispossessed. The depression had reached its nadir: banks were failing across the country; troops were actually deployed in many major cities to guard against riots; the economy seemed at a near-standstill. Lovecraft's fears of a culture-destroying revolution seemed quite realistic, and they no doubt account for the urgent, even harried tone of his essay.

"Some Repetitions on the Times" survives only in an autograph manuscript, and Lovecraft appears to have made no effort whatever to prepare it for publication. Perhaps he felt that he was not enough of an authority on the subject, but in that case why write the treatise at all? There is no evidence that he even showed it to any of his colleagues, with whom he conducted long debates in letters about the economic situation. In any case, Lovecraft had by this time landed wholly in the (moderate) socialist camp—economically, at least.

In this essay Lovecraft finally realised that business leaders—and, for that matter, the ordinary run of politicians—were simply not going to deal with economic realities with the vigour and radicalism they required; only direct government intervention could solve the immediate problem. "It is by this time virtually clear to everyone save self-blinded capitalists and politicians that the old relation of the individual to the needs of the community has utterly broken down under the impact of intensively productive machinery." What is the solution? In purely economic terms Lovecraft advocated the following proposals:

1. Governmental control of large accumulations of resources (including utilities) and their operation not on a basis of profit but strictly on need;

2. Fewer working hours (but at higher pay) so that all who were capable of working could work at a livable wage;
3. Unemployment insurance and old age pensions.

None of these ideas was, of course, Lovecraft's original contribution—they had been talked about for years or decades, and the very title of Lovecraft's essay, "Some Repetitions on the Times," makes it clear that he is simply echoing what others had said over and over again. Let us consider the history of these proposals in greater detail.

The least problematical was the last. Old age pensions had been instituted in Germany as early as 1889, in Australia in 1903, and in England tentatively in 1908 and definitively by 1925. In 1911–14 unemployment insurance came to England. In the United States, the Social Security Act was signed by Roosevelt on August 14, 1935, although disbursement of money did not begun until 1940.

Government control of large accumulations of wealth has always been a pipe-dream in this country—plutocrats will always be plutocrats—but government control (or at least supervision) of utilities and other institutions was by no means a radical conception in the 1930s. The Roosevelt administration did not undertake such an action until 1934, when the Federal Communications Commission (FCC) was formed to regulate interstate telephone and telegraph rates. By 1935 the Federal Power Commission was governing interstate sale of electric power (natural gas came under control in 1938), the Public Utility Holding Company Act had authorised the Securities and Exchange Commission (SEC) to curb abuses by holding companies (specifically those governing utilities), banks came under federal regulation, and higher taxes were imposed on the wealthy. This was certainly not socialism—although reactionary politicians and businessmen constantly bandied that word about to frighten the electorate and to preserve their own wealth—but it was at least a step in that direction. Of course, many foreign countries exercised actual governmental ownership of public utilities, whereas the United States continues to this day to settle only for governmental supervision. As for what Lovecraft in "Some Repetitions on the Times" calls "bald assertion of governmental control over large accumulations of resources [and] a potential limitation of private property beyond certain liberal limits"—I have trouble imagining that he believed this to be a political reality even during the depression; but evidently he did so.

The most striking of Lovecraft's proposals is the limitation of working hours so that all who were capable of working could work. This idea enjoyed a brief popularity among political theorists and reformers, but in the end the rabid opposition of business doomed it. In April 1933 Senator Hugo Black of Alabama and William Connery, chairman of the House Labor Committee, proposed a bill for a thirty-hour week so that more people could be employed. Roosevelt did not favour it and countered with the NIRA (National Industrial Recovery Act), which ultimately created the NRA (National Recovery Administration). This established a minimum wage of $12 a week for a forty-hour week. But, although hailed initially as a landmark in cooperation between government, labour, and business, the NRA quickly ran into trouble because its director, General Hugh Samuel Johnson, believed that businesses would of their own accord adopt codes of fair competition and fair labour practice, something that naturally did not happen. The NRA became the object of criticism from all sides, especially among labour unions and small businesses. Less than two years after it was enacted, on May 27, 1935, it was struck down by the Supreme Court as unconstitutional and was officially abolished on January 1, 1936. Many of its labour provisions, however, were ultimately reestablished by other legislation.

Although the movement for shorter working hours continued to the end of the depression, it never regained the momentum it had had in the early 1930s, prior to its coopting by the NRA.[16] The forty-hour work week has now been enshrined as a sacrosanct tenet of business, and there is not much likelihood that shorter hours—the chief component of Lovecraft's (and others') plans for full employment—will ever be carried out.

Roosevelt, of course, realised that unemployment was the major problem to be dealt with in the short term (at least 12,000,000 were unemployed in 1932—nearly a quarter of the work force), and one of the first things he did upon gaining office was to establish various emergency measures in an attempt to relieve it. Among these was the CCC (Civilian Conservation Corps), which would enlist young men from the ages of seventeen to twenty-four for the reforestation of parks, flood control, power development, and the like. Incredibly, Lovecraft's friend Bernard Austin Dwyer, although thirty-eight at the time, was accepted for the CCC and in late 1934 went to Camp 25 in Peekskill, New York, where he eventually became editor of the camp newsletter.

Some have wondered why Lovecraft himself never made an attempt to sign on to some such program. But he was never strictly speaking unemployed: he always had revision work and very sporadic sales of original fiction, and perhaps he feared that he would lose even these modest sources of income if he joined a government-sponsored work program. What of the WPA (Works Progress Administration), instituted in the summer of 1935? This mostly generated blue-collar construction jobs obviously unsuited for Lovecraft, but the Federal Writers' Project was an important subdivision of the WPA and resulted in the production of a number of significant works of art and scholarship. Lovecraft could perhaps have worked on the guide to Rhode Island published in 1937, but he never made any effort to do so.

Once Lovecraft had jumped on the New Deal bandwagon, he defended its policies, at least privately, from attacks on both sides of the political spectrum. Attacks from the right were, of course, the more vociferous, and Lovecraft faced a good deal of it in his own hometown. In the spring of 1934 the conservative *Providence Journal* wrote a series of editorials hostile to the new administration, and Lovecraft responded with a lengthy letter to the editor, titled "The Journal and the New Deal," dated April 13, 1934. As with "Some Repetitions on the Times," I wonder what compelled Lovecraft to write this treatise; or, rather, how he expected the newspaper to publish even a fraction of this 4000-word screed. The piece does, however, begin to evince that scornful sarcasm which enters into much of Lovecraft's later political writing (mostly in letters) as he found himself becoming increasingly exasperated with the slowness of reform and the ferocity of right-wing sniping:

> And so, though a sincere admirer of the Journal and Bulletin's news and liter-ary standards, a third-generation subscriber without other daily informative pabu-lum, and a product of an hereditarily Republican and conservative background, the writer must register dissent from the heated periods of the editorial genius whose alarm for the public liberties is so touching. It is impossible not to see in such an alarm the blind defensive gesture of vested capital and its spokesmen as distinguished from the longer-range thought which recogises historic change, val-ues the essence instead of the surface forms of human quality, and tests its apprais-als by standards deeper than those of mere convention and recent custom.

One perhaps unintended effect of the economic crisis was to deflect Lovecraft's attention from other social evils. The 18th Amendment was repealed on December 6, 1933. A year and a half earlier Lovecraft had already announced that his enthusi-asm for prohibition was a thing of the past,[17] but he made it clear that this was only because he realised that the law against liquor was essentially unenforceable:

> As for prohibition, I was originally in favour of it, & would still be in favour of anything which could make intoxicating liquor *actually* difficult to get or retain. I see absolutely no good, & a vast amount of social harm, in the practice of alcohol drinking. It is clear, however, that under the existing governmental attitude (i.e., in the absence of a strong fascistic policy) prohibition can scarcely be enforced, & can scarcely be even imperfectly half-enforced, without an altogether dispropor-tionate concentration of energy & resources—so that the repeal of the 18th amendment at this trying historic period was hardly worth fighting. In other words, the burden of fighting the alcohol evil was so heavy as to form a new evil greater than the original one—like getting crippled from the recoil of a huge mus-ket shot off at a relatively insignificant rat. The present age is so full of perils & evils—principally economic—infinitely worse than alcohol, that we cannot spare the strength just now for a fight against this minor enemy.[18]

Lovecraft was surely not pleased at the repeal, but this reference to alcoholism as a "relatively insignificant rat" certainly contrasts with his fulminations against drink-ing a decade and a half earlier.

Where Lovecraft departed most radically from the Roosevelt administration itself as well as from the main stream of American opinion was in his suggestions for political reform. In effect, he saw economics and politics as quite separate phenomena requiring separate solutions. While proposing the spreading of economic wealth to the many, he concurrently advocated the restricting of political power to the few. This should come as no surprise, given Lovecraft's early (and romanticised) support for the English aristocracy and monarchy, his later readings in Nietzsche, and his own intellectual superiority. And yet, because Lovecraft enunciated his view somewhat misleadingly—or, perhaps, in a deliberately provocative way—he has taken some criticism from later commentators.

In the first place, Lovecraft's "oligarchy of intelligence and education" (as he termed it in "Some Repetitions on the Times") was not actually an aristocracy or even an oligarchy in the strictest sense. It was indeed a democracy—but merely a democracy that recognised the ill effects of universal suffrage if the electorate consisted (as in fact it does) largely of the uneducated or the politically naive. Lovecraft's argument was a very simple one, and was again an outgrowth of his realisation of the socioeconomic complexities brought on by the machine age: governmental decisions are now too complex for anyone other than a sophisticated specialist to understand.

> Today all government involves the most abstruse & complicated technology, so that the average citizen is absolutely without power to form any intelligent estimate of the value of any proposed measure. Only the most highly trained technicians can have any real idea of what any governmental policy or operation is about— hence the so-called "will of the people" is merely a superfluity without the least trace of value in meeting & dealing with specific problems.[19]

He discussed the matter with pungent cynicism to Robert E. Howard:

> Democracy—as distinguished from universal opportunity and good treatment—is today a fallacy and impossibility so great that any serious attempt to apply it cannot be considered as other than a mockery and a jest. . . . Government "by popular vote" means merely the nomination of doubtfully qualified men by doubtfully authorised and seldom competent cliques of professional politicians representing hidden interests, followed by a sardonic farce of emotional persuasion in which the orators with the glibbest tongues and flashiest catch-words herd on their side a numerical majority of blindly impressionable dolts and gulls who have for the most part no idea of what the whole circus is about.[20]

How little things have changed.

The first thing that should be done about this situation, in Lovecraft's view, was to restrict the vote "to those able to pass rigorous educational examinations (emphasising civic and economic subjects) and scientific intelligence tests" ("Some Repetitions on the Times"). It need not be assumed that Lovecraft automatically included himself in this number; in "Some Repetitions on the Times" he declared himself a "rank layman" and went on to say: "No non-technician, be he artist, philosopher, or scientist, can even begin to judge the labyrinthine governmental problems with which these administrators must deal." Lovecraft did not seem entirely aware of the difficulty of ensuring that these tests be fair to all (although I suspect he would have little patience with modern complaints that many intelligence tests are culturally biased), but he maintained that such a restriction of the vote would indeed be fair because—as we shall see presently—educational opportunities would be vastly broadened under his political scheme.

This whole idea—that the common people in the United States are not intelligent enough for democracy to work—was not nearly as radical in Lovecraft's time as it now seems. In the early 1920s Charles Evans Hughes, Harding's secretary of state, had already proposed the notion of a meritocracy in government—even though the thoroughly corrupt and inept Harding administration was about as far from putting that notion into practice as any could have been. Walter Lippmann in *Public Opinion* (1922) and its sequel, *The Phantom Public* (1925), had come close to this idea also. Lippmann's very complex views are difficult to summarise in brief compass, but essentially he felt that the common person was no longer able to make intelligent decisions on specific courses of action relating to public policy, as had been possible in earlier stages of democracy in the United States, when political, social, and economic decisions were less complex. Lippmann did not renounce democracy or even majority rule; rather, he believed that a democratic elite of administrators and technicians should have a relatively free hand in actual decision-making, with the public to act as a kind of umpire over them. There is no evidence that Lovecraft read Lippmann: I have found only one mention of him in letters, and that is an admission of his ignorance of Lippmann's work. In any case, Lovecraft's distrust of democracy had already emerged much earlier, first perhaps from readings in Nietzsche, and then by plain observation.

And yet, Lovecraft's elitism on this point (if indeed it is such), although it might now be associated with various conservative thinkers with whom he would otherwise have little in common, has recently been echoed by the unimpeachably liberal Arthur Schlesinger, Jr, who in a discussion of George F. Kennan writes:

> More nonsense has been uttered in this country over the perils of elitism than on almost any other subject. All government known to history has been government by minorities, and it is in the interests of everyone, most especially the poor and powerless, to have the governing minority composed of able, intelligent, responsive, and decent persons with a large view of the general welfare. There is a vast difference between an elite of conscience and an elite of privilege—the difference that Thomas Jefferson drew between the "natural aristocracy" founded on "virtue and talents" and the "artificial aristocracy founded on wealth and birth,"

adding that the natural aristocracy is "the most precious gift of nature" for the government of society.[21]

It is unfortunate that Lovecraft occasionally used the term fascism to denote this conception; it does not help much that he says on one occasion, "Do not judge the sort of fascism I advocate by any form now existing."[22] Lovecraft never actually renounced Mussolini, but his support of him in the 1930s does not seem quite as ardent as it was when Mussolini first rose to power in 1922. The problem was, however, that by the 1930s the term fascism connoted not only Mussolini but various English and American extremists with whom Lovecraft had no intention of aligning himself. It is true that he rather discouragingly says on one occasion that "I have my eye on Sir Oswald Moseley [sic] & his element of British fascists,"[23] since Mosley—who had founded the British Union of Fascists in 1932—quickly revealed himself to be an anti-Semite and pro-Hitlerian who spent much of World War II in a British prison for subversive activities. But the American fascists of the middle to late thirties were a very different proposition, and Lovecraft regarded them on the whole not so much as dangerous radicals as mere buffoons who could do little harm to the political fabric. They were not by any means a coordinated group, but even individually they represented various threats to the government with which both the administration and political thinkers (even armchair ones like Lovecraft) had to come to terms.

The first was the redoubtable Senator Huey P. Long of Louisiana. Elected governor in 1928, Long quickly achieved popularity by appealing for a radical redistribution of wealth. Then, in 1934, as a senator he formed the Share Our Wealth Society in an attempt to put his theories into practice. If it be thought that Long's political vision was actually similar to Lovecraft's in its union of economic socialism and political fascism, it should be made very clear that Long was not a socialist by any means—he did not believe in collectivism but instead yearned nostalgically for a small-town America in which everyone would be an individualistic small business person—and his fascism was of an utterly ruthless sort that rode roughshod over his opponents and in the end led to his being shot on September 8, 1935, and his death two days later.

Then there was the Reverend Charles E. Coughlin, who in his weekly radio programme ("The Golden Hour of the Little Flower") had, since 1930, fulminated against both communism and capitalism, attacking bankers specifically. In late 1934 he conceived of a wealth distribution scheme by forming the National Union for Social Justice.

Lovecraft took frequent note of Long and Coughlin, and in the end he finally repudiated them—not for their economic policies (with which he was more in agreement than otherwise), but for their genuinely fascistic political tactics. But he never regarded them as serious threats. He wrote airily in early 1937 that "I doubt whether the growing Catholic-fascist movement will make much headway in Amer-ica"[24] (an explicit reference to Coughlin) and later remarked, in regard to a broad group of pro-Nazi organisations in America: "Granting the scant possibility of a Franco-like revolt of the Hoovers and Mellons and polite bankers, and conceding that—despite Coughlinism, the Black Legion, the Silver Shirts, and the K.K.K.—the soil of America is hardly very fertile for any variant of Nazism, it seems likely that the day of free and easy plutocracy in the United States is over."[25] He might have been less sanguine had he seen how Coughlin—who was already becoming increasingly anti-Semitic by 1936—sloughed off his social justice pretence in 1938 and came out forthrightly as a pro-Nazi, attracting millions in the process.

Lovecraft knew that Roosevelt was trying to steer a middle course between both right- and left-wing extremism; and on the whole he approved that course. Just after the 1932 election he remarked that a vote for the Socialist Norman Thomas "would have been simply thrown away."[26] And yet, he supported Upton Sinclair's radical senatorial campaign in 1934 and said that he would vote for Sinclair if he were a Californian.[27] He said nothing, though, about the vicious attacks on Sinclair by Re-publicans that led to his defeat. Nevertheless, although he yearned for Roosevelt to progress still farther and faster with reform, it quickly became obvious to him that the New Deal was the only series of measures that had any real hope of actually passing, given the violent resistance on both sides of the political spectrum:

> That is why we must go slowly and cautiously, lending our support to *anything headed in the right direction which has a real chance of adoption,* even if it does not suit us as exactly as some other plan which has less chance of adoption. . . . The New Deal, in spite of its present internal inconsistencies and frankly experi-mental phases, probably represents as great a step in the right direction as could *now* command any chance of support . . .[28]

He referred to Coughlin, Sinclair, and Long as "salutary irritants"[29] who would help push Roosevelt more to the left (something that in fact happened following the midterm elections of 1934, which gave Congress a more liberal slant). But in early 1935 he was announcing that he wanted something "considerably to the left of the New Deal,"[30] although he did not think it was practicable; and by the summer of 1936 he expressed a naive irritation that the administration was "too subservient to capitalism"[31]—as if Roosevelt had any intention of ushering in real socialism (even of a liberal, non-Marxist variety) instead of merely shoring up capitalism!

The death-knell of capitalism was indeed being rung by many political think-ers of the day, as was entirely natural in the wake of the depression, capitalism's most signal disaster. John Dewey's thunderous declaration—"Capitalism must be destroyed"—is prototypical.[32] Some of Lovecraft's younger colleagues—Frank Long, R. H. Barlow, Kenneth Sterling—were wholeheartedly espousing communism, to the point that at the very end of his life Lovecraft expostulated in mock horror, "Damme, but are all you kids going bolshevik on grandpa?"[33]

And yet, as time went on Lovecraft increasingly lost patience with the social and political conservatism of the middle-class milieu in which he found himself. He came to understand the *temperament* that led fiery youths like Long and Barlow to communism without being himself entirely inclined in that direction. Lovecraft was of course well aware that Providence was a bastion of Republicanism; by the time the election of 1936 he claimed to have nearly a family feud on his hands, as Annie Gamwell and her friends remained firmly opposed to Roosevelt, leading Lovecraft to explode:

> The more I observe the abysmal, inspissated *ignorance* of the bulk of allegedly cultivated people—folks who think a lot of themselves and their position, and who include a vast quota of university graduates—the more I believe that something is radically wrong with conventional education and tradition. These pompous, self-complacent "best people" with their blind spots, delusions, prejudices, and callousness—poor devils who have no conception of their orientation to human history and the cosmos—are the victims of some ingrained fallacy regarding the development and direction of cerebral energy. They don't lack brains, but have never been taught how to get the full benefit of what they have.[34]

Turning specifically to politics:

> As for the Republicans—how can one regard seriously a frightened, greedy, nostalgic huddle of tradesmen and lucky idlers who shut their eyes to history and science, steel their emotions against decent human sympathy, cling to sordid and provincial ideals exalting sheer acquisitiveness and condoning artificial hardship for the non-materially-shrewd, dwell smugly and sentimentally in a distorted dream-cosmos of outmoded phrases and principles and attitudes based on the bygone agricultural-handicraft world, and revel in (consciously or unconsciously) mendacious assumptions (such as the notion that *real liberty* is synonymous with the single detail of *unrestricted economic license,* or that a rational planning of resource-distribution would contravene some vague and mystical "American heritage" . . .) utterly contrary to fact and without the slightest foundation in human experience? Intellectually, the Republican idea deserves the tolerance and respect one gives to the dead.[35]

How little things have changed.

When the election actually occurred—with another landslide for Roosevelt against the hapless Alf Landon and a third-party candidate, William Lemke, a stooge of Coughlin and Francis E. Townsend, the proponent of old age pensions—Lovecraft could not help gloating:

> It amuses me to see the woebegone state of the staid reactionary reliques with whom I am surrounded. Around election-time I came damn near having a family

feud on my hands! Poor old ostriches. Trembling for the republic's safety, they actually thought their beloved Lemke or Langston or Langham (or whatever his name was) had a chance! However, the alert university element was not so blind—indeed, one of the professors said just before the election that his idea of a bum sport was a man who would actually *take* one of the pro-Lansdowne (or whatever his name was) bets offered by the white-moustached constitution-savers of the Hope Club easy-chairs. Well—even the most stubborn must some day learn that the tide of social evolution can't be checked for ever. King Canute & the waves![36]

Lovecraft's last few months were perhaps spent in satisfaction, with the thought that Roosevelt could now continue his reforms and achieve a genuine moderate socialist state; it must have been a comforting thought as he lay dying.

What Lovecraft was seeking, in the totality of his speculations on this subject, was the *economic and political reform* that was so cryingly needed, but also *cultural continuity.* He saw no conflict in this, since he wholly rejected the Marxist notion that culture is an inextricable product of socioeconomic forces, and that the alteration of the one inevitably entails the alteration of the other. In "Some Repetitions on the Times" he could not speak with sufficient loathing about the horrors of the Russian revolution and urges, a little frantically, that it is "worth going to any length to escape" a duplication of its effects in America:

> What the Soviets have done is to ensure a meagre livelihood to the least competent classes by destroying the whole background of tradition which made life endurable for persons of a higher degree of imagination and richer store of cultivation. It is their claim that they could not have guaranteed security to the humble without this wholesale destruction of accustomed ideas, but we may easily see that this is but a thin veil for a purely theoretical fanaticism bearing all the earmarks of a new religion—a fetichistic cult woven around the under-man's notion of trans-valuated social values and around a fantastically literal application and extension of the groping theories and idealistic extravagances of the late Karl Marx.

This may sound self-serving—Lovecraft wants the cultural tokens of his civilisation to be preserved even with fairly radical political and economic reforms—but then, his economic suggestions were, at least on paper, capable of implementation without serious disturbance of the cultural fabric.

Nevertheless, toward the very end of his life Lovecraft did indeed come to see the need for social and economic justice beyond any mere worry of a violent overthrow by the dispossessed. Capitalism was the implacable enemy, and it must go. The whole economic structure must be changed: "I am likewise no friend of aimless idleness—but I do not see why a savage and feverish scramble for bare necessities, *made artificially hard after machinery has given us the means of easier production,* is necessarily superior to a reasonable amount of sensible work plus an intelligently outlined programme of cultural development."[37] Here again Lovecraft was coming to terms with technology—and, now, realising that it can be beneficial as well as deleterious. The machine can be the liberating friend of mankind, and it can allow society to end poverty and physical hardship *instantly* through a rational redistribution of resources; but old-time capitalism still rules the minds of business and government leaders alike. Lovecraft, finally abandoning his worries about a revolution of "under-men," came to regard the whole issue of full employment as a simple matter of human dignity:

> I agree that most of the motive force behind any contemplated change in the economic order will necessarily come from the persons who have benefited least by the existing order; but I do not see why that fact makes it necessary to wage the struggle otherwise than as *a fight to guarantee a place for everybody* in the social fabric. The just demand of the citizen is that society assign him a place in its complex mechanism whereby he will have equal chances for education at the start, and a guarantee of just rewards for such services as he is able to render (or a proper pension if his services cannot be used) later on.[38]

But the forces of reaction were relentless:

> The greatest peril to civilised progress—aside from an annihilative war—is some kind of basically reactionary system with enough grudging concessions to the dispossessed to make it *really work after a fashion,* and thus with the capacity to postpone indefinitely the demand of the masses for their real rights—educational, social, and economic—as human beings in a world where the great resources should be cornered by none. . . . Unsupervised capitalism is through. But various Nazi and fascist compromises can be cooked up to save the plutocrats most of their spoils while lulling the growing army of the unpropertied with either a petty programme of *panem et circenses,* or else a system of artificially created and distributed jobs at starvation wages on the C.C.C. or W.P.A. idea. A regime of that sort, spiced with the right brand of hysterical flag-waving, sloganeering, and verbal constitution-saving, might conceivably be as stable and popular as Hitlerism—and that is what the younger and more astute babbitts of the Republican party are quietly and insidiously working toward.[39]

It is as if Lovecraft had a crystal ball and saw Ronald Reagan in it.

As the 1930s advanced Lovecraft became more and more concerned not only with the problems of economics and government but with the place of art in modern society. I have already shown how the notion of civilisation was the central guiding principle behind all his shifts in political allegiance; and as he matured he became convinced that art could not retreat unthinkingly into the past but must—as he himself had done on an intellectual level—come to some sort of terms with the machine age if it were to survive and remain a living force in society. This created an immediate problem, for as early as 1927 Lovecraft had concluded: "The future civilisation of mechanical invention, urban concentration, and scientific standardisation of life and thought is a monstrous and artificial thing which can never find embodiment either in art or in religion. Even now we find art and religion completely divorced from life and subsisting on retrospection and reminiscence as its vital material."[40] If the machine age is inherently unsuited for artistic expression, what is one to do? Lovecraft's answer to this was a little curious, but entirely in consonance with his broadly conservative outlook. We need not rehearse his antipathy to what he considered such freakish artistic tendencies as imagism, stream-of-consciousness, or the recondite allusiveness of Eliot's *Waste Land,* which were all, to his mind, symptoms of the general decline of this phase of Western culture. Avant-garde movements in painting and architecture similarly met with his disapproval. Lovecraft's solution— spelled out in the essay "Heritage or Modernism: Common Sense in Art Forms," written in late 1934—was a *conscious* antiquarianism:

> When a given age has no new *natural* impulse toward change, is it not better to continue building on the established forms than to concoct grotesque and meaningless novelties out of thin academic theory?
>
> Indeed, under certain conditions is not a policy of frank and virile antiquarianism—a healthy, vigorous revival of old forms still justified by their relation to life—infinitely sounder than a feverish mania for the destruction of familiar things and the laboured, freakish, uninspired search for strange shapes which nobody wants and which really mean nothing?

This too is conveniently self-serving, but Lovecraft is acute in puncturing the pompous theorisings of artists and architects who were resolutely dictating the spirit of the age:

> If the moderns were *truly* scientific, they would realise that their own attitude of *self-conscious theory* removes them absolutely from all kinship with the creators of genuine artistic advances. Real art must be, above all else, *unconscious and spontaneous*—and this is precisely what modern functionalism is *not.* No age was ever truly "expressed" by theorists who sat down and deliberately mapped out a technique for "expressing" it.

The real issue Lovecraft was facing was how to steer a middle course between "high" culture, which in its radicalism was consciously being addressed to an increasingly small coterie of devotees, and "popular" culture—notably the pulps— which was adhering to false, superficial, and outmoded standards through the inevitable moral conservatism such forms of culture have always displayed. This may be the primary reason for Lovecraft's lack of commercial success in his lifetime: his work was not conventional enough for the pulps but not daring enough (or daring enough in the right way) for the modernists. Lovecraft correctly recognised that capitalism and democracy gave rise to this split in the nineteenth century:

> Bourgeois capitalism gave artistic excellence and sincerity a death-blow by en-
> throning cheap *amusement-value* at the expense of that *intrinsic excellence* which
> only cultivated, non-acquisitive persons of assumed position can enjoy. The de-
> terminant market for written . . . and other heretofore aesthetic material ceased to
> be a small circle of truly educated persons, but became a substantially larger . . .
> circle of mixed origin numerically dominated by crude, half-educated clods whose
> systematically perverted ideals . . . prevented them from ever achieving the tastes
> and perspectives of the gentlefolk whose dress and speech and external manners
> they so assiduously mimicked. This herd of acquisitive boors brought up from the
> shop and the counting-house a complete set of artificial attitudes, oversimplifica-
> tions, and mawkish sentimentalities which no sincere art or literature could grat-
> ify—and they so outnumbered the remaining educated gentlefolk that most of the
> purveying agencies became at once reoriented to them. Literature and art lost most
> of their market; and writing, painting, drama, etc. became engulfed more and
> more in the domain of *amusement enterprises.*[41]

The principal foe, again, is capitalism, in that it inculcates values that are actively
hostile to artistic creation:

> . . . in the past did capitalism award its highest benefits to such admittedly superior
> persons as Poe, Spinoza, Baudelaire, Shakespeare, Keats, and so on? Or is it just
> possible that the *real* beneficiaries of capitalism are *not* the truly superior, but
> merely *those who choose to devote their superiority to the single process of per-
> sonal acquisition rather than to social service or to creative intellectual or aesthetic
> effort* . . . those, and the lucky parasites who share or inherit the fruits of their nar-
> rowly canalised superiority?[42]

America, of course, is especially bad in that the nineteenth century brought to the
fore a psychology that vaunted money- or possession-grubbing as the chief gauge
of human worth. This is something Lovecraft had always repudiated, and his new
views on economics only emphasised his sentiments:

> . . . I always despised the bourgeois use of *acquisitive power* as a measure of hu-
> man character. I have never believed that the securing of material resources ought
> to form the central interest of human life—but have instead maintained that *per-
> sonality* is an independent flowering of the intellect and emotions wholly apart
> from the struggle for existence. . . .
> . . . Now we live in an age of easy abundance which makes possible the fulfil-
> ment of all moderate human wants through a relatively slight amount of labour.
> What shall be the result? Shall we still make resources *prohibitively hard to get*
> when there is really a plethora of them? . . . If "stamina" and "Americanism" de-
> mand a state of constant anxiety and threatened starvation on the part of every or-
> dinary citizen, then they're not worth having![43]

But what then is to be done? Even if economic reform is effected, how does one change a society's *attitude* in regard to the relative value of money as opposed to the development of personality? The solution was—again on paper—simple: education. The shorter working hours proposed in Lovecraft's economic scheme would allow for a radically increased leisure time for all citizens, which could be utilised profitably in education and aesthetic appreciation. As he states in "Some Repetitions on the Times": "Education . . . will require amplification in order to meet the needs of a radically increased leisure among all classes of society. It is probable that the number of persons possessing a sound general culture will be greatly increased, with correspondingly good results to the civilisation." This was a common proposal—or dream—among the more idealistic social reformers and intellectuals. Did Lovecraft really fancy that such a Utopia of a broadly educated populace that was willing or able to enjoy the aesthetic fruits of civilisation would actually come about? It certainly seems so; and yet, we cannot hold Lovecraft responsible for failing to predict either the spectacular recrudescence of capitalism in the generations following his own or the equally spectacular collapse of education that has produced a mass audience whose highest aesthetic experiences are pornography, television miniseries, and sporting events.

It is an open question whether Lovecraft's entire economic, political, and cultural system—moderate socialism; restriction of the vote; increased education and aesthetic appreciation—is inherently unworkable (perhaps people are simply not good enough—not sufficiently intelligent, unselfish, and culturally astute—to function in such a society) or whether it may be effected if the people and government of the United States ever make a concerted effort to head in that direction. The prospects at the moment certainly do not look good: a fair number of his economic proposals (Social Security, unemployment insurance, fair labour and consumer laws) are now well established, but his political and cultural goals are as far from realisation as ever. Needless to say, a fairly broad segment of the population does not even acknowledge the validity or propriety of Lovecraft's recommendations, so is not likely to work toward bringing them about.

The interesting thing about these speculations of the 1930s is that they gradually enter into his fiction as well as his letters and essays. We have seen that "The Mound" (1929–30) contains searching parallels between the political and cultural state of the underground mound denizens and Western civilisation; and in *At the Mountains of Madness* (1931) there is a fleeting mention that the government of the Old Ones was probably socialistic. These tentative political discussions reach their culmination with "The Shadow out of Time."

The Great Race is a true utopia, and in his description of its political and economic framework Lovecraft is manifestly offering his view as to the future of mankind:

The Great Race seemed to form a single, loosely knit nation or league, with major institutions in common, though there were four definite divisions. The political and economic system of each unit was a sort of fascistic socialism, with major resources rationally distributed, and power delegated to a small governing board elected by the votes of all able to pass certain educational and psychological tests. . . .

Industry, highly mechanised, demanded but little time from each citizen; and the abundant leisure was filled with intellectual and aesthetic activities of various sorts.

This and other passages can be seen as virtually identical to those in Lovecraft's later letters on the subject and with "Some Repetitions on the Times." The note about "highly mechanised" industry is important in showing that Lovecraft has at last—as he had not done when he wrote "The Mound" (1929–30) and even *At the Mountains of Madness*—fully accepted mechanisation as an ineradicable aspect of modern society, and has devised a social system that will accommodate it.

Lovecraft's specific responses to contemporary mainstream literature are certainly worth studying in detail. Around 1922 he made a concerted effort (perhaps egged on by Frank Belknap Long and other younger associates) to keep up on the fashionable highbrow literature of the day, although we have seen that he admitted never actually having read Joyce's *Ulysses*. By the 1930s Lovecraft grudgingly felt that perhaps another refresher course was necessary, but he was rather less enthusiastic than before—it was less important to him to be literarily contemporary (even though he always remained scientifically and philosophically contemporary), since he was generally out of sympathy with the now entrenched trend of modernism. In 1930 he called Dreiser "*the* novelist of America,"[44] even though by this time Dreiser was little more than an elder statesman with his best work decades behind him (his 1925 behemoth, *An American Tragedy,* received generally mixed reviews, even from such devoted advocates as H. L. Mencken). Sinclair Lewis—whose *Babbitt* and *Main Street* he presumably read, if one gauges by the frequency with which those terms are peppered through his writings in his *épater le bourgeois* period—he considered more a social theorist or even propagandist than a creative artist, although he felt that Lewis's receiving the Nobel Prize in 1930 was "not as bad as it might be."[45] He mentioned F. Scott Fitzgerald, the laureate of the Jazz Age, only twice in all the correspondence I have seen, and in a manner that is both disparaging and suggestive that he never actually read Fitzgerald.[46] He did not run a temperature over Willa Cather, although he read her historical novel *Shadows on the Rock* (1931) for its Quebec setting.[47] Aside from "A Rose for Emily," it does not seem as if Lovecraft read much of William Faulkner, although he wanted to read more. Gertrude Stein he understandably dismissed: "I must admit that I've never read any book of hers, since scattered fragments in periodicals discouraged any interest I might otherwise have acquired."[48] Hemingway came in for random discussion, but only to be scorned for the "machine-gun fire" of his prose; but Lovecraft added cogently:

> I refuse to be taken in by the goddam bunk of this aera just as totally as I refused to fall for the pompous, polite bull of Victorianism—and one of the chief fallacies of the present is that smoothness, even when involving no sacrifice of directness, is a defect. The best prose is vigorous, direct, unadorn'd, and closely related (as is the best verse) to the language of actual discourse; but it has its natural rhythms and smoothness just as good oral speech has. There has never been any prose as good as that of the early eighteenth century, and anyone who thinks he can improve upon Swift, Steele, and Addison is a blockhead.[49]

This is certainly a good attack, in principle, on the skeletonic prose of Hemingway or Sherwood Anderson; but whether Lovecraft himself followed some of its recommendations is more open to question. Even his later prose can hardly be called "unadorn'd"; and although some of his friends remarked that his writing (in correspondence, at least) did in fact duplicate his speech, this is only because Lovecraft was generally given to formality in both writing and discourse.

Lovecraft was relatively conservative on British novelists, choosing those writers who had already well established themselves in the early part of the century. He defended Galsworthy against J. Vernon Shea's iconoclastic attack by remarking: "Galsworthy, I think, will survive. His style at times halts one, but the substance is there."[50] The day before he discovered the robbery of his Brooklyn flat in 1925, he was reading Joseph Conrad's *Lord Jim* and came away tremendously impressed. He admitted having previously read "only the shorter and more minor productions" of the author (among which one hopes *Heart of Darkness* might have been included, although Lovecraft never mentions it), but now he declares:

> Conrad is at heart supremely a poet, and though his narration is often very heavy and involved, he displays an infinitely potent command of the soul of men and things, reflecting the tides of affairs in an unrivalled procession of graphic pictures which burn their imagery indelibly upon the mind. . . . No other artist I have yet encountered has so keen an appreciation of the essential *solitude* of the high-grade personality—that solitude whose projected overtones form the mental world of each sensitively organised individual . . .[51]

This may be a trifle self-serving, too, since Lovecraft axiomatically regarded himself as one of those solitary, high-grade personalities (as, indeed, he was). Hardy he considered overrated and sentimental—a rather surprising judgment (made, apparently, on the basis of *Tess of the d'Urbervilles* and *Jude the Obscure*) on a writer whose bleakness of vision Lovecraft might have been expected to appreciate. D. H. Lawrence, too, he not surprisingly thought overrated: "his fame was fortuitously boosted by the fact that he was a biassed neurotic in an age generally permeated by the same neurosis."[52] This was not an uncommon accusation in Lovecraft's day, and indeed there is some validity in it. Interestingly enough, Lovecraft once declared, "Writers I'd call morbid are D. H. Lawrence & James Joyce, Huysmans & Baudelaire";[53] but this did not stop him from relishing the latter two as powerful weird writers. Aldous Huxley's fiction did not appeal to him, but he did charitably refer to him as an "arresting social thinker."[54] He admitted that he had not read *Brave New World* (1932),[55] and it is unlikely that he would have cared for it if he had, for (as he remarked in "Some Notes on Interplanetary Fiction") "Social and political satire [in science fiction] is always undesirable." I find no mention of Evelyn Waugh or Virginia Woolf anywhere in Lovecraft. He did, incredibly, admit to reading "extracts" of Joyce's *Anna Livia Plurabelle* (a short piece published separately in 1928 and eventually incorporated into *Finnegans Wake*) without much actual enjoyment, but he went on to say, a little surprisingly: "And yet there is no more powerful or penetrant writer living than Joyce when he is not pursuing his theory to these ultimate extremes."[56]

As it is, the chief contemporary novelist of the day, for Lovecraft, was neither American nor British but French—Marcel Proust. Although he never read more than the first two volumes in English (*Swann's Way* and *Within a Budding Grove*) of *Remembrance of Things Past,* he nevertheless doubted that "the 20th century has so far produced anything to eclipse the Proustian cycle as a whole."[57] Proust occupied the ideal middle ground between stodgy Victorianism and freakish modernism; and Lovecraft's fondness for Derleth's mainstream work rested in large part on his belief that it reflected that sense of delicate reminiscence which was Proust's own chief feature.

Lovecraft, indeed, repeatedly vaunted the entire French novelistic tradition as far superior to the English or American:

> The French are the real masters of that field—Balzac, Gautier, Flaubert, de Maupassant, Stendhal, Proust . . . Nobody can beat them unless it is in the 19th century Russians—Dostoievsky, Chekhov, Turgeniev—& they reflect a racial temper so unlike ours that we really have much difficulty in appraising them. On the whole, I believe that Balzac is the supreme novelist of western Europe.[58]

There is much truth to this, but part of Lovecraft's preference may have been his relative coolness for the eighteenth-century British novelists, who reflected so different a world from the polished British essayists and historians of the period on whom he doted, and his utter detestation of Dickens, whose sentimentality he abhorred and whom he even claimed did not draw character well: "Dickens never drew a real human being in all his career—just a pageant of abstractions, exaggerations, & general characters. Each 'character' is merely an abstraction of a single human instinct. Character—motivation—values—all false, artificial, & conventional."[59] Lovecraft would probably not be much impressed if one were to counter that Dickens wasn't aiming for "realism" as such, and that his characters are meant to be "larger than life." On one occasion Lovecraft could even give some moderate praise to writers he did not otherwise care for merely as a stick with which to beat Dickens over the head: "I certainly loathe sentimental hypocrites like Dickens and Trollope far more than honest portrayers and intelligent interpreters like Zola and Fielding and Smollett and Flaubert and Hemingway."[60]

Lovecraft could be pretty shrewd in assessing the real merits of the popularly acclaimed novels of his day. At a time when all the world (especially August Derleth) was vaunting Thornton Wilder's *Bridge of San Luis Rey* (1927) as a masterwork, Lovecraft, who read the novel several years after its publication, remarked more soberly: "That book is clever & striking, but undeniably artificial & in places even mawkish. It was absurdly overrated upon its appearance, & now seems to be receding into something more like its proper niche."[61] Even though the novel won the Pulitzer Prize, this judgment now seems sound. Sometimes there is a virtue in not being so "desperately contemporary," as Lovecraft once quoted Brown University President W. H. P. Faunce. And yet, he could waste five days reading Hervey Allen's enormous best-seller *Anthony Adverse*—solely, it appears, because of its portrayal of the late eighteenth century (and, perhaps, because of Lovecraft's admiration of Allen's landmark biography of Poe, *Israfel* [1926]). Lovecraft, of course, had no intention of keeping up with best-sellers or even with critically acclaimed recent works; not only was the inclination not there, but his very lean purse prohibited purchase of expensive new books of doubtful permanent value.

And yet, even if Lovecraft did not enjoy much of the actual prose work of his day, he had a healthy respect for the social realism that had become the characteristic style of the novels of the 1920s and 1930s. He expressed regret—sincerely, I think—at his own inability to write this sort of realism, because of his lack of wide experience in life and, perhaps more importantly, his inability (or disinclination) to invest the ordinary phenomena of life with the *importance* and *vitality* that a realistic writer must be able to do:

> When I say that I can write nothing but weird fiction, I am not trying to exalt that medium but am merely confessing my own weakness. The reason I can't write other kinds is not that I don't value & respect them, but merely that my slender set of endowments does not enable me to extract a compellingly acute personal sense of interest & drama from the natural phenomena of life. I know that these natural phenomena are more important & significant than the special & tenuous moods which so absorb me, & that an art based on them is greater than any which fantasy could evoke—but I'm simply not big enough to react to them in the sensitive way necessary for artistic response & literary use. God in heaven! I'd certainly be glad enough to be a Shakespeare or Balzac or Turgeniev *if I could!* . . . I respect realism more than any other form of art—but must reluctantly concede that, through my own limitations, it does not form a medium which I can adequately use.[62]

There is nothing new here, but it leads to two celebrated and resounding utterances:

> Time, space, and natural law hold for me suggestions of intolerable bondage, and I can form no picture of emotional satisfaction which does not involve their defeat—especially the defeat of time, so that one may merge oneself with the whole historic stream and be wholly emancipated from the transient and the ephemeral.[63]

> There is no field other than the weird in which I have any aptitude or inclination for fictional composition. Life has never interested me so much as the escape from life.[64]

That last utterance in particular is in great danger of misinterpretation, since one might easily conclude from it—if one knew nothing else about its author—that Lovecraft was an escapist who had no active interest in the world. It should by now be sufficiently obvious that this is manifestly false: even if his late and consuming interest in the problems of society, economics, and government were not evidence enough, then the intense pleasure he took at the very real sites he witnessed on his far-flung travels emphatically proves that Lovecraft was one for whom the real world existed. It is simply that the mundane activities of human beings were not intrinsically interesting to him (recall *In Defence of Dagon:* "Man's relations to man do not captivate my fancy"), and that he required a literature that might allow for a sort of imaginative overlay upon the events of the real world. Lovecraft wanted to see *beyond* or *through* reality—or, more specifically, *behind* it, temporally and imaginatively. And yet, his own most characteristic work is indeed realism except where the supernatural enters.

Lovecraft's views on contemporary poetry are a little mixed. Although he flayed T. S. Eliot's *Waste Land* in 1923, he grudgingly went to see Eliot give a reading of some of his poetry in Providence in February 1933. He reported that the reading was "interesting if not quite explicable."[65] But regarding poetry as a whole, Lovecraft came to a perhaps surprising conclusion: ". . . *verse* is spectacularly and paradoxically *improving;* so that I do not know any age since that of Elizabeth in which poets have enjoy'd a better medium of expression."[66] I think, though, that the remark needs interpretation and contextualisation. Lovecraft was contrasting the present age of poetry in comparison with what he regarded as the hollowness and insincerity of his favourite whipping-boy, late Victorianism; and he did not come out and say that there actually *were* as many great poets in his day as in that of Elizabeth, merely that there was the *possibility* of greatness. The above remark is followed by this: "One can but wish that a race of major bards surviv'd to take advantage of the post-Victorian rise in taste and fastidiousness." In other words, poets like Tennyson and Longfellow would have had the potential to be authentically great if they had lived longer and shed the crippling affections—both in terms of style (inversions, investing of spurious glamour upon certain words and conceptions) and aesthetic orientation (sentimentality, hypocrisy, excessive prudishness)—that doomed their work to flawed greatness at best and mediocrity at worst. As it was, Lovecraft thought that Yeats was "probably the greatest living poet,"[67] and the only other poet whom he placed even remotely in his class was, interestingly, Archibald MacLeish, whom he heard lecture in Providence in January 1935 and whom he said "comes about as near to a major poet as this hemisphere can now boast."[68] MacLeish was, in spite of being influenced by Eliot and Pound, relatively conservative, and even his free verse is rhythmical, metaphorical, and full of compact imagery—just the sort of thing Lovecraft appreciated. Lovecraft seemed genuinely fond of MacLeish's long narrative poem, *Conquistador* (1932).

It might be thought that one could accurately gauge Lovecraft's opinion of modern literature by examining certain passages in the document known as "Suggestions for a Reading Guide"—the final chapter of Lovecraft's revision of Renshaw's *Well Bred Speech* (1936), which was excised from the published version. But in fact it is abundantly clear that he has listed in this bulky article a good many works of literature that he has not read, and on whose merits he is relying only on the word of others, or by general reputation. Hence, among British novelists he lists Galsworthy, Conrad, Bennett, Lawrence, Maugham, Wells, Huxley, and some others; among British poets, Masefield, Housman, Brooke, de la Mare, Bridges, and T. S. Eliot. The Irish Yeats he again calls "the greatest living poet." Among American novelists, we find Norris, Dreiser, Wharton, Cather, Lewis, Cabell, Hemingway, Hecht, Faulkner, and Wolfe; among American poets, Frost, Masters, Sandburg, Millay, and MacLeish. But consultation of his letters shows that, while he had indeed read a good many of these, others he either was planning to read but apparently never did or knew merely by reputation. In hindsight this list may perhaps seem, even by the standards of 1936, a little old-fashioned; but Lovecraft felt that in an elementary treatise of this kind it was better to be conservative and list those authors who had genuinely stood the test of time. He opens his discussion of twentieth-century literature in English with the caveat: "Crossing into the present century, we are confronted by a flood of books and authors whose relative merits are still undetermined . . ."

Lovecraft also fleetingly turned his attention to another medium—film—but again his judgment was mixed. I have shown that he enthusiastically watched the early films of Chaplin, Douglas Fairbanks, and others in the teens; but as the twenties advanced he lost interest, seeing films only when Sonia or Frank Long or others dragged him to them. Although talkies were introduced in 1927, Lovecraft took no notice of them until 1930: "Despite the recent improvement in quality in some films—due to the new talking device—the majority are as inane & insipid as before . . ."[69] I would not care to dispute Lovecraft's judgment on the films he actually saw at this time.

But it appears that Lovecraft was harbouring at least one misconception or prejudice that hampered his appreciation of film as an independent aesthetic mode. Of course, many of the films of his day—even those now regarded by misplaced nostalgia as "classic"—were extraordinarily crude and technologically backward; and Frank Long did not help matters any by taking Lovecraft to an endless series of vapid musicals or romantic comedies on the latter's successive trips to New York. But Lovecraft seemed to feel that films based on literary works should be rigidly faithful to those works, and any departure from the text should be regarded as an inherent flaw.

This prejudice comes into play specifically in regard to Lovecraft's evaluation of horror films. In one choice passage he roundly abuses one relatively obscure work and two "classics":

> "The Bat" made me drowse back in the early 1920's—and last year an alleged "Frankenstein" on the screen *would* have made me drowse had not a posthumous sympathy for poor Mrs. Shelley made me see red instead. Ugh! And the screen "Dracula" in 1931—I saw the beginning of that in Miami, Fla.—but couldn't bear to watch it drag to its full term of dreariness, hence walked out into the fragrant tropic moonlight![70]

The Bat (in spite of Lovecraft's mention of "early 1920's") must be the silent film of 1926, and is really more of a mystery than a horror film (it is an adaptation of Mary Roberts Rinehart's best-selling mystery novel *The Circular Staircase*). Lovecraft elaborated upon his disapproval of *Frankenstein* to Barlow: "I saw the cinema of 'Frankenstein', & was tremendously disappointed because no attempt was made to follow the story." But Lovecraft went on to remark: "However, there have been many worse films—& many parts of this one are really quite dramatic when they are viewed independently & without comparison to the episodes of the original novel." But he concluded ruefully, "Generally speaking, the cinema always cheapens & degrades any literary material it gets hold of—especially anything in the least subtle or unusual."[71] I believe that last utterance still carries a good deal of truth.

Lovecraft expressed keen regret at not seeing *The Cabinet of Dr. Caligari* (1922) both on its initial release and on several revivals; it is quite likely that he would have enjoyed this startling work of German Expressionist cinema. He noted seeing *King Kong* (1933), but said only that it had "good mechanical effects."[72]

Lovecraft's abuse of *Dracula* came in the context of his refusal to grant Farnsworth Wright permission for radio dramatisation rights to "The Dreams in the Witch House." Although Lovecraft occasionally listened to the radio for news and liked to "fish" for distant channels for imaginative stimulation, he had little respect for radio shows as an art form, specifically horror programs.

> What the public consider "weirdness" in drama is rather pitiful or absurd— according to one's perspective. As a thorough soporific I recommend the average

popularly "horrible" play or cinema or radio dialogue. They are all the same—flat, hackneyed, synthetic, essentially atmosphereless jumbles of conventional shrieks and mutterings and superficial, mechanical situations.

One other medium Lovecraft sampled on a single occasion was television. On October 22, 1933, he wrote to Clark Ashton Smith: "Saw an interesting demonstration of *television* in a local department store yesterday. Flickers like the biograph pictures of 1898"[73] (a reference to the old film technique used from 1895 to 1913, chiefly by D. W. Griffith). Television was at this time still in its infancy. The first public demonstration of television had occurred in 1926, and General Electric had broadcast a dramatic presentation in 1928. RCA made tests in 1931 and the next year began experimental broadcasts; but mechanical difficulties caused blurry images, which no doubt prompted Lovecraft's comment. Although interest in television continued to increase throughout the decade, the first television sets for public use did not appear until 1939.

One other social issue—the place of sex and sexual orientation in life and literature—did, incredibly enough, on rare occasions come up for discussion in the last decade of Lovecraft's life. Lovecraft does indeed seem to be among the most asexual individuals in human history, and I do not think this was a mere façade: certainly his letter to Sonia prior to his marriage (published as "Lovecraft on Love") evokes only snickers today, and would probably have seemed extreme in its asceticism even in its own day; but there is every reason to believe that Lovecraft himself abided by its precepts, to the point that it surely became one (if only one) cause of his wife's refusal to continue the marriage.

We have also seen that Lovecraft exhibited quick prejudice against homosexuals when he met one in Cleveland in 1922. By 1927 his views had changed little; in a discussion with Derleth about Oscar Wilde (who, let us recall, was a clear source for Lovecraft's Decadent aesthetics), he unleashed this remarkable passage:

> As a man, however, Wilde admits of absolutely no defence. His character, notwithstanding a daintiness of manners which imposed an exterior shell of decorative decency and decorum, was as thoroughly rotten and contemptible as it is possible for a human character to be ... So thorough was his absence of that form of taste which we call a moral sense, that his derelictions comprised not only the greater and grosser offences, but all those petty dishonesties, shiftinesses, pusillanimities, and affected contemptibilities and cowardices which mark the mere "cad" or "bounder" as well as the actual "villain". It is an ironic circumstance that he who succeeded for a time in being the Prince of Dandies, was never in any basic sense what one likes to call a *gentleman*.[74]

(As an aside, let us turn to "The Shadow over Innsmouth," where we find Capt. Obed Marsh described as a "great dandy" of whom "people said he still wore the

frock-coated finery of the Edwardian age." Marsh too had introduced sexual irregularities into his community.)

Six years later Lovecraft intoned: "So far as the case of homosexualism goes, the
primary and vital objection against it is that it is naturally (physically and involuntar-
ily—not merely 'morally' or aesthetically) repugnant to the overwhelming bulk of
mankind . . ."[75] How Lovecraft arrived at this view is a mystery; but I suppose it was
common enough then—as it is now, sadly enough. No one need censure him for not
revealing a tolerance toward homosexuality that is still a relative rarity in our own
time. The point has been raised that many of Lovecraft's own colleagues were gay,
but he was surely either unaware of the fact (as in the case of Samuel Loveman) or
their homosexuality had presumably not yet made itself evident (as in the case of
R. H. Barlow). Lovecraft never commented on Hart Crane's homosexuality on the
few occasions he met him; but again, perhaps Crane made no overt demonstration of
it in Lovecraft's presence. He may have done so covertly, but Lovecraft was probably
so ignorant of the matter that he perhaps did not recognise it for what it was.

Nevertheless, on at least one occasion (late 1929) Lovecraft felt sufficiently informed on the subject of "normal" sexual relations to give friendly advice to one
even more ignorant than he: Woodburn Harris, a resident of rural Vermont who
evidently expressed some astoundingly naive and ignorant views on the subject of
female sexuality. Lovecraft scientifically avers:

> a) the desire is *more slowly excited* than in the male;
>
> b) but, once excited, it is *certainly just as strong*, and according to a large
> group of physiologists, much stronger.
>
> c) eroticism is *more of a motivating force* in the female than in the male—&
> there is a more persistent tendency to regard it sentimentally or cosmically.
>
> d) females, in the absence of the male, experience desires & frustrations just
> as intense as those of the isolated male—hence the savage sourness of old maids,
> the looseness of modern spinsters, & the infidelity or tendency thereto of wives left
> alone by their husbands for more than a week or two.[76]

There is a great deal more, but this is enough to suggest that Lovecraft has arrived
at his views jointly by a reading of various anthropological and psychological studies
of sex and by actual sexual experience with Sonia. In the course of this letter Lovecraft mentions such things as Havelock Ellis's *Little Essays in Love and Virtue*
(1922) and other contemporary authorities, whom he presumably read or at least (as
he frankly admits to doing in other matters) read representative reviews of their
work. There is also a long discussion about the "many & complex causes of change
in erotic standards" in his time—a largely neutral discussion in which such things as
"decline of illusions of religion & romantic love," "discovery of effective contracep-
tive methods," and "economic independence of women" are listed in sequence.

What is more, the question of the role of sex in literature found Lovecraft much more tolerant in his final decade. Of course, there is virtually no sex in the whole length and breath of his own work: heterosexual sex is rendered moot by the near-total absence of female characters, while homosexual sex, either between men or between women, would have been unthinkable given Lovecraft's views on the subject. This is what makes Lovecraft's comment in 1931—"I can't see any differ-ence in the work I did before marriage & that I did during a matrimonial period of some years"[77]—somewhat unhelpful. One must look very hard even to find hints of sex in the fiction: the undescribed "orgiastic licence" of the worshippers of Cthulhu in the Louisiana bayou, in "The Call of Cthulhu" is perhaps the only remotely ex-plicit reference, while the suggestions in "The Dunwich Horror" (Lavinia Whateley mating with Yog-Sothoth) and "The Shadow over Innsmouth" (the Innsmouth folk mating with the fish-frogs) are so oblique as almost to pass unno-ticed. Not a word is said of Edward and Asenath Derby's sexual relations in "The Thing on the Doorstep," perhaps because they are irrelevant to the story; but noth-ing is even said about the potential anomalies of sex reversal. Ephraim Waite takes over the body of his daughter Asenath: what are his sentiments when he becomes a woman, and especially when he marries Derby? If, as this story suggests, Lovecraft regards the mind or personality (rather than the body) as the essence of an individ-ual, is this marriage homosexual? What does Derby feel when his mind is thrown into the rotting body of his wife? If someone were to write a story on this basic premise today, it is unlikely that such issues would be avoided.

But, as I say, Lovecraft loosened up on the subject, at least where works by other writers were concerned. From one perspective, he felt the need to continue battling against censorship (as he had done in "The Omnipresent Philistine" [1924]), an issue that was coming to the fore as the 1920s—an age of sexual awak-ening, liberation, and perhaps decadence in both life and literature—progressed. His chief opponent, predictably, was the rigid theist Maurice W. Moe.

Lovecraft was addressing the issue of "that peculiar rage felt by persons over forty . . . concerning the free presentation of erotic matters in art and literature"[78] (he himself was seven months before forty when writing this), and—aside from predictably finding one more opportunity to trash the Victorian age ("the whole structure of Victorian art and thought and sexual morality was based upon a tragic sham")—specified seven different types or methods of sexual discussion in art:

1. Impersonal and serious descriptions of erotic scenes, relationships, motiva-tions, and consequences in real life.

2. Poetic—and other aesthetic—exaltations of erotic feelings.

3. Satirical glimpses of the erotic realities underlying non-erotic pretences and exteriors.

4. Artificial descriptions or symbols designed to stimulate erotic feelings, yet without a well-proportioned grounding in life or art.

5. Corporeal nudity in pictorial or sartorial art.

6. Erotic subject-matter operating through the medium of wit and humour.

7. Free discussion of philosophic and scientific issues involving sex.

He illustrated these seven methods with the following examples: 1) Theodore Dreiser, Ernest Hemingway, James Joyce; 2) Catullus, Walt Whitman; 3) James Branch Cabell, Voltaire, Henry Fielding; 4) Pierre Louys, the Marquis de Sade; 5) Giorgione, Praxiteles, or modern bathing-suit designers; 6) the dramatists of the Restoration; 7) Havelock Ellis, Auguste Forel, Richard von Kraft-Ebing, Freud. Of these, he declared that numbers 1, 2, 3, and 7 were not debatable at all—there was no question of censorship in these cases, and any imposition of it is barbarous and uncivilised; 5 was outside the present question because it was not, properly speaking, an erotic phenomenon at all ("No one but a ridiculous ignoramus or a warped Victorian sees anything erotic in the healthy human body . . . Only fools, jokers or perverts feel the urge to put overalls on Discobulus or tie an apron around the Venus of the Medici!"—the use of "perverts" here is exquisite); 6 was genu- inely debatable, but even here Lovecraft did not think that much of a case for ac- tual censorship could be made. Point 4 was the one on which he and Moe agreed; but Lovecraft turned the matter ingeniously to his advantage so as to enunciate his own moral and aesthetic foci: "These things are like Harold Bell Wright and Eddie Guest in other fields—pap and hokum, and emotional short-cuts and fakes." Lovecraft nevertheless said he would not actually censor a copy of Sacher- Masoch's *Venus in Furs* if he received one as a present, but would turn around and sell it for a young fortune!

The matter came up for discussion three years later in connexion with Donald Wandrei's unpublished mainstream novel *Invisible Sun,* a work that contained some fairly explicit depictions of sexual activity, although they were presented as part of an overall depiction of the general amoralism of modern youth. Here it was Derleth (who also read the work in manuscript) who found these passages objectionable. Although it is exactly in the course of this discussion that Lovecraft made his com- ment that homosexuality is "naturally" repugnant, he went on to say (not having yet read Wandrei's novel): "although I detest all sexual irregularities *in life itself,* as violations of a certain harmony which seems to me inseparable from high-grade liv- ing, I have a scientific approval of perfect realism in *the artistic delineation of life.*"[79] After reading the novel, Lovecraft generally defended Wandrei's use of sexual situa- tions (including a soliloquy in which a female character fantasises about sex and ends up masturbating to climax, and another scene where a college party leads to public sexual intercourse), remarking: "Concerning the element of repulsiveness—I repeat that this is only a logical outcome of that repudiation of natural & age-old aesthetic attitudes concerning certain departments of life which (though neither new nor moral) arrogates to itself the title of 'new morality' . . ."[80]

I do not wish to say a great deal about Lovecraft's later metaphysics or ethics, for they do not appear to have undergone much significant change since the later 1920s. One thing may be worth emphasising here—the remarkable if complex *unity* of nearly all phases of his thought. It is clear that Lovecraft had worked out an all-encompassing philosophical system in which each part logically (or at least psychologically) implied the other.

Beginning with metaphysics, Lovecraft espoused cosmicism in its broadest form: the universe, even if not theoretically infinite in space and time (Einstein's notion of curved space is noted), is still of such vastness that the human sphere assumes a role of utter negligibility when compared to the cosmos. Science also establishes the extreme unlikelihood of the immortality of the "soul" (whatever that may be), the existence of a deity, and nearly all other tenets espoused by the religions of the world. Ethically, this means that values are relative either to the individual or to the race, but that (and I have already displayed that this argument is fallacious and contradictory) there is one anchor of fixity for human beings in this cosmic flux—the cultural traditions in which each individual was raised. Aesthetically, the cosmicism/traditionalism dichotomy implies conservatism in art (repudiation of modernism, functionalism, etc.) and, in the realm of weird fiction, the suggestion of the simultaneously terrifying and imaginatively stimulating gulfs of space and time. Many of Lovecraft's other predilections—antiquarianism, gentlemanliness of comportment, even perhaps racialism (as an aspect of cultural traditionalism)—can be harmonised within this complex of beliefs.

How Lovecraft's late political and economic views harmonise with his general philosophy is perhaps a little harder to gauge. That there is no contradiction between Lovecraft's fervent, even compulsive interest in these matters in the last five years of his life and his general cosmicism—which purports to minimise human importance and human effort—is made clear by a single statement in 1929, even though the subject of discussion here is art: "Art, then, is really very important . . . though it abrogates its function and ceases to be art as soon as it becomes self-conscious, [or] puffed with illusions of *cosmic* significance, (as distinguished from local, human, emotional significance) . . ."[81] The distinction between cosmic and human significance is critical: we may not matter a whit to the cosmos, but we matter sufficiently to ourselves to fashion the fairest political and economic system that we can.

Now and then Lovecraft spoke more personally on his beliefs, desires, and reasons for living—still in a generally philosophical mode, but with no expectation of persuading anyone to adopt his views. One very poignant utterance was made to August Derleth in 1930:

> I am perfectly confident that I could never adequately convey to any other human being the precise reasons why I continue to refrain from suicide—the reasons, that

is, why I still find existence enough of a compensation to atone for its dominantly burthensome quality. These reasons are strongly linked with architecture, scenery, and lighting and atmospheric effects, and take the form of vague impressions of adventurous expectancy coupled with elusive memory—impressions that certain vistas, particularly those associated with sunsets, are avenues of approach to spheres or conditions of wholly undefined delights and freedoms which I have known in the past and have a slender possibility of knowing again in the future. Just what those delights and freedoms are, or even what they approximately resemble, I could not concretely imagine to save my life; save that they seem to concern some ethereal quality of indefinite expansion and mobility, and of a heightened perception which shall make all forms and combinations of beauty simultaneously visible to me, and realisable by me. I might add, though, that they invariably imply a total defeat of the laws of time, space, matter, and energy—or rather, an individual independence of these laws on my part, whereby I can sail through the varied universes of space-time as an invisible vapour might . . . upsetting none of them, yet superior to their limitations and local forms of material organisation. . . . Now this all sounds damn foolish to anybody else—and very justly so. There is no reason why it should sound anything except damn foolish to anyone who has not happened to receive precisely the same series of inclinations, impressions, and background-images which the purely fortuitous circumstances of my own especial life have chanced to give me.[82]

Much as I admire the logician in Lovecraft—the fierce foe of religious obscurantism, the rationalist and materialist who absorbed Einstein and retained a lifelong belief in the validity of scientific evidence—I think a passage like this, personal and even mystical in its way, gets closer to what Lovecraft was all about; for this is an honest and sincere exposure of his *imaginative life,* and—while there is nothing here that contradicts his general metaphysics and ethics—it humanises Lovecraft and shows that, beyond the cold rationalism of his intellect, he was a man whose emotions responded deeply to many of the varied phenomena of life. *Persons* may not have moved him—he may have genuinely loved no one in his life but his closest family members—but he felt intensely and profoundly many things that most of us pass over with scarcely a thought.

The opening sentence of this utterance—a reflection of his abiding acknowledgement of Schopenhauer's belief in the fundamental wretchedness of existence—may be of relevance in considering another series of statements that has caused a certain amount of controversy: his letters to Helen Sully.

L. Sprague de Camp has interpreted these statements as revealing a profound depression on Lovecraft's part in his later years; and, taken out of context—or perhaps without an awareness of their import—they could indeed be interpreted as such. Consider the following:

In actual fact, there are few total losses & never-was's which discourage & exasperate me more than the venerable E'ch-Pi-El. I know of few persons whose attainments fall more consistently short of their aspirations, or who in general have less to live for. Every aptitude which I wish I had, I lack. Everything which I value, I have either lost or am likely to lose. Within a decade, unless I can find some job paying at least $10.00 per week, I shall have to take the cyanide route through inability to keep around me the books, pictures, furniture, & other familiar objects which constitute my only remaining reason for keeping alive. . . . The reason I have been more "melancholy" than usual in the last few years is that I am coming to distrust more & more the value of the material I produce. Adverse criticism has of late vastly undermined my confidence in my literary powers. And so it goes. Decidedly, Grandpa is not one of those beaming old gentlemen who radiate cheer wherever they go![83]

This certainly sounds pretty bad, but—although there are perhaps no actual falsehoods in any of it—a consideration of its context, and of some passages I have omitted, may allow us to take a different view.

Reading the entirety of Lovecraft's letters to Sully (we do not have her side of the correspondence), it becomes readily apparent that Sully was a high-strung, hypersensitive woman who was experiencing a series of disappointments (among them unfortunate love affairs) and was looking for Lovecraft to lend her some fortitude and encouragement. Lovecraft makes frequent reference to her "recent sombre reflections" and "feeling of oppression,"[84] and—in the very letter in which the above extract is drawn—even quotes some phrases in Sully's letter in which she described herself as feeling "hopeless, useless, incompetent, and generally miserable" and Lovecraft as a "beautifully balanced, contented person." Lovecraft's tactic—which may or may not have been successful—was two-pronged: first, suggest that "happiness" as such was a relatively little-realised goal among human beings; and second, suggest that he was in a far worse position than herself, so that if *he* can be tolerably contented, so much more should she be.

As to the first point:

Of course, real *happiness* is only a rare & transient phenomenon; but when we cease to expect this extravagant extreme, we usually find a very tolerable fund of mild contentment at our disposal. True, people & landmarks vanish, & one grows old & out of the more glamorous possibilities & expectancies of life; but over-against these things there remains the fact that the world contains an almost inexhaustible store of objective beauty & potential interest & drama . . .[85]

Lovecraft goes on to say that the best way to gain this mild contentment is to abolish one's emotions, take an objective view of things, etc. etc.—things Sully probably did not especially want to hear and would probably have been unable or unwilling to carry out in any case. As her "sombre reflections" continued, Lovecraft felt that self-deprecation was the only option to make his correspondent feel better; hence the passage I quoted above. But here are some parts I did not quote:

Meanwhile, of course, I certainly *do* get a lot of pleasure from books, travel (when I *can* travel), philosophy, the arts, history, antiquarianism, scenery, the sciences, & so on . . . & from such poor attempts in the way of aesthetic creation (= fantastic fiction) as I can kid myself into thinking I can sometimes achieve. . . . I'm no pining & picturesque victim of melancholy's romantic ravages. I merely shrug my shoulders, recognise the inevitable, let the world march past, & vegetate along as painlessly as possible. I suppose I'm a damned sight better off than millions. There are dozens of things I can actually enjoy.

But the point is, that I'm probably *a thousand times worse off than you are* . . . The gist of my "sermon" is that if analysis & philosophy can make *me* tolerably resigned, it *certainly* ought to produce even better results with one not nearly so gravely handicapped.

And Lovecraft ends with the rousing peroration, "So—as a final homiletic word from garrulous & sententious old age—for Tsathoggua's sake cheer up!" Again, I am not clear how well Lovecraft succeeded in relieving Sully of her depression; but certainly the passages in his letters to her cannot be taken straightforwardly as evidence of any depression of his own. Very little of the rest of his correspondence of this period corroborates such an impression.

The one area of Lovecraft's thought that has—justifiably—aroused the greatest outrage among later commentators is his attitude on race. My contention is, however, both that Lovecraft has been criticised for the wrong reasons and that, even though he clearly espoused views that are illiberal, intolerant, or plain wrong scientifically, his racism is at least logically separable from the rest of his philosophical and even political thought.

Lovecraft retained to the end of his days a belief in the biological inferiority of blacks and also of Australian aborigines, although it is not clear why he singled out this latter group. Even the 9th edition of the *Encyclopaedia Britannica*—where he obtained most of the information on Australia for "The Shadow out of Time"—declared that the aborigines' "mental faculties, through probably inferior to those of the Polynesian copper-coloured race, are not contemptible. They have much acuteness of perception for the realations of individual objects . . . The grammatical structure of some North Australian languages has a considerable degree of refinement."[86] Nevertheless, the general thrust of the article could lead someone like Lovecraft to believe that the race is irremediably mired in savage primitivism.

In any event, Lovecraft advocated an absolutely rigid colour line against intermarriage between blacks and whites, so as to guard against "miscegenation." This view was by no means uncommon in the 1920s, and many leading American biologists and psychologists wrote forebodingly about the possibility that racial intermixture could lead to biological abnormalities.[87] Of course, laws against interracial marriage survived in this country until an embarrassingly recent time.

Lovecraft's views on the matter no doubt affected his judgment of the celebrated Scottsboro case. In March 1931 nine black youths between the ages of thirteen and twenty-one were charged with the rape of two white women while riding on a freight train near Scottsboro, Alabama. In two weeks the defendants were found guilty by an all-white jury and sentenced to the electric chair. Lovecraft made no mention of the case at this time. After the convictions, the Communist-backed International Labor Defense took up the case, and in November 1932 the U.S. Supreme Court ordered a new trial on the grounds that the defendants had not received adequate counsel. The trial began in March 1933. The first defendant was again sentenced to death, while the trial of the others was postponed indefinitely because of the furore that erupted. Two years later, on April 1, 1935, the U.S. Supreme Court reversed the conviction because blacks were systematically barred from the jury. In subsequent trials in 1936–37 five of the defendants were convicted and sentenced to long prison terms; the other four defendants were dismissed.

In May 1933 Lovecraft remarked to J. Vernon Shea, who clearly believed in the defendants' innocence: "Naturally nobody wants to kill the poor niggers unless they were guilty . . . but it doesn't seem to me that their innocence is at all likely. This is no low-grade lynching incident. A very fair court has passed on the case . . ."[88] Lovecraft charitably recommended mere life imprisonment for the suspects rather than execution, so that any "mistake" in their conviction could be rectified. In February 1934 Lovecraft, continuing to argue over the case with Shea, made the remarkable claim: "It doesn't seem natural to me that well-disposed men would deliberately condemn even niggers to death if they were not strongly convinced of their guilt."[89] To be fair to Lovecraft, there was little suspicion at the time that the alleged victims were fabricating the whole story, even though we now know that that was indeed the case; but it is dismaying how Lovecraft could be so oblivious of the deep-seated racism that routinely resulted in African-Americans in the South (and elsewhere) being convicted on poor evidence by white juries.

But, as we have seen earlier, Lovecraft in the course of time was forced to back down increasingly from his claims to the superiority of the Aryan (or Nordic or Teuton) over other groups aside from blacks and aborigines:

> No anthropologist of standing insists on the uniformly advanced evolution of the Nordic as compared with that of other Caucasian and Mongolian races. As a matter of fact, it is freely conceded that the Mediterranean race turns out a higher percentage of the aesthetically sensitive and that the Semitic groups excel in sharp, precise intellection. It may be, too, that the Mongolian excels in aesthetick capacity and normality of philosophical adjustment. What, then, is the secret of pro-Nordicism amongst those who hold these views? Simply this—that ours is a Nordic culture, and that the roots of that culture are so inextricably tangled in the national standards, perspectives, traditions, memories, instincts, peculiarities, and physical aspects of the Nordic stream that no other influences are fitted to mingle

in *our* fabric. We don't despise the French *in France or Quebec,* but we don't want them grabbing *our* territory and creating foreign islands like Woonsocket and Fall River. The fact of this uniqueness of every separate culture-stream—this dependence of instinctive likes and dislikes, natural methods, unconscious apprais-als, etc., etc., on the physical and historical attributes of a single race—is too obvi-ous to be ignored except by empty theorists.[90]

This passage is critical. Now that his race has been stripped of any recognisable superiority over others (although, of course, the "concessions" he made as to the distinguishing features of other races are merely simple-minded stereotypes), how could Lovecraft continue to defend segregation? He did so by asserting—from an illegitimate generalisation of his own prejudices—a wildly exaggerated degree of incompatibility and hostility among different cultural groups. And there is a subtle but profound hypocrisy here also: Lovecraft trumpeted "Aryan" conquests over other races (European conquest of the American continent, to name only one ex-ample) as justified by the inherent strength and prowess of the race; but when other "races" or cultures—the French-Canadians in Woonsocket, the Italians and Por-tuguese in Providence, the Jews in New York—made analogous incursions into "Aryan" territory, he saw it as somehow contrary to Nature. He was backed into this corner by his claim that the Nordic is *"a master in the art of orderly living and group preservation"*[91]—and he therefore cannot account for the increasing hetero-geneity of "Nordic" culture.

Lovecraft was, of course, entirely at liberty to feel personally uncomfortable in the presence of aliens; he was even, I believe, at liberty to wish for a culturally and racially homogeneous society. This wish is, in itself, not pernicious, just as the wish for a racially and culturally diverse society—such as the United States has now become—is not in itself self-evidently virtuous. Each has its own advantages and drawbacks, and Lovecraft clearly preferred the advantages of homogeneity (cul-tural unanimity and continuity, respect for tradition) to its drawbacks (prejudice, cultural isolationism, fossilisation). Where Lovecraft went astray philosophically is in attributing his own sentiments to his "race" or culture at large: "We can *like* a fool or a boor even when we laugh at him. There is nothing *loathsome* or *mon-strous* to us in weak thinking or poor taste. But for the cringing, broken, unctuous, subtle type we have a *genuine horror—a sense of outraged Nature*—which excites our deepest nerve-fibres of mental and physical repugnance."[92] That repeated "we" is rhetorically clever but transparently fallacious.

In my view, Lovecraft leaves himself most open to criticism on the issue of race not by the mere espousal of such views but by his lack of openmindedness on the issue, and more particularly his resolute unwillingness to study the most up-to-date findings on the subject from biologists, anthropologists, and other scientists of un-questioned authority who were, through the early decades of the century, systematically destroying each and every pseudo-scientific "proof" of racialist theories. In every other aspect of his thought—metaphysics, ethics, aesthetics, politics—Lovecraft was constantly digesting new information (even if only through newspaper reports, magazine articles, and other second-hand sources) and readjusting his views accordingly. Only on the issue of race did his thinking remain relatively static. He never realised that his beliefs had been largely shaped by parental and societal influence, early reading, and outmoded late nineteenth-century science. The mere fact that he had to defend his views so vigorously and argumentatively in letters—chiefly to younger correspondents like Frank Long and J. Vernon Shea—should have encouraged him to rethink his position; but he never did so in any significant way.

The brute fact is that by 1930 every "scientific" justification for racism had been demolished. The spearhead of the scientific opposition to racism was the anthropologist Franz Boas (1857–1942), but I find no mention of him in any of Lovecraft's letters or essays. The intelligentsia—among whom Lovecraft surely would have wished to number himself—had also largely repudiated racist assumptions in their political and social thought. Indeed, such things as the classification of skulls by size or shape (dolichocephalic, brachycephalic, etc.)—which Lovecraft and Robert E. Howard waste much time debating in their letters of the early 1930s—had been shown to be preposterous and unscientific even by the late nineteenth century. At least Lovecraft did not generally utilise intelligence tests (such as the Stanford-Binet test perfected in 1916) to "prove" the superior brain-capacity of whites over non-whites—something that, remarkably enough, has experienced a recrudescence in our own day.

And yet, ugly and unfortunate as Lovecraft's racial views are, they do not materially affect the validity of the rest of his philosophical thought. They may well enter into a significant proportion of his fiction (miscegenation and fear of aliens are clearly at the centre of such tales as "The Lurking Fear," "The Horror at Red Hook," and "The Shadow over Innsmouth"), but I cannot see that they affect his metaphysical, ethical, aesthetic, or even his late political views in any meaningful way. These views do not stand or fall on racialist assumptions. I certainly have no desire to brush Lovecraft's racism under the rug, but I do not think that the many compelling positions he advocated as a thinker should be dismissed because of his clearly erroneous views on race.

If Lovecraft's racism has been the one aspect of his thought that has been subject to the greatest censure, then within that aspect it is his qualified support of Hitler and his corresponding suspicion of Jewish influence in America that has—again justifiably—caused even greater outrage. He argued the matter at length with J. Vernon Shea in the early 1930s, and the late date of this discussion emphatically refutes the claims of many of Lovecraft's apologists (among whom, surprisingly, can be numbered L. Sprague de Camp, who otherwise has been criticised for so openly displaying Lovecraft's racialist comments, especially during his New York period) that he somehow "reformed" at the end of his life and shed many of the beliefs he had spouted so carelessly in his earlier years. Some of his comments are acutely embarrassing:

> [Hitler's] vision is of course romantic & immature, & coloured with a fact-ignoring emotionalism. . . . There surely *is* an actual Hitler peril—yet that cannot blind us to the honest rightness of the man's basic urge. . . . I repeat that there is a great & pressing need behind every one of the major planks of Hitlerism—racial-cultural continuity, conservative cultural ideals, & an escape from the absurdities of Versailles. The crazy thing is not what Adolf wants, but the way he sees it & starts out to get it. I know he's a clown, but by God, I *like* the boy![93]

These points are elaborated at great length in this and other letters. According to Lovecraft, Hitler is right to suppress Jewish influence in German culture, since "no settled & homogeneous nation ought (a) to admit enough of a decidedly alien race-stock to bring about an actual alteration in the dominant ethnic composition, or (b) tolerate the dilution of the culture-stream with emotional & intellectual elements alien to the original cultural impulse." Hitler is, according to Lovecraft, wrong in the extremism of his hostility toward anyone with even a small amount of Jewish blood, since it is culture rather than blood that should be the determining criterion. It is remarkable and distressing to hear Lovecraft praising Hitler's "conservative cultural ideals," since—in spite of his vociferous protests that his brand of fascistic socialism would assure complete freedom of thought, opinion, and art—this reference must allude to Hitler's philistine objections to and suppression of what he deemed "degenerate" art. Admittedly, much of this art was of that modernist school that Lovecraft despised, although even so one cannot imagine him wishing to censor it; and it is quite likely that his own weird fiction might have come under such a ban if it had been written in Germany.

The whole question of American and British support for Hitler is one that has received surprisingly little scholarly study. Certainly, Lovecraft was not alone among the intellectual classes prior to 1937 in expressing some approbation of Hitler; and just as certainly, Lovecraft cannot possibly be considered of the same stripe as the American pro-Nazi groups in this country (which, as we have already seen, he scorned and repudiated), much less such organisations as the Friends of the New Germany or the German-American Bund, who largely attracted a small number of disaffected German-Americans and were even operated for the most part by German Nazis. It is true that the German-American Bund, established in 1936 as the successor to the Friends of the New Germany, published much literature that warned in foreboding terms of Jewish control of American government and culture, in tones that (as we shall see presently) are not entirely dissimilar to Lovecraft's; but this literature began appearing years after Lovecraft's views on the matter were already solidified. Lovecraft cannot even be lumped indiscriminately with the common run of American anti-Semites of the 1930s, most of whom were extreme political conservatives who sought to equate Jewishness with Bolshevism.[94] My feeling is that Lovecraft came by his overall economic and political views, as well as his racial stance, by independent thought on the state of the nation and the world. His beliefs are so clearly and integrally an outgrowth of his previous thinking on these issues that the search for some single intellectual influence seems misguided.

Harry Brobst provides some evidence of Lovecraft's awareness of the horrors of Hitler's Germany toward the very end of his life. He recalls that a Mrs Sheppard (the downstairs neighbour of Lovecraft and Annie Gamwell at 66 College) was a German native and wished to return permanently to Germany. She did so, but (in Brobst's words) "it was at that time that Nazism was beginning to flower, and she saw the Jews beaten, and she was so horrified, upset, distraught that she just left Germany and came back to Providence. And she told Mrs. Gamwell and Lovecraft about her experiences, and they were both very incensed about this."[95]

Lovecraft indeed took note of the departure of Mrs Alice Sheppard in late July 1936, observing that she dumped upon Lovecraft some very welcome volumes from her library. He stated, however, that she was planning to settle in Germany for three years, then return to live out her life in Newport, Rhode Island.[96] I find, however, no mention in any letters of her abrupt return, nor any expression of horror at any revelations she may have conveyed. But references to Hitler do indeed drop off radically in the last year of Lovecraft's life, so it is conceivable that Lovecraft, having heard accounts from Mrs Sheppard, simply clammed up about the matter in the realisation that he had been wrong. It would be a comforting thought.

Lovecraft's point about Jewish domination of German culture leads directly to his assessment of what he felt was happening in this country, specifically in its literary and publishing capital, New York:

> As for New York—there is no question but that its overwhelming Semitism has totally removed it from the American stream. Regarding its influence on literary & dramatic expression—it is not so much that the country is flooded directly with Jewish authors, as that Jewish publishers determine just which of our Aryan writers shall achieve print & position. That means that those of us who least express our own people have the preference. Taste is insidiously moulded along non-Aryan lines—so that, no matter how intrinsically good the resulting body of literature may be, it is a special, rootless literature which does not represent us.[97]

Lovecraft went on to mention Sherwood Anderson and William Faulkner as writers who, "delving in certain restricted strata, seldom touch on any chord to which the reader personally responds." If this is not a case of generalising from personal experience, I don't know what is! I have trouble believing that Lovecraft was actually serious on this point, but the frequency with which he spoke of it must mean that he was. Newspaper reporting in New York also angered him:

> . . . not a paper in New York dares to call its soul its own in dealing with the Jews & with social & political questions affecting them. The whole press is absolutely enslaved in that direction, so that on the whole length & breadth of the city *it is impossible to secure any public American utterance—any frank expression of the typical mind & opinions of the actual American people—on a fairly wide & potentially important range of topics.* . . . Gawd knows I have no wish to injure any race under the sun, but I *do* think that something ought to be done to free American expression from the control of *any* element which seeks to curtail it, distort it, or remodel it in any direction other than its natural course.[98]

But what *is* the "natural course" of American expression? And why did Lovecraft axiomatically believe that he and people like him were the "actual American people" (which means that others who did not share his views were necessarily "un-American")? Lovecraft is again being haunted by the spectre of change: Faulkner and Sherwood Anderson don't write the way the more conservative novelists write or used to write, so they are deemed "unnatural" or unrepresentative.

The degree to which matters of race were central to Lovecraft's own sense of "placement" and comfort is made clear in a late letter:

> In my opinion the paramount things of existence are those whose mental and imaginative landmarks—language, culture, traditions, perspectives, instinctive responses to environmental stimuli, etc.—which gives to mankind the illusion of significance and direction in the cosmic drift. Race and civilisation are more important, according to this point of view, than concrete political or economic status; so that the weakening of any racial culture by political division is to be regarded as an unqualified evil . . .[99]

I am inclined to think that Lovecraft exaggerated the actual "racial" aspect of this sentiment—as similarly when he stated, as late as 1930, "I am hitched on to the cosmos not as an isolated unit, but as a Teuton-Celt"[100]—but in any case it was his view. What he wanted was simply *familiarity*—the familiarity of the milieu in a racially and culturally homogeneous Providence that he had experienced in youth. In stating that even art must satisfy our "homesickness . . . for the things we have known" ("Heritage or Modernism"), Lovecraft was testifying to the homesickness he himself felt when, as an "unassimilated alien"[101] in New York or even in latter-day Providence, he witnessed the increasing urbanisation and racial heterogeneity of his region and his country. Racialism was for him a bulwark against acknowledging that his ideal of a purely Anglo-Saxon America no longer had any relevance and could never be recaptured.

More generally, the increasing racial and cultural heterogeneity of his society was for Lovecraft the chief symbol of *change*—change that was happening too fast for him to accept. The frequency with which, in his later years, he harps on this subject—"change is intrinsically undesirable";[102] "Change is the enemy of everything really worth cherishing"[103]—speaks eloquently of Lovecraft's frantic desire for social stability and his quite sincere belief (one, indeed, that has something to recommend it) that such stability is a necessary precondition of a vital and profound culture.

Lovecraft's final years were characterised both by much hardship (painful rejections of his best tales and concomitant depression over the merit of his work; increasing poverty; and, toward the very end, the onset of his terminal illness) and by moments of joy (travels all along the eastern seaboard; the intellectual stimulus of correspondence with a variety of distinctive colleagues; increasing adulation in the tiny worlds of amateur journalism and fantasy fandom). But to the end, Lovecraft continued to wrestle, mostly in letters, with the fundamental issues of politics, economics, society, and culture, with a breadth of learning, acuity of logic, and a deep humanity born of wide observation and experience that could not have been conceived by the "eccentric recluse" who had so timidly emerged from self-imposed hermitry in 1914. That his largely private discussions did not have any influence on the intellectual temper of the age is unfortunate; but his unceasing intellectual vigour, even as he was descending into the final stages of cancer, is as poignant a testimonial to his courage and to his devotion to the life of the mind as anyone could wish. Lovecraft himself, at any rate, did not think the effort wasted.

For the time being "The Shadow out of Time" remained in manuscript; Lovecraft was so unsure of its quality that he didn't know whether to type it up or tear it up. Finally, in a kind of despair, he sent the notebook containing the handwritten draft to August Derleth at the end of February 1935—as if he no longer wished to look at it. Derleth sat on it for months without, evidently, making even the attempt to read it.

Meanwhile the fifth proposal by a publisher to issue a collection of Lovecraft's stories emerged in mid-February—this time through the intercession of Derleth. He had importuned his own publishers, Loring & Mussey (who issued both his Judge Peck detective novels and his *Place of Hawks*) to consider a volume of Lovecraft's tales. Already by early March Derleth was suggesting to Lovecraft that he write an introduction to the collection, even though Lovecraft had not even sent to Loring & Mussey any actual stories but only a list of them. The publishers took their time making a decision. Things didn't look good by the end of May: "Mussey is indecisive; his wife (who is in the business) doesn't like the stories & wants to turn them down; & Loring hasn't read them."[1] A definite rejection came in the middle of July. Lovecraft's response was typical: "This about finishes me with writing. No more submissions to publishers."[2]

Lovecraft meant what he said. He had already announced to Derleth at the beginning of 1935, "I send nothing to W T now";[3] so that when E. Hoffmann Price, to whom the idea of not submitting a finished story must have appeared a species of lunacy, continually badgered Lovecraft to send in "The Thing on the Doorstep" (still unsubmitted anywhere) to *Weird Tales,* Lovecraft was not much inclined to listen. As early as February 1934 Price said he would himself send the story to Farnsworth Wright, but clearly he never did. In August 1935 Price again urged Lovecraft to collaborate, the proceeds to go to a trip to California where he could see Clark Ashton Smith and other Pacific coast associates; but of course Lovecraft declined.

Meanwhile, in the tiny world of fandom, the humble little *Fantasy Fan* ceased publication after the February 1935 issue, to the lamentations of all parties. It really was a very useful forum for the expression of readers' views on weird and fantasy fiction, and the work it published—fiction, poetry, and articles—was on the whole substantially better than what followed it. The loss was doubly unfortunate for Lovecraft, for not only did it cause the suspension of the serialisation of "Supernatural Horror in Literature" in midstream but it also prevented the appearance of a biographical article on Lovecraft written by F. Lee Baldwin.

This item was, however, transferred to Julius Schwartz's *Fantasy Magazine*, where it appeared in April 1935 as "H. P. Lovecraft: A Biographical Sketch". Much of the content of the article was drawn quite directly from Lovecraft's letters to Baldwin, although Lovecraft also noted that Baldwin had sent him a question-naire to answer.[4] It was the first of what would be many articles in the fan maga-zines appearing just before and just after Lovecraft's death. It also featured a fine linoleum cut of Lovecraft by Duane W. Rimel.

William L. Crawford had a wild idea of reviving the *Fantasy Fan* and installing Lovecraft as editor; Lovecraft actually tentatively accepted the offer, but he was pretty certain that Crawford could never pull off the project. In the spring of 1935 Crawford proposed a variety of book ideas to Lovecraft—the issuance of *At the Mountains of Madness* or "The Shadow over Innsmouth" as a booklet, or both to-gether in one volume. This undertaking, however, took a long time to reach fruition.

In March 1935 Lovecraft heard from Lloyd Arthur Eshbach (1910–2003), the editor of an amateur magazine called the *Galleon*. Although Eshbach published a good many science fiction stories in the pulps in the 1930s, he specifically con-ceived the *Galleon* as a general magazine that would not focus on the weird or on science fiction. Lovecraft did not think he had anything that Eshbach would want, but in the end two pieces of his were published in the magazine: the poem "Back-ground" (sonnet XXX of *Fungi from Yuggoth*) in the May–June 1935 issue, and the story "The Quest of Iranon" in the July–August 1935 issue. Later in the year it was decided that the magazine would become purely a regional Pennsylvania en-terprise, and Esbach resigned as editor, returning another *Fungi* sonnet, "Harbour Whistles," that had been accepted. Eshbach later went on to do more work in the fantasy and science fiction fields as author and editor.

In August Duane W. Rimel proposed editing and publishing a fan magazine entitled, of all things, the *Fantaisiste's Mirror* that would resume the serialisation of "Supernatural Horror in Literature." Rimel was teaming up with Emil Petaja (1915–2000), a Montana fan with whom Lovecraft had come in touch at the end of 1934. They presumably corresponded to the end of Lovecraft's life, although not many of Lovecraft's letters to him have come to light. Petaja went on to become a minor writer in the science fiction field. The Rimel-Petaja magazine was never published.

Lovecraft continued to be the hub of an increasingly wide network of fans and writers in both the amateur and weird fiction fields. One name very little known until recently, precisely because his prime concern was not the weird, is Lee McBride White (1915–1989). Although born in Monroe, North Carolina, White spent most of his life in Alabama. He had written to Lovecraft through *Weird Tales* as early as 1932, while he was a senior in high school; but, after a three-year silence during which he attended Howard College (now Samford University) in Birmingham, White seemed to lose his interest in the weird and became devoted to general literature, mostly in a modernist vein. He worked on several college literary publications, and in later life was a journalist. He wrote one book, *The American Revolution in Notes, Quotes, and Anecdotes* (1975).

Because of White's literary orientation, he did not associate much with other members of Lovecraft's correspondence circle, even though Lovecraft himself occasionally tried to put White in touch with potentially congenial individuals. The letters to White are full of Lovecraft's opinions on contemporary mainstream literature, and toward the end there emerges a very interesting discussion of John Donne and the Metaphysical poets (then experiencing a revival thanks to their seeming anticipation of many modernist tendencies). Lovecraft revised an untitled poem White wrote about Donne, although commenting that he was "an anti-Donnite" who believed that Donne was "not primarily a poet—but rather a thinker & minute analyser of human nature"—exactly the same criticism he had levelled at T. S. Eliot, who, not surprisingly, was a leading advocate of the Metaphysical poets.

William Frederick Anger (1920–1997) was a more typical late correspondent of Lovecraft's. A devotee of weird fiction (and, apparently, little else), he came in touch with Lovecraft in the summer of 1934. A Californian who later became one of the few fans or writers to visit Clark Ashton Smith in person, Anger and his colleague Louis C. Smith (about whom almost nothing is known) had ambitious plans that in the end came to nothing. First they proposed an index to *Weird Tales*—a prophetic idea, anticipating T. G. L. Cockcroft's index by almost thirty years—but never completed it; in any case, it appeared to be not so much an index as a simple listing of the tables of contents of every issue. Then, in the summer of 1935, they conceived the notion of producing a mimeographed edition of Lovecraft's *Fungi from Yuggoth*. Although this project too ran aground very quickly, it gains importance for one feature that I shall explore a little later. The only thing Anger and Smith seem actually to have accomplished is a brief article on E. Hoffmann Price (whom Lovecraft had put in touch with them) in the *Fantasy Fan* for December 1934. Lovecraft's correspondence with Anger exclusively concerns weird fiction and the fantasy fan circuit, and if nothing shows how gentlemanly he could be to anyone who wrote to him: the correspondence continued to the very end of his life.

A much more significant later colleague was Donald A. Wollheim (1914–1990). A New York City resident (he lived for most of his life in Rego Park, a district in Queens), Wollheim in 1935 took over a fan magazine started by Wilson Shepherd, the *International Science Fiction Guild Bulletin,* and renamed it the *Phantagraph,* continuing it into 1946. Although a very slim publication (some issues consisted of only four pages), the *Phantagraph* might perhaps be—largely because of its relative regularity of issuance and its longevity—the most significant fanzine since the *Fantasy Fan*. Lovecraft published a number of minor items—mostly prose poems and sonnets from the *Fungi*—in its pages from 1935 onward, and Wollheim continued to print such items well after Lovecraft's death. The correspondence to Wollheim has not surfaced, so it is impossible to gauge its duration (it commenced probably no earlier than 1935) or its substance. Wollheim of course went on in later years to become an important figure in the fantasy and science fiction community, chiefly as the editor of the *Avon Fantasy Reader* (1947–52) and of many other science fiction anthologies. He also wrote a number of science fiction novels for juveniles.

In addition to new correspondents, colleagues old and new began descending upon Lovecraft in person throughout 1935. The first was Robert Ellis Moe (1912–1992?), the eldest son of Lovecraft's longtime amateur associate Maurice W. Moe. Lovecraft had met Robert in 1923, when the latter was eleven; now, at twenty-three, he had secured a position at the General Electric Company in Bridgeport, Connecticut, and, having a car, paid Lovecraft a visit in Providence on March 2–3. Lovecraft gave him the usual tour of Providence and Newport antiquities, and they stopped at Warren, Bristol, East Greenwich, and Wickford also. Three days after Moe left, Lovecraft took a solitary twelve-mile walk to the Quinsnicket area north of Providence.[5]

Sometime in early March Lovecraft received another visitor:

> One night last week I was reading the paper in my study when my aunt entered to announce (with a somewhat amused air) a caller by the name of Mr. Kenneth Sterling. Close on her heels the important visitor appeared . . . in the person of a little Jew boy about as high as my waist, with unchanged childish treble & swarthy cheeks innocent of the Gilette's [*sic*] harsh strokes. He *did* have long trousers—which somehow looked grotesque upon so tender an infant.

Sterling (1920–1995) was not quite fifteen at this time. He was a member of a fan organisation called the Science Fiction League, and his family had recently moved to Providence, where he was attending Classical High School. Knowing that a master of weird fiction lived in the city, Sterling with the boldness of youth took the liberty of introducing himself in the most direct imaginable way. But when they began actually discussing both science and science fiction, Lovecraft's amusement turned to admiration:

> Damme if the little imp didn't talk like a man of 30—correcting all the mistakes in the current science yarns, reeling off facts & figures a mile a minute, & displaying the taste & judgment of a veteran. He's already sold a story to *Wonder* . . ., & is bubbling over with ideas. . . . Hope he won't prove a nuisance—but I wouldn't for the world discourage him in his endeavours. He really does seem like an astonishingly promising brat—& means to become a research biologist.[6]

Sterling did in fact visit Lovecraft with some frequency over the next year or so, but in the fall of 1936 he went to Harvard, where he gained a B.S. in 1940; three years later he earned a medical degree at Johns Hopkins. He would spend many years on the staffs of the Columbia University College of Physicians and Surgeons and the Department of Veterans Affairs Medical Center in the Bronx. His interest in weird and science fiction would fade rather quickly, but one notable item would emerge from it.

Robert Moe returned for another visit on April 27–28, at which time the Lovecraft took him again to Newport and then to New Bedford, with its abundance of whaling memories (but the whaling museum was closed). Later they explored an area of southern Massachusetts and southeastern Rhode Island that Lovecraft—because of his own lack of a vehicle—had never seen before: "Splendid unspoiled countryside with rambling stone walls & idyllic white-steepled villages of the old New England type. Of the latter the two best specimens—Adamsville & Little Compton Commons—are both in Rhode Island. Adamsville contains the world's only known monument to a *hen*—perpetuating the fame of the Rhode Island Red . . ."[7] This rural area is pretty much the same today. They returned via Tiverton, Fall River (which Lovecraft rightly declares to be "a lousily ugly mill city just over the line in Mass."), and Warren, where they had a dinner consisting entirely of ice cream.

Lovecraft went to see Edward H. Cole in Boston on May 3–5, and in spite of the unusually cold weather managed at least to get to beloved Marblehead. Amateurdom was the subject of much discussion, as the NAPA was heating up with a variety of controversies and feuds from which Lovecraft attempted to remain aloof (although quietly supporting those individuals he felt most honourable and most likely to further the amateur cause) but into which he would in the course of time get dragged in spite of himself. But at the moment Lovecraft was a mere observer of the fray.

On May 25 Charles D. Hornig, the erstwhile editor of the *Fantasy Fan,* stopped by to visit Lovecraft in Providence. He was given the usual historic tour, which he seemed to appreciate the more because it reminded him of his own hometown of Elizabeth, New Jersey. Ken Sterling was on hand for most of the festivities.

By this time, however, Lovecraft was already in the midst of planning for another grand southern tour—the last, as it happened, he would ever take. For in early May Barlow had invited him down to Florida for another stay of indefinite length. Lovecraft was naturally inclined to accept, and only money stood in the way; but by May 29 Lovecraft concluded optimistically, "Counting sestertii, & I think I can make it!"[8]

The trip began on June 5. Reaching New York in the early afternoon, he found time so short that he did not look up anyone, not even Frank Long. Instead, he spent some time writing postcards in Prospect Park, Brooklyn, before catching the 9.40 P.M. bus to Washington. Arriving there at 6.15 A.M. on the 6th, he immediately caught another bus to Fredericksburg, managing to get six hours of exploring and postcard-writing there before catching a late bus to Charleston, which he reached on the morning of the 7th. By spending two nights on buses, Lovecraft saved two nights' expense in hotels or YMCAs. He did spend the night of the 7th in the Charleston YMCA after a full day of sightseeing. The next day was apparently spent in Charleston also, as Lovecraft could not bear to leave the place after only a single day; but late that day he must have caught another bus to Jacksonville, where he stayed in a hotel (the Aragon, apparently) before catching another bus the next morning (the 9th) for DeLand.

Once again we are in the position of not knowing much of Lovecraft's activities during his unprecedentedly long stay with Barlow (June 9–August 18). Correspondence to others is our sole guide, and this time we do not even have the supplements of any memoirs—either written at the time or later—by Barlow himself. In a postcard to Donald and Howard Wandrei written in July, Lovecraft gives some idea of his activities:

> Programme much the same as last year, except that Bob's father—a retired colonel—is home. Bob's brother Wayne—a fine chap of 26—has been here on a furlough from Ft. Sam Houston, Texas, but has now returned to his 2nd Lieutenanting. ¶ Bob has built a cabin in an oak grove across the lake from the house, & is busy there with various printing projects—of some of which you'll hear later on.... ¶ Last month we explored a marvellous tropical river near the Barlow place. It is called Black Water Creek, & is lined on both sides by a cypress jungle with festoons of Spanish moss. Twisted roots claw at the water's edge, & palms lean precariously on every hand. Vines & creepers—sunken logs—snakes & alligators—all the colour of the Congo or Amazon.[9]

The trip to Black Water Creek took place on June 17. The cabin is of some interest, since it appears that Lovecraft actually did some work on it. Barlow later declared that Lovecraft "helped to creosote [it] against termites,"[10] and by August 4 Lovecraft was noting: "The edifice is now quite complete, & not long ago I cleared a road to it through the scrub palmetto growths."[11]

Of the printing projects Lovecraft mentioned, we know one in particular—an edition of Long's collected poetry written subsequent to *The Man from Genoa* (1926), entitled *The Goblin Tower*. Lovecraft helped to set type on this slim pamphlet, which Barlow managed to print and bind by late October.[12] Lovecraft took the occasion to correct Long's faulty metre in some of the poems. Barlow was bursting with ideas for other projects, chiefly a collection of Clark Ashton Smith's poems entitled *Incantations;* but, as with so many other of his ambitious endeavours, this venture hung fire for years before finally coming to nothing.

One other idea Barlow had evolved at about this time was a volume of C. L. Moore's best stories. Catherine Lucile Moore (1911–1987) first appeared in *Weird Tales* in November 1933 with the striking fantasy "Shambleau"; she wrote under a gender-concealing name because she did not wish to reveal to her employers (she worked for the Fletcher Trust Co. in Indianapolis) that she had an alternate source of income, which during these lean times might give them an excuse to fire her. She went on to publish several more stories in *Weird Tales*—"Black Thirst" (April 1934), "The Black God's Kiss" (October 1934), "Black God's Shadow" (December 1934)—that evocatively combined exotic romance, even sexuality, with otherworldly fantasy. Lovecraft was not long in recognising their merit:

> These tales have a peculiar quality of cosmic weirdness, hard to define but easy to recognise, which marks them out as really unique. "Black God's Shadow" isn't up to the standard—but you can get the full effect of the distinctive quality in "Shambleau" and "Black Thirst". In these tales there is an indefinable atmosphere of vague *outsideness* & *cosmic dread* which marks weird work of the best sort.[13]

Barlow had contemplated a book of Moore's work in the spring of 1935, but wished her to revise some of her work for the volume; he entrusted Lovecraft with the delicate task of making this request to her. Lovecraft felt very awkward doing so, but he must have sufficiently praised Moore's work in his first letter to her (probably around April) that she took no offence. A substantive correspondence ensued, Lovecraft continually beseeching her not to kowtow to pulp standards and to preserve her aesthetic independence, even if it meant economic losses in the short term. Unusually for him, he kept all her responses; unfortunately, Lovecraft's letters to her now exist, for unknown reasons, only in fragments. Had he lived longer, he would have taken heart in her subsequent career, for she became one of the most distinctive and respected voices in the next generation of science fiction and fantasy writers.

Barlow's negotiations with Moore about the volume do not seem to have progressed very far, and it must have been dropped when Barlow, with his incandescent temperament, found other projects more compelling. But he had at least put Moore and Lovecraft in touch, and both were very likely grateful for it.

Aside from printing, some actual writing was accomplished by the pair. Once again they engaged in a whimsy, although unlike "The Battle That Ended the Century" this one was not distributed until after Lovecraft's death. "Collapsing Cosmoses" is a story fragment of scarcely 500 words, but has some moments of piquant humour nonetheless. The idea was for each author to write every other paragraph or so, although on occasion Lovecraft only wrote a few words before yielding the pen back to his younger colleague, so that considerably more than half the piece is Barlow's, as are a fair number of the better jokes.

As a satire on the space-opera brand of science fiction popularised by Edmond Hamilton, E. E. "Doc" Smith, and others, "Collapsing Cosmoses" is undeniably effective; the fact that it is unfinished makes little difference, for the absurdity of the plot would have precluded any neat resolution in any event. The opening (by Lovecraft) tells the whole story:

> Dam Bor glued each of his six eyes to the lenses of the cosmoscope. His nasal tentacles were orange with fear, and his antennae buzzed hoarsely as he dictated his report to the operator behind. "It has come!" he cried. "That blur in the ether can be nothing less than a fleet from outside the space-time continuum we know. Nothing like this has ever appeared before. It must be an enemy. Give the alarm to the Inter-Cosmic Chamber of Commerce. There's no time to lose—at this rate they'll be upon us in less than six centuries. Hak Ni must have a chance to get the fleet in action at once."

Later, when Hak Ni leads his fleet into space, he hears a sound, "which was something like that of a rusty sewing-machine, only more horrible" (this is by Barlow). Certainly, it would have been an entertainment of this piece had gone on a little longer, but the authors had made their point, and Barlow probably lost patience and dragged Lovecraft to some other activity. He printed the item in the second issue of *Leaves* (1938).

But perhaps the most important function that Barlow performed was neither printing nor writing, but typing. By mid-July Derleth had still given no report on the autograph manuscript of "The Shadow out of Time"; and, although Robert Bloch had expressed interest in seeing it, Barlow was still more enthusiastic about it, so Lovecraft asked Derleth to send it down to Florida. By early August Lovecraft was expressing a certain irritation that neither Derleth nor Barlow had apparently made much of an effort to read the thing: "The bad handwriting is perhaps partly responsible for their inattention; but in addition to that the story must lack interest, else they would be carried along in spite of the difficult text."[14] Now this is all pretty unreasonable, and a clear indication of the near-complete despair into which he had fallen in regard to his own work; but very shortly he was forced, delightedly, to eat his words. For in fact Barlow was surreptitiously preparing a typescript of the story.

Lovecraft was completely bowled over by Barlow's diligence and generosity in this undertaking, and he seems not to have suspected anything when Barlow asked him to copy over one page (page 58 of the autograph), probably because it was unusually hard to read. This one-page text—with the note at the bottom, "Copied Aug. 15, 1935"—was all that survived of any manuscript of the story until the recent discovery of the original autograph draft. Although Lovecraft generously wrote that Barlow's transcript was "accurately typed,"[15] he later admitted, "I fear Barlow's text had many errors, some of which greatly misrepresent my style—since I recall doing quite a bit of correction on my copy."[16] Barlow also failed to prepare even a single carbon (Lovecraft usually prepared two). Nevertheless, Lovecraft sent the typescript on the usual round of readers.

Lovecraft clearly had a wonderful time in Florida, if for no other reason than the climate. It was not that central Florida was *hot,* in an absolute sense—the hottest it got was 88°, while correspondents from the Northwest and Northeast reported still higher temperatures—but that the absence of *low* temperatures (it was never below 80° during his entire visit) prevented Lovecraft from experiencing that debilitating enervation he felt during northern winters. In early August he noted with amazement, "At present I'm feeling so well that I scarcely know myself!"[17]

The Barlows were again insistent that Lovecraft stay on as long as he liked. They even wanted him to stay all winter, and even move down permanently (perhaps being housed in the cabin that Robert had built), but both these plans were clearly impracticable. Lovecraft appreciated the gesture, but would have felt helpless without his books and papers for any extended period of time.

Lovecraft finally moved along on August 18. The Barlows took him as far as Daytona Beach, where they were spending a fortnight; from there he caught a bus to St Augustine. The antiquity of the place was a balm to him after nearly three months of rustic modernity. On the 20th (Lovecraft's forty-fifth birthday) Barlow came up unexpectedly, and Lovecraft showed him the sights—including a newly discovered Indian burying ground north of the town, where the skeletons were preserved as they were buried.[18] By the 26th Lovecraft was in Charleston; on the 30th he was in Richmond for a day; the 31st saw him in Washington, the 1st of September in Philadelphia, and the 2nd in New York, where he holed up with the Wandrei brothers, who had obtained a flat above New York's oldest bar, Julius's, at 155 West 10th Street. He finally reached home on September 14.

One thing Lovecraft did in Charleston and Richmond was finish what he called a "composite story"—a round-robin weird tale entitled "The Challenge from Beyond." This was the brainchild of Julius Schwartz, who wanted two round-robin stories of the same title, one weird and one science fiction, for the third anniversary issue of *Fantasy Magazine* (September 1935). He initially signed up C. L. Moore, Frank Belknap Long, A. Merritt, Lovecraft, and a fifth undecided writer for the weird version, and Stanley G. Weinbaum, Donald Wandrei, E. E. "Doc" Smith, Harl Vincent, and Murray Leinster for the science fiction version. It was something of a feat to have harnessed all these writers—especially the resolutely professional A. Merritt—for such a venture, in which each author would write a section building upon what his or her predecessor had done; but the weird version did not go quite according to plan.

Moore initiated the story with a rather lacklustre account of a man named George Campbell who, while camping alone in the Canadian wilderness, comes upon a curious quartzlike cube for whose exact nature and purpose he cannot account. Long then wrote what Lovecraft called "a rather clever development";[19] but this left Merritt in the position of actually developing the story. Merritt balked, saying that Long had somehow deviated from the subject-matter suggested by the title, and refused to participate unless Long's section were dropped and Merritt allowed to write one of his own. Schwartz, not wanting to lose such a big name (Long, not having such an impressive reputation, was apparently considered expendable), weakly went along with the plan. Merritt's own version is pretty inane and fails to move the story along in any meaningful way: Campbell is merely impressed with the bizarrerie of the object ("It was alien, he knew it; not of this earth. Not of earth's life"), and while peering into it finds his mind sucked into the core of the object. Lovecraft, next on the list, realised that he would have to take the story in hand and actually make it go somewhere.

Notes to Lovecraft's segment survive and make interesting reading—if only for the amusing drawings of the alien entities he introduces into the tale (giant worm- or centipede-like creatures) and for the clear borrowings he has made from the plot of "The Shadow out of Time." For this segment of "The Challenge from Beyond" is nothing more than an adaptation of the central conception of that story—mind-exchange. Here the exchange is effected by the cubes, which draw the mind of anyone who looks into it and flings it back to the transgalactic world of the centipede creatures, where it is somehow housed in a machine; by the reverse method one of the centipedes casts his mind into the body of the mind so captured. Campbell manages to figure out what has happened to him because he has, handily enough, read "those debatable and disquieting clay fragments called the Eltdown Shards" which tell the whole story of this centipede race and their explorations of space via the cubes.

Lovecraft need scarcely be held responsible for pillaging his own recently completed story for the core of the plot of "The Challenge from Beyond"; for the latter was clearly a sporting venture of no conceivable literary consequence. The anomaly, however, is that this mind-exchange idea actually got into print months before its much better utilisation in "The Shadow out of Time" did. Lovecraft's segment is about three to four times as long as that of any other writer's, taking up about half the story. Robert E. Howard, who had been talked into taking the fourth instalment, displays Campbell (in the body of a centipede) suddenly reviving from a fainting fit to engage in an orgy of slaughter against his slimy opponents, while Long—whom Lovecraft had talked into coming back on board the project after he had walked away in a huff when Schwartz had dumped his initial instalment—concludes the story by showing the centipede-bodied Campbell becoming a god on the distant planet while the human-bodied alien degenerates into mindless bestiality. It's all good fun of a sort, although even Lovecraft's segment—clearly the most substantial of the lot (it has actually been published separately as a self-contained narrative)—cannot claim much aesthetic value. The science fiction version is, if possible, even worse.

Another story on which Lovecraft worked around this time—Duane W. Rimel's "The Disinterment"—is, however, a very different proposition. This tale—very similar in atmosphere to some of Lovecraft's early macabre stories, especially "The Outsider"—is to my mind either wholly written by Lovecraft or a remarkably faithful imitation of Lovecraft's style and manner. Rimel has emphatically maintained that the story is largely his, Lovecraft acting only as a polisher; and correspondence between the two men—especially Lovecraft's enthusiastic initial response to the story—seems to support this claim. Consider a passage in Lovecraft's letter to Rimel of September 28, 1935: "First of all, let me congratulate you on the story. Really, it's *splendid*—one of your best so far! The suspense & atmosphere of dread are admirable, & the scenes are very vividly managed. . . . I've gone over the MS. very carefully with a view to improving the smoothness of the prose style—& I hope you'll find the slight verbal changes acceptable."[20] The critical issue is what to make of that final sentence (the manuscript or typescript, with Lovecraft's putative corrections, does not survive). The fact that Lovecraft refers to "slight verbal changes" should not lead us to minimise his role in the tale, since this may simply be another instance of his customary modesty. It is, moreover, odd that Rimel subsequently wrote nothing even remotely as fine (or, at any rate, as Lovecraftian) as this tale. Rimel (or Lovecraft) has taken the hackneyed "mad doctor" trope and shorn it of its triteness and absurdity by a very restrained portrayal, one that suggests far more than it states; and although the "surprise" ending—a man whose body is afflicted with leprosy finds that his head has been severed and reattached to the body of some other person (apparently a black man)—is hardly a surprise to the alert reader, it follows the lead of many Lovecraft stories in which the narrator cannot bring himself to state, unequivocally and definitively, the hideous truth until the very last line. The prose seems to me remarkably Lovecraftian:

> It was on the evening following my half-recovery that the dreams began. I was tormented not only at night but during the day as well. I would awaken, screaming horribly, from some frightful nightmare I dared not think about outside the realm of sleep. These dreams consisted mainly of ghoulish things; graveyards at night, stalking corpses, and lost souls amid a chaos of blinding light and shadow. The terrible *reality* of the visions disturbed me most of all: it seemed that some *inside* influence was inducing the grisly vistas of moonlit tombstones and endless catacombs of the restless dead. I could not place their source; and at the end of a week I was quite frantic with abominable thoughts which seemed to obtrude themselves upon my unwelcome consciousness.

"The Disinterment" was initially rejected by Farnsworth Wright but then, in early 1936, accepted; it was not published in *Weird Tales*, however, until the January 1937 issue. Rimel went on to have one more story, "The Metal Chamber," in *Weird Tales* (March 1939), but neither this nor any of Rimel's other published stories aside from "The Tree on the Hill" appear to bear any significant amount of Lovecraft prose, even though Lovecraft seems to have been looking over and perhaps lightly touching up a number of Rimel's other stories of the period.

More travel loomed on Lovecraft's horizon. He spent September 20–23 in Massachusetts with Edward H. Cole, but this time the trip was not entirely for pleasure: the two men were entrusted with the melancholy duty of scattering the ashes of the old amateur Jennie E. T. Dowe (1841–1919), the mother of Edith Miniter, in the Wilbraham region where she was born. The trip had been in the offing for more than a year, but kept being delayed because of obligations by either Cole or Lovecraft; W. Paul Cook was to have accompanied them but was unable at the last moment to go. Some of the ashes were scattered in the Dell cemetery, the rest in the rose garden of the then-deserted house, Maplehurst, where Lovecraft himself had stayed in 1928 with Miniter. This was, of course, the "Dunwich" region, and Lovecraft was heartened to find that "Nothing had changed—the hills, the roads, the village, the dead houses—all the same."[21]

On the 22nd Cole and his family took Lovecraft to Cape Cod, going through Hyannis and Chatham, the latter being the easternmost point of Massachusetts. The next day the party explored Lynn and Swampscott, on the North Shore, and Lovecraft went home that evening.

One more trip that Lovecraft managed before the cold drove him indoors for the winter was a day's journey on October 8 to New Haven, where he and Annie were taken by a friend in a car. Lovecraft had passed through the town on a number of occasions but had never stopped there. He was delighted, particularly with the Yale campus and its imitation Gothic quadrangles—

> each an absolutely faithful reproduction of old-time architecture & atmosphere, & forming a self-contained little world in itself. The Gothic courtyards transport one in fancy to mediaeval Oxford or Cambridge—spires, oriels, pointed arches, mullioned windows, arcades with groined roofs, climbing ivy, sundials, lawns, gardens, vine-clad walls & flagstoned walks—everything to give the young occupants the massed impression of their accumulated cultural heritage which they might obtain in Old England itself. To stroll through these quadrangles in the golden afternoon sunlight; at dusk, when the lights in the diamond-paned casements flicker up one by one; or in the beams of a mellow Hunter's Moon; is to walk bodily into an enchanted region of dream. It is the past—& the ancient mother land—brought magically to the present time & place. . . . Lucky is the youth whose formative years are spent amid such scenes! I wandered for hours through this limitless labyrinth of unexpected elder microcosms, & mourned the lack of further time.[22]

Lovecraft yearned to visit New Haven again, but he never got the chance.

Even this was not quite the end of his year's travels, for at 6 A.M. on October 16 Sam Loveman reached Providence from the New York boat, and the two friends spent two days in Boston exploring bookshops, museums, antiquities, and the like. Lovecraft lamented the destruction of two more old houses in the North End ("Pickman's Model") area.

In mid-October 1935 Lovecraft broke his self-imposed rule against collaboration by revising a story by William Lumley entitled "The Diary of Alonzo Typer." Lumley had produced a hopelessly illiterate draft of the tale and sent it to Lovecraft, who, feeling sorry for the old codger, rewrote the story wholesale while still preserving as much of Lumley's conceptions and even his prose as possible. Lumley's version still survives, although it would be a blessing for his reputation if it did not. We are here taken to some spectral house, evidently in upstate New York (Lumley was a resident of Buffalo), where strange forces were called up by the Dutch family that had re-sided there. The narrator, an occult explorer, attempts to fathom the mysteries of the place, but in Lumley's version the tale ends quite inconclusively, with the explorer awaiting some mysterious fate while thunder and lighting rage all around. Some parts of his account are unintentionally comical, as when the narrator goes to a hill and recites a chant he finds in a strange book but is disappointed that not much hap-pens; he concludes laconically, "Better luck next time."[23]

Lovecraft, while preserving as much as he could of this farrago of nonsense—including such of Lumley's inventions as the *Book of Forbidden Things,* "the seven lost signs of terror," the mysterious city Yian-Ho, and the like—at least made some coherent sense of the plot. The result, however, is still a dismal failure. Lovecraft felt the need to supply a suitably cataclysmic ending, so he depicted the narrator coming upon the locus of horror in the basement of the house, only to be seized by a mon-ster at the end while heroically (or absurdly) writing in his diary: "Too late—cannot help self—black paws materialise—am dragged away toward the cellar. . . ."

To compound the absurdity, Lovecraft was hoping to foist the typing of the story on to someone else, but noted that his autograph version was so hopelessly interlined that no one but he could type it—something he found singularly ironic given the story's title. Lovecraft thought that Lumley would dump the thing upon some fan or semi-professional magazine like *Marvel Tales,* but Lumley enterpris-ingly sent it to Farnsworth Wright, who accepted it in early December for $70.00.[24] Wright noticed the traces of Lovecraft's style in the piece, and one won-ders whether this had anything to do with the long delay in its publication (it ap-peared in *Weird Tales* only in February 1938). Lovecraft magnanimously let Lumley keep the entire $70.00.

He may have been in a generous mood at this time because of some remark-able financial developments of his own. Probably during Lovecraft's stay in New

York in early September, Julius Schwartz had come to a gathering of the weird fiction gang at Donald Wandrei's apartment. The exact date of this event is unclear: Schwartz did meet Lovecraft at Frank Long's on September 4,[25] but this was in connexion with "The Challenge from Beyond"; and Schwartz is clear that he met Lovecraft at Wandrei's, not Long's.[26] In any event, Schwartz, who was attempting to establish himself as an agent in the weird and science fiction fields, had been in touch with F. Orlin Tremaine, editor of *Astounding,* who was wanting to broaden the scope of the magazine to include some weird or weird/science material. Schwartz asked Lovecraft whether he had any tales that might fit into this purview, and Lovecraft replied that *At the Mountains of Madness* had been rejected by Wright and had not been submitted elsewhere. Schwartz, recalling the incident fifty years after the fact, thinks that Lovecraft must have given him the story on the spot; but this seems highly unlikely, unless the typescript happened to have been lent to Wandrei or some other New York colleague at that time. In any event, Schwartz eventually got the story and took it to Tremaine, probably in late October. Here is his account of what transpired:

> The next time I went up to Tremaine, I said, roughly, "I have in my hands a 35,000 word story by H. P. Lovecraft." So he smiled and said roughly to the equivalent, "You'll get a check on Friday." Or "It's sold!" . . .
>
> Now I'm fairly convinced that Tremaine never read the story. Or if he tried to, he gave up.

What this shows is that Lovecraft was by this time sufficiently well known in the weird/science fiction pulp field that Tremaine did not even need to read the story to accept it; Lovecraft's name on a major work—whose length would require it to be serialised over several issues—was felt to be a sufficient drawing card. Tremaine was true to his word: Tremaine paid Schwartz $350.00; after keeping his $35.00 agent's fee, he sent the rest to Lovecraft.

Lovecraft was of course pleased at this turn of events, but in less than a week he would have reason to be still more pleased. In early November he learned that Donald Wandrei had submitted "The Shadow out of Time"—which presumably had found its way to him on Lovecraft's circulation list—to Tremaine, and that story was also accepted, for $280.00. In all likelihood Tremaine scarcely read this tale either.

There has been considerable confusion over the exact details of this remarkable double sale. Schwartz and Wandrei have each maintained that he alone was responsible for selling both stories, but Lovecraft's letters clearly state that Schwartz sold the one and Wandrei the other. Wandrei's whole account in his memoir, "Lovecraft in Providence" (1959), is highly suspect, since he reports that after sounding out Tremaine about the prospect of publishing the two stories, he wrote to Lovecraft immediately and asked Lovecraft to send him the typescripts without delay;

but no such exchange is found in the extant letters between Lovecraft and Wandrei. All we find is a postcard, on November 3, in which Lovecraft has already received a cheque from Street & Smith:

> What's this I hear about philanthropic agenting activities behind Grandpa's back? A couple of days ago certain rumours began to filter in from Sonny & little Meestah Stoiling [Kenneth Sterling]—& this morning a $280 cheque from S & S confirmed the most extreme reports. Yuggoth, what a stroke! Hope you took out a good commission—if you didn't, Grandpa'll have to send you one! ¶ No doubt you heard that Leedle Shoolie [Julius Schwartz] managed to sell the "Mts. of Madness" to S & S for a sum which nets me $315. The coincidence of *two* such stories successfully landing is almost unbelievable, since neither has anything in common with the policy & formulae of *Astounding*. I thought they had not the slightest shadow of a chance with Tremaine. The combined sum—595—comes as a crisis-postponing life-saver at this juncture . . . & I certainly wish such marketing could keep up![27]

This surely tells us all we need to know. The financial boon was certainly marked: Lovecraft put it in graphic but perhaps not exaggerated terms when he wrote, "I was never closer to the bread-line than this year."[28] Elsewhere he bluntly stated: "The recent cheques were indeed life-savers—so much so that I fear they can't be translated into travel, or anything less prosaic than food & rent!"[29] Aside from $105 for "Through the Gates of the Silver Key" and $32.50 from the London agency Curtis Brown for a proposed reprinting of "The Music of Erich Zann" that never transpired,[30] Lovecraft had had no sales of original fiction in 1934 or 1935. In late 1935 we even read of Lovecraft having to conserve on ink: he felt unable to make repeated purchases of his usual Skrip ink, at 25¢ a bottle, and was trying to get by on Woolworth's 5¢ brand.[31] In a short time we shall see that even these two welcome checks from Street & Smith could scarcely save Lovecraft and Annie from severe economies in the coming spring.

Meanwhile, William L. Crawford, who must have heard from Lovecraft about the *Astounding* acceptances, contemplated submitting "The Shadow over Innsmouth"—which he had by this time resolved to issue as a booklet—to *Astounding*.[32] Lovecraft had no objection in principle, although he warned Crawford that this might be a case of going to the well once too often, and he also knew that "The Shadow over Innsmouth" was much less allied to the realm of science fiction than the two tales that had been taken. Nothing more is heard of this matter, and it is not clear that Crawford actually submitted the story to *Astounding;* if he did, it was of course rejected.

Lovecraft's jubilation at the *Astounding* sales would later turn sour when he saw the actual stories in print; but that was months in the future. It is very evident that, just as a rejection—or even an unfavourable report from an associate—would plunge Lovecraft into depression and self-doubt about his abilities as a writer, so this double acceptance directly stimulated him into renewed composition. On November 5–9 he reeled off a new tale, "The Haunter of the Dark."

This last original story by Lovecraft came about almost as a whim. Robert Bloch had written a story, "The Shambler from the Stars," in the spring of 1935, in which a character—never named, but clearly meant to be Lovecraft—is killed off. Lovecraft was taken with the story, and when it was published in *Weird Tales* (September 1935), a reader, B. M. Reynolds, praised it and had a suggestion to make: "Contrary to previous criticism, Robert Bloch deserves plenty of praise for *The Shambler from the Stars.* Now why doesn't Mr. Lovecraft return the compliment, and dedicate a story to the author?"[33] Lovecraft took up the offer, and his story tells of one Robert Blake who ends up a glassy-eyed corpse staring out his study window.

But the flippancy of the genesis of "The Haunter of the Dark" should not deceive us; it is one of Lovecraft's more substantial tales. Robert Blake, a young writer of weird fiction, comes to Providence for a period of writing. Looking through his study window down College Hill and across to the far-away and vaguely sinister Italian district known as Federal Hill, Blake becomes fascinated by one object in particular—an abandoned church "in a state of great decrepitude." Eventually he gains the courage actually to go to the place and enter it, and he finds all sort of anomalous things within. There are copies of strange and forbidden books; there is, in a large square room, an object resting upon a pillar—a metal box containing a curious gem or mineral—that exercises an unholy fascination upon Blake; and, most hideously, there is the decaying skeleton of an old newspaper reporter whose notes Blake reads. These notes speak of the ill-regarded Starry Wisdom church, whose congregation gained in numbers throughout the nineteenth century and was suspected of satanic practices of a very bizarre sort, until finally the church was shut down by the city in 1877. The notes also mention a "Shining Trapezohedron" and a "Haunter of the Dark" that cannot exist in light. Blake concludes that the object on the pillar is the Shining Trapezohedron, and in an "access of gnawing, indeterminate panic fear" he closes the lid of the object and flees the place.

Later he hears anomalous stories of some lumbering object creating havoc in the belfry of the church, stuffing pillows in all the windows so that no light can come in. Things come to a head when a tremendous electrical storm on August 8–9 causes a blackout for several hours. A group of superstitious Italians gathers around the church with candles, and they sense some enormous dark object appearing to fly out of the church's belfry:

> Immediately afterward an utterly unbearable foetor welled forth from the unseen heights, choking and sickening the trembling watchers, and almost prostrating those in the square. At the same time the air trembled with a vibration as of

flapping wings, and a sudden east-blowing wind more violent than any previous blast snatched off the hats and wrenched the dripping umbrellas of the crowd. Nothing definite could be seen in the candleless night, though some upward-looking spectators though they glimpsed a great spreading blur of denser blackness against the inky sky—something like a formless cloud of smoke that shot with meteor-like speed toward the east.

Blake's diary tells the rest of the tale. He feels that he is somehow losing control of his own sense of self ("My name is Blake—Robert Harrison Blake of 620 East Knapp Street, Milwaukee, Wisconsin. . . . I am on this planet"; and still later: "I am it and it is I"); his perspective is all confused ("far is near and near is far"); finally he sees some nameless object approaching him ("hell-wind—titan blur—black wings—Yog-Sothoth save me—the three-lobed burning eye. . . ."). The next morning he is found dead—of electrocution, even though his window was closed and fastened.

What, in fact, has happened to Blake? His poignant but seemingly cryptic diary entry "Roderick Usher" tells the whole story. Just as in "Supernatural Horror in Literature" Lovecraft analysed Poe's "The Fall of the House of Usher" as a tale which "displays an abnormally linked trinity of entities at the end of a long and isolated family history—a brother, his twin sister, and their incredibly ancient house all sharing a single soul and meeting one common dissolution at the same moment," so in "The Haunter of the Dark" we are led to believe that the entity in the church—the Haunter of the Dark, described as an avatar of Nyarlathotep—has possessed Blake's mind but, at the moment of doing so, is struck by lightning and killed, and Blake dies as well. Just as, in "The Call of Cthulhu," the accidental sinking of R'lyeh saves the world from a monstrous fate, so here a random bolt of electricity is all that prevents a creature of spectacular power from being let loose upon the planet.

Many of the surface details of the plot were taken directly from Hanns Heinz Ewers's "The Spider," which Lovecraft read in Dashiell Hammett's *Creeps by Night* (1931). This story involves a man who becomes fascinated with a strange woman he sees through his window in a building across from his own, until finally he seems to lose hold of his own personality. The entire story is told in the form of the man's diary, and at the end he writes: "My name—Richard Bracquemont, Richard Bracquemont, Richard—oh, I can't get any farther . . ."[34] It is not entirely clear that Lovecraft has improved on Ewers.

"The Haunter of the Dark" does not involve any grand philosophical principles—Lovecraft does not even do much with the basic symbolism of light and dark as parallel to good and evil or knowledge and ignorance—but it is simply an extremely well-executed and suspenseful tale of supernatural horror. There are only hints of the cosmic, especially in Blake's diary ("What am I afraid of? Is it not an avatar of Nyarlathotep, who in antique and shadowy Khem even took the form of man? I remember Yuggoth, and more distant Shaggai, and the ultimate void of the black planets"), but otherwise the tale is notable chiefly for its vivid evocation of Providence.

Many of the landmarks described in the story are manifestly based upon actual sites. The view from Blake's study, as is well known, is nothing more than a poignant description of what Lovecraft saw out of his own study at 66 College Street:

> Blake's study . . . commanded a splendid view of the lower town's outspread roofs and of the mystical sunsets that flamed behind them. On the far horizon were the open countryside's purple slopes. Against these, some two miles away, rose the spectral hump of Federal Hill, bristling with huddled roofs and steeples whose remote outlines wavered mysteriously, taking fantastic forms as the smoke of the city swirled up and enmeshed them.

A passage almost identical to this can be found in Lovecraft's letters to Bloch and others as he moved into 66 College Street in May 1933. Moreover, this exact view can be seen today from such a vantage point as Prospect Terrace on the brow of College Hill.

The church that figures so prominently in the tale is—or was—real: it is St John's Catholic Church on Atwell's Avenue in Federal Hill (recently condemned and now destroyed). This church was in fact situated on a raised plot of ground, as in the story, although there was (at least prior to its demolition) no metal fence around it. It was, in Lovecraft's day, very much a going concern, being the principal Catholic church in the area. The description of the interior and belfry of the church is quite accurate. Lovecraft heard that the steeple had been destroyed by lightning in late June of 1935 (he was not there at the time, being in Florida visiting Barlow); and instead of rebuilding the steeple, the church authorities decided merely to put a rather stubby cap on the brick tower.[35] This incident no doubt started his imagination working.

The end of 1935 saw Lovecraft's fourth—and last—Christmas visit to Frank Long and the rest of the New York gang. Oddly enough, the letters or postcards he must have written to Annie Gamwell do not survive, so we have to piece together the details of the visit from letters to others. Lovecraft apparently left Providence on Sunday, December 29, and stayed till January 7. Amid the usual round of socialising with old friends (Long, Loveman, the Wandreis, Talman, Leeds, Kleiner, Morton), he met some new figures: his new correspondent Donald A. Wollheim; Arthur J. Burks, the pulp writer whose "Bells of Oceana" (December 1927) he rightly considered one of the best things ever to appear in *Weird Tales;* and Otto Binder, half of a collaborative team (with his brother Earl) that published weird and science fiction tales under the name Eando (= "E. and O.") Binder. He met Seabury Quinn for the first time since 1931 and attended a dinner of the American Fiction Guild, an organisation that Hugh B. Cave had for years been trying to get him to join.

On two occasions Lovecraft went to the new Hayden Planetarium of the American Museum of Natural History, where he was quite taken with the sophisticated displays, including a gigantic orrery that depicts the planets revolving around the sun at their actual relative speeds, and a dome capable of depicting the celestial vault as seen at any hour, in any season, from any latitude, and at any period of history. Lovecraft bought two 25¢ planispheres and charitably gave them to Long and Donald Wandrei, so that they would make fewer mistakes in citing the constellations in their stories.

Just before his trip Lovecraft heard dim reports of a Christmas surprise that Barlow had prepared for him—a pamphlet reprinting "The Cats of Ulthar." Lovecraft had suspected nothing when, around October, Barlow had casually asked whether there had been any misprints in the *Weird Tales* appearance of the story;[36] he had replied in the negative and let it go at that. Given his fastidiousness about the accurate printing of his work, it is therefore no surprise that the first thing he asked Barlow when he heard about the pamphlet was: "Bless my soul, Sir, but what's this your Grandpa hears about a Yuletide brochure publish'd without permission or proofreading?"[37] But his fears were groundless: when he actually saw the booklet at Frank Long's, he was not only overwhelmingly delighted at Barlow's generosity, but relieved to find it a very soundly printed text.

The Cats of Ulthar is one of the choicest items for the Lovecraft collector. Forty copies of a "regular" edition (bearing the imprint of The Dragon-Fly Press, Cassia, Florida) were printed and bound, and two copies were printed on what Barlow calls Red Lion Text. One of these copies (Lovecraft's) is in the John Hay Library; the whereabouts of the other is unknown. Lovecraft's praises of the appearance of this charming item are justified: "Let me repeat my congratulations anent the taste and accuracy of the brochure. The Dragon-Fly Press is surely coming along!"[38]

Another booklet that seems to have emerged at this time is *Charleston*. This is a mimeographed pamphlet that exists in two "editions," if they can be called that. H. C. Koenig was planning a trip to Charleston in early 1936 and asked Lovecraft for a brief description of some of the highlights of the place. Lovecraft, always willing to expatiate on the city he loved second only to Providence, wrote a long letter on January 12 that combined a potted history of Charleston with a specific walking tour. This letter actually does no more than paraphrase and abridge Lovecraft's superb (and at the time still unpublished) 1930 travelogue, "An Account of *Charleston*," leaving out the archaic usages and also some of the more interesting but idiosyncratic personal asides. Koenig was so taken with this letter that he typed it up and mimeographed it, running off probably fewer than 25 copies. When Lovecraft received the item, he found a number of mistranscriptions that he wished to correct; meanwhile Koenig had asked Lovecraft to rewrite the beginning and ending so as to transform the piece from a letter into an essay. After these corrections and changes were made, Koenig ran off about 30–50 copies of the new version, "binding" it (as he had done with the first version) in a cardboard folder with the words "CHARLESTON / By H. P. Lovecraft" typed on it.

The actual date of these editions is difficult to specify. Lovecraft mentioned receiving the first (letter) version on April 2[39] and the second version in early June.[40] One other anomaly is that a brochure on Charleston, printed by the Electrical Testing Laboratories (where Koenig worked) in the spring of that year, contained Lovecraft's hand-drawn illustrations of Charleston houses and other architectural details. The president of the laboratories had seen the illustrations (which Lovecraft had included as separate sheets to accompany his letter) just as the brochure was going to press, and he had asked Koenig (but not Lovecraft) permission to print them. Lovecraft was tickled at his first published appearance as an artist in thirty years[41]—the first occasion being the astronomy articles he wrote for the *Providence Tribune* (1906–08), which contained hand-drawn star charts. This Charleston item has not been located.

Not long after returning from New York, Lovecraft—although overwhelmed by revision work, a growing feud in the NAPA, and (ominously) a severe case of what he called "grippe," which involved "headache, nausea, weakness, drowsiness, bad digestion, and what the hell"[42]—still managed to find time to lapse into one more collaborative fiction venture—this time with Kenneth Sterling. The result is the interesting if insubstantial science fiction tale "In the Walls of Eryx."

Sterling has stated that the idea of the invisible maze was his, and that this core idea was adapted from Edmond Hamilton's celebrated story (which Lovecraft liked), "The Monster-God of Mamurth" (*Weird Tales,* August 1926), which concerns an invisible building in the Sahara Desert. Sterling wrote a draft of 6000–8000 words; Lovecraft entirely rewrote the story ("in very short order," Sterling declares) on a small pad of lined paper (perhaps similar to the one on which he had written "The Shadow out of Time"), making it about 12,000 words in the process.[43] Sterling's account suggests that the version as we have it is entirely Lovecraft's prose, and indeed it reads as such; but one suspects (Sterling's original draft is not extant) that, as with the collaborated tales with Price and Lumley, Lovecraft tried to preserve as much of Sterling's own prose, and certainly his ideas, as possible.

The authors have made the tale amusing by devising nasty in-jokes on certain mutual colleagues (e.g., farnoth-flies = Farnsworth Wright of *Weird Tales;* effjay weeds and wriggling akmans = Forrest J Ackerman); I suspect these are Lovecraft's jokes, since they are roughly similar to the punning names he devised for "The Battle That Ended the Century." The narrative, however, turns into a *conte cruel* when the hapless protagonist, trapped in the invisible maze whose opening he can no longer locate, reveals his deteriorating mental and physical condition in the diary he writes as he vainly seeks to escape.

The already hackneyed use of Venus as a setting for the tale is perhaps its one significant drawback. It should be noted that the spectacle of a human being walking without much difficulty (albeit with an oxygen mask and protective suit) on the surface of Venus was not preposterous in its day. There was much speculation as to the surface conditions of the planet, some astronomers believing that the planet was steamy and swampy like our own Palaeozoic age, others believing that it was a barren desert blown by dust storms; still others thought the planet covered with huge oceans of carbonated water or even with hot oil. It was only in 1956 that radio waves showed the surface temperature to be a minimum of 570° F, while in 1968 radar and radio observations at last confirmed the temperature to be 900° F and the surface atmospheric pressure to be at least ninety times that of the earth.[44]

Lovecraft's handwritten version of the story was presumably typed by Sterling, since the existing typescript is in an otherwise unrecognisable typewriter face. The byline reads (surely at Lovecraft's insistence) "By Kenneth Sterling and H. P. Lovecraft." The story was submitted to *Astounding Stories, Blue Book, Argosy, Wonder Stories,* and perhaps *Amazing Stories* (all these names, except the last, are crossed out on a sheet prefacing the typescript). Finally it was published in *Weird Tales* for October 1939.

Lovecraft, according to Sterling, had helped his young friend on this story because he wished to give him some practical advice and encouragement in story writing, although both Lovecraft and Sterling sensed even then that the latter's career lay in science and not literature. Sterling had, however, previously published a story entitled "The Bipeds of Bjhulhu" (*Wonder Stories,* February 1936), whose title was consciously meant to evoke Cthulhu, although there are no Lovecraftian touches in the tale itself.

Less than a month after Lovecraft recovered from his bout of "grippe," he reported to his correspondents that his aunt Annie was stricken with a much severer case, one that ultimately involved hospitalisation (beginning March 17), then a two-week stay at the private convalescent home of one Russell Goff (April 7–21). Here is one more of the relatively few occasions in which Lovecraft is guilty of deceit, but in this case it is entirely understandable. In fact, Annie Gamwell was suffering from breast cancer, and her hospital stay involved the removal of her right breast.[45] It is not a subject someone like Lovecraft would wish to discuss openly even to close associates.

The result for Lovecraft was a complete disruption of his schedule. Even before Annie's actual hospital stay, her illness (which had become serious by February 17) caused Lovecraft to have "no time to be aught save a combined nurse, butler, & errand boy";[46] then, with the hospital stay, things went from bad to worse, causing Lovecraft to find an analogy to his troubles only in Milton:

> All my own affairs went absolutely to hell—letters unanswered, borrowed books piled up unread, N.A.P.A. duties shifted to others, revision jobs unperformed, fiction-writing a thing of the past . . .
>
> > With ruin upon ruin, rout on rout—
> > Confusion worse confounded.[47]

Lovecraft added graciously, "But it was a damn sight worse on my aunt than on me!" He went on to note rather harrowingly: "My own programme is totally shot to pieces, & I am about on the edge of a nervous breakdown. I have so little power of concentration that it takes me about an hour to do what I can ordinarily do in five minutes—& my eyesight is acting like the devil." The weather didn't help any, remaining anomalously chilly until well into July.

The one thing Annie's illness and hospital stay brought out was the severe state of the family finances—something made graphically real by one of the saddest documents ever written by Lovecraft, a diary that he kept while Annie was away and which he would bring to her every few days in order to give an account of his activities. Amidst constant references to "wrestling with correspondence" (both his own and Annie's) and intermittently attempting to do his own revision work, we receive an unvarnished account of the perilous state of the household finances (made severer by the expenses of the hospital, a private nurse, and the like) and the severe economies—especially in food—which Lovecraft was compelled to practise.

On March 20 we learn that Lovecraft had gone back to a bad habit of Clinton Street days—eating canned food cold—for we now hear of his "experiment[ing] with *heating*" a can of chile con carne. It gets worse. On March 22 some twenty-minute eggs plus half a can of baked beans made "a sumptuous repast." Around March 24 Lovecraft felt the necessity to use canned goods that had been lying around for at least three years, since they had been brought over from Barnes Street. These included Zocates (a type of canned potato), Protose (a vegetarian substitute for meat made by Kellogg), and even some canned brown bread. On the 26th he made a potato salad with the Zocates and some old mayonnaise and salt; but finding it "a bit lacking in taste," he added a touch of ketchup—"which made an absolutely perfect & highly appetising blend." On March 29 he began using up some old Chase & Sanborn coffee that would otherwise go bad, even though he liked Postum better. Dinner on March 30 was cold hot dogs, biscuits, and mayonnaise.

On April 10 Lovecraft began experimenting with a tin of ten-year-old Rich's Cocoa and found that it had "acquired an earthy taste": "However, I shall use it up somehow." He was true to his word: over the next three days he mixed it with condensed milk and resolutely drank it. Afterward he found a tin of Hershey's Cocoa, a nearly full container of salt from Barnes Street, and a can of Hatchet diced carrots on the top shelf of a kitchen cabinet and set these down for eventual use, also beginning to eat the canned brown bread, which seemed all right.

The entire effect of all this economising and eating of old and possibly spoiled food can only be conjectured. Is it any wonder that on April 4 Lovecraft admitted to feeling so tired during the middle of the day that he had to rest instead of going out, and that on April 13 he found, after a nap, that "I was too weak & drowsy to do anything"? It should, of course, be emphasised that the meals prepared during this period did not represent his normal eating habits, although these latter were themselves ascetic enough. I shall have more to say about this later.

As I have suggested, one of the things Lovecraft had to do during Annie's illness was to tend to her own correspondence. She had many friends in Providence with whom she stayed in touch either in person or by correspondence, and when they found that she was in the hospital they wrote many cards of condolence. Lovecraft felt obligated to answer every one of them, thanking them for their concern and giving updates on Annie's condition.

One such individual who evolved into a rather quaint correspondent of her own—or, at least, inspired in Lovecraft a charmingly piquant series of letters—is Marion F. Bonner, who lived at The Arsdale at 55 Waterman Street. Bonner appears to have known Annie from at least the time they moved into 66 College Street, which was not at all far from her own residence, and in a memoir she states that she visited them often at their home; but if Lovecraft wrote any letters to her prior to Annie's illness, they do not survive.

In the course of this correspondence Lovecraft revealed his fondness for cats, and he filled the margins of his letters with the most delightful drawings of cats gambolling with each other or playing with balls of yarn or other activities so heartwarmingly written about in his old essay "Cats and Dogs." Bonner, discussing the Kappa Alpha Tau fraternity, writes:

> Whenever I told him of any cat in down-town Providence, suggesting election into above fraternity, he almost always knew of it. Possibly these endeavors of mine earned me the election into the "Fraternity" as an honorary member, "with complimentary purrs." At one time he wrote in a brochure on cats, which he presented to me, that the said brochure was "not yet published." The latter is now in the possession of the John Hay Library of Brown University.[48]

I do not know exactly what this brochure is; it may simply be some transcription of "Cats and Dogs." No such item survives, as far as I know, in the John Hay Library.

The reference to cats in downtown Providence makes one think of Lovecraft's celebrated account of Old Man, an incredibly aged cat whom he knew nearly his whole life. The description is too good not to quote:

> So I hadn't spoken about "Old Man" and my dreams of him! Well—he was a great fellow. He belonged to a market at the foot of Thomas Street—the hill street mentioned in "Cthulhu" as the abode of the young artist—and could usually (in later life) be found asleep on the sill of a low window almost touching the ground. Occasionally he would stroll up the hill as far as the Art Club, seating himself at the entrance to one of those old-fashioned courtyard archways (formerly common everywhere) for which Providence is so noted. At night, when the electric lights make the street bright, the space within the archway would remain pitch-black, so that it looked like the mouth of an illimitable abyss, or the gateway of some nameless dimension. And there, as if stationed as a guardian of the unfathomed mysteries beyond, would crouch the Sphinxlike, jet-black, yellow-eyed, and incredibly ancient form of Old Man. I first knew him as a youngish cat in 1906, when my elder aunt lived in Benefit St. nearby, and Thomas St. lay on my route downtown from her place. I used to pat him and remark what a fine boy he was. I was sixteen then. The years went by, and I continued to see him off and on. He grew mature—then elderly—and finally cryptically ancient. After about ten years—when I was grown up and had a grey hair or two myself—I began calling him "Old Man". He knew me well, and would always purr and rub around my ankles, and greet me with a kind of friendly conversational "e-ew" which finally became hoarse with age. I came to regard him as an indispensable acquaintance, and would often go considerably out of my way to pass his habitual territory, on the chance that I might find him visible. Good Old Man! In fancy I pictured him as an hierophant of the mysteries behind the black archway, and wondered if he would ever invite me *through* it some midnight . . . wondered, too, if I could ever could back to earth alive after accepting such an invitation. Well—more years slipped away. My Brooklyn period came and went; and in 1926, a middle-aged relique of thirty-six, with a goodly sprinkling of white in my thatch, I took up my abode in Barnes Street—whence my habitual downtown route led straight down Thomas St. hill. And there by the ancient archway Old Man still lingered![49]

The cat continued to live until at least 1928, when Lovecraft—seeing him no more and almost dreading to ask the proprietors of the market about the matter—finally learned that he had died. After this Lovecraft dreamed of him even more than before—he would "gaze with aged yellow eyes that spoke secrets older than Aegyptus or Atlantis." An entry in the commonplace book (#153) is about Old Man, and

Lovecraft reported that he had lent it to Bernard Austin Dwyer for use; but Dwyer wrote no story about Old Man and neither, regrettably, did Lovecraft.

Meanwhile R. H. Barlow was importuning Lovecraft with a variety of publishing projects. One in which Lovecraft was not directly involved but on which he supplied generous encouragement was Barlow's own NAPA journal, the *Dragon-Fly*. Two very creditable issues appeared, dated October 15, 1935, and May 15, 1936. They do not contain any material by Lovecraft, although in response to Barlow's request he had somewhat half-heartedly offered him "The Haunter of the Dark," rightly believing that Barlow would find it too long to use. The weird is not significantly present in the contents, although the first issue contains Barlow's striking tale "A Dream"; otherwise it includes poetry by Elizabeth Toldridge, August Derleth, Eugene B. Kuntz, and Ernest A. Edkins, essays by J. Vernon Shea and Edkins, and some epigrams ("The Epigrams of Alastor") by Clark Ashton Smith. The second issue's chief feature is a fine story by Barlow, "Pursuit of the Moth," and a long essay on "What Is Poetry?" by Edkins. The printing is a little uneven at times, but the typesetting is generally accurate and attractive.

More relevant to Lovecraft was Barlow's idea of printing the complete *Fungi from Yuggoth*. Once it became clear that William Frederick Anger and Louis C. Smith would not come through on their mimeographed edition, Lovecraft asked Smith to send to Barlow the typescript he had lent him; Smith took his time doing so, but eventually did. Barlow began setting up type on the volume in late 1935. In the summer of 1936, however, he reiterated a suggestion he had already made in the summer of 1935[50]—adding the sonnet "Recapture," written just before the other thirty-five *Fungi* sonnets, to the cycle. Barlow had prepared a new typescript of the cycle, placing "Recapture" at the end; but Lovecraft, looking over this sequence, felt that "'Recapture' better be *#34*—with 'Evening Star' as *35* & 'Continuity' as *36*. 'Recapture' seems somehow more *specific & localised* in spirit than either of the others named, hence would go better before them—allowing the Fungi to come to a close with more diffuse ideas."[51] It is remarkable that Lovecraft himself had not thought of adding "Recapture" to the series, and that the *Fungi* took six and a half years to reach the form we have come to know. Although Barlow ended up typesetting a good many of the *Fungi*, this was another project that never came to fruition.

By this time, however, Barlow had come up with yet another scheme—nothing less than The Collected Poetical Works of H. P. Lovecraft. When Lovecraft first heard of this project, in early June 1936, he laughed off the idea of anything approaching a complete edition of his poetry, since he would pay heavy blackmail to keep his general amateur verse in the oblivion of long-forgotten amateur journals. He did, however, prepare a list of his *weird* verse which he would not be wholly opposed to seeing reprinted; it is as follows:

Fungi from Yuggoth and Other Verses
by H. P. Lovecraft

Fungi from Yuggoth, I–XXXVI

Aletheia Phrikodes?

The Ancient Track
Oceanus?
Clouds?
Mother Earth?
The Eidolon?
The Nightmare Lake?
The Outpost
The Rutted Road?
The Wood
Hallowe'en in a Suburb?
The City
The House

Primavera
October

To a Dreamer
Despair?

Nemesis

This is a very instructive list. It is, of course, not a complete list of even his weird poetry: such things as "Astrophobos," the lengthy "Psychopompos," "Despair" (if its plangent pessimism can be said to have carried it over into the weird), "Bells," and any number of other published poems, as well as several unpublished ones (including the very striking "The Cats" and the Poe hoax, "To Zara," which Lovecraft did in fact send to Barlow at this time merely for examination), are omitted. The question-marks, denoting poems about whose merits Lovecraft was uncertain, seem generally to apply to the earlier verse, while most of the poems of the 1929–30 burst of poetry writing are preserved (but, surprisingly, the fine sonnet "The Messenger" is left off the list). Lovecraft explicitly specified "Aletheia Phrikodes," the central section of "The Poe-et's Nightmare," since he now resolved not to have the comic framework (which, as I have remarked, seems to undercut the cosmic central section) reprinted.

It need hardly be said that this project too never materialised, although perhaps the fault was not entirely Barlow's: a family breakup was impending, causing him to leave Florida and indefinitely lose touch with much of his weird fiction collection and printing material. Nevertheless, when Lovecraft was faced with these successive waves of book ideas by Barlow, he delivered a stern lecture—a lecture that many individuals in the science fiction and fan community ought to take to heart:

> You get me wrong about that *one-thing-at-a-time-&-finish-what-you-start* advice. I'm not urging you to *do anything more.* Indeed, I'm urging you to do *less!* My main point is that you ought to *stop starting new things* until you've finished up what's already under way. Not that you ought to hurry with the latter. Go easy, & avoid overstrain. But simply *choose the existing jobs to work at when you feel like working at anything at all.* That's the only way they'll ever get done. It's better to *finish one job* than to get a dozen started & have them all stalled at various stages. . . . Simply limit your plans to things you know you can finish. Many things—perhaps this new volume of verse—ought not to be started at all. How about "Incantations"—copy for which Klarkash-Ton says he has sent in? Wasn't that to follow "The Goblin Tower" on your programme? *There's* a volume fifty times more deserving of publication than this crap of mine! Take an old man's advice & put your energies . . . into the few things that count most![52]

In fairness to Barlow, however, he really was accomplishing a good deal—writing some fine stories, completing two issues of the *Dragon-Fly* as well as *The Goblin Tower* and *The Cats of Ulthar,* establishing an impressive collection of published work and manuscripts by leading pulp weird writers, pursuing his career as a pictorial artist, and many other things—all with very bad eyesight that needed constant medical attention and a family situation that would cause serious disruptions in his life for years. Some of his projects are so prophetic that they can only inspire amazed head-shaking even today: a *Collected Poetical Works of H. P. Lovecraft,* although in the planning stages in the early 1990s, did not appear until 2001.

At exactly this point, however, Lovecraft was distracted by another débâcle that nearly drove him to give up writing altogether. In mid-February he had seen the first instalment of *At the Mountains of Madness* in the February 1936 *Astounding* and professed to like it; in particular, he had words of praise for the interior illustrations by Howard Brown, which clearly indicated that Brown had actually read the story and had based his descriptions of the Old Ones upon the text. Lovecraft went so far as to say: "The illustrator drew the nameless Entities precisely as I had imagined them . . ."[53] He made no mention of the fact that he received the cover design for the issue—or, rather, noting it, never alluded to the fact that *Weird Tales* never gave him a cover during his entire lifetime. (The Canadian issue of *Weird Tales* for May 1942 gave Lovecraft the cover for "The Shadow over Innsmouth.") But the attractiveness of the illustrations soon soured when Lovecraft actually studied the text.

Although he purchased the third and last instalment (April 1936) as early as March 20,[54] Lovecraft apparently did not consult it in detail until the end of May. It was only then that he discovered the serious tampering that the *Astounding* editors had performed on the story, particularly the last segment. Lovecraft went into a towering rage:

> But hell & damnation! . . . In brief, that goddamn'd dung of a hyaena Orlin Tremaine has given the "Mts." the worst hashing-up any piece of mine ever received—in or out of Tryout! I'll be hanged if I can consider the story as published at all—the last instalment is a joke, with whole passages missing. . . .
>
> But what I think of that decayed fish Tremaine wouldn't go in a wholesome family paper! I'll forgive him *real misprints,* as well as the lousy spelling used by Street & Smith—but *some* of the things on his "style sheet" are beyond tolerance! (He changes "Great God!" to "Great *Heavens!*")
>
> Why, for example, are *Sun, Moon,* & even *Moonlight* (!!) always *capitalised?* Why must the damn fool invariably change my ordinary animal name to its capitalised scientific equivalent? (dinosaurs = "Dinosauria" &c) Why does he change *subterrene* to *subterrane,* when the latter has no existence as an adjective? Why, in general, an overcapitalising & *overpunctuating* mania? . . . I pass over certain affected changes in sentence-structure, but see red again when I think of the *paragraphing.* Venom of Tsathoggua! Have you seen the damn thing? *All my paragraphs cut up into little chunks* like the juvenile stuff the other pulp hacks write. Rhythm, emotional modulations, & minor climactic effects thereby destroyed. . . . Tremaine has tried to make "snappy action" stuff out of old-fashioned leisurely prose. . . .
>
> But the *supremely* intolerable thing is the way the text is cut in the last instalment—to get an old serial out of the way quickly. Whole passages . . . are left out—the result being to decrease vitality & colour, & make the action mechanical. So many important details & impressions & touches of sensation are missing from the concluding parts that the effect is that of a flat ending. After all the adventure & detail *before* the encounter with the shoggoth in the abyss, the characters are shot up to the surface without any of the gradual experiences & emotions which make the reader *feel* their return to the world of man from the nighted aeon-old world of the Others. All sense of the *duration & difficulty* of the exhausted climb is lost when it is dismissed objectively in only a few words, with no hint of the fugitives' reactions to the scenes through which they pass. . . .[55]

There is more, but this is surely enough; and volumes could be written on it.

In the first place, what this passage does is to show how conscious Lovecraft was of the emotional and psychological effect of prose, right down to the level of punctuation, and the need (in serious literature as opposed to pulp hackwork) to ground a weird or wonder tale in the most careful realism both of scene and of mood in order for it to convince an adult reader. Perhaps Lovecraft is trying to have his cake and eat it too in writing a story containing very advanced philosophical and scientific conceptions in "old-fashioned leisurely prose" and then expecting it to appear intact in a science fiction pulp magazine. Moreover, he later realised that the fault was in some sense his for not insisting (as he had done at the very beginning of his relationship with *Weird Tales*) on the stories' being printed without alteration or not being printed at all.

In the second place, Lovecraft was entirely within his rights to complain about the *nature* of the changes made, many of which seem needless even for a pulp magazine. The most serious alterations are the paragraphing and the cuts toward the end. The first is perhaps marginally justifiable—on pulp standards—because *Astounding* was, like most pulps, printed in two rather narrow columns per page, making Lovecraft's long paragraphs even longer and providing little relief for the eye of the generally juvenile and ill-educated readership of the magazine. Almost every one of his paragraphs has been cut into two, three, or more smaller paragraphs. The cuts at the end seem also quite arbitrary and in parts rather ridiculous. They only amount to about 1000 words, or perhaps one or two printed pages. Some of Lovecraft's most powerful and poignant utterances here have been rendered almost comical. The sentence "We had passed two more penguins, and heard others immediately ahead" becomes the flat "We had heard two more penguins." The mere omission of ellipses at one point (the celebrated ". . . poor Lake, poor Gedney . . . and poor Old Ones!" becomes "Poor Lake. Poor Gedney. And poor Old Ones!") is a significantly weakening effect.

Lovecraft was, of course, wrong in attributing the changes directly to F. Orlin Tremaine. It is not even clear that Tremaine even saw or approved of them; rather, they were probably done by various subeditors or copyeditors—among them Carl Happel and Jack DuBarry[56]—who were evidently expected to make as many copy-editing changes as they could in order to justify their positions. This may account for some of the changes, although no doubt someone in the *Astounding* offices really did think that the ending of the story was dragging on and needed abridging.

What Lovecraft therefore did—aside from considering the story to be essentially unpublished—was to purchase three copies of each instalment and laboriously correct the text either by writing in the missing portions and connecting the paragraphs together by pencil or by eliminating the excess punctuation by scratching it out with a penknife. This whole procedure took the better part of four days in early June. All this may seem somewhat anal retentive, but Lovecraft wished to lend these three copies to colleagues who had not seen the typescript when it was circulated and would otherwise be reading only the adulterated *Astounding* text. Unfortunately, Lovecraft did not in fact correct many of the errors, some (e.g., the Americanisation of his British spellings) perhaps because he considered them insignificant, others because he did not notice them (such as two small omissions in the first instalment, which he does not seem to have gone over carefully), and some because he was basing his corrections not upon the typescript—his one carbon was apparently lent to someone—but the autograph manuscript. He had made a number of changes in the autograph when preparing his typescript, but in the five-year interval between writing and publication he had forgotten some of these changes, so that in some cases he restored the original autograph reading instead of the revised reading of the typescript. The result is that a good many of the approximately 1500 errors in the *Astounding* text were not corrected by Lovecraft or were corrected erroneously. The only means to prepare a text that is even partially accurate is to go by the typescript, following Lovecraft's corrected copies in those instances (e.g., the erroneous hypothesis about the Antarctic continent being two land masses separated by a frozen sea) where demonstrable revisions were made on the now non-extant typescript sent to *Astounding*.

On top of this, the story itself was received relatively poorly by the readers of the magazine. This negative response has perhaps been exaggerated by later critics, but certainly there were a sufficient number of readers who failed to understand the point of the tale or felt it inappropriate for *Astounding*. The letters start appearing in the April 1936 issue, and they were generally praiseworthy rather than otherwise: only Carl Bennett's philistine "*At the Mountains of Madness* would be good if you leave about half the description out of it" qualifies as a genuine knock. Lovecraft's new colleague Lloyd Arthur Eshbach contributed general praise of Lovecraft but did not seem to have read the actual story.

In May the letters were uniformly praiseworthy, and there were at least a half-dozen of them. August Derleth was the only associate of Lovecraft's who wrote in, but others who were mere fans wrote letters of commendation. Some of these may not have been very astute ("*At the Mountains of Madness* is one keen yarn," opines Lyle Dahibrun), but in this issue there is not a word of criticism.

In the June issue the letters that comment on Lovecraft divide into four praiseworthy and three critical, with one neutral. Here, however, are some of the most piquant attacks. Although James L. Russell declared that the story "will make history" and that Lovecraft "is excelled only by Edgar Allen [*sic*] Poe in creating a desired mood in his readers" and Lew Torrance refers to Lovecraft's "superb style," Robert Thompson observed with pungent sarcasm: "I am glad to see the conclusion to *At the Mountains of Madness* for reasons that would not be pleasant to Mr. Lovecraft." But Cleveland C. Soper, Jr, was the most devastating:

> ... why in the name of science-fiction did you ever print such a story as *At the Mountains of Madness* by Lovecraft? Are you in such dire straits that you *must* print this kind of drivel? In the first place, this story does not belong in Astounding Stories, for there is no science in it at all. You even recommend it with the expression that it was a fine word picture, and for that I will never forgive you.

> If such stories as this—of two people scaring themselves half to death by look-
> ing at the carvings in some ancient ruins, and being chased by something that even
> the author can't describe, and full of mutterings about nameless horrors, such as the
> windowless solids with five dimensions, Yog-Sothoth, etc.—are what is to constitute
> the future yarns of Astounding Stories, then heaven help the cause of science-fiction!

Much of this is reminiscent of Forrest J Ackerman's attack on Clark Ashton Smith in the *Fantasy Fan*. Although it is scarcely worth going into Soper's misconceptions (as Lovecraft once said many years earlier of an amateur journalist's attack on him, "It refuted itself"[57]), such myopic criticisms would frequently be aimed at Lovecraft by subsequent generations of science fiction readers, writers, and critics.

Of the relatively few (and on the whole negative) comments on Lovecraft in the July issue, one must by all accounts be quoted: "*At the Mountains of Madness* was rather dry, although a pretty girl and the appearance of the Elders [*sic*] would have made it an excellent story for a weird magazine." I do not know if Mr Harold Z. Taylor is being subtly sarcastic here, but I doubt it.

"The Shadow out of Time" appeared in the June 1936 issue of *Astounding*. Lovecraft incredibly said that "It doesn't seem even nearly as badly mangled as the Mts.,"[58] and the one surviving annotated copy of the issue bears relatively few cor-rections; but the recently unearthed autograph manuscript makes it abundantly clear that this story suffered the same reparagraphing that *At the Mountains of Madness* received, and yet Lovecraft has failed to make the necessary restorations. Other errors are apparently due to Barlow's inability to read Lovecraft's handwrit-ing when he prepared the typescript. It is a mystery why Lovecraft did not com-plain more vociferously about the corruption of this text, even though no actual passages of significance were dropped. My feeling is that he may have felt so in-debted to both Barlow (for typing the story) and Wandrei (for submitting it) that any complaints might have struck him as a sign of ingratitude. In any event, in a short time other matters would distract him from such a relatively harmless matter.

"The Shadow out of Time" was received much more unfavourably than *At the Mountains of Madness* by readers. The August 1936 issue (the only one that con-tains any significant comment on the story) contains a barrage of criticism: "*At the Mountains of Madness* . . . was bad enough: but when I began to read *The Shadow out of Time* I was so darned mad that I was tempted to leave the story unfinished" (Peter Ruzella, Jr); "I'm fed up with Lovecraft and this is the worst yet. I think *The Shadow out of Time* is the height of the ridiculous" (James Ladd); "Lovecraft's *The Shadow out of Time* was very disappointing" (Charles Pizzano). Other com-ments were less hostile, and meanwhile some individuals either came to Lovecraft's defence in regard to the attacks received by *At the Mountains of Madness* or had generous praise for the new story. Corwin Stickney, then perhaps already in touch with Lovecraft through Willis Conover, declared hotly: "Say, what's the matter with your readers' literary tastes, anyhow? Lovecraft's *At the Mountains of Madness* is perhaps the best-written story ever to find its way into Astounding's pages . . ." Calvin Fine disputed Cleveland C. Soper's view of that novel, while John V. Baltadonis flatly declared: "*The Shadow out of Time* is the best story in the issue." But the most perspicacious comment—and the lengthiest comment on Lovecraft in all the issues of *Astounding*—came from one W. B. Hoskins, who started by claiming that Lovecraft is one of "only three or four authors who could qualify as authors *only,* not merely as authors of science-fiction," and went on rather poetically to say:

> Lovecraft does much the same thing in his stories that Tschaikowsky does in his music—his climaxes are obvious, yet you always get a kick out of them. In my own case, at least, his description is so convincing that I wonder: Is this man chiseling his stories out of fresh, uncut granite, or is he merely knocking away the detritus of some age-old carving? His lore has all the somber ring of truth. You get the general idea. I like Lovecraft.

This may not place Mr Hoskins in the company of F. R. Leavis or Harold Bloom, but it certainly negates the claim that Lovecraft's work was universally panned in *Astounding.*

Lovecraft, however, had little time to bother with the reaction of his work in the magazine: he knew that he was not likely to write very much more that would find favour with *Astounding*. In any case, other events closer to home were occupying his attention.

The only viable amateur organisation, the NAPA, was reaching levels of spite and vindictiveness rarely seen even in the teens, when the UAPA and NAPA were violently hostile to each other, when the two separate factions of the UAPA were bickering over which was the legitimate association, and when Lovecraft himself was embroiled in extraordinarily bitter controversies with James F. Morton, Anthony F. Moitoret, Ida C. Haughton, and others. The locus of this new feuding was Hyman Bradofsky, whose *Californian* offered unprecedented space for lengthy prose contributions and whom Lovecraft had supported in his successful bid for the presidency of the NAPA for the 1935–36 term. Lovecraft had presumably got in touch with Bradofsky at least by 1934, since this is when his first contributions to the magazine appear; he wrote some fifty letters to Bradofsky, but only one has been published.

I am not entirely clear why Bradofsky created so much hostility among other members. He was evidently accused of being high-handed in various procedural matters relating to the NAPA constitution, and he himself apparently responded to criticism in a somewhat testy manner. Whether Bradofsky's being a Jew had anything to do with it is similarly unclear; I suspect that this was a factor, although Lovecraft never acknowledges it. In any case, it is certainly to Lovecraft's credit that he came to Bradofsky's defence, since by all accounts many of the attacks upon him were highly unjust, capricious, and snide. As examples of these attacks Lovecraft mentioned a magazine containing harsh criticism of Bradofsky which was mailed to every NAPA member except Bradofsky himself, and another magazine that contained a rather lame story by Bradofsky with sneering annotations added.

Lovecraft responded to all this, on June 4, with "Some Current Motives and Practices." It is, in its way, a noble document, as Lovecraft censured Bradofsky's opponents—or, rather, the thoroughly despicable tactics they are using against him—refuted the attacks by vindicating Bradofsky's conduct, and in general pleaded for a return to civilised standards in amateurdom:

> It is again appropriate, as on many past occasions, to ask whether the primary function of amateur journalism is to develop its members in the art of expression or to provide an outlet for crude egotism and quasi-juvenile spite. Genuine criticism of literary and editorial work, or of official policies and performances, is one thing. It is a legitimate and valuable feature of associational life, and can be recognised by its impersonal approach and tone. Its object is not the injury or denigration of any person, but the improvement of work considered faulty or the correction of policies considered bad. The zeal and emphasis of the real critic are directed solely toward the rectification of certain definite conditions, irrespective of the individuals connected with them. But it takes no very acute observer to perceive that the current floods of vitriol and billingsgate in the National Amateur Press Association have no conceivable relationship to such constructive processes.

Lovecraft did not mention the names of any of the attackers, but he knew that one of Bradofsky's chief opponents was Ralph W. Babcock, an otherwise distinguished amateur who had somehow developed a furious hostility toward the NAPA president. In a letter to Barlow, Lovecraft noted wryly that his salvo might well "arouse some squawking & feather-ruffling in the roosts of Great Neck, L.I.,"[59] a direct reference to Babcock.

Lovecraft, of course, felt at liberty to speak out on the matter because he was, with Vincent B. Haggerty and Jennie K. Plaisier, one of the Executive Judges of the NAPA for this 1935–36 term. And yet, he evidently regarded it as impolitic to have "Some Current Motives and Practices" actually published in an amateur paper, so he arranged with Barlow to mimeograph enough copies to send to all NAPA members. Lovecraft wrote out the essay in a relatively neat hand, but at that he still complained that Barlow had made mistranscriptions when he typed out the text. The result was, like "The Battle That Ended the Century," two long (8½ × 14") sheets, each with type on only one side of the page. Barlow must have distributed the item by the end of June. I cannot sense that it had any particular effect. The next election was, in any event, held in early July, and Bradofsky was elected Official Editor, although he shortly afterward resigned on what he claimed were physician's orders. Lovecraft felt that "the convention gave young Babcock rather a trouncing."[60]

Frank Belknap Long and
Lovecraft in Brooklyn

Charles W. "Tryout" Smith
and W. Paul Cook

Lovecraft's home from 1933 to 1937 at 65 Prospect Street,
Providence (moved from 66 College Street)

William E. Hart

Robert H. Barlow

St. John's Catholic Church, 352 Atwells Avenue, Providence (demolished; featured in "The Haunter of the Dark")

Donovan K. Loucks

Lovecraft's gravestone in Swan Point Cemetery, Providence

25. THE END OF ONE'S LIFE
(1936–1937)

In early June Robert E. Howard wrote to his friend Thurston Tolbert: "My mother is very low. I fear she has not many days to live."[1] He was correct: on the morning of June 11, Hester Jane Ervin Howard, who had failed to recover from an operation performed the previous year, fell into a coma from which her doctors said she would never emerge. Howard got into his car and shot himself in the head. He died eight hours later; his mother died the next day, leaving Howard's aged father, Dr I. M. Howard, doubly bereaved. Robert E. Howard was thirty years old.

At a time when telephones were not as common as now, the news spread relatively slowly. Lovecraft only heard of it around June 19, when he received a postcard written three days earlier by C. L. Moore. This postcard does not survive, and I do not know how Moore heard the news before any of Lovecraft's other colleagues. Whatever the case, Lovecraft—who hoped against hope that the news was some sort of joke or error—got the full story a few days later from Dr Howard.

Lovecraft was overwhelmed with shock and grief:

> Damnation, what a loss! That bird had gifts of an order even higher than the readers of his published work could suspect, and in time would have made his mark in real literature with some folk-epic of his beloved southwest. He was a perennial fount of erudition and eloquence on this theme—and had the creative imagination to make old days live again. Mitra, what a man! . . . I can't understand the tragedy—for although R E H had a moody side expressed in his resentment against civilisation (the basis of our perennial and voluminous epistolary controversy), I always thought that this was a more or less impersonal sentiment . . . He himself seemed to me pretty well adjusted—in an environment he loved, with plenty of congenial souls . . . to talk and travel with, and with parents whom he obviously idolised. His mother's pleural illness imposed a great strain upon both him and his father, yet I cannot think that this would be sufficient to drive his tough-fibred nervous system to self-destructive extremes.[2]

Lovecraft was not the only one who could not understand the tragedy—other friends and later scholars and biographers have also been mightily puzzled. This is scarcely the place for a posthumous psychoanalysis of Robert E. Howard, even if such a thing could be done with any sort of accuracy. Suffice it to say that the facile attribution of an Oedipus complex to Howard is highly problematical, not least because it begs the question by assuming the actual existence of the Oedipus complex, which many psychologists have now come to doubt.[3] Lovecraft later came to feel that Howard's extreme emotional sensitivity caused him somehow to refuse to accept the loss of a parent "as part of the inevitable order of things."[4] There is something to this, and some Howard scholars have also seen an obsession with death in much of his work. Whatever the cause, Lovecraft had lost a colleague of six years' standing who—although the two never met—meant a great deal to him.

In the short term Lovecraft assisted Dr Howard as best he could, by sending various items—including his letters from Howard—to a memorial collection at Howard Payne College in Brownwood, Texas (Lovecraft calls it Howard's alma mater, but Howard spent less than a year there). Lovecraft's own letters to Howard met a more unfortunate fate, and appear to have been inadvertently destroyed by Dr Howard sometime in the late 1940s. But extensive extracts of them had been transcribed under August Derleth's direction; a relatively small proportion of them was actually published in the *Selected Letters,* but the joint correspondence, in two large volumes, has now appeared.

Howard left such a staggering number of unpublished manuscripts that not only are all his book publications posthumous, but—in spite of his voluminous appearances in pulps of all sorts—far more of his work has been issued since his death than before. One of the first such items was *The Hyborian Age* (Los Angeles: LANY Coöperative Publications, 1938), Howard's clever "history" of the world before, during, and after the lifetime of Conan. This publication featured, as an introduction, a letter Lovecraft had sent to Donald A. Wollheim, probably in September 1935, accompanying Howard's piece.

Almost immediately Lovecraft wrote a poignant memoir and brief critical appraisal, "In Memoriam: Robert Ervin Howard," that appeared in *Fantasy Magazine* for September 1936. It contains, in somewhat more formalised diction, much of the substance of his letter to E. Hoffmann Price of June 20, embodying his initial reactions to Howard's death. A shorter version of this article, "Robert Ervin Howard: 1906–1936," appeared in the *Phantagraph* for August 1936. R. H. Barlow wrote a touching sonnet, "R. E. H.," that formed his first and last appearance in *Weird Tales* (October 1936). That issue contained a wealth of tributes to Howard in the letters column, one of which was of course from Lovecraft.

Various outings in spring and summer and visits by a number of friends old and new during the latter half of the year made 1936 not quite the disaster it had been up to then. On May 4 the Rhode Island Tercentenary celebration began with a parade in colonial costumes that began at the Van Wickle Gates of Brown University, scarcely a hundred yards from Lovecraft's door. Later, at the Colony House, there was a reenactment of the "tragic sessions of the rebel legislature"[5] three hundred years earlier in which the signers were each portrayed by lineal descendants. Lovecraft was one of the few to get into the building to see the ceremony—he had

"had work not to hiss the rebels & applaud the loyal minority who stood firmly by his Majesty's government"! Later Governor Curley of Massachusetts presented to Governor Green of Rhode Island a copy of the revocation of Roger Williams's banishment of 1635. "After 300½ years, I am sure that Roger highly appreciates this mark of consideration!"[6]

The summer was anomalously late in arriving, but the week of July 8 finally brought temperatures in the 90s and saved Lovecraft "from some sort of general breakdown."[7] In six days he accomplished more than in the six week previous. On July 11 he took a boat trip to Newport, doing considerable writing on the lofty cliffs overlooking the ocean.

As for guests, first on the agenda was Maurice W. Moe, who had not seen Lovecraft since the latter's fat days of 1923. Moe came with his son Robert for a visit on July 18–19, and since Robert had come in his car, they had convenient transport for all manner of sightseeing. They went to the old fishing village of Pawtuxet (then already absorbed into the Providence city limits), drove through Roger Williams Park, and visited the Warren-Bristol area that Robert and Lovecraft had seen in March of the previous year. At Warren they had another all-ice cream dinner. Maurice could only finish two and a half pints, Robert barely managed three, and Lovecraft finished three and could have eaten three more.

Moe was not much involved with amateurdom at this time, but he nevertheless managed to talk Lovecraft into becoming involved in a round-robin correspondence group, the Coryciani, similar to the old Kleicomolo and Gallomo. Although Moe was evidently the leader of this group, it had been founded by John D. Adams; Natalie H. Wooley, an amateur journalist and correspondent of Lovecraft's since at least 1933 about whom almost nothing is known, was also involved. The focus of the group's activities was the analysis of poetry, although in the one letter by Lovecraft that survives (July 14, 1936) there is a discussion—evidently in response to another member's query—as to what Lovecraft might do on his last hour of life:

> For my part—as a realist beyond the age of theatricalism & naive beliefs—I feel quite certain that my own known last hour would be spent quite prosaically in writing instructions for the disposition of certain books, manuscripts, heirlooms, & other possessions. Such a task would—in view of the mental stress—take at least an hour—& it would be the most useful thing I could do before dropping off into oblivion. If I *did* finish ahead of time, I'd probably spend the residual minutes getting a last look at something closely associated with my earliest memories—a picture, a library table, an 1895 Farmer's Almanack, a small music-box I used to play with at 2½, or some kindred symbol—completing a psychological circle in a spirit half of humour & half of whimsical sentimentality. Then—nothingness, as before Aug. 20, 1890.[8]

July 28 saw the arrival of no less important a guest than R. H. Barlow, who was forced to leave his Florida home because of family disruptions that ultimately sent him to live with relatives in Leavenworth, Kansas. Barlow stayed more than a month in Providence, taking up quarters at the boarding-house behind 66 College and not leaving until September 1. During this time he was quite unremitting in his demands on Lovecraft's time, but the latter felt obliged to humour him in light of the superabundant hospitality he himself had received in Florida in 1934 and 1935:

> Ædepol! The kid took a room at the boarding-house across the garden, but despite this degree of independence was a constant responsibility. He *must* be shewn to this or that museum or bookstall . . . he *must* discuss some new fantasy or chapter in his future monumental novel . . . & so on, & so on. What could an old man do—especially since Bobby was such a generous & assiduous host himself last year & the year before?[9]

In fairness to Barlow, this letter was written to a revision client who was demanding work on which Lovecraft was very late, so that perhaps he was merely making excuses; there is every reason to believe that he was delighted with Barlow's company and was glad of the visit. To Elizabeth Toldridge—whom Barlow had visited frequently when in Washington some months earlier attending art classes at the Corcoran Gallery—Lovecraft declared, "I was so glad to see him that I forgave him the fierce moustache & side-whiskers!"[10] It was at this time that Lovecraft and Barlow discovered that they were sixth cousins—having a common ancestry in John Rathbone or Rathbun (b. 1658).

Still another visitor descended upon Providence on August 5—the redoubtable Adolphe de Castro, who had just been to Boston to scatter his wife's ashes in the sea. By now a broken man—in his seventies, with no money, and his beloved wife dead—de Castro was still trying to foist various unrealistic projects upon Lovecraft. Two years previous he had pleaded with Lovecraft to work on a collection of miscellaneous historical and political essays entitled *The New Way,* in one essay of which he purported to have discovered the "true" facts about the parents of Jesus—derived from "Germanic [*sic*] and Semitic sources." Lovecraft, in looking over this piece, found elementary errors in the sections dealing with Roman history, so was naturally sceptical about the rest; in any case, he felt unable to conduct any revision on the work except over a very long period of time—a tactful way of telling de Castro that he really did not want to work on the thing at all. De Castro, however, did not get the message and sent the manuscript to Lovecraft anyway in November 1934; Lovecraft returned it to him in the summer of 1935, saying that he would look it over only after a first reviser had done a major overhauling of its factual basis. Whether as a joke or not, Lovecraft suggested that de Castro consider publishing the chapters on Jesus as historical fiction rather than as a work of scholarship.

All this was forgotten, however, when de Castro came to Providence. Trying to cheer the old boy up, Lovecraft and Barlow took him on August 8 to St John's Churchyard in Benefit Street, where the spectral atmosphere—and the fact that Poe had been there courting Sarah Helen Whitman ninety years before—impelled the three men to write acrostic "sonnets" on the name Edgar Allan Poe. (These were, of course, one line shorter than an actual sonnet.) The full title of Lovecraft's is "In a Sequester'd Providence Churchyard Where Once Poe Walk'd"; Barlow's is titled "St. John's Churchyard"; de Castro's, merely "Edgar Allan Poe." Of these three Barlow's may well be the best. But de Castro—whose poem is rather flat and sentimental—was the canniest of the bunch, for he later revised his poem and submitted it to *Weird Tales,* where it was quickly accepted, appearing in the May 1937 issue. When Lovecraft and Barlow learnt this, they too submitted their poems—but Farnsworth Wright wanted to use only one. Lovecraft and Barlow were forced to dump their pieces on the fan magazines—specifically the *Science-Fantasy Correspondent,* where they appeared in the March–April 1937 issue.

News of the poetical escapade spread quickly among Lovecraft's colleagues, and Maurice W. Moe not only composed his own sonnet (not especially distinguished) but duplicated all four in a hectographed booklet for his classes, under the title *Four Acrostic Sonnets on Edgar Allan Poe* (1936). August Derleth saw this item and decided to reprint Moe's poem in the anthology he was co-editing with Raymond E. F. Larsson, *Poetry out of Wisconsin* (1937). Still later, toward the end of the year, Henry Kuttner added his own piece—which is easily the best of the lot. Unfortunately, it remained unpublished for many years.[11]

De Castro left shortly after the churchyard visit. Barlow hung around for another three weeks, and he and Lovecraft visited Newport on the 15th and Salem and Marblehead on the 20th (Lovecraft's forty-sixth birthday). On the way up they picked up Kenneth Sterling, who was staying in Lynn recovering from an operation prior to his entry into Harvard that fall.

Another literary project on which Lovecraft and Barlow probably worked during his stay in Providence was "The Night Ocean." We are now able to gauge the precise degree of Lovecraft's contribution to this tale, as Barlow's typescript, with Lovecraft's revisions, has now surfaced. Prior to this discovery, all we had to go on were various remarks in letters and certain other documents. Lovecraft told Hyman Bradofsky (who published the tale in the Winter 1936 issue of the *Californian*) that he "ripped the text to pieces in spots";[12] but in a letter to Duane W. Rimel upon appearance of the work, he waxed eloquent about its merits: "The kid is coming along—indeed, the N.O. is one of the most truly artistic weird tales I've ever read."[13] It would be uncharacteristic of Lovecraft so to praise a story in which he had had a very large hand; and sure enough, Lovecraft's contribution probably amounts to no more than 10%. He was in any event correct that Barlow had been "coming along," as the latter's "A Dim-Remembered Story" (*Californian,* Summer

1936) is a superbly crafted tale but one that does not seem to bear any revisory hand by Lovecraft at all. The story is in fact dedicated to Lovecraft, and each of its four sections is prefaced by a half-line of the celebrated *Necronomicon* couplet, "That is not dead which can eternal lie, / But with strange aeons even death may die"; but otherwise it bears little stylistic or conceptual similarity to Lovecraft's work. Lovecraft waxed enthusiastic about it when he read it: "Holy Yuggoth, but it's a masterpiece! *Magnificent* stuff—will bear comparison to the best of C A S! Splendid rhythm, poetic imagery, emotional modulations, & atmospheric power. Tsathoggua! But *literature* is certainly your forte, say what you will! . . . You've rung the bell this time! All the cosmic sweep of Wandrei's early work—& infinitely more substance. Keep it up!"[14] Indeed, it is possible that Lovecraft was commenting not on a manuscript but upon the printed version, which would conclusively militate against Lovecraft's revisory hand in the tale. Even though Lovecraft urged Barlow to send the story to Farnsworth Wright, he went on to add, "Previous amateur appearance is no barrier to W T publication," as if the tale had already been scheduled for publication in the *Californian* or had in fact already appeared there. Barlow does not appear to have submitted the story to *Weird Tales*. Lovecraft repeated his praise for it in a "Literary Review" that appeared in the very same issue of the *Californian* as "The Night Ocean" itself.

It is difficult to deny that "The Night Ocean" is one of the most pensively atmospheric tales produced by anyone in the Lovecraft circle. It comes very close—closer, perhaps, than any of Lovecraft's own works with the exception of "The Colour out of Space"—to capturing the essential spirit of the weird tale, as he wrote of some of Blackwood's works in "Supernatural Horror in Literature": "Here art and restraint in narrative reach their very highest development, and an impression of lasting poignancy is produced without a single strained passage or a single false note. . . . Plot is everywhere negligible, and atmosphere reigns untrammelled." The plot of the story—an artist occupies a remote seaside bungalow for a vacation and senses strange but nebulous presences on the beach or in the ocean—is indeed negligible, but the artistry is in the telling: the avoidance of explicitness—one of the besetting sins of Lovecraft's later works—is the great virtue of the tale, and at the end all the narrator can conclude is that

> . . . a strangeness . . . had surged up like an evil brew within a pot, had mounted to the very rim in a breathless moment, had paused uncertainly there, and had subsided, taking with it whatever unknown message it had borne. . . . I had come frighteningly near to the capture of an old secret which ventured close to man's haunts and lurked cautiously just beyond the edge of the known. Yet in the end I had nothing.

"The Night Ocean" is a richly interpretable story that produces new insights and pleasures upon each rereading. It is the last surviving piece of fiction on which Lovecraft is known to have worked.

James F. Morton visited Lovecraft in Providence on September 11–13, and Robert Moe stopped by on September 19–20, although he was now coming chiefly to court Eunice French (1915–1949), a philosophy student at Brown. A surviving photograph of Lovecraft and French must have been taken at this time, presumably by Moe.

The revision client to whom Lovecraft made his mock-complaint about Barlow was his old amateur colleague Anne Tillery Renshaw, who had gone from being a professor to running her own school, The Renshaw School of Speech, in Washington, D.C. In early 1936 she made Lovecraft a proposal: she wished him to revise and edit a booklet she was writing entitled *Well Bred Speech,* designed for her adult education classes. Lovecraft was, of course, entirely willing to work on the project, not only because it would be intrinsically interesting but because it would presumably bring in revenue at a time when revision work was apparently lean and sporadic.

Lovecraft received at least a partial draft of the text by mid-February and came to realise that "the job is somewhat ampler than I had expected—involving the furnishing of original elements as well as the revision of a specific text"; but—in spite of his aunt's illness at this time—he was willing to undertake the task if he received clear instructions on how much expansion he should do. He breezily added, "Rates can be discussed later—I fancy that any figure you would quote (with current precedent in mind) would be satisfactory."[15] Later, after all the work was finished, he felt that Renshaw would be a cheapskate if she paid him anything less than $200. In the end, he received only $100, but this seems to have been his own fault, since his own final price was $150, which he reduced to $100 because of his tardiness.[16]

Renshaw responded to Lovecraft's initial queries on February 28, but—because of Annie's hospital stay and the attendant congestion of his schedule—he did not reply until March 30. By this time, however, he had done work on chapters 2 (Fifty Common Errors) and 4 (Terms Which Should Own a Place in Your Conversation); all the revisions he had made were done from resources of his own personal library, since he had no time to go to the public library. Hitherto Lovecraft had merely corrected an existing text by Renshaw; now he realised that it was time for original work to begin, and he again wished specific instructions on how much of this work—particularly on bromides, words frequently mispronounced, and a reading guide—he should do. Indeed, he held out a slim hope that Renshaw, irritated at his dilatoriness, might relieve him of his duties and dump the book on someone else, like Maurice W. Moe.

Renshaw disillusioned Lovecraft on that last point: in her response on April 6, she clarified her intentions and set a deadline of May 1 for the entire project. This would, presumably, allow the book to be printed in time for the opening of the fall semester. Lovecraft, however, was still engulfed in attending to Annie, coming to terms with the *Astounding* debacle, absorbing the death of Robert E. Howard, dealing with the NAPA contretemps, and receiving his various guests of the late summer and fall. As a result, he did not reply to Renshaw until September 19, and then only after a letter from her on September 15 made such a reply mandatory. Lovecraft had, indeed, been doing work piecemeal on the text in August, during Barlow's stay: "Well—I did a lot of work in the small hours after the kid had retired to his trans-hortense cubicle (& then he thought it funny that Grandpa didn't get up till noon!), but what headway could such stolen snatches make against a schedule-congestion which had things *already* half shot to hades?"[17] But this was clearly inadequate: faced with a new deadline of October 1, Lovecraft worked for *sixty hours without a break* on or around the time he wrote this letter.

Much of both Renshaw's and Lovecraft's work on *Well Bred Speech* survives in manuscript and allows us to gauge precisely how much each contributed to most parts of the text. It should be said at the outset that the book overall is not exactly a work of towering scholarship; but without Lovecraft's assistance it would have been totally hopeless. Renshaw may or may not have been an able teacher (her specialty, it appears, was elocution as opposed to grammar or literature); but as a writer she falls considerably below the level one can reasonably expect even for an instructor of adult education courses. It is true that the work's purpose is relatively humble; and Lovecraft's assessment of it, and of Renshaw, was quite charitable, as when he wrote to another colleague who had expressed amusement that an English professor would need help on a book on English usage: "A teacher may know the elements of correct speech, yet lack altogether the ability to *formulate* the material in a neat & effective fashion. Using good phraseology & *organising a treatise* are two different matters. In this case the author's lack of time is the main factor."[18] This is, as we shall see, a very charitable assessment indeed.

The contents of the finished book is as follows:

    I. The Background of Speech [history of human language]
   II. Fifty Common Errors [errors of grammar and syntax]
  III. Words Frequently Mispronounced
  IV. Terms Which Should Own a Place in Your Conversation
   V. Increasing Your Vocabulary
  VI. Bromides Must Go [on clichés]
 VII. Tone Training [on elucution]
VIII. Conversational Approaches
  IX. Speech in Social Usage
   X. What Shall I Read?

The first thing Lovecraft had to do was to put the work in order, since Renshaw's draft was very much out of sequence and did not progress logically. Then there was the question of amplification: although Lovecraft admitted that he was given carte blanche by Renshaw for additions, he wished to be entirely clear on the matter before undertaking significant work. As it happens, much of his work turned out to be for naught.

Chapter I is an extraordinarily brief account—all of two and a half printed pages—on the development of the language faculty in human beings. Lovecraft clearly wrote a good portion of it (no manuscript of it survives); indeed, it seems to embody much of what Lovecraft had written to Renshaw in his letters of February 24 and March 30, when he successfully persuaded her to give up the notions that language was a "divine revelation" to humans and that the English language has its origins in Hebrew!

Chapter II (also non-extant in manuscript) seems largely by Renshaw, although some of the examples of erroneous usage (e.g., "Mr. Black is an *alumni* of Brown University") are probably by Lovecraft; some of them repeat the strictures found in his old piece on "Literary Composition" (1920).

Chapter III survives in manuscript, and it can be seen that Lovecraft has written nearly the whole of it. His list of mispronounced words at the end of the chapter is a little truncated in the published version, and his very long list of words with more than one acceptable pronunciation has been excised altogether.

Chapter IV, in the printed text, follows a typescript prepared by Renshaw and somewhat revised by Lovecraft. The bulk of the chapter is a list of terms—chiefly drawn from history, literature, and economics—and their definitions and connotations; some are largely or entirely by Lovecraft.

Chapter V similarly follows a text initially written by Renshaw and exhaustively revised and augmented (especially at the end) by Lovecraft.

Chapter VI is also a text initially written by Renshaw, but Lovecraft has made so many additions that it is now largely his. The manuscript lists an enormous number of bromides, but this has been radically cut down in the published version. Renshaw had, indeed, asked for only fifty specimens;[19] Lovecraft has supplied nearly six times as many. Incredibly, he asked for this list to be returned to him (as it evidently was) for future use of his own!

Chapter VII, VIII, and IX are ones in which Lovecraft admitted to having little or no expertise (or interest), so presumably (the manuscript does not survive for any of these chapters) he only polished up an existing text by Renshaw. Random portions do, however, bear traces of his style.

Chapter X, whose manuscript is extant, is the most interesting—and unfortunate. In the published version, the first two paragraphs of the text are by Renshaw (slightly revised by Lovecraft), while the rest of the text—sixteen printed pages—is by Lovecraft. This does not, however, tell the whole story; for he had written a chapter some two or three times as long (it has been published posthumously as "Suggestions for a Reading Guide"), but Renshaw—perhaps concerned about space or about some seemingly technical parts of this section or about its possible disproportion in relation to the rest of the work—has essentially gutted it and made it vastly less useful than it could have been. I wish to discuss this chapter in detail before commenting on some features in the previous ones.

We have seen that Lovecraft here supplies his fairly conservative opinions on modern literature, and that he had certainly not read all the works he mentions. In fact, however, "Suggestions for a Reading Guide" is a comprehensive—and on the whole quite sound—reading list of the highlights of world literature from antiquity to the present as well as the most up-to-date works in all the sciences and arts. It would have been an exceptionally useful pedagogical tool for its day if it had appeared intact.

Renshaw has preserved a good deal of Lovecraft's recommendations of classical literature, although she reduces Lovecraft's citation of the four great Greek playwrights (Aeschylus, Sophocles, Euripides, and Aristophanes) to only Aeschylus. About half of Lovecraft's paragraph on mediaeval literature is preserved, but his discussion of Malory's *Morte d'Arthur* and (much to his chagrin, no doubt) the *Arabian Nights* is omitted. The paragraph on Renaissance literature is reduced to Lovecraft's discussions of Shakespeare, Bacon, and Spenser. Almost the whole of his paragraph on seventeenth-century literature is excised, except for a reduced section on Milton; and Renshaw has so bumblingly edited this passage that Milton's name never gets mentioned.

For eighteenth-century literature, Renshaw keeps Lovecraft's discussion of the English novel and English poetry but drops his recommendations on the English essayists (who were, of course, his favourites of this period). The paragraph on nineteenth-century English literature is preserved largely intact, but incredibly Renshaw drops Lovecraft's entire discussion of French literature of this period— and we have already seen how high he ranked Balzac as a novelist. Scandinavian and Russian literature of the nineteenth century survives more or less whole.

Lovecraft's discussion of the twentieth century does not fare so well. While preserving most of his mentions of British writers, she cuts out the passage on Irish literature—including the mention of Yeats as the "greatest living poet" and the citation of Dunsany as well as of Joyce. The entire discussion of the American novel is dropped, and only Lovecraft's mentions of the leading American poets is preserved. Lovecraft should, I suppose, have predicted that Renshaw would cut most of his discussion of "lighter" literature, including an entire half-paragraph on weird and detective fiction.

The greatest disfigurement is in Lovecraft's subsequent recommendations—

on dictionaries, literary histories, literary criticism, language, history, and the sciences. This last section—covering mathematics, physics, chemistry, geology, geography, biology, zoology, human anatomy and physiology, psychology, anthropology, economics, political science, and education—is all gone. Renshaw keeps only a small bit of Lovecraft's discussion of philosophy (including only his recommendation of Will Durant's *The Story of Philosophy*), and drops his discussion of works on ethics, aesthetics, the various arts (including music), and technology. Lovecraft's concluding remarks are also highly truncated.

Although "Suggestions for a Reading Guide" does contain recommendations of a fair number of titles from Lovecraft's own library, he did do considerable work at the public library to find the soundest and most up-to-date works on some of the technical subjects. It is, indeed, of some interest to trace some autobiographical connexions in this section—some insignificant, some perhaps less so. Among the music books Lovecraft mentions is "Isaacson's *Face to Face with the Great Musicians*"—a work by none other than his old amateur foe Charles D. Isaacson, who had gone on to write a number of popular works on music. He cannot help ridiculing Carlyle, whom he quite correctly characterises as "having a choppy, artificial style suggestive of the modern news-magazine *Time*." He is obliged to speak kindly of the hated Dickens, but recommends only *David Copperfield*. But perhaps the most charming autobiographical allusion is a passage toward the end on how the impecunious reader may go about assembling a book collection:

> Acquire as many books of the right sort as you can afford to house, for ownership means easy and repeated access and permanent usefulness. Don't be a foppish hoarder of fine bindings and first editions. Get books for what's in them, and be glad enough of that. Marvellous bargains can be found on the dime counters of second-hand shops, and a really good library can be picked up at surprisingly little cost. The one great trouble is housing when one's quarters are limited; though by using many small bookcases—cheap sets of open shelves—in odd corners one can stow away a gratifying number of volumes.

As for the rest of the book, Lovecraft has received considerable criticism for being outdated in some of his recommendations, especially in regard to pronunciation; but it is not at all clear that he deserves such censure. On page 22 of the published book, he records four preferred pronunciations: *con-cen´trate* to *con´centrate; ab-do´-men* to *ab´-do-men; ensign* to *ensin;* and *profeel* to *profyle*. The *Oxford English Dictionary* of 1933 supports Lovecraft on the last three of these. It is possible that American usage had changed in regard to these words, as well as on the other ones on the enormous list that was not used; but Lovecraft is by no means as antiquated as he has been accused of being.

Nevertheless, *Well Bred Speech* cannot possibly be called a work of any great merit; and it is something one wishes Lovecraft had not spent such back-breaking effort working on at this time. Lovecraft read the proofs of the book later in the year, and—although it bears a copyright date of 1936—it is not clear that it actually came out before the end of the year. But it was presumably available for the beginning of the second semester of Renshaw's school. In 1937 Renshaw published another book, *Salvaging Self-Esteem: A Program for Self-Improvement.* Since it found its way into Lovecraft's library, it was presumably published sometime in the spring. There is, mercifully, no evidence that Lovecraft worked on this item.

"Suggestions for a Reading Guide" was finally published in 1966. The first two paragraphs—basically by Renshaw, with light editing by Lovecraft—had also been previously revised by R. H. Barlow. The title was probably supplied either by Barlow or August Derleth.

In his final year Lovecraft continued to attract new—and mostly young— correspondents who, unaware of his increasing ill health, were thrilled to receive actual letters from this giant of weird fiction. Most of them continued to reach him through *Weird Tales,* but several got in touch through the increasingly complex network of the science fiction and fantasy fan circuit.

Among the most promising of these was Henry Kuttner (1915–1958). A friend of Robert Bloch's, he had published only a single poem in *Weird Tales* ("Ballad of the Gods" in February 1936) before writing to Lovecraft early in 1936. Lovecraft later confessed that several colleagues thought that he had either ghost-written or extensively revised Kuttner's "The Graveyard Rats" (*Weird Tales,* March 1936),[20] but this story had already been accepted before Lovecraft heard from Kuttner. It is, in fact, difficult to believe how anyone could have mistaken this story for Lovecraft's: although an entertaining (if not very plausible) tale of grue involving the caretaker of a cemetery who is despatched by the huge rats that burrow into coffins and remove the mortal remains, its only conceivable connexions with Lovecraft are its setting (Salem) and its very dim echoes of "The Rats in the Walls"; the style is not even very Lovecraftian.

Kuttner had, however, by this time already written a tale whose first draft— rejected by *Weird Tales*—may have been consciously Lovecraftian. In his second letter to Kuttner, on March 12, Lovecraft offered a lengthy criticism of "The Salem Horror"; and it is clear that Kuttner made major changes in the story based upon these comments. What is uncertain, however, is whether the first draft had been as consciously Lovecraftian—or, rather, had contained a "new" mythical god, Nyogtha, and a quotation from the *Necronomicon* in which the attributes of this god are specified—as it now stands. Nothing in Lovecraft's letter would lead one to think so, although a comment in his previous letter, in reference to various stories by Kuttner that Lovecraft had not yet seen—"I appreciate the compliment implied in the use of some of my settings & dramatic entities"[21]—suggests that perhaps some allusions already were present in the initial draft.

Kuttner's geographical, historical, and architectural knowledge of Salem was all wrong, and Lovecraft set about correcting it; his letter is full of drawings of representative Salem houses, a map of the city, and even sketches of various types of headstones found in the older cemeteries. Lovecraft remarks that "Derby St. is a slum inhabited by Polish immigrants,"[22] and Kuttner has indeed set the final version of "The Salem Horror" in Derby St. Other parts of Lovecraft's letter suggest that significant overhauling to the basic plot and incidents of the story were also done, since Lovecraft felt (as he had done with some of Bloch's early tales) that the story was "a little *vaguely motivated.*"[23]

Lovecraft's letters to Kuttner predictably discuss almost nothing but weird fiction, but one small detail proved to be of great moment in the subsequent history of weird, fantasy, and science fiction. In May he casually asked Kuttner to pass on some photographs of Salem and Marblehead to C. L. Moore once Kuttner himself had finished with them;[24] and it was in this casual way that Moore and Kuttner became acquainted. Marrying in 1940, the couple went on to write some of the most distinguished work of the "Golden Age" of science fiction. It is now nearly hopeless to untangle the novels and tales that may have been written predominantly by Moore and those written largely by Kuttner; they collaborated on nearly every work of fiction until Kuttner's death in 1958. Indeed, in his very last letter to Kuttner, written in February 1937, Lovecraft already commented that Kuttner and Moore were collaborating on some unspecified "dual masterpiece."[25] However the authorship of their works is apportioned, such works as "Judgment Night" (1943), *Earth's Last Citadel* (1943), and "Vintage Season" (1946) well fulfil the high expectations Lovecraft had for both his younger colleagues.

One of the most distinctive of Lovecraft's late associates—not so much for what he accomplished at the time as for what he did later—was Willis Conover, Jr (1920–1996). In the spring of 1936, as a fifteen-year-old boy living in the small town of Cambridge, Maryland, Conover had conceived the idea of a Junior Science-Fiction Correspondence Club, where like-minded fans from all over the country would write letters to each other; this idea metamorphosed quickly into a magazine, the *Science-Fantasy Correspondent,* on which Conover began actively working in the summer. In addition to publishing the work of fans, Conover wished to lend prestige to his magazine by soliciting minor pieces from professionals. He could not, of course, pay anything: he and his printer, Corwin F. Stickney of Belleville, New Jersey, could scarcely afford the printing bills for each issue. Still, Conover had ambitious plans, and he wrote letters to August Derleth, E. Hoffmann Price, and many other leading writers in the field—including, in July 1936, Lovecraft.

In a brief but cordial response on July 9, Lovecraft wished Conover well in his venture and, although having no prose contribution available (that is, no unpublished story short enough for inclusion in a fan magazine), did send him the poem "Homecoming" (sonnet V of *Fungi from Yuggoth*); later Lovecraft discovered to his dismay that this sonnet, which he thought unpublished, had actually appeared in the January 1935 *Fantasy Fan.*

A more significant development occurred in late August, when Conover expressed regret that the *Fantasy Fan* serialisation of "Supernatural Horror in Literature" had ended so abruptly. It was Lovecraft who casually suggested that Conover continue the serialisation in his own magazine from the point where it had left off (the middle of chapter eight), and Conover jumped at this idea. This item could not be accommodated in the first issue of the *Science-Fantasy Correspondent* (November–December 1936), but by September Lovecraft had already sent Conover the same annotated copy of the *Recluse* (with additions written on separate sheets) that he had lent (and received back) from Hornig.

In early December Conover asked Lovecraft to prepare a "short summary" of the first eight chapters of "Supernatural Horror in Literature," for the benefit of those readers who had not seen the earlier appearances. Lovecraft agreed, but was unclear what Conover meant by "short"; in any event, as he began preparing the summary, he found it difficult to condense those eight chapters (about 18,000 words) into a compass that would convey any meaning. In the end, he wrote a 2500-word summary that ably abstracts the essence of this very dense essay. One actual addition is highly amusing: in speaking of Walpole's *Castle of Otranto,* Lovecraft berated its "brisk, cheerful style (like much of the pulp magazine 'weird' fiction of today)"—a slam at the pulps that Lovecraft had elaborated at great length in late letters to E. Hoffmann Price, August Derleth, C. L. Moore, and many others.

Shortly after this time, however, Conover took over Julius Schwartz's *Fantasy Magazine,* since Schwartz wished to abandon fan editing to become a full-time agent in the science fiction field. Conover then decided to reprint "Supernatural Horror in Literature" from the beginning. The second issue of the *Science-Fantasy Correspondent* was dated January–February 1937, but did not contain any segment of the essay; Conover had, however, typed out the whole of it and sent it to Lovecraft, who managed to correct at least the first half of it by mid-February 1937, after which he became too ill to do any further work. No more issues of Conover's magazine appeared, however; some of the material was later transferred to Stickney's *Amateur Correspondent* (including what is apparently the best of three separate manuscript versions of "Notes on Writing Weird Fiction"), but Conover lost interest in the field at about this time—perhaps, indeed, as a direct consequence of Lovecraft's death.

We know so much about the relationship between Conover and Lovecraft—

which is, in all frankness, a fairly minor one in the totality of Lovecraft's life, although clearly it was significant to Conover—not only because Lovecraft's letters to him survive, but because of the volume Conover published in 1975 entitled *Lovecraft at Last*. This book is not only one of the finest examples of modern book design, but a poignant, even wrenching testimonial to the friendship between a middle-aged—and dying—man and a young boy who idolised him. Although the two never met, the correspondence was warm from the beginning. Some of it is a trifle silly, as Lovecraft indulged Conover in some of his juvenile tastes: he patiently answered Conover's inane questions regarding some figures in Lovecraft's invented pantheon ("Incidentally, how is your stooge Yog-Sothoth? And where do you keep him at night?"[26]) and claimed that he would soberly cite Conover's mythical book *Ghorl Nigral* in a story (he thankfully never did so, chiefly because he did not write any original stories in the last six months of his life). No doubt Lovecraft was remembering his own enthusiasm as a boy reading the *Argosy* and *All-Story,* and he did recognise in Conover an unusual level of competence (he praised the *Science-Fantasy Correspondent* for its near-total lack of typographical errors) and diligence.

There were other fan editors and publishers with whom Lovecraft came in touch at this time. One of them was Wilson Shepherd (1917–1985), Wollheim's colleague on the *Phantagraph.* Lovecraft had already learnt something of Shepherd just prior to beginning his brief correspondence with him in the spring of 1936, but it was not at all to Shepherd's credit. In March R. H. Barlow had presented to Lovecraft a sheaf of letters between himself and Shepherd, dating to 1932, in which Shepherd had apparently tried to bamboozle Barlow out of a part of his magazine collection. Shepherd had claimed that he had a complete file of *Weird Tales,* among other things, and agreed to part with the issues for 1923–25 (which Barlow lacked) in exchange for eight bound volumes of *Amazing Stories.* Barlow sent the *Amazings* but received in return an assortment of very ordinary magazines which he already had, but no issues of *Weird Tales.* When Barlow protested, Shepherd offered him a complete set of "*Science Fiction Magazine* and its sister magazine INTERPLANETARY STORYS" [*sic*], two nonexistent magazines. Barlow at this point came to the conclusion that he was dealing with either a thief or an insane person. It is not clear what the upshot of this whole deal was, but in the spring of 1936 Barlow had asked Lovecraft to prepare a précis of this correspondence to circulate to other colleagues, and the result is a sober but unwittingly hilarious piece entitled "Correspondence between R. H. Barlow and Wilson Shepherd of Oakman, Alabama, Sept.–Nov. 1932." It is probable, incidentally, that Shepherd never had a complete set of *Weird Tales,* which even at that time was pretty rare.

Lovecraft did not know what to make of Shepherd; to Barlow he expressed the belief that he was "a poor white or illiterate hill-billy grades below even [William L.] Crawford—jest an Allybammy cracker with the amorality of a Faulkner peas-

ant."[27] Although he referred to Shepherd as "Share-Cropper Shep" to other correspondents, Lovecraft dealt with him cordially enough when actually coming into
direct touch with him in April 1936. He offered Shepherd advice on improving the
typography and design of the *Phantagraph;* he sent "The Nameless City" for printing in the semi-professional magazine that Wollheim and Shepherd were planning,
Fanciful Tales; and he even revised two poems by Shepherd, "Death" and "Irony"
(which Lovecraft retitled "The Wanderer's Return"). Neither of these poems
amounts to much, but in Lovecraft's version they at least scan and rhyme.

Shepherd (in conjunction with Wollheim) gave Lovecraft a nice forty-sixth
birthday present in return for his various kindnesses. He issued a broadside containing the poem "Background" (titled "A Sonnet") as the sole contribution to
Volume XLVII, No. 1 of a magazine called the *Lovecrafter.* It is a very appropriate tribute, for this poem—sonnet XXX of *Fungi from Yuggoth*—certainly reflects the essence of Lovecraft's imaginative life. Lovecraft was delighted at the
birthday gift, and was also relieved at the absence of typographical errors.

He was less happy with the sole issue of the Wollheim-Shepherd *Fanciful
Tales of Time and Space* appeared. Dated Fall 1936, it contained the much-
rejected "The Nameless City," along with pieces by Rimel, David H. Keller,
Robert E. Howard, Derleth, and others; but the Lovecraft contribution contained
at least fifty-nine misprints. "That is surely something of a record!"[28] Lovecraft
bemoaned (later a correspondent caught still more errors). But he himself may
have been partly to blame, for he read proofs of several pages of the story as Shepherd sent them to him. Lovecraft was, however, a bad proofreader of his own material (he was much better when proofreading others' work). To pick one example at
random, he failed to notice that the unidentified typist of "The Thing on the Doorstep" had not only made serious misreadings, but severely erred in making section
divisions in the story. And yet, this was the typescript that was sent to *Weird Tales*
and ultimately printed in this erroneous condition.

Still another new correspondent, Nils Helmer Frome (1918–1962), is an interesting case. Born in Sweden but spending most of his life in Fraser Mills, British Columbia (a northern suburb of Vancouver), Frome has the distinction of being Canada's first active science fiction fan.[29] In the fall of 1936 Frome evidently
solicited some contributions from Lovecraft for his fan magazine *Supramundane
Stories,* but the first issue—initially planned for October 1936 but later dated December [1936]–January 1937—did not contain any work by him. The second
(and last) issue, dated Spring 1938, contained Lovecraft's "Nyarlathotep" as well
as a version of his essay on weird fiction, which Frome titled "Notes on Writing
Weird Fiction—the 'Why' and 'How.'" Lovecraft had also sent Frome the prose-
poem "What the Moon Brings" (1922), but upon the folding of *Supramundane
Stories* the piece was passed on to James V. Taurasi, who used it in his fanzine,

Cosmic Tales, for April–May–June 1941. Frome also let some of his letters from Lovecraft appear in *Phantastique/The Science Fiction Critic* for March 1938.

Lovecraft did not know quite what to make of Frome. He was no doubt pleased to have a correspondent in a country that still retained its loyalty to the British throne, but Frome was a strange, mystical character who believed in numerology, fortune-telling, the immortality of the soul, and other conceptions Lovecraft found preposterous. And yet, Frome seemed to be a man of such keen native intelligence that Lovecraft strove to instruct and aid him as best he could. While nearly on his deathbed, he sent to Frome a list of recent books on the sciences (culled largely from "Suggestions for a Reading Guide") that would, he hoped, clear up the many misconceptions about the universe Frome had. How successful Lovecraft was in his educational efforts, it is difficult to say. Frome eventually lost touch with fandom and died before his forty-fourth birthday.

Two final fan editors with whom Lovecraft exchanged a few letters were James Blish (1921–1975) and William Miller, Jr (b. 1921), two youths living in East Orange, New Jersey. They were publishing a fanzine entitled the *Planeteer,* whose first issue was dated November 1935 (Nils Frome did the artwork for some of its covers); but they do not seem to have come into touch with Lovecraft until the summer of 1936. At that time they inevitably asked Lovecraft for a contribution, and he sent them the poem "The Wood," which had hitherto appeared only in the *Tryout* for January 1929. Although the pages containing the poem were set up, this issue— which was dated September 1936, and which had by this time absorbed the fanzine *Tesseract* and had become retitled *Tesseract Combined with The Planeteer*—was never completed. (The next year the young Sam Moskowitz bought the uncompleted copies—about fifteen or so—and sold them for five or ten cents each.[30])

What scraps of correspondence we have to Blish and Miller (Lovecraft wrote to them jointly) is pretty insignificant and deals with Lovecraft disillusioning them as to the reality of the *Necronomicon* and then, in response to a suggestion by the two boys, suggesting rather half-heartedly that he might write, not the whole *Necronomicon* (for he had already cited a passage from page 751 of the tome in "The Dunwich Horror"), but perhaps an excerpt or chapter from it (as Clark Ashton Smith had done in "The Coming of the White Worm," purportedly a chapter from the *Book of Eibon*) or producing a sort of "abridged and expurgated" version.

Although Miller vanished into oblivion shortly after this time, Blish did not. He went on to become one of the most important science fiction writers of his generation, and such works as *Doctor Mirabilis* (1964), *Black Easter* (1968), and *The Day After Judgment* (1972) are among the most philosophically challenging of their kind. Lovecraft's influence on Blish cannot be said to be especially significant, but Blish certainly seems to have remembered his brief association for the whole of his own tragically abbreviated life.

In addition to writers, editors, and publishers, Lovecraft also heard from weird artists. Chief among these was Virgil Finlay (1914–1971), whose work in *Weird Tales* Lovecraft had admired for several months prior to coming in touch with him. Finlay is indeed now recognised as perhaps the greatest pictorial artist to emerge from the pulps, and his stunning pen-and-ink work is unmistakable in its precision and imaginative scope. Lovecraft first heard from him in September 1936, and their correspondence was cordial even though Lovecraft in the end wrote only five letters and one postcard to him. Willis Conover had secretly arranged for Finlay to draw the celebrated portrait of Lovecraft as an eighteenth-century gentleman to head the first instalment of "Supernatural Horror in Literature" in the *Science-Fantasy Correspondent,*[31] a portrait that, after the demise of that fanzine, appeared on the cover of *Amateur Correspondent* for April–May 1937.

Finlay was responsible for what proved to be Lovecraft's penultimate creative utterance. Hearing Finlay's lament on the decline of the old custom of writing verses on current works of art and literature, Lovecraft included one in his letter of November 30: "To Mr. Finlay, upon His Drawing for Mr. Bloch's Tale, 'The Faceless God'" (Finlay's illustration for "The Faceless God" in *Weird Tales* for May 1936 was regarded by many as the best work of art ever to appear in the magazine). Lovecraft prefaced the sonnet by the remark, "I could easily scrawl a sonnet to one of your masterpieces if you weren't too particular about quality,"[32] leading one to believe that he wrote the poem on the spot while writing the letter. This may well be the case, although the poem also appears in a letter to Barlow of the same date. In any case, it is a fine sonnet, the more remarkable if it really was the work of a few impromptu minutes.

About a week later Lovecraft wrote what might be definitively his last work— another sonnet, titled on one manuscript as "To Clark Ashton Smith, Esq., upon His Fantastic Tales, Verse, Pictures, and Sculptures" and on another manuscript as "To Klarkash-Ton, Lord of Averoigne." This too is a fine evocation of Smith's variegated creative work, although it is excelled by Smith's own poignant elegy to Lovecraft written a few months later.

In October 1936 Lovecraft got in touch with Stuart Morton Boland (1909–1973), a young librarian in San Francisco. In his own account of his brief association with Lovecraft, Boland states that he had initially sent to Robert E. Howard a reproduction of an illuminated manuscript that he had seen in Budapest and that Howard had passed this on to Lovecraft, wondering whether this was anything like what the *Necronomicon* was supposed to be. When Boland came home months later, he found a long letter by Lovecraft awaiting him.[33] There is, however, no mention of Boland in the surviving Lovecraft-Howard correspondence, and in any case Howard's last letter to Lovecraft appears to have been written on May 13, leading one to wonder why another five months passed before Boland and Love-craft got into direct communication.

In any event, Boland was knowledgeable in Mesoamerican lore, and in reply to Lovecraft's query as to whether there might be any similarity between his invented pantheon and actual gods of the Aztecs or Mayans, Boland sent an annotated list of some of the more peculiar deities (*"Chiminig-Agua:* A violent deity and keeper of the Cosmic Light. Creator of the colossal Black Avians that distribute light about the Universe during the daytime and who gobbled it up every night"[34]). Lovecraft, although pleased with this exotic folklore, found that it would require "a great deal of interpretation and modification" for fictional use. He had always maintained that synthetic "gods" were much more amenable than actual deities for such a purpose, since their attributes could be moulded to suit the precise requirements of the story.

Brief as his association was, Boland seized on one aspect of Lovecraft's work that has eluded many of his self-styled disciples:

> . . . I got the impression that the Lovecraft Theology was a source of considerable amusement and secret mirth to him . . . He seemed to be bubbling over with a deep Jovian inner laughter because supposedly intelligent readers of his tales took his gods for granted as real existing powers. I further sensed that his attitude was that Man *"created god in his own image and likeness"* to serve his own ends and purposes. I felt a sardonic impulse at play here, but one which with all its burden of tremendous knowledge faced the future with a courage and fortitude un-matched in my experience.[35]

It was in November 1936 that Lovecraft heard from an individual whom he correctly identified as "a genuine find."[36] Fritz Leiber, Jr (1910–1992) was the son of the celebrated Shakespearean actor Fritz Leiber, Sr, whom Lovecraft had seen around 1912 playing in Robert Mantell's company when it came to the Providence Opera House. The son was also interested in drama, but was increasingly turning toward literature. He had been reading the weird and science fiction pulps from an early age, and much later he testified that "The Colour out of Space" in the Sep-tember 1927 *Amazing* "gave me the gloomy creeps for weeks."[37] Then, when *At the Mountains of Madness* and "The Shadow out of Time" appeared in *Astound-ing,* Leiber's interest in Lovecraft was renewed and augmented—perhaps because these works probed that borderline between horror and science fiction that Leiber himself would later explore in his own work. And yet, he himself was too diffident to write to Lovecraft, so his wife Jonquil did so care of *Weird Tales;* for a time Lovecraft was corresponding quasi-separately to both of them.

In mid-December Leiber sent Lovecraft his poem cycle, *Demons of the Up-per Air,* and a novella or short novel, "Adept's Gambit." Both profoundly im-pressed Lovecraft, especially the latter. This first tale of Fafhrd and the Gray Mouser—two swashbuckling characters (modelled upon Leiber himself and his friend Harry O. Fischer [1910–1986], with whom Lovecraft also corresponded briefly) who roamed some nebulous fantastic realm in search of adventure—must have been scintillating, for Lovecraft wrote a long letter commenting in detail about it and praising it effusively:

> My appreciation & enjoyment of "Adept's Gambit" as a capturer of dark currents from the void form an especially good proof of the story's essential power, since the style & manner of approach are almost antipodal to my own. With me, the transition to the unreal is accomplished through humourless pseudo-realism, dark suggestion, & a style full of sombre menace & tension. You, on the other hand, adopt the light, witty, & sophisticated manner of Cabell, Stephens, the later Dunsany, & others of their type—with not a few suggestions of "Vathek" & "Ouroboros" [E. R. Eddison's *The Worm Ouroboros*]. Lightness & humour impose a heavy handicap on the fantaisiste, & all too often end in triviality—yet in this case you have turned liabilities to assets & achieved a fine synthesis in which the breezy whimsicality ultimately builds up rather than dilutes or neutralises the tension & sense of impending shadow.[38]

The published version of "Adept's Gambit" (in Leiber's collection, *Night's Black Agents*, 1947) apparently differs somewhat from the version Lovecraft saw. The nature of Lovecraft's remarks leads one to believe that the story was set more firmly in Graeco-Roman antiquity than it now is. Indeed, the fact that Lovecraft pointed out so many anachronisms and actual errors in the historical setting probably led Leiber to make the story less an historical fantasy and more of a pure fantasy. In the draft Lovecraft read there were also references to his myth-cycle; these were also excised in the final draft. The original manuscript of "Adept's Gambit" has recently surfaced, but it has yet to be published and has not been made available to me.

Leiber has testified frequently and eloquently to the importance of his brief but intense relationship with Lovecraft. Writing in 1958, he confessed: "Lovecraft is sometimes thought of as having been a lonely man. He made my life far less lonely, not only during the brief half year of our correspondence but during the twenty years after."[39] Elsewhere he has even stated that Lovecraft was "the chiefest influence on my literary development after Shakespeare"[40]—a statement I shall want to examine more detailedly later. Here it can be said that Leiber is the one colleague of Lovecraft's who can even remotely be considered his literary equal—more so than August Derleth, Robert E. Howard, Robert Bloch, C. L. Moore, Henry Kuttner, or even James Blish. Leiber's subsequent career—with such landmark works of fantasy and science fiction as *Gather, Darkness!* (1950), *Conjure Wife* (1953), *The Big Time* (1958), *A Specter Is Haunting Texas* (1969), *Our Lady of Darkness* (1977), and dozens of Fafhrd and Gray Mouser stories—is as distinguished as that of any writer in these fields during the past half-century; but like Dunsany and Blackwood, the very mass and complexity of his work seems to have deterred critical analysis, so that Leiber remains merely a revered but ill-understood figure. He learned much from Lovecraft, but like the best of Love-craft's associates and disciples, he became his own man and his own writer.

Finally, let us consider the case of Jacques Bergier (pseudonym of Yakov Mik-hailovich Berger, 1912–1978). This Russian-born Frenchman, living in Paris in the late 1930s, claimed in later years to have corresponded with Lovecraft; indeed, he presents us with the charming anecdote of having asked Lovecraft how he had so realistically portrayed Paris in "The Music of Erich Zann," to which Lovecraft is supposed to have replied that he had visited that city—"in a dream, with Poe."[41] This is all very quaint, but it may be apocryphal. Lovecraft never mentions Bergier in any correspondence I have ever seen. Bergier did write a letter to *Weird Tales,* published in the March 1936 issue, in which he singles out Lovecraft for praise ("By all means, give us more stories by H. P. Lovecraft. He is the only writer of today who is really *haunted"*), so it is just conceivable that Bergier had asked Farnsworth Wright to for-ward a letter to his idol. Bergier also wrote a letter to *Weird Tales* about Lovecraft after the latter's death, without mentioning any correspondence with him; but per-haps it would have been out of place to do so. Lovecraft had no foreign-language correspondents to my knowledge. In any event, Bergier certainly did in later years spearhead the effort to disseminate Lovecraft's work in France.

Lovecraft both lamented and delighted in his burgeoning correspondence. To Willis Conover he wrote in September 1936:

> As for the curtailment of my correspondence . . . this will not mean any abrupt pol-icy of arrogant and neglectful silence. It will mean rather a cutting down of the *length and promptness* of such letters as do not absolutely demand space and speed. I immensely enjoy the new points of view, varied ideas, and diverse reac-tions offered by a wide correspondence, and would be infinitely reluctant to have any drastic or large-scale elimination.[42]

About three months later he was telling Barlow: "I find my list has grown to 97 now—which surely calls for some pruning. . . . but how the hell can one get out of epistolary obligations without becoming snobbish & uncivil?"[43] No greater testi-monial to Lovecraft's flexibility of mind, openness to new information and new impressions, and gentlemanliness of behaviour is required than these two quota-tions. He was dying, but he was still seeking to learn and still adhering to the stan-dards of civilised discourse.

Late in 1936 Lovecraft finally saw something he never thought he would see—a published book bearing his name. But predictably, the entire venture was, from first to last, an error-riddled débâcle. It is certainly little consolation that *The Shadow over Innsmouth* has, by virtue of its being the only actual book published and released in Lovecraft's lifetime, become a valued collectors' item.

William L. Crawford's first book publication was a peculiar little booklet in which Clark Ashton Smith's "The White Sybil" (yes, Smith misspelled "Sibyl") was issued jointly with David H. Keller's "Men of Avalon"; this item emerged under the imprint of Fantasy Publications in 1934. I have already mentioned that Crawford had a variety of plans for issuing either *At the Mountains of Madness* or "The Shadow over Innsmouth" or both as a booklet. In a later article Crawford maintains that he had wanted to do *Mountains* but found it too long, whereupon Lovecraft had suggested "Innsmouth";[44] but Lovecraft's correspondence belies this simple scenario and suggests that Crawford was proposing all manner of schemes for the two stories—including prior serialisation in either *Marvel Tales* or *Unusual Stories* before their book appearance. Finally—presumably after learning of the acceptance of *Mountains* by *Astounding*—Crawford focused on "Innsmouth." The process began in early 1936, and the book was typeset by the *Saxton Herald,* the local paper in Everett, Pennsylvania. Lovecraft began reading proofs later that spring, finding them full of mistakes but laboriously correcting them as best he could; some pages were apparently so bad that they had to be reset virtually from scratch.

It was Lovecraft who, in late January or early February, urged Crawford to use Frank Utpatel as an artist for the book.[45] He had remembered that Utpatel (1905–1980), a Midwesterner of Dutch origin, had been encouraged by his friend August Derleth to do some pen-and-ink drawings for the story as early as 1932, when Derleth was trying to market the tale on his own. The two drawings Utpatel had made at that time no longer existed, and in any event Crawford and Utpatel decided that the illustrations for the book would be in the form of woodcuts. Utpatel executed four woodcuts, one of which—a spectacularly hallucinatory depiction of Innsmouth's decaying roofs and spires, rather suggestive of El Greco—was also used for the jacket illustration. Lovecraft had initially sent Utpatel a set of pictures of some unspecified New England seaport (it may indeed have been Newburyport, the town that had partly inspired the setting), but in mid-February providentially found in the newspaper—as an advertisement by a bank urging depositors to be thrifty and keep their property in good condition[46]—a picture that came very close to capturing his idea of the crumbling town. Lovecraft was delighted with the resultant illustrations by Utpatel, as well he should be, even though the bearded Zadok Allen was portrayed as clean-shaven.

The illustrations, in the end, proved to be perhaps the only worthy item in the book, for certainly the text itself was seriously mangled. The fact that Lovecraft read proofs did not seem to make much difference, for new errors were evidently introduced in making the corrections he indicated, as frequently occurs in a linotype process where an entire line has to be reset even if a single error occurs in it. Lovecraft did not receive a copy of the book until November[47]—a point worth noting, since the copyright page of the book itself gives the date of April 1936 (the title page supplies Crawford's new imprint, Visionary Publishing Co.). Lovecraft claimed to have found 33 misprints in the book, but other readers found still more. He managed to persuade Crawford to print an errata sheet—whose first version was itself so misprinted as to be virtually worthless[48]—and also found the time and effort to correct many copies of the book manually. He did so by a method somewhat analogous to that used to correct the *Astounding* serialisation of *At the Mountains of Madness:* erroneous or supernumerary words, letters, or punctuation marks would be removed with a knife, and corrections written in with a sharp pencil. It seems as if copies bearing such corrections are more numerous than those that do not.

This may have to do with the fact that, although 400 copies of the sheets were printed, Crawford had the money to bind only about 200. Lovecraft declared that Crawford had actually borrowed money from his father for the entire enterprise;[49] indeed, at about the time *The Shadow over Innsmouth* came out, Crawford incredibly asked Lovecraft for a $150 loan to continue *Marvel Tales.*[50] The book—although advertised in both *Weird Tales* and some of the fan journals—sold slowly (it was priced at $1.00), and shortly after its publication Crawford was forced to give up printing and publishing for seven years; at some point during this time the remaining unbound sheets were destroyed. So much for Lovecraft's "first book."

Lovecraft's own career as a practising fiction writer was certainly not going very well. In late June Julius Schwartz, evidently intent on following up the success of placing *At the Mountains of Madness* with *Astounding,* had proposed what Lovecraft considered a wild and impractical idea of placing some of his stories in England. Lovecraft sent him "a lot of manuscripts"[51] (leading one to think that Schwartz may have had a mind to approach book publishers), and in order to exhaust the American market for as-yet unpublished stories, he finally submitted "The Thing on the Doorstep" and "The Haunter of the Dark" to *Weird Tales*—the first stories he had personally submitted since the rejection of *At the Mountains of Madness* in 1931, with the exception of "In the Vault" in 1932. Lovecraft claimed to be surprised that Farnsworth Wright accepted these stories immediately, but he should not have been. Readers of the magazine had been clamouring for his work for years and had to be satisfied with reprints. In 1933 *Weird Tales* had published one original story ("The Dreams in the Witch House") and two reprints; in 1934, one original story (if the collaboration "Through the Gates of the Silver Key" can count as such) and one reprint; in 1935, no original stories and one reprint; in 1936, one original story ("The Haunter of the Dark" in December) and three reprints. (These figures exclude the several revisions that appeared at this time.)

The exact tone of Lovecraft's letter to Wright when submitting these stories is of interest. It is as if he is almost asking for rejection:

Young Schwartz has persuaded me to send him a lot of manuscripts for possible placement in Great Britain, and it occurs to me that I'd better exhaust their cisatlantic possibilities before turning them over to him. Accordingly I am going through the formality of obtaining your official rejection of the enclosed—so that I won't feel I've overlooked any theoretical source of badly-needed revenue.[52]

I doubt that Wright took any great pity on Lovecraft for that last note about much-needed revenue; he simply wanted new Lovecraft stories that he could successfully publish (*At the Mountains of Madness* and "The Shadow over Innsmouth" apparently did not fall into that category), and perhaps he was even concerned—after seeing the two *Astounding* appearances—that Lovecraft was finally preparing to abandon *Weird Tales* altogether. Wright could not possibly have known that Lovecraft would write no more original fiction. Lovecraft, for his part, was simply shielding himself psychologically from rejection by paradoxically assuming—or claiming to assume—that the stories were certain to be rejected.

In fact, Lovecraft had reached a psychological state that made the writing of any new stories nearly impossible. As early as February 1936—three months after the writing of his last original tale, "The Haunter of the Dark," and several months before the contretemps over his stories in *Astounding*—he was already admitting:

[*At the Mountains of Madness*] was written in 1931—and its hostile reception by Wright and others to whom it was shewn probably did more than anything else to end my effective fictional career. The feeling that I had failed to crystallise the mood I was trying to crystallise robbed me in some subtle fashion of the ability to approach this kind of problem in the same way—or with the same degree of confidence and fertility.[53]

Lovecraft was already speaking of his fictional career in the past tense. In late September 1935 he had announced to Duane W. Rimel, "I may be experimenting in the wrong medium altogether. It may be that poetry instead of fiction is the only effective vehicle to put such expression across"[54]—a remark modified about a half-year later when he hypothesised that "*fiction* is *not* the medium for what I *really want to do.* (Just what the right medium would be, I don't know—perhaps the cheapened and hackneyed term 'prose-poem' would hint in the general direction.)"[55]

We have some dim hints of new stories being written—or at least contemplated—around this time, but clearly nothing came of them. Ernest A. Edkins writes:

Just before his death Lovecraft spoke to me of an ambitious project reserved for some period of greater leisure, a sort of dynastic chronicle in fictional form, dealing with the hereditary mysteries and destinies of an ancient New England family, tainted and accursed down the diminishing generations with some grewsome variant of lycanthropy. It was to be his *magnum opus,* embodying the results of his profound researches in the occult legends of that grim and secret country which he knew so well, but apparently the outline was just beginning to crystallize in his mind, and I doubt if he left even a rough draft of his plan.[56]

We have to take Edkins's word on this matter, for his correspondence with Lovecraft has not surfaced and this plot-germ is never mentioned anywhere else. It sounds rather like a horrific version of *The House of the Seven Gables,* and—if genuine—suggests that Lovecraft was contemplating a move away from the science fiction/horror compound that he had evolved in much of his later work.

An actual story that Lovecraft is supposed to have written late in life is mentioned by one Lew Shaw:

> Lovecraft had written a story about a true incident. At one time there was a young woman, a chambermaid in the hotel on Benefit Street, who left and married into wealth. Sometime afterward, she returned to visit the hotel as a guest. When she found herself discourteously treated and snubbed, she departed but put a "curse"on the hotel, on all those who had humiliated her, and on everything concerned with the hotel. In short order, ill luck apparently befell all and the hotel itself burned down. Furthermore, it had never been possible, somehow, for anyone to rebuild on the site.[57]

Shaw claims that Lovecraft wrote the story but failed to prepare a carbon of it. He sent it to a magazine but was apparently lost in the mails.

There is much reason to suspect this entire account. In the first place, the story sounds like nothing Lovecraft would have written—the idea is hackneyed, and the protagonist would uncharacteristically have been a woman. Secondly, it is inconceivable that Lovecraft would have prepared a story without his usual two carbons. In the case of his essay on Roman architecture in late 1934, he wrote the piece by hand and sent it to Moe without typing it at all. Lew Shaw claims to have actually met Lovecraft on the street, in the company of a friend "who was interested in science-fiction" and knew Lovecraft; this might conceivably have been Kenneth Sterling, but Sterling never mentions this matter in either of his two memoirs. Shaw also claims to be of the Brown Class of 1941; but there is no one of that name in that class listed in the Brown University alumni directory. There is a Lewis A. Shaw in the Class of 1948, and a Lew Shaw who received a Ph.D. in 1975, but that is all. My feeling is that Lew Shaw (probably a pseudonym) is perpetrating a hoax.

This brings us to the final, and perhaps the saddest, episode in Lovecraft's career as a "professional" writer. In the fall of 1936 Wilfred B. Talman proposed acting as agent to market either a collection of tales or a new novel to William Morrow & Co., where Talman evidently had some connexions. Lovecraft casually gave Talman a free hand in the matter, declaring first that "I am done with all direct contact with publishers," and then (about the novel idea), "A full-length novel to order (acceptance not being guaranteed) would be quite a gamble—although I'd enjoy attempting such a thing if I could get the time."[58] Talman apparently interpreted that last remark rather more forcefully than Lovecraft intended; for Morrow, although declining a short-story collection, expressed some interest in a novel. The firm wished Lovecraft to submit the first 15,000 words, acceptance being predicated upon this portion.

At this point Lovecraft got alarmed and backed off. Of course, he had nothing to submit, and could not have written the first 15,000 words of a novel without having a clear idea of where the rest of it was going. Also, he did not want Morrow to dictate an ending, as it seemed inclined to do. In effect, it appears—in spite of Lovecraft's urging Talman in early November that "it would perhaps be best to avoid the making of any promises"[59]—that Talman had already half committed Lovecraft to such a work. Lovecraft knew that he was "all out of the fictional mood now—having written nothing original in a year," and that he would have to start by writing some short stories before he could work up to a novel.

Talman must have written a somewhat irritated reply, perhaps because he had been forced to renege on whatever commitment he had made with Morrow. Lovecraft was effusively contrite: "I genuflect. I grovel. And my regret is of the most acute & genuine, as distinguished from the formal & perfunctory, sort. Damn it all! But you can at least justify yourself with the firm by telling them—with my cordial permission—that your client is a muddled old fool who doesn't know enough to say what he means the first time!"[60] Lovecraft gave approval for Talman "to give [Morrow] a reasonably strong promise of a synopsis sooner or later, & much less definite suggestions regarding a complete or fractional novel-manuscript in the remote future." The matter was still being discussed as late as mid-February 1937, but by then Lovecraft was in no shape to do anything about it. Talman seems much more to blame in this whole fiasco than Lovecraft, for the latter's offhand remarks in his letters could not possibly have been plausibly interpreted as committing Lovecraft to the composition of a substantial work of fiction.

It is difficult to know exactly when Lovecraft realised that he was dying. The summer of 1936 finally brought the temperature up to a level where he could actually enjoy being outdoors and have the energy to accomplish his work. Barlow's visit was certainly delightful, even though it entailed a sixty-hour session with *Well Bred Speech* after his departure. The fall saw Lovecraft still taking long walks, and resulted in his seeing several sections of terrain he had never before seen in his life. One expedition—on October 20 and 21—took him to the east shore of Narragansett Bay, in an area called the Squantum Woods. Here, during his walk on the 20th, he met two small kittens, one of whom became very playful and allowed Lovecraft to carry him on his journey; the other was hostile and aloof, but tagged along reluctantly because it did not wish to lose its mate. On October 28 Lovecraft went to an area of the Neutaconkanut woods three miles northwest of College Hill:

> From some of its hidden interior meadows—remote from every sign of nearby human life—I obtained truly marvellous glimpses of the remote urban skyline—a dream of enchanted pinnacles & domes half-floating in air, & with an obscure aurea of mystery around them.... Then I saw the great yellow disc of the Hunter's Moon (2 days before full) floating above the belfries & minarets, while in the orange-glowing west Venus & Jupiter commenced to twinkle.[61]

The presidential election in November cheered him; he had seen a glimpse of Roosevelt on the morning of October 20 during a campaign rally in downtown Providence.

Christmas was a festive occasion. Lovecraft and Annie again had a tree, and the two of them had dinner at the boarding-house next door. Naturally they gave each other gifts, and Lovecraft received one outside gift which he certainly did not expect but which he professed to find quite delightful: a long-interred human skull, found in an Indian graveyard and sent to him by Willis Conover. Conover has received much criticism for sending this item at this time, but of course he could not have known of the state of Lovecraft's health; and Lovecraft's pleasure at receiving this mortuary relic seems entirely sincere.

The entire winter was unusually warm, allowing Lovecraft to continue neighbourhood walks into December and even January. Various letters of this time certainly bespeak no intimations of mortality. With the Leibers he had been discussing the feasibility of editing a high-grade weird magazine sometime in the future, and he wrote to Jonquil in mid-December: "I shall probably be available—if still living at so advanced an age—for that good-weird-magazine editorship which Mr. Leiber has in mind!"[62] Ruminating on politics with Henry George Weiss, the communist with whom Lovecraft now found he shared many views in common, he wrote as late as early February: "The next few years in America will be intensely interesting to watch"[63]—as if he were confident that he would be around to watch them.

In early January, however, Lovecraft admitted to feeling poorly—"grippe" and bum digestion, as he put it. By the end of the month he was typing his letters—always a bad sign. Then, in mid-February, he told Derleth that he had an offer (of which nothing is known) for a revised version of some old astronomical articles (presumably the *Asheville Gazette-News* series), which caused him to unearth his old astronomy books and explore new ones. (In mid-October 1936 he had been delighted to attend a meeting of the Skyscrapers, a newly formed amateur astronomy group in Providence.) He added at the end of this letter: "Funny how early interests crop up again toward the end of one's life."[64]

Lovecraft was at this time finally receiving the attention of a doctor, who prescribed three separate medications. On February 28 he made a feeble response to

Talman's continued queries about the Morrow book deal: "Am in constant pain, take only liquid food, and so bloated with gas that I can't lie down. Spend all time in chair propped with pillows, and can read or write only a few minutes at a time."[65] Two days later Harry Brobst, who was much on the scene during this time, wrote to Barlow: "Our old friend is quite ill—and so I am writing this letter for him. He has seemed to grow progressively weaker the last few days."[66] On a postcard sent to Willis Conover on March 9, Lovecraft wrote in pencil: "Am very ill & likely to be so for a long time."[67]

The nature of Lovecraft's various illnesses is ill understood, at least in terms of their aetiology. This may be because Lovecraft waited so long to have them examined by a competent medical authority. On his death certificate the principal cause of death was given as "Carcinoma of small intestine"; a contributory cause was "chronic nephritis," or kidney disease.

Cancer of the small intestine is relatively rare, colon cancer being much more common; as a result, this cancer frequently goes undetected for years, even when patients are examined. Lovecraft, of course, was never examined until a month before his death, at which time it was too late to do anything except relieve his pain—and even massive doses of morphine seemed to offer little alleviation. It can be hypothesised why Lovecraft did not go to a doctor earlier, since he first experienced a serious bout of what he called indigestion as early as October 1934 ("I was in bed—or dragging betwixt there & the kitchen & bathroom—a week, & have thereafter been distinctly flabby & shaky"[68]). Lovecraft's habitual term for this condition—"grippe"— is simply an antiquated layman's term for the flu, although it is quite clear (and was probably clear to Lovecraft) that that is not what he had. But Lovecraft's phobia of doctors and hospitals may have been of very long standing. Recall that his mother's death was caused by a gall bladder operation from which she was unable to recover. Although it was probably Susie's general physical and psychological debilitation that led to her death, rather than any medical malfeasance, perhaps Lovecraft gained a fear and suspicion of doctors from this point onward.

The causes of intestinal cancer are various. Chief among them is diet: a high-fat, low-fiber diet results in the greater absorption of animal proteins in the digestive tract, and cancer can result in this manner. Interestingly enough, in view of the amount of canned food Lovecraft ate, studies have shown that modern food additives and preservatives may actually inhibit intestinal cancer.[69] In other words, it was not that the preservatives in the canned food Lovecraft ate caused his cancer, but that their possible absence may have done so.

It is a difficult question whether Lovecraft's kidney problems were related to or actually produced by his cancer or were a separate phenomenon entirely; the latter seems quite possible. Chronic nephritis is a now antiquated term for a variety of kidney ailments. In all likelihood, Lovecraft had chronic glomerulonephritis (formerly known as Bright's disease)—the inflammation of the renal glomeruli (small bulbs of blood capillaries in the kidney). If unrelated to the cancer, the cause of this ailment is not entirely clear. In some cases it is a function of a breakdown of the immune system; in other cases, poor nutrition may be a factor.[70] In other words, poor diet may have caused or contributed to both his cancer and his renal failure, hence it is worth examining once more his eating habits, especially as they evolved toward the end of his life.

In a letter to Jonquil Leiber written three months before his death, Lovecraft outlined the average content of his two daily meals:

(a) *Breakfast* . . .
Doughnut from Weybosset Pure Food Market 0.015
York State Medium Cheese (for sake of round numbers).................0.060
Coffee + Challenge Brand Condensed Milk + $C_{12}H_{22}O11$ 0.025
$\qquad\qquad\qquad\qquad\qquad\qquad$ Total Breakfast..............0.100

(b) *Dinner* . . .
1 can Rath's Chili con Carne* 0.100
2 slices Bond Bread 0.025
Coffee (with accessories as noted above) 0.025
Slice of cake or quadrant (or octant) oif pie.......................................0.050
$\qquad\qquad\qquad\qquad\qquad$ Total Dinner....................0.200
$\qquad\qquad\qquad\qquad$ Grand Total for Entire Day..........0.30
$\qquad\qquad\qquad\qquad\qquad\qquad\qquad\qquad\qquad$ 7
$\qquad\qquad\qquad\qquad$ Average Total per Week...............2.10

(*or Armour's Corned Beef Hash or baked beans from delic., or Armour's Frankfort Sausage or Boiardi Meat Balls and Spaghetti or chop suey from delicatessen or Campbell's Vegetable Soup, etc., etc. etc.)[71]

This table's chief purpose was to show how Lovecraft could eat on 30¢ a day or $2.10 a week; as Lovecraft had written some months earlier to Willis Conover, if the remnants of his inheritance didn't help to augment (minimally) the income from revision (sporadic) and original fiction (nearly non-existent except from accidents like the *Astounding* sales), "I wouldn't be eating very much."[72] But the brute fact of the matter is that Lovecraft was *not* eating very much, and that much of his diet was indeed high-fat (cheese, ice-cream, cake, pie). August Derleth maintained that it is a "myth" that Lovecraft died of starvation; but clearly his poor diet contributed significantly to his early death.

I have delayed discussion of Lovecraft's anomalous sensitivity to cold till now because I am convinced that it has some relation to his worsening cancer, although it is perhaps now impossible to ascertain what that relation may be. It has previously been thought that Lovecraft suffered from a supposed ailment called poikilothermia. This is, however, not a disease but merely a physiological property of certain animals, whereby their body temperature varies with the external environment; in other words, this property applies to cold-blooded animals such as reptiles. Mammals are all homeothermic, or capable of maintaining a constant body temperature (within narrow limits) regardless of the external environment.

Now there is no explicit evidence that Lovecraft's actual body temperature decreased during the cold, although it could have; since he was never hospitalised when suffering from exposure to cold, no tests exist on what his body temperature was in such a state. We only have various anecdotes as to his symptoms on such occasions: disturbed cardiovascular and respiratory functions (he had to pant when exposed to cold during a Christmas visit to New York); swelling of feet (customarily an indication of poor blood circulation); difficulty in the manipulation of hands;[73] headache and nausea,[74] sometimes leading to vomiting;[75] and in extreme cases (perhaps three or four times in his life), actual unconsciousness. I have no idea what this concatenation of symptoms signifies.

What could have caused this condition? There does not seem to be any actual illness coinciding with these symptoms, but one hypothesis can perhaps be made. Body temperature is, in mammals, almost certainly regulated by the central nervous system. Experiments with animals have shown that a lesion in the caudal section of the hypothalamus can result in homeothermic animals becoming quasi-poikilothermic: they do not sweat in hot weather, nor do they shiver in cold weather.[76] Lovecraft, of course, *did* admit to sweating profusely in hot weather, but claimed nevertheless that he had nearly unbounded energy on these occasions. Nevertheless, I believe it is at least possible that some sort of damage to the hypothalamus—which does not affect intellectual or aesthetic capacity in any way—caused Lovecraft's sensitivity to cold.

And yet, Lovecraft makes it abundantly clear that his "grippe" really did improve whenever the weather warmed up. This, at any rate, was the case during the winter of 1935–36. This fact may have led Lovecraft to believe that his digestion problems were some by-product of his sensitivity to cold, which he apparently believed to be non-treatable; if so, it could have contributed to his failure to see a doctor until the very end.

Lovecraft's last month of life is agonising merely to read about; what it must have been like to experience can scarcely be imagined. This period has been made suddenly more vivid by a document that was long thought to be lost or even apocryphal: a "death diary" of his condition that Lovecraft kept until he could scarcely hold a pen. We do not have the actual document: Annie Gamwell gave it to R. H. Barlow after Lovecraft's death, and it has subsequently been lost; but Barlow copied out selected portions of it in a letter to August Derleth. These selections, in addition to Lovecraft's medical record and the recollections of two doctors who treated him, give us a stark account of his last days.[77]

Lovecraft began keeping the diary at the very beginning of 1937. He notes lingering digestive trouble throughout the first three weeks of January. There is one curious note on January 27: "revise Rimel story." He finished the revision the next day. This is a story entitled "From the Sea," which Lovecraft returned to Rimel in mid-February "with such minor changes as I think are needed."[78] The story was apparently never published and presumably does not now survive. However minor the revisions, it is the last piece of fiction on which Lovecraft worked.

Dr Cecil Calvert Dustin was brought in on February 16. According to his recollections, he could tell immediately that Lovecraft was suffering from terminal cancer, so that he probably prescribed a variety of painkillers (Lovecraft states three different "nostrums" given to him). Lovecraft's condition did not improve, and the medications did not even appear to alleviate his pain. He took to sleeping propped up in the morris-chair, since he could not lie down comfortably. Also, there was enormous distension in his abdomen. This is an edema in the peritoneal cavity caused by his kidney disease.

On February 27th Annie told Dr Dustin that Lovecraft was much worse. When Dustin came over, he claims to have notified Lovecraft that his condition was terminal. Lovecraft, of course, kept up a good front to his colleagues, saying merely that he would be out of commission for an indefinite period; but perhaps he assumed that this euphemism would be correctly understood. On March 1 Annie asked Dustin to call in a specialist in internal medicine. Dustin contacted Dr William Leet, but clearly not much could be done at this stage. The diary entry for March 2 tells the story: "pain—drowse—intense pain—rest—great pain." On March 3 and 4 Harry Brobst and his wife paid a visit; Brobst, with his medical knowledge, must have immediately known of the nature of Lovecraft's condition, although he too put up a good front when writing to mutual colleagues.

On March 6 Dr Leet came over and found Lovecraft in the bath: immersions in hot water appeared to alleviate the pain somewhat. On this day Lovecraft suffered "hideous pain." By March 9 Lovecraft was unable to take any food or drink. Leet called the next day and advised that Lovecraft check into Jane Brown Memorial Hospital. He was taken there that day in an ambulance and placed in what was then Room 232 (the rooms were renumbered during an expansion of the hospital in the 1960s).[79] Lovecraft's diary ends on March 11; presumably he was unable to hold a pen thereafter.

For the next several days Lovecraft had to be fed intravenously, as he continued vomiting up all nourishment, even liquids. On March 12 Annie wrote to Barlow:

> I have intended to write you a gay little letter, long since, but now I am writing a sad little letter telling you that Howard is so pitifully ill & weak. . . . the dear fellow grows weaker & weaker—nothing can be retained in his stomach. . . .
>
> Needless to say he has been pathetically patient & philosophical through it all. . . .[80]

On March 13 Harry Brobst and his wife came to visit Lovecraft in the hospital. Brobst asked Lovecraft how he felt; Lovecraft responded, "Sometimes the pain is unbearable." Brobst, in parting, told Lovecraft to remember the ancient philosophers. Lovecraft smiled—the only response Brobst received.[81]

On March 14 Lovecraft's edema was so severe that a stomach tap drained six and three-fourths quarts of fluid. That day Barlow, having received Annie's letter, telegraphed her from Leavenworth, Kansas: "WOULD LIKE TO COME AND HELP YOU IF AGREEABLE ANSWER LEAVENWORTH TO-NIGHT."[82]

Howard Phillips Lovecraft died early in the morning of March 15, 1937. He was pronounced dead at 7.15 A.M. That evening Annie telegraphed a reply to Barlow:[83]

HOWARD DIED THIS MORNING NOTHING TO DO THANKS

26. THOU ART NOT GONE (1937–2010)

On the evening of March 15 the *Providence Evening Bulletin* ran an obituary, full of errors large and small; but it made mention of the "clinical notes" Lovecraft kept of his condition while in the hospital—notes that "ended only when he could no longer hold a pencil." This feature was picked up by the wire services, and an obituary entitled "Writer Charts Fatal Malady" appeared in the *New York Times* on March 16. Frank Long, Lovecraft's best friend, learnt of his death from reading this obituary.

A funeral service was held on March 18 at the chapel of Horace B. Knowles's Sons at 187 Benefit Street. Only a small number of friends and relatives were there—Annie, Harry Brobst and his wife, and Annie's friend Edna Lewis. These individuals then attended the actual burial at Swan Point Cemetery, where they were joined by Edward H. Cole and his wife and Ethel Phillips Morrish, Lovecraft's second cousin. The Eddys had planned to come but arrived after the gravesite ceremony was over. Lovecraft's name was inscribed only on the central shaft of the Phillips plot, below those of his father and mother: "their son / HOWARD P. LOVECRAFT / 1890–1937." It took forty years for Lovecraft and his mother to receive separate headstones.

News of Lovecraft's death spread a little faster than that of Robert E. Howard, but some of his closest colleagues still did not hear of it for weeks. Donald Wandrei had written Lovecraft a long letter on March 17, concluding: "What of your own winter? Did you make a holiday visit to Belknap, or indulge in explorations farther south? Have you written, or are you writing, any new tales?"[1] And yet, it was Wandrei who, when he eventually did learn of the matter, passed the news on to August Derleth. Derleth noted that he read Wandrei's letter "on my way into the marshes below Sauk City, where I had intended to spend an afternoon reading Thoreau's *Journal.* Instead, I sat at a railroad trestle beside the brook and considered ways and means of putting together Lovecraft's best works and bringing them out in book form."[2]

Derleth told Clark Ashton Smith, but Smith had already heard from Harry Brobst. "The news of Lovecraft's death seems incredible and nightmarish, and I cannot adjust myself to it. . . . It saddens me as nothing has done since my mother's death . . ."[3] Recall that neither Smith nor Derleth had ever met Lovecraft but had merely corresponded with him for fifteen and eleven years, respectively.

The outpouring of grief from both the weird fiction and the amateur press was instantaneous and overwhelming. The June 1937 issue of *Weird Tales* contained only the first wave of letters from colleagues and fans alike. Farnsworth Wright prefaced the letters with the touching note: "We admired him for his great literary achievements, but we loved him for himself; for he was a courtly and noble gentleman, and a dear friend. Peace be to his shade!" It is remarkable how perfect strangers such as Robert Leonard Russell, who knew Lovecraft only from his work, could write: "I feel, as will many other readers of *Weird Tales,* that I have lost a real friend." Many real friends—from Hazel Heald to Robert Bloch to Kenneth Sterling to Clark Ashton Smith to Henry Kuttner—also wrote moving letters. Kuttner wrote: "I've been feeling extremely depressed about Lovecraft's death. . . . He seemed, somehow to have been an integral part of my literary life . . ." In the August 1937 issue Robert A. W. Lowndes, who exchanged exactly two letters with Lovecraft, wrote: " . . . it may seem somewhat strange for me to say that it is as though I had lost a beloved friend of many years' acquaintance. Yet this is the case . . ." Jacques Bergier, in the September 1937 issue, concluded: "The passing of Lovecraft seems to me to mark an end of an epoch in the history of American imaginative fiction . . ."

As for amateurs, Walter J. Coates wrote an affecting obituary in *Driftwind* for April 1937. Perhaps the most significant tribute was a special issue of the *Californian* (Summer 1937) prepared by Hyman Bradofsky, full of memoirs, poetry by Lovecraft, the first significant publication of his letters ("By Post from Providence"—excerpts of his letters to Rheinhart Kleiner on amateur affairs), and a moving eulogy by Bradofsky:

> Great as was Howard Lovecraft in heart and mind, we of today are unable to evaluate him at his true worth. Time and the march of events will bring increased understanding of him and of his tangible legacies. . . .
>
> Lovecraft's passing is a distinct loss to this writer. When we visit Boston we will not see him. That hurts, when we force ourselves to realize it. But Lovecraft lives on in his work; lives, too, in the memory of those who knew him, and lives well.[4]

Edward H. Cole revived his amateur journal, the *Olympian,* after a twenty-three-year hiatus to produce a superb Autumn 1940 issue containing poignant memoirs by Ernest A. Edkins, James F. Morton, Cole himself, and W. Paul Cook. Cook's piece was an early version of his full-length memoir, *In Memoriam: Howard Phillips Lovecraft: Recollections, Appreciations, Estimates* (1941), which remains the finest memoir ever written about Lovecraft.

One of the most remarkable phenomena about Lovecraft's passing is the number of poetic tributes it inspired. Henry Kuttner, Richard Ely Morse, Frank Belknap Long, August Derleth, Emil Petaja, and many others wrote fine elegies; but the best without question is Clark Ashton Smith's "To Howard Phillips Lovecraft," written on March 31, 1937 and published in *Weird Tales* for July. Its conclusion can only be quoted:

And yet thou art not gone
Nor given wholly unto dream and dust:
For, even upon
This lonely western hill of Averoigne
Thy flesh had never visited,
I meet some wise and sentient wraith of thee,
Some undeparting presence, gracious and august.
More luminous for thee the vernal grass,
More magically dark the Druid stone
And in the mind thou art for ever shown
As in a wizard glass;
And from the spirit's page thy runes can never pass.[5]

R. H. Barlow, of course, had been the first to hear the news of Lovecraft's death, and he immediately caught a bus from Kansas City to Providence, arriving a few days after Lovecraft's interment. He had done this because of a document Lovecraft had written some months before his death: "Instructions in Case of Decease." Annie had been horrified to catch sight of Lovecraft writing this melancholy if very businesslike set of notes, but felt obligated to follow its strictures.[6] It begins: "All files of weird magazines, scrap books not wanted by A. E. P. G. and all original mss. to R. H. Barlow, my literary executor."

"Instructions in Case of Decease" is not, of course, a legal document, and no one has ever claimed that it is: it was not drafted by a lawyer or in the presence of a lawyer, it does not represent a codicil to Lovecraft's 1912 will, and it was never filed for probate; indeed, the document itself does not survive in its original form but only in a handwritten transcription by Annie Gamwell, who wished to keep the original for sentimental purposes. Nevertheless, Annie sought to follow its particulars as best she could; accordingly, on March 26 she had at least the note about Barlow's literary executorship made legal by a formal contract, part of which reads:

> WHEREAS, the late Howard P. Lovecraft was the nephew of the said Mrs. Gamwell; and
> WHEREAS, the said Howard P. Lovecraft expressed a wish and desire that the said Mr. Barlow should have his manuscripts (typewritten and long-hand), completed and uncompleted, and note books and should attend to the arrangements with respect to publishing and republishing the said manuscripts, published or unpublished; and
> WHEREAS, the said Mrs. Gamwell desires to carry out the wish of her said late nephew, Howard P. Lovecraft. . . .
> The said Mr. Barlow agrees to arrange for the publication or republication of said manuscripts, either typed or in long-hand, at his own expense and to pay the

said Mrs. Gamwell all receipts that he shall receive from said publications or otherwise, less a three per cent (3%) commission of the gross amount received.

Barlow accordingly took away many books and manuscripts, distributing some of
the former to Lovecraft's colleagues in accordance with the "Instructions." Some
papers—chiefly letters to Lovecraft by his associates—Barlow deposited immediately in the John Hay Library of Brown University, which was initially somewhat
grudging in accepting the material (it was not properly catalogued for another
thirty years). After a year or two, his personal life still troubled, Barlow felt that he
should deposit the remaining manuscripts and effects, and in the course of the next
several years did so; this included all story manuscripts except "The Shadow out of
Time," Lovecraft's complete file of *Weird Tales* (to which Barlow eventually
added portions of his own file to cover the period after Lovecraft's death), and
much other matter. It should be noted that Lovecraft's "Instructions" give Barlow
outright ownership of his manuscripts and some of his other effects; it is not simply
that Barlow is to work toward securing the publication of any of this material, as
would be customary for a literary executor. So Barlow was within his rights to do
with the material what he wished; and it is to his eternal credit that he decided so
unhesitatingly to deposit most of this material in a public institution.

Because of his frequent moves across the country and his consequent tardiness
or negligence in answering letters, Barlow inadvertently created considerable ill-will
among Lovecraft's colleagues. He also later admitted that he had erred in not making public the statement regarding himself in Lovecraft's "Instructions," since
some parties believed that Barlow had pilfered Lovecraft's property. In the winter
of 1938–39 he was jolted to receive this letter from Clark Ashton Smith: "R. H.
Barlow: Please do not write me or try to communicate with me in any way. I do not
wish to see you or hear from you after your conduct in regard to the estate of a late
beloved friend. Clark Ashton Smith."[7] Donald Wandrei seemed particularly to
have a bee in his bonnet about Barlow, and damned his memory to his own dying
day.

And yet, Barlow was in some ways the most significant figure in the posthumous recognition of Lovecraft. His depositing Lovecraft's papers in the John Hay
Library has made much of the Lovecraft scholarship of the past four decades possible, and he continually urged many colleagues to donate their own letters and
other materials from Lovecraft to the library. Barlow did not, indeed, manage to
get much of Lovecraft's work into print: his edition of the *Notes & Commonplace
Book,* published in 1938 by The Futile Press (run by Claire and Groo Beck in
Lakeport, California), is full of errors, although less so than Derleth's various editions. Barlow, of course, did not have the means to undertake full-scale publication
of Lovecraft's major stories; and we have already seen that it was another individual

who, quite literally at the moment he heard of Lovecraft's death, conceived of a plan of doing so.

August Derleth perhaps felt that he himself had been—or should have been— deemed Lovecraft's literary executor on the strength of two comments Lovecraft had made to him in various letters. In 1932 Lovecraft had remarked rather wist- fully (but prophetically): "Yes—come to think of it—I fear there might be some turbulent doings among an indiscriminately named board of literary heirs handling my posthumous junk! Maybe I'll dump all the work on you by naming you soul heir."[8] Then, in late 1936, when Derleth was again hounding Lovecraft about the marketing of a book of his tales, Lovecraft had stated rather wearily: "As for trying to float a volume of Grandpa's weird tales some day—naturally I shall have bless- ings rather than objections to offer, but I wouldn't advise the expenditure of too much time & energy on the project."[9] Derleth used this remark as the ultimate basis for his later work on Lovecraft's behalf.

Derleth wasted no time. By the end of March 1937 he had already mapped out the venture in broad details and enlisted the aid of Donald Wandrei. In short order he evolved the following scheme: he would assemble three volumes, the first con- taining Lovecraft's most significant tales, the second containing the remaining fic- tion and perhaps some poetry and essays, and the third containing letters. Derleth maintained that it was Wandrei who suggested that all Lovecraft's work, especially the letters, be preserved;[10] but this idea would presumably have followed logically in any event.

Where did Barlow fit into these plans? The thinking on Derleth's part appears to have been: if Barlow wishes to cooperate, fine; if not, he had better not interfere. As it happens, Barlow lent what aid he could in the assembling of what became *The Outsider and Others.* By late March Derleth was asking Barlow to send him Lovecraft's annotated copies of *Astounding* containing *At the Mountains of Mad- ness,*[11] since he knew that the printed text was corrupt. Since all the contents of the volume consisted of previously published material, Derleth assembled copy himself by preparing tearsheets of the stories (in many cases, however, taking them from the poorest published sources—e.g., the *Fanciful Tales* text of "The Nameless City" with its fifty-nine bad misprints—since these were the easiest to hand) and having his personal secretary, Alice Conger, prepare a mammoth typescript, which ultimately came to 1500 pages. It contained thirty-six stories plus "Supernatural Horror in Literature."

It was at this point that Derleth made a critical decision. He had first submit- ted the volume to Charles Scribner's Sons:

> Scribner's were at that time my own publishers, and, while sympathetic to the pro- ject and cognizant of the literary value of Lovecraft's fiction, rejected the manu- script because the cost of producing so bulky a book, combined with the public's

then sturdy resistance to buying short story collections and the comparative obscurity of H. P. Lovecraft as a writer, made the project financially prohibitive. Simon & Schuster, to whom the manuscript was next submitted, likewise rejected, for similar reasons.[12]

This process, Derleth says elsewhere,[13] took several months, and he was unwilling to waste more time submitting to other publishers. But did it never occur to Derleth to offer a smaller volume, with perhaps a dozen of Lovecraft's best stories? Might not Scribner's or Simon & Schuster have accepted such an offer? But Derleth seemed fixated on his three-volume conception, so he did the inevitable: he formed, with Wandrei, his own small press, Arkham House, and issued the volume himself.

In the short term *The Outsider and Others,* which emerged in December 1939, certainly attracted the attention of the publishing world. Many regarded as a noble curiosity—a kind of monument to friendship regardless of the actual contents of the book. Derleth complained that, in spite of ads taken out in *Weird Tales* and the fan publications, the volume took a full four years to sell out its 1268 copies; but what can he have expected from generally impecunious weird fiction enthusiasts who were loath to spend $5.00 (the average price for a volume being then $2.00) for 550 pages of 9-point type? *The Outsider and Others* is unreadable today, and is nothing but a collector's item. It is, to be sure, a landmark in publishing, but of a decidedly mixed sort: at the very time that it launched what was for many years the most prestigious small press in the weird fiction community, it effected the ghettoisation of Lovecraft and his type of weird tale. Had Lovecraft been issued by Scribner's or some other mainstream house, then the entire history of his critical recognition, and the entire subsequent history of weird fiction, would have been very different. It is not clear how many other writers would have escaped the genre ghetto: whether Clark Ashton Smith or Robert E. Howard or Henry S. Whitehead would have followed Lovecraft into the mainstream is very much in doubt. But certainly Lovecraft would not have been quite the literary curiosity he became over the next several decades. One develops the strong suspicion, however, that Derleth simply did not want to give up his control of Lovecraft, as he would in part have done if a mainstream house had published his work. For the next thirty years Derleth effectively owned Lovecraft, even though he had little right to do so.

And yet, *The Outsider and Others* received very cordial reviews. It is no surprise that, in the *Providence Journal,* B. K. Hart sang its praises, nor that Will Cuppy enthusiastically if uncritically lauded the book in the *New York Herald Tribune.* What is indeed surprising is that Thomas Ollive Mabbott, then the world's leading Poe scholar, wrote a glowing review in *American Literature* (March 1940)—the first review, or mention, of Lovecraft in an academic journal. "Time will tell if his place be very high in our literary history; that he has a place seems certain."[14] Four years later, writing in a fan magazine, Mabbott was still more enthusiastic: "I have never quite been sure *how* great he was; though I do feel he was a great writer."[15] One other notice possibly inspired by *The Outsider* was an article by William Rose Benét in which he mentioned in passing that his brother Stephen Vincent "was entirely familiar with the work of H. P. Lovecraft long before that little-known master of horror was brought to the attention of the critics."[16]

Meanwhile Derleth, in spite of the slow sales of *The Outsider,* was pushing on with the next Lovecraft omnibus. He also published a volume of his own stories and one by Clark Ashton Smith to keep the Arkham House imprint in the public eye. At the same time he was vigorously marketing to *Weird Tales* those of Lovecraft's stories that had not appeared there, including many that Farnsworth Wright had rejected. This pace of magazine publication picked up when Wright died in 1940. His place was taken over by Dorothy McIlwraith, who edited the magazine until it folded in 1954. McIlwraith seemed a trifle less finical than Wright, accepting Lovecraft's longer stories but publishing them in appallingly butchered abridgements: "Medusa's Coil" (January 1939), "The Mound" (November 1940), *The Case of Charles Dexter Ward* (May and July 1941), "The Shadow over Innsmouth" (January 1942). Derleth turned all the proceeds of these fiction sales to Annie Gamwell; they amounted to nearly $1000.[17]

Annie died of cancer on January 29, 1941. She was, really speaking, the last direct familial link to Lovecraft, for among Annie's own heirs Ethel Phillips Morrish was only a second cousin (albeit one who recalled Lovecraft from the age of four) and Edna Lewis was only a friend. She was pleased with Derleth's devotion and also had considerable fondness for Barlow, although toward the end she seemed to become a little frazzled and wished that all the various individuals interested in her nephew could work harmoniously together.

Beyond the Wall of Sleep came out from Arkham House in 1943; the print run, because of war restrictions, was only 1217. It was nearly the same size as its predecessor and sold for the same price; it too took years to go out of print. Its chief features were the two unpublished novels, *The Dream-Quest of Unknown Kadath* and *The Case of Charles Dexter Ward,* which Derleth or his secretary transcribed (inaccurately) from the autograph manuscripts supplied by Barlow. This volume also received relatively cordial reviews in the mainstream press: a laudatory but comically error-riddled one in the *New York Times Book Review* by William Poster, another enthusiastic one by Will Cuppy in the *New York Herald Tribune,* and a rather lukewarm one by the comic novelist Peter de Vries, of all people, in the *Chicago Sun Book Week.*

By this time, however, Derleth realised that the volume of letters would have to be postponed: he had received thousands upon thousands of pages of correspondence from Lovecraft's associates, and Donald Wandrei's entry into the army in

1942 severely limited the amount of time he had to work on the editing of the letters. In 1944 Derleth issued a "stop-gap" volume, *Marginalia.* In one way it was
prophetic: aside from containing a few revisions, essays, juvenilia, and fragments, it
featured a large number of memoirs and other writings commissioned by Derleth
from Lovecraft's colleagues. In this way there began a flood of Lovecraft memora-
bilia that has proceeded almost to the present day. This is certainly one of Derleth's
most significant contributions to Lovecraft studies: valuable insights have been
provided by these memoirs, the authors of many of which died not long after their
writing. One of the best pieces in *Marginalia* was not a memoir but a formal essay,
"His Own Most Fantastic Creation," by Winfield Townley Scott. Scott had taken
over B. K. Hart's role as literary editor of the *Providence Journal,* and he had already written several keen articles on Lovecraft and discussed Lovecraft regularly
in his column, "Bookman's Gallery." In "His Own Most Fantastic Creation"
Scott, using many primary documents, wrote the first important biographical study
of Lovecraft, one that still retains considerable value today.

The title of Scott's essay was derived from a review by Vincent Starrett, who
around this time began paying attention to his old correspondent in brief articles
and reviews. His review of *Beyond the Wall of Sleep* contains some celebrated remarks:

> But to me Lovecraft himself is even more interesting than his stories; he was his
> own most fantastic creation—a Roderick Usher or C. Auguste Dupin born a cen-
> tury too late. . . He was an eccentric, a dilettante, and a *poseur par excellence;* but
> he was also a born writer, equipped with a delicate feeling for the beauty and mys-
> tery of words. The best of his stories are among the best of their time, in the field
> he chose to make his own.[18]

Although this is meant in affectionate flattery, I think it has caused considerable
mischief and has fostered the illusion that Lovecraft was a freak who should be
more regarded for his "eccentricities" than for his literary work.

In the meantime the fan world had not been idle. At the beginning this community paid tribute to Lovecraft not so much with memoirs or criticism as with
publications: hence, Corwin F. Stickney issued a small brochure of Lovecraft's
poetry, *HPL* (1937); Wilson Shepherd issued a "Limited Memorial Edition" of *A
History of the Necronomicon* (1937); Barlow compiled the *Notes & Commonplace Book* (1938); William H. Evans mimeographed the first thirty-three sonnets
of *Fungi from Yuggoth* for the Fantasy Amateur Press Association (FAPA) in
1943 (there is no explanation as to why he left off the final three sonnets; presumably he was working from an incomplete typescript).

But in 1942 a significant event occurred: Francis T. Laney founded the *Acolyte,* the most noteworthy fan magazine since the *Fantasy Fan* and one that during
its four-year run published a number of valuable rare works by Lovecraft and astute

memoirs and studies of him. Laney had been drawn into the fan world by Duane W. Rimel,[19] and he, Rimel, and F. Lee Baldwin (whose interest had been rekindled) were the guiding forces behind the quarterly magazine. Crude in appearance as it is (the first issue was run off on ditto and is now virtually illegible; the other issues were mimeographed), it generated much worthwhile material. Laney later had a violent reaction against the fan world, recorded in his piquant autobiography, *Ah, Sweet Idiocy!* (1948). Another magazine, A. Langley Searles's *Fantasy Commentator,* also generated much valuable critical material about Lovecraft.

Other fan publishers issued Lovecraft's obscurer stories, poems, essays, and even letters, as well as quaint tributes to him. One of the strangest and most affecting was J. B. Michel's "The Last of H. P. Lovecraft," in the *Science Fiction Fan* for November 1939. Michel had never known Lovecraft but had gone with Donald A. Wollheim to 66 College Street. Annie Gamwell had allowed the two young men to examine Lovecraft's study, which remained unaltered since his death. Michel concludes with a poignant and half-hostile peroration that shows how Lovecraft was already becoming a myth:

> Lovecraft, for all his giant knowledge and piercing, calculating intellect, was the deadly enemy of all that to me is everything, an inflexible Jehovah-man, a gaunt, prophet-like high priest of dark rites and darker times, clad in funereal robes and funereal visage, gazing with suppressed hate upon a great new world which placed more value upon the sanitary condition of a bathroom fixture than all the greasy gold and jewels, the bones and dirt-crushed half knowledge of a thousand and a thousand-thousand kingdoms of the hoary past, whose faithful chronicler he was and in which he lived.[20]

A much more sensible piece was J. Chapman Miske's "H. P. Lovecraft: Strange Weaver" (*Scienti-Snaps,* Summer 1940), a surprisingly sane, accurate, and balanced biographical article. "For Lovecraft was eccentric to the point of being born 'out of his due time'. Not freakish, simply different, by temperament, tastes, and, to certain degrees, actions. . . . Lovecraft is dead, but the strange patterns he wove will always be appreciated by a small but intelligent group."[21]

Meanwhile Lovecraft's work was being disseminated beyond the confines of the small press. In December 1943 F. Orlin Tremaine, the erstwhile editor of *Astounding,* contacted Derleth about reprinting Lovecraft in paperback for his company, Bartholomew House. Derleth prepared a list of tales, but Tremaine thought it too long and prepared one of his own. The result was *The Weird Shadow over Innsmouth and Other Stories of the Supernatural* (1944), the first Lovecraft paperback volume. It contained only five stories. Tremaine requested an initial print run of 100,000, and, incredibly, it must have sold well, for by November 1944 he was proposing a second volume. Interestingly enough, one of his ideas was to issue *At the Mountains of Madness* and "The Shadow out of Time"—the two stories he had bought for *Astounding*—together in one volume. This plan did not material-ise, but what did emerge in 1945 was *The Dunwich Horror,* containing only three long stories.[22]

Lovecraft was also beginning to appear in important anthologies. The most important of all was the inclusion of "The Rats in the Walls" and "The Dunwich Horror" in Herbert A. Wise and Phyllis Fraser's *Great Tales of Terror and the Supernatural,* a landmark volume—probably the finest anthology of weird tales ever published—issued by the Modern Library (now an imprint of Random House) in 1944. It was reprinted frequently and published also in England. Also significant was Donald A. Wollheim's *The Portable Novels of Science* (1945), issued by Viking Press and including "The Shadow out of Time."

The year 1945 was both very good and very bad for Lovecraft. In this year Derleth published *H. P. L.: A Memoir* through the publisher Ben Abramson, who also simultaneously issued Derleth's edition of *Supernatural Horror in Litera-ture.* Derleth's small monograph can hardly be called a biography, and it is only fleshed out to the length of a small book by the inclusion of several items by Love-craft in a large appendix. Of its three large chapters two are biographical and one critical; all three are quite undistinguished. Although Derleth had by this time the enormous resources of Lovecraft's letters at his disposal, he was too busy as a writer and publisher to make careful use of them; he was, in any event, not a scholar in any sense. The work was really nothing more than a means of popularising Love-craft, and in this sense it may perhaps have succeeded modestly.

Also in 1945 the World Publishing Company issued Derleth's compilation of Lovecraft's *Best Supernatural Stories.* William Targ of World had approached Derleth about the idea in May 1944; he wished a collection of about 120,000 words. Derleth, realising the importance of the venture, solicited many colleagues' opinions as to their favourite Lovecraft tales; in the end the selection was good, aside from the unfortunate "In the Vault" and "The Terrible Old Man." The vol-ume appeared in April 1945; a second printing appeared in September and a third in June 1946. By the end of 1946, 67,254 copies had been sold in hardcover—a remarkable figure. From this point on sales tapered off, although by mid-1949 sales had reached 73,716.[23] The paper used for the first three printings is very poor in quality; that for the fourth printing (September 1950) is much better.

Parenthetically, it appears that the emergence of the *Best Supernatural Stories* put an end to efforts by Winfield Townley Scott to market a collection of Love-craft's stories with E. P. Dutton.[24] In 1942 Scott had also queried with Knopf for a collection, but this too came to nothing.[25] Whether Derleth would even have al-lowed such a thing is, of course, very much in question.

What made 1945 a bad year, however, was a review that some of these items received. In 1944 Edmund Wilson had written "A Treatise on Tales of Horror," in which he expressed great disdain for most weird stories with the exception of Henry James's *The Turn of the Screw* and a few others. It is clear that Wilson had a prejudice toward genre fiction generally and imaginative fiction in particular, although I must confess that his several attacks on the detective story seem to me pretty much on the mark. But when his article appeared, many readers objected that he had failed to consider the new phenomenon, H. P. Lovecraft. Securing such books as *Marginalia, Best Supernatural Stories,* and *H. P. L.: A Memoir,* he rendered his verdict in a *New Yorker* article on November 24, 1945, entitled "Tales of the Marvellous and the Ridiculous."

The title says it all:

> I regret that, after examining these books, I am no more enthusiastic than before. . . . the truth is that these stories were hack-work contributed to such publications as *Weird Tales* and *Amazing Stories,* where, in my opinion, they ought to have been left.
>
> The only real horror in most of these fictions is the horror of bad taste and bad art. Lovecraft was not a good writer. The fact that his verbose and undistinguished style has been compared to Poe's is only one of the many sad signs that almost nobody any more pays real attention to writing.[26]

And so on. It is scarcely worth dissecting the errors and misconceptions in even the above passage, let alone the piece as a whole. Wilson should have realised that Lovecraft's tales, regardless of their merits, were not "hack-work" because they were at least written with a sincerity of purpose lacking in most work of this kind; and as for the comparison with Poe, Wilson cannot comprehend how T. O. Mabbott (who wrote a fine appreciation of Lovecraft in *Marginalia*) actually likes Lovecraft: evidently the leading Poe scholar of his generation is lacking in critical judgment on the very issue of Lovecraft's similarity to Poe! The fact is that Wilson has merely tossed off a book review without much thought behind it—a point emphasised by the number of factual errors made in the piece, a result of his extreme carelessness in reading some of Lovecraft's tales. Certainly, on the basis of this review Wilson would not deserve the title—which he does indeed deserve on the basis of his work as a whole—of America's leading literary critic of the period.

What is interesting, however, is the praise of Lovecraft that sneaks through Wilson's hostility almost in spite of himself. He first echoes Vincent Starrett in saying "Lovecraft himself, however, is a little more interesting than his stories," citing his erudition and praising "Supernatural Horror in Literature"; he finds Lovecraft's letters full of wit and humour; and at the end he even concludes:

> But Lovecraft's stories do show at times some traces of his more serious emotions and interests. He had a scientific imagination rather similar, though much inferior, to that of the early Wells. The story called "The Colour out of Space" more or less predicts the effects of the atomic bomb, and "The Shadow out of

Time" deals not altogether ineffectively with the perspectives of geological eons and the idea of controlling time-sequence.

What is abundantly clear is that Wilson actually found Lovecraft the man rather fascinating—and his work perhaps a little more disturbing than he cared to indicate.

There is, indeed, a curious and little-known sequel to Wilson's evaluation of Lovecraft. In his play, *The Little Blue Light* (1950), there are clear references to Lovecraft at various points. When a friend of Wilson's, David Schvchavadze, later made note of these allusions, Wilson "livened up considerably and produced a book of Lovecraft's correspondence, which he had obviously read and enjoyed."[27] (This must have been after 1965, when the first volume of *Selected Letters* appeared.) Wilson, unfortunately, never had occasion to voice his reevaluation of Lovecraft in print.

It is difficult to gauge the actual effect of Wilson's attack on Lovecraft's subsequent critical reputation. Certainly Derleth must have fumed over it, and not long after this time he seems to have ceased sending out Arkham House books to mainstream reviewers, thereby augmenting the ghettoisation of Lovecraft and weird fiction generally. And yet, as early as the summer of 1946 Fred Lewis Pattee wrote an almost excessively flattering review of the Ben Abramson *Supernatural Horror in Literature* in *American Literature,* referring to the amazing concision of the essay ("One's first impression is that it is a remarkable piece of literary compression"), declaring (contrary to the opinion of many later critics) that "he has omitted nothing important," and concluding generally, "It is a brilliant piece of criticism."[28] Then, in 1949, Richard Gehman wrote an article on science fiction for the *New Republic* in which he took no notice whatever of Wilson in declaring that "Howard Phelps [*sic!*] Lovecraft was the first notable modern practitioner of science-and-fantasy in this country."[29] After this, however, critical articles and reviews begin to trail off and would not resume until the 1970s.

But Lovecraft's own work was continuing to be disseminated widely. Philip Van Doren Stern arranged for a paperback edition of Lovecraft, *The Dunwich Horror and Other Weird Tales,* to be published with the Editions for the Armed Services.[30] This volume, costing 49¢, appeared probably in late 1945 or early 1946, and introduced Lovecraft to large numbers of servicemen still stationed in Europe after the war. It is an excellent collection of twelve of Lovecraft's best tales. Avon issued a paperback in 1947, *The Lurking Fear and Other Stories.*

In 1945 Derleth published another volume, *The Lurker at the Threshold*—"by H. P. Lovecraft and August Derleth." This volume is the first of his sixteen "posthumous collaborations" with Lovecraft, and opens up what is perhaps the most disreputable phase of Derleth's activities: his promulgation of the "Cthulhu Mythos." The history of this long and sordid affair is very involved, but requires treatment in detail.

We have seen that as early as 1931 Derleth had become fascinated with Lovecraft's pseudomythology, seeking not only to add to it but investing it with the name "The Mythology of Hastur." Indeed, it was exactly at this time that Derleth wrote the initial drafts of several stories, both on his own and in collaboration with Mark Schorer, which—though most were published much later—put the seal on his radically different treatment of the mythos. One story in particular, "The Horror from the Depths" (written with Schorer in the summer of 1931; published in *Strange Stories* for October 1940 as "The Evil Ones"), is very illuminating. Farnsworth Wright rejected this tale not only because he thought it too derivative of Long's *Horror from the Hills* but because

> you have lifted whole phrases from Lovecraft's works, as for instance: "the fright-ful *Necronomicon* of the mad Arab Abdul Alhazred," "the sunken kingdom of R'lyeh," "the accursed spawn of Cthulhu," "the frozen and shunned Plateau of Leng," etc. Also you have taken the legends of Cthulhu and the Ancient Ones directly out of Lovecraft. This is unfair to Lovecraft.[31]

When Derleth relayed Wright's complaints to Lovecraft, the latter gave them short shrift: "I *like* to have others use my Azathoths & Nyarlathoteps—& in return I shall use Klarkash-Ton's Tsathoggua, your monk Clithanus, & Howard's Bran." Derleth seemed to use this single sentence as justification for his subsequent "additions" to Lovecraft's mythos, but he seems to have failed to notice the very preceding sentence: "The more these synthetic daemons are mutually written up by different authors, the better they become as general background-material."[32] The term "background-material" is critical here: whereas writers like Clark Ashton Smith and Robert E. Howard really did use various elements of Lovecraft's mythos merely as random allusions to create atmosphere, Derleth set about resolutely writing whole stories whose very core was a systematic (and, accordingly, tedious) exposition of the mythos as he conceived it.

Relatively few of the stories Derleth was writing at this time actually got into print before Lovecraft's death, since they were repeatedly rejected. "Lair of the Star-Spawn" made it into *Weird Tales* for August 1932; its mention of the Tcho-Tcho people was picked up by Lovecraft in "The Shadow out of Time." "The Thing That Walked on the Wind," also written in 1931, was published in *Strange Tales* for January 1933. This tale actually does refer to the various components of the Lovecraft mythos in a random and allusive way, and is a relatively competent piece of work. One comment made by Derleth to Barlow in reference to it in 1934 is of supreme interest: "According to the mythology as I understand it, it is briefly this: the Ancient or Old Ones ruled the universes—from their authority revolted the evil Cthulhu, Hastur the Unspeakable, etc., who in turn spawned the Tcho-

Tcho people and other cultlike creatures."³³ This, in essence, is the "Derleth Mythos." Virtually all the elements are here, chiefly the good-vs.-evil scenario (the "Ancient or Old Ones" become the "Elder Gods" in later tales) and the "revolt" of Cthulhu, etc. The notion of the gods as elementals is already faintly present in "The Thing That Walked on the Wind."

Derleth put the seal on his disfigurement of Lovecraft's mythos in the story "The Return of Hastur," begun in 1932 but put aside and not finished until April 1937. It was published in *Weird Tales* for March 1939 after being initially rejected by Wright. Some correspondence between Derleth and Clark Ashton Smith concerning the tale is highly revealing. Even before reading the story, Smith—responding to Derleth's attempts to systematise the mythos—commented:

> As to classifying the Old Ones, I suppose that Cthulhu can be classed both as a survival on earth and a water-dweller; and Tsathoggua is a subterranean survival. Azathoth, referred to somewhere as "the primal nuclear chaos", is the ancestor of the whole crew but still dwells in outer and ultra-dimensional space, together with Yog-Sothoth, and the demon piper Nyarlathotep, who attends the throne of Azathoth. I shouldn't class any of the Old Ones as *evil:* they are plainly beyond all limitary human conceptions of either ill or good.³⁴

Smith was clearly responding to Derleth's attempt to shoehorn the mythos entities into elementals. Then, a little later, Smith wrote: "A deduction relating the Cthulhu mythos to the Christian mythos would indeed be interesting; and of course the *unconscious* element in such creation is really the all-important one. However, there seems to be no reference to *expulsion* of Cthulhu and his companions in 'The Call.'"³⁵ Here again Smith is trying to steer Derleth on to the right track, since he knew Lovecraft repudiated Christianity. Then, after reading "The Return of Hastur," Smith wrote: "One reaction, confirmed rather than diminished by the second reading, is that you have tried to work in too much of the Lovecraft mythology and have not assimilated it into the natural body of the story."³⁶ Derleth was very fond of making lengthy catalogues of mythos entities and terms in his tales, as if their mere citation would serve to create horror; he also hammered home his conception of the mythos in story after story, since he had evidently come to the conclusion— one that some politicians of today have also discovered—that if one repeats something often enough, no matter how false, people begin to believe it. Smith's strictures had absolutely no effect on Derleth, who assumed that his views were self-evidently correct and was seeking only commendation and support for them.

It would have been bad enough for Derleth to expound his conception of the Mythos in his own fiction—for it could conceivably have been assumed that this was his (legitimate or illegitimate) elaboration upon Lovecraft's ideas. But Derleth went much further than this: in article after article he attributed his views to Lovecraft, and this is where he stands most culpable. In this way Derleth impeded the proper understanding of Lovecraft for thirty years, since he was looked upon as the "authority" on Lovecraft and as his appointed spokesman. The first published article in which Derleth propounded his views was in "H. P. Lovecraft, Outsider," published in an obscure little magazine, *River,* for June 1937. By this time Derleth had conveniently found the fictitious "All my stories . . ." quotation supplied by Farnese, which he would use repeatedly to bolster his conception of the mythos. The critical passage in this article is as follows:

> After a time there became apparent in his tales a curious coherence, a myth-pattern so convincing that after its early appearance, the readers of Lovecraft's stories began to explore libraries and museums for certain imaginary titles of Lovecraft's own creation, so powerful that many another writer, with Lovecraft's permission, availed himself of facets of the mythos for his own use. Bit by bit it grew, and finally its outlines became distinct, and it was given a name: the Cthulhu Mythology: because it was in *The Call of Cthulhu* that the myth-pattern first became apparent.[37]

The disingenuousness of the passive voice here ("it was given a name") is evident: it was Derleth who had given the mythos this name. Later, citing the "All my stories . . ." quotation, Derleth commented that this formula is "remarkable for the fact that, though it sprang from the mind of a professed religious unbeliever, it is basically similar to the Christian mythos, particularly in regard to the expulsion of Satan from Eden and the power of evil."

The charade continued. In "A Master of the Macabre" (*Reading and Collecting,* August 1937), an article that had begun as a review of the Visionary *Shadow over Innsmouth* but awkwardly turned into a memorial tribute, Derleth cites *both* the fake "All my stories . . ." quotation and the *real* one ("All my tales are based on the fundamental premise that common human laws and interests and emotions have no validity or significance in the vast cosmos-at-large"), which, as any intelligent person should have been able to tell, directly contradicts the fake one!

Derleth completed his co-opting of Lovecraft with *The Lurker at the Threshold* and its successors. Here he has taken two separate fragments by Lovecraft ("Of Evil Sorceries Done in New England . . ." and "The Round Tower"), totalling about 1200 words, and incorporated them into a 45,000-word novel. There was no explanation of this in the novel itself, but by the time Derleth published a collection of these "posthumous collaborations," *The Survivor and Others* (1957), he wrote on the copyright page: "Among . . . Lovecraft['s papers] were various notes and/or outlines for stories which he did not live to write. Of these, the most complete was the title story of this collection. These scattered notes were put together by August Derleth, whose finished stories grown from Lovecraft's suggested plots, are offered here as a final collaboration, post-mortem." There is considerable prevarication here. "The Survivor" is based upon some very sketchy notes (mostly dates) written on a newspaper cartoon. "The Lamp of Alhazred" (1954) is actually an affecting tribute to Lovecraft, taking many passages directly from Lovecraft's letters, especially the one about his rambles in Neutaconkanut Hill in the fall of 1936. But all the other stories are derived from entries in the commonplace book. "Wentworth's Day" is based upon this plot-germ: "Hor. Sto.: Man makes appt. with old enemy. Dies—body keeps appt." "The Peabody Heritage" is based upon this: "Members of witch-cult were buried face downward. Man investigates ancestor in family tomb & finds disquieting condition." "The Fisherman of Falcon Point" comes from this: "Fisherman casts his net into the sea by moonlight—what he finds." The most amusing of the lot is "The Ancestor." Here Derleth stumbled upon Lovecraft's "A List of Basic Underlying Horrors Effectively Used in Weird Fiction" and, thinking these Lovecraft's own plot-germs rather than conceptions extracted from published works, wrote a story that turned out to be an unwitting plagiarism of Leonard Cline's *The Dark Chamber*. What is also interesting is how many of these "posthumous collaborations" turn out to be "tales of the Cthulhu Mythos," even though the plot-germs themselves gave not the remotest indication of such a thing.

Derleth published these stories at every opportunity—in magazines, in his anthologies, and in his collections of Lovecraft miscellany. It is scarcely to be wondered, given how secretive Derleth was about the genesis of these works, that hostile critics would use them as ammunition with which to attack Lovecraft. Damon Knight's "The Tedious Mr. Lovecraft" (*Fantasy and Science Fiction*, August 1960) is one such example. (Knight, however, later went on to reprint *The Dream-Quest of Unknown Kadath* in an anthology of fantasy tales.) Even today, when the truth about these "posthumous collaborations" has long been known, careless critics still cite them as work by Lovecraft, and careless publishers continue to reprint them—sometimes even omitting Derleth's name altogether and leaving Lovecraft as the sole author!

As early as the 1940s Derleth had become obsessed by the "Cthulhu Mythos," writing story after story. Two volumes, *The Mask of Cthulhu* (1958) and *The Trail of Cthulhu* (1962), containing stories published in the 1940s and 1950s, feature some of his worst writing. Like many later pastichists, Derleth somehow seemed to fancy that the highest tribute he could pay to Lovecraft was to write half-baked ripoffs of Lovecraft's own stories; hence, "The Whippoorwills in the Hills" (*Weird Tales*, September 1948) lifts passages almost directly from "The Rats in the Walls"; "Something in Wood" (*Weird Tales*, March 1948) is a rewrite of "The Call of Cthulhu"; "The Sandwin Compact" (*Weird Tales*, November 1940), "The House in the Valley" (*Weird Tales*, July 1953), and "The Watcher from the Sky" (*Weird Tales*, July 1945) are all near-plagiarisms of "The Shadow over Innsmouth," a story that seemed to fascinate Derleth. Nearly every one of these stories contains a catechism about the Elder Gods, elementals, the "expulsion" of the "evil" Cthulhu, Yog-Sothoth, and Hastur (now deemed, by Derleth, the half-brother to Cthulhu, whatever that means).

It may sound odd to say so, but Derleth really had no genuine feel for the weird. All his work in this domain is either highly conventional (tales of ghosts, haunted houses, etc.) or clumsy pastiche. Many of these Lovecraft-inspired tales are, in addition, poor not in their deviation from Lovecraft's own conceptions (some later work that so deviates is highly meritorious, as we shall see), but in the basic craft of fiction-writing: they are written carelessly and hastily, with very poor, ham-fisted attempts to imitate Lovecraft's style (Derleth frequently maintained that Lovecraft's prose was easy to mimic!), clumsy development, laughable attempts at verisimilitude by long catalogues of esoteric terms, and flamboyant conclusions in which good triumphs in the nick of time over evil (in the final tale of the "novel" *The Trail of Cthulhu* Cthulhu ends up being nuked!). These tales really are subject to the very flaws that critics have falsely attributed to Lovecraft—verbosity, artificiality, excessive histrionics, and the like.

Derleth tried as much as possible to sound like Lovecraft but failed pitiably. For some bizarre reason, he set nearly all his "Cthulhu Mythos" tales in New England, which he had never seen, and as a result was totally unconvincing in his atmosphere. He attempted to mimic Lovecraft's archaistic prose when presenting old documents but produced comical errors. He was fond of pomposities such as the following: "I have come out of the sky to watch and prevent horror from being spawned again on this earth. I cannot fail; I must succeed."[38] But it is too painful to make a catalogue of Derleth's shortcomings; they are now all too apparent for all to see.

What is of some interest is that several early scholars simply refused to pay attention to Derleth's tendentious interpretation of the mythos and produced some fine analyses on their own. Three individuals stand out in particular. Fritz Leiber's "A Literary Copernicus," which appeared in Derleth's second Lovecraft miscellany volume, *Something about Cats and Other Pieces* (1949), is a revision of several previous pieces that had appeared in the *Acolyte* and elsewhere; it may still stand as the best general article on Lovecraft. Leiber boldly declared, ". . . I believe it is a mistake to regard the beings of the Cthulhu mythos as sophisticated equivalents of the entities of Christian demonology, or to attempt to divide them into balancing Zoroastrian hierarchies of good and evil."[39] Matthew H. Onderdonk wrote several articles in the 1940s, including some pioneering studies of Lovecraft's philosophical thought that emphasised his mechanistic materialism and atheism and sought to harmonise the prodigal creation of "gods" in his fiction with this outlook. George T. Wetzel wrote a series of articles in the 1950s culminating in "The Cthulhu Mythos: A Study" (1955), in which he paid no attention to Derleth and merely studied the themes and motifs running through Lovecraft's work. But they were lone voices, and almost all other commentators thoughtlessly accepted Derleth's pronouncements as if they came from Lovecraft himself.

One final issue, partly related to his promulgation of the "Cthulhu Mythos," is Derleth's control over the Lovecraft copyrights. This is an extraordinarily complicated situation and has yet to be resolved, but a few notes can be set down here. Lovecraft's will of 1912 naturally made no provision for a literary estate, so any such estate by default ended up in the control of his sole surviving relative, Annie Gamwell, upon his death. Annie, as we have seen, formalised Lovecraft's wish to have Barlow deemed his literary executor, but this conferred no control over the copyrights to Lovecraft's work. When Annie herself died, her estate passed to Ethel Phillips Morrish and Edna Lewis.

Derleth from the beginning claimed *de facto* ownership of Lovecraft's work by virtue of publishing it in book form, but his control is almost certainly fictitious. He became angry at Corwin Stickney for publishing his small *HPL* pamphlet in 1937, even though this booklet of eight sonnets was published in an edition of 25 copies. He repeatedly badgered anthologists into paying him reprint fees for Lovecraft stories, and most did so simply to stay on good terms with him. Derleth indeed claimed that he had sunk $25,000 of his own money into Arkham House in its first decade,[40] and I am willing to believe it; but I also maintain that Arkham House would never have stayed afloat at all had it not been for the sales generated from Lovecraft's work.

What, then, were Derleth's claims for ownership of Lovecraft's copyrights? He initially tried to maintain that Annie Gamwell's will had conferred such rights, but that will states clearly that Derleth and Wandrei are to receive merely the remaining proceeds from *The Outsider and Others*—not the literary rights to the material therein. Arkham House then claimed that something called "the Morrish-Lewis gift" (presumably a document signed by Ethel Phillips Morrish and Edna Lewis) grants Arkham House blanket permission to publish Lovecraft's work; but this document, which was finally produced in court, does not in any sense transfer copyright to Arkham House.

Finally, Derleth claimed to have purchased from *Weird Tales* the rights to forty-six Lovecraft stories published in that magazine. There is indeed a document to this effect, dated October 9, 1947; but the question is: what rights could have been transferred in this manner? *Weird Tales* could only have transferred rights to those stories where they controlled all rights (not merely first serial rights); but Lovecraft declared frequently that, although initially selling all rights to *Weird Tales* because he did not know any better, by April 1926 he began reserving his rights.[41] Now there is no documentary evidence of this (i.e., no contracts from *Weird Tales* in which only first serial rights are purchased), but there is considerable circumstantial evidence to support Lovecraft's claim. Recall the Carl Swanson incident of 1932: Swanson had wanted to reprint stories from *Weird Tales,* and Farnsworth Wright had told Lovecraft not only that he (Wright) would not give Swanson second serial rights to any stories he owned, but that he "did not favour the second sale of those tales in which I hold later rights."[42] Wright would not have made such a statement if he had held all rights.

If April 1926 is the cut-off, there are thirteen stories for which *Weird Tales* owned all rights (not counting "Under the Pyramids," which was presumably written on a work-for-hire contract). But of these thirteen, seven had already appeared in amateur (uncopyrighted) journals, hence were in the public domain the moment they were published. Therefore, Derleth in truth purchased the rights to only six stories. And yet, he continued to act as if he controlled *all* of Lovecraft's works, going so far as to state in 1949:

> As representatives of the estate of H. P. Lovecraft, it is the duty and obligation of Arkham House to prevent any such publication [i.e., unauthorised publication of Lovecraft's works]; luckily, Supreme Court decisions have clearly supported every stand Arkham House has taken, and not even a letter by H. P. Lovecraft may be published without the consent of Arkham House.[43]

Derleth later backed down from this outrageous claim (and I have no idea what "Supreme Court decisions" could have bolstered it); indeed, Derleth did nothing when many fans published works by Lovecraft in magazines. Moreover, when Sam Moskowitz wished to publish "The Whisperer in Darkness" in his anthology, *Strange Signposts* (1966), he refused to pay anything for it. Derleth threatened to sue; Moskowitz dared him to go ahead; Derleth did nothing.

Derleth, in effect, relied upon bullying and upon his self-appointed role as Lovecraft's publisher and disciple. He even went so far as to claim that the "Cthulhu Mythos" was an Arkham House property, and in this way badgered the pulp writer C. Hall Thompson from developing his own offshoot of the mythos, set in New Jersey. As late as 1963 Derleth was claiming: "I should point out that the Mythos and its pantheon of Gods etc. are under copyright and may not be used in fiction without the express permission of Arkham House."[44] Admittedly, this statement was made in a personal letter written to some young fan who was attempting to write "Cthulhu Mythos" tales; but Derleth did declare in print four years later: "the title 'Necronomicon' is a literary property and may not be used without permission."[45]

This whole issue is, of course, now moot, for it is widely acknowledged that Lovecraft's entire work went into the public domain at the end of the seventieth year following his death, i.e. January 1, 2008.

One interesting upshot of all this involves Lovecraft's ex-wife. Sonia had left for California in 1933, and in 1936 she married Dr Nathaniel Davis. Incredibly, she did not hear of Lovecraft's death until 1945, when Wheeler Dryden informed her of it. This seemed to rekindle her interest in her ex-husband, for she resumed contact with some Lovecraft associates, especially Samuel Loveman. She began preparing a memoir of Lovecraft and even contemplated publishing some unspecified materials by Lovecraft which she possessed (not her letters, since she had burned these long before). Derleth, hearing of the venture, shot back a stern letter:

> ... I hope you are not going ahead regardless of our stipulations to arrange for publication of anything containing writings of any kind, letters or otherwise, of H. P. Lovecraft, thus making it necessary for us to enjoin publication and sale, and to bring suit, which we will certainly do if any manuscript containing works of Lovecraft does not pass through our office for the executor's permission.[46]

Sonia was indeed deterred by this from publishing whatever Lovecraft materials she had, but she did go ahead and write her memoir, which appeared in the *Providence Sunday Journal* for August 22, 1948 as "Howard Phillips Lovecraft as His Wife Remembers Him." It was heavily edited by Winfield Townley Scott. As further edited by Derleth, it appeared in *Something about Cats and Other Pieces* (1949). Her full, unedited version did not see print until 1985.

Robert Hayward Barlow died by his own hand on January 2, 1951. After essentially being pushed out of his literary executorship by Derleth and Wandrei, Barlow had begun to pursue other interests. Moving to California and taking courses at Berkeley, he emigrated to Mexico in 1942 and became a professor of anthropology at the University of Mexico. He remains a revered and distinguished figure there for the landmark work he did in the study of the native Indian languages of the region. He had also evolved into a very fine poet. But word leaked out about his homosexuality, and to forestall exposure he committed suicide. He was thirty-two years old. It was a tragic waste, for—although not in the field of weird fiction—he had fully justified Lovecraft's predictions of his precocious genius, and would have accomplished far more had he lived.

The 1950s were a somewhat quiescent decade for Lovecraft. Much of his work fell out of print in the United States except for random appearances in anthologies. One surprising development occurred, however: the publication of Lovecraft's work in Europe. The British publisher Victor Gollancz, passing through New York, contacted Derleth and asked about the possibility of issuing Lovecraft in England. Gollancz published two volumes in 1951, *The Haunter of the Dark and Other Tales of Horror* and *The Case of Charles Dexter Ward*. Both received relatively favourable reviews, suggesting that British critics were a little less predisposed to dislike the weird on principle than American critics of the day were. *Punch* declared: "Lovecraft was undoubtedly a minor master of cosmic horror."[47] An unsigned review of *The Case of Charles Dexter Ward* in the *Times Literary Supplement* has now been assigned to the distinguished novelist Anthony

Powell. While not entirely favourable, Powell does conclude: "There are, however, undeniably some eerie moments among the corpses."[48] The mystery writers Francis Iles (Anthony Berkeley Cox) and Edmund Crispin praised Lovecraft.[49] Both Gollancz volumes did remarkably well: *The Haunter of the Dark* went through five hardcover printings through 1977 and five paperback printings with Panther Books; *The Case of Charles Dexter Ward* was reprinted by Panther in 1963 and went through four printings through 1973. The Avon *Lurking Fear* was reprinted in paperback by World Distributors in 1959, attracting a new generation of British weird enthusiasts.

Still more remarkable than British interest in Lovecraft is the foreign response. In 1954 two books of Lovecraft's stories were published in France; editions in Germany, Italy, Spain, and South America followed rapidly. The leader of the French movement was Jacques Bergier, who may or may not have corresponded with Lovecraft. These early volumes attracted the attention of Jean Cocteau, who contributed to a symposium in the *Observer* and remarked of the first French volume, *La Couleur tombée du ciel,* "Mr. Lovecraft, who is American, invents a terrifying world of space-time; his somewhat loose style has gained by translation into French."[50] This remark echoes that of Lovecraft's early French translator Jacques Papy, who actually found Lovecraft's style so offensive that he wilfully omitted many words and phrases so as to produce a more "elegant" and simplified French version. It is perhaps true that Lovecraft's dense style cannot be well accommodated in French, but the majority of French readers who have read only Papy's translations (which continue to be reprinted to the present day) cannot be said to have read Lovecraft. Criticism abroad also followed these early volumes, and was on the whole much more astute than American or English criticism.

The fan movement continued to be active in the 1950s. Here George T. Wetzel was the spearhead. As early as 1946 he had begun compilation of a new bibliography of Lovecraft: Francis T. Laney and William H. Evans (receiving assistance from Barlow and other individuals) had assembled one in 1943, but it was very preliminary. Wetzel spent years combing through amateur journals, while Robert E. Briney concentrated on professional appearances. The result—the seventh and last volume of Wetzel's *Lovecraft Collectors Library* (1955)—is a landmark, and the foundation for all subsequent bibliographic work on Lovecraft. The first five volumes of the *Lovecraft Collectors Library* contained obscure stories, poems, and essays by Lovecraft; the sixth, essays about him, including memoirs reprinted from Edward H. Cole's special *Olympian* issue. These volumes were all humbly produced on mimeograph, but they began that resurrection of Lovecraft's lesser work which continues in the small press today.

On a more academic front, the Swiss scholar Peter Penzoldt devoted some remarkably astute pages to Lovecraft in *The Supernatural in Fiction* (1952), which could be called the first significant treatise in the field since "Supernatural Horror in Literature," and which itself draws upon Lovecraft's monograph for many of its theoretical presuppositions. Lovecraft also entered a textbook for the first time (if we discount "Sleepy Hollow To-day") when "The Music of Erich Zann" was included in James B. Hall and Joseph Langland's *The Short Story* (1956), complete with study questions at the end.

In 1950 the first academic paper had emerged—James Warren Thomas's "Howard Phillips Lovecraft: A Self-Portrait," a master's thesis written at Brown University. While Thomas did extensive research into Lovecraft's New York period (based, of course, largely upon the letters to his aunts), he let his horror at Lovecraft's racism colour his views, so that he called Lovecraft "narrow and prejudiced and strait-laced and lacking in ordinary human feeling . . ." Thomas wished to publish his thesis and asked Barlow (who still had legal control of the papers at the John Hay Library) and Derleth for permission to quote Lovecraft's letters. Derleth was violently opposed to publication, since the work would cast Lovecraft in a very bad light, and he essentially squelched the project. The thesis finally did appear in gutted form in the University of Detroit literary magazine, *Fresco,* serialised over four issues (Fall 1958–Summer 1959). The Spring 1958 issue of *Fresco* had been entirely devoted to Lovecraft, and contains a few pieces of interest.

By 1959 Derleth had gathered enough material to publish another miscellany volume, *The Shuttered Room and Other Pieces.* This set the stage for a resurgence of interest in Lovecraft in the 1960s. It is unclear how Derleth gained the funds to reissue Lovecraft's major work in three volumes, *The Dunwich Horror and Others* (1963), *At the Mountains of Madness and Other Novels* (1964), and *Dagon and Other Macabre Tales* (1965). He declared that publishing these books caused significant delays in other projects,[51] but he also went on to cite the early film adaptations of Lovecraft, which must have generated some income for Arkham House. In any event, Derleth decided to keep these three books in print. In 1963 he also finally issued a slim volume of *Collected Poems* (it of course never pretended to be Lovecraft's "complete" poetry), delayed for years by Frank Utpatel's dilatoriness in producing illustrations; but it was well worth the wait, for Utpatel's line drawings—particularly for *Fungi from Yuggoth*—are stunning.

Meanwhile, in 1965, Derleth at last brought out the much-delayed first volume of *Selected Letters.* The project took so long because Derleth and Wandrei continued to receive new batches of letters that disturbed the chronological sequence they had established; money also was probably lacking. The second volume emerged in 1968, the third in 1971. Although full of mistranscriptions and bizarre editorial decisions regarding abridgements (in one instance only the greeting and closing of a letter were included, the body of the text entirely excised), the appearance of this set was a landmark. But Derleth had by this time developed a kind of hostility to the mainstream press (both because of some unfavourable reviews of early Arkham House books and, perhaps, also because his own mainstream reputation—culminating in 1945 with an article on him by Sinclair Lewis in *Esquire*—had steadily declined with the passing of the years), and so the appearance of the letters was noted only in the science fiction and fantasy community. Derleth also compiled one final miscellany volume, *The Dark Brotherhood and Other Pieces* (1966), an anthology, *Tales of the Cthulhu Mythos* (1969), and *The Horror in the Museum and Other Revisions* (1970).

Some word should be said of the early media adaptations of Lovecraft. Although "The Dunwich Horror" was adapted for radio on the CBS series "Suspense" as early as 1949 (being just the sort of melodramatic, atmosphereless rendition that Lovecraft feared when he denied radio dramatisation rights for "The Dreams in the Witch House"), it was in the early 1960s that Lovecraft became a sudden media presence. At that time three films emerged in quick succession: *The Haunted Palace* (1964), *Die, Monster, Die* (1965), and *The Shuttered Room* (1967). The first was part of Roger Corman's Poe series, and a Poe-related title was affixed to it even though it was clearly an adaptation of *The Case of Charles Dexter Ward* (and credited as such). The second is an adaptation of "The Colour out of Space," while the third adapts a "posthumous collaboration." All are interesting experiments (Vincent Price appears in the first, Boris Karloff in the second, Gig Young in the third), although none of them could be called intrinsically good films in their own right; ironically, the best is perhaps *The Shuttered Room*. Then came *The Dunwich Horror* (1970), a grotesque fiasco with the implausibly handsome Dean Stockwell playing Wilbur Whateley, the lovely Sandra Dee playing a character that has no existence in the original story, and the Old Ones being played, apparently, by hippies on an acid trip.

Criticism in this decade was almost non-existent, although the *Selected Letters* was laying the seed for future work. Jack L. Chalker's anthology, *Mirage on Lovecraft* (1965), is very insubstantial. Perhaps the best item remained unfortunately unpublished: Arthur S. Koki's "H. P. Lovecraft: An Introduction to His Life and Writings," a large master's thesis for Columbia (1962) that used primary documents in presenting the course of Lovecraft's life. Foreign interest, however, continued to be strong. A German collection of tales, *Cthulhu: Geistergeschichten* (1968), was translated by the distinguished poet H. C. Artmann. Then, in 1969, the prestigious French journal *L'Herne* devoted its entire twelfth issue to Lovecraft, featuring translations of works by him, translations of American critical articles, and many original French pieces.

One work of criticism does indeed call for attention: Colin Wilson's *The Strength to Dream: Literature and the Imagination* (1961). Wilson had gained celebrity by publishing, at the age of twenty-four, the challenging sociological study,

The Outsider (1956). Now, turning his attention to weird and science fiction, he stumbled upon Lovecraft; his reaction was very bizarre. "In some ways, Lovecraft is a horrifying figure. In his 'war with rationality,' he brings to mind W. B. Yeats. But, unlike Yeats, he is sick, and his closest relation is with Peter Kürten, the Düsseldorf murderer . . . Lovecraft is totally withdrawn; he has rejected 'reality'; he seems to have lost all sense of health that would make a normal man turn back halfway."[52] How the inoffensive Lovecraft could possibly have caused Wilson to have this extreme reaction would be an interesting psychological study. It scarcely needs saying that Wilson's entire blast is a tissue of nonsense, derived from an extraordinarily superficial reading of Lovecraft's works (to the point that he has misconstrued the very plot of "The Shadow out of Time") and a shockingly careless study of his life and thought. But Wilson later admitted that he is a cheerful optimist and was gravely offended by what he took to be Lovecraft's pessimism (evidently Wilson, who claims some sort of standing as a philosopher, could not distinguish between pessimism and Lovecraft's very different brand of "indifferentism").

Derleth, who had provided Wilson some source material for *The Strength to Dream,* was gravely offended by Wilson's remarks. He challenged Wilson to write his own "Lovecraftian" novel, and the latter in short order produced *The Mind Parasites* (1967), the American edition of which Arkham House published. In the introduction Wilson grudgingly admitted that his treatment of Lovecraft in *The Strength to Dream* had been "unduly harsh"; but elsewhere he continued to aver that Lovecraft is an "atrocious writer" whose work is "finally interesting as case history rather than literature."[53] The true fact of the matter is, of course, that Wilson is appalled by Lovecraft's dark vision and its implicit repudiation of Wilson's own naive belief in some future development of the human species.

And yet, *The Mind Parasites* is a highly compelling piece of work, even though its premise—that a kind of "mind cancer" has afflicted the human race since about 1780, thereby producing artists who have a bleak, pessimistic outlook on life—is quite preposterous even as fiction. But Wilson has done what a true pastichist has to do: use Lovecraft's conceptions as a springboard for his own vision. To date, almost no "Cthulhu Mythos" writers have followed Wilson in this regard. Wilson wrote two sequels to *The Mind Parasites, The Philosopher's Stone* (1969) and *The Space Vampires* (1976); the former actually has a somewhat greater Lovecraftian content than *The Mind Parasites,* but it is a bit of a literary shambles and an excess of pompous philosophising, while *The Space Vampires* goes to the opposite extreme in being merely a science fiction/horror adventure story with relatively little relation to Lovecraft. Wilson, who has continued on occasion to write ignorantly on Lovecraft (see his introduction to the Creation Press edition of *Crawling Chaos: Selected Works 1920–1925* [1993]), has also destroyed his reputation as an intellectual with a variety of credulous works on the occult, since he sees certain occult phenomena as foreshadowing that future advancement of the human species which is the core of what he calls his philosophy. Wilson, much more than Lovecraft, is a curiosity of intellectual history.

If criticism was in short supply in the 1960s, a new generation of fiction writers was taking up the "Cthulhu Mythos." Interestingly, two of the most dynamic figures were English, J. Ramsey Campbell (b. 1946) and Brian Lumley (b. 1937). Campbell is by far the more interesting figure. Around 1960, when he was only fourteen, he began writing stories based on Lovecraft. He sent these boldly to August Derleth, without revealing his age. Derleth saw merit in Campbell's work, but advised him to drop the New England settings in his tales (Campbell had never been to New England) and set them in England instead. In this way Campbell evolved a British counterpart to Lovecraft's fictional milieu. Derleth published Campbell's *The Inhabitant of the Lake and Less Welcome Tenants* in 1964, when Campbell was eighteen. These pastiches are certainly written with a verve not found in much work of their kind, but they are still very derivative. Campbell realised the fact, and he almost immediately proceeded to turn violently away from Lovecraft and evolve his own style. By 1967 he began producing the tales that would fill his second collection, *Demons by Daylight* (1973), which in its way is one of the most significant volumes of weird fiction since *The Outsider and Others:* it introduced a radically new Ramsey Campbell, one who had evolved a dreamlike, hallucinatory style of his own and a very modern subject-matter involving sexual tension, alienation, and aberrant psychology. Campbell has gone on to become perhaps the leading writer of weird fiction since Lovecraft.

Lumley's fate has not been so happy. He began publishing stories in the late 1960s (some in Derleth's small magazine, the *Arkham Collector,* which was a successor to the fine but short-lived *Arkham Sampler* of 1948–49 and which lasted for ten issues between 1967 and 1971), and his first collection, *The Caller of the Black,* appeared from Arkham House in 1971. Several other novels and story collections have followed. Lumley's work is derivative not so much of Lovecraft as of Derleth: he has swallowed the "Derleth Mythos" whole and produces unwitting parodies of Lovecraft by mimicking Derleth's Elder Gods, elementals, etc. In the novel *Beneath the Moors* (1974) one character actually has a genial chat with Bokrug, the water-lizard from "The Doom That Came to Sarnath"! In *The Burrowers Beneath* (1974) Lumley formalises Derleth's good-vs.-evil scenario of Elder Gods vs. Old Ones by affixing upon the latter the ridiculous acronym CCD (Cthulhu Cycle Deities). Lumley has thankfully abandoned the "Cthulhu Mythos" and gone on to write multi-volume cycles of novels mixing fantasy and horror, whose unreadability is only matched by their inexplicable popularity.

A very different work altogether is *Dagon* (1968), a novel by the distinguished poet, novelist, and short story writer Fred Chappell. This grim tale of psychological horror deftly uses Lovecraftian elements as backdrop. Although a fine novel, it received relatively poor reviews, but it won a prize when translated into French.[54] Chappell has in recent years written several more stories based on Lovecraft's work or using Lovecraft as a character; some are collected in *More Shapes Than One* (1991).

August Derleth died on July 4, 1971, leaving unfinished a final "posthumous collaboration," a prospective novel entitled *The Watchers out of Time*. How exactly one is to evaluate Derleth's stewardship of Lovecraft will depend upon one's assessment of the four basic aspects of this stewardship: 1) the publication of Lovecraft's work; 2) the criticism of his life and work; 3) the dissemination of the "Cthulhu Mythos"; and 4) the control of Lovecraft's copyrights. On the latter three of these counts, there can be no doubt that Derleth deserves far more censure than praise. On only the first count can he possibly gain approbation, and even here there is room for debate. It has frequently been stated by Derleth's partisans that he was not only the person who "put Lovecraft on the map" literarily, but the only one who could have done so: Barlow could not have done anything significant, and without Derleth's aid Lovecraft's work would have fallen into oblivion. This is highly questionable. I have already mentioned that Derleth made, to my mind, a fundamental error in deciding so quickly to publish Lovecraft himself, thereby preventing his work from reaching a mainstream audience and perhaps affecting the entire course of weird fiction in the latter half of this century. It cannot conclusively be stated that Lovecraft's work would never have been rediscovered had Derleth not done so: I think it quite possible that scholars of the pulps would have recognised its merit sooner or later—probably sooner. Moreover, the papers at the John Hay Library would no doubt have been examined by some enterprising scholar whether or not Lovecraft's work was readily available. Of course, the brute fact is that Derleth *did* rescue Lovecraft's work, and that is something that cannot be taken away from him. But his legacy is nonetheless a decidedly mixed one.

Sad to say, it seemed to require Derleth's death to bring on the next stage of Lovecraft scholarship. The first half of the 1970s was an extraordinarily fertile period, both in terms of the publication of Lovecraft's stories and criticism of his life and work. Beagle Books (later subsumed by Ballantine) began an extensive publication of Lovecraft in paperback in 1969; amusingly enough, however, only four of the eleven volumes of their "Arkham Edition of H. P. Lovecraft" contained works by Lovecraft; the other volumes featured the "posthumous collaborations," a reprint of Derleth's anthology, *Tales of the Cthulhu Mythos,* and, appallingly enough, Derleth's *Mask of Cthulhu* and *Trail of Cthulhu*. What is more, the Beagle/Ballantine editions did not even contain many of Lovecraft's best stories, since the paperback rights to these were owned by Lancer Books, which had issued two fine editions, *The Dunwich Horror and Others* (1963) and *The Colour out of Space* (1965), and kept them in print into the early 1970s (they were reprinted in 1978 by Jove). What is more, two volumes of Lovecraft's "dreamland" tales were edited in 1970 by Lin Carter in his Adult Fantasy series for Ballantine, some of the contents of which overlap those of the Beagle editions. Nevertheless, the various Beagle/Ballantine editions sold nearly a million copies and definitively made Lovecraft a posthumous member of the counterculture. He became fashionable reading among high school and college students, and rock musicians began making covert allusions to him. (In the late 1960s there had even been a rock band named H. P. Lovecraft that issued two albums. Derleth reported that they substantially augmented sales of Arkham House books.[55]) The Beagle/Ballantine editions received a lengthy review in *Time* magazine in 1973, in which the reviewer Philip Herrera, although making some foolish errors, did succeed in a half-parodic imitation of Lovecraft's style. There are also a few keen reflexions:

> Well did he know that true terror lies in the tension between our scientific age's rationalism and our primordial sense of individual powerlessness—of being enmeshed in something vast, inexplicable and appallingly evil. For this reason he eschewed the stock devices of werewolves and vampires for a more intimate horror. . . .
>
> It is true that some of Lovecraft's stories of the Cthulu [*sic*] Mythos—*The Call of Cthulu, At the Mountains of Madness*—rank high among the horror stories of the English language. But Great Cthulu only knows why perfectly good, independent writers from the late August Derleth to Colin Wilson have seized and elaborated on the Mythos in their work.[56]

Foreign translations—collections as well as magazine and anthology appearances—became common at this time, as Lovecraft appeared in Dutch, Polish, Swedish, Norwegian, Rumanian, and Japanese. (There may in fact have been Japanese translations as early as the 1940s.) Foreign criticism continued apace, the leading contribution being Maurice Lévy's *Lovecraft ou du fantastique* (1972), a revision of a 1969 dissertation for the Sorbonne. It may be the single best monograph on Lovecraft, and it is unfortunate that it took sixteen years for an English translation to appear.

The fan world was tremendously active. Among the highlights was a somewhat crudely produced but very substantial anthology, *HPL* (1972), edited by Meade and Penny Frierson, with fine pieces by George T. Wetzel, J. Vernon Shea, and many others. One of the most important contributions was Richard L. Tierney's "The Derleth Mythos," a one-page article that began the destruction of Derleth's conception of the mythos. This work was substantially fostered by Dirk W. Mosig in his landmark essay "H. P. Lovecraft: Myth-Maker" (1976), which received widespread dissemination both here and abroad.

Other fan work of the time was rather less distinguished. Darrell Schweitzer produced a respectable small anthology of criticism, *Essays Lovecraftian* (1976), but it received poor distribution. Also out of the fan community, although professionally published, was Lin Carter's *Lovecraft: A Look Behind the "Cthulhu Mythos"* (1972), which made some egregious factual errors and wholly adopted the "Derleth Mythos," but nevertheless presented an adequate "history" of the mythos, especially after Lovecraft's death.

In 1973 Joseph Pumilia and Roger Bryant founded the Esoteric Order of Dagon, an amateur press association in which members each produced humble magazines devoted to Lovecraft or weird fiction. Although in many cases the journals were very crude both in physical appearance and in contents, a surprising amount of substantial work appeared in them, including penetrating work by Kenneth W. Faig, Jr, Ben P. Indick, David E. Schultz, and others. Faig perhaps established himself as the leading scholar of Lovecraft during the early 1970s, doing a tremendous amount of biographical and bibliographical work in Providence. Much of this research was embodied in a huge unpublished monograph, "Lovecraftian Voyages" (1973). Also at this time R. Alain Everts was doing prodigious work in tracing Lovecraft's surviving colleagues, but only a small portion of his research has seen print. Two bibliographies appeared, David A. Sutton's *Bibliotheca: H. P. Lovecraft* (1971) and Mark Owings and Jack L. Chalker's *The Revised H. P. Lovecraft Bibliography* (1973), but neither added much to Wetzel's work.

All this work culminated in 1975 with the near-simultaneous emergence of three substantial books about Lovecraft: L. Sprague de Camp's *Lovecraft: A Biography* (Doubleday); Frank Belknap Long's *Howard Phillips Lovecraft: Dreamer on the Nightside* (Arkham House); and Willis Conover's *Lovecraft at Last* (Carrollton-Clark).

It would, I suppose, be uncharitable of me to speak ill of de Camp's work, for it is without question the first significant full-scale biography of Lovecraft and embodies more research than any other published volume up to that time. De Camp spent three or four years working on his biography—consulting papers at the John Hay Library, interviewing old colleagues of Lovecraft, and reading Lovecraft's obscurer writings. And yet, what strikes one about his bulky work is its sketchiness: very complicated matters are passed over with misleading brevity, and much of the biography develops a fragmented and random character because de Camp has not really pondered the interrelations between Lovecraft's life, work, and thought. There are, to be sure, any number of mistakes of fact, but the biography's failings go far beyond such surface details: it seriously errs in its very conception.

De Camp admitted that he was temperamentally nothing like Lovecraft: not sensitive to environment, looking to the future rather than the past, a go-getter "professional" writer intent on sales rather than on aesthetic expression, etc. etc.

These differences are embarrassingly evident. Whenever de Camp encounters some facet of Lovecraft's personality that he cannot understand or does not share, he immediately undertakes a kind of half-baked posthumous psychoanalysis. Hence he refers to Lovecraft's sensitivity to place as "topomania"—as if no one could be attached to the physical tokens of his birthplace without being considered neurotic.

Perhaps the worst failing of de Camp's biography is his treatment of Lovecraft's philosophical thought—or, rather, the absence thereof. Although a popular writer on science, de Camp was not a trained philosopher and was entirely incapable of tracing the sources or evolution of Lovecraft's world view and the degree to which it structured his literary work. Many readers would be excused if, after reading de Camp's work, they concluded that Lovecraft had no world view at all. At the same time, de Camp harped upon Lovecraft's racial views all out of proportion to their significance in his general philosophy, and without even a proper understanding of their origin or purpose.

As for de Camp's literary criticism, the most charitable thing that can be said of it is that it is a trifle amateurish. De Camp had little appreciation of literature beyond the level of popular entertainment, and he accordingly took great umbrage when Lovecraft properly trashed pulp fiction as the hackwork that it was—perhaps because de Camp's own science fiction and fantasy is not much above this level. De Camp's highest praise for a Lovecraft tale is that it is a "rousing good yarn."

It is not surprising, therefore, that de Camp's book received widespread condemnation in the fan press. De Camp responded to this barrage of criticism by claiming loftily that he had merely offended the Lovecraft "cult" by knocking their idol down a few notches; but the facts are more complex than this. It is not that de Camp violated the canons of "objectivity" by passing value judgments—this is the proper function of any biographer; it is that these value judgments were arrived at through inadequate understanding and false perspective. The fact that many of these judgments were antipodally at variance with the views of all Lovecraft's close friends should have suggested to de Camp that there was something wrong with his assessments.

And yet, for all its inadequacies, de Camp's biography did do some good. Although it gave ammunition to several reviewers to attack Lovecraft (notable among these were Ursula K. Le Guin and Larry McMurtry, whose ignorant snipes ended up casting more ridicule upon themselves than upon Lovecraft), the volume did indeed give Lovecraft wider exposure in the general literary world and helped to interest an entirely new legion of enthusiasts and scholars in Lovecraft the man and writer. One of these was myself: I devoured the volume at the age of seventeen and felt that there was much work to be done on this strange and little-known writer.

Frank Long's *Howard Phillips Lovecraft: Dreamer on the Nightside,* although it emerged roughly at the same time as de Camp's biography, was in fact written as a direct response to it: Long read much of de Camp's work in manuscript and confessed to me that he so objected to the portrayal of Lovecraft that he found there that he felt the need to write his own version. Long's is, of course, nothing more than an extended memoir, not a formal biography; and it is flawed on several counts. Minor failings such as silly forays into literary criticism, an unconvincing attempt to recall Lovecraft's exact words on a given occasion, and an embarrassing question-and-answer session in which Lovecraft is made to expound his views on various subjects can be set aside. What cannot be ignored is the imprecision of Long's memory and the haste with which he wrote his book; the result was that the manuscript had to be exhaustively revised by Arkham House's editor, James Turner, to such a degree that as it stands it is virtually a collaborative work. Long should have written this memoir many years earlier; by 1974 his memories of Lovecraft had lapsed to the point that many of his comments are highly unreliable. Nevertheless, the picture of Lovecraft that emerges from this ungainly book is far more accurate than that found in de Camp: here at least is a Lovecraft that is recognisable and bears some kinship with the man we find from his letters, essays, and stories.

Unquestionably the finest of the trilogy of books on Lovecraft to appear in 1975 is Willis Conover's *Lovecraft at Last.* I have already spoken of this heartfelt memoir of a boy and the older man he revered, and of the unstinting labour and expense Conover put into this volume so that it has already become a legend in modern book design. It presents perhaps the truest portrait of Lovecraft of the three books, since of course many of its words are by Lovecraft himself, in the form of his letters to Conover. It also provides a fascinating glimpse into the little-known world of fantasy fandom of the 1930s.

In 1976 the final two volumes of *Selected Letters* appeared under the editorship of James Turner. The completed five-volume set is certainly a monument, in spite of its errors and abridgements, and it has materially aided in the renaissance of scholarship during the last two decades. It was just at this time that I myself was becoming involved in the field, so that my perspective must now change from that of an historian to that of a spectator and, later, a participant.

Dirk W. Mosig, a German professor of psychology, was at this time the leading scholarly figure in the field and the focus of a growing international interest in Lovecraft. The actual articles Mosig published in his relatively brief career are not at all reflective of his importance, for they are either general biographical articles or psychoanalytical approaches to Lovecraft utilising the theories of Jung. Mosig was, like Lovecraft himself, a tremendous letter-writer, and he prodigally dispersed his comprehensive knowledge of Lovecraft to all parties; he moreover lent considerable assistance to editors and publishers overseas, so that previously unavailable material by and about Lovecraft began appearing in translation. I can attest that Mosig was the most significant influence on my own understanding of Lovecraft, even though my views have departed from his in some particulars. Perhaps Mosig's greatest failing was, paradoxically, his enthusiasm: he was so taken with Lovecraft that he could see few flaws in either his character or his work (he defended even Lovecraft's poetry). Around 1978, a variety of personal difficulties led to Mosig's abrupt departure from the field.

But by this time several others had, through Mosig's influence, become interested in Lovecraft. One of the leading figures was Donald R. Burleson, a professor of mathematics and English who began writing careful studies of the topographical and literary sources behind Lovecraft's tales. This phase of his work culminated in *H. P. Lovecraft: A Critical Study* (1983), still perhaps the single best overview of Lovecraft's work. From this point on, however, Burleson developed radically and controversially into a deconstructionist critic who keenly probed Lovecraft by means of the most contemporary and sophisticated critical tools available; and his monograph, *Lovecraft: Disturbing the Universe* (University Press of Kentucky, 1990), remains the most challenging book yet written on Lovecraft.

Barton L. St Armand, professor of English at Brown University, took a more orthodox academic approach but produced no less scintillating results. He had already written an admirable master's thesis on Lovecraft at Brown (1966), and went on to produce such fine pieces as "Facts in the Case of H. P. Lovecraft" (1972; on *The Case of Charles Dexter Ward*), "H. P. Lovecraft: New England Decadent" (1974; a study of Lovecraft's fusion of Puritanism and Decadence), and *The Roots of Horror in the Fiction of H. P. Lovecraft* (1977), a long study of "The Rats in the Walls." St Armand's work is distinguished for its literary polish and its critical sophistication, and must be pondered deeply by all students of Lovecraft.

Not all work, academic or otherwise, was quite this meritorious. Such things as John Taylor Gatto's Monarch Notes study of Lovecraft (1977) and Darrell Schweitzer's *The Dream Quest of H. P. Lovecraft* (1978) are scarcely worth the paper they are printed on. Less contemptible is Philip A. Shreffler's *H. P. Lovecraft Companion* (1977), although it is largely a series of plot summaries of Lovecraft's stories and an annotated glossary of characters and places cited in the fiction.

By this time my own work was beginning to see fruition. I had initially begun by assembling a volume reprinting important critical statements on Lovecraft from the 1940s to the 1970s, *H. P. Lovecraft: Four Decades of Criticism* (1980), which appears to have been the first work on Lovecraft from an academic publisher. The next year my bibliography of Lovecraft and Lovecraft criticism—compiled with the assistance of many individuals in the Lovecraft community, especially Mosig and David E. Schultz—was published. During this time, while attending Brown University, I had begun a comparison of the manuscripts of Lovecraft's entire work—but chiefly his fiction—with the published editions, finding to my horror thousands of errors in the standard Arkham House editions of the tales. After protracted negotiations with Arkham House, I finally arranged for the publication of corrected texts of Lovecraft's fiction, which emerged in four volumes over five years: *The Dunwich Horror and Others* (1984), *At the Mountains of Madness and Other Novels* (1985), *Dagon and Other Macabre Tales* (1986), and *The Horror in the Museum and Other Revisions* (1989). If anything I have done on Lovecraft deserves to survive, it is this edition; for it makes possible the analysis of Lovecraft's work based upon what he actually wrote.

The specialty publisher Necronomicon Press, founded by Marc A. Michaud in 1976, offered an abundant forum for much of my work and the work of other Lovecraft scholars. The journal *Lovecraft Studies,* founded in 1979, generated considerable work of value. The press also issued a good number of Lovecraft's obscure or unpublished works in small pamphlets (notably David E. Schultz's landmark critical edition of the *Commonplace Book* [1987]), as well as several important monographs, among them Kenneth W. Faig, Jr's *The Parents of Howard Phillips Lovecraft* (1990) and Richard D. Squires's study of the Lovecraft family in Rochester (1995).

In 1981 Robert M. Price founded the fanzine *Crypt of Cthulhu* as a kind of lighter version of *Lovecraft Studies;* nevertheless, much valuable work appeared in its pages, especially by Price himself, who examined the "Cthulhu Mythos" from his academic perspective as a professor of religious studies. Lately, however, Price has become convinced that Derleth's conception of the mythos is not all wrong; he has also become, incongruously, a deconstructionist. His later work has accordingly not been well received.

Lovecraft Studies and *Crypt of Cthulhu* afforded a forum for the most significant Lovecraft criticism of the 1980s, including Steven J. Mariconda's studies of Lovecraft's prose style, Paul Montelone's philosophical studies of Lovecraft's tales, and fine papers on a variety of topics by Mike Ashley, Peter Cannon, Stefan Dziemianowicz, Jason C. Eckhardt, Norman R. Gayford, Robert H. Waugh, and others.

Much of the recent work on Lovecraft achieved a sort of symbolic culmination in 1990, the centennial of his birth. During this time several important books emerged from academic presses: Peter Cannon's *H. P. Lovecraft* (1989) for Twayne's United States Authors Series; Burleson's *Lovecraft: Disturbing the Universe;* my *H. P. Lovecraft: The Decline of the West* (Starmont House, 1990). The H. P. Lovecraft Centennial Conference, taking place at Brown University on August 17–19, brought together nearly all the leading scholars in the field as well as some from overseas. The proceedings of the conference were published the next year, as was an important anthology of original essays, *An Epicure in the Terrible,* edited by David E. Schultz and myself and published by Fairleigh Dickinson University Press.

The centennial conference was such an epochal event that it seemed to result in a kind of exhaustion among Lovecraft scholars. In the past decade relatively little criticism of great substance has appeared. Part of this dearth is the result of the nearly simultaneous collapse of *Lovecraft Studies* (which became highly irregular after 1999 and was defunct by 2005) and *Crypt of Cthulhu* (which came to an end in 2003). Efforts to revive both these journals have so far come to nothing, and I have now begun a new publication, *The Lovecraft Annual* (2007f.), although its infrequent appearance cannot generate sustained interest. In the meantime, other scholars have come to the fore. The critically acclaimed French writer Michel Houellebecq published a lively if controversial volume, *H. P. Lovecraft: Contre le monde, contre la vie* (1991), contending (falsely to my mind) that Lovecraft's racism is central to his world view and to his fiction; it was translated into English in 2005 as *H. P. Lovecraft: Against the World, Against Life.* Arkham House can take pride in the issuance of Peter Cannon's superbly edited *Lovecraft Remembered* (1998), a virtually definitive collection of memoirs of Lovecraft. The Finnish scholar Timo Airaksinen has issued a dense but idiosyncratic study, *The Philosophy of H. P. Lovecraft* (1999), while Robert H. Waugh has gathered his Lovecraftian essays in *The Monster in the Mirror: Looking for H. P. Lovecraft* (2006). David E. Schultz and I wrote what we hope is a helpful reference work, *An H. P. Lovecraft Encyclopedia* (2001). Scholars in France (William Schnabel, Philippe Gindre), Italy (Pietro Guarriello, Lorenzo Mastropierro), and Germany (Marco Frenschkowski, Joachim Körber) continue to do outstanding work.

But if Lovecraft criticism has to some extent lagged, the publication and dissemination of his work worldwide has reached levels that even the scholars of the 1970s could not have imagined. Shortly after the publication of *H. P. Lovecraft: A Life* (1996), I was approached by Penguin Books to prepare annotated editions of Lovecraft's stories for Penguin Classics. Three such volumes appeared, in 1999, 2001, and 2004; nearly simultaneously, two volumes of *The Annotated H. P. Lovecraft* appeared from Dell in 1997 and 1999. The Penguin editions no doubt laid the groundwork for the epochal appearance of a volume of Lovecraft's *Tales* in the Library of America in 2005—a volume that sold 25,000 copies within a few months. Lovecraft's enshrinement in the American canon can be said to have become definitive with the publication of this book. While a few reviews (mostly in right-wing venues such as the *New Criterion*) continued to carp at Lovecraft in the manner of Edmund Wilson, the great majority of reviewers welcomed his ascent into the company of Melville, Fitzgerald, and Faulkner. Simultaneously, the Modern Library issued a slim volume of what it termed the "definitive" text of *At the Mountains of Madness,* along with "Supernatural Horror in Literature." Ballantine/Del Rey has, of course, continued to issue both mass-market and trade paperbacks of Lovecraft's work, the latter beginning with the egregiously subtitled *The Best of H. P. Lovecraft: Blood-curdling Tales of Horror and the Macabre* (1982) and continuing to the present day; but unlike the Penguins or the Library of America edition, the Ballantine editions continue to reprint the corrupt Arkham House texts.

Meanwhile, other bodies of Lovecraft's work have appeared. My edition of *The Ancient Track: Complete Poetical Works,* originally scheduled for publication by Necronomicon Press, was issued by Night Shade Books in 2001. I edited Lovecraft's *Collected Esssays* (2004–06) in five volumes for Hippocampus Press.

The last frontier in the publication of Lovecraft's work is the issuance of his thousands of letters. While the *Selected Letters* was a prodigious enterprise, it quickly became clear to David E. Schultz—who had begun the electronic transcription of Lovecraft's letters so early as 1990—and myself that the only sensible way to issue Lovecraft's letters was to group them by individual correspondent. Necronomicon Press began such an undertaking by issuing the letters to Richard F. Searight (1992), Robert Bloch (1993), and others, but the project foundered soon thereafter. Schultz and I released two volumes of letters—*Mysteries of Time and Spirit* (2002) and *Letters from New York* (2005)—with Night Shade Books, along with two volumes—*Letters to Rheinhart Kleiner* (2003) and *Letters to Alfred Galpin* (2005)— with Hippocampuss Press; *O Fortunate Floridian: H. P. Lovecraft's Letters to R. H. Barlow* appeared in 2007 from University of Tampa Press, which also issued a radically expanded and updated version of my bibliography of Lovecraft in 2009. We are now undertaking the ambitious programme of editing the entirety of Lovecraft's correspondence, in an estimated twenty-five volumes, with Hippocampus; the first four volumes of this informal series, *Essential Solitude: The Letters of H. P. Lovecraft and August Derleth* and *A Means to Freedom: The Letters of H. P. Lovecraft and Robert E. Howard,* appeared in 2008 and 2009, respectively.

Foreign publications have been even more impressive. A meticulously edited four-volume edition of Lovecraft's *Tutti i racconti* (1989–92), prepared by Giuseppe Lippi, is only one of several competing "collected" editions of Lovecraft's work. In Germany, a ten-volume *Gesammelte Werke* (1999–2004) has appeared. A four-volume Greek collected edition (1990) has also appeared. There have been dozens of editions in Spain and Latin America, as well as in such languages as Bengali, Turkish, Hungarian, Estonian, Catalan, Portuguese, Russian, and Polish. There is no question that Lovecraft is now a figure in world literature, and is likely to remain there for some time.

Lovecraft is remarkable in continuing to appeal on both a scholarly and a popular level. One sign of the latter is the widespread distribution of a role-playing game, *The Call of Cthulhu,* first issued by Chaosium, Inc. in 1981 and continuing to the present day with many additions and modifications. While it is somewhat incongruous to adapt Lovecraft's sophisticated, atmospheric tales to the somewhat mechanical action format of a role-playing game, this venture has at least brought Lovecraft to the attention of many young people who might not otherwise have been exposed to his work. More recently, Chaosium published a number of anthologies of "Cthulhu Mythos" tales edited by Robert M. Price; Price also compiled other anthologies for another small press, Fedogan & Bremer, which also issued two volumes of pastiches of Lovecraft's "The Shadow over Innsmouth" edited by Stephen Jones. It cannot be said that much of the material in these volumes is of towering literary value, but it at least keeps Lovecraft's name alive. Another volume, *Lovecraft's Legacy* (1990), edited by Robert E. Weinberg and Martin H. Greenberg, contains a few stories of merit. Arkham House's James Turner produced a revised version of Derleth's *Tales of the Cthulhu Mythos* (1990), following up Ramsey Campbell's innovative *New Tales of the Cthulhu Mythos* (1980), and then edited the innovative anthology *Cthulhu 2000* (1995). Two of the most striking recent works of Lovecraftian fiction are William Browning Spencer's *Résumé with Monsters* (1995) and Donald Tyson's enormous *Alhazred* (2006); the former is a complex novel of Lovecraftian obsession, and the latter is a compulsively readable biographical fantasy about the author of the *Necronomicon.*

Indeed, Mythos writing has proliferated to such an extent—chiefly through such venues as Mythos Books (which has issued sound work by such writers as Stanley C. Sargent, Gary Myers, Michael Cisco, and others), Hippocampus Press (see the work of W. H. Pugmire, perhaps the leading Lovecraftian author writing today), and others—that even the otherwise censorious S. T. Joshi, whose *The Rise and Fall of the Cthulhu Mythos* (2008) was in part intended to inhume the more unworthy pastiches of Lovecraft's work, was tempted to assemble *Black Wings: New Tales of Lovecraftian Horror* (PS Publishing, 2010). My purpose in compiling this volume—whose most notable contributions include stories by such leading contemporary writers as Caitlín R. Kiernan, Jonathan Thomas, Nicholas Royle, Laird Barron, and Michael Shea—is to present less obvious and more searching imitations or adaptations of Lovecraft's ideas. Whether I have succeeded is for readers to determine.

Rather less reputably, occultists of various stripes have embraced Lovecraft in the belief—already evinced by Lovecraft's strange colleague William Lumley—that he either literally believed in the reality of Cthulhu, Yog-Sothoth, etc., or, while consciously denying such things, was tapping various mystical sources of knowledge through his subconscious. Much of this work is pathetically inaccurate and fails to take cognisance of Lovecraft's materialist philosophy—or, rather, while taking outward cognisance of it, has a ready-made excuse for ignoring it (Lovecraft saw the truth but couldn't admit it even to himself!). Such work begins as early as

Lovecraft's French enthusiast Jacques Bergier, who discusses Lovecraft in a work written with Louis Pauwels entitled *Le Matin des magiciens* (1959; translated as *The Morning of the Magicians*). Kenneth Grant and others have traced fanciful relationships between Lovecraft and Aleister Crowley.

The occultists have been unusually fascinated with the *Necronomicon,* which they refuse to believe is mythical. As if to fulfil their expectations, a man going by the name of Simon has actually written a book entitled *The Necronomicon: The Book of Dead Names* (1977), using one of the several false derivations of the Greek word. This book, first published in an oversize hardcover format that makes it look uncannily like a high-school yearbook, has also appeared in paperback. Not to be outdone, other individuals have issued books bearing the name *Necronomicon,* although most of these are conscious hoaxes. One such volume, published by Owlswick Press in 1976, purports to be the original Arabic text of the hideous tome; but in fact it consists of about three pages of Aramaic script repeated over and over again. The artist H. R. Giger has produced a spectacular collection of his art under the title *Necronomicon* (1977). His set designs for the science fiction film *Alien* (1979) are markedly Lovecraftian. The best of the fake *Necronomicons* is one produced under the editorship of George Hay (1978), with a long, exquisitely tongue-in-cheek introduction by Colin Wilson. This volume has been translated into French and Italian.

One of the most interesting developments in recent years is the emergence of Lovecraft as a character in fiction. By far the best works of this kind are two by the leading Lovecraft scholar Peter Cannon. The first, *Pulptime* (1984), is a delightful novella in which Lovecraft, Frank Long, and the Kalems become involved with the aged Sherlock Holmes. The second, *The Lovecraft Chronicles* (2004), is a richly evocative work that imagines the transformation of Lovecraft's life and career if he had actually issued a volume with Knopf in 1933. Richard A. Lupoff's *Lovecraft's Book* (1985) is substantially less interesting, being marred by a poor understanding of the details of Lovecraft's life. Many short stories using Lovecraft as a character have also been written. The volume was presented in a radically abridged version upon first publication, and Lupoff has recently printed his unabridged text under its original title, *Marblehead* (2007).

In the arcane realm of Lovecraftian humour Peter Cannon has also excelled. *Scream for Jeeves* (1994) is a series of three stories exquisitely mingling the styles and themes of Lovecraft and (of all people) P. G. Wodehouse. Cannon's other works of Lovecraftian humour are collected in *Forever Azathoth and Other Horrors* (1999).

Another noteworthy phenomenon is the persistent interest in Lovecraft exhibited by a select group of mainstream writers, especially those whose work is on the borderline of the fantastic. The chief figure here is Jorge Luis Borges. In his slim monograph, *An Introduction to American Literature,* first published in Spanish in 1967 and translated into English in 1971, Borges devoted as much space to Lovecraft as he does to Poe, Hawthorne, or Faulkner. His remarks were at times curious: "He studiously imitated the style of Poe with its sonorities and pathos, and he wrote co[s]mic nightmares [*orig:* "pesadillas cosmicas"]."[57] Borges then wrote a story, "There Are More Things," subtitled "To the Memory of H. P. Lovecraft." This appeared in the *Atlantic Monthly* for July 1975 and was reprinted in *The Book of Sand* (1977), in the afterword to which he somewhat uncharitably calls Lovecraft "an unconscious parodist of Poe."[58] An interesting case has been made that Thomas Pynchon's *Crying of Lot 49* (1966) was in part influenced by "The Call of Cthulhu."[59] John Updike mentions a Mr and Mrs Lovecraft in *The Witches of Eastwick* (1984), set in Rhode Island, and Lovecraft comes in for mention in various of Paul Theroux's travel writings. Umberto Eco dropped a reference to Cthulhu into *Foucault's Pendulum* (Italian edition 1988; English translation 1989), and includes a few more references in his Charles Eliot Norton lectures, *Six Walks in the Fictional Woods* (1994). Woody Allen made a joking reference to Lovecraft in a humorous piece in the *New Republic* for April 23, 1977 ("The Lunatic's Tale"), while S. J. Perelman made a mention in "Is There a Writer in the House?" (*New Yorker,* March 20, 1978). A little more ambiguously, Gore Vidal claimed that Norman Mailer's novel *Ancient Evenings* was a cross between Lovecraft and James Michener.[60] It is not clear that this remark was meant to praise any of the writers in question. In a sense these references seem to be made precisely because Lovecraft retains a kind of "famous obscurity": while many readers now know his name, they know little about him; and the very citation of his name—which many, from Lovecraft's own day to the present, have considered so piquant as to be a pseudonym—can help create an ambiance of strangeness or sardonic humour.

Media adaptations have picked up in recent years, although their quality is very variable. After "Pickman's Model" and "Cool Air" appeared on successive weeks in Rod Serling's "Night Gallery" television series (December 1 and 8, 1971), little work was done for over a decade. Then, spectacularly, Stuart Gordon and Brian Yuzna released a gaudy film entitled *H. P. Lovecraft's Re-Animator* (1985). Let it pass that one of Lovecraft's worst stories was chosen for adaptation: it was only as a springboard for an entertaining, if insubstantial, display of reanimated corpses performing the most surprising activities. The film contained a considerable amount of good humour, something unfortunately lacking in its loose sequel, *H. P. Lovecraft's From Beyond* (1986). But the series returned to form with *Bride of Re-Animator* (1990; directed by Yuzna alone), an outrageously hilarious venture that is more faithful to the original story than the first film. Gordon has gone on to adapt several other Lovecraft stories, including the oddly titled *Dagon* (2002), in reality an adaptation of "The Shadow over Innsmouth." *The Curse* (1987), an adaptation of "The Colour out of

Space" directed by David Keith, is surprisingly effective in spite of the fact that the setting has been transferred to the South. But such potboilers as *The Unnamable* (1988) and its several spinoffs and *The Lurking Fear* (1994) had best be passed over in merciful silence. Somewhat better is *The Resurrected* (1992), a tolerably faithful adaptation of *The Case of Charles Dexter Ward.*

One striking performance is *Cast a Deadly Spell,* an HBO television special aired in 1991; it was initially going to be called *Lovecraft.* In this highly effective two-hour film, Fred Ward plays a tough private eye, H. Phil Lovecraft, who in an alternate-world Los Angeles is on the hunt for the Old Ones. Although not explicitly based on any single Lovecraft story, this program—in spite of its occasional lapses into self-parody—comes surprisingly close to capturing the essence of Lovecraft. A sequel to this telecast had very little Lovecraftian content.

Some of the most effective "Lovecraftian" films are those that are only inspired by Lovecraft rather than based on a specific work. John Carpenter has frequently acknowledged his admiration for Lovecraft, and this is very evident in such of his films as *The Fog* (Rank/Avco Embassy, 1979) and *The Thing* (Universal, 1982). The latter draws heavily upon *At the Mountains of Madness,* as is fitting given that it is an adaptation of John W. Campbell's "Who Goes There?" Carpenter's *In the Mouth of Madness* (1995) is laced with Lovecraftian motifs and conceptions. The Italian directors Dario Argento and Lucio Fulci also make frequent nods to Lovecraft in their films.

Lovecraft is now the focal point of such interest in the film community that an H. P. Lovecraft Film Festival is held annually in October in Portland, Oregon. Its organiser, Andrew Migliore, and John Strysik have compiled the splendid volume, *The Lurker in the Lobby* (1999; rev. ed. 2005), a comprehensive guide to Lovecraft-related films. Lurker Films has also issued a number of effective DVDs of Lovecraftian films and television segments.

There have also been a fair number of comic book adaptations in recent years, some passable, some quite otherwise. One of the best is a fine rendering of "The Call of Cthulhu" by the British artist John Coulthart, included in the otherwise very uneven Lovecraft tribute volume, *The Starry Wisdom* (1994), edited by D. M. Mitchell.

An entirely different issue of immense complexity is that of Lovecraft's influence upon subsequent weird and science fiction. I now do not refer to actual pastiches or "Cthulhu Mythos" tales; it should be evident by now that these do not amount to much. It was Lovecraft's bad luck to have attracted, by and large, self-styled disciples whose actual literary talents were pretty slim. And yet, although Lovecraft is now recognised as the dominant voice in American weird fiction during the first half of the century, his influence is perhaps less than one might think it to be; but the explanation for this lies not with his own work as with the tendencies in fantastic fiction since his death.

For a variety of reasons, the pulp magazines suffered a slow death following the end of World War II. The paperback book took off at this time, and such fields as mystery fiction and science fiction did well in this new venue; for some reason, weird fiction did not. Of course, weird fiction had never been written in any great quantity, and for most of its long run *Weird Tales* remained the only magazine devoted solely to horror. But after the war writers largely abandoned the weird and went into the neighbouring fields of mystery and science fiction instead. This is typified by Lovecraft's two leading protégés, Robert Bloch and Fritz Leiber.

Bloch's stories of the 1940s continued to draw upon Lovecraft sporadically, but gradually he turned his attention to the crime or suspense story. *The Scarf* (1947), *Psycho* (1959), and *The Dead Beat* (1960) are what give Bloch his deservedly high place in this field, and they exhibit little if any Lovecraft influence. Later on, of course, Bloch did write an affectionate homage to Lovecraft in the short novel *Strange Eons* (1977), but this is an avowed pastiche and, although more substantial than some other works of its kind, does not rank high in literary merit. Bloch continued to write about Lovecraft throughout his career, but his fictional work is in many ways quite consciously un-Lovecraftian except in his absorption of Lovecraft's strictures (expressed in his early letters) toward restraint and suggestion rather than flamboyance and excess.

Leiber's case is still more interesting. Although he too wrote a fine Lovecraft pastiche late in his career, "The Terror from the Depths" (1976), the Lovecraft influence manifests itself much more subtly in the rest of his work. Several stories in his first collection, *Night's Black Agents* (1947), utilise Lovecraftian themes, but in such a way that they remain Leiber's own work. "The Sunken Land" is influenced by several Lovecraft stories, but chiefly "The Call of Cthulhu"; "Diary in the Snow" reflects some conceptions from "The Shadow out of Time" and "The Whisperer in Darkness"; even Leiber's famous "Smoke Ghost" may be drawn in part from Lovecraft's conception of Nyarlathotep. The novel *Conjure Wife* (1953) might perhaps be thought to reflect "The Dreams in the Witch House" in its "updating" of the witchcraft theme, but the relation is quite tenuous. In effect, Leiber has learnt much by Lovecraft's example, and in his early career he was perhaps so saturated with Lovecraft's work that some elements emerged subconsciously. None of these tales can by any stretch of the imagination be called pastiches; they are emphatically original, but with key elements borrowed or adapted from Lovecraft.

But beyond this, there is little concrete influence of Lovecraft upon later work in the field. This is largely because weird writers chose to go into a very different direction from the visionary cosmicism of Lovecraft, Machen, and Blackwood. The emphasis became focused upon the mundane, and the incursion of the weird into an ordinary scenario. In some cases this resulted in utter flatness and lack of imagination; but in the best writers it produced work that was very close to the better mainstream work. Perhaps the leading American writer of weird fiction of the 1940s and 1950s—although she was never considered a "horror writer"—was Shirley Jackson (1916–1965), but neither her short stories nor her novels (notably *The Haunting of Hill House,* 1959) exhibit the least trace of Lovecraftian influence. Both Charles Beaumont or Richard Matheson, two other significant figures of this period, surely read Lovecraft (Beaumont wrote the screenplay to *The Haunted Palace*), but their work too reveals few traces of Lovecraft. In England, Robert Aickman's superb "strange stories" of the 1960s and 1970s owe almost nothing to Lovecraft, but are in the tradition of the British ghost story of M. R. James and the psychological ghost story of Walter de la Mare and L. P. Hartley.

When the "horror boom" began in the 1970s, its most popular practitioner, Stephen King, brought Lovecraft back to the forefront with such stories as "Jerusalem's Lot" (in *Night Shift,* 1978), an avowed pastiche. King's other novels and tales drop references to Lovecraft from time to time, and he has spoken of him with tolerable kindness in his informal critical survey of the field, *Danse Macabre* (1981); but the whole tenor of King's work—with its emphasis on family relationships, very conventional supernaturalism (much of it derived from previous works in the field, movies, and comic books), and psychological aberrations—is antipodal to Lovecraft. The other bestselling writers—Clive Barker, Peter Straub, Anne Rice—similarly owe little to Lovecraft, although Rice's *The Tale of the Body Thief* (1992) explicitly cites "The Thing on the Doorstep" and may have been partly inspired by it. Straub wrote an avowed take-off of "The Dunwich Horror" in the novel *Mr. X* (1999), but it is at best an indifferent success.

Ramsey Campbell's later work shows traces of Lovecraft, especially such novels as *The Hungry Moon* (1986), *Midnight Sun* (1990), and *The Darkest Part of the Woods* (2002). But Campbell's vision, too, is generally lacking in cosmicism, and his dominant work is emphatically oriented toward the anomalies inherent in neurosis (in this sense the chilling non-supernatural novel *The Face That Must Die* [1979] is his most characteristic work, and one of his best) or in the complexities of human relationships, which Campbell treats with a deftness and sensitivity far superior to the maudlin sentimentalism of King. And yet, Campbell has recently assembled all the Lovecraft-inspired tales written over his entire career in *Cold Print* (1993);[61] it is a surprisingly large volume.

One of the most interesting cases is T. E. D. Klein. As a senior at Brown University he wrote a penetrating if discursive honours thesis on Lovecraft and Lord Dunsany, then went on to write some of the most distinguished weird fiction of his generation. Such works as "The Events at Poroth Farm" (1972) and its novel-length expansion, *The Ceremonies* (1984), have a pervasive but very attenuated

Lovecraft influence while remaining emphatically Klein's own work. Klein retains an admiration for Lovecraft, but his only avowed "Cthulhu Mythos" tale is "Black Man with a Horn" (in Campbell's *New Tales of the Cthulhu Mythos*), a powerful piece of work that is much more Klein than Lovecraft. His lack of productivity in recent years is one of the tragedies of modern weird fiction. Another writer who has sadly fallen silent is Thomas Ligotti, whose "The Last Feast of Harlequin" (published in 1990 but written many years earlier) is a striking evocation of Lovecraft; other of Ligotti's works also feature a persistent if nebulous Lovecraftian undercurrent, but this most distinctive of contemporary horror writers incorporates Lovecraft as one of many influences in his work, which nonetheless remains profoundly and hallucinatingly original.

It is perhaps not a paradox to say that Lovecraft may have had more of an influence on fantasy or science fiction than upon weird fiction. This is because these former fields have taken over that cosmicism which weird fiction seems to have abandoned. However, many science fiction writers have responded to Lovecraft with considerable hostility: John Brunner, Avram Davidson, Isaac Asimov, and Damon Knight have heaped much abuse on him, probably because of his dense style and his emphasis on pure horror. And yet, John W. Campbell, Jr—whose magazine *Unknown* (later *Unknown Worlds;* 1939–43) was consciously conceived to be as different from the Lovecraft type of tale as possible—nevertheless wrote "Who Goes There?" (1938), a novelette that, although very different from Lovecraft stylistically, clearly betrays the influence of *At the Mountains of Madness*. Traces of Lovecraft can probably be found in the work of A. E. Van Vogt, Philip K. Dick, and several other science fiction writers of the 1940s to 1970s. Ray Bradbury wrote a letter praising Lovecraft in *Weird Tales* for November 1939 ("Lovecraft again proved his wizardry of words by chilling me with a draft of 'Cool Air'"), but has admitted that he has consciously avoided imitating Lovecraft in his later work in fantasy and science fiction. Still, an influence can perhaps be found in such of his horror tales as "Skeleton" and "The Fog Horn." Arthur C. Clarke admitted to great enthusiasm for Lovecraft's two tales in *Astounding*,[62] and Lovecraft's conceptions are perhaps detectable in such of Clarke's novels as *Childhood's End* (1953) and even *2001: A Space Odyssey* (1968), with their notion (similar to that of "The Shadow out of Time") of aliens guiding the intellectual development of the human species. Gene Wolfe wrote a Lovecraft pastiche in *Lovecraft's Legacy,* and probably other Lovecraftian traces can be found in his novels. Lovecraft is a definite presence in the dark work of Charles Stross.

What is one to make of H. P. Lovecraft the man and writer? Certainly, judgments of him will differ in accordance with individual temperament. To those stolid bourgeois citizens who believe that "success" in life means working for a living, having a loving spouse and adoring children, and having a normal, wholesome out-look on life, Lovecraft will seem shiftless, freakish, and rather repulsive. Many derogations of Lovecraft's character—including those pronounced by his previous biographer—stem from this perspective. But it is to be wondered whether the re-markable literary work Lovecraft has left us—remarkable and compelling precisely because of its defiance of normality and convention—could have been written by a normal, wholesome individual whose attitudes do not depart in any way from those inculcated in us by mass "culture." Might it not also be the case that what passes for normality and wholesomeness is profoundly abnormal and unwholesome?—profoundly aberrant to the full play of intellect and imagination that is the only means of distinguishing ourselves from the other living creatures on this planet?

It should also be stressed that one's final picture of Lovecraft must be based largely upon the last ten or so years of his existence; for it was at this time that he shed many of the prejudices and dogmatisms that his early upbringing and seclu-sion had engendered, and when he produced his most characteristic work. In those ten years I see very little to criticise and very much to praise. Let us then assess some key elements of Lovecraft's beliefs, personal comportment, and work.

There will scarcely be anyone who will not disagree with one or the other com-ponent of Lovecraft's philosophical thought. Some will be offended by his atheism; others by his "fascism"; others by his emphasis on cultural traditionalism; and so on. But few can deny that Lovecraft's views were well conceived, modified by con-stant reading and observation, and sharpened by vigorous debates with correspon-dents. No one wishes to claim for Lovecraft a leading place among philosophers—he remained, by his own admission, a layman in this discipline. But he pondered philosophical issues more rigorously than most creative writers, and he also made his creative work the direct outgrowth of his philosophy.

The matter of Lovecraft's erudition is worth pondering. Many of his colleagues professed amazement at his encyclopaedic knowledge, but there is some truth to the contention that many of these individuals were themselves not very learned—few people in the realms of amateur journalism or weird fiction are—and were therefore easily impressed. Nevertheless, Lovecraft did absorb a prodigious fund of knowl-edge over his lifetime, and was perhaps the more well-rounded precisely because of his relative lack of formal schooling, which prevented his specialising in a small number of narrow fields. He always had good library resources at his disposal, and he made good use of them. In the end, he became a near-authority on colonial archi-tecture, eighteenth-century literature, and weird fiction, and had a thorough grasp of classical literature, philosophy, English and American history, and several other realms; most impressively, he had a keen knowledge of many sciences (especially astronomy, physics, chemistry, biology, and anthropology)—something obtrusively lacking in many creative artists. His discourses on these subjects, mostly in letters, perhaps sound the more impressive because of his tremendous *rhetorical* skill; but there is a foundation of genuine knowledge underlying them.

Lovecraft's rank as an "amateur" writer and his scorn of professionalism has rightly been seen as an outgrowth of his belief in aristocracy and his scorn of money-grubbing. Such attitudes are looked upon with vast disdain and hostility in this country, but they have been common among the educated classes throughout human history. Lovecraft began with the eighteenth-century view of art as an elegant amusement; after passing through his Decadent phase in the early 1920s, he came to believe that art was pure self-expression and that writing for money was not so much vulgar (although it was indeed that) as a business—a business, moreover, that held an unfortunate but illusory and mocking similarity to real writing. Certainly we would all like to have seen Lovecraft enjoy in his own lifetime a little more of the fame that his work has achieved since his death; but that work might never have achieved that fame had he not maintained his aesthetic integrity so keenly. Lovecraft towers above other writers of the pulp magazines, not only because of his native talent but because he refused to buckle down to editors' whims and write what they wanted or alter a tale to suit their needs. For this he should be praised, not censured. The hackwork of Seabury Quinn, E. Hoffmann Price, and hundreds of other hacks whose stories have achieved merciful oblivion is a sufficient warning of what might have happened to Lovecraft had he not held firm to his principles.

In broader terms, Lovecraft's disdain of money certainly subjected him to personal hardship, but it was hardship that he willingly underwent for the sake of his art. I see no reason to doubt that Lovecraft really did have a poor head for business, as he himself stated repeatedly. Whether this is judged a flaw of character will depend upon whether one regards the acquisition of money as in itself a good, or whether one believes that other values hold a higher moral or aesthetic worth.

Related to this is Lovecraft's inability to hold a regular job and his consequent poverty. Again, this is a very American concern, reflecting a bourgeois contempt (or envy) of those who do not operate conventionally within the narrow range of economic society. It was, certainly, unfortunate that Lovecraft never received suitable job training in young adulthood; but this was not so much his fault as that of his mother and aunts, who—with the death of Whipple Phillips in 1904 and the consequent collapse of the family finances—should have realised that Lovecraft would in the course of time need to be able to support himself. There is every indication that in the last decade of his life he had overcome any highbrow opposition to regular work and sought—or at least hoped he could find—some means of employment that would allow him the leisure to write what he wished. That he never came upon such employment is scarcely surprising in someone who, with no previous job experience, was seeking to find work in the depression. And yet, Lovecraft worked very hard—even if most of his work was on his correspondence and on rather poorly paying freelance revision. He did manage to get by with the money earned from revision and sporadic sales of original fiction; and with this income he did travel fairly widely up and down the eastern seaboard of the United States. He went to his grave with his books, furniture, and other possessions around him to lend stability and comfort to his environment, and his wide correspondence and personal magnetism attracted a larger band of devoted friends, associates, and disciples than many more outgoing persons can claim.

And yet, even on these points—his "obsessive" need for familiar possessions, his apparent desire to keep relationships at a distance, his seeming fear of change—Lovecraft has received criticism. There are a number of very complex issues here. Lovecraft's "sense of place"—his passionate devotion to his various residences, his hometown, his region, his country, and his culture—was certainly pronounced, and it is what gives his fiction the textural depth and realism it has. I do not know that it was so pronounced as to be considered somehow pathological: at a time when frequent moving from place to place is far less common than now, many probably felt as Lovecraft did. This attachment to familiar things grew, I believe, out of an extraordinarily keen aesthetic sensibility that yearned for an harmonious and stable milieu; for it was exactly this milieu that would provide the springboard for Lovecraft's imaginative ventures into the farthest reaches of the cosmos.

As for keeping relationships at a distance, the brute fact is that Providence—then and now not a town known for its intellectuals—did not offer the sort of stimulating give-and-take of argument that his far-flung correspondence offered. Lovecraft made every effort to meet his pen friends, and indeed met a good many of those who lived on the East Coast. Many others undertook the effort and expense to visit him in Providence, something they would not likely have done had they not sensed a deep mutual regard.

The one personal relationship—aside from his troubled involvement with his mother—that was definitively a failure was his marriage to Sonia; and here, certainly, Lovecraft does leave himself open to abundant criticism. His treatment of his wife can only be called shabby. And yet, she herself seems to have gone into the marriage—as many women do—with the resolute determination to remould him to her taste, and Lovecraft naturally rebelled. He did so not because he was an "ingrained bachelor," but because he was his own person and resented not being taken for what he was. My feeling remains that it was a mistake for him to have married at all; but perhaps this was something he had to experience at first hand to realise that it was a mistake.

I scarcely imagine that Lovecraft's attitudes on sex require much discussion. Probably they were unusually reserved even in their own day, and in our oversexed society nowadays they seem little short of bizarre. Lovecraft confessed that he was among the least sensuous of individuals, but in this he was very much like his idol

Poe; and, during a time of great upheavals in sexual relations, it allowed him to retain his quiet dignity of bearing and shielded him from descending to prostitution, extra-marital affairs, and other ignominies that other writers have ill resisted.

The fact is that Lovecraft made every effort to overcome, and did in fact largely overcome, the severe emotional crippling inflicted upon him by his mother—the mother who had both showered doting affection upon him and called him "hideous"; the mother who indulged him in each new whim but publicly lamented his economic uselessness; the mother who no doubt instilled in him a distaste for sex that only aided in the collapse of his marriage. It is, in fact, remarkable how sane and balanced Lovecraft became in later years—he really had been tried in the fire, both by his mother and by his New York experience, and came out pure gold. If he remained somewhat emotionally reserved, he revelled in the play of his intellect and displayed an aesthetic sensitivity—to landscape, to literature, to art, to dreams, to the pageant of history—that few have ever equalled.

His "pose" as an eighteenth-century gentleman was, in the first place, a function of his cultural conservatism and, in the second place, clearly adopted out of tongue-in-cheek humour in his later years. (Lovecraft is frequently not given sufficient credit for being a jester—whimsical or sardonic as the case may be.) He certainly believed in continuity of culture, and certainly believed that the eighteenth century represented a high-water mark in Anglo-American culture—something on which it is not easy to dispute him. But he was flexible enough to adopt moderate socialism as the only economic solution to the problems engendered by unrestrained capitalism, and his theorisings on this issue are compelling and retain value even today. His hostility to democracy—or, rather, universal suffrage—will be less easily tolerated, since few political theorists in this country have had the courage to defy this most sacred of American dogmas; but his words on this issue also have much to recommend them.

It can scarcely be denied that cultural conservatism was a large factor in his racism. This is, without question, the one true black mark on his character; and it is so not because he was morally wrong (there might be some debate on this point) but intellectually wrong. He ascribed to views about races and cultures that were false, and that had been proven to be false before and during the course of his lifetime. It was the one area of his thought where he failed to reveal openness to new evidence. I repeat that his basic desire for a culturally homogeneous society is not in itself wrong, just as the currently fashionable view of a culturally heterogeneous society is not intrinsically and axiomatically right; there are virtues and drawbacks to each. Where Lovecraft erred was in conceiving that his simple-minded stereotypes were the product of scientific study of racial distinctions and in believing that different races and cultures were unalterably opposed and could not mix without disaster. It is possible that the highly developed aesthetic sensibility I mentioned earlier—a sensibility that craved harmony and stability—had much to do with his racial theories, or at least had much to do with the sense of discomfort he felt around racial and cultural aliens; but whatever the case, his views on the subject are embarrassing and contemptible. But they have also been blown out of proportion: discussions of race take up a relatively small proportion of his entire correspondence, and enter his creative work only fleetingly and tangentially.

Turning to Lovecraft's work, I cannot hope to offer a comprehensive assessment of it—it is too rich and complex for that—but shall only discuss some elements that are directly related to his life and thought. At its core is *cosmicism*—the depicting of the boundless gulfs of space and time and the risible insignificance of humanity within them. This is something Lovecraft expressed more powerfully than any writer before or since, and it is his one distinctive contribution to literature. And yet, his fiction has paradoxically been criticised by myopic critics precisely on the grounds that it lacks "normal" human characters and relationships— that it is cold, impersonal, and remote. It is exactly that, and that is its great virtue. It is difficult to be cosmic and human at the same time. If one wants affecting pictures of married bliss or children at play or people working at the office, one does not turn to the fiction of Lovecraft or Poe or Bierce or any other horror writer except perhaps the soap-opera supernaturalism of Stephen King or Charles L. Grant. And yet, the poignancy with which Lovecraft's characters react to the perception of cosmic insignificance gives to his work a genuine emotional resonance. When the narrator of "The Shadow over Innsmouth" learns that he is one of the monsters he has been fleeing so ardently; when Peaslee in "The Shadow out of Time" sees the manuscript he must have written millions of years ago: there are few moments in all literature that provide a reader with such a complex network of emotions—horror, bafflement, pity, sublimity, and much else besides.

Related to this complaint about the absence of "normal" people is the claim that Lovecraft had a "tin ear for dialogue." The absence of idle chatter in his stories is another great virtue, for it not only creates a concision that only Poe has equalled, but it again shifts the focus of the tale from the human characters to where it belongs— the weird phenomenon itself, which Lovecraft knew to be the true "hero" of his tales. Lovecraft boldly challenged that most entrenched dogma of art—that human beings should necessarily and exclusively be the centre of attention in every aesthetic creation—and his defiance of the "humanocentric pose" is ineffably refreshing.

The aspect of Lovecraft's work that has caused the most controversy is his style—termed, by its critics, "turgid," "artificial," "verbose," or "labored," as the case may be. Again, it is a matter of taste and preference. Although Lovecraft admired the straightforward elegance of Addison and Swift, he knew that he himself had early absorbed writers who wrote more densely—Samuel Johnson, Edward Gibbon, Edgar Allan Poe, and later Lord Dunsany (although his prose is actually very pure and

"Addisonian" in spite of its exotic subject-matter) and Arthur Machen—so that this style, though seemingly artificial, came to him naturally, as any reader of his letters can testify. There is, to be sure, an increased rhetorical element in his tales, but it is clear that the effect Lovecraft was seeking was a kind of incantation whereby the atmosphere generated by language creates an awed sense of the strange reality of the unreal. And now that the bare-bones prose of Hemingway and Sherwood Anderson has ceased to be regarded as self-evidently the best and only correct style for all works of fiction regardless of subject, having yielded to the richness of Gore Vidal, Robertson Davies, Thomas Pynchon, and others, we are perhaps more willing than a generation ago to give Lovecraft his due as a writer in the "Asianic" style.

What makes Lovecraft's style so distinctive is its mingling of scientific precision and lush Poe-esque rhetoric. Whether one likes the result or not is strictly dependent upon one's temperament: many—especially those in the science fiction community, who are used to a more stripped-down style that emphasises ideas over atmosphere—will not like it, and that is their prerogative. But surely no reader can claim that in its final refinement—during the last ten years of his life—this style could not achieve tremendously powerful emotive effects. Lovecraft was unquestionably master, not slave, of his style. He knew exactly what he was doing. Of course it is a somewhat heavy style for those who are not used to verbal and atmospheric richness; it takes effort and intelligence to read it. Scarcely any good writer is "easy" to read. Those who call Lovecraft "verbose" because of this density of style are antipodally wrong: in fact, this density achieves incredible compactness of expression, so that even his near-novel-length works have all the unity of effect of a short story. There is rarely a wasted word in Lovecraft's best stories; and every word contributes to the final outcome.

What is remarkable about Lovecraft is that, in spite of his prodigal invention of "gods" in his fiction, his is among the most secular temperaments in all human history. Religion has no place in his world view except as a sop to the ignorant and timid. The "gods" in his tales are symbols of all that lies unknown in the boundless cosmos, and the randomness with which they can intrude violently into our own realm is a poignant reflection of the tenuousness of our fleeting and inconsequential existence. Let it pass that his imitators have failed to perceive this symbolism, or felt content to play with unwitting frivolity with the varied mythic elements in his tales; these derivative treatments can have little effect upon our valuation of Lovecraft. In David E. Schultz's felicitous formulation, Lovecraft was creating an *antimythology*—an imaginary mythology that mocked the very things that religion and myth claim to do for humanity. We are *not* the centre of the universe; we do *not* have a special relationship with God (because there is no God); we will vanish into oblivion upon our deaths. It is scarcely to be wondered that many readers and writers have been unable to endure these withering conceptions.

Lovecraft was, of course, an uneven writer, as all writers are. In the works of his first decade of fiction writing there are many mediocrities, some outright failures, and some genuine triumphs ("The Rats in the Walls" being perhaps the most notable of them). But in the last decade the triumphs far outweigh the failures and mediocrities. And yet, it is still remarkable that Lovecraft's entire fictional corpus (exclusive of revisions) can be accommodated comfortably into three large volumes. No writer in the field of weird or science fiction, save Poe, has achieved such distinction and recognition on so small a body of work. But, if we are to gauge by the scholarship of the last twenty years, that work is inexhaustibly rich in substance.

Other bodies of his work, with one exception, perhaps require less attention. As an essayist Lovecraft was only occasionally effective. Certainly, his early amateur essays were of the greatest formative value in allowing him to exercise his rhetorical skills and hone his style; but they are intrinsically of little value, crippled as many of them are by dogmatism and limited perspective. Lovecraft did not write many essays in his later years—his creative energies had clearly turned to fiction—but some of these are considerable value, if only ancillary to his fiction and his general philosophy. Few have denied the value of "Supernatural Horror in Literature" both as an historical-critical study and as an index to Lovecraft's own theory and practice of fiction writing; while such other pieces as "Cats and Dogs," "Notes on Writing Weird Fiction," "Some Notes on a Nonentity," and several others are ones we would be much the poorer without.

Of Lovecraft's poetry little need be said. Even the best of it—the late verse, including *Fungi from Yuggoth*, "The Ancient Track," "The Messenger," and others—is only an adjunct to his fiction. Much of Lovecraft's early poetry is entirely forgettable, and the motive for its composition seems less aesthetic than psychological—the attempt of a man to retreat imaginatively into the eighteenth century and out of a twentieth century he loathed. Lovecraft later came to be very much a part of his time, although having great reservations—as any intelligent person would—regarding many trends that were causing what he perceived to be the decline of his civilisation; but his poetry never fully recovered. Some of his satiric verse is tart and effective, and comes closest to the Augustan forms he strove to mimic. Long before his death Lovecraft came to realise that his proper medium was prose, and he wisely cultivated it and let his verse writing rest.

Of his letters much more must be said. It is a frequent complaint among critics that Lovecraft "wasted" his time writing so many letters when he could have been writing more stories instead. There are several false assumptions underlying this complaint. First, it assumes that Lovecraft should have led his life for us, not for himself; if he had written no stories but only letters, it would have been our loss but his prerogative. Second, it overlooks the degree to which gentlemanly courtesy—usually regarded as a positive quality—governed his actions, so that a letter received required a response. Third, it ignores Lovecraft's stated purpose behind his letter-writing—as a replacement for conversation and (especially in light of the absence of stimulating company in Providence) the vital need to expand his intellect and imagination by debating issues with individuals whose opinions differed provocatively from his own. And fourth, it assumes that Lovecraft would indeed have written more stories if he had not written so many letters, something that is not at all clear given the degree to which his fiction writing was dependent upon inspiration, mood, and positive reinforcement.

There is, finally, the very real possibility that Lovecraft's letters will come to be recognised as his greatest literary and personal achievement. It is not simply the sheer quantity of letters he wrote (no more than 10% of which probably survive) that is important, but their intellectual breadth, rhetorical flourish, emotional intimacy, and unfailing courtesy that make them among the most remarkable literary documents of their time. Horace Walpole may have gained transient fame for *The Castle of Otranto,* but his true literary greatness now properly resides in his correspondence; a similar fate may overtake Lovecraft, even though his fiction is vastly richer than Walpole's. The ideal situation, to my mind, is that Lovecraft comes to be valued equally for his tales and for his letters, something that might well occur now that his letters are being published in unabridged form.

How is one, finally, to account for the continued appeal of H. P. Lovecraft? There now seems less dispute that Lovecraft somehow belongs in the canon of American and world literature; a reviewer of Burleson's *Disturbing the Universe* remarked pointedly: "It's getting to where those who still ignore Lovecraft will have to go on the defensive."[63] The attacks of Edmund and Colin Wilson have been forgotten, and Lovecraft is cited in encyclopaedias and other reference works with some cordiality.

But why do people read Lovecraft at all, and what leads a good many of them to develop a kind of compulsive fascination with both his work and the man himself? There is no denying that Lovecraft appeals on many levels, to many differing types of readers, from teenage boys to college professors to highbrow novelists. For young boys, it is Lovecraft's very exoticism—the absence of those disturbing creatures, girls, and the family scenario altogether; the depiction of boundless space, not in the science-fictional sense of a place of infinite possibilities for human action but of infinite horror and dread; the apparent luridness of some of his monsters, from fish-frogs to ten-foot cones to humans degenerating into cannibals; a prose style that can seem hallucinatory as a drug-delirium—that seems to cast an ineffable appeal; and there is still the half-mythical figure of Lovecraft himself, the gaunt "eccentric recluse" who slept during the day and wrote all night. As one matures, one sees different things in Lovecraft the man and writer—the philosophical depth underlying the surface luridness of his work; the dignity, courtesy, and intellectual breadth of his temperament; his complex role in the political, economic, social, and cultural trends of his age. Perhaps it is useless, and foolish, to deny that Lovecraft is an oddity—neither he nor his work is "normal" in any conventional sense, and much of the fascination that continues to surround him resides exactly in this fact. But both his supporters and his detractors would do well to examine the facts about both his life and his work, and also the perspective from which they make their own pronouncements and evaluations of his character. He was a human being like any of us—neither a lunatic nor a superman. He had his share of flaws and virtues. But he is dead now, and no amount of praise or blame will have any effect upon the course of his life. His work alone remains.

Chapter 16: The Assaults of Chaos

1. "Diary: 1925" (ms., JHL).

2. HPL to LDC, 13–16 September 1922; *Letters from New York,* 24.

3. HPL to MWM, 15 June 1925; *Letters from New York,* 143.

4. HPL to LDC, 23–24 September 1925 (ms., JHL).

5. See note 3.

6. HPL to LDC, 7 August 1925; *Letters from New York,* 164.

7. HPL to AEPG, 26 February 1925; *Letters from New York,* 114.

8. See note 3 (*Letters from New York,* 144).

9. HPL to LDC, 11 April 1925; *Letters from New York,* 119.

10. HPL to LDC, 28 May 1925; *Letters from New York,* 132.

11. HPL to LDC, 30–31 July 1925; *Letters from New York,* 159.

12. HPL to LDC, 1 September 1925 (ms., JHL).

13. HPL to LDC, 22 October 1925; *Letters from New York,* 227.

14. HPL to LDC, 14–19 November 1925 and 22–23 December 1925; *Letters from New York,* 247, 255.

15. HPL to LDC, 28 May 1925; *Letters from New York,* 133.

16. Sonia H. Davis, Letter to Samuel Loveman (1 January 1948), quoted in Gerry de la Ree, "When Sonia Sizzled," in Wilfred B. Talman et al., *The Normal Lovecraft,* 29.

17. Cook, *In Memoriam,* in *Lovecraft Remembered,* 115.

18. HPL to LDC, 29 November 1924; *Letters from New York,* 102.

19. HPL to AEPG, 26 February 1925; *Letters from New York,* 113.

20. See note 9.

21. HPL to LDC, 28–30 September 1925; *Letters from New York,* 213.

22. Hart, "Walkers in the City," 8.

23. RK, "After a Decade and the Kalem Club," *Californian* 4, No. 2 (Fall 1936): 47.

24. Eric Rhode, *A History of the Cinema from Its Origins to 1970* (New York: Hill & Wang, 1976), 39.

25. HPL to LDC, 27 July 1925; *Letters from New York,* 151.

26. HPL to AEPG, 10 February 1925; *Letters from New York,* 111.

27. *SL* 2.18–19 (note 3).

28. HPL to LDC, 2 April 1925; *Letters from New York,* 116.

29. HPL to LDC, 11 April 1925; *Letters from New York,* 118.

30. HPL to LDC, 6 July 1925; *Letters from New York,* 149.

31. HPL to LDC, 19–23 August 1925; *Letters from New York,* 182.

32. HPL to LDC, 18 September 1925 (ms., JHL).

33. HPL to LDC, 24–27 October 1925; *Letters from New York,* 231.

34. See note 28.

35. HPL to LDC, 11 April 1925 (ms., JHL [this portion not in *Letters from New York*]).

36. HPL to LDC, 10 September 1925 (ms., JHL).

37. HPL to LDC, 25 [actually 26] May 1925; *Letters from New York,* 128–29.

38. HPL to LDC, 28 May 1925; *Letters from New York,* 129–30. The drawing by HPL that I go on to discuss is reproduced on p. 130.

39. HPL to LDC, 6 July 1925; *Letters from New York,* 146.

40. HPL to LDC, 14–15 October 1925; *Letters from New York,* 218.

41. Ibid. (*Letters from New York,* 219).

42. HPL to LDC, 20 October 1925; *Letters from New York,* 225.

43. HPL to LDC, 24–27 October 1925; *Letters from New York,* 232–33.

44. HPL to LDC, 24 August 1925; *Letters from New York,* 185.

45. HPL to LDC, 22 October 1925; *Letters from New York,* 226.

46. HPL to LDC, 2 April 1925; *Lettes from New York,* 117.

47. Hart, 10.

48. HPL to LDC, 21 April 1925 (ms., JHL).

49. Davis, *Private Life,* 27.

50. HPL to LDC, 20 May 1925; *Letters from New York,* 125.

51. HPL to LDC, 6 July 1925; *Letters from New York,* 148.

52. HPL to MWM, 15 June 1925 (ms., JHL).

53. HPL to LDC, [20 July 1925] (ms., JHL).

54. HPL to LDC, 18 September 1925; *Letters from New York,* 195.

55. HPL to LDC, 27 July 1925; *Letters from New York,* 154.

56. HPL to FBL, 2 August 1925 (*SL* 2.20).

57. HPL to Bernard Austin Dwyer, 26 March 1927 (*SL* 2.116).

58. Davis, *Private Life,* 12.

59. HPL to CAS, 9 October 1925 (*SL* 2.28).

60. "The Incantation from Red Hook" (probably a letter to Wilfred B. Talman), in *The Occult Lovecraft* (Saddle River, NJ: Gerry de la Ree, 1975), 28.

61. HPL to LDC, 27 July 1925; *Letters from New York,* 155.

62. Ibid.

63. HPL to LDC, 8 August 1925; *Letters from New York,* 167.

64. HPL to AD, 26 November 1926; *Essential Solitude,* 1.52.

65. See Robert M. Price, "The Humor at Red Hook," *CoC* No. 28 (Yuletide 1984): 9.

66. Davis, *Private Life,* 11.

67. Ibid., 20.

68. Ibid., 26–27.

69. Sonia H. Davis to Winfield Townley Scott, 24 September 1948 (ms., JHL).

70. HPL to LDC, 6 July 1925; *Letters from New York,* 148.

71. HPL to LDC, 11 January 1926; *Letters from New York,* 269.

72. HPL to LDC, 27 March 1926 (ms., JHL).

73. Long, *Dreamer on the Nightside,* 227.

74. See note 71 (*Letters from New York,* 271).

75. HPL to JVS, 19 November 1931 (AHT).

76. Long, 228–29.

77. HPL to LDC, 13 August 1925; *Letters from New York,* 171–72.

78. HPL to LDC, 29–30 September 1924; *Letters from New York,* 68.

79. "Little Sketches About Town," *New York Evening Press* (29 August 1924): 9; rpt. in HPL's *From the Pest Zone: Stories from New York* (New York: Hippocampus Press, 2003), 106.

80. See Elaine Schechter, *Perry Street—Then and Now* (New York, 1972).

81. HPL to LDC, 20 August 1924; *Letters from New York,* 60–61.

82. See further my article, "Lovecraft and Dunsany's *Chronicles of Rodriguez*" (*CoC,* Hallowmass 1992), in *Primal Sources,* 177–81.

83. HPL to LDC, 23–24 September 1925; *Letters from New York,* 197.

84. HPL to LDC, 12–13 September 1925; *Letters from New York,* 191.

85. HPL to LDC, 13 August 1925; *Letters from New York,* 172.

86. HPL to LDC, 8 August 1925 (ms., JHL).

87. HPL to CAS, 20 September 1925 (*SL* 2.26).

88. CAS to HPL, 11 March 1930 (ms., JHL).

89. HPL to LDC, 2 December 1925; *Letters from New York,* 251.

90. HPL to LDC, 13 December 1925; *Letters from New York,* 252.

91. HPL to LDC, 2 October 1925 (ms., JHL).

92. HPL to LDC, 27 August 1925; *Letters from New York,* 187.

93. The date is derived from Bernard Hubertus Maria Vlekke and Henry Beets, *Hollanders Who Helped Build America* (New York: American Biographical Company, 2nd ed. 1942), 223, which contains a biography of Talman whose information was presumably provided by Talman himself.

94. Ibid. (*Letters from New York,* 186–87).

95. HPL to LDC, 22–23 December 1925; *Letters from New York,* 158.

96. HPL to LDC, 19–23 August 1925 (ms., JHL).

97. HPL to LDC, 1 September 1925 (ms., JHL).

98. HPL to LDC, 8 September 1925 (ms., JHL).

99. HPL to LDC, 12–13 September 1925; *Letters from New York,* 190.

100. HPL to LDC, 28–30 September 1925; *Letters from New York,* 204.

101. Ibid. (*Letters from New York,* 209).

102. Ibid. (*Letters from New York,* 210).

103. HPL to FBL, 21 March 1924 (*SL* 1.332).

104. HPL to LDC, 22 October 1925; *Letters from New York,* 227.

105. HPL to LDC, 14–19 November 1925; *Letters from New York,* 247.

106. Ibid. (*Letters from New York,* 249).

107. HPL to JFM, 5 January 1926 (*SL* 2.36).

108. Lovecraft to LDC, 5 March 1926 and 6 March 1926 (mss., JHL).

109. Lovecraft to LDC, 12–13 April 1926 (ms., JHL).

110. *SL* 2.36 (note 107).

111. HPL to the Gallomo, [April 1920]; *Letters to Alfred Galpin,* 73.

112. HPL to LDC, 29–30 September 1924; *Letters from New York,* 63.

113. HPL to Vincent Starrett, 6 December 1927 (*SL* 2.211).

114. HPL to LDC, 13 December 1925; *Letters from New York,* 253.

115. HPL to LDC, 26 January 1926; *Letters from New York,* 275.

116. HPL to JVS, 5 February 1932 (*SL* 4.15).

117. See AD, "Introduction," *Supernatural Horror in Literature* (New York: Ben Abramson, 1945), 9–11.

118. Review of *Supernatural Horror in Literature* (Ben Abramson, 1945), *American Literature* 18 (1946): 175.

119. See *The Supernatural in Fiction* (1952); portions reprinted in my *H. P. Lovecraft: Four Decades of Criticism* (1980), 63f. (but cf. my note ad loc.).

120. See *Elegant Nightmares: The English Ghost Story from LeFanu to Blackwood* (Athens: Ohio University Press, 1978), 32.

121. Lovecraft to CAS, [16 January 1932] (ms., JHL).

122. HPL to LDC, 6 January 1926 (postcard); *Letters from New York,* 266.

123. HPL to LDC, 11 January 1926; *Letters from New York,* 272.

124. HPL to Henry Kuttner, 29 July 1936; *Letters to Henry Kuttner* (West Warwick, RI: Necronomicon Press, 1990), 21.

125. Arthur Machen, "Novel of the White Powder," in *Tales Horror and the Supernatural* (New York: Alfred A. Knopf, 1948), 55.

126. Poe, *Collected Works,* 3.1243.

127. Hart, "Walkers in the City," 11–16.

128. HPL to LDC, 19–23 August 1925; *Letters from New York,* 182.

129. HPL to LDC, 7 August 1925 (ms., JHL).

130. HPL to LDC, 12 February 1926 (ms., JHL).

131. HPL to LDC, 6 March 1926; *Letters from New York,* 281–82.

132. "When Sonia Sizzled," 29.

133. HPL to LDC, 27 March 1926; *Letters from New York,* 282–83.

Chapter 17: Paradise Regain'd

1. HPL to Arthur Harris, 22 July 1924 (ms., JHL).

2. HPL to LDC, 2 April 1925; *Letters from New York,* 116.

3. HPL to CAS, 15 October 1927 (*SL* 2.176).

4. HPL to LDC, 14–19 November 1925 (ms., JHL).

5. HPL to LDC, 27 July 1925 (ms., JHL).

6. HPL to LDC, 8 August 1925; *Letters from New York,* 168.

7. Scott, "His Own Most Fantastic Creation," in *Lovecraft Remembered,* 18. In his copy of *Marginalia* (where Scott's essay first appeared), now owned by Kenneth W. Faig, Jr, Benjamin Crocker Clough, a reviewer for the *Providence Journal,* has written: "So he [Loveman] told me, and I told WTS. 'Phial' I'm not sure of."

8. Hart, "Walkers in the City," 10.

9. HPL to MWM, 15 June 1925; *Letters from New York,* 144.

10. HPL to LDC, 22–23 December 1925; *Letters from New York,* 254.

11. Scott, "His Own Most Fantastic Creation," in *Lovecraft Remembered,* 18–19.

12. Koki, 159.

13. Long, *Dreamer on the Nightside,* 167.

14. HPL to LDC, 29 March 1926; *Letters from New York,* 288–89.

15. HPL to LDC, 1 April 1926; *Letters from New York,* 290–91.

16. HPL to LDC, 6 April 1926; *Letters from New York,* 293.

17. HPL to LDC, 12–13 April 1926; *Letters from New York,* 299–300.

18. Davis, *Private Life,* 14.

19. Ibid., 20.

20. Ibid., 27.

21. Ibid., 23.

22. George Gissing, *The Private Papers of Henry Ryecroft* (1903; rpt. New York: E. P. Dutton, 1907), 54.

23. Gissing, 47; Davis, *Private Life,* 23.

24. Gissing, 56.

25. Gissing, 166.

26. Gissing, 280–81.

27. HPL to AD, 16 January 1931 (*SL* 3.262).

28. HPL to MWM, [2 July] 1929 (*SL* 3.5, 8).

29. Davis, *Private Life,* 27.

30. Sonia H. Davis to Samuel Loveman, 4 January 1948 (ms., JHL).

31. HPL to DW, 10 February 1927; *Mysteries of Time and Spirit,* 35.

32. HPL to Bernard Austin Dwyer, 26 March 1927 (*SL* 2.117).

33. See note 31.

34. HPL to DW, 27 March 1927; *Mysteries of Time and Spirit,* 63.

35. HPL to DW, 12 April 1927; *Mysteries of Time and Spirit,* 74.

36. Davis, *Private Life,* 11.

37. HPL to LDC, 12–13 April 1926; *Letters from New York,* 301.

38. HPL to FBL, 1 May 1926 (*SL* 2.46–47).

39. Lévy, *Lovecraft: A Study in the Fantastic,* 23.

40. Cook, *In Memoriam,* in *Lovecraft Remembered,* 116.

41. de Camp (*Lovecraft: A Biography,* 259) maintains that Sonia was delayed by an "appointment to discuss a prospective new job." I do not know what the source of this statement is; perhaps it comes from de Camp's interview with Sonia.

42. Cook, *In Memoriam,* in *Lovecraft Remembered,* 116–17.

43. HPL to FBL, 1 May 1926 (ms., JHL [this portion not in *SL*]).

44. HPL to JFM, 16 May 1926 (*SL* 2.50).

45. HPL to the Gallomo, [April 1920] (*Letters to Alfred Galpin,* 87–88); HPL to RK, 21 May 1920 (*SL* 1.114–15).

46. Guy de Maupassant, "The Horla," *Tales of Supernatural Terror,* ed. and tr. Arnold Kellett (London: Pan, 1972), 114–17.

47. Robert M. Price, "HPL and HPB: Lovecraft's Use of Theosophy" (*CoC,* Roodmas 1982), in Price's *H. P. Lovecraft and the Cthulhu Mythos* (Mercer Island, WA: Starmont House, 1990), 12–19.

48. HPL to CAS, 17 June 1926 (*SL* 2.58).

49. See HPL to AD, 5 June 1936 (*SL* 5.263).

50. HPL's first letter to de Castro (ms., JHL) is dated November 15, 1925; but this appears to be a stenographic error on HPL's part. In what appears to be de Castro's first extant letter to HPL (20 November 1927; ms., JHL) he writes: "My friend, Mr. Samuel Loveman, was kind enough to mention that you might be inclined to aid me in bringing out one or the other of my labors which sadly need revision."

51. Steven J. Mariconda, "On the Emergence of 'Cthulhu'" (*LS,* Fall 1987), in *On the Emergence of "Cthulhu,"* 59 (citing the *New York Times,* 1 March 1925).

52. HPL to LDC, 14–19 November 1925; *Letters from New York,* 247.

53. HPL to Bernard Austin Dwyer, [January 1928] (*SL* 2.217).

54. HPL to AD, 16 May 1931; *Essential Solitude,* 336.

55. HPL to FBL, 22 February 1931 (*SL* 3.293).

56. HPL to Farnsworth Wright, 5 July 1927 (*SL* 2.150).

57. See David E. Schultz, "The Origin of Lovecraft's 'Black Magic' Quote," *CoC* No. 48 (St John's Eve 1987): 9–13. For more on this, and on the whole subject of the Cthulhu Mythos as elaborated by HPL and others, see my *The Rise and Fall of the Cthulhu Mythos* (Poplar Bluff, MO: Mythos Books, 2008).

58. See David E. Schultz, "From Microcosm to Macrocosm: The Growth of Lovecraft's Cosmic Vision," in Schultz and Joshi, *An Epicure in the Terrible,* 212.

59. John Milton, *Paradise Lost* 1.26.

60. HPL to Duane W. Rimel, 23 July 1934 (*SL* 5.10–11).

61. DW, "Lovecraft in Providence," in *Lovecraft Remembered,* 313.

62. RHB, "[Memories of Lovecraft (1934)]," *On Lovecraft and Life,* 14.

63. For an exhaustive discussion of the topography of the story and other elements, see Robert D. Marten, "The Pickman Models," *LS* No. 44 (2004): 42–80.

64. HPL to AD, 25 October 1926; *Essential Solitude,* 1.44.

65. HPL to AD, 26 August 1926, 27 September 1926; *Essential Solitude,* 1.33, 37.

66. HPL to AD, 8 September 1926; *Essential Solitude,* 1.36.

67. HPL to AD, 2 September 1926; *Essential Solitude,* 1.34.

68. HPL to Wilfred B. Talman, 21 July 1926 (*SL* 2.61).

69. Talman, *The Normal Lovecraft,* 8.

70. HPL to FBL, 26 October 1926 (*SL* 2.79).

71. Davis, *Private Life,* 20.

72. HPL to LDC, [15 September 1926] (ms., JHL).

73. Ibid.

74. HPL to FBL, 26 October 1926 (*SL* 2.87).

75. HPL to Fritz Leiber, 15 November 1936 (*SL* 5.354).

76. HPL to the Gallomo, [April 1920] (*SL* 1.106).

77. Kenneth W. Faig, Jr, "'The Silver Key' and Lovecraft's Childhood" (*CoC,* St John's Eve 1992), in *The Unknown Lovecraft,* 148–82.

78. HPL to AD, 26 November 1926; *Essential Solitude,* 1.52.

79. HPL to AD, 26 July 1927; *Essential Solitude,* 1.100.

80. HPL to AD, 4 August 1928; *Essential Solitude,* 1.150–51.

81. HPL to AD, [2 August 1929]; *Essential Solitude*, 1.206.

82. HPL to FBL, 6 September 1927 (*SL* 2.164).

83. HPL to AD, 6 November 1931 (*SL* 3.433).

84. See my article, "Lovecraft and Dunsany's *Chronicles of Rodriguez*" (*CoC*, Hallowmass 1992), in *Primal Sources*, 177–81.

85. HPL to AD, [early December 1926] (*SL* 2.94).

Chapter 18: Cosmic Outsideness

1. HPL to CAS, 21–22 January 1927 (*SL* 2.99).

2. HPL to AD, [early December 1926] (*SL* 2.94).

3. HPL to Wilfred B. Talman, 19 December 1926 (*SL* 2.95).

4. de Camp, *Lovecraft: A Biography*, 280.

5. See Peter Cannon, "The Influence of *Vathek* on H. Lovecraft's *The Dream-Quest of Unknown Kadath*," in Joshi, *Four Decades*.

6. See my article "The Dream World and the Real World in Lovecraft" (*CoC*, Lammas 1983), in *Primal Sources*, p 90–103. Giuseppe Lippi has attempted to defend HPL on this point; see "Lovecraft's Dreamworld Revisited." *LS* No. 26 (Spring 1992): 23–25.

7. HPL to CAS, 7 November 1930 (*SL* 3.212).

8. HPL to Alfred Galpin, 26 January 1918 (*SL* 1.54–55).

9. HPL to FBL, [February 1927] (*SL* 2.100).

10. HPL to DW, 29 January 1927; *Mysteries of Time and Spirit*, 21.

11. HPL to AD, 9 February 1927; *Essential Solitude*, 1.68.

12. HPL to AD, 20 February 1927; *Essential Solitude*, 1.71.

13. HPL to CAS, 21 January 1927 (*SL* 2.99).

14. HPL to LDC, 24 August 1925; *Letters from New York*, 185.

15. *Rhode Island: A Guide to the Smallest State* (Boston: Houghton Mifflin, 1937), 290.

16. HPL to LDC, 15 September 1925; *Letters from New York*, 193.

17. HPL to FBL, 11 June 1926 (*SL* 2.57).

18. See Richard Ward, "In Search of the Dread Ancestor: M. R. James' 'Count Magnus' and Lovecraft's *the Case of Charles Dexter Ward*," *LS* No. 36 (Spring 1997): 14–18.

19. HPL to LDC, 4 October and 25 November 1925 (mss., JHL).

20. See M. Eileen McNamara and S. T. Joshi, "Who Was the Real Charles Dexter Ward?" *LS* Nos. 19/20 (Fall 1989): 40–41, 48. Most of the information in this article is derived from discussions with Mauran's widow, Grace Mauran.

21. "Facts in the Case of H. Lovecraft" (1972), in Joshi, *Four Decades*, 178.

22. HPL to RHB, [19 March 1934]; *O Fortunate Floridian*, 120.

23. HPL to CAS, 24 March 1927 (*SL* 2.114).

24. HPL to Richard Ely Morse, 13 October 1935 (ms., JHL).

25. HPL to FBL, 26 October 1926 (*SL* 2.81).

26. HPL to LDC, 1 September 1925 (ms., JHL).

27. HPL to JVS, [30 October 1931] (*SL* 3.429).

28. "A Literary Copernicus" (1949), in Joshi, *Four Decades*, 50.

29. Sam Moskowitz, "The Lore of H. Lovecraft," *Explorers of the Infinite: Shapers of Science Fiction* (Cleveland: World Publishing Co., 1963), 255.

30. Sam Moskowitz to S. T. Joshi, 11 June 1994. Moskowitz maintained, however, that he believed he read of the submission of "The Colour out of Space" to *Weird Tales* in a Lovecraft letter prior to writing his article.

31. "You're undoubtedly correct in predicting that Wright will have little use for 'The Colour Out of Space'. I shall probably try it on him as a matter of routine, but do not expect the thing to achieve the dignity of fully

professional print." HPL to AD, 29 April [1927]; *Essential Solitude*, 1.85.

32. HPL to Farnsworth Wright, 5 July 1927 (*SL* 2.151).

33. HPL to CAS, 17 October 1930 (AHT).

34. HPL to Wilfred B. Talman, 29 April 1927 (ms., JHL).

35. HPL to AD, 16 May 1927; *Essential Solitude*, 1.88.

36. HPL to AD, [21 October 1927]; *Essential Solitude* 1.111. See also HPL to DW, 19 May 1927 (*Mysteries of Time and Spirit*, 106), where HPL refers to the magazine as *Mystery Magazine*.

37. HPL to DW, 1 July 1927; *Mysteries of Time and Spirit*, 130.

38. HPL to AD, [15 April 1927]; *Essential Solitude*, 1.83.

39. HPL to DW, 27 March 1927; *Mysteries of Time and Spirit*, 61.

40. HPL to AD, 2 September 1926; *Essential Solitude*, 1.34.

41. HPL to AD, 13 August 1926 and 31 October 1926; *Essential Solitude*, 1.30, 46–47.

42. HPL to DW, 13 March 1927; *Mysteries of Time and Spirit*, 54.

43. HPL to JFM, 1 April 1927 (*SL* 2.123).

44. HPL to DW, 21 April 1927; *Mysteries of Time and Spirit*, 92–93.

45. HPL to CAS, 12 May 1927 (*SL* 2.127).

46. HPL to CAS, 24 June 1927 (*SL* 2.148). Chambers's weird work (excluding *The Slayer of Souls*) has now been gathered in *The Yellow Sign and Other Stories* (Oakland, CA: Chaosium, 2000).

47. M. R. James, "An M. R. James Letter" [to Nicholas Llewelyn Davies, 12 January 1928], *Ghosts & Scholars* 8 (1986): 28–33.

48. DW to HPL, 27 September 1928; *Mysteries of Time and Spirit*, 227.

49. HPL to JFM, 1 April 1927 (*SL* 2.122).

50. HPL to DW, 2 November 1930; *Mysteries of Time and Spirit*, 261.

51. DW, *Sanctity and Sin: The Collected Poems and Prose Poems of Donald Wandrei* (New York: Hippocampus Press, 2008), 74.

52. HPL to FBL, 10 February 1928 (*SL* 2.223).

53. HPL to DW, 21 April 1927; *Mysteries of Time and Spirit*, 85.

54. HPL to AD, 19 October 1926; *Essential Solitude*, 1.43.

55. DW to HPL, 22 June 1927; *Mysteries of Time and Spirit*, 118.

56. DW to HPL, 20 June 1927; *Mysteries of Time and Spirit*, 117.

57. DW, "Lovecraft in Providence," in *Lovecraft Remembered*, 315.

58. HPL to DW, [2 August 1927]; *Mysteries of Time and Spirit*, 138.

59. HPL to AD, 20 July 1929; *Essential Solitude*, 1.201–2.

60. DW to HPL, 30 June 1927; *Mysteries of Time and Spirit*, 119.

61. Wandrei, "Lovecraft in Providence," in *Lovecraft Remembered*, 304–5.

62. HPL to LDC, [17 July 1927] (ms., JHL).

63. HPL to MWM, 30 July 1927 (*SL* 2.157).

64. Ibid.

65. Ibid.

66. HPL to CAS, 17 October 1930 (*SL* 3.192).

67. DW to HPL, [11 August 1927]; *Mysteries of Time and Spirit*, 147.

68. HPL to DW, 23 August 1927; *Mysteries of Time and Spirit*, 152.

69. Cook, *In Memoriam*, in *Lovecraft Remembered*, 109.

70. "The Trip of Theobald," *Tryout* (September 1927).

71. HPL to LDC, [1 September 1927] (postcard) (ms., JHL).

72. HPL to FBL, [November 1927] (*SL* 2.181–84).

73. HPL to Wilfred B. Talman, 28 December 1927 (*SL* 2.214).

74. Paul Fatout, *Ambrose Bierce: The Devil's Lexicographer* (Norman: University of Oklahoma Press, 1951), 8.

75. HPL to FBL, 20 May 1926 (*SL* 2.53).

76. HPL to AD, 7 November 1926; *Essential Solitude,* 1.48.

77. HPL to Farnsworth Wright, 22 December 1927 (AHT).

78. HPL to AD, 7 November 1926; *Essential Solitude,* 1.48.

79. HPL to AD, 2 March [1927]; *Essential Solitude,* 1.72.

80. HPL to AD, 11 October 1926; *Essential Solitude,* 1.40.

81. HPL to LDC, [5 June 1928] (postcard) (ms., JHL).

82. HPL to LDC, [27 June 1928] (postcard) (ms., JHL).

83. HPL to DW, 29 February 1928; *Mysteries of Time and Spirit,* 208.

84. HPL to AD, 20 June 1930; *Essential Solitude,* 1.267.

85. HPL to Wilfred B. Talman, 1 June 1928 (*SL* 2.243).

86. HPL to LDC, 25 June 1928 (ms., JHL).

87. HPL to LDC, 15 June 1928 (ms., JHL).

88. HPL to DW, [20 January 1928]; *Mysteries of Time and Spirit,* 202.

89. HPL to FBL, [December 1927] (*SL* 2.202).

90. HPL to FBL, 24 September 1927 (*SL* 2.171–72).

91. Long, "The Space-Eaters," in *Tales of the Cthulhu Mythos,* ed. AD (rev. ed. Sauk City, WI: Arkham House, 1990), 88–89.

92. HPL to Bernard Austin Dwyer, [November 1927] (*SL* 2.189).

93. Virgil, *The Poems of Virgil,* Translated into English Verse by James Rhoades (London: Humphrey Milford/Oxford University Press, 1921), 151.

94. *SL* 2.191 (note 92).

95. *SL* 2.197 (note 92).

96. HPL to DW, 24 November 1927 (*SL* 2.200).

97. "'The Thing in the Moonlight': A Hoax Revealed," *CoC* No. 53 (Candlemas 1988): 12–13.

98. HPL to CAS, 27 November 1927 (*SL* 2.201).

99. HPL to DW, [27 September 1927]; *Mysteries of Time and Spirit,* 166.

100. HPL to MWM, 17 December 1914 (AHT).

101. See further my essay, "Lovecraft, Regner Lodbrog, and Olaus Wormius" (*CoC,* Eastertide 1995), in *Primal Sources,* 145–53.

102. *SL* 2.207 (note 89).

103. "Bob Davis Recalls: New Light on the Disappearance of Ambrose Bierce," *New York Sun* (17 November 1927): 6. For more on Danziger/de Castro, including his relations with HPL, see Chris Powell, "The Revised Adolphe Danziger de Castro," *LS* No. 36 (Spring 1997): 18–25.

104. Adolphe de Castro to HPL, 20 November 1927 (ms., JHL).

105. Adolphe de Castro to HPL, 5 December 1927 (ms., JHL).

106. HPL to LDC, 23 May 1928 (ms., JHL).

107. *SL* 2.208 (note 89).

108. *SL* 2.207 (note 89).

109. Adolphe de Castro to HPL, 1 April 1928 (ms., JHL).

110. HPL to DW, 5 April [1928]; *Mysteries of Time and Spirit,* 217.

111. Adolphe de Castro to HPL, 8 December 1927 (ms., JHL).

112. HPL to LDC, 23 May 1928 (ms., JHL).

113. Lewis Mumford, review of *Portrait of Ambrose Bierce, New York Herald Tribune Books* (24 March 1929): 1.

114. Napier Wilt, review of *Portrait of Ambrose Bierce, New Republic* (8 May 1929): 338.

115. Carey McWilliams, review of *Portrait of Ambrose Bierce, New York Evening Post* (30 March 1929): 10M.

116. HPL to Farnsworth Wright, 22 December 1927 (*SL* 2.212). The printed text reads "can" for "cane." Neither sounds very pleasant if broken over one's head.

117. A complete list of de Castro's books is as follows: *The Monk and the Hangman's Daughter* (with Ambrose Bierce) (Chicago: F. J. Schulte, 1892); *In the Confessional and the Following* (New York & San Francisco: Western Authors' Publishing Association, 1893); *A Man, a Woman, and a Million* (London: Sands & Co., 1902); *Jewish Forerunners of Christianity* (New York: E. P. Dutton, 1903; rpt. 1926 as *Jesus Lived: Hebrew Evidences of His Existence and the Rabbis Who Believed in Him* [London: John Murray, 1904]); *Children of Fate: A Story of Passion* (New York: Brentano's, 1905); *After the Confession and Other Verses* (New York: Adolphe Danziger, 1908; London: Henry J. Drane, 1908); *Helen Polska's Lover; or, The Merchant Prince* (New York: Adolphe Danziger, 1909; London: Henry J. Drane, 1909); *In the Garden of Abdullah and Other Poems* (Los Angeles: Western Authors Publishing Association, 1916); *The World Crucified: A Photoplay of the Mundane Activity of Christ in Six Apotheoses* (Los Angeles: Western Authors Publishing Association, 1921); *Portrait of Ambrose Bierce* (New York: Century Co., 1929); *The Painter's Dream* (Los Angeles: Western Authors' Association, 1940); *The Hybrid Prince of Egypt; Plus, Song of the Arabian Desert* (Los Angeles: Western Authors Association, 1950); *Die Werte des Lebens: Beitrag zur Ethik des Ramban, Maimonides* (n.d.). At the end of *Jewish Forerunners* de Castro lists several monographs as apparently published, although he gives no dates or publishers (*Labor Unions and Strikes in Ancient Rome, The Position of Laboring Men among the Ancient Hebrews, Jesus, the Pharisee, Oriental Aphorisms, Two Great Jews*); but I can find no evidence that these were actually published.

118. Zealia Bishop, "H. Lovecraft: A Pupil's View," in *Lovecraft Remembered*, 265.

119. HPL to JFM, 23 May 1927 (*SL* 2.129).

120. HPL to AD, 6 October [1929]; *Essential Solitude*, 1.222.

121. HPL to Zealia Bishop, 9 March 1928 (*SL* 2.232).

122. HPL to Zealia Bishop, 28 August 1929 (*SL* 3.15).

123. HPL to Zealia Bishop, 1 May 1928 (*SL* 2.238).

Chapter 19: Fanlights and Georgian Steeples

1. Davis, *Private Life*, 21.

2. HPL to AD, 2 May 1928; *Essential Solitude*, 1.141.

3. HPL to DW, [7 May 1928] (postcard); *Mysteries of Time and Spirit*, 219.

4. HPL to JFM, 10 May 1928 (*SL* 2.239).

5. HPL to LDC, 29–30 April 1928 (ms., JHL).

6. Davis, *Private Life*, 21.

7. "Observations on Several Parts of America" (1928).

8. See note 5.

9. HPL to LDC, 14 May 1928 (ms., JHL).

10. *Weird Tales* 12, No. 2 (August 1928): 281.

11. HPL to DW, 23 November 1928; *Mysteries of Time and Spirit*, 231.

12. See note 5.

13. HPL to LDC, [3 May 1928] (postcard) (ms., JHL).

14. HPL to RHB, 30 September 1936 (ms., JHL); *O Fortunate Floridian*, 362.

15. HPL to LDC, [12 June 1928] (postcard) (ms., JHL).

16. HPL to Zealia Bishop, 28 July 1928 (*SL* 2.245). The article is an unsigned item, "Literary Persons Meet in Guilford," *Brattleboro Daily Reformer* (18 June 1928): 1.

17. Vrest Orton, "A Weird Writer Is in Our Midst," *Brattleboro Daily Reformer* (16 June 1928): 2. The final paragraph, as quoted

here, was omitted in *Lovecraft Remembered,* 409. The article was discovered by Donald R. Burleson.

18. HPL to LDC, 24 June 1924 (postcard) (ms., JHL).

19. HPL to LDC, 19 June 1928 (ms., JHL).

20. HPL to LDC, 1 July 1928 (ms., JHL).

21. HPL to LDC, 11 July 1928 (ms., JHL).

22. See note 7.

23. Ibid.

24. HPL to AD, 21 November [1930]; *Essential Solitude,* 1.290.

25. Letter to Edwin Baird, [c. October 1923]; *Weird Tales* (March 1924).

26. "The Mythic Hero Archetype in 'The Dunwich Horror,'" *LS* No. 4 (Spring 1981): 3–9.

27. HPL to AD, [27 September 1928]; *Essential Solitude,* 1.158.

28. HPL to LDC, 1 July 1928 (ms., JHL).

29. See Burleson, "Humour beneath Horror: Some Sources for 'The Dunwich Horror' and 'The Whisperer in Darkness,'" *LS* No. 2 (Spring 1980): 5–15.

30. See W. Paul Cook, *In Memoriam,* in *Lovecraft Remembered,* 129; Burleson, "Humour beneath Horror."

31. HPL to CAS, 31 August 1928 (*SL* 2.246).

32. HPL to Farnsworth Wright, 21 November 1933 (*SL* 4.322).

33. HPL to MWM, 19 January [1931] (AHT).

34. MWM to HPL, 3 August 1938 (ms., JHL).

35. MWM to HPL, 29 January 1931 (ms., JHL).

36. HPL to AD, [November 1928]; *Essential Solitude,* 1.166.

37. T. Everett Harré, "Introduction" to *Beware After Dark!* (New York: Macaulay, 1929), 11.

38. HPL to Farnsworth Wright, 15 February 1929 (*SL* 2.260).

39. HPL to Carl F. Strauch, [5 November 1931], *Lovecraft Annual* 4 (2010): 55.

40. HPL to Elizabeth Toldridge, 1 July [1929] (ms., JHL).

41. HPL to Elizabeth Toldridge, 8 March 1929 (*SL* 2.315); "any" printed as "my" in *SL.*

42. HPL to Elizabeth Toldridge, 20 November 1928 (ms., JHL).

43. HPL to DW, 12 September 1929; *Mysteries of Time and Spirit,* 243–44.

44. HPL to JFM, 30 July 1929 (*SL* 3.10).

45. HPL to MWM, 4 August 1927 (ms., JHL). The recipient of the letter has until recently been thought to have been Alfred Galpin.

46. HPL to Wilfred B. Talman, [18 August 1929] (postcard); in *The Normal Lovecraft,* 10.

47. Davis, *Private Life,* 21.

48. Koki, 209–10.

49. See Nelson Manfred Blake, *The Road to Reno: A History of Divorce in the United States* (New York: Macmillan, 1962), 189–202.

50. HPL to MWM, [2 July] 1929 (*SL* 3.5–6).

51. HPL to LDC, 5 April [1929] (ms., JHL).

52. HPL to LDC, 12 April 1929 (ms., JHL).

53. Ibid.

54. HPL to LDC, 30 April 1929 (ms., JHL).

55. HPL to LDC, 2 May 1929 (ms., JHL).

56. Ibid.

57. HPL to LDC, 3–4 May 1929 (ms., JHL).

58. HPL to LDC, 6 May 1929 (ms., JHL).

59. "Travels in the Provinces of America" (1929).

60. Ibid.

61. HPL to LDC, [11 May 1929] (postcard) (ms., JHL).

62. Appropriately enough, the Lovecraft scholar Robert H. Waugh lived on Huguenot Street for many years.

63. HPL to LDC, 13–14 May [1929] (ms., JHL).

64. HPL to LDC, 14–15 May 1929 (ms., JHL).

65. HPL to LDC, [15 May 1929] (postcard) (ms., JHL).

66. HPL to LDC, [17 August 1929] (postcard) (ms., JHL).

67. HPL to MWM, 1 September 1929 (*SL* 3.19).

68. HPL to Elizabeth Toldridge, [1 July 1929] and 16 September 1929 (mss., JHL).

69. HPL to AD, 8 July 1929; *Essential Solitude,* 1.200.

70. See "Travels in the Provinces of America."

71. HPL to REH, 14 August 1930 (*SL* 3.166).

72. HPL to FBL, 3 November 1930 (*SL* 3.204).

73. HPL to Emil Petaja, 31 May 1935 (*SL* 5.173).

74. Robert M. Price, "Lost Revisions?," *CoC* No. 17 (Hallowmass 1983): 42.

75. HPL to AD, [17 November 1929]; *Essential Solitude,* 1.230.

76. HPL to the Editor of the *Sunday Journal,* 5 October 1926 (*SL* 2.73).

77. John Hutchins Cady, *The Civic and Architectural Development of Providence 1636–1950* (Providence, RI: The Book Shop, 1957), 239–40.

78. HPL to AD, [mid-January 1930]; *Essential Solitude,* 1.244.

79. See HPL to JFM, 30 July 1929 (*SL* 3.11).

80. HPL to JFM, 6 December 1929 (*SL* 3.90).

81. HPL to LDC, [6 May 1929] (postcards) (ms., JHL).

82. B. K. Hart, *The Sideshow,* ed. Philomela Hart (Providence: Roger Williams Press, 1941), 56–58.

83. Winfield Townley Scott, "A Parenthesis on Lovecraft as Poet" (1945), in Joshi, *Four Decades of Criticism,* 213.

84. HPL to AD, [February 1930]; *Essential Solitude,* 1.249.

85. HPL to JFM, 30 October 1929 (*SL* 3.55).

86. HPL to FBL, [November 1927] (*SL* 2.186).

87. HPL to JFM, [12 March 1930] (*SL* 3.128).

88. HPL to AD, [early January 1930]; *Essential Solitude,* 1.242.

89. HPL to RHB, 13 June 1936; *O Fortunate Floridian,* 342.

90. HPL to Elizabeth Toldridge, [January 1930] (*SL* 3.116).

91. HPL to Zealia Bishop, 26 January 1930 (*SL* 3.114–15).

92. William Bolitho, "Pulp Magazines," *New York World* (4 January 1930): 11.

93. HPL to AD, [mid-January 1930]; *Essential Solitude,* 1.244.

94. RHB, ms. note on the T.Ms. of "The Mound" (JHL).

95. HPL to Elizabeth Toldridge, 20 December 1929 (*SL* 3.97).

96. HPL to Woodburn Harris, 25 February–1 March 1929 (*SL* 2.309).

97. HPL to AD, [late February 1930]; *Essential Solitude,* 1.251.

98. Zealia Bishop, "H. Lovecraft: A Pupil's View," in *Lovecraft Remembered,* 271.

99. Long, *Dreamer on the Nightside,* xiii–xiv.

100. FBL to HPL, [c. 19 March 1930] (ms., JHL).

101. HPL to RHB, 26 June 1934; *O Fortunate Floridian,* 143.

102. HPL to FBL, 17 October 1930 (*SL* 3.187).

103. HPL to FBL, [14–16 March 1930] (*SL* 3.130).

104. HPL to Woodburn Harris, 9 November 1929 (*SL* 3.58).

105. HPL to LDC, 28 April 1930 (ms., JHL).

106. HPL to AD, [29 April 1930] (post-card); *Essential Solitude,* 1.261.

107. HPL to LDC, 13–14 May 1930 (ms., JHL).

108. Wandrei, "Lovecraft in Providence," in *Lovecraft Remembered,* 309.

109. See note 107.

110. HPL to JFM, 15 May 1930 (*SL* 3.150).

111. HPL to DW, 21 April 1927; *Mysteries of Time and Spirit,* 89.

112. HPL to RHB, [24 May 1935], *O Fortunate Floridian,* 276; HPL to CAS, [6 August 1930] (ms., JHL).

113. [Notes to "Medusa's Coil"].

114. HPL to FBL, [November 1930] (AHT).

115. HPL to LDC, 20–21 May 1930 (ms., JHL).

116. HPL to LDC, 24–26 May 1930 (ms., JHL).

117. HPL to LDC, 21–22 May 1930 (ms., JHL).

118. See note 116.

119. Hart Crane, "The Tunnel" (ll. 79–82), section VII of *The Bridge* (1930); *The Poems of Hart Crane* (New York: Liveright, 1986), 99.

120. HPL to LDC, 11 June 1930 (ms., JHL).

121. HPL to AD, [mid-July 1930]; *Essential Solitude,* 1.272.

122. HPL to Elizabeth Toldridge, [c. 3 September 1930] (*SL* 3.164).

123. HPL to JFM, 24 October 1930 (*SL* 3.197).

124. HPL to JFM, [29 December 1930] (*SL* 3.249); HPL to JFM, 18 January 1931 (*SL* 3.266).

125. Steven J. Mariconda, "Tightening the Coil: The Revision of 'The Whisperer in Darkness,'" *LS* No. 32 (Spring 1995): 12–17.

126. HPL to AD, [4 November 1927]; *Essential Solitude,* 1.113.

127. HPL to LDC, [12 June 1928] (ms., JHL).

128. HPL to FBL, 14 March 1930 (*SL* 3.130).

129. HPL to JFM, [15 March 1930] (AHT).

130. HPL to Elizabeth Toldridge, 1 April 1930 (*SL* 3.136).

131. Long, "Some Random Memories of H. L.," in *Lovecraft Remembered,* 186.

132. HPL to AD, 7 June 1930; *Essential Solitude,* 1.265.

Chapter 20: Non-Supernatural Cosmic Art

1. HPL to JFM, 30 October 1929 (*SL* 3.46).

2. Quoted in *Why I Am Not a Christian* (New York: Simon & Schuster, 1957), 104.

3. HPL to Elizabeth Toldridge, 24 April 1930 (*SL* 3.146).

4. *Scepticism and Animal Faith* (New York: Scribner's, 1923), vii.

5. John Passmore, *A Hundred Years of Philosophy* (1957; 2nd ed. 1966; rpt. Harmondsworth: Penguin, 1968), 228.

6. HPL to FBL, 20 February 1929 (*SL* 2.265).

7. Ibid. (*SL* 2.261).

8. Ibid. (*SL* 2.266–67).

9. HPL to FBL, 22 November 1930 (*SL* 3.228).

10. Bertrand Russell, *Human Knowledge: Its Scope and Limits* (New York: Simon & Schuster, 1948), 23.

11. HPL to JFM, 30 October 1929 (*SL* 3.53).

12. HPL to FBL, 22 November 1930 (*SL* 3.226).

13. HPL to MWM, 3 August 1931 (*SL* 3.390–91).

14. *SL* 3.39 (note 11).

15. HPL to FBL, [April 1928] (*SL* 2.234).

16. HPL to AD, 21 November 1930 (*SL* 3.222).

17. HPL to JFM, 6 November 1930 (*SL* 3.208).

18. HPL to AD, 25 December 1930 (*SL* 3.244).

19. HPL to Elizabeth Toldridge, 10 June 1929 (*SL* 2.356–57).

20. *SL* 3.244 (note 18).

21. HPL to JFM, [January 1931] (*SL* 3.253).

22. HPL to Woodburn Harris, 9 November 1929 (*SL* 3.78).

23. Ibid. (*SL* 3.58–59).

24. HPL to AD, 26 March 1927 (*SL* 2.120).

25. HPL to JFM, 19 October 1929 (*SL* 3.32).

26. HPL to Woodburn Harris, 25 February–1 March 1929 (*SL* 2.305).

27. HPL to AD, 5 October 1928; *Essential Solitude,* 1.160.

28. HPL to LDC, 4–6 November 1924; *Letters from New York,* 86.

29. See note 27.

30. HPL to Elizabeth Toldridge, 3 September 1929 (*SL* 3.20).

31. Louis Berman, *The Glands Regulating Personality* (New York: Macmillan, 1921 [rev. ed. 1928]), 23.

32. HPL to Woodburn Harris, 25 February–1 March 1929 (*SL* 2.298).

33. HPL to FBL, 22 February 1931 (*SL* 3.293–96).

34. HPL to AD, 20 November 1931 (*SL* 3.434).

35. "Behind the Mountains of Madness: Lovecraft and the Antarctic in 1930," *LS* No. 14 (Spring 1987): 3–9.

36. HPL to FBL, 17 October 1930 (*SL* 3.186–87).

37. HPL to CAS, 17 October 1930 (*SL* 3.193).

38. Fritz Leiber, "A Literary Copernicus" (1949), in Joshi, *Four Decades,* 57.

39. "Demythologizing Cthulhu," in *H. P. Lovecraft and the Cthulhu Mythos.*

40. CAS to HPL, [c. mid-December 1930]; *Letters to H. P. Lovecraft,* 23.

41. Jules Zanger, "Poe's Endless Voyage: *The Narrative of Arthur Gordon Pym,*" *Papers on Language and Literature* 22, No. 3 (Summer 1986): 282.

42. HPL to AD, 24 March [1931]; *Essential Solitude,* 1.325.

43. HPL to JVS, 7 August 1931 (*SL* 3.395).

44. HPL to DW, 8 March 1932; *Mysteries of Time and Spirit,* 301.

45. HPL to DW, [22 October 1927]; *Mysteries of Time and Spirit,* 174.

46. HPL to AD, [late March? 1931]; *Essential Solitude,* 1.327.

47. HPL to LDC, 16 July 1931 (ms., JHL).

48. *SL* 3.395–96 (note 43).

49. HPL to AD, 16 April 1931; *Essential Solitude,* 1.329–30.

50. HPL to AD, 9 May 1931; *Essential Solitude,* 1.334.

51. HPL to AD, [5 June 1929]; *Essential Solitude,* 1.195.

52. HPL to AD, 4 March 1932; *Essential Solitude,* 2.460–61.

53. HPL to CAS, [20 November 1931] (*SL* 3.435).

54. HPL to DW, [27 November 1931]; *Mysteries of Time and Spirit,* 291.

55. See ch. 12, note 25.

56. HPL to FBL, 17 October 1930 (*SL* 3.187).

57. HPL to Henry Kuttner, 16 April 1936 (*SL* 5.236).

58. HPL to AD, 2 April [1928]; *Essential Solitude,* 1.140.

59. HPL to JFM, 19 October 1929 (*SL* 3.31).

60. HPL to AD, 10 December 1931; *Essential Solitude,* 1.419–20.

61. "Lovecraft and *Strange Tales,*" *CoC* No. 74 (Lammas 1990): 3–11.

62. HPL to AD, 23 December 1931; *Essential Solitude,* 1.429.

63. HPL to AD, 21 January 1932; *Essential Solitude,* 2.442–43.

64. HPL to AD, 2 February 1932; *Essential Solitude,* 2.446.

65. See CAS to AD, 16 February 1932 (ms., SHSW); quoted in Smith's *Letters to H. P. Lovecraft,* 34n3.

66. See note 64 (*Essential Solitude,* 2.448).

67. HPL to AD, 29 February [1932]; *Essential Solitude,* 2.459.

68. HPL to Farnsworth Wright, 18 February 1932 (*SL* 4.17).

69. Farnsworth Wright to AD, 17 January 1933 (ms., SHSW).

70. HPL to F. Lee Baldwin, 21 August 1934 (ms., JHL).

71. HPL to FBL, 8 November 1923 (*SL* 1.258).

72. REH, "On Reading—and Writing," in *The Last Celt,* ed. Glenn Lord (West Kingston, RI: Donald M. Grant, 1976), 51.

73. REH to HPL, [c. December 1930]; *A Means to Freedom: The Letters of H. P. Lovecraft and Robert E. Howard* (New York: Hippocampus Press, 2009), 1.100.

74. HPL to Kenneth Sterling, 14 December 1935 (*SL* 5.214).

75. HPL to AD, [28 January 1932]; 2 February [1932]; 29 March [1934], 29 April 1934; *Essential Solitude,* 2.446, 448, 628, 632.

76. HPL to Robert Bloch, [late June 1933]; *Letters to Robert Bloch,* 23.

77. HPL to CAS, 3 December 1929 (*SL* 3.87).

78. *The End of the Story* (Collected Fantasies, Volume 1) (San Francisco: Night Shade Books, 2006), 82.

79. HPL to REH, 14 August 1930 (*SL* 3.166).

80. CAS to AD, 4 January 1933 (ms., SHSW).

81. HPL to AD, 16 May 1931; *Essential Solitude,* 1.336.

82. HPL to FBL, 20 February 1929 (*SL* 2.274).

83. See A. Langley Searles, "Fantasy and Outré Themes in the Short Fiction of Edward Lucas White and Henry S. Whitehead," in *American Supernatural Fiction,* ed. Douglas Robillard (New York: Garland, 1996), 64–72.

84. "All his papers were found in perfect order, but this was soon disturbed by hands which destroyed his files of correspondence with Lovecraft and others." RHB, "Henry S. Whitehead," *Jumbee and Other Uncanny Tales* (Sauk City, WI: Arkham House, 1944), ix.

85. HPL to FBL, 3 November 1930 (*SL* 3.205).

86. HPL to JVS, 28 August 1931 (AHT).

Chapter 21: Mental Greed

1. HPL to LDC, 5 May 1931 (ms., JHL).

2. HPL to AD, 9 May 1931; *Essential Solitude,* 1.332–33.

3. HPL to AD, 23 May 1931; *Essential Solitude,* 1.342.

4. HPL to AD, [25 May 1931] (postcard); *Essential Solitude,* 1.346.

5. HPL to AD, 23 December 1931; *Essential Solitude,* 1.432.

6. HPL to RHB, 25 February 1932; *O Fortunate Floridian,* 24.

7. HPL to LDC, 11–12 June 1931 (ms., JHL).

8. HPL to AD, 17 June 1931; *Essential Solitude,* 1.349.

9. HPL to LDC, 22 June 1931 (ms., JHL).

10. Ibid.

11. HPL to LDC, 23–24 June 1931 (ms., JHL).

12. HPL to LDC, 8–10 July 1931 (ms., JHL).

13. Ibid.

14. HPL to AD, 3 August 1931; *Essential Solitude,* 1.353.

15. HPL to AD, 2 September 1931; *Essential Solitude,* 1.372.

16. HPL to Edward H. Cole, 31 December 1931 (ms., JHL).

17. HPL to JVS, 10 November 1931 (ms., JHL).

18. HPL to DW, [2 January 1932] (postcard); *Mysteries of Time and Spirit,* 294.

19. HPL to AD, 16 January 1931; *Essential Solitude,* 1.308.

20. HPL to REH, 7 November 1932 (*SL* 4.104).

21. HPL to AD, 16 May 1931; *Essential Solitude,* 1.338.

22. HPL to AD, 18 August 1931; *Essential Solitude,* 1.363.

23. HPL to AD, 18 September, and 30 September 1931; *Essential Solitude,* 1.383, 390. HPL to Wilfred B. Talman, 2 April [1932] (ms., JHL).

24. HPL to AD, 19 November [1932]; *Essential Solitude,* 2.526.

25. HPL to JVS, 5 February 1932 (ms., JHL).

26. HPL to Wilfred B. Talman, 5 March 1932 (*SL* 4.27).

27. HPL to JVS, 22 March 1932 (ms., JHL).

28. Enclosed in letter to Richard F. Searight, 31 August 1933; *Letters to Richard F. Searight,* 12.

29. See note 19.

30. See note 15 (*Essential Solitude,* 1.370).

31. HPL to AD, 9 October 1931; *Essential Solitude,* 1.393–94.

32. HPL to Lee Alexander Stone, 18 September 1930 (*SL* 3.170–71).

33. HPL to FBL, [April 1931] (AHT).

34. HPL to Wilfred B. Talman, 28 October 1930 (*SL* 3.199).

35. HPL to Wilfred B. Talman, 10 December 1930 (*SL* 3.239–40).

36. "Lovecraft's Cosmic Imagery," in Schultz and Joshi, *An Epicure in the Terrible,* 192.

37. "Through Hyperspace with Brown Jenkin", in Joshi, *Four Decades of Criticism,* 146.

38. HPL to AD, 14 May [1932]; *Essential Solitude,* 2.478.

39. HPL to AD, 6 June 1932; *Essential Solitude,* 2.482–83.

40. HPL to E. Hoffmann Price, 20 October 1932 (*SL* 4.91).

41. HPL to AD, 16 May 1931; *Essential Solitude,* 1.339.

42. HPL to CAS, 3 October 1933 (*SL* 4.270–71).

43. HPL to Elizabeth Toldridge, 15 April 1929 (ms., JHL).

44. HPL to Elizabeth Toldridge, 24 October 1930 (*SL* 3.198).

45. *SL* 4.71 (note 42).

46. "An Interview with Harry K. Brobst," *LS* Nos. 22/23 (Fall 1990): 24–26.

47. "All but one or two of the considerable number of letters that I received from him have been either lost or passed on to others . . ." Edkins, "Idiosyncrasies of HPL" (1940), in *Lovecraft Remembered,* 93.

48. HPL to RHB, [22 August 1934]; *O Fortunate Floridian,* 166–67.

49. HPL to RHB, 29 January [1936]; *O Fortunate Floridian,* 317.

50. HPL to Carl Ferdinand Strauch, 16 February 1932, *Lovecraft Annual* 4 (2010): 65.

51. HPL to AD, 21 April 1932; *Essential Solitude,* 2.473.

52. HPL to AD, 6 June 1932; *Essential Solitude,* 2.480.

53. Ibid. (*Essential Solitude,* 2.481).

54. HPL to DW, [2 August 1927]; *Mysteries of Time and Spirit,* 138.

55. HPL to AD, 9 September 1931; *Essential Solitude,* 1.381.

56. HPL to JVS, 13 October 1932 (*SL* 4.87).

57. E. Hoffmann Price, "The Man Who Was Lovecraft," in *Lovecraft Remembered,* 289–90.

58. HPL to JFM, 5 July 1932 (*SL* 4.47).

59. HPL to MWM, 12 July 1932 (*SL* 4.48–49).

60. Harold S. Farnese to AD, 11 April 1937 (ms., SHSW); quoted in David E. Schultz, "The Origin of Lovecraft's 'Black Magic' Quote," *CoC* No. 48 (St John's Eve 1987): 9.

61. It is reproduced facing *SL* 4.159.

62. Harold S. Farnese to AD, 11 April 1937 (see note 60).

63. HPL to Harold S. Farnese, 22 September 1932 (*SL* 4.70–71).

64. See note 60.

65. HPL to JVS, 13 October 1932 (ms., JHL; this portion not included in *SL*).

66. Cook, *In Memoriam,* in *Lovecraft Remembered,* 131.

67. Muriel E. Eddy, *The Gentleman from Angell Street* (1961), in *Lovecraft Remembered,* 61–63. This matter is not mentioned at all in Eddy's 1945 memoir.

68. HPL to Duane W. Rimel, 19 November 1934 (*SL* 5.72).

69. Hazel Heald to AD, 30 September 1944; quoted in a footnote in *The Horror in the Museum and Other Revisions* (Sauk City, WI: Arkham House, 1970), 27.

70. HPL to AD, [mid-August 1932]; *Essential Solitude,* 2.497.

71. HPL to RHB, 10 April 1934 (*SL* 4.403).

72. HPL to E. Hoffmann Price, 20 October 1932 (ms., JHL).

73. HPL to Richard Ely Morse, 28 July 1932 (*SL* 4.229).

74. HPL to REH, 24 July–5 August 1933 (*SL* 4.222).

75. HPL to CAS, 26 March 1935 (*SL* 5.130).

76. E. Hoffmann Price, "The Man Who Was Lovecraft," in *Lovecraft Remembered,* 291.

77. E. Hoffmann Price to HPL, 10 October 1932 (ms., JHL).

78. First printed in *CoC* No. 10 (1982): 46–56.

79. HPL to E. Hoffmann Price, 3 October 1932 (*SL* 4.74–75).

80. HPL to JVS, 24 March 1933 (*SL* 4.158).

81. HPL to E. Hoffmann Price, 6 April 1933 (*SL* 4.175).

82. "The Man Who Was Lovecraft," in *Lovecraft Remembered,* 291.

83. *SL* 4.178 (note 81).

84. E. Hoffmann Price to Farnsworth Wright, 7 August 1933 (ms., JHL).

85. Farnsworth Wright to H. Lovecraft, 17 August 1933 (ms., JHL); quoted in *Letters to Robert Bloch,* 31n.

86. HPL to Farnsworth Wright, 14 November 1933 (*SL* 4.319).

87. Earl C. Kelley to HPL, 29 February 1932 (ms., JHL).

88. HPL to RHB, 22 August 1934; *O Fortunate Floridian,* 168.

89. HPL to E. Hoffmann Price, 7 December 1932 (*SL* 4.116–17).

90. HPL to Duane W. Rimel, 12 September 1934 (*SL* 5.33).

91. HPL to CAS, 4 April 1932 (*SL* 4.37).

92. HPL to RHB, 9 April 1933; *O Fortunate Floridian,* 59.

93. HPL to Alfred Galpin, 4 November 1933; *Letters to Alfred Galpin,* 196–97.

94. Davis, *Private Life,* 17.

95. HPL to AEPG, 27–28 December [1932] (ms., JHL).

96. HPL to AEPG, [2 January 1933] (postcard) (ms., JHL).

97. HPL to RHB, 18 February 1933; *O Fortunate Floridian,* 51.

98. HPL to RHB, [17 December 1933]; *O Fortunate Floridian,* 90.

99. HPL to DW, 21 February 1933; *Mysteries of Time and Spirit,* 319.

Chapter 22: In My Own Handwriting

1. HPL to Carl F. Strauch, 31 May 1933 *Lovecraft Annual* 4 (2010): 100–101.

2. HPL to Carl F. Strauch, 5 June 1933, *Lovecraft Annual* 4 (2010): 102.

3. HPL to AD, 5 June 1933; *Essential Solitude*, 2.580.

4. See note 2.

5. In *Marginalia* (1944), facing 214.

6. HPL to Carl F. Strauch, 18 March 1933, *Lovecraft Annual* 4 (2010): 97–98.

7. Davis, *Private Life*, p 22–23.

8. HPL to Alfred Galpin, 24 June 1933 (*SL* 4.215).

9. Price, "The Man Who Was Lovecraft," in *Lovecraft Remembered*, 293.

10. HPL to JVS, 25 September 1933 (*SL* 4.250).

11. HPL to Elizabeth Toldridge, 28 August 1933 (ms., JHL).

12. HPL to RHB, [2 December 1933] (postcard); *O Fortunate Floridian*, 89.

13. HPL to Allen G. Ullman, 16 August 1933 (ms., JHL).

14. HPL to Duane W. Rimel, 16 April 1935 (ms., JHL).

15. *Weird Tales* 22, No. 6 (December 1933): 776.

16. HPL to RHB, [24 May 1935]; *O Fortunate Floridian*, 274.

17. HPL to Charles D. Hornig, 7 August [1933] (postcard) (ms.).

18. HPL to Willis Conover, 1 September 1936; *Lovecraft at Last* (Arlington, VA: Carrollton-Clark, 1975), 86. HPL's mention that some of the "interpolated portions" may be "illegible" (*Lovecraft at Last*, 97) suggests that at least some of the insertions were handwritten.

19. HPL to RHB, [16 March 1935]; *O Fortunate Floridian*, 219.

20. HPL to RHB, [21 October 1933]; *O Fortunate Floridian*, 82.

21. Derleth prepared a poor text for *Beyond the Wall of Sleep* (1943) as well as for an annotated separate edition (Arkham House/Villiers, 1963). I prepared a corrected text for *Autobiographical Writings* (1992) and *Miscellaneous Writings* (1995).

22. Talman, "The Normal Lovecraft," 8.

23. When AD found this document, he was unaware what it was and thought it represented plot-germs by Lovecraft; he wrote up Lovecraft's plot description of *The Dark Chamber* into the "posthumous collaboration" entitled "The Ancestor."

24. HPL to RK, 23 April 1921 (*SL* 1.128).

25. HPL to CAS, 17 October 1923 (*SL* 1.256).

26. HPL to FBL, 24 July 1923 (*SL* 1.238).

27. HPL to CAS, [28 October 1934] (*SL* 5.64).

28. HPL to CAS, [22 October 1933] (*SL* 4.289).

29. Ibid. (*SL* 4.289–90).

30. HPL to Robert Bloch, 27 April 1933; *Letters to Robert Bloch*, 10.

31. HPL to F. Lee Baldwin, 16 October 1933 (ms., JHL).

32. For more on Baldwin see Josephine Richardson et al., *Within the Circle: In Memoriam F. Lee Baldwin 1913–1987* (Glenview, IL: Moshassuck Press, 1988).

33. For a selection of Rimel's weird writing see *To Yith and Beyond* (Glenview, IL: Moshassuck Press, 1990).

34. HPL to Richard F. Searight, 31 August 1933; *Letters to Richard F. Searight*, 9.

35. HPL to Richard F. Searight, 15 January 1934; *Letters to Richard F. Searight*, 16.

36. Ibid., 17.

37. Helen V. Sully, "Memories of Lovecraft: II," in *Lovecraft Remembered*, 278.

38. HPL to CAS, [25 July 1933] (postcard) (ms.).

39. HPL to Helen V. Sully, 24 November 1933 (ms., JHL).

40. See HPL to DW, 16 January 1932; *Mysteries of Time and Spirit*, 297–98. This novel, along with Wandrei's unpublished mainstream novel *Invisible Sun* (written 1932–33), are forthcoming.

41. AD, *Place of Hawks* (New York: Loring & Mussey, 1935), 91–92.

42. HPL to E. Hoffmann Price, 26 November 1932 (*SL* 4.113).

43. Wandrei, *The Eye and the Finger* (Sauk City, WI: Arkham House, 1948), 55.

44. Howard, *Cthulhu* (New York: Baen, 1987), 57.

45. HPL to Robert Bloch, [late June 1933]; *Letters to Robert Bloch*, 22.

46. HPL to Robert Bloch, [November 1933]; *Letters to Robert Bloch*, 41.

47. *Something about Cats and Other Pieces*, 117–18.

48. Ibid., 117.

49. HPL to F. Lee Baldwin, 31 January 1934 (*SL* 4.350).

50. HPL to E. Hoffmann Price, 12 January 1933 (*SL* 4.133).

51. HPL to JVS, 28 September 1931 (*SL* 3.416).

52. HPL to AD, 12 November 1926; *Essential Solitude*, 1.49.

53. HPL to Willis Conover, 1 September 1936 (*SL* 5.304).

54. HPL to Bernard Austin Dwyer, [1932] (*SL* 4.4).

55. HPL to JVS, 5 February 1932 (*SL* 4.15).

56. HPL to Willis Conover, 10 January 1937 (*SL* 5.384).

57. HPL to Fritz Leiber, 9 November 1936 (*SL* 5.341).

58. *SL* 5.384 (note 56).

59. HPL to E. Hoffmann Price, 24 March 1933 (*SL* 4.163).

60. HPL to AD, 27 October 1934; *Essential Solitude*, 2.663.

61. HPL to AEPG, [28 December 1933] (postcard) (ms., JHL).

62. HPL to AEPG, [1 January 1934] (postcard) (ms., JHL).

63. Samuel Loveman, "Lovecraft as a Conversationalist," in *Lovecraft Remembered*, 210–11.

64. HPL to AEPG, [4 January 1934] (postcard) (ms., JHL).

65. HPL to AEPG, [8 January 1934] (postcard) (ms., JHL).

66. HPL to C. L. Moore, [7 February 1937] (*SL* 5.400–401).

67. HPL to RHB, 12 March [1932]; *O Fortunate Floridian*, 25.

68. HPL to CAS, 3 October 1933 (ms., JHL). See, in general, Will Murray, "Mearle Prout and 'The House of the Worm,'" *CoC* No. 18 (Yuletide 1983): 29–30, 39.

69. Walter, "Three Hours with H. Lovecraft," in *Lovecraft Remembered*, 42.

70. HPL to RHB, [19 March 1934]; *O Fortunate Floridian*, 114.

71. HPL to Elizabeth Toldridge, 25 March 1933 (*SL* 4.166).

72. HPL to RHB, 10 April 1934; *O Fortunate Floridian*, 124.

73. Barlow, "The Wind That Is in the Grass," in *O Fortunate Floridian*, xxix.

74. Stephen J. Jordan, "Lovecraft in Florida," *LS* Nos. 42–43 (Autumn 2001): 34, 42.

75. Barlow, "[Memories of Lovecraft (1934)]," *On Lovecraft and Life*, 11.

76. HPL to Helen V. Sully, 26 May 1934 (ms., JHL).

77. Barlow, "The Wind That Is in the Grass," in *O Fortunate Floridian*, xxx.

78. HPL to AD, [early June 1934] (postcard); *Essential Solitude*, 2.643.

79. See, in general, S. T. Joshi, "RHB and the Recognition of H. P. Lovecraft," *CoC* No. 60 (Hallowmass 1988): 46–47.

80. HPL to RHB, [1? October 1934] (postcard); *O Fortunate Floridian*, 184.

81. HPL to RHB, 29 June 1934; *O Fortunate Floridian*, 146.

82. HPL to RHB, 21 July 1934; *O Fortunate Floridian*, 153.

83. HPL to E. Hoffmann Price, 31 August 1934 (*SL* 5.24–25).

84. HPL to RHB, 7 September 1934; *O Fortunate Floridian*, 176.

85. HPL to E. Hoffmann Price, 7 August 1934 (ms., JHL).

86. HPL to Duane W. Rimel, 22 January 1934 (ms., JHL).

87. HPL to Duane W. Rimel, 15 February 1934 (ms., JHL).

88. HPL to Duane W. Rimel, 13 May 1934 (ms., JHL).

89. See Duane W. Rimel, "A History of the Chronicle of Nath," *Etchings and Odysseys* No. 9 (1986): 80.

90. HPL to Duane W. Rimel, 23 July 1934 (ms., JHL).

91. "About Rimel . . . I think you're wrong. *I* have not extensively revised any of his *recent* verses; & if they are not his own, the modelling agency is Klarkash-Ton & not Grandpa! I know that he has submitted these to C A S & received assistance, but according to C A S the amount of change made has not been considerable." HPL to RHB, 25 September 1934; *O Fortunate Floridian,* 180.

92. Ibid.

93. Ibid. (*O Fortunate Floridian,* 179).

94. HPL to Kenneth Sterling, 14 December 1935; cited in Sterling's "Caverns Measureless to Man," in *Lovecraft Remembered,* 376.

95. HPL to Edward H. Cole, [20 November 1934] (postcard) (ms., JHL).

96. HPL to REH, 27–28 July 1934 (*SL* 5.12).

97. It is so dated in AHT.

98. HPL to AD, 30 December 1934; *Essential Solitude,* 2.674.

99. HPL to AEPG, [31 December 1934] (postcard) (ms., JHL).

100. HPL to CAS, [13 December 1933] (*SL* 4.328–29).

101. HPL to F. Lee Baldwin, 27 March 1934 (ms., JHL).

102. HPL to AD, [February 1928]; *Essential Solitude,* 1.135.

103. HPL to JVS, 8 November 1933 (ms.).

104. HPL to RHB, [26 October 1934]; *O Fortunate Floridian,* 187.

105. HPL to JVS, 4 February 1934 (*SL* 4.362–64). See Darrell Schweitzer, "Lovecraft's Favorite Movie," *LS* Nos. 19/20 (Fall 1989): 23–25, 27.

106. John L. Balderston, *Berkeley Square* (New York: Macmillan, 1929), 98.

107. HPL to AD, 7 August 1935; *Essential Solitude,* 2.705.

108. HPL to CAS, [11 November 1930] (*SL* 3.217).

109. HPL to CAS, [2 March 1932] (*SL* 4.25–26).

110. HPL to E. Hoffmann Price, 18 November 1934 (*SL* 5.71).

111. Ibid. (*SL* 5.70).

112. HPL to E. Hoffmann Price, 30 December 1934 (*SL* 5.86).

113. HPL to Wilfred B. Talman, 10 November 1936 (*SL* 5.346).

114. The rediscovery of the manuscript, after its whereabouts were unknown for nearly sixty years, is itself an enthralling tale. See the introduction to the annotated edition of *The Shadow out of Time* (New York: Hippocampus Press, 2001).

Chapter 23: Caring about the Civilisation

1. HPL to Jennie K. Plaisier, 8 July 1936 (*SL* 5.279).

2. HPL to C. L. Moore, [7 February 1937] (*SL* 5.405).

3. HPL to C. L. Moore, [c. mid-October 1936] (*SL* 5.322).

4. HPL to JFM, 18 January 1931 (*SL* 3.271).

5. HPL to Woodburn Harris, 25 February–1 March 1929 (*SL* 2.290).

6. Ibid. (*SL* 2.308).

7. *SL* 5.321 (note 3).

8. HPL to REH, 7 November 1932 (*SL* 4.104–5).

9. REH to HPL, [6 March 1933]; *A Means to Freedom,* 2.546.

10. HPL to REH, 24 July–5 August 1933 (*SL* 4.222–23).

11. HPL to FBL, 27 February 1931 (*SL* 3.304).

12. HPL to REH, 16 August 1932 (*SL* 4.58–59).

13. Ibid. (*SL* 4.61).

14. HPL to Alfred Galpin, 27 October 1932 (*SL* 4.92–93).

15. HPL to Elizabeth Toldridge, 28 October 1932 (ms., JHL).

16. See Benjamin Kline Hunnicutt, *Work without End: Abandoning Shorter Hours for the Right to Work* (Philadelphia: Temple University Press, 1988).

17. HPL to REH, 25 July 1932 (*SL* 4.51).

18. HPL to RHB, [17 December 1933]; *O Fortunate Floridian,* 92.

19. HPL to Elizabeth Toldridge, 23 March 1931 (*SL* 3.346).

20. *SL* 4.106–7 (note 8).

21. Arthur Schlesinger, Jr, "The Radical," *New York Review of Books* (11 February 1993): 6.

22. HPL to JFM, [3 February 1932] (*SL* 4.13).

23. HPL to JVS, 8–11 November 1933 (ms.).

24. HPL to Henry George Weiss, 3 February 1937 (*SL* 5.392).

25. *SL* 5.402 (note 2).

26. HPL to Elizabeth Toldridge, 22 December 1932 (*SL* 4.124).

27. HPL to CAS, [30 September 1934] (*SL* 5.41).

28. Ibid. (*SL* 5.40).

29. HPL to JVS, 13 March 1935 (*SL* 5.122).

30. HPL to JVS, 10 February 1935 (ms., JHL).

31. HPL to C. L. Moore, [August 1936] (*SL* 5.297).

32. See Edward Robb Ellis, *A Nation in Torment: The Great American Depression 1929–1939* (New York: Coward-McCann, 1970), 211.

33. HPL to RHB, 27 December 1936; *O Fortunate Floridian,* 387.

34. HPL to JFM, 25 July 1936 (*SL* 5.283).

35. *SL* 5.293–94 (note 31).

36. HPL to RHB, 30 November 1936; *O Fortunate Floridian,* 369.

37. *SL* 5.323 (note 3).

38. HPL to Kenneth Sterling, 18 October 1936 (*SL* 5.330).

39. *SL* 5.325–26 (note 3).

40. HPL to AD, 20 February 1927 (*SL* 2.104–5).

41. *SL* 5.397–98 (note 2).

42. *SL* 5.329 (note 3).

43. HPL to CAS, 28 October 1934 (*SL* 5.60–62).

44. HPL to MWM, 18 June 1930 (*SL* 3.155).

45. HPL to Elizabeth Toldridge, 23 November 1930 (*SL* 3.236).

46. See HPL to DW, [22 October 1927] and 23 November 1928; *Mysteries of Time and Spirit,* 173, 231.

47. HPL to JVS, 5 February 1932 (*SL* 4.15).

48. HPL to Lee McBride White, 15 October 1936; "Letters to Lee McBride White," *Lovecraft Annual* 1 (2007): 60.

49. HPL to MWM, 26 March 1932 (*SL* 4.32–33).

50. HPL to JVS, 24 March 1933 (*SL* 4.158).

51. HPL to LDC, 25 May 1925; *Letters from New York,* 126–27.

52. HPL to Lee McBride White, 31 May 1935; *Lovecraft Annual,* 36.

53. HPL to MWM, 18 June 1930 (*SL* 3.155).

54. See note 52.

55. HPL to RHB, 21 March [1932]; *O Fortunate Floridian,* 27.

56. HPL to JVS, 5 February 1932 (*SL* 4.14).

57. HPL to JVS, 25 September 1933 (*SL* 4.259).

58. See note 52 (*Lovecraft Annual,* 37).

59. HPL to Richard F. Searight, 16 April 1935; *Letters to Richard F. Searight,* 57.

60. HPL to MWM, 4 January 1930 (*SL* 3.107).

61. HPL to JVS, 13 September 1931 (*SL* 3.414).

62. HPL to E. Hoffmann Price, 29 September 1933 (*SL* 4.267–68).

63. HPL to AD, 21 November 1930 (*SL* 3.220).

64. HPL to JVS, 7 August 1931 (*SL* 3.395).

65. HPL to JVS, 24 March 1933 (*SL* 4.159).

66. HPL to MWM, 26 March 1932 (*SL* 4.33).

67. HPL to JVS, 16 November 1932 (*SL* 4.110).

68. HPL to Elizabeth Toldridge, 12 February 1935 (*SL* 5.106).

69. HPL to LDC, 27–28 May 1930 (ms., JHL).

70. HPL to Farnsworth Wright, 16 February 1933 (*SL* 4.154–55).

71. HPL to RHB, 10 July 1932; *O Fortunate Floridian,* 33.

72. HPL to JVS, 30 July 1933 (ms., JHL).

73. HPL to CAS, 22 October 1933 (ms.).

74. HPL to AD, 20 January 1927; *Essential Solitude,* 1.64–65.

75. HPL to AD, 16 February 1933; *Essential Solitude,* 2.545–46.

76. HPL to Woodburn Harris, 9 November 1929 (*SL* 3.72).

77. HPL to JVS, [13 October 1931] (*SL* 3.425).

78. HPL to MWM, 4 January 1930 (*SL* 3.103).

79. HPL to AD, 9 February 1933; *Essential Solitude,* 2.542.

80. HPL to AD, 14 March 1933; *Essential Solitude,* 2.553.

81. HPL to Elizabeth Toldridge, 3 September 1929 (*SL* 3.24).

82. HPL to AD, 25 December 1930 (*SL* 3.243).

83. HPL to Helen V. Sully, 15 August 1935 (ms., JHL [not printed in its entirety in *SL*]).

84. HPL to Helen V. Sully, 28 June 1934 (ms., JHL [not printed in its entirety in *SL*]).

85. Ibid. (*SL* 4.418).

86. "Australia" (by Roger Acton), *Encyclopaedia Britannica,* 9th ed. (Chicago: The Werner Co., 1900), 3.112.

87. See Gossett, *Race,* 387f.

88. HPL to JVS, 29 May 1933 (*SL* 4.195).

89. HPL to JVS, 4 February 1934 (*SL* 4.367).

90. HPL to JFM, 18 January 1931 (*SL* 3.276).

91. HPL to JVS, 25 September 1933 (*SL* 4.253).

92. *SL* 3.277 (note 90).

93. HPL to JVS, 25 September 1933 (*SL* 4.257).

94. See Morris Schonbach, *Native American Fascism During the 1930s and 1940s: A Study of Its Roots, Its Growth and Its Decline* (New York: Garland, 1985), 269.

95. "An Interview with Harry Brobst," 29.

96. HPL to RHB, 23 July 1936; *O Fortunate Floridian,* 356.

97. HPL to JVS, 30 July 1933 (*SL* 4.230–31).

98. HPL to JVS, 8–11 November 1933 (*SL* 4.307).

99. HPL to Elizabeth Toldridge, 26 February 1932 (*SL* 4.19).

100. HPL to AD, 25 December 1930 (*SL* 3.245).

101. HPL to CAS, 15 October 1927 (*SL* 2.176).

102. HPL to JVS, 8–11 November 1933 (ms.).

103. HPL to Helen V. Sully, 28 October 1934 (*SL* 5.50).

Chapter 24: Close to the Bread-Line

1. HPL to RHB, [24 May 1935]; *O Fortunate Floridian,* 273.

2. HPL to AD, 15 July 1935; *Essential Solitude,* 2.703.

3. HPL to AD, 16 February 1935; *Essential Solitude,* 2.678.

4. HPL to Richard F. Searight, 31 May 1935; *Letters to Richard F. Searight,* 58.

5. HPL to RHB, [16 March 1935]; *O Fortunate Floridian,* 222–23.

6. Ibid. (*O Fortunate Floridian,* 216–17).

7. HPL to RHB, [11 May 1935]; *O Fortunate Floridian,* 263.

8. HPL to RHB, 29 May 1935; *O Fortunate Floridian,* 278.

9. HPL to Donald and Howard Wandrei, [July 1935] (postcard); *Mysteries of Time and Spirit,* 355.

10. Barlow, "The Wind That Is in the Grass," in *O Fortunate Floridian,* xxix.

11. HPL to Richard F. Searight, 4 August 1935; *Letters to Richard F. Searight,* 61.

12. HPL to RHB, [25 October 1935] (postcard); *O Fortunate Floridian,* 303.

13. HPL to William Frederick Anger, 28 January 1935 (*SL* 5.92–93).

14. HPL to Duane W. Rimel, 4 August 1935 (ms., JHL).

15. HPL to AD, 19 August 1935; *Essential Solitude,* 2.705–6.

16. HPL to AD, [23 October 1935]; *Essential Solitude,* 2.711.

17. See note 14.

18. HPL to DW, 24 August 1935; *Mysteries of Time and Spirit,* 360.

19. HPL to Duane W. Rimel, 28 September 1935 (*SL* 5.200).

20. Ibid. (ms., JHL [this portion not in *SL*]).

21. HPL to RHB, 26 September 1935; *O Fortunate Floridian,* 293.

22. HPL to RHB, 21 October 1935; *O Fortunate Floridian,* 301.

23. Lumley's original version has been printed in *CoC* No. 10 (1982): 21–25.

24. HPL to AD, 4 December 1935; *Essential Solitude,* 2.719.

25. HPL to RHB, 5 September 1935; *O Fortunate Floridian,* 291.

26. See Will Murray's interview, "Julius Schwartz on Lovecraft," *CoC* No. 76 (Hallowmass 1990): 14–18.

27. HPL to DW, [3 November 1935] (postcard); *Mysteries of Time and Spirit,* 365–66.

28. HPL to JVS, 5 December 1935 (*SL* 5.210).

29. HPL to Natalie H. Wooley, 30 December 1935 (*SL* 5.220).

30. HPL to AD, 6 November [1934]; *Essential Solitude,* 2.664.

31. HPL to Duane W. Rimel, 12 November 1935 (ms., JHL).

32. HPL to DW, 10 November 1935; *Mysteries of Time and Spirit,* 368.

33. *Weird Tales* 36, No. 5 (November 1935): 652.

34. Hanns Heinz Ewers, "The Spider," in *Creeps by Night,* ed. Dashiell Hammett (New York: John Day Co., 1931), 184.

35. HPL to Richard F. Searight, 24 December 1935; *Letters to Richard F. Searight,* 70.

36. HPL to RHB, 21 October 1935; *O Fortunate Floridian,* 300.

37. HPL to RHB, [27 December? 1935]; *O Fortunate Floridian,* 309.

38. HPL to RHB, 29 January 1936; *O Fortunate Floridian,* 314.

39. Diary (1936) (ms., JHL).

40. HPL to RHB, 4 June 1936; *O Fortunate Floridian,* 338.

41. HPL to RHB, 11 March 1936; *O Fortunate Floridian,* 326.

42. See note 38.

43. Sterling, "Caverns Measureless to Man," in *Lovecraft Remembered,* 374–77.

44. See Eric Burgess, *Venus: An Errant Twin* (New York: Columbia University Press, 1985), 11–13.

45. See her death certificate, issued by the Rhode Island Department of Public Health, which reports (in 1941) a "Removal of rt breast" during an operation "5 yrs ago."

46. See note 41 (*O Fortunate Floridian,* 321).

47. HPL to JVS, 19 May 1936 (ms., JHL).

48. Marian F. Bonner, "Miscellaneous Impressions of H.P.L.," in *Lovecraft Remembered,* 28.

49. HPL to Duane W. Rimel, 22 December 1934 (*SL* 5.81–82).

50. HPL to William Frederick Anger, 22 July 1935 (ms., University of Minnesota).

51. HPL to RHB, 13 June 1936; *O Fortunate Floridian,* 341–42.

52. Ibid. (*O Fortunate Floridian,* 343).

53. HPL to AD, 11 February 1936; *Essential Solitude,* 2.725.

54. Diary (1936) (ms., JHL).

55. HPL to RHB, 4 June 1936; *O Fortunate Floridian,* 335–36.

56. See note 26.

57. HPL to Edward H. Cole, 13 May 1918 (ms., JHL).

58. See note 55.

59. See note 55 (*O Fortunate Floridian,* 337).

60. HPL to Edward H. Cole, 15 August 1936 (ms., JHL).

Chapter 25: The End of One's Life

1. REH, *Selected Letters 1931–1936* (West Warwick, RI: Necronomicon Press, 1991), 79.

2. HPL to E. Hoffmann Price, 20 June 1936 (*SL* 5.272–73).

3. This point is made astutely by Marc A. Cerasini and Charles Hoffman in *Robert E. Howard* (Mercer Island, WA: Starmont House, 1987), 12.

4. HPL to E. Hoffmann Price, 5 July 1936 (*SL* 5.276).

5. HPL to Elizabeth Toldridge, 8 May 1936 (ms., JHL).

6. Ibid.

7. HPL to RHB, 23 July 1936; *O Fortunate Floridian,* 355.

8. HPL to the Coryciani, 14 July 1936 (ms., JHL).

9. HPL to Anne Tillery Renshaw, 19 September 1936 (ms., JHL).

10. HPL to Elizabeth Toldridge, 31 July 1936 (ms., JHL).

11. All five poems are included in David E. Schultz's article, "In a Sequester'd Churchyard," *CoC* No. 57 (St John's Eve 1988): 26–29.

12. HPL to Hyman Bradofsky, 4 November 1936 (ms.).

13. HPL to Duane W. Rimel, 20 February 1937 (ms., JHL).

14. HPL to RHB, 9 July 1936; *O Fortunate Floridian,* 351.

15. HPL to Anne Tillery Renshaw, 24 February 1936 (ms., JHL).

16. HPL, marginal note on Anne Tillery Renshaw to HPL, 2 October 1936 (ms., JHL).

17. HPL to Anne Tillery Renshaw, 19 September 1936 (ms., JHL).

18. HPL to Richard F. Searight, 12 June 1936; *Letters to Richard F. Searight,* 78.

19. See n. 17.

20. HPL to Duane W. Rimel, 1 April 1936 (ms., JHL).

21. HPL to Henry Kuttner, 16 February 1936; *Letters to Henry Kuttner,* 7.

22. HPL to Henry Kuttner, 12 March 1936; *Letters to Henry Kuttner,* 11.

23. Ibid., 9.

24. HPL to Henry Kuttner, 18 May 1936; *Letters to Henry Kuttner,* 16.

25. HPL to Henry Kuttner, 8 March 1937; *Letters to Henry Kuttner,* 30.

26. *Lovecraft at Last,* 75.

27. HPL to RHB, 11 March 1936; *O Fortunate Floridian,* 325.

28. HPL to Elizabeth Toldridge, 4 December 1936 (*SL* 5.368).

29. See Sam Moskowitz, ed., *Howard Phillips Lovecraft and Nils Helmer Frome* (Glenview, IL: Moshassuck Press, 1989).

30. Sam Moskowitz to S. T. Joshi, 23 February 1995.

31. *Lovecraft at Last,* 141.

32. "Letters to Virgil Finlay," *Fantasy Collector's Annual* (1974): 12.

33. Stuart M. Boland, "Interlude with Lovecraft," *Acolyte* 3, No. 3 (Summer 1945): 15.

34. Ibid., 16.

35. Ibid.

36. HPL to RHB, 11 December 1936; *O Fortunate Floridian,* 383.

37. Fritz Leiber, "Through Hyperspace with Brown Jenkin: Lovecraft's Contribution to Speculative Fiction," in Joshi, *Four Decades of Criticism,* 145.

38. HPL to Fritz Leiber, 19 December 1936; in *Fritz Leiber and H. P. Lovecraft: Writers of the Dark,* ed. Ben J. S. Szumskyj and S. T. Joshi (Holicong, PA: Wildside Press, 2003), 38–39.

38. Fritz Leiber, "My Correspondence with Lovecraft," in *Lovecraft Remembered,* 301.

40. Leiber, "Foreword" to *The Book of Fritz Leiber* (1974); cited in Bruce Byfield, *Witches of the Mind: A Critical Study of Fritz Leiber* (West Warwick, RI: Necronomicon Press, 1991), 11.

41. Jacques Bergier, "Lovecraft, ce grand génie venu d'ailleurs," *Planète* No. 1 (October–November 1961): 43–46.

42. HPL to Willis Conover, 23 September 1936 (*SL* 5.307).

43. HPL to RHB, 3 January 1936 [i.e. 1937]; *O Fortunate Floridian,* 393.

44. William L. Crawford, "Lovecraft's First Book," in *Lovecraft Remembered,* 365.

45. HPL to Frank Utpatel, 8 February 1936 (ms., JHL).

46. HPL to Frank Utpatel, 13 March 1936 (ms., JHL).

47. HPL to AD, 18 November 1936; *Essential Solitude,* 2.759.

48. HPL to DW, 8 November 1936; *Mysteries of Time and Spirit,* 384.

49. See n. 46.

50. HPL to Duane W. Rimel, 20 December 1936 (ms., JHL).

51. HPL to Farnsworth Wright, 1 July 1936 (*SL* 5.274).

52. Ibid. (*SL* 5.274–75).

53. HPL to E. Hoffmann Price, [12 February 1936] (*SL* 5.223–24).

54. HPL to Duane W. Rimel, 28 September 1935 (*SL* 5.199).

55. HPL to E. Hoffmann Price, 16 March 1936 (*SL* 5.230).

56. Ernest A. Edkins, "Idiosyncrasies of H.P.L.," in *Lovecraft Remembered,* 94–95.

57. Lew Shaw, "The Day He Met Lovecraft," *Brown Alumni Monthly* 72, No. 7 (April 1972): 3.

58. HPL to Wilfred B. Talman, 6 October 1936 (*SL* 5.318).

59. HPL to Wilfred B. Talman, 2 November 1936 (*SL* 5.339).

60. HPL to Wilfred B. Talman, 10 November 1936 (*SL* 5.344).

61. HPL to RHB, 30 November 1936; *O Fortunate Floridian,* 375–76.

62. HPL to Jonquil Leiber, 20 December 1936 (*SL* 5.379).

63. HPL to Henry George Weiss, 3 February 1937 (*SL* 5.391).

64. HPL to AD, 17 February 1937 (*SL* 5.412).

65. HPL to Wilfred B. Talman, 28 February 1937 (*SL* 5.419).

66. "The Last Days of H. Lovecraft: Four Documents," *LS* No. 28 (Spring 1993): 36.

67. *Lovecraft at Last,* 245.

68. HPL to Duane W. Rimel, 8 October 1934 (ms., JHL).

69. Thomas J. Slaga, "Food Additives and Contaminants as Modifying Factors in Cancer Induction," in *Nutrition and Cancer: Etiology and Treatment,* ed. Guy R. Newell and Neil M. Ellison (New York: Raven Press, 1981), 279–80.

70. Stewart Cameron, *Kidney Disease: The Facts,* 2nd ed. (Oxford: Oxford University Press, 1986), ch. 8.

71. HPL to Jonquil Leiber, 20 December 1936 (*SL* 5.381).

72. HPL to Willis Conover, 23 September 1936 (*SL* 5.307).

73. HPL to JFM, [November 1925] (*SL* 2.30).

74. HPL to JFM, 1 April 1927 (*SL* 2.122).

75. HPL to JFM, 14 January 1930 (*SL* 3.110).

76. See John Bligh, *Temperature Regulation in Mammals and Other Vertebrates* (Amsterdam: North-Holland Publishing Co., 1973).

77. See, in general, R. Alain Everts, *The Death of a Gentleman: The Last Days of Howard Phillips Lovecraft* (Madison, WI: The Strange Co., 1987). The "death diary" is transcribed on pp. 25–28.

78. HPL to Duane W. Rimel, [20 February 1937] (ms., JHL).

79. M. Eileen McNamara, M.D., "Where Lovecraft Died," *CoC* No. 76 (Hallowmass 1990): 6–7.

80. "The Last Days of H. Lovecraft," 36.

81. "An Interview with Harry K. Brobst," 32.

82. "The Last Days of H. Lovecraft," 36.

83. Ibid.

Chapter 26: Thou Art Not Gone

1. DW to HPL, 17 March 1937; *Mysteries of Time and Spirit,* 391.

2. Derleth, *Arkham House: The First Twenty Years* (Sauk City, WI: Arkham House, 1959), i.

3. CAS to AD, 23 March 1937; in Smith's *Letters to H. P. Lovecraft,* 54.

4. Hyman Bradofsky, "Amateur Affairs," *Californian* 5, No. 1 (Summer 1937): 28–29.

5. Smith, *Complete Poems and Translations* (New York: Hippocampus Press, 2007–08), 2.474.

6. Barlow, "The Wind That Is in the Grass," in *O Fortunate Floridian,* xxxii–xxxiii.

7. Quoted in my introduction to Barlow's *On Lovecraft and Life,* 21n.

8. HPL to AD, 14 April 1932; *Essential Solitude,* 2.472.

9. HPL to AD, 16 December 1936; *Essential Solitude,* 2.760.

10. *Arkham House: The First Twenty Years,* ii.

11. AD to RHB, 21 March 1937 (ms., JHL).

12. *Arkham House: The First Twenty Years,* ii.

13. [Unsigned], "Horror Story Author Published by Fellow Writers," *Publishers' Weekly* 137, No. 8 (24 February 1940): 890–91.

14. *American Literature* 12, No. 1 (March 1940): 136.

15. Thomas O. Mabbott, letter to the editor, *Acolyte* 2, No. 3 (Summer 1944): 25.

16. William Rose Benét, "My Brother Steve," *Saturday Review of Literature,* 15 November 1941, 25.

17. Derleth, "Myths about Lovecraft," *Lovecraft Collector* No. 2 (May 1949): 3.

18. Starrett, *Books and Bipeds* (New York: Argus Books, 1947), 120–22.

19. Rimel, "A Fan Looks Back" (1944); rpt. in Rimel's *To Yith and Beyond* (Glenview, IL: Moshassuck Press, 1990), 50.

20. J. B. Michel, "The Last of H. P. Lovecraft," *Science Fiction Fan* 4, No. 4 (November 1939): 7.

21. J. Chapman Miske, "H. P. Lovecraft: Strange Weaver," *Scienti-Snaps* 3, No. 3 (Summer 1940): 9, 12.

22. See David E. Schultz, "The Bart House Paperbacks," *CoC* No. 65 (St John's Eve 1989): 27–28.

23. See David E. Schultz, "Lovecraft's *Best Supernatural Stories,*" *CoC* No. 66 (Lammas 1989): 15–17.

24. See John Macrae to Winfield Townley Scott, 3 January, 6 January, and 27 January 1944 (mss., JHL).

25. See Emily M. Morrison to Winfield Townley Scott, 2 February, 11 February, and 25 May 1942 (mss., JHL).

26. "Tales of the Marvellous and the Ridiculous" (1945), rpt. in Joshi, *H. P. Lovecraft: Four Decades of Criticism* (1980), 46–49.

27. David Chavchavadze, quoted in L. Sprague de Camp, "H. Lovecraft and Edmund Wilson," *Fantasy Mongers* No. 1 (1979): 5.

28. Fred Lewis Pattee, review of *Supernatural Horror in Literature, American Literature* 18, No. 2 (May 1946): 175.

29. Richard B. Gehman, "Imagination Runs Wild," *New Republic* (17 January 1949): 17.

30. Derleth, "H. P. Lovecraft: The Making of a Literary Reputation 1937–1971," *Books at Brown* 25 (1977): 16.

31. Farnsworth Wright to AD, 13 July 1931 (ms., SHSW).

32. HPL to AD, 3 August 1931; *Essential Solitude*, 1.353.

33. AD to RHB, 15 June 1934 (ms., JHL).

34. CAS to AD, 13 April 1937; *Letters to H. P. Lovecraft*, 58.

35. CAS to AD, 21 April 1937; *Letters to H. P. Lovecraft*, 62.

36. CAS to AD, 28 April 1937; *Letters to H. P. Lovecraft*, 64.

37. AD, "H. P. Lovecraft, Outsider," *River* 1, No. 3 (June 1937): 88.

38. *The Trail of Cthulhu* (1962; rpt. New York: Beagle Books, 1971), 70.

39. *Something about Cats and Other Pieces*, 294.

40. *Arkham House: The First Twenty Years*, ix.

41. HPL to DW, 14 May 1936; *Mysteries of Time and Spirit*, 376.

42. HPL to Wilfred B. Talman, 5 March 1932 (*SL* 4.27).

43. AD, "Myths about Lovecraft," 4.

44. AD to Thomas R. Smith, 10 July 1963 (ms., SHSW).

45. Mark Owings, *The Necronomicon: A Study* (Baltimore: Mirage Press, 1967), title page.

46. AD to Sonia H. Davis, 21 November 1947; cited in Gerry de la Ree, "When Sonia Sizzled," in *The Normal Lovecraft*, 29.

47. E. O. D. K[eown], "Sabbat-Night Reading," *Punch* (28 February 1951): 285.

48. *Times Literary Supplement* (22 February 1952): 137.

49. See Derleth, "H. P. Lovecraft: The Making of a Literary Reputation," 19.

50. "Books of 1954: A Symposium," *Observer* (26 December 1954): 7.

51. Derleth, "H. P. Lovecraft: The Making of a Literary Reputation," 20.

52. Wilson, *The Strength to Dream* (Boston: Houghton Mifflin, 1962), 1–2.

53. Wilson, "Prefatory Note" to *The Philosopher's Stone* (1969; rpt. New York: Warner Books, 1981), 18.

54. See Fred Chappell, "Remarks on *Dagon*," *H. P. Lovecraft Centennial Conference: Proceedings*, ed. S. T. Joshi (West Warwick, RI: Necronomicon Press, 1991), 44.

55. Derleth, "H. P. Lovecraft: The Making of a Literary Reputation," 23.

56. Philip Herrera, "The Dream Lurker," *Time* (11 June 1973): 99–100.

57. Cited in St Armand, "Synchronistic Worlds: Lovecraft and Borges," in *An Epicure in the Terrible*, 299.

58. Borges, *The Book of Sand*, tr. Norman Thomas di Giovanni (New York: E. Dutton, 1977), 124.

59. See Jeffrey L. Meikle, "'Other Frequencies': The Parallel Worlds of Thomas Pynchon and H. P. Lovecraft," *Modern Fiction Studies* 27 (1981): 287–94.

60. Cited in Rhoda Koenig's review of *Ancient Evenings, New York Magazine* (25 April 1983): 71.

61. Not to be confused with an earlier (1987) edition of the same title.

62. See Clarke's *Astounding Days: a Science Fictional Autobiography* (New York: Bantam, 1990), 128–32.

63. *American Literature* 63 (June 1991): 374.

BIBLIOGRAPHY

I. PRIMARY

A. Manuscript Archives

H. P. Lovecraft Papers, John Hay Library, Brown University, Providence, RI.

August Derleth Papers, State Historical Society of Wisconsin, Madison, WI.

B. Books and Pamphlets

i. Letters

Dreams and Fancies. Ed. August Derleth. Sauk City, WI: Arkham House, 1962.

E'ch-Pi-El Speaks: An Autobiographical Sketch. Saddle River, NJ: Gerry de la Ree, 1972.

Essential Solitude: The Letters of H. P. Lovecraft and August Derleth. Ed. David E. Schultz and S. T. Joshi. New York: Hippocampus Press, 2008. 2 vols.

Letters from New York. Ed. S. T. Joshi and David E. Schultz. San Francisco: Night Shade Books, 2005.

Letters to Alfred Galpin. Ed. S. T. Joshi and David E. Schultz. New York: Hippocampus Press, 2005.

Letters to Henry Kuttner. Ed. David E. Schultz and S. T. Joshi. West Warwick, RI: Necronomicon Press, 1990.

"Letters to John T. Dunn." Ed. S. T. Joshi, David E. Schultz, and John H. Stanley. *Books at Brown* 28–29 (1991–92 [1995]): 157–223.

Letters to Rheinhart Kleiner. Ed. S. T. Joshi and David E. Schultz. New York: Hippocampus Press, 2003.

Letters to Richard F. Searight. Ed. David E. Schultz and S. T. Joshi, with Franklyn Searight. West Warwick, RI: Necronomicon Press, 1992.

Letters to Robert Bloch. Ed. David E. Schultz and S. T. Joshi. West Warwick, RI: Necronomicon Press, 1993.

Letters to Samuel Loveman and Vincent Starrett. Ed. S. T. Joshi and David E. Schultz. West Warwick, RI: Necronomicon Press, 1994.

Lord of a Visible World: An Autobiography in Letters. Ed. S. T. Joshi and David E. Schultz. Athens: Ohio University Press, 2000.

A Means to Freedom: The Letters of H. P. Lovecraft and Robert E. Howard. Ed. S. T. Joshi, David E. Schultz, and Rusty Burke. New York: Hippocampus Press, 2009. 2 vols.

Mysteries of Time and Spirit: The Letters of H. P. Lovecraft and Donald Wandrei. Ed. S. T. Joshi and David E. Schultz. San Francisco: Night Shade Books, 2002.

O Fortunate Floridian: H. P. Lovecraft's Letters to R. H. Barlow. Ed. S. T. Joshi and David E. Schultz. Tampa: University of Florida Press, 2007.

Selected Letters. Ed. August Derleth and Donald Wandrei (Vols. I–III); ed. August Derleth and James Turner (Vols. IV–V). Sauk City, WI: Arkham House, 1965–76. 5 vols.

Uncollected Letters. Ed. S. T. Joshi. West Warwick, RI: Necronomicon Press, 1986.

Yr Obt Servt: Some Postcards of Howard Phillips Lovecraft Sent to Wilfred Blanch Talman. Ed. R. Alain Everts. Madison, WI: The Strange Co., 1988.

ii. Fiction

The Annotated H. P. Lovecraft. Ed. S. T. Joshi. New York: Dell, 1997.

At the Mountains of Madness: The Definitive Text. New York: Modern Library, 2005.

At the Mountains of Madness and Other Novels. Ed. August Derleth. Sauk City, WI: Arkham House, 1964. (Rev. ed. by S. T. Joshi, 1985.)

The Battle That Ended the Century (with R. H. Barlow). [DeLand, FL: R. H. Barlow, 1934.]

Best Supernatural Stories of H. P. Lovecraft. Ed. August Derleth. Cleveland: World Publishing Co., 1945.

Beyond the Wall of Sleep. Ed. August Derleth and Donald Wandrei. Sauk City, WI: Arkharn House, 1943.

The Call of Cthulhu and Other Weird Stories. Ed. S. T. Joshi. New York: Penguin, 1999.

The Cats of Ulthar. Cassia, FL: The Dragon-Fly Press, 1935.

Dagon and Other Macabre Tales. Ed. August Derleth. Sauk City, WI: Arkhain House, 1965. (Rev. ed. by S. T. Joshi, 1986.)

The Dreams in the Witch House and Other Weird Stories. Ed. S. T. Joshi. New York: Penguin, 2004.

The Dunwich Horror and Others. Ed. August Derleth. Sauk City, WI: Arkharn House, 1963. (Rev. ed. by S. T. Joshi, 1984.)

The Fiction. [Ed. S. T. Joshi.] New York: Barnes & Noble, 2008.

From the Pest Zone: Stories from New York. Ed. S. T. Joshi and David E. Schultz. New York: Hippocampus Press, 2003.

A History of the Necronomicon. Oakman, AL: Wilson H. Shepherd (The Rebel Press), [1937]. West Warwick, RI: Necronomicon Press, 1977 (rev. ed. 1980).

The Horror in the Museum and Other Revisions. [Ed. August Derleth.] Sauk City, WI: Arkham House, 1970. (Rev. ed. by S. T. Joshi, 1989.)

More Annotated H. P. Lovecraft. Ed. Peter Cannon and S. T. Joshi. New York: Dell, 1999.

The Outsider and Others. Ed. August Derleth and Donald Wandrei. Sauk City, WI: Arkharn House, 1939.

The Shadow out of Time. Ed. S. T. Joshi and David E. Schultz. New York: Hippocampus Press, 2001.

The Shadow over Innsmouth. Everett, PA: Visionary Publishing Co., 1936.

The Shadow over Innsmouth. Ed. S. T. Joshi and David E. Schultz. West Warwick, RI: Necronomicon Press, 1994 (rev. ed. 1997).

The Shunned House. Athol, MA: W. Paul Cook (The Recluse Press), 1928. [Printed but not bound or distributed.] Dover, 1973.

Tales. Ed. Peter Straub. New York: Library of America, 2005.

Tales of H. P. Lovecraft. Ed. Joyce Carol Oates. Hopewell, NJ: Ecco Press, 1997. New York: HarperCollins, 2000.

The Thing on the Doorstep and Other Weird Stories. Ed. S. T. Joshi. New York: Penguin, 2001.

iii. Essays and Miscellany

The Annotated Supernatural Horror in Literature. Ed. S. T. Joshi. New York: Hippocampus Press, 2000.

Autobiographical Writings. Ed. S. T. Joshi. West Warwick, RI: Necronomicon Press, 1992.

The Californian: 1934–1938. Ed. Marc A. Michaud. West Warwick, RI: Necronomicon Press, 1977.

Charleston. [New York: H. C. Koenig, 1936; rev. ed. 1936.]

Collected Essays. Ed. S. T. Joshi. New York: Hippocampus Press, 2004–06. 5 vols.

Commonplace Book. Ed. David E. Schultz. West Warwick, RI: Necronomicon Press, 1987. 2 vols.

The Conservative: Complete 1915–1923. Ed. Marc A. Michaud. West Warwick, RI: Necronomicon Press, 1976.

The Conservative. Ed. S. T Joshi. West Warwick, Rl: Necronomicon Press, 1990.

The Dark Brotherhood and Other Pieces. [Ed. August Derleth.] Sauk City, WI: Arkham. House, 1966.

European Glimpses. Ed. S. T. Joshi. West Warwick, Rl: Necronomicon Press, 1988.

First Writings: Pawtuxet Valley Gleaner 1906. Ed. Marc A. Michaud. West Warwick, RI: Necronomicon Press, 1976 (rev. ed. 1986).

Further Criticism of Poetry. Louisville, KY. Press of George G. Fetter Co., 1932.

In Defence of Dagon. Ed. S. T. Joshi. West Warwick, RI: Necronomicon Press, 1985.

Juvenilia 1897–1905. Ed. S. T. Joshi. West Warwick, RI: Necronoirdcon Press, 1984.

Looking Backward. Haverhill, MA: C. W, Smith, [1920]. West Warwick, RI: Necronomicon Press, 1977.

Lovecraft at Last (with Willis Conover). Arlington, VA: Carrollton-Clark, 1975.

The Lovecraft Collectors Library. Ed. George T. Wetzel. North Tonawanda, NY: SSR Publications, 1952–55. 7 vols.

Marginalia. Ed. August Derleth and Donald Wandrei. Sauk City, WI: Arkham. House, 1944.

The Materialist Today. North Montpelier, VT: Driftwind Press, [1926].

Miscellaneous Writings. Ed. S. T. Joshi. Sauk City, WI: Arkham House, 1995.

The Notes & Commonplace Book . . . [Ed. R. H. Barlow.] Lakeport, CA: The Futile Press, 1938.

The Occult Lovecraft. Ed. Anthony Raven. Saddle River, NJ: Gerry de la Ree, 1975.

Science versus Charlatanry: Essays on Astrology (with J. F. Hartmann). Ed. S. T. Joshi and Scott Connors. Madison, WI: The Strange Co., 1979.

The Shuttered Room and Other Pieces. Ed. August Derleth. Sauk City, Wl: Arkham House, 1959.

Some Current Motives and Practices. [DeLand, FL: R. H. Barlow, 1936.]

Something about Cats and Other Pieces. Ed. August Derleth. Sauk City, WI: Arkham House, 1949.

Supernatural Horror in Literature. New York: Ben Abramson, 1945 (rev. ed. 1945). New York:

To Quebec and the Stars. Ed. L. Sprague de Camp. West Kingston, RI: Donald M. Grant, 1976.

Uncollected Prose and Poetry. Ed. S. T. Joshi and Marc A. Michaud. West Warwick, RI: Necronomicon Press, 1978–82. 3 vols.

United Amateur Press Association: Exponent of Amateur Journalism. [Privately printed, 1915.]

The Vivisector. [Ed. S. T. Joshi.] West Warwick, RL Necronomicon Press, 1990.

Writings in The Tryout. Ed. Marc A. Michaud. West Warwick, RI: Necronomicon Press, 1977.

Writings in The United Amateur *1915–1925.* Ed. Marc A. Michaud. West Warwick, RI: Necronomicon Press, 1976.

iv. Poetry

The Ancient Track: Complete Poetical Works. Ed. S. T. Joshi. San Francisco: Night Shade Books, 2001.

Collected Poems. [Ed. August Derleth.] Sauk City, WI: Arkham House, 1963.

The Crime of Crimes. Llandudno, Wales: A[rthur] Harris, [1915].

The Fantastic Poetry. Ed. S. T Joshi. West Warwick, RI: Necronomicon Press, 1990.

Fungi from Yuggoth. [Washington, DC?:] FAPA [Fantasy Amateur Press Association] (Bill Evans), 1943.

HPL. [Bellville, NJ: Corwin F. Stickney, 1937.]

Medusa and Other Poems. Ed. S. T. Joshi. Mount Olive, NC: Cryptic Publications, 1986.

Saturnalia and Other Poems. Ed. S. T. Joshi. [Bloomfield, NJ:] Cryptic Publications, 1984.

A Winter Wish. Ed. Tom Collins. Chapel Hill, NC: Whispers Press, 1977.

II. SECONDARY

A. Bibliographies, Catalogues, and Indices

Joshi, S. T. *H. P. Lovecraft and Lovecraft Criticism: An Annotated Bibliography.* Kent, OH: Kent State University Press, 1981. Rev. ed. as *H. P. Lovecraft: A Comprehensive Bibliography.* Tampa: University of Tampa Press, 2009.

Joshi, S. T., and L. D. Blackmore. *H. P. Lovecraft and Lovecraft Criticism: An Annotated Bibliography: Supplement 1980–1984.* West Warwick, RI: Necronomicon Press, 1985.

———. *An Index to the Fiction and Poetry of H. P Lovecraft.* West Warwick, RI: Necronomicon Press, 1992.

———. *An Index to the Selected Letters of H. P. Lovecraft.* West Warwick, RI: Necronomicon Press, 1980 (rev. ed. 1991).

————. *Lovecraft's Library: A Catalogue.* West Warwick, RI: Necronomicon Press, 1980. Rev. ed. New York: Hippocampus Press, 2002.

Wetzel, George, ed. *The Lovecraft Collectors Library,* Volume Seven: Bibliographies. North Tonawanda, NY: SSR Publications, 1955.

B. Books about Lovecraft

Airaksinen, Timo. *The Philosophy of H. P. Lovecraft.* New York: Peter Lang, 1999.

Barlow, R. H. *On Lovecraft and Life.* Ed. S. T. Joshi. West Warwick, R.I: Necronomicon Press, 1992.

Beckwith, Henry L. P., Jr. *Lovecraft's Providence and Adjacent Parts.* West Kingston, RI: Donald M. Grant, 1979 (rev. ed. 1986).

Burleson, Donald R. *H. P. Lovecraft. A Critical Study.* Westport, CT: Greenwood Press, 1983.

————. *Lovecraft: Disturbing the Universe.* Lexington: University Press of Kentucky, 1990.

Cannon, Peter. *The Chronology out of Time: Dates in the Fiction of H. P Lovecraft.* West Warwick, RI: Necronomicon Press, 1986.

————. *H. P. Lovecraft.* Boston: Twayne, 1989.

————, ed. *Lovecraft Remembered.* Sauk City, WI: Arkham House, 1998.

Carter, Lin. *Lovecraft: A Look behind the "Cthulhu Mythos."* New York: Ballantine Books, 1972. Mercer Island, WA: Starmont House, 1993.

Colavito, Jason. *The Cult of Alien Gods: H. P. Lovecraft and Extraterrestrial Pop Culture.* Amherst, NY: Prometheus Books, 2005.

Connors, Scott, ed. *A Century Less a Dream: Selected Criticism on H. P. Lovecraft.* Holicong, PA: Wildside Press, 2002.

Cook, W. Paul. *In Memoriam: Howard Phillips Lovecraft: Recollections, Appreciations, Estimates.* North Montpelier, VT: The Driftwind Press, 1941. West Warwick, RI: Necronomicon Press, 1977 (rev. ed. 1991).

Davis, Sonia H. *The Private Life of H. P, Lovecraft.* Ed. S. T. Joshi. West Warwick, RI: Necronomicon Press, 1985 (rev. ed. 1992).

de Camp, L. Sprague. *Lovecraft: A Biography.* Garden City, NY: Doubleday, 1975.

Derleth, August. *H.P.L.: A Memoir.* New York: Ben Abramson, 1945.

————. *Some Notes on H. P. Lovecraft.* [Sauk City, WI:] Arkham House, 1959. West Warwick, RI: Necronoinicon Press, 1982.

Eddy, Muriel E. *The Gentleman from Angell Street.* [Providence: Privately Printed,] 1961.

Everts, R. Alain. *The Death of a Gentleman: The Last Days of Howard Phillips Lovecraft.* Madison, WI: The Strange Co., 1987.

Faig, Kenneth W., Jr. *H. P. Lovecraft: His Life, His Work.* West Warwick, RI: Necronomicon Press, 1979.

———. *The Parents of Howard Phillips Lovecraft.* West Warwick, RI: Necronomicon Press, 1990.

———. *The Unknown Lovecraft.* New York: Hippocampus Press, 2009.

Frierson, Meade and Penny, ed. *HPL.* [Birmingham, AL: The Editors, 1972.]

Grant, Donald M., and Thomas P. Hadley, ed. *Rhode Island on Lovecraft.* Providence: Grant-Hadley, 1945.

Harms, Daniel, and John Wisdom Gonce III. *The Necronomicon Files: The Truth Behind the Legend.* San Francisco: Night Shade Books, 1998.

Houellebecq, Michel. *H. P. Lovecraft: Contre le monde, contre la vie.* Monaco: Editions du Rocher, 1991. Tr. by Dorna Khazeni (as *H. P. Lovecraft: Against the World, Against Life*). San Francisco: Believer Books, 2005.

Jones, Stephen. *H. P. Lovecraft in Britain.* Birmingham: British Fantasy Society, 2007.

Joshi, S. T. *A Dreamer and a Visionary: H. P. Lovecraft in His Time.* Liverpool: Liverpool University Press, 2001.

———. *H. P. Lovecraft.* (Starmont Reader's Guide 13.) Mercer Island, WA: Starmont House, 1982.

———. *H. P. Lovecraft: A Life.* West Warwick, RI: Necronomicon Press, 1996.

———. *H. P. Lovecraft: The Decline of the West.* Mercer Island, WA: Starmont House, 1990.

———. *Primal Sources: Essays on H. P. Lovecraft.* New York: Hippocampus Press, 2003.

———. *The Rise and Fall of the Cthulhu Mythos.* Poplar Bluff, MO: Mythos Books, 2008.

———. *Selected Papers on Lovecraft.* West Warwick, RI: Necronomicon Press, 1989.

———. *A Subtler Magick: The Writings and Philosophy of H. P. Lovecraft.* San Bernadino, CA: Borgo Press, 1996.

———, ed. *Caverns Measureless to Man: 18 Memoirs of Lovecraft.* West Warwick, RI: Necronomicon Press, 1996.

———, ed. *H. P. Lovecraft: Four Decades of Criticism.* Athens: Ohio University Press, 1980.

————, ed. *The H. P. Lovecraft Centennial Conference: Proceedings.* West Warwick, RI: Necronornicon Press, 1991.

————, ed. *H. P. Lovecraft in the Argosy: Collected Correspondence from the Munsey Magazines.* West Warwick, RI: Necronomicon Press, 1994.

Joshi, S. T., and Marc A. Michaud, ed. *H. P. Lovecraft in "The Eyrie."* West Warwick, RI: Necronomicon Press, 1979.

Joshi, S. T., and David E. Schultz. *An H. P. Lovecraft Encyclopedia.* Westport, CT: Greenwood Press, 2001. New York: Hippocampus Press, [2004].

Lévy, Maurice. *Lovecraft ou du fantastique.* Paris: Christian Bourgois (Union Générale d'Editions), 1972. Tr. by S. T. Joshi (as *Lovecraft: A Study in the Fantastic*). Detroit: Wayne State University Press, 1988.

Long, Frank Belknap. *Howard Phillips Lovecraft: Dreamer on the Nightside.* Sauk City, WI: Arkham House, 1975.

Mariconda, Steven J. *On the Emergence of "Cthulhu" and Other Observations.* West Warwick, RI: Necronomicon Press, 1995.

Migliore, Andrew, and John Strysik, ed. *The Lurker in the Lobby: A Guide to the Cinema of H. P. Lovecraft.* Seattle: Armitage House, 1999. San Francisco: Night Shade Books, 2005.

Mosig, Dirk W. *Mosig at Last: A Psychologist Looks at H. P. Lovecraft.* West Warwick, RI: Necronomicon Press, 1997.

Pearsall, Anthony. *The Lovecraft Lexicon.* Tempe, AZ: New Falcon Publications, 2005.

Price, Robert M. *H. P. Lovecraft and the Cthulhu Mythos.* Mercer Island, WA: Starmont House, 1990.

St Armand, Barton Levi. *H. P. Lovecraft: New England Decadent.* Albuquerque, NM: Silver Scarab Press, 1979.

————. *The Roots of Horror in the Fiction of H. P. Lovecraft.* Elizabethtown, NY. Dragon Press, 1977.

Schultz, David E., and S. T. Joshi, ed. *An Epicure in the Terrible: A Centennial Anthology of Essays in Honor of H. P. Lovecraft.* Rutherford, NJ: Fairleigh Dickinson University Press, 1991.

Schweitzer, Darrell, ed. *Essays Lovecraftian.* Baltimore: T-K Graphics, 1976. Rev. ed. as *Discovering H. P. Lovecraft.* Mercer Island, WA: Starmont House, 1987. Rev. ed. Holicong, PA: Wildside Press, 2001.

Shreffler, Philip A. *The H. P. Lovecraft Companion.* Westport, CT: Greenwood Press, 1977.

Squires, Richard D. *Stern Fathers 'neath the Mould: The Lovecraft Family in Rochester.* West Warwick, RI: Necronomicon Press, 1995.

Szumskyj, Ben J. S., and S. T. Joshi, ed. *Fritz Leiber and H. P. Lovecraft: Writers of the Dark*. Holicong, PA: Wildside Press, 2003.

Talman, Wilfred B. [et al.]. *The Normal Lovecraft*. Saddle River, NJ: Gerry de la Ree, 1973.

Van Hise, James, ed. *The Fantastic Worlds of H. P. Lovecraft*. Yucca Valley, CA: James Van Hise, 1999.

Waugh, Robert H. *The Monster in the Mirror: Looking for H. P. Lovecraft*. New York: Hippocampus Press, 2006.

Wetzel, George T., and R. Alain Everts. *Winifred Virginia Jackson—Lovecraft's Lost Romance*. [Madison, WI: R. Alain Everts, 1976.]

C. Articles in Books and Periodicals

i. Memoirs and Biographical Articles

Baldwin, F. Lee. "H. P. Lovecraft: A Biographical Sketch." *Fantasy Magazine* 4, No. 5 (April 1935):108–10, 132.

Barlow, Robert H. "The Wind That Is in the Grass: A Memoir of H. P. Lovecraft in Florida." In Lovecraft's *Marginalia* (q.v.). In *O Fortunate Floridian* (q.v.), pp. xxix–xxxiv.

Bishop, Zealia. "H. P. Lovecraft: A Pupil's View." In Bishop's *The Curse of Yig*. Sauk City, WI: Arkham House, 1953, pp. 139–51.

Bloch, Robert. "Out of the Ivory Tower." In Lovecraft's *The Shuttered Room and Other Pieces* (q.v.), pp. 171–77.

Boland, Stuart. "Interlude with Lovecraft." *Acolyte* 3, No. 3 (Summer 1945): 15–18.

Bradofsky, Hyman. "Amateur Affairs." *Californian* 5, No. 1 (Summer 1937): 28–31.

Brobst, Harry K. "An Interview with Harry Brobst" (conducted by Will Murray). *Lovecraft Studies* Nos. 22/23 (Fall 1990): 24–42, 21.

Cole, Edward H. "Ave atque Vale!" *Olympian* No. 35 (Autumn 1940): 7–22.

Crawford, William L. "Lovecraft's First Book." In Lovecraft's *The Shuttered Room and Other Pieces* (q.v.), pp. 287–90.

Davis, Sonia H. "Memories of Lovecraft: I." *Arkham Collector* No. 4 (Winter 1969): 116–17.

Derleth, August. "Addenda to 'H. P. L.: A Memoir.'" In Lovecraft's *Something about Cats and Other Pieces* (q.v.), pp, 247–77.

———. "H. P. Lovecraft, Outsider." *River* 1, No. 3 (June 1937): 88–89.

————. "A Master of the Macabre." *Reading and Collecting* 1, No. 9 (August 1937): 9–10.

Eddy, C. M., Jr. "Walks with H. P. Lovecraft." In Lovecraft's *The Dark Brotherhood and Other Pieces* (q.v.), pp. 262–67.

Edkins, E. A. "Idiosyncrasies of HPL." *Olympian* No. 35 (Autumn 1940): 1–7.

Everts, R. Alain. "Howard Phillips Lovecraft and Sex; or, The Sex Life of a Gentleman." *Nyctalops* 2, No. 2 (July 1974): 19.

————. "Mrs. Howard Phillips Lovecraft." *Nyctalops* 2, No. 1 (April 1973): 45.

Faig, Kenneth W., Jr. "Howard Phillips Lovecraft: The Early Years 1890–1914." *Nyctalops* 2, No. 1 (April 1973): 3–9, 13–15; 2, No. 2 (July 1974): 34–44.

Galpin, Alfred. "Memories of a Friendship." In Lovecraft's *The Shuttered Room and Other Pieces* (q.v.), pp. 191–201.

Hart, Mara Kirk. "Walkers in the City: George Willard Kirk and Howard Phillips Lovecraft in New York City, 1924–1926." *Lovecraft Studies* No. 28 (Spring 1993): 2–17.

Houtain, George Julian. "20 Webster Street." *Zenith* (January 1921): 5.

Isaacson, Charles D. "Concerning the Conservative." *In a Minor Key* No. 2 [1915]: [10–11].

Keller, David H. "Lovecraft's Astronomical Notebook." *Lovecraft Collector* No. 3 (October 1949): 1–4.

————. "Shadows over Lovecraft." *Fantasy Commentator* 2, No. 7 (Summer 1948): 237–46.

Kleiner, Rheinhart. "After a Decade and the Kalem Club." *Californian* 4, No. 2 (Fall 1936): 45–47. *Lovecraft Studies* No. 28 (Spring 1993): 34–35.

————. "Howard Phillips Lovecraft." *Californian* 5, No. 1 (Summer 1937): 5–8.

————. "A Memoir of Lovecraft." In Lovecraft's *Something about Cats and Other Pieces* (q.v.), pp. 218–28.

Leiber, Fritz. "My Correspondence with Lovecraft." *Fresco* 8, No. 3 (Spring 1958): 30–33.

Lockhart, Andrew Francis. "Little Journeys to the Homes of Prominent Amateurs." *United Amateur* 15, No. 2 (September 1915): 27–28, 34.

Long, Frank Belknap. "Some Random Memories of H. P. L." In Lovecraft's *Marginalia* (q.v.), pp. 332–37.

Loveman, Samuel. "Howard Phillips Lovecraft." In Lovecraft's *The Shuttered Room and Other Pieces* (q.v.), pp. 229–33.

————. "Lovecraft as a Conversationalist." *Fresco* 8, No. 3 (Spring 1958): 34–36.

————. "Of Gold and Sawdust." In Lovecraft's *The Occult Lovecraft.* Saddle River, NJ: Gerry de la Ree, 1975, pp. 21–22.

Macauley, George W. "Lovecraft and the Amateur Press." *Fresco* 8, No. 3 (Spring 1958): 40–44.

McNamara, M. Eileen, and S. T. Joshi. "Who Was the Real Charles Dexter Ward?" *Lovecraft Studies* Nos. 19/20 (Fall 1989): 40–41, 48.

Moe, Maurice W. "Howard Phillips Lovecraft: The Sage of Providence." *O-Wash-Ta-Nong* [2, No. 2] [1937]: [3].

Morton, James F. "'Conservatism' Gone Mad." *In a Minor Key* No. 2 [1915]: [15–16].

————. "A Few Memories." *Olympian* No. 35 (Autumn 1940): 24–28.

Munn, H. Warner. "HPL." *Whispers* 3, No. 1 (December 1976): 24–28 (Part 1); 4, No. 1–2 (October 1979): 88–95 (Part II; as "HPL: A Reminiscence").

Munro, Harold W. "Lovecraft, My Childhood Friend." *Etchings and Odysseys* No. 2 (May 1983): 103–5.

Murray, Will. "Julius Schwartz on Lovecraft." *CoC* No. 76 (Hallowmass 1990): 14–18.

Orton, Vrest. "A Weird Writer Is in Our Midst." *Brattleboro Daily Reformer* (16 June 1928): 2.

Price, E. Hoffmann. "The Man Who Was Lovecraft." In Lovecraft's *The Shuttered Room and Other Pieces* (q.v.), pp. 278–89.

Price, Robert M. "Did Lovecraft Have Syphilis?" *CoC* No. 53 (Candlemas 1988): 25–26.

Rimel, Duane W. "Lovecraft as I Knew Him." *CoC* No. 18 (Yuletide 1983): 9–11.

Scott, Winfield Townley. "His Own Most Fantastic Creation: Howard Phillips Lovecraft." In Lovecraft's *Marginalia* (q.v.), pp. 309–31. Rev. ed. in Scott's *Exiles and Fabrications.* Garden City, NY: Doubleday, 1961, pp. 50–72.

Shea, J. Vernon. "H. P. Lovecraft: The House and the Shadows." *Magazine of Fantasy and Science Fiction* 30, No. 5 (May 1966): 82–99. West Warwick, RI: Necronomicon Press, 1982.

Sterling, Kenneth. "Caverns Measureless to Man." *Science-Fantasy Correspondent* No. 1 (1975): 36–43.

————. "Lovecraft and Science." In Lovecraft's *Marginalia* (q.v.), pp. 351–54.

Sully, Helen. "Memories of Lovecraft: II." *Arkham Collector* No. 4 (Winter 1969): 117–19.

Walter, Dorothy C. "Lovecraft and Benefit Street." *Ghost* No. 1 (Spring 1943): 27–29.

————. "Three Hours with H. P. Lovecraft." In Lovecraft's *The Shuttered Room and Other Pieces* (q.v.), pp. 178–90.

Wandrei, Donald. "The Dweller in Darkness: Lovecraft, 1927." In Lovecraft's *Marginalia* (q.v.), pp. 362–69.

————. "Lovecraft in Providence." In Lovecraft's *The Shuttered Room and Other Pieces* (q.v.), pp. 124–40.

ii. Critical Articles

Burleson, Donald R. "H. P. Lovecraft: The Hawthorne Influence." *Extrapolation* 22, No. 3 (Fall 1981): 262–69.

————. "Humour beneath Horror: Some Sources for 'The Dunwich Horror' and 'The Whisperer in Darkness.'" *Lovecraft Studies* No. 2 (Spring 1980): 5–15.

————. "The Mythic Hero Archetype in 'The Dunwich Horror.'" *Lovecraft Studies* No. 4 (Spring 1981): 3–9.

Carter, Lin. "H. P. Lovecraft: The Books." In Lovecraft's *The Shuttered Room and Other Pieces* (q.v.), pp. 212–49. Rev. ed. (by Robert M. Price and S. T. Joshi) in Schweitzer, *Discovering H. P. Lovecraft* (q.v.), 2001 ed., pp. 107–47.

Clore, Dan. "Metonyms of Alterity: A Semiotic Interpretation of *Fungi from Yuggoth*." *Lovecraft Studies* No. 30 (Spring 1994): 21–32.

Derleth, August. "H. P. Lovecraft: The Making of a Literary Reputation, 1937–1971." *Books at Brown* 25 (1977): 13–25.

Eckhardt, Jason C. "Behind the Mountains of Madness: Lovecraft and the Antarctic in 1930." *Lovecraft Studies* No. 14 (Spring 1987): 31–38.

Evans, Timothy H. "A Last Defense against the Dark: Folklore, Horror, and the Uses of Tradition in the Works of H. P. Lovecraft." *Journal of Folklore Research* 42, No. 1 (January–April 2005): 99–135.

————. "Tradition and Illusion: Antiquarianism, Tourism and Horror in H. P. Lovecraft." *Extrapolation* 45, No. 2 (Summer 2004): 176–95.

Faig, Kenneth W., Jr. "'The Silver Key' and Lovecraft's Childhood." *CoC* No. 81 (St John's Eve 1992): 11–47.

Fulwiler, William. "E. R. B. and H. P. L." *ERB-dom* No. 80 (February 1975): 41, 44.

————. "'The Tomb' and 'Dagon': A Double Dissection." *CoC* No. 38 (Eastertide 1986): 8–14.

Gayford, Norman R. "Randolph Carter: An Anti-Hero's Quest." *Lovecraft Studies* No. 16 (Spring 1988): 3–11; No. 17 (Fall 1988): 5–13.

Hazel, Faye Ringel. "Some Strange New England Mortuary Practices: Lovecraft Was Right." *Lovecraft Studies* No. 29 (Fall 1993): 13–18.

Joshi, S. T. "Autobiography in Lovecraft." *Lovecraft Studies* No. 1 (Fall 1979): 7–19.

———. "The Development of Lovecraftian Studies 1971–1982." *Lovecraft Studies* No. 8 (Spring 1984): 32–36 (as "Lovecraft in the Foreign Press 1971–1982"); No. 9 (Fall 1984): 62–71; No. 10 (Spring 1985): 18–28; No. 11 (Fall 1985): 54–65.

———. "Lovecraft and the *Regnum Congo*." *CoC* No. 28 (Yuletide 1984): 13–17.

———. "The Rationale of Lovecraft's Pseudonyms." *CoC* No. 80 (Eastertide 1992): 15–24, 29.

———. "Topical References in Lovecraft." *Extrapolation* 25, No. 3 (Fall 1984): 247–65.

Keffer, Willametta. "Howard P(seudonym) Lovecraft: The Many Names of HPL." *Fossil* No. 158 (July 1958): 82–84.

Kleiner, Rheinhart. "A Note on Howard P. Lovecraft's Verse." *United Amateur* 18, No. 4 (March 1919): 76.

Livesey, T. R. "Dispatches from the Providence Observatory: Astronomical Motifs and Sources in the Writings of H. P. Lovecraft." *Lovecraft Annual* 2 (2008): 3–87.

Mabbott, T. O. "Lovecraft as a Student of Poe." *Fresco* 10, No. 3 (Summer 1960): 22–24.

Mariconda, Steven J. "H. P. Lovecraft: Art, Artifact, and Reality." *Lovecraft Studies* No. 29 (Fall 1993): 2–12.

Marten, Robert D. "Arkham Country: In Rescue of the Lost Searchers." *Lovecraft Studies* No. 39 (Summer 1998): 1–20.

Mosig, Dirk W. "H. P. Lovecraft: Myth-Maker." *Whispers* 3, No. 1 (December 1976): 48–55.

———. "Lovecraft: The Dissonance Factor in Imaginative Literature." *Gothic* 1 (1979): 20–26. *CoC* No. 33 (Lammas 1985): 12–23.

Murray, Will. "Behind the Mask of Nyarlathotep." *Lovecraft Studies* No. 25 (Fall 1991): 25–29.

———. "The Dunwich Chimera and Others: Correlating the Cthulhu Mythos." *Lovecraft Studies* No. 8 (Spring 1984):10–24.

———. "Lovecraft and *Strange Tales*." *CoC* No. 74 (Lammas 1990): 3–11.

Nelson, Dale J. "Lovecraft and the Burkean Sublime." *Lovecraft Studies* No. 24 (Spring 1991):2–5.

Onderdonk, Matthew H. "Charon—in Reverse; or, H. P. Lovecraft versus the 'Realists' of Fantasy." *Fantasy Commentator* 2, No. 6 (Spring 1948): 193–97.

Fresco 8, No. 3 (Spring 1958): 45–51. *Lovecraft Studies* No. 3 (Fall 1980): 5–10.

———. "The Lord of R'lyeh." *Fantasy Commentator* 1, No. 6 (Spring 1945):103–14. *Lovecraft Studies* No. 7 (Fall 1982): 8–17.

Price, Robert M. "Demythologizing Cthulhu." *Lovecraft Studies* No. 8 (Spring 1984): 3–9, 24.

———. "Higher Criticism and the *Necronomicon*." *Lovecraft Studies* No. 6 (Spring 1982): 3–15.

St Armand, Barton L., and John H. Stanley. "H. P. Lovecraft's *Waste Paper:* A Facsimile and Transcript of the Original Draft." *Books at Brown* 26 (1978): 31–47.

Schultz, David E. "Lovecraft's *Fungi from Yuggoth*." *CoC* No. 20 (Eastertide 1984): 3–7.

———. "Lovecraft's New York Exile: Its Influence on His Life and Writings." *CoC* No. 30 (Eastertide 1985): 8–14.

———. "The Origin of Lovecraft's 'Black Magic' Quote." *CoC* No. 48 (St John's Eve 1987): 9–13.

———. "Who Needs the Cthulhu Mythos?" *Lovecraft Studies* No. 13 (Fall 1986): 43–53.

Starrett, Vincent. *Books and Bipeds*. New York: Argus Books, 1947, pp. 119–22, 203–4.

Tierney, Richard L. "The Derleth Mythos." In Frierson, *HPL* (q.v.). *CoC* No. 24 (Lammas 1984): 52–53.

Waugh, Robert H. "Documents, Creatures, and History in H. P. Lovecraft." *Lovecraft Studies* No. 25 (Fall 1991): 2–10.

———. "Dr. Margaret Murray and H. P. Lovecraft: *The Witch-Cult in Western Europe*." *Lovecraft Studies* No. 31 (Fall 1994): 2–10.

———. "The Structural and Thematic Unity of *Fungi from Yuggoth*." *Lovecraft Studies* No. 26 (Fall 1992): 2–14.

Wetzel, George T. "The Mechanistic-Supernatural of Lovecraft." *Fresco* 8, No. 3 (Spring 1958): 54–60.

Wilson, Colin. *The Strength to Dream: Literature and the Imagination*. London: Victor Gollancz, 1961; Boston: Houghton Mifflin, 1962, pp. 1–10, 111–15.

Wilson, Edmund. "Tales of the Marvellous and the Ridiculous." *New Yorker* 21, No. 41 (24 November 1945): 100, 103–4, 106. In Wilson's *Classics and Commercials: A Literary Chronicle of the Forties*. New York: Farrar, Straus, 1950, pp. 286–90.

D. Unpublished Works

Faig, Kenneth W., Jr. "Lovecraftian Voyages." [1973.]

Koki, Arthur S. "H. P. Lovecraft: An Introduction to His Life and Writings." M.A. thesis: Columbia University, 1962.

Thomas, James Warren. "Howard Phillips Lovecraft: A Self-Portrait." M.A. thesis: Brown University, 1950.

E. Lovecraft in Fiction

Campbell, Ramsey, ed. *New Tales of the Cthulhu Mythos.* Sauk City, WI: Arkham House, 1980.

Cannon, P[eter] H. *Pulptime.* Buffalo, NY: Weirdbook Press, 1984.

―――. *Scream for Jeeves: A Parody.* New York: Wodecraft Press, 1994.

―――. *The Lovecraft Chronicles.* Poplar Bluff, MO: Mythos Books, 2004.

Chappell, Fred. *Dagon.* New York: Harcourt, Brace & World, 1968.

Derleth, August, ed. *Tales of the Cthulhu Mythos.* Sauk City, WI: Arkharn House, 1969. (Rev. ed. by James Turner, 1990.)

Jones, Stephen, ed. *Shadows over Innsmouth.* Minneapolis: Fedogan & Bremer, 1994.

Lupoff, Richard A. *Lovecraft's Book.* Sauk City, WI: Arkham House, 1985.

Hay, George, ed. *The Necronomicon.* Jersey, UK: Neville Spearman, 1978.

Schevill, James. *Lovecraft's Follies.* Chicago: Swallow Press, 1971.

Weinberg, Robert, and Martin H. Greenberg, ed. *Lovecraft's Legacy.* New York: Tor, 1990.

F. Works on Supernatural Fiction

Birkhead, Edith. *The Tale of Terror.* London: Constable, 1921.

Bourke, Joanna. *Fear: A Cultural History.* Emeryville, CA: Shoemaker & Hoard, 2005.

Carroll, Noël. *The Philosophy of Horror.* New York: Routledge, 1990.

Derleth, August. *Arkham House: The First Twenty Years 1939–1959: A History and Bibliography.* Sauk City, WI: Arkham House, 1959.

―――. *Thirty Years of Arkham House 1939–1969.* Sauk City, WI: Arkham House, 1970.

Joshi, S. T. *The Evolution of the Weird Tale.* New York: Hippocampus Press, 2004.

―――. *The Modern Weird Tale.* Jefferson, NC: McFarland, 2001.

————. *Sixty Years of Arkham House*. Sauk City, WI: Arkham House, 1999.

————. *The Weird Tale*. Austin: University of Texas Press, 1990.

Joshi, S. T., and Stefan Dziemianowicz, ed. *Supernatural Literature of the World: An Encyclopedia*. Westport, CT: Greenwood Press, 2005. 3 vols.

Moskowitz, Sam. *Under the Moons of Mars: A History and Anthology of "The Scientific Romance" in the Munsey Magazines 1912–1920*. New York: Holt, Rinehart & Winston, 1970.

Railo, Eino. *The Haunted Castle*. London: Routledge, 1927.

Weinberg, Robert. *The Weird Tales Story*. West Linn, OR: FAX Collector's Editions, 1977.

G. General Works

Ayer, A. J. *Language, Truth and Logic*. 1936 (rev. ed. 1946). New York: Dover, 1952.

Balderston, John L. *Berkeley Square: A Play in Three Acts*. New York: Macmillan, 1929.

Bell, Leland V. *In Hitler's Shadow: The Anatomy of American Nazism*. Port Washington, NY: Kennikat Press, 1973.

Breach, R. W. *A History of Our Own Times: Britain 1900–1964*. Oxford: Pergamon Press, 1968.

Bulfinch, Thomas. *Bulfinch's Mythology*. 1855. New York: Modern Library, n.d.

Calder, Ritchie. *Man and the Cosmos: The Nature of Science Today*. Harmondsworth: Penguin, 1970.

Cashman, Sean Dennis. *America in the Age of the Titans: The Progressive Era and World War I*. New York: New York University Press, 1988.

Chapman, Walker. *The Loneliest Continent: The Story of Antarctic Discovery*. Greenwich, CT: New York Graphic Society, 1964.

Cohen, Stanley. *Rebellion against Victorianism: The Impetus for Cultural Change in 1920s America*. New York: Oxford University Press, 1991.

Crane, Hart. *The Poems of Hart Crane*. Ed. Marc Simon. New York: Liveright, 1986.

De Grand, Alexander. *Italian Fascism: Its Origins and Development*. Lincoln: University of Nebraska Press, 1982.

Derleth, August. *Evening in Spring*. New York: Scribner's, 1941.

————. *Place of Hawks*. New York: Loring & Mussey, 1935.

Elliot, Hugh. *Modern Science and Materialism*. London: Longmans, Green, 1919.

Ellis, Havelock. *On Life and Sex.* New York: New American library, 1957.

Ellis, Edward Robb. *A Nation in Torment: The Great American Depression 1929–1939.* New York: Coward-McCann, 1970.

Faig, Kenneth W., Jr. *Some of the Descendants of Asaph Phillips and Esther Whipple of Foster, Rhode Island.* Glenview, IL: Moshassuck Press, 1993.

Field, Edward, ed. *State of Rhode Island and Providence Plantations at the End of the Century: A History.* Boston: Mason Publishing Co., 1902. 3 vols.

Fiske John. *Myths and Myth-Makers: Old Tales and Superstitions Interpreted by Comparative Mythology.* 1872. Rpt. Boston: Houghton Mifflin, 1902.

Frazer, Sir James George. *The Golden Bough: The Roots of Religion and Folklore.* London. Macmillan, 1890. 2 vols.

Gissing, George. *The Private Papers of Henry Ryecroft.* 1903. Rpt. New York. E. P. Dutton, 1907.

Gohau, Gabriel. *A History of Geology.* Rev. & tr. Albert V. Carozzi and Marguerite Carozzi. New Brunswick, NJ: Rutgers University Press, 1991.

Gossett, Thoma F. *Race: The History of an Idea in America.* Dallas: Southern Methodist University Press, 1963.

Grimm, Brothers. *The Complete Grimm's Fairy Tales.* New York: Pantheon, 1944.

Haeckel, Ernst. *The Riddle of the Universe at the Close of the Nineteenth Century.* Tr. Joseph McCabe. New York: Harper & Brothers, 1900.

Harris, Marvin. *The Rise of Anthropological Theory: A History of Theories of Culture.* New York: Thomas Y. Crowell Co., 1948.

Huxley, Thomas Henry. *Man's Place in Nature and Other Anthropological Essays.* New York: D. Appleton & Co., 1894.

Jeans, Sir James. *The Universe around Us.* New York: Macmillan, 1929.

Kaufmann, Walter. *Nietzsche: Philosopher, Psychologist, Antichrist.* Princeton: Princeton University Press, 1950 (4th ed. 1974).

Kevles, Daniel J. *In the Name of Eugenics: Genetics and the Uses of Human Heredity.* New York: Knopf, 1985.

Krutch, Joseph Wood. *The Modern Temper: A Study and a Confession.* New York: Harcourt, Brace, 1929.

Mackie, J. L. *Ethics: Inventing Right and Wrong.* Harmondsworth: Penguin, 1977.

McLoughlin, William G. *Rhode Island: A Bicentennial History.* New York: W. W. Norton; Nashville: American Association for State and Local History, 1978.

Moorhouse, Geoffrey. *Imperial City: The Rise and Rise of New York*. London: Hodder & Stoughton, 1988.

Morison, Samuel Eliot; Commager, Henry Steele; and Leuchtenburg, William E. *The Growth of the American Republic*. 7th ed. New York. Oxford University Press, 1980. 2 vols.

Murray, Margaret Alice. *The Witch-Cult in Western Europe: A Study in Anthropology*. Oxford: Clarendon Press, 1921.

Nietzsche, Friedrich. *On the Genealogy of Morals; Ecce Homo*. Tr. Walter Kaufmann and R. J. Hollingdale. New York: Vintage, 1969.

———. *Twilight of the Idols; The Anti-Christ*. Tr. R. J. Hollingdale. Harmondsworth: Penguin, 1968.

Noll, Mark A. *A History of Christianity in the United States and Canada*. Grand Rapids, MI: William B. Eerdmans, 1992.

Parrish, Michael E. *Anxious Decades: America in Prosperity and Depression 1920–1941*. New York: W. W. Norton, 1992.

Passmore, John. *A Hundred Years of Philosophy*. 1957 (rev. ed. 1966). Rpt. Harmondsworth. Penguin, 1968.

Poe, Edgar Allan. *Collected Works*. Ed. Thomas Ollive Mabbott. Cambridge, MA: Harvard University Press, 1969–78. 3 vols.

Reynolds, Quentin. *The Fiction Factory, or, From Pulp Row to Quality Street: The Story of 100 Years of Publishing at Street & Smith*. New York: Random House, 1955.

Rhode, Eric. *A History of the Cinema from Its Origins to 1970*. New York: Hill & Wang, 1976.

Russell, Bertrand. *Human Knowledge: Its Scope and Limits*. New York: Simon & Schuster, 1948.

———. *The Selected Papers of Bertrand Russell*. New York: Modem Library, 1927.

Santayana, George. *The Life of Reason*. New York: Charles Scribner's Sons, 1905. 5 vols.

———. *Scepticism and Animal Faith*. New York: Charles Scribner's Sons, 1923.

Schneer, Cecil J. *Mind and Matter: Man's Changing Concepts of the Material World*. New York: Grove Press, 1969.

Schonbach, Morris. *Native American Fascism during the 1930s and 1940s: A Study of Its Roots, Its Growth and Its Decline*. (Ph.D. diss.: UCLA, 1958.) New York: Garland, 1985.

Schopenhauer, Arthur. *Essays of Arthur Schopenhauer.* Tr. T. Bailey Saunders. New York: Willey Book Co., [1914].

Skinner, Charles M. *Myths and Legends of Our Own Land.* Philadelphia: J. B. Lippincott Co., 1896. 2 vols.

Smith, William Benjamin. *The Color Line: A Brief in Behalf of the Unborn.* New York: McClure, Phillips & Co., 1905.

Spencer, Truman J. *The History of Amateur Journalism.* New York: The Fossils, 1957.

Spengler, Oswald. *The Decline of the West.* Tr. Charles Francis Atkinson. New York: Alfred A. Knopf, 1926–28. 2 vols.

Taylor, A. J. P. *English History 1914–1945.* New York: Oxford University Press, 1965.

Turner, James. *Without God, Without Creed: The Origins of Unbelief in America.* Baltimore: Johns Hopkins University Press, 1985.

Twain, Mark [Samuel Langhorne Clemens]. *What Is Man?* 1906. Rpt. *What Is Man and Other Irreverent Essays.* Ed. S. T. Joshi. Amherst, NY: Prometheus Books, 2008.

Tylor, Edward Burnett. *Primitive Culture.* 1871. Rpt. (from the 2nd [1873] ed.) New York: Harper & Row, 1958 (as *The Origins of Culture* [Volume 1] and *Religion in Primitive Culture* [Volume 2]).

Whitney, Charles A. *The Discovery of Our Galaxy.* New York: Knopf, 1971.

Books by S. T. Joshi

Books Written

An Index to the Selected Letters of H. P. Lovecraft (1980; rev. 1991)

Lovecraft's Library: A Catalogue (1980; rev. 2002)

H. P. Lovecraft and Lovecraft Criticism: An Annotated Bibliography (1981; rev. 2009)

H. P. Lovecraft (Starmont Reader's Guide 13) (1982)

Selected Papers on Lovecraft (1989)

The Weird Tale (1990)

John Dickson Carr: A Critical Study (1990)

H. P. Lovecraft: The Decline of the West (1990)

An Index to the Fiction and Poetry of H. P. Lovecraft (1992)

Lord Dunsany: A Bibliography (with Darrell Schweitzer) (1993)

Lord Dunsany: Master of the Anglo-Irish Imagination (1995)

The Core of Ramsey Campbell: A Bibliography & Reader's Guide (with Ramsey Campbell and Stefan Dziemianowicz) (1995)

H. P. Lovecraft: A Life (1996)

A Subtler Magick: The Writings and Philosophy of H. P. Lovecraft (1996)

Sixty Years of Arkham House (1999)

Ambrose Bierce: An Annotated Bibliography of Primary Sources (with David E. Schultz) (1999)

The Modern Weird Tale (2001)

A Dreamer and a Visionary: H. P. Lovecraft in His Time (2001)

Ramsey Campbell and Modern Horror Fiction (2001)

An H. P. Lovecraft Encyclopedia (with David E. Schultz) (2001)

God's Defenders: What They Believe and Why They Are Wrong (2003)

Primal Sources: Essays on H. P. Lovecraft (2003)

The Evolution of the Weird Tale (2004)

The Angry Right (2006)

Gore Vidal: A Comprehensive Bibliography (2007)

Emperors of Dreams: Some Notes on Weird Poetry (2008)

Classics and Contemporaries: Some Notes on Horror Fiction (2009)

H. L. Mencken: An Annotated Bibliography (2009)

Junk Fiction: America's Obsession with Best-sellers (2009)

Books Edited

H. P. Lovecraft in "The Eyrie" (with Marc A. Michaud) (1979)

H. P. Lovecraft: Four Decades of Criticism (1980)

Sonia H. Davis, The Private Life of H. P. Lovecraft (1985; rev. 1993)

Donald Wandrei, Collected Poems (1988)

Clark Ashton Smith, Nostalgia of the Unknown: The Complete Prose Poetry (with Marc & Susan Michaud and Steve Behrends) (1988)

Robert E. Howard, Selected Letters 1923-1936 (with Glenn Lord, Rusty Burke, and Steve Behrends) (1989–91; 2 vols.)

The H. P. Lovecraft Centennial Conference: Proceedings (1991)

An Epicure in the Terrible: A Centennial Anthology of Essays in Honor of H. P. Lovecraft (with David E. Schultz) (1991)

The Count of Thirty: A Tribute to Ramsey Campbell (1993)

H. P. Lovecraft in the Argosy: Collected Correspondence from the Munsey Magazines (1994)

Caverns Measureless to Man: 18 Memoirs of Lovecraft (1996)

Bram Stoker, Best Ghost Stories (with Richard Dalby and Stefan Dziemianowicz) (1997)

Henry Ferris, A Night with Mephistopheles (1997)

Arthur Machen, The Line of Terror and Other Essays (1997)

Algernon Blackwood, The Complete John Silence Stories (1998)

Ambrose Bierce, A Sole Survivor: Bits of Autobiography (with David E. Schultz) (1998)

Documents of American Prejudice (1999)

Great Weird Tales (1999)

Ambrose Bierce, *Collected Fables* (2000)

Sir Arthur Quiller-Couch, *The Horror on the Stair and Other Weird Tales* (2000)

Civil War Memories (2000)

W. C. Morrow, *The Monster Maker and Other Stories* (with Stefan Dziemianowicz) (2000)

Ambrose Bierce, *The Unabridged Devil's Dictionary* (with David E. Schultz) (2000)

Robert W. Chambers, *The Yellow Sign and Other Stories* (2000)

Atheism: A Reader (2000)

Ambrose Bierce, *The Fall of the Republic and Other Political Satires* (with David E. Schultz) (2000)

Rudyard Kipling, *The Mark of the Beast and Other Horror Tales* (2000)

From Baltimore to Bohemia: The Letters of H. L. Mencken and George Sterling (2001)

Arthur Machen, *The Three Impostors and Other Stories* (2001)

Robert Hichens, *The Return of the Soul and Other Stories* (2001)

Clark Ashton Smith, *The Black Diamonds* (2002)

Great Tales of Terror (2002)

H. L. Mencken, *H. L. Mencken on American Literature* (2002)

Algernon Blackwood, *Ancient Sorceries and Other Weird Stories* (2002)

H. L. Mencken, *H. L. Mencken on Religion* (2002)

Ramsey Campbell, *Ramsey Campbell, Probably* (2002)

Clark Ashton Smith, *The Last Oblivion: Best Fantastic Poems* (with David E. Schultz) (2002)

R. H. Barlow, *Eyes of the God: The Weird Fiction and Poetry of R. H. Barlow* (with Douglas A. Anderson and David E. Schultz) (2002)

Ambrose Bierce, *A Much Misunderstood Man: Selected Letters of Ambrose Bierce* (with David E. Schultz) (2003)

George Sterling, *The Thirst of Satan: Poems of Fantasy and Terror* (2003)

Lord Dunsany, *The Pleasures of a Futuroscope* (2003)

Arthur Machen, *The White People and Other Stories* (2003)

Fritz Leiber and H. P. Lovecraft: Writers of the Dark (with Ben J. S. Szumskyj) (2003)

H. L. Mencken, *Mencken's America* (2004)

Lord Dunsany, *In the Land of Time and Other Fantasy Tales* (2004)

Lord Dunsany, *The Collected Jorkens* (2004–05; 3 vols.)

Arthur Machen, *The Terror and Other Stories* (2005)

M. P. Shiel, *The House of Sounds and Others* (2005)

Clarence Darrow, *Closing Arguments: Clarence Darrow on Religion, Law, and Society* (2005)

M. R. James, *Count Magnus and Other Ghost Stories* (2005)

Supernatural Literature of the World: An Encyclopedia (with Stefan Dziemianowicz) (2005; 3 vols.)

The Shadow of the Unattained: The Letters of George Sterling and Clark Ashton Smith (with David E. Schultz) (2005)

In Her Place: A Documentary History of Prejudice against Women (2006)

The Short Fiction of Ambrose Bierce: A Comprehensive Edition (with Lawrence I. Berkove and David E. Schultz) (2006; 3 vols.)

M. R. James, *The Haunted Dolls' House and Other Ghost Stories* (2006)

Icons of Horror and the Supernatural (2007; 2 vols.)

Clark Ashton Smith, *Complete Poetry and Translations*, Vol. 3 (with David E. Schultz) (2007)

Warnings to the Curious: A Sheaf of Criticism on M. R. James (with Rosemary Pardoe) (2007)

The Agnostic Reader (2007)

American Supernatural Tales (2007)

Donald Wandrei, *Sanctity and Sin: The Collected Poems and Prose Poems of Donald Wandrei* (2008)

Clark Ashton Smith, *The Complete Poetry and Translations* (with David E. Schultz) (2008–09; 3 vols.)

Icons of Unbelief: Atheists, Agnostics, and Secularists (2008)

Mark Twain, *What Is Man? and Other Irreverent Essays* (2009)

H. L. Mencken, *Mencken on Mencken: Uncollected Autobiographical Writings* (2010)

EDITIONS OF WORKS BY H. P. LOVECRAFT

Uncollected Prose and Poetry (with Marc A. Michaud) (1978–82; 3 vols.)

Science vs. Charlatanry: Essays on Astrology (with Scott Connors) (1979)

Saturnalia and Other Poems (1984)

The Dunwich Horror and Others (1984)

Juvenilia: 1897–1905 (1984)

In Defence of Dagon (1985)

At the Mountains of Madness and Other Novels (1985)

Medusa and Other Poems (1986)

Dagon and Other Macabre Tales (1986)

Uncollected Letters (1986)

The Horror in the Museum and Other Revisions (1989)

The Conservative (1990)

The Fantastic Poetry (1990; rev. 1993)

Letters to Henry Kuttner (with David E. Schultz) (1990)

Letters to Richard F. Searight (with David E. Schultz and Franklyn Searight) (1992)

Autobiographical Writings (1992)

Letters to Robert Bloch (with David E. Schultz) (1993)

The H. P. Lovecraft Dream Book (with David E. Schultz and Will Murray) (1994)

The Shadow over Innsmouth (with David E. Schultz) (1994; rev. 1997)

Letters to Samuel Loveman and Vincent Starrett (with David E. Schultz) (1994)

Miscellaneous Writings (1995)

The Annotated H. P. Lovecraft (1997)

More Annotated H. P. Lovecraft (with Peter Cannon) (1999)

The Call of Cthulhu and Other Weird Stories (1999)

Lord of a Visible World: An Autobiography in Letters (with David E. Schultz) (2000)

The Annotated Supernatural Horror in Literature (2000)

The Shadow out of Time (with David E. Schultz) (2001)

The Ancient Track: Complete Poetical Works (2001)

The Thing on the Doorstep and Other Weird Stories (2001)

Mysteries of Time and Spirit: The Letters of H. P. Lovecraft and Donald Wandrei (with David E. Schultz) (2002)

From the Pest Zone: Stories from New York (with David E. Schultz) (2003)

Letters to Alfred Galpin (with David E. Schultz) (2003)

Collected Essays (2004–06; 5 vols.)

The Dreams in the Witch House and Other Weird Stories (2004)

Letters from New York (with David E. Schultz) (2005)

Letters to Rheinhart Kleiner (with David E. Schultz) (2005)

Essential Solitude: The Letters of H. P. Lovecraft and August Derleth (with David E. Schultz) (2008; 2 vols.)

A Means to Freedom: The Letters of H. P. Lovecraft and Robert E. Howard (with David E. Schultz and Rusty Burke) (2009; 2 vols.)

BOOKS TRANSLATED

Maurice Lévy, *Lovecraft: A Study in the Fantastic* (1988)

MAGAZINES EDITED

Lovecraft Studies (1979–2005; 45 issues)

Studies in Weird Fiction (1986–2005; 27 issues)

Necrofile: The Review of Horror Fiction (1991–99; 32 issues)

The New Lovecraft Collector (1993–99; 26 issues)

Dead Reckonings (2007–)

The Lovecraft Annual (2007–)

Studies in the Fantastic (2008–09; 2 issue)

The Weird Fiction Annual (2010–)